ELIZABETH J

Born in 1923, Elizabeth Jane Howard was awarded the John Llewellyn Rhys Memorial Prize for her book *The Beautiful Visit*. Her subsequent novels were *The Long View, The Sea Change, After Julius, Odd Girl Out, Something in Disguise* and *Getting it Right*. She has also written fourteen television scripts, a biography of Bettina von Arnim with Arthur Helps, a cookery book with Fay Maschler (reissued as *Cooking for Occasions* by Macmillan in 1994), and two film scripts; and has edited two anthologies and published a book of ghost stories. She is currently working on the Cazalet Chronicle, a quartet of novels the first volume of which, *The Light Years*, was published in 1990, followed by *Marking Time* in 1991 and *Confusion* in 1993. *Casting Off* will be published by Macmillan in November 1995.

Also by Elizabeth Jane Howard

The Beautiful Visit
After Julius
Odd Girl Out
Something in Disguise
Getting It Right
Mr Wrong
The Light Years
Marking Time
Confusion

ELIZABETH JANE
HOWARD

THE LONG VIEW

With an introduction by John Bayley

THE SEA CHANGE

With an introduction by Sybille Bedford

PAN BOOKS

The Long View First published 1956 by Jonathan Cape Ltd
and first published by Pan Books 1995
The Sea Change First published 1959 by Jonathan Cape Ltd
and first published by Pan Books 1995

This combined edition published 1995 by Pan Books
an imprint of Macmillan General Books
25 Eccleston Place, London SW1W 9NF

Associated companies throughout the world

ISBN 0 330 34588 5

1 3 5 7 9 10 8 6 4 2

A CIP catalogue record for this book is available from the British Library

Typeset by Centracet Limited, Cambridge
Printed and bound in Great Britain

The Long View

For
E.M.

INTRODUCTION

In an essay of the early thirties a witty and benevolent critic, Desmond MacCarthy, observed that all women's fiction began with the same sentence: 'Robina was glad she had lighted a fire.' He was being deliberately unfair of course. It was the period of *The Waves* and *Mrs Dalloway*, of *Lolly Willowes*, *A View from the Harbour*, *The Weather in the Streets*, *The Death of the Heart* – to name but a few; and Desmond MacCarthy was himself the friend and warm admirer of the talented novelists who had produced these masterpieces. But he had a point. Less talented writers were inclined to be indulgent with themselves, to feel that feminine consciousness, like a new green growth, had only to be seen uncoiling and expanding to give the reader a new sort of aesthetic satisfaction, and one far removed from the mechanical plots and ideological contrivances of men.

There is an important distinction looming in the background here, one which attends all novel writing at all times and is not confined to any difference between the masculine and the feminine. Some novelists – Graham Greene for example – are natural manipulators, whose characters are stereotyped to behave in particular ways in exciting or unusual situations. Some novelists appear to let their characters develop naturally, so that they surprise the reader, or even cease to interest him, because their individuality is not established for a particular purpose but seems to come and go, opaque at some moments and clear at others. When managed in a masterly fashion, as it is in *The Long View*, this creative process can be very rewarding indeed.

It is also very difficult to do, and to control. Control in the kind of novel Desmond MacCarthy was thinking of tends to be exercised all too simply, by the perpetual presence of the writer as heroine as consciousness. Robina was glad she had lighted a fire, and then she was distracted about this, and delighted about that, and wondering if she was really in love with Charles, and so forth. A modern Robina is found in the novels of a writer like Margaret Drabble, and her consciousness is carefully assessed in relation to the outlook and feelings of a changing society. Nowadays she is sensitive and caring, and the reader is invited to care for and with her; but while this can easily be done, and a large measure of interest taken, there lurks somewhere in the presiding consciousness an equally large measure of complacency, a lack of sharpness and detachment. Indeed the reader is invited to find such an absence of sharpness admirable in itself, a sign that being warm and caring are virtues in our society, which the novel's consciousness must imitate and embody.

That may be all very well, but an alternative strategy is to cast a cold eye, or seem to do so. Elizabeth Jane Howard does not require us to sympathise in a facile way with her Antonia, or to become instantly intimate with her. The art of the novel does indeed lie in making us take the long view. We come gradually to know, to like, to respect the heroine, and our sense of her varies in the reversed perspective so that at times she seems a stranger and at times familiar, sometimes vulnerable and touching, sometimes distant and difficult to understand. It is as if Anna Karenina were to be revealed gradually from the moment of her death back into her girlhood, so that we begin to understand (in a way that Tolstoy of course never tells us, leaving us instead to make our own inferences) how a certain kind of personality comes into existence. Antonia is not a 'portrait'; she is not on display like Dorothea Brooke in George Eliot's *Middlemarch*, or Henry James's Isobel Archer in *The Portrait of a Lady*. The indirection with which the reader is made increasingly aware of her is a technical triumph, and one of a very unusual sort, depending neither on the calm relationship in which the author demonstrates her heroine to the reader, nor the intimate one in which the reader is invited to enter the heroine's stream of consciousness.

The triumph is created by means as subtle as they are unobtrusive. We first know the heroine as Mrs Fleming, and we do not even know she is the heroine; she seems a capable and helpful person arranging a dinner party and coping as best she can with a house and husband and grown-up children. Gradually she becomes a pronoun – she – but without losing that indeterminate mildness ('Mrs Fleming said mildly . . .') which seems inappropriate to the persona of a heroine. Gradually, as she is younger and more unformed, and as time is carrying us steadily backwards, she becomes Antonia, the young girl of the novel's final section. But she could never be like Desmond MacCarthy's Robina, thrust upon us by the author, a girl in the company of whose consciousness we have to remain as if we had been brought together by a too-officious hostess.

Antonia is not mysterious: she is more interesting than that. Her passivity and her helpfulness have been exploited by life, by the conditions and expectations such a girl grows up with. But here again Elizabeth Jane Howard quietly confounds the reader's own expectations of how he or she is required to react, for this is neither a case of *pitié pour les femmes* nor of the hard but rewarding growth of experience, the *ingénue* learning with pleasures and pains about the world of men and marriage. Rather it illustrates, and in a complex and scrupulous way, how instinctive is the process by which we co-operate with destiny, finding 'what something hidden from us chose' and making a life of it without too much surprise or reflection. Antonia's marriage is beautifully suggested in its desolation and its humdrum intimacy. Her husband Conrad becomes a part of her without ever letting her become a part of him. With most marriages in novels there is a blur left, as it were, in the area of the two partners' closeness. The novelist finds himself having to concentrate upon one individuality or the other. The achievement of *The Long View* is to dissolve the heroine in the necessities and acceptances of marriage, and yet retain her, by means of the backward look, as a personality on her own.

Conrad himself has much to do with this. A remarkable and wholly convincing projection in himself, he is also a symbolic figure of man in marriage, accepted as such by his wife, who, we infer, comes to depend on and to need just that side of him which is ill-suited to the domestic relation. The woman accepts, the man chooses: but her acceptance is not necessarily of what he chooses, which is why they have two children he never wanted. There is a great deal of buried humour in this situation, which the narrative insists on no more than it does on the symbolic role of wife and husband – she prepared to accept what happens, he determined to create everything for himself in his own life, his wife included. He takes a mistress on the same terms, and we see the process undergoing there its own variations. Equably, without bitterness or insistence, the novel shows how many women find it hard to resist a man like Conrad, just because he is so capable of loving them 'for themselves', that is, of creating a self for them which they can welcome and inhabit with love. Young Imogen, the mistress, is pleased to destroy her drawings, because Conrad had given her an image of herself which no longer requires them. 'Sweet to myself that am so sweet to you' as the Victorian poet Coventry Patmore put it with his usual rather embarrassing insight. Yet there is something touching in the process, and the novel admirably reveals how it is a potential for growth and joy, as well as for sterility and imprisonment. This novel is also far too realistic to tread mechanically in any of the now well-worn paths of 'women's lib'.

It is a sad novel, but with a sadness well earned and never exploited. Humour and fun are never far away, and even when, quite early on, Antonia finds herself sitting at her solitary dinner-table with her married life over, she is not a pitiable figure but a strong resigned mild one, who will do her best to help her children survive the usual ghastly mistakes in love and marriage, or their modern equivalents; and who will go on being as cheerful as she can. None the less, the cocktail party she goes to before that solitary dinner has tragic overtones and moving effects of a very original kind. She has met there someone who seemed as unhappy as herself, who seemed to intuit for that reason what her unhappiness was. She was frightened by the way in which he had recognised what was wrong with her, and as she sits down to her supper she is overwhelmed with a sense of the 'passionate gravity' of the present.

> If she had known, then, how to find the man who had so frightened her at Leila's party, she would have gone to him. But she did not know.

The past stretches behind into the rest of the book, the future is unknown. But its promise still exists, for anyone who is prepared to take the long view.

John Bayley, 1986

PART ONE

1950

1

This, then, was the situation. Eight people were to dine that evening in the house at Campden Hill Square. Mrs Fleming had arranged the party (it was the kind of unoriginal thought expected of her, and she sank obediently to the occasion) to celebrate her son's engagement to June Stoker. The guests were asked at a quarter to eight for eight. On arrival the men would be politely wrenched from their overcoats, their hats, umbrellas, evening papers, and any other more personal outdoor effects by the invaluable Dorothy, until, reduced to the uniformity of their dinner jackets, they would be encouraged to ascend the steep curving staircase to the drawing-room. The women must climb to Mrs Fleming's bedroom on the second floor, where she would afterwards find strange powder spilled on her dressing-table, mysterious hairs of no colour she associated with the heads of her guests caught in her ivory comb, and a composite smell of unremarkable scents. When the women had confirmed before Mrs Fleming's mirror whatever they had thought a little while earlier of themselves before their own; when one of them, perhaps, had made public some small disparaging discovery about her appearance, and heard it indifferently denied, they would troop cautiously down the stairs (it was easy to tread on one another's skirts round the sharp vertiginous corners) to the drawing-room, where they would find the men drinking, and eating glazed dazed little pieces of food. June Stoker would be introduced to a company which had otherwise long ceased to discover anything about themselves likely to increase either their animation or their intimacy, and her immediate future with Julian Fleming (a honeymoon in Paris and a flat in St John's Wood) outlined.

In due course they would descend to the dining-room and eat oysters and grouse and cold orange soufflé, and drink (in deference to June Stoker) champagne. The conversation would consist of an innocuous blend of the world situation, and the St John's Wood situation of June Stoker and Julian Fleming. In neither case would enough curiosity or information be supplied to provoke real interest. After the soufflé the women would retire to the drawing-room (or Mrs Fleming's bedroom) to match up June's potential experience with their own: and the men would continue over brandy (or port if Mr Fleming turned up at his own house in time to decant it) to turn the Korean situation to economic, not to say financial, account. The party would merge again in the drawing-room, until, at eleven, the prospect of another day exactly like the one just spent, would transport them in their mind's eye to the last-minute hitches of the evening – their garage doors sticking; urgent incomprehensible telephone messages left by their foreign servants; their reading-lamps fused – perhaps even the necessity of discussing with one familiar person the threadbare subject of something done mutually and without pleasure. Then they would leave the delightful party: Julian would see June home; and Mrs Fleming would be left in the drawing-room scattered with ash trays, brandy glasses, exhausted cushions, and, possibly – Mr Fleming.

That, reflected Mrs Fleming, was the only factor of the evening in the least uncertain; and even then there was merely the alternative. Either he would stay, or he would go. How the alternative reduces one's prospect and petrifies the imagination in a way that the possibility can never do. Possibilities, innumerable and tightly packed, could shower forth like mushroom spore between such alternatives as being here, or there; alive, or dead; and old, or young.

Mrs Fleming shut the book she had not been reading, uncoiled herself from the sofa, and went upstairs to dress for dinner.

The view, even from the second floor of the house, was beautiful and disturbing. From the front windows the steeply declining square crammed with lawn and bushes, and the massive trees, which were fading and yellowing in the chill silent sunlight, filled the eye, so that the houses straight across the square were scarcely visible, and a little to the right down the hill were quite out of sight. At the bottom were no houses: the square opened straight on to the main road, like the 'fourth wall' of a theatre, or the 'Terrible Zone'. The effect from Mrs Fleming's bedroom was mysterious and satisfying: the great metropolis knowing its place, and rumbling distantly back and forth.

From the back windows the view was almost a miniature of the front: but instead of the square, narrow strips of back gardens dropped away until only the black tops of their walls could be seen. Beyond the gardens was a sloping row of mews cottages, all a little different from each other, and beyond them lay London, under a sky left hyacinth by the vanishing sun. She glanced down at the mews attached to her garden and observed that her daughter had returned from work. A man's hand, at least not Deirdre's (her daughter did not like women), twitched the scarlet curtains together. Mrs Fleming was genuinely without curiosity, salacious or moral, about her daughter's private life, knowing only that it was conducted with a dramatic symmetry of conflict. There were always two men involved – one dull, devoted creature whose only distinction was his determination to marry her, in the face of a savage series of odds (the other, more attractive, but even more unsatisfactory young man). She suspected that Deirdre was not happy, but the suspicion was an easy one; and since Deirdre herself was clearly convinced that a mutual ignorance was all that held them tolerably apart, Mrs Fleming never attempted to force her daughter's lack of confidence. She supposed that whoever had twitched the curtains was probably coming to dinner, but she could not remember his name . . .

Louis Vale let himself into his ground-floor flat in Curzon Street, slammed the metallic door, threw his briefcase on to the bed or divan (he preferred to call it a bed), and turned on his bath. His room, one of an enormous block, resembled the cell of some privileged prisoner. Bare but very expensive essentials were symmetrically arranged in a room so small and so dark that colour, untidiness, or time-wasting trivia of any kind would have been lost or unusable in it. Everything possible was flush with the walls. The cupboard for his clothes, the shelf for his alcohol, the wireless: even the lights clung like white bulbous leeches to the grey paint. There was a cringing armchair and a small double-tier table on which lay an ash tray, a telephone, and the current copy of *The Architectural Review*. The curtains were grey: he never drew them. His bathroom, equipped like a small operating theatre for the business of bathing and shaving, and now slowly suffusing with steam, was a bright uncompromising white. He emptied his pockets, flung off his clothes, and bathed. Ten minutes later he was in his dinner jacket swallowing whisky and water. There was a single drawer set into the wall above the head of his bed. It had no handle and opened with a minute key. Inside the drawer were three unsealed white envelopes. He selected one, shook out of it a latch-key, and locked the drawer.

He parked his car outside the mews in Hillsleigh Road, and let himself into Deirdre Fleming's flat. It was very small, and, he observed with distaste, in a transitional, very feminine state of untidiness. A pile of clothes lay in one corner of the room awaiting the laundry or cleaners. Plates and glasses (the ones they had used two nights ago) were stacked on the draining board by the sink. The bed, or divan (Deirdre preferred to call it a divan), had been stripped of sheets and was now loosely covered by its loose cover. Two half-written letters lay on the table with an unaddressed brown paper parcel. The waste paper basket was full. The only chair was hung with stockings, almost dry, laid on dirty tea-cloths. In a large saucepan he discovered the wreck of an old chicken soaking in water. He read the letters. One was to her father, thanking him for the cheque he had given her on her birthday – and the other, he found with quickening interest, was to him. She felt she must write to him, he read, since he would never allow her to talk. She knew that she irritated him, but he made her so unhappy that she could not remain silent. She knew that he did not really love her, as, if he did, surely he would understand her better. If he really knew the effect that he had upon her when he failed to ring up or to stick to any arrangement, and thought her simply absurd, would he please tell her; but she could not really believe that he knew. He could not possibly want to make anyone so unhappy: she knew what he was really like underneath – an entirely different person to the one he made himself out to be. She knew that his work meant more . . .

Here she had stopped. Here we go again, he thought wearily, and put the letter back on the table, with a sudden vision of Deirdre naked, trying not to cry, and waiting to be loved. She has to be stripped of her self-respect in order to dress me in it. By the time she has grown out of being a romantic, I shan't want her. I am a stinking cad to go on living on her emotional capital. Perhaps, he concluded without much conviction, I thought that she would infuse me with her belief. If she had succeeded, I should have made it worth her while – but she will not succeed. She hasn't got what it takes, and I haven't got what it makes.

Suddenly, old and sad about her, he drew the curtains, so that she should think he had been in the dark, and had not noticed her letter. Then he lay down on the uncomfortable bed, and slept.

He heard her cautiously intruding upon his sleep: opening the door carelessly, shutting it with elaborate calm; trying the ceiling light – on, and off – and then lighting the standard lamp. He felt her motionless in the middle of the room, watching him, and nearly opened his eyes, to interrupt her private heart about him – then remembered the letter, and remained still. He heard her move towards him and halt – heard her fingers on the paper; her sudden little breath which had always charmed him, and the indeterminate noises of concealment. Then, because he did not want to be woken up by her, he opened his eyes . . .

June Stoker emerged from the Plaza Cinema in a dim tear-soaked daze, stopped a taxi and asked it to go to Gloucester Place as quickly as possible. She felt in a confused way that she was late: not for anything in particular – her dinner was not until a quarter to eight, and she intended skipping the Thomases' drinks party – but simply late: what in fact she always felt when she had been doing something secretly of which she was rather ashamed. For she would *die* sooner than tell her mother how she had spent the afternoon; alone in a cinema watching a film which in any company at all she would have condemned as sob stuff. To her it seemed frightfully, frightfully sad, and possibly even quite true, if one was that sort of girl. To June the essence of romance suggested the right man in the wrong circumstances – but somehow she could not imagine Julian in those circumstances, in spite of his father, whose behaviour really did seem to be rather odd. She was rather afraid of meeting him: even Julian, who was so calm about everything, seemed a little uncertain about the prospect. His mother had been easy, although June supposed you couldn't really tell in one meeting. Mothers-in-law were supposed to be awful, but one need not see them much. She opened her compact, and powdered her nose. Anyone observant could tell that she had been crying. She looked exactly as though the tears had sprung from all over her face, and not simply from her eyes. She would slip into her room and say that she had a headache. She had a sort of headache now she came to think of it. Home. But it won't *be* my home much longer, she realized: I shall have a different name, and a different house, and all my clothes will be new (well, nearly all), and Mummy won't possibly be able to ask me where I am going all the time; but I *do hope* Julian will ask me when he comes back from the office: and we shall have our friends to dinner – I'll be a marvellous cook, he'll keep finding unsuspected qualities in me . . . I wonder what it will be like spending a whole fortnight alone with Julian . . .

She had paid the taxi and shut herself into the lift. She would have to ring Julian to tell him to pick her up at home, instead of at the Thomases'. She wondered what the dinner party with his parents would be like. Full of awfully clever and interesting people to whom she would not be able to think of anything to say. She sighed, and felt for her latch-key.

Angus, her Aberdeen, yapped mechanically round her feet, and of course her mother called her into the drawing-room. She was having tea with her old school friend, Jocelyn Spellforth-Jones. June first submitted to being told by her mother that she was late, that she looked hot, and that she never shut doors behind her, and then to a general and very unappetizing invitation from Jocelyn Spellforth-Jones to 'tell her all about it'. Nobody but Mummy would think of telling Jocelyn anything: perhaps that is why she always wants to know so badly, thought June, the inevitable blush searing her face and neck, as she protested weakly that there was nothing much to tell, really. Mrs Stoker looked with mock despair at her best friend. Jocelyn returned the look, and invited Angus to search her. He was a sensible little dog and declined. Jocelyn then reminded Mrs Stoker of how absurd they had been when they were June's age, and told a really revolting story about a set of blue china bunnies which she had insisted when she married on transporting from her bedroom mantelpiece in her old home, to a shelf built especially for the purpose by her new bed. Mrs Stoker remembered the bunnies perfectly, and June felt she might reasonably escape. Murmuring something about a headache, she rose to her feet. Immediately, her mother began bombarding her with questions. Had she found a pair of shoes? Did she remember the Thomases? What had Marshall's said about her nighties? Well, what *had* she been doing all afternoon, and why did she suddenly have a headache? June blushed and lied and eventually fled to her bedroom feeling cross and tired.

Everything in her bedroom was pale peach coloured. She

liked this; but when she had suggested repeating the colour in their flat, Julian had said that cream was more suitable. It was more neutral, he had said, and she expected that he was right. She slipped out of her pink woollen dress, kicked off her shoes, and emptied her bag on to the end of her bed. Angus (he was getting much too fat) waddled aimlessly round her shoes and then jumped on to his chair which was covered with a greasy car rug of the Hunting Stewart tartan.

If she had not spent most of the afternoon in tears, June would certainly have cried now. Just when everything ought to be marvellous, it somehow actually wasn't. Of course it was largely that awful woman sitting there with Mummy and talking about her marriage with a deathly mixture of silliness and nastiness – and Mummy (although of course she wasn't really like that) at least putting up with it – not noticing it. What was there to *say* about Julian anyway? He worked in an office, advertising things; she didn't know much about it, and honestly it didn't sound awfully interesting, and 'they' said that in view of his uncle, and his general ability for the position, he was certain to be a director before he was thirty. Which, 'they' said, was very good indeed. Julian would not have been able to marry so young without such a prospect, and to start with they would certainly have to be careful. She tried hard to imagine what being careful meant, but she could only think of cottage pies, and not going to the Berkeley. Julian was determined to keep his car, and she simply could not set her own hair. It was dark brown, thick, and rather wiry – frightful hair – although her friends said how lucky she was to have a natural wave. But Julian . . . Well, he was rather good looking, and they thought the same about things, like not believing much in God, and thinking circuses were rather cruel, and not bringing up children in a new-fangled way – and – all that kind of thing. Masses of things really. They had met at a dance and got engaged in Julian's car by the Serpentine. That evening was only a month ago; it had been simply wonderful, and she had thought about it so much since then, that now she could not remember it properly – which was a bore. One ought to remember the night of one's engagement. Julian had seemed a little nervous – she had liked that – and he had talked very fast about them, except when he had touched her, and then he had not talked at all. She could still remember his fingers on the back of her neck just before he kissed her. He had never held her head again in the same way, and she had not dared ask him in case, when he did, it would be different. She lived nostalgically on that little shiver, and the hope that it would return and envelop her when circumstances permitted.

Well, in a week she would be married, and everyone, except that foul Jocelyn (and she didn't matter), was being very nice about it. After all she was an only child: Mummy, for all her frenzied co-operation, would probably be a bit lonely when it was all over, and Julian was the only son. Rather rotten for parents worrying away for years and then getting left. She wondered whether Mrs Fleming minded. Julian did not seem to be especially what her mother described as 'close' to his mother. Perhaps Mrs Fleming preferred Julian's sister. Or perhaps she concentrated on her extraordinary (probably glamorous) husband. One heard all kinds of things about him. He did not seem to lead much of a family life, which had made Mummy like Mrs Fleming much more than she would otherwise have done. June knew that her mother distrusted women of her own age who did not look it; but Mr Fleming's frequent absences from both of his houses made Mummy sorry for Mrs Fleming.

She had been sitting in front of her pink dressing-table removing her make-up; her clear red lipstick, and the film of pink powder which bloomed unbecomingly on her flushed face. She wore no rouge – if one blushed much it was fatal – and her eyelashes were dark and thick like a child's. She scraped her hair back from her wide, shallow forehead, and fastened it with a piece of old pink chiffon. She looked attractive because she was so young, and because she was so young, she felt, like this, very unattractive. How should she employ these rites with a husband always about? What would he think when he first saw her like this? Impossible to pin up her hair and put cream on her face at night: but how could one expect to remain attractive if one never did these things? She would ask Pamela, who had been married for nearly a year: but Pamela looked ravishing, different, of course, but still ravishing without any make-up at all, while she simply looked like a schoolgirl who was not allowed to know better. And then, as if to convince herself that she no longer was a schoolgirl, she ran to her door and shot its bolt, peeled off her remaining clothes, and lit a cigarette. Now, she thought, she resembled some awful French picture. She certainly did not look like a schoolgirl. Now she would ring up Julian.

Only when she reached the telephone did she realize with a shock which filled her brown eyes with sudden tears of discretion, that she would not, even if he asked her, tell Julian that she had spent the afternoon alone in a cinema.

She pulled the counterpane round her shoulders, and lifted the receiver.

Mr Fleming replaced the telephone on its shelf, and sank back into his bath. He had had an exceedingly tiring afternoon, and he felt much the better for it. He regarded his wife's dinner for their son calmly, and decided that he would arrive late. One of his secret pleasures was the loading of social dice against himself. He did not seem for one moment to consider the efforts made by kind or sensitive people to even things up: or if such notions ever occurred to him, he would have observed them with detached amusement, and reloaded more dice.

An unorthodox master at his public school had once written neatly across the corner of his report: 'Brilliant, but bloody minded.' This had delighted Mr Fleming at the time, and he had stuck to the formula ever since. It had really got him a very long way. Throughout his several astonishingly successful careers (he had roared through the examinations for chartered accountancy, fought a courageous war in the service of the Navy – ending up in the trade, gambled his prize money on the Stock Exchange with spectacular luck or ingenuity, and almost as casually begun his term as law student) he had concentrated on himself with a kind of objective ferocity; until now, at an age which merely added to his fascination, he had constructed a personality as elaborate, mysterious, and irrelevant, as a nineteenth-century folly. In turn, he had cultivated information, power, money, and his senses, without ever allowing one of them to influence him exclusively. His incessant curiosity enabled him to amass a quantity of knowledge which his ingenuity and judgement combined to disseminate, or withhold, to the end of power over ideas and people. He made money out of both without people clearly recognizing it, since they were usually so dazzled by his attention that their own ends were blinded. He had a heart when he cared to use it. But on the whole, he did not care in the least about other people, and neither expected nor desired them to care about him. He cared simply and overwhelmingly for himself: and he felt now that he was at last a man after his own heart. The only creature in the world who caused him a moment's disquiet was his wife, and this, he thought, was only because he had at one period in their lives allowed her to see too much of him. This indirectly had resulted in their children: who, though clearly a case for Shaw's theory of eugenics, were, in his opinion, otherwise the consequence of mistaken social exuberance. The boy bored him. He had no doubt that Julian was marrying an exceptionally, even a pathetically, dull young woman; and the only mitigating feature of the affair, Julian's extreme youth, was not likely, in view of his work and disposition, to count for very much. He would probably attempt to extricate himself at thirty, or thereabouts, by which time he would have two or three brats, and a wife, who, drained of what slender resources had first captivated him, would at the same time be possessed of a destructive knowledge of his behaviour. This would inevitably lead to his leaving her (if indeed he were to achieve it) for entirely the wrong reasons.

He considered his daughter to be a more subtle disaster. She was undoubtedly attractive, but although not a fool, she was not equipped with enough intellectual ballast for her charms. Hers was an impulsive intelligence, and she had not the reason either to sustain or to reject her impulses. She would confuse her life with men who exploited her, and work that did not; until, her attractions waning, and her judgement impelled by fear, she would marry. This last, short of a miracle. Mr Fleming believed only in miracles wrought by himself: 'by hand' he would explain with an ingenuous expression, that appeared on his face quite devilish. All this was the result of his wife trying to be a good mother; and he, he was perfectly sanguine about it, trying not to be a father of any kind.

Innumerable women had enquired why he had married his wife; and it had fascinated him to hear the varying degrees of curiosity, solicitude, and spite with which they contrived to put the damaging little question. It had fascinated him no less to reply (throwing contemptuously aside such repertorial excuses as youth or inexperience) with fantastic, and apparently circumstantial detail; in such a way as to defer their hopes, excite their interest, or disprove their theories: discovering, each time (and he never told the same story twice), that there was no limit or horizon to the human capacity of belief. He did it, he considered, in the best possible taste. He never deprecated his wife, even by implication. He simply added, as it were, another storey to the structure of his personality, and invited the lady in question to put herself temporarily in possession: there she might perch precariously, in what she could be easily persuaded was an isolated castle in a rich and strange air.

He was bathed; he was dressed.

In the bedroom he regarded a tangle of sheets, damp silky hair, and bare sulking arms, with faint, with very faint, interest. When he had said hours ago that he would not be dining with her, she had started to make emotional capital out of it. His remark that to her monotony was the spice of life had reduced her to an injured dramatic silence which he knew very well she expected him to break. Instead he put two five-pound notes and some small change on the dressing-table, secured them by her bottle of Caron, and left. It amused him to see how women reacted to this: he always maintained that the theatrical insult of pennies thrown upon the stage related strictly to the value of the coins. Sovereigns would produce a different result. The sentimental women (they were legion) returned the notes and kept the change. The professional kept the lot and never alluded to it. The romantic and inexperienced returned the lot and discussed it for weeks with varying degrees of tortuous indignation (he had learned to avoid them). One woman had left it lying on an hotel dressing-table for days, and then, when they had left the hotel, announced that it was a tip for the chambermaid; and one had kept the notes and sent the change back to him as a donation to the cause of his sensibility.

He collected a taxi and drove to his club for a drink and a little telephoning. The time had come, he felt, to make several, drastic changes . . .

Leila Talbot telephoned her house to tell her maid to tell her nanny that the children were not to wait up for her as she would be late at the hairdresser, to ring up the Thomases to say that she would be late for her drink (oh dear, and they had asked her to be early), and to ring up the Flemings to say that she would be late for dinner as she would be late at the Thomases'. Then, with a little groan of pride at her administrative ability, she cautiously encased herself in the electric hair-drying machine. Most people were late without warning people; they had no manners nowadays . . .

I should like to be really rude to him. Really outrageous, Joseph Fleming thought, his gouty fingers struggling with his black tie. He had disliked his elder brother so intensely for so many years that even at the prospect of seeing him he indulged in a preliminary orgy of hate. His mind ebbed and flowed and broke again over the rock of his brother's insolence, his success with other men, with any woman, with money (his profession seemed exasperatingly to combine streams of women and the acquisition of money), and finally with that collective mystery, the world. He did not like Mrs Fleming either; but then, he did not like women, he disliked other men liking them, and he loathed anyone who had ever liked his brother.

It was characteristic of Joseph that he suffered badly from gout, particularly in his hands, without drinking red wine. He knew that the angry variations upon which he was now engaged, would make him very hungry; that he would eat too much too fast at dinner, and that he would spend a night sleepless with indigestion. It was also characteristic of him that however little he thought he wanted to go to dinner at Campden Hill Square to meet some hard-boiled chit that damned young puppy his nephew was to marry (and probably a small crowd of dreary people he had so frequently met there before), nothing would have induced him to miss it. As it was, he believed he had one of his gargantuan colds coming . . . but still, he would go, although how anybody could expect the evening to be enjoyable was utterly beyond him.

2

THEY all sat round the table eating oysters. June said she adored them. Leila Talbot said how exciting it was to eat them for the first time every September. Joseph said that he had met somebody at his club who had lived in New Zealand where all one had to do was to put one's hand into a pool and pull them out. Mr Fleming had remarked that if they were quite so easily come by, he did not think that he would want them. Deirdre said anyway there ought to be *some* compensation for living in New Zealand. Louis, who had been very silent, said that he had been born there, and that, with Deirdre subsiding into an agony of sensibility, was that.

Mrs Fleming, as a result of formal interest, learned that

Louis Vale was an architect, a member of the Georgian Group, and a contributor to several sympathetic journals on such subjects as the ground plans of great houses long since demolished. The conversation flowered, as monologues of intelligent young men on the subject of their careers to an intelligent and sympathetic woman will do; until, at the point when Deirdre was softening under the influence of her lover acquitting himself so well (she had not listened to what Louis had been saying, but only to the effect of what he had said), and Joseph, unable to command Leila Talbot's attention against such competition, was rumbling and snarling inside like a volcano, Mr Fleming leaned forward and, with deceptive delicacy, asked Louis what he was designing, or doing.

Louis, pulled up – floundered – said that he taught second-year students, and that (he spoke very fast) he was designing prefabricated public conveniences . . . to be used, of course, all over the country.

During the moments that followed, Georgian, or what they conceived to be Georgian, images fell to ruins in the pit of a silence so small but so deep, that at the end of it all of them were made violently aware of one another, as people who have survived an earthquake. Joseph thought: Stevenson could have written him: only Stevenson. He's a villain – an intellectual villain.

Deirdre, subject to a battery of emotion – hatred of her father, and resentment of her mother – suddenly saw Louis separate from herself; as he must have been before she knew him – as he was now, without her; the part of him that was recoiling from her father might envelop him to the exclusion of herself. A waste of emotional despair overcame her; so that for a moment she was positively, destructively, beautiful – her eyelids weighted to Botticellian proportions – her baroque mouth simplified by her unhappiness. Instinctively, she glanced at her mother; but every thread of her face was controlled. *Her* thoughts, *her* feelings were so much her own business, that she had no time for those belonging to anyone else. But miraculously, she had. She leaned forward, and with perfect conventional manipulation, she restored Louis's faith in himself. Architecture was again safe: Joseph was again possessed of Leila Talbot; and Mr Fleming, unmoved, proceeded to dissect June, who, almost everyone knew, including Mr Fleming, was hardly fair prey . . . it was indeed a minute admission on his part. June was quickly reduced to the public uttermost depths of an unformed mind. Dark green and bright red reminded her of holly, which reminded her of Christmas, which reminded her of her childhood. Had she been less simple, she would have realized that these reactions were uniform. If she had been more adept she would have prevented these discoveries relating to herself. As she was (and Mr Fleming intended she should be), she blushed amid high school clichés and indestructible platitudes which she had read and spoken since she had been taught to read and speak: but her limitations and her embarrassment were so routine that they afforded Mr Fleming little pleasure. She was a nice, ignorant, repressed, anxious, unimaginative girl, designed perfectly to reproduce herself; and regarding her, Mr Fleming found it difficult to believe in *The Origin of Species*.

Julian enjoyed his grouse, and wondered what the hell he was going to *do* with June in Paris. After all, there were limits, pretty stringent ones, if she'd never been to bed with anyone before. He approved of that, but it made the prospect of a honeymoon with her something of an ordeal. He reviewed his own experience rather defiantly to reassure himself: the local intellectual tart at Oxford; that extraordinary woman he had met at a shoot in Norfolk; and Mrs Travers, who had been at least forty, and infinitely stimulating. It was odd that although he had been to bed with her four times, he still thought of her as Mrs Travers. Sometimes he tried saying 'Isobel' carelessly to himself, but he never felt happy about it. Mrs Travers had had a husband, a lover who lived in her house, and a stream of young men. She was very good tempered, and told them all extremely careless lies; but as long as they pretended to believe her, she was very kind to them. From her he had learned that everything took twice as long as he had thought necessary; but except for her irritating habit (when she was otherwise carried away) of calling him Desmond, the incident had proved as enjoyable as it had been educative.

Fortified by these fleeting exaggerated recollections, he considered grandly whether he had better not sack Harrison. Harrison was their office manager, and had been for nearly twenty years. Julian was not really in a position to sack him, but anyone with any imagination could see that Harrison's methods were hopelessly antiquated, and that his sole concern (that of keeping down overheads) was beginning seriously to cramp developments, and even giving the firm a bad name. Harrison owed his position to a crablike ingenuity with Uncle Joseph, consisting chiefly in a nauseating Dickensian act of worthless feudal memories, which Julian's uncle, who could never remember anything, greatly enjoyed. Well, in Paris he could think about sacking Harrison. He half wished that Paris was over; June said that she did not really speak French, and neither of them knew anyone there at all well – still they would have the car, and they could go to films. June said that French films were much better than English or American ones – she was saying it now to his father; and he, damn him, was asking her why she thought so. Poor darling, she was blushing, and of course she didn't know why. Suddenly protective about her, he felt for her hand which was nervously twisting her napkin under the table. When he touched her, she turned to him with such a radiance of gratitude that for a moment he knew that he loved her.

Mrs Fleming, while she listened to Deirdre's difficult, attractive young man, examined her husband's face, which was now blatantly, almost insultingly, expressionless, as he enquired into June's prejudices and predilections. It was a lack of expression so complete, that although she had observed it many hundred times, she was never able to believe it; and she searched now a little more urgently than usual (perhaps because she wanted to protect June?) for some trace of his mind on his face. But his large pale forehead was smooth; his pale blue, nearly round eyes had not even the familiar intense quality of glass eyes; and his lips – so unlike one another, so little a pair that it was impossible to think of them as a mouth – touched one another and parted for food and speech as though they had no interest in either. She believed that at such moments his mind was working furiously; but the insulation was so practised and complete that she was never certain. He was probably bored. After their first three years she had spent the remaining twenty fighting the battle of his boredom, and, she realized suddenly now, never with any hope of success; since from the first he had been freakishly and inexorably ranged against her. It had been he who had suggested this dinner party; he had resisted her slightest attempt to enliven it with less accountable guests; and she, in the solitary and dangerous position of knowing half his mind, had not persevered.

Now, suddenly finished with June, he was leaning towards Deirdre and saying in his soft pedantic voice: 'But you, my dear Deirdre, never answer letters until your recipient's anticipation has been blunted by despair. You will never make a Clarissa. You will lose your voice on the telephone, and your virtue, unable to prevaricate by any civilized means, will turn uneasily in its double grave.'

And Deirdre, who knew her father well enough not then to thank him for his birthday present, replied: 'My dear Papa, of what possible interest can my voice or my virtue be to you?'

To which, with the faintest gleam of malicious acknowledgement, he said: 'None, excepting that I am a student of strife,' and stared gently at his orange soufflé.

Mrs Fleming hastily relinquished Louis Vale for Deirdre's reinstatement. How many times had she sat at this table blocking her husband's sorties – a little too soon, and he was resentful; a little too late, and the guests were damaged; perhaps, worst of all, at exactly the right moment, when he felt challenged to more murderous and ingenious attacks: always upon people without the wit or assurance to respond (as he might have liked) against him. She had threatened once to throw him out of countenance, but ignoring the impossibility of such a proposition, he had silenced her by saying simply that the situation between two people married was so painfully familiar to them, that the need for it to be an enigma to everyone else was surely obvious. She was not exactly afraid of him, but in twenty-three years he had literally exhausted her, and she had therefore never attempted publicly to confound him. He must, she supposed, have had a trying afternoon. She turned now to Joseph, who, she knew, disliked her in a simple uncompromising manner that she found pathetic and sometimes even endearing.

Louis, aware that he had been thrown into the breach, gathered together the warp and woof of his aggression and his self-control; sized up Mr Fleming (and got him wrong) – and was immediately outfaced by Mr Fleming selecting the works of Bellamy, to which he brought the full weight and variety of his mind. Soon they were lost in the heights of Tiahuanaco. Deirdre unwisely attempted to introduce the Pyramids, but Mr Fleming waved them gently aside as so many castle puddings, and continued to expound and elaborate Bellamy's theories with an amiable brilliance of which, earlier, Louis would not have thought him capable.

Leila Talbot was a woman who talked to men about themselves and to women about other people. When she was doing neither, she applied stern concentration to her own appearance, or a more frivolous appraisement to the appearance of any other woman present (she was seldom alone). She had accounted for June – she had observed that June was inexperienced or conscientious or rich enough to wear her best stockings with a long dress; that she veered unhappily and unsuccessfully between Victorian and Edwardian family heirlooms and 'costume jewellery'; that she clearly experienced trouble with her hair; and that she had lost weight since she had bought the buff-coloured jersey silk she was wearing. Now, Leila, as she ate her soufflé, turned, as on these occasions she always did, to her hostess. She had known Mrs Fleming for a very long time and their friendship, never intimate, uncharged by either competition or sympathy of interest, afforded them none the less a certain pleasure as women who have known each other for anything more than twenty years, without either side divulging any of the ephemeral misleading details of their private lives. Even when Mrs Talbot's husband was killed in an air crash, she had not confided to Mrs Fleming how little she had cared, and how guilty she had felt for not caring; but Mrs Fleming had been quietly imaginatively kind to her at the time, she remembered. Leila kept any speculations about Mrs Fleming's life with her husband to herself, which was more than she did for anyone else. Mrs Fleming, she felt, stimulated the best in her, and though this meant that she did not want to see too much of Mrs Fleming, she enjoyed being accepted as reserved, disinterested in personal affairs, reliable, and more intelligent than she was.

At the moment, however, she was characteristically concerned with her friend's appearance: with her hair, which though still dark and thick, was laced with single pure white hairs apparent now even in the candelight – showing more, Leila thought, because she wore it gathered neatly to the back of her head without a parting; with her skin, which was smooth, and of an even parched colour; with her eyes, which looked as though they had once been a brilliant temporary blue, and had bleached to the texture of water by some violent light. Except for her eyes, none of her features was remarkable – but the absolute regularity of their disposition gave her a kind of distinction, a pleasing and rare elegance, perhaps more prevalent, at any rate more consciously aimed at, in the time of Jane Austen, than now. That was the answer, Leila concluded, to her mysteriously ageless quality; she was quite simply out of another age . . . and now she was fast on the way to becoming a grandmother. Leila considered her own three children, all identically unattractive, sized ten, twelve, and fourteen, like horrible mass-produced clothes, and thanked God that at least they were far from an age when they would be likely to bombard her with grandchildren.

Her speculations were finally brought to an end by her hostess's eye. The four women went upstairs, and having seen them on the way to her bedroom, Mrs Fleming retired alone to the drawing-room to make the coffee.

There were four cups on the tray by the fire, which meant that Mr Fleming was performing the same operation on the floor below. Mrs Fleming made excellent coffee, but never to her husband's liking. When he made it, it became mysteriously a foreign drink, tasting of its colour, and unbelievably hot, so that one half-expected the brittle cups to explode. She made her coffee, and thought she thought of nothing at all: but when June entered the room, and, on her invitation, advanced rather timidly to share the long stool, she realized that her husband, and Julian, and Deirdre, had been running through her head like some endless unsatisfactory fugue, which would not, could not, stop, unless it was resolved or interrupted.

June seemed nervously to expect this tête-à-tête to become a cross-examination of her ability to look after Julian. In vain did Mrs Fleming discourse with mild kindness of Paris and the new flat; June closed each attempt with defensive assertions about her domestic, and even maternal, talents. When she asked whether she might be taught to make coffee like Mrs Fleming, to whom the gaucherie of such ingratiation was both alarming and disagreeable, Deirdre joined them, remarking that Leila was telephoning the Thomases', where she thought she might have left her cigarette case. She then asked affectionately for some of her mother's perfectly filthy coffee. 'You make it like some health-giving tea, and Papa makes it like a drug: same coffee, same apparatus. I don't know how you do it.'

Mrs Fleming said: 'I expect people's natures obtrude upon their coffee,' and smiled at June, who looked as though Deirdre had dropped a brick on her. 'The cigarettes,' she said severely to her daughter, 'are on the mantelpiece.'

Deirdre reached for the box, handed it to June, and lit their cigarettes.

'Are dozens of horrible presents still rolling in?' she asked, with a kind of commiseration that was none the less aggressive.

'Quite a lot.' June smiled unhappily. She was terrified of Deirdre, and did not like her.

'I haven't given you anything yet. What would you like?'

Stretched on the rack of this heartless generosity, June was reduced to saying that Deirdre had better ask Julian.

'Oh, *Julian*. He never really *wants* anything.' She rose suddenly, and threw her barely smoked cigarette into the fire. 'Mamma, may I have some brandy?'

'They can't find it, but they are looking. If they fail, I shall work steadily backwards over yesterday!' Leila left the door ajar, and sank into a chair.

Mrs Fleming murmured: 'It sounds like a play by Mr Priestley,' and handed her coffee.

'Thank you. Yes, I should love some. But really, it is too depressing. This is the case that I only found last week, after losing it for all that time before.'

June thought that obviously Leila's mother had never told her that she always left doors open. She shivered, and Mrs Fleming, who had been warming glasses, gave her some brandy.

Deirdre continued mercilessly: 'We were trying to decide what I should give June for a wedding present.'

'Oh my dear, it's a dreadful problem. But, I warn you, what you get in the way of revolting objects and fulsome congratulation when you are married is nothing to what you get when you have a baby. Could I have a cigarette?'

Deirdre supplied her, lit another herself, looked at it, and laid it on an ash tray.

'Dreadful books about its age and weight at every conceivable moment, and ghastly yellow knitted matinee coats (why *are* they so often yellow?) and letters from hospitals, and photographs of other people's babies so that you can see exactly how awful it's going to look when it's larger, and little brushes and combs and things covered with pixies; a sort of undercurrent of Margaret Tarrant and Walt Disney, glazed with God. Oh! I shall send you two dozen Harrington Squares.'

Mrs Fleming was amused; and June, though faintly shocked, was laughing, when Deirdre, with a sudden clumsy movement, knocked her brandy glass over on to the hearth, where it smashed to the stem. Ignoring it, she walked to the door. 'The most appalling draught,' she said, and returned to the broken glass.

Mrs Fleming was about to speak; looked at her daughter's stormy face, and was silent. Something is very wrong: but I shall never know what it is until it doesn't matter whether I know or not; which is probably quite right. I only think I can save her some needless extravagance of the heart; or perhaps I only think I ought to save her. Oh dear, oh dear, what a mistake it is to listen to one's thoughts. But it is a mistake of such infinite variety that making it constitutes a chief pleasure in life. Aloud, she said: 'Clear away the bits, darling. You know what your father feels about anything broken.'

'I don't believe he feels about anything until it *is* broken.'

But she picked up every single fragment that she could see, and wrapped them in the evening paper.

Leila and June were happily engaged upon the absorbing and uncontroversial subject of how much too expensive everything was. Deirdre's mouth curled, and she looked desperately round the room. She has his capacity for boredom, thought Mrs Fleming anxiously, I wonder whether she has . . .

But at that moment the men entered the room: returned from the mysterious technical conversations about money, about sex, about the murderous propensities of the North Korean – having discussed the fundamentals as superficially as the women in the drawing-room discussed the superficialities fundamentally. After half an hour's uneasy amalgamation, the party broke up.

Mr Fleming showed no signs of breaking with them, but accompanied them to the door in an obtrusively hostly manner; leaving Mrs Fleming in the drawing-room. He was sure she was tired, he said . . .

Julian shut June into the car and walked round to his door saying something that she could not hear. As soon as he had switched on the ignition she asked him what he had said. (This was a ritual they were to repeat until the tedium of it provoked them to conduct all their quarrels in cars.) Now, however, he thought it rather sweet of her to care what he had said.

'I said it's a good thing we have this hill to start on, because she hasn't been charging properly for weeks.'

He released the brake and they slid down the hill, jolting a little as the motor started.

'What about Paris?' June asked.

'What about it?'

'Not being able to start.'

'Oh *that*. She's going on charge tomorrow morning.'

There was a pause, and then June said carefully: 'I like your mother. But all your family are a bit frightening.'

'Oh well, the only course open to in-laws is to be frightening or dull. It's better if they start frightening, I should think.'

'But your mother *is* nice,' persisted June, wanting to know how nice Julian thought his mother.

However, he answered indifferently: 'She's all right. A perfectly blameless creature. My father is no joke though.'

'Everybody is to *him*.'

'You know, I believe that's true. That's *clever* of you!'

He said it with such surprise that she might have laughed, but she was so young, and knew so little about people, that she was hurt, and said: 'I do know about people. People are my thing.'

'Oh darling! People are your thing!'

The chain of lights down Bayswater Road were strung before them like Douglas's bad sonnet on London.

'Aren't they pretty?'

'What?'

'The lights all down the centre of the road.'

'Awfully pretty. No policemen about, are there?' He began to drive fast.

A minute later, June asked: 'Did you have a tiring day?'

'Not specially. Tiresome. Clearing things up.'

She waited for him to ask her what sort of day she had had,

so that she could tell him quickly about the cinema; but he did not ask her. They were at Marble Arch, and he said: 'Damn. I should have turned left.'

Outside her house, he switched off the engine and took off his hat. She had planned at Marble Arch to tell him at this moment – quickly – just before he kissed her, because his wanting to kiss her would make it all seem less shameful or less absurd: but his deliberation, which seemed to her both practised and heartless, frightened her again. She did not know that he was deliberate simply because he was nervous.

So she did not tell him.

Deirdre and Louis left hurriedly together. They left Leila and Joseph waiting for the taxi for which Julian had telephoned. Louis left with regret, and Deirdre with relief exacerbated by Louis's obvious reluctance to finish the evening. She knew that he had been impressed by both of her parents; but while this was something that part of her passionately required, she as passionately wanted to be regarded by Louis 'for herself' as women say, which means for some elusive attraction which they do not feel they possess.

They walked in silence the few yards up the hill and round the corner to the Hillsleigh Road mews outside which stood Louis's car. The sight of it threw Deirdre into a state of defiance which was very like panic. She determined to say nothing aloud; but her secret self gabbled and implored, alternately abject and bitter: her immense distrust of everyone which began with herself completed its circle, until, by the time they were arrived outside her door and Louis's car, nothing she said would have had any meaning, and she might have said anything, if Louis had not forestalled her.

'I'll see you safely inside, and then, I *think*, home to my own bed. Darling,' he added. He had been praying (in more measured terms) that Deirdre would also be tired – be calm, but tired. Now, however, she swung round on him, her hand on the uncomfortably high door-knob, her eyes dilated, blazing with entreaty. He moved nearer to her, ready to want her, but she flung out the fingers of her left hand in a minutely passionate denial (she had hands like her mother's – elegant, eloquent hands); her eyebrows rose and settled in quivering drifts of humiliation, and she turned away from him to the door.

For a moment he was really afraid of her . . . of her perilous depths of emotion, which seemed to sweep her desolate of pride, and to strand them both in a desert of anxious silence and nervous hands: then he remembered the letter, and thought angrily that her sense of drama made her ridiculous, and life with her intolerable – why even her despair was in some sort erotic, so what could she *expect* him to feel?

Trying to eliminate the exasperation from his voice, he said: 'But I shall see you tomorrow evening,' and then, when she did not reply: 'Deirdre, what is it?' (That surely gives her an opening.)

Without looking at him, she said: 'It is having to *ask* you to stay. I find that unbearable. Being forced to ask you. Then it simply makes you think that . . .'

She had spoken very slowly, as though her words were difficult to choose, and when they became easy, she stopped, obviously afraid of where they might lead her.

Louis thought: Women are sensitive to temperature in exact proportion to the amount they are bored. He was extremely cold himself. Aloud, he said: 'Well darling Deirdre, quite often, I am glad to say, you *do* want to go to bed with me. And, quite as often, you think you don't, and find you do. If you just want to talk to me, couldn't it wait until tomorrow? I do promise you, I shall listen far better . . .'

'But I have something to tell you!' she cried, as though this cleared and precipitated the whole situation.

Christ, that damned letter, he thought: remembered how young she was, how little versed in the subtle laws of emotional demand and supply, and resolved to be gentle with her, but to go through with it in such a way that she would never abandon them again to further situations of the kind.

'Right, well if only you'll open the door, I will walk up into your parlour.'

She opened the door, started up the steep rickety stairs, and then, before she reached the top, she turned round to him, and said with an effort of lightness: 'My dear Louis, I do assure you that in this particular instance, *I* am the fly.'

He noticed then that she was shaking from head to foot, and with a kind of unwilling fear, for the first time he took her seriously. The letter, he remembered, had not been finished . . .

'Since she *knows* that I live in Chiltern Court, and she in Pelham Crescent, why does she expect me to share a cab with her? In order to have someone to chatter at, and pay the fare for her, damn her.' Joseph eyed Leila Talbot morosely as they waited for the cab; and managed during those interminable minutes, to pin this feminine contrivance on his brother. He particularly disliked Mrs Talbot because she was not only a woman, but a widow, and he regarded all widows with egocentric suspicion: irrespective of their age, they were predatory and *passée* like man-eating tigresses. The fact that Mrs Talbot throughout the evening had divided her attentions among her fellow diners with indifferent partiality only made him angrier, and he rationalized her behaviour venomously as yet another instance of her cunning.

Their drive in the taxi was therefore not enjoyable. Leila was both nervous and bored. She attempted three or four topics sufficiently uninteresting to merit some sort of reply, but he grunted her out of countenance. She knew he was passionately interested in something . . . (was it coins or caves?) but serious conversation in a taxi cab was to her an anachronism.

At Pelham Crescent she thanked him, made some move to pay her share of the fare, and then without in the least meaning it, said as she climbed out: 'I know there was something frightfully important that I wanted to tell you, but I simply can't remember what it is.' There was a pause, and then she said, 'I shall have to ring you up.'

She immediately forgot this, but Joseph pondered it with exhaustive distrust all the way to Chiltern Court and throughout his ensuing indigestible night.

Mr Fleming bolted the door on the last of his guests, and walked thoughtfully to the ebony table where he had earlier observed a pile of envelopes addressed to him. He put them in his pocket, returned to the door, unbolted it, and climbed the stairs to the drawing-room.

She looked up from her book – he suspected that she had not been reading it – and he shut the door gently behind him . . .

3

MRS FLEMING sat perfectly still where Mr Fleming had left her. Her mind remained as motionless as her body: poised for some movement which she felt must be collected and designed if she were not to perish. All the words and thoughts and shivering sensation attributed to a shock of this kind poured through her, rejected by the age of her reason as inadequate. The fear of doing, or saying, or being something annihilating to the pride which she had guarded for so long, through the agonizing sequence of smash and grab and compromise against which she had been ranged, was paralysing in its strength. It was not a simple question of tears, or vituperation, of the beautifully easy blame which children and political agitators release in their predicaments: she had no violent facile conviction to support her; no private place where she could vanish from self-consciousness: no godlike creature brimming with objective love and wisdom to whom she could turn . . . simply the skeleton of perhaps twenty-five years ahead of her on to which she must graft some fabric of her life.

So she sat, perfectly still amid the coffee cups and brandy glasses, until, long after the fire had died, and a fine even chill had settled imperceptibly on the room like ashes, she became aware that she was very, very cold; and that he had been gone nearly three hours.

Waking was like being born: 'We are worthless to one another,' he was saying – but not once – again and again, and tears were streaming down her face.

She considered leaving Julian to breakfast downstairs alone, and then as sleep and the damning reiteration receded, realized the folly of such an indulgence. She had woken at her usual hour, and as she proceeded with the routine of beginning the day, she reflected how inexorably people as they grew older become set in the mechanics of their lives. When Dorothy arrived with tea and lemon juice, she was already in a very hot bath.

In her bath she discovered two things: that her mind, usually able to play freely on her favourite theme of relating ideas she had read to things she had seen, or people she had encountered (often resolving in some grandiloquent notion – frivolous, but pleasant exercise to one who enjoyed the morning), was now leashed in an immediate introspective manner to herself. It crowded in a frenzy of ghoulish anticipation, round the naked reclining body of Mrs Fleming; as though she had suffered some accident, and it was awaiting unhelpfully further developments; her removal from the scene – her actual death.

The other discovery was her age. One applied age to other people, generally and precisely: they were older than they looked; they were only twenty-two; they were remarkable for forty-three: but the growing up with oneself – the stiffening of the body and the loosening of the mind; the selection and rejection of what could or could not be done, or said, or thought; the accretion of experience and habit was so gradual: there was such a quantity of these moving pictures, that one did not seem (and was not) very different from another, until something happened which forced the whole private collection upon their owner; discrepancies of behaviour and appearance shouted down the years which make age, echoing in vault after vault of memory that they had changed – that they were new – that they were old. That she was forty-three.

She brushed and combed and dressed her hair, wondering at what age people were most vulnerable: when they were very young, with a daring beautiful resilience, in love with themselves and anyone who loved them; or later, when experience could be compared, and future opportunity was diminished; or later still, in the middle of the wood, where the trees ahead so horribly resembled the trees behind, and the undergrowth of their past caught and clung and tore at them as they moved on. Perhaps they were most vulnerable of all very late, when the end at least, even for the short-sighted, was inexorably in sight – the small clearing in which to lie down and be still and sleep like the dead.

She put on enough make-up to render her face familiar to those who did not really know it, and went down to breakfast with her son.

Julian, balked of his *Times* by the number of congratulatory letters his engagement still provoked, was in his usual early morning temper. When Mrs Fleming arrived he was annihilating toast, and ripping envelopes which he cast from him unread in silent resentment. He hated writing letters, and, being a consistent young man, he hated getting them.

'I say, Mamma, were you afflicted like this when you married?'

Mrs Fleming finished pouring her coffee before she replied: 'I expect it was worse, because people had more leisure; but mercifully I cannot remember it at all.'

There was a short silence, during which Mrs Fleming

thought how old Julian must think her not to remember the letters she had got when she was married. Then, he said:

'I really think June might cope with them. She hasn't got to work all day.'

'She has all her own letters, and her clothes, not to mention the new flat. Anyway, can you imagine how outraged some of your friends would be if they were answered by her. Really, Julian, your sense of indecorum is . . .'

'Remarkably developed: you might be a bloody Bohemian,' he finished. It was the remark of one of his great-uncles thus frivolously handed down. It did not make either of them laugh; it was a kind of ritualistic trap into which from time to time they and Deirdre fell.

'Oh well, Porky can answer then.' He began sweeping them into jagged heaps.

Mrs Fleming said: 'I sometimes wonder whether even she likes being called that.'

'Porky? Well she's been called it for twenty-two years; she must be used to it. She's the only secretary in the office with a nickname. I expect you'd find she's proud of it.' He got up from the table in a cloud of envelopes. 'Women like Porky, Mamma, get used to *anything*. They have to. I'll be out to dinner,' and he went.

No, she wouldn't, she couldn't tell Julian.

She went upstairs to write to her husband that Julian need not be worried by their private affairs until after he was married and back from Paris. 'Of course, he need never be *worried* . . .' she wrote: 'but he need not even be told. I imagine that you will attend his wedding.' This last was, in their currency, a desperate plea that he should attend: so complex, dull, and indirect had become thoughts and desires between them.

The familiar uncertainty which these uncharacteristic demands always induced stopped her now for consideration, and her consideration was interrupted by the telephone. Her heart made a violent unpleasurable leap, and she picked up the receiver.

But it was Louis Vale.

He sounded very much older than he was, older, and more responsible. He wondered whether he might see her. Well, yes, it was rather. He knew that it sounded extremely odd, but could she possibly lunch with him? He meant odd because it was such short notice and she hardly knew him, he added. He spoke with the kind of calmness which suggested long-term agitation. Mrs Fleming proposed that he lunch at Campden Hill Square. He accepted with a gratitude which, she detected, at the back of his manners, was desperate. He thanked her thoroughly, but noncommittally, for her dinner the night before, and rang off.

'I believe if I had not asked him here, he had keyed himself up to propose it.' Then suddenly she thought of Deirdre, and in unthinking panic dialled the number of the place where she worked. It was engaged, and while she waited for the line, Louis telephoned again. This time he sounded really embarrassed. He knew that it was a preposterous thing to ask, but would she very much mind not telling anyone that he was coming to lunch? *Anyone?* Of course, he didn't expect her deliberately to rush about telling people, but he hadn't made it at all clear that he wanted to see her privately . . . by the way, he was not inconveniencing her, was he: she would be alone? She reassured him, and then asked if he knew whether Deirdre was at work? No, it wasn't one of her office days, he replied, and then said: 'As a matter of fact she's out for the day. She'll be back in the evening, I think.' Mrs Fleming, relieved, said that she would expect him at twelve thirty. 'You are exceedingly kind. Exceedingly kind,' he repeated, and rang off.

'I suppose he wants to discuss Deirdre. But really, what a fuss.' She felt the slight irritation which so often succeeds unwarranted panic; signed the letter to her husband, addressed it to his club, and went downstairs to arrange about luncheon.

Louis arrived at twelve twenty-five.

The first thing they each privately observed of the other was that he and she looked as though they had not slept. He put this down to her age, and she to his youth and obviously nervous disposition. They drank sherry and tried to make allowances for one another (she had looked such a very attractive woman the night before: now she seemed parched – drained of her particular degree of attractiveness – daylight, and unromantic clothes?): and she tried to walk them through the conversational prelude to whatever it was he had really come to talk about (he looked positively haggard; as though he had been humiliatingly drunk, or killed somebody by accident, or been told that he was to die six months hence), until finally she found that they were both looking desperately at the clock, in an effort to calculate and arrange the time. She realized then that he wanted to begin, but was afraid, and that he was considering their removal to the dining-room in a few minutes.

'Would you rather wait until we go downstairs before telling me whatever it is you want to tell me, or would you rather start now? We are lunching at one.'

He looked at the clock again, and back at her. She had a way of looking at him at the end of her sentence – an absolutely direct unimpassioned gaze, which lent a kind of dignity and significance to her most commonplace remarks, and which seemed to him then the most intricate blend of charm and good manners. If he had not been so desperately nervous and generally sick at the prospect before him, he might have enjoyed lunching with her. As it was . . .

'The difficulties are,' he said, 'that if I don't begin very soon, I shall not have the courage to begin at all; but if I start, and we are interrupted, I shall find it . . . the whole thing will become . . .' He flicked the ash off his cigarette on to the carpet, and pounced on it with his foot. 'Oh, damn, what an awful thing to do . . .' He was too much distressed to say anything more, and the general situation began to rock and tremble and lose its balance.

Mrs Fleming said: 'If you will carry it, I think we had better move our lunch up here where it is much warmer, and we shall not be disturbed by Dorothy.'

He stumbled gratefully to his feet, and carefully carried two vast trays round the narrow corners on the stairs, while Mrs Fleming established their privacy with Dorothy. Eventually, they were seated on either side of the fire with food on their plates and whisky in Louis's glass. Mrs Fleming began calmly eating her lunch which she did not in the least want. The moment had suddenly arrived.

'If you accept the fact that at least I think I am right to tell you all this, perhaps you will forgive the way I tell it. You see, I've thought and thought and rehearsed in my mind how to begin, and it all seems hopeless now. I think, in spite of the shock, I'd better try to be simple and brief.'

'I must, of course, reserve my judgement of whether you are right to tell me at all.'

'You must, of course, do that.' He drank some of his whisky, and stared at his untouched food.

'Deirdre has started a child. The child is undoubtedly mine. Apparently she has known about it for some time, but she only told me last night. She has not said so, but I know that she wants me to marry her. She didn't tell me about the child sooner, and she hasn't said that she wants to marry me, because she knows that I do not want to marry her.'

There was a little silence: he cleared his throat and looked at her. She was not looking at him, and there was no expression on her face. Oh God, I could not have put it worse, he thought. Where has she gone from here? He raced along all the possible avenues of her mind in vain pursuit. He found nothing; he could feel nothing.

'Of course, there are one or two ways out of this situation,' he said, 'but they are not so simple as one might think. Possibly they seem more complicated to me than they would to you.'

Mrs Fleming drank a little water.

'Listen,' he said; her silence was stripping his mind to a point where he felt she ought not to remain alone in the room with it. 'I haven't come here to justify my behaviour or elude my responsibilities. But there is no point in my telling you this unless I tell *all* of it, and you believe me.'

'Why *are* you telling me?'

'Because I honestly don't know what to do,' he said. 'I've got to do something, and you seemed to me . . . last night, that is . . . someone who would know what to do. In any crisis. Last night. Do you despise me very much for that?'

She felt him almost unconsciously trying to lighten the atmosphere, which, in the circumstances, was hardly his prerogative, and said: 'Do you know why it is so easy to make decisions for other people? It is not simply because one is objective. It is because if I make a decision for you, I shall not have to carry it out. If I make a wrong decision, the responsibility will still be yours.'

'Yes?'

'Perhaps you had better describe your behaviour and responsibilities. I am not very clear about how you regard either.'

He thought this was sarcasm, and looked at her expecting to see it dirtying her face; but it was not; and he thought again— She is simply exact in her language, and I hope to God I shall be honest and accurate to her. Aloud, he said:

'The obvious solution in a sense would be for me to marry her. The trouble about that is that I don't love her, and I should make her very unhappy. I don't want to marry anyone at the moment, and I am not faithful to Deirdre even now. But I don't think it would be dishonest to say that she doesn't love me. She has made something of me in her mind, which I do not in the least resemble, and she suffers frequently from my failure to be what she wants to think I am. All things being equal, she would eventually have despaired of me, and created the same image of another man.' He paused, and tried in the silence to gauge her interest and disapproval; but again, he could not. He could only feel that she was very intent.

'Another solution would be for her not to have the child. I'm afraid last night that I began by assuming that she would not want to have it, and, of course, I offered to arrange all that for her. But I found her absolutely determined to go on with it. Before I say anything more outrageous, I do want to tell you that although I do not love Deirdre, I care very much about her; I do feel responsible for her, and am prepared, if that seems the best thing for her, to marry her. I am also, of course – I know I said this before – prepared to see to – to look after . . .'

'It is not, in fact, a question of love or money,' Mrs Fleming said calmly.

He looked up sharply from his cigarette-case (he had not attempted to eat), his rather dully tragic features enlivened by dismay. Whatever she offered – comfort, resentment, advice, assistance – might well be beyond his intellectual powers to grasp. Louis had always applied the best of his mind, his intelligence, perseverance, and intuition to his career, confining his private relations (and this was easy) largely to women whose emotions and senses dominated their lives. He was, in fact, at twenty-seven, in a fair way to becoming a success; in the case of this particular piece of human mass production 'untouched by human heart'. Faced with a predicament, however, he was sincerely concerned to employ principles, which, although he did not thoroughly understand them, were not, he knew, necessarily conducive to his advancement. He was only twenty-seven.

Something of this penetrated Mrs Fleming's mind as she sat making coffee and trying to understand him. She had suggested coffee in lieu of the food that neither of them seemed to want, in a manner which allowed them to be silent while she made it.

Taken separately, people were not difficult, if one took the trouble to take them separately. It was people in relation to one another that baffled her. What had brought her daughter to her knees before this young man? She tried to consider this; but the jokes about village girls and bad limericks about abortionists . . . *mariages de convenance* . . . the very short-term bliss of ignorance, and fragments of the conversation she had had so late in the night with her husband, dispersed untidily . . . nothing, she felt, is so unhelpful as experience when it seems irrelevant . . . and she needed to be single-minded with a fixed point of view – like Pinero or Elgar.

With some curiosity, she asked: 'What do you expect me to say to you?'

'If I knew that, I should not be waiting here, because the whole thing would not seem so immensely difficult. I thought you would probably want to ask me more about it. You might just want to tell me how badly I have behaved towards your daughter.'

'Your assumption that Deirdre does not love you seems to me rather unfair.'

'Perhaps it is. Perhaps she does love me.'

His willingness to agree, shifted a little more moral ground under Mrs Fleming's feet. Morality, she felt, was like sand. She said:

'It seems to me something you should know. Presumably this child was an accident.'

He put his coffee cup carefully back in its saucer before replying, and, in the instant of his doing it, Mrs Fleming's heart sank.

'I'm sure that it was,' he said.

For the first time she really liked him.

'I think perhaps that I had better talk to Deirdre.'

'Oh.' She could not tell whether he was more apprehensive or relieved. 'Of course, she doesn't know that I have talked to you.'

'I suppose she would mind that very much,' said Mrs Fleming.

'I'm afraid so. Would it be at all possible for you to discover what is happening . . . I don't really know whether she talks to you I'm afraid . . .' he was tentative, apologetic.

'No, she does not talk to me at all, and that would be very difficult. I'll try, but something must be done about this you know. I cannot leave it because you are afraid that she will be angry with you. Deirdre is only nineteen.'

'I only meant that if I am to marry her, it would be better not to start with her feeling . . .'

'But you *have* talked to me behind her back. Much better

tell her that yourself. I shall do everything I can to persuade her *not* to marry you.'

He looked astounded.

'My dear Mr Vale,' Mrs Fleming said gently, 'it is not possible to teach children not to make the classical mistakes. But children should not be brought into the world at all for reasons of social blackmail or moral compensation: only if they are wanted by the people who beget them. I do know this. Neither the children nor the parents ever recover from the guilt of compulsion. You do not want to marry Deirdre, and you are therefore very unlikely to make her happy. You most certainly do not want this child. I shall try to make both these things very plain to her.'

There was a short silence, and then he stubbed out his cigarette and said: 'Yours is not a usual point of view. You seem, forgive me saying so, extremely certain.'

She answered: 'I have two very good reasons.' And for the first time he observed that she did not look at him.

They parted with mutual respect and relief; with Mrs Fleming promising to telephone Louis when she had seen Deirdre. ('The aspirin of social intercourse', somebody had once described the telephone to her.)

Now, she stood alone in the narrow hall. The little new air that the opening and shutting of the front door had introduced hurried round her, and then settled, with the faint tinkling of the small chandelier, to the weight and texture of the house: becoming not quite transparent, and not absolutely cold: an atmosphere with a suggestion of consommé, set in the familiar silence of a London house on a foggy afternoon.

In the basement, Dorothy, having dismissed the morning daily, would be sitting in an ancient basket chair seemingly made of brambles, as whenever she sat in it, it snarled her stockings and cardigans. She nevertheless refused to exchange it for anything more comfortable; and padded it from time to time with cushions filled with dust or oozing an occasional improbably exotic feather. In this chair she sat every afternoon of the week (except when she went to Brixton to see a sister suffering from mistaken, but absolutely intractable illusions of grandeur). She sat chain-smoking Goldflakes, with the wireless belching incessant quantities of entertainment and information: knitting some huge pale pink or lemon coloured garment which mysteriously disappeared on completion to be replaced by another (she was never seen wearing one). On a chair opposite her sat a colossal common cat. Both of them endured the wireless with impartial indifference – hoots of canned laughter – dreadful news – unintelligible plays – sentimental songs – jokes – orchestrated signature tunes – the vicarious excitement of football and racing commentaries – comforting heart-to-heart talks on silage, national health, or chicken incubators . . . not a muscle of their faces moved; no shred of the information they must both have absorbed ever escaped either of them, or appeared to influence their lives in any way.

At four o'clock, the wireless would be turned off, Dorothy would make tea, and the cat would leap lightly through a small and widely barred window.

Above the basement, however, the house was thickly quiet, patient and desolate. Mrs Fleming returned quickly to the drawing-room. The letter that she had written to her husband lay on her desk beside her diary. The diary reminded her that she was to have tea (that horrible unnecessary meal designed to make unsatisfied women still more unsatisfactory) with Mrs Stoker at Gloucester Place. The wedding was, after all, only a week off, and there was much to arrange. She had nearly two hours in which to start upon the immense and baffling task of clearing up.

As she climbed the further two flights to the top floor where Deirdre had slept until she had moved to the mews, and Julian had a room for six more nights, she reflected, a little wearily, that at least the house had always possessed far too many stairs . . .

4

TEN hours later, Mrs Fleming sat in her bedroom watching her daughter's mews. She sat in the dark, except for a small electric fire which burned with a heartless local heat and neither warmed nor illumined her.

It was long past midnight; she had left Deirdre nearly an hour ago, but the light in the mews still burned, and Mrs Fleming had reached a point of fatigue and anxiety when she felt constrained to watch a light which in reality could tell her nothing. If it was put out, or if it continued to burn, she would not really know whether Deirdre slept, or wept, or went out, or tried to do anything more desperate. The last, she told herself again, Deirdre would not do. Deirdre's unhappiness was an acutely vital business: she was half in love with it – she did not want it to end. She did not possess the matters of fact to render her hopeless. It was therefore futile to watch the light; but Mrs Fleming drew her coat round her shoulders and watched. It had been a frightful day. The panic and agony at the back of her mind had lain in wait for just such a moment as this – to catch her tired and alone, free of other people's superable problems. It had been a frightful day, she told herself soothingly, and this curiously comforted her.

She remembered that in her youth, she had been enjoined always to think of others less fortunate than herself; relativity in any misfortune had been employed as a successful counter-irritant by her family. She had always resisted the sadistic complacency of such a creed, but now, although she did not approach the dangers inherent in comparison, she was none the less thankful that there were people who patently needed thinking about.

After such a day, she could ruminate on the general predicament of mothers and daughters: June and her mother, and she with Deirdre. The ghastly sterility behind the scene she had witnessed between Mrs Stoker and June at tea had struck her with terrifying force. They had seemed two women bound together, having in common nothing in particular, and everything in general; who, were they not related, would not willingly have spent five minutes in each other's company; but who, because of their relationship, had spent nineteen years, irritating, modifying, interfering with, decrying and depending upon each other. The scene had begun by Mrs Stoker announcing with a kind of angry roguishness that she knew how June had spent the previous afternoon; and had ended, interminable minutes later, with June scarlet and near to tears, crying why shouldn't she go to a cinema if she wanted to, she had her own life to lead – and leaving the room. As she had returned soothing noises to Mrs Stoker's circle of apologies, excuses, and aggression, Mrs Fleming had tried to consider her relationship with Deirdre; but what she found she felt about her own daughter appeared so uncertain and intangible, that she had stopped in fright. She felt simply unhappy, embarrassed and inadequate; and very much afraid for Deirdre. (She also made a private resolution never again to have tea with Mrs Stoker in her beige and peach-pink flat.)

Now she had seen Deirdre – they had gone through the whole business – they had broken down fence after fence of suspicion and reserve, and found nothing but a waste of tears and shame. For Deirdre's utter inability to see the affair in relation to anyone but herself had filled Mrs Fleming with a kind of miserable shame which amounted almost to revulsion. She discovered that she was caring about her daughter with deliberation; finding reasons for her love, bolstering it with all the protective sense she possessed. This, she was well aware, was not what Deirdre wanted. Deirdre had seemed to expect a violent parental outcry, emotional, and totally uncomprehending, of what she evidently considered to be uniquely mitigating factors of her affair. 'You don't understand!' she had cried over and over again: long after, if she had thought about it, she must have seen that Mrs Fleming did.

Louis, whom Deirdre described as heartless (Mrs Fleming suspected that this was part of his attraction), had assessed both Deirdre's nature and the situation with surprising accuracy. It was impossible, Mrs Fleming thought wearily, not to blame herself for the whole affair. One wanted children; had them, and brought them up: and then, in spite of all the calculations of time and care, they defeated one by producing a result which seemed, to say the least, almost mathematically incorrect. It was Deirdre's attitude that demoralized her: this wilful manipulation of circumstances, followed by complete subjection to them. She had wanted to shake Deirdre – to utter some of the bracing platitudes with which her own youth had been so frequently braced. She remembered that at one point she had said things of the kind: had earnestly implored Deirdre to pull herself together, to think a little about Louis and the child; to remember that life seldom finished for anyone at nineteen – above all to control herself and *think*. Deirdre had stared at her with resentful streaming eyes, and then reiterated that if Louis was really determined not to marry her – if he couldn't see how desperately right that would be – she would still have the child, because she would never love anyone else, and at least then she would have the child: adding inconsequently that a lot of very nice people were illegitimate, so if Mummy fussed about that . . .

Apart from what either of them felt about illegitimacy, Mrs Fleming had interrupted, there was the question of supporting and educating the child: bastards, in her opinion, tended to be rather more expensive than the ordinary kind – if one was to protect them adequately from that section of society unable to distinguish between cause and effect. Deirdre had seemed thoroughly shocked.

'You are talking like Papa! *Have* you talked to him?'

'Of course not,' Mrs Fleming had replied; and caught herself wondering for how many years she would have said 'of course'. From that moment, however, things had seemed a little easier between them: until Mrs Fleming, after a general discourse on the folly of marrying without mutual enthusiasm, had made the mistake of mentioning that Louis was not absolutely unprepared to marry Deirdre, if Deirdre really saw no alternative. Then they were off again: 'Why not? Why *not*?' and more tears. But Mrs Fleming saw that Deirdre's ground had shifted, had dissolved a little; and began to see her reasonably, as very young, and pregnant, and pathetic.

After some comforting, however, Deirdre's pendulum had swung again: she blew her nose defiantly and said:

'Of course I could marry Miles,' and when her mother simply stared at her, trying to think who on earth Miles was – she said: '*You* know Miles. He's been around for ages wanting to marry me – *he* doesn't mind anything: he wouldn't even mind Louis's child.'

Mrs Fleming said sharply:

'Have you told him about it?'

'No: but of course I would if I married him. It would be all right I suppose as long as he didn't get *duller* married, but I've an awful feeling that he would and then I might literally *die* of boredom.'

This necessitated more desperate advice; giving it, she did not feel that it would be taken, but having given it she thought that perhaps her daughter had merely been determined to shock her at all costs.

It had all ended by Deirdre promising to consider carefully everything that her mother had said. Mrs Fleming had tried very hard to get her to sleep in the house that night, but had failed so immediately, that she thought it wiser not to persist. She had left Deirdre with two sleeping pills and a box of cigarettes.

Back in the house, she had attempted to telephone Louis, but had found him out.

No, certainly she could not tell Deirdre.

This meant another letter to her husband. The thought of writing again to him faintly nauseated her, recalling the Duchesse de Praslin; but at least, she reflected, *her* letters enjoyed the dignity of the post . . .

5

THE very early morning was the worst time: the frightful half-conscious moments when catching up with the present – becoming awake and aware – lacerated sleep; when half the mind craved oblivion and the delusions surrounding it, and the other half struggled and sought for complete consciousness, until the whole painful situation took possession of mind and body; the present day leapt suddenly into life, and as suddenly, sleep was gone. It was then that she would find herself in tears, which seemed terrible to her because she could not remember their beginning. Then, she found, she wept because she found herself weeping . . .

She lay, watching the ribs of shallow sunlight which fell listlessly on the carpet, trying to make them symmetrical, or to complete some pattern: encouraging her mind with all the minute detail of the room that she could see or hear without turning her head, as though she was ill or a prisoner. The Morris wallpaper of green leaves and clear red berries which she had chosen years ago in a determined effort to make this room, at least, uncompromisingly her own (William Morris, her husband had then said, made him howl with laughter), was remarkably satisfying. When she felt safer, and steadier, she could risk looking at her watch, or finding a handkerchief: it was odd how the smallest movement made too soon after tears provoked them again.

It was seven o'clock, and she found her handkerchief.

In the bath, she found herself, via random speculation on Deirdre and Julian, facing the next hurdle with which her particular brand of introspective honesty was bound to face her. She had wondered whether Deirdre and Julian would ever succeed, if they were to try, in communicating to each other their feelings about Louis and June: and had come to the conclusion that they would fail, or that they would not try, because their ideas and requirements concerning people were utterly dissimilar. Then, suddenly, as she was idly turning over the thought that the word 'love' had as many implications as the word 'light', her mind was blocked by the petrifying fear that the first word meant nothing to her – absolutely nothing. What, for instance, did she feel for her husband, about whom she was extremely unhappy? Did she love him? Or was she subject simply to fear and pride: of being left alone, and of other people seeing this happen to her? She had been taught, she realized, to regard life in four stages. One stored extreme youth, in order to expend it in the twenties; and one banked the middle part of one's life, in order that one might live on a minimum of the accrued interest in one's old age. One was, in fact, permitted a butterfly extravagance with youth or beauty or pleasure for a shorter time in relation to one's whole life than a butterfly in relation to its metamorphosis from an egg to a caterpillar to a chrysalis. There was something wrong somewhere. But then, she had never regarded marriage, or ideal marriage, or perhaps simply her own marriage, in the light of saving up, or banking.

While she dressed, she reflected that after twenty-three years she could hardly expect her husband to desire her – even were she as desirable as she knew she had been twenty-three years ago: that it would be indeed remarkable if after twenty-three years there were segments of her mind which he had not either thoroughly assimilated or ignored because he disapproved of them; that her accomplishments during that time had progressed by the twilight of nature, and thus imperceptibly – there was no sudden glare or sunlight of achievement upon her ability now to run two houses and bring up two children, to decorate herself, or anything surrounding her: that Mr Carroll's penetrating remark about running very hard to stay in the same place applied to marriage as to so much else; but that the achievement of this naturally got one nowhere; and that therefore there was no earthly reason why she should expect the same man to continue spending a day in her ageing and familiar company.

She breakfasted, and dispatched Julian. There was a postcard from Leila Talbot which she said she had written ages ago and forgotten to post asking her to a cocktail party that evening. Mrs Fleming noticed that she was asked by herself, and wondered how long this had been so, or whether Leila knew that now this was the way she should always be asked to parties. The curtains in Deirdre's flat were still drawn. Dorothy was in a bad temper about the number of silver-fish that wriggled deathlessly all over the basement. These curious creatures appeared from nowhere at unspecified intervals, infuriating Dorothy, and delighting her cat, who killed them by dozens with a kind of oriental dispassionate intensity.

Mrs Fleming arranged for the death of the silver-fish, and went to the very top of her house, to the floor where Julian and Deirdre kept their possessions. For two hours she struggled with the infantile, schoolgirl, and adolescent welter of her daughter's things. Objects such as a one-eyed rather nebulous animal called Strickland were revealed (she recalled how passionately Deirdre had wanted to be renamed Strickland); a scrap-book half-filled with pressed wild flowers, little jars filled with green dust (a relic of the days when Deirdre had feverishly made face-cream from white of egg, and sold it to unsuspecting and spotty school friends); a letter from a quite hideous little boy who had lived across the square, saying that he was collecting enough string to tie her to a tree in Kensington Gardens; a brush and comb bag embroidered with Mrs Fleming's initials, in red and green – unfinished – and stuck with a rusty needle; four mercifully unfinished diaries (she did not read more than the first sentence of each): 'Elizabeth Tomkinson will always be my greatest nearest friend.' 'I am afraid that I am more sensitive than anyone else I know,' and so on. Mrs Fleming threw them away. There were boxes and boxes of clothes, half-knitted jerseys, unstrung beads, lipstick cases, and theatre programmes. These, she felt, must be sorted by Deirdre herself. Almost everything was either half broken or half finished. When she had reached the gymkhana ballet era of Deirdre's life, Dorothy suddenly appeared with a cup of warm brown tea – a mark of forgiveness and solicitude which Mrs

Fleming knew she must accept to the dregs. Dorothy felt that people *ought* to want tea: if they refused it, they did not know what was good for them; they were poorly, and needed more tea than ever. She stood over Mrs Fleming now, repeating everything she had said about the silver-fish; to show Mrs Fleming that she was no longer angry, but that the silver-fish had been important enough to warrant anger two hours ago. Dorothy's cat, who always accompanied her, ostensibly out of affection, but really, Mrs Fleming thought, with the subconscious desire to trip her up, had gone comfortably to sleep in a cardboard lid on John Gielgud and some metal hair curlers. 'I'll leave my boy with you,' Dorothy said, pretending that she had any control over him, and departed.

Mrs Fleming slowly drank the tea, and permitted the other side of her mind its elaborate (and, she secretly felt, more convincing) point of view. Why should anybody expect to collect one either in the prime of life, or, worse, before one had had time to reach a prime, cut a pattern for one, pin one down for years and years until one had entirely become a compromise of their original ideal, and their increasing indifference; if at the end, one found oneself the wrong creature in solitude? It was too late to mourn any private intentions she might once have had towards herself – she had been loved, and touched and fashioned; dominated, protected, and ignored, until even her enjoyment of the wallpaper that her husband despised was coloured by the fact that he despised it. Even the few occasions when she had thought that she had asserted herself were direct results of her association with him. The wear and pull and take of human relations suddenly appalled her: she did not feel able, at forty-three, to assume an equal share of responsibility about them. It is fatal, she thought, to grow up with anybody: one must remain young with them, or begin old. I was not grown up when I married – I was very little older than Deirdre – different, but very little older. I could manage the whole situation now, if only I could start at the beginning: what is difficult, is the end of a situation that I began so badly.

Dorothy called reproachfully that Miss June was on the

telephone. Mrs Fleming, who had heard it ring, apologized for not hearing, and went down to speak to her future daughter-in-law.

In spite of the fact that she spent a great deal of her life on the telephone, June used the instrument rather as a means to general than specific communication. This, for anyone who disliked telephones, was one of her most tiresome habits: Mrs Fleming, who had not previously encountered it, was now plunged into a stream of disjointed small talk; apologies for not having written about the dinner party, speculations about the forthcoming wedding, and even a short account of the canker in Angus's ears. Among all this, Mrs Fleming gathered that June had to go that afternoon to the new flat where various irrevocable decisions about its decoration must be made: that Julian was unable or unwilling to accompany her; that they did not agree about pink or cream distemper; and that in any case June felt unable alone to select either a pink or a cream. As she had not yet seen the flat, June thought that perhaps Mrs Fleming might be free that afternoon to look at it and advise her. It would be frightful if, by herself, she went and chose the wrong pink or cream. Mrs Fleming accepted this depressing aesthetic responsibility, wondering how many years ago she would passionately have persuaded June to use and enjoy colour.

During luncheon, a woman, nearly in tears, and with a Viennese accent, telephoned and asked for Mr Fleming. On hearing that he was away, she uttered some tragic exclamation in German, broke down altogether, and rang off.

Mrs Fleming arrived at the flat before June.

The third floor could be reached by a lift, which resembled a cavity in a tooth; exuding an air of breathless discomfort which, she felt, would ascend a pinnacle of agony if she touched it. She walked up, and, having rung the bell, stood in a draughty vomit-coloured gloom, mentally adding unpunctuality to her knowledge of June.

June arrived panting in a pink woollen dress and a beaver lamb coat that was a little too short for her. She groped about in her bag for the latch-key, explaining and apologizing; feverishly at a disadvantage. She had vaguely meant Mrs Fleming to be reassured and gratified by this plan of seeing the flat, and now it was all going wrong: she was not, as her mother would put it 'gaining Mrs Fleming's confidence', or approval, or anything of the kind. Her mother constantly said, 'Oh June, don't be so *silly*'; and now, when she least wanted to, here she was being very silly indeed – oh thank *goodness*, the key – but she was by then so nervous that she was unable to turn it in the lock.

Mrs Fleming, remembering the scene at tea with Mrs Stoker, and conscience-stricken at her conclusions before June's arrival, opened the door for her, and they entered the flat.

It was small; it was cheerless; it was unexpectedly dark. The three rooms were so designed that any piece of furniture of the slightest use must either crowd or ridicule their proportions. It would, Mrs Fleming thought, afford passable comfort for people about four feet high. She exhausted herself, however, by creating the flat's advantages to June, who, in turn, pointed out such disabilities as she could envisage: these were varied, and surprising, in that none of them had occurred to Mrs Fleming, and now stuck the needle of her taste into the groove of June's practical requirements. They both wanted so desperately to be kind.

When they had thoroughly surveyed the dirty almost empty rooms, they perched uncertainly upon a pair of trestles left by the decorators in the bedroom, and June produced shade cards of distemper and paint. The colours began with those suited to the strings of pastel wooden beads which confound so many small babies; proceeded to a selection of the heartless vivacity associated with tiny village sweets; and ended with the monumental drabness, the grandiose olive, mud, and damp chocolate, endured in so many institutions. There was, as June said, so very much to choose from – although one honestly wouldn't actually be able to *live* with very many of the shades. Mrs Fleming suggested mixing a colour and getting it matched, but June, clearly terrified at the idea, said that there was no time, as the painters had to start work the next morning, if the decoration was to be finished by the time she and Julian returned from Paris.

A silence ensued, during which June fingered unpleasantly possible pinks, and Mrs Fleming noticed her pretty nails. Eventually, as it seemed that the silence was not to be broken by a choice being made, Mrs Fleming, after the impulse of finding them attractive had waned, remarked on the pretty nails.

June blushed deeply, and dropped the shade card on to the floor.

'Oh, honestly, they aren't really. I mean Julian hasn't noticed them.'

'I'm sure that he has.' Mrs Fleming detected that the nails might be symbolic, and that the fact that Julian had not observed their attraction had rushed suddenly into June's mind, tugging a stream of similar omissions in its wake. She intended reassurance, but she was immediately confounded.

June had descended from her trestle to pick up the card which had skidded out of reach across the dirty parquet floor. Now she seemed to crumple, she was actually on the floor, twisting the card in her hands, and looking away from Mrs Fleming.

'I do sometimes feel,' she said, attempting to weight her sudden panic with the appearance of habit, 'sometimes – not always, of course – that he ought to notice things like – well, anything that he finds . . .' the card fell on to her lap, 'I mean people *always* notice what is bad about one, don't they? Even if they don't *say* anything, they notice everything. And if, when people marry, they don't notice any of the good things – at the beginning, I mean – then they'll just get used to them, and only notice the bad things. It's something that has been worrying me for a long time,' she added hesitantly, having just discovered what had been worrying her.

Mrs Fleming, treading water very gently, said:

'People very seldom say all that they feel.'

'But how does one know that they feel anything?'

'Julian wants to marry you. You know that.'

'I don't believe he really does! I don't believe he really *wants me* at all! I might be anyone, and *he* might be anyone. It's – oh, awful!' Her eyes were so full of tears that it seemed impossible they should remain in her eyes.

Mrs Fleming, not daring to move, lest she unwittingly propel June still further out of her depths, sat silent.

'People don't – I thought that when two people were marrying each other they were frightfully happy. Like discovering something – oh, you know, marvellous. I thought that was the point of it: like the very end of books – not simply the next thing you do in your life – except with Julian I think it is.'

'You haven't begun your marriage yet: this is the worst part . . .'

But June turned suddenly to her like a creature whose instincts were at bay; a hunted exhausted expression which utterly subdued any such middle-aged claptrap, and shamed Mrs Fleming out of continuing it.

'I'm not at all clever or interesting. I'm not beautiful, or even especially pretty. I do see all that quite clearly. I can't really see why he should want to marry me.' She found it difficult to speak: her slow painful blush spreading, it seemed, all over her body, as she saw more and more of herself for the first time in her life. 'But if he *does* want to marry me, surely he ought to find at least one particular reason? If I don't seem special to him in any kind of way, I shall always be the same, shan't I? And nobody will find anything special about me because it won't be there. He – he doesn't seem to *expect* anything – and Mummy says I'm dull, so I'm afraid – I'm afraid,' she repeated, and a tear dropped on to the colour card of paints. She ignored her tears with unexpected arrogance.

Mrs Fleming, recognizing this piece of honesty, took refuge in curiosity.

'Do you tell Julian why you want to marry him?'

'I?' She seemed really startled. 'I – I thought that I could – oh, cook, and things like that. Look after him, you know. It isn't that part of it – the separate bits of our lives. It's – living together – not his work, or this flat, but our *lives*. I don't mean bed, of course,' she added rapidly, and Mrs Fleming saw that she did not: that that aspect seemed set by itself; so mysteriously remote, so utterly unpredictable, that to June it was meaningless.

What was there to say? That they were like two people on a desert island – aware that food was a necessity, and consequently prepared to eat berries which might equally sustain or poison them? But they were not on a desert island. June, Mrs Fleming thought, is perhaps a pathetic version of the princess who must sleep until anyone cared to discover her – and then kiss her awake. But the princess's pride had been protected by the magic forest of brambles, and June had no such protection: a foolish mother who had no thought for her but marriage, and who therefore set her, without purpose or interest, in an arid waste where anyone might approach her – where she was no attainment, because even the most indifferent could attain her. But is Julian so indifferent? Have I been so foolish a parent that any household seems preferable to mine? Julian, however, had been free to live where he chose, and he had apparently chosen June. This act of folly, for so it appeared to her now, did not seem to be graced by a spark of romantic selection, desire, or bravado – seemed nothing more, as June had said, than the next thing these two were to do in their lives. They seemed to have no reason behind them; no intentions before, but simply to have drifted in a vacuum of social intercourse as close to one another as the vacuum would allow, with the consequences that society presumably expected of them.

Looking at June (she was frowning in an effort to check her tears which seemed now to have become the very texture of her face), Mrs Fleming wondered what on earth was expected of either of them. The fundamental unnecessity of the situation perplexed her, but her proximity to Julian, and now to June, prevented her from objective criticism. 'What a piece of work is a man,' indeed – but one could not criticize any piece of work with which one was not in sympathy, and here all she could do was cry down their marriage, without, at least in June's case, presenting her with an alternative. However, there seemed nothing else to be done; and, very hesitantly, she suggested that, in view of June's uncertainty about Julian's feelings, and even, Mrs Fleming ventured, possibly June's feelings about the whole affair, it might perhaps be wise to postpone the marriage until . . . But here the appearance of June forestalled her. She looked as though someone was attempting to take a toy, of which she was very afraid, away from her.

'Oh no!' she cried; and, 'It's all ***arranged***! I didn't mean . . .' She got up, and walked to the window.

'You must think me frightfully silly,' she said a moment later, and Mrs Fleming's heart sank.

'No, I did not think that, at all.'

'Saying all those awful things. After all, you are Julian's mother.' This, almost as though Mrs Fleming had been deliberately concealing the fact.

For a moment Mrs Fleming considered retorting that indeed she was, and for that reason was justifiably anxious; but she realized, before the sentence cleared her mind, the danger of saying anything of the kind. The marriage would go forward; and June would merely be convinced that her mother-in-law opposed it. She could perhaps talk to Julian – a prospect which filled her with weary alarm, as she had not attempted it since the night before he went to prep school – but here and now she must perforce revert to clap-trap. She rose to her feet.

'Not at all,' she said. 'Everyone gets exhausted with being engaged. I remember feeling exactly the same.'

June glanced at her uncertainly, but Mrs Fleming's face preserved a good-natured blank which comfortably reduced June's earlier revelations to a small (but understandable) display of nerves.

It remained to choose the pink or cream. June, whose judgement was now apparently reinforced, selected the cream for the drawing-room and pink for the bedroom. 'It's a compromise!' she exclaimed to Mrs Fleming as though presenting her with an original triumphant achievement.

She really is awfully understanding for a mother-in-law, June thought relaxing in her cab. She felt *much* better: oh, as though there had been a thunderstorm, or she'd passed an examination at school, or arranged some flowers and somebody had asked whether Mummy had done them (Mummy was absolutely *wonderful* with flowers).

Mrs Fleming, having successfully evaded sharing a taxi with June, drove back to Campden Hill Square, repeating again and again with a kind of horrified revulsion: 'I did *not* feel like that. I *never* felt like it. I did not: I did *not*.'

6

LEILA TALBOT gave cocktail parties distinguished, so far as Mrs Fleming was concerned, in one respect. With remarkably few exceptions, they were attended by a stream of people one had never met at her house before, and who, experience proved, one would never meet again. Mrs Fleming, having gone to parties at Pelham Crescent for nearly twenty years, had by now run her speculative gamut about them: she had assumed that Leila must give parties every night, and wondered how she contrived to have so many friends; she had once, before a bad attack of influenza, conceived the morbid notion that they were all really the same people whom she was unable to identify or remember; she had considered the statistics of cocktail party gate-crashing – but with all these reflections, and many too idle to record, she had never reached any satisfactory conclusion. What mystified her most was the way these ceaseless streams of guests seemed to know their hostess with exactly the same enigmatic degree of intimacy: it was impossible to tell whether they also had known her for twenty years, or whether they had merely met her the previous week. Sometimes, Mrs Fleming thought that they had perhaps known her very well twenty years *ago* – had perhaps played together as children – but then she reflected that even Leila could hardly have played with, and then reassembled, quite so many and such diverse people (apart from their hostess, they had little in common). It was possible, occasionally, to observe some specific professional or cultural undertow; such as doctors when Leila had been working as an almoner and playing a lot of golf – or architects when, after her husband's death, she had nearly built a house in the Isle of Wight (in order, Mr Fleming had remarked, that she might more decently conceal her lack of grief). There was usually one man, whose satisfied isolation from everybody else – whose apparent lack of personality coupled to his rather eager familiarity with the contents of the cocktail cabinet – proclaimed him to the interested and observant as Leila's current lover. Leila invariably called him 'darling', whoever he was, and never introduced him to anybody. He moved about the room in an anonymous haze – he always knew where everything was, from angostura to the lavatory – and, *he* was hardly ever the same man from party to party – which was confusing to the observant, although they might have comforted themselves with the oral reflection that Leila never called two people 'darling' at one party.

There were about a dozen people assembled when she arrived, only one of whom she knew, as having vaguely occupied the background of Leila's life; a bright thin stringy woman, parched with sunburn, looking now with her dry bleached hair like an old little girl of fourteen; although she had herself told Mrs Fleming that she had had two husbands and four children.

The professional undertow at this party seemed to be cultural administration of one kind or another: people were being introduced to each other either as Mr Gordion the painter, who was now engaged upon organizing the exhibition of British Sea Shells for the '51 Festival – or, alternatively, as Mr White, who, having run the house organs for the Ministries of Wealth and Welfare during the war, and been Secretary to the Association for the Prevention of Internal Anxiety after it, was now entrusted with the delicate task of designing a ton of plastic tropical fish, to be dropped from aeroplanes on to the artificial lakes in public parks at the opening of the Festival.

Mrs Fleming, having met four people engrossed in discussing these and similar activities, having refused three cigarettes and accepted a glass of Tio Pepe from a sallow little man whose anonymity was if anything enhanced by a soft ginger beard, found herself sitting in a large armchair, on one arm of which perched Leila's stringy friend.

'But it's ages since I *rode* a bicycle!' she was exclaiming, throwing one stringy little leg over the other, and staring brightly into the face of an enormous man in a bow tie and striped trousers, who laughed with a kind of baritone lechery and said, 'You should try, my dear Esmé, you should try.'

More people were arriving, and Leila forestalled the ginger beard's determination to offer Mrs Fleming her fourth cigarette. 'She doesn't smoke, darling. See if Nanny has managed to open the American nuts.'

Somebody standing alone by the fireplace threw a half-smoked cigarette sharply into the fire. The gesture caught Mrs Fleming's attention, reminding her suddenly of Deirdre after dinner two nights ago. It had been, she realized, the beginning of all the subsequent revelations: the first occasion of Deirdre's distress, which even then, had meant almost nothing. Now, a cigarette thrown away unfinished had for her a private significance, which means, she thought, that in a room containing approximately fifteen people, the private significances must occur in such quantity as to drive Providence mad . . .

Leila interrupted her with a young couple called Fenwick who had just arrived. 'They're house-hunting, and are mad about Campden Hill.'

Mrs Fleming found herself embarked upon a discussion of houses in that area. The Fenwicks were recently married, and frequently said so. It seemed the only fact of which they were sure, as the necessity they evidently felt for substituting 'we' for 'I', made both of them so tentative, hesitant, and self-conscious, that their plans and requirements were a perpetual compromise.

Mrs Fleming politely battled with the pair of them, feeling that they would be much better alone together, or alone separately, until they had learned how to be together with other people; feeling also more and more like a social worker, until the arrival even of Leila's twelve-year-old daughter brought a merciful relief.

Mrs Fleming could never believe that Maureen was as unattractive as she looked: she looked like a small pig dressed by Daniel Neal; but her repertoire of unattractiveness was considerably more extensive than any pig's. She now stood bulging and hostile in front of Mrs Fleming.

'What foul earrings,' she remarked; 'just like bird's mess – give me some of that.'

Mrs Fleming favoured her with her famous glassy stare reserved for revolting children, and did not reply; but young Mr Fenwick smiled weakly and said: 'It's not good for little girls.'

'Go on, give me some. You'll be drunk if you drink all that. Give me the olive, then.'

Mr Fenwick gave her the olive. He wanted his wife to see how good he was with children. Maureen ate it, and spat the stone back into his glass. 'It looks like a piece of rat's mess in your glass. I say, have you noticed the piece of rat's mess in your glass?' Delighted with this, she proceeded round the room extracting other people's olives, and repeating her performance with them. The Fenwicks smiled guardedly at one another, and murmured something about a difficult age.

'Nonsense!' Mrs Fleming heard herself say – so clearly above the room's conversation – that in some confusion she turned away from the Fenwicks to meet the eye of someone standing across the room by the fireplace. He gazed at her for a moment with enquiring interest: she felt that he had heard her say 'Nonsense!' and that he faintly wanted to know what she found so positively nonsensical; then somebody moved and he was obscured from her.

The Fenwicks had retreated: culturally administrative talk hemmed her in, and she felt isolated in the midst of the noise.

'The beauty of the whole design is that it can be executed *entirely* in paper.'

There was an appreciative grunt.

'With a little plastic, of course.'

'Of course.'

'Of course, there was trouble with the insurance people, but I said to Braithwaite – you know Braithwaite?'

'We did all those posters on hygiene together.'

'Of *course* you did– Well I said to Braithwaite, "My dear chap, that's *your* department's job to departmentalize. Not mine." My department, I mean. I mean one cannot be eternally hamstrung on a point like selection of materials because another department can't delegate responsibility. What is Braithwaite *for*? I mean, we all know he's a good chap, keen and conscientious and all that, but he will *not* delegate. I don't know whether you found that with the hygiene job. He will try and do it all himself. Puts everyone's back up – after all, he's not *supposed* to *know* anything.'

'Good Lord, no!'

They both smiled indulgently, while the ginger beard filled up their glasses.

'But it's fascinating in the big cities. They walk up and down all night – literally all night, below one's windows, and one can't get a wink of sleep. They *never* go to bed.'

'My *dear* Esmé!'

She laughed brightly, and fitted a cigarette into her holder. 'I adored Spain. Every inch.'

Mrs Fleming accepted a second glass of sherry. She could see nobody to whom she wished to talk: indeed the room seemed fuller than usual of people she would prefer to leave unmet, but she felt she could hardly continue sitting in the most comfortable chair, drinking in a silence which in any case Leila would probably observe and inappropriately break. Perhaps she should go home and see Julian. She looked down at her sherry. At that moment, there was a loud thud, a sound of breaking glass, and a wail from Maureen. Everybody turned in the direction of the fireplace. Two people picked Maureen up, now howling and shouting, 'He tripped me up. You beast! You tripped me up!'

She was immediately removed bleeding at the nose by Leila. The room seemed clearer, and Mrs Fleming saw the man whose eye she had met, collecting pieces of glass off the carpet, and putting them into what looked like the *Radio Times*. It was only then that she identified him as the one who had thrown the cigarette into the fire. When he had finished, he ran his hand over the carpet, and rose slowly to his feet. He was tall, and immensely thin. Then he picked a cigarette-box off the mantelpiece and walked over to her.

'Do you smoke?'

'No, thank you.'

'Do you drink?'

'I don't smoke, because I do drink.' She indicated her glass.

'I must sit down.' He cast about him for an empty chair, which there was not. He picked a plate of nuts and a vase of flowers off a small table, gave the nuts to her, and put the flowers on the mantelpiece. When he returned, he had a glass in his hand.

'So do I. But I don't suppose you like nuts. Shall I put them on the floor?'

'Your talents in that direction are remarkably useful.'

He smiled then, rather tiredly, and said, 'Oh yes. I never spill things; I only trip them up, or dispose of them.'

There was an amiable silence between them. Then he said:

'I don't find alcohol very insulating.'

She noticed that he was drinking brandy. 'Do you want to be insulated?'

His hand, which had lain stretched out along the arm of her chair, closed up, and he said: 'Well, yes, at times. Everybody wants to be insulated at times.'

'From what?'

'Oh – from "the thousand natural shocks", I suppose.' He had retracted altogether; he had decided not to talk about that. He smiled.

His hands were very large, but unmuscular: with long bony

fingers; not a good or a bad shape, but noticeable, because they were unusually large, and in proportion.

Someone was extolling Ernest Hemingway's new book, and someone else was decrying it. They listened for a minute; then Mrs Fleming said: 'Somebody told me that he was writing another book, but that in the middle of it he was told that he had only a little while to live, so he abandoned the first work, and wrote a second: and now he has been told that he will not die.'

He looked up suddenly, and she saw that he was both astonished and angry. 'How do you know that?'

'I do not know. I cannot even remember who told me. I don't expect that it is true.'

'In any case, his state of mind – or body, can have nothing to do with the intrinsic merit of the work. Either it is a good book, or a bad one. Whether he was dying when he wrote it, or thought himself dying, can have nothing to do with the book afterwards.'

Mrs Fleming said mildly: 'If it was true, it must have had a good deal to do with the book while he was writing it.' She could not understand what she had said that had so disturbed him. 'Anyway, I have not read it. Do you write books?'

'No. I wrote one book a long time ago; a reference book, bristling with information that nobody wants, and so heavy that the average student would not have wanted to lug it home from the library. The kind of book one finds being auctioned by the yard at sales. It cost twenty-five shillings even then, and was fearfully dull. Before I wrote it, I used to wonder who wrote them.' He had a habit of smiling when he had finished speaking: the rather tired illumination of his features was his full stop.

'What was it about?'

He considered her gravely for a moment. 'No, if I tell you, it will spoil the story. You do not write books?' He was not really asking her; he was sure she did not.

'No. I don't do anything. My life is rather an indirect business.'

Again, she saw him regarding her with a shock of interest or enquiry (what was it – passionate curiosity, disapproval, agreement with what was surely this time a rather gauche remark?). At any rate she found these sudden halts, with the full weight of his mind upon her, a little unnerving, and, as she turned away from him silently, he spoke.

'It is clear to me that you do not like nuts.' He disposed of them. 'Would you prefer dinner?'

'Thank you, but I am already dining. Do you know the time?'

'I no longer wear a watch, but I'll find out.'

Before he had returned, Leila was upon her, saying:

'Lunch, we simply must have lunch; but I suppose it will have to be after the wedding. What a thoroughly nice girl – how *sensible* of Julian. You must be so relieved. Did you meet Erasmus White? I meant you to – over there, not listening to Percy. Twenty-five to eight, darling. I won't keep you – I *so* understand how you feel about punctuality.'

So when he returned, she knew the time.

She told him that she was going, and wished for a fleeting instant that she was not. They shook hands; and then he said with an impassivity that made the words more startling:

'Of course, no amount of alcohol would insulate either of us as we are at present.'

She stared at him, wanting to laugh at or dislike him, but she could do neither; she was simply, horribly, afraid: she was so frozen with terror, that she could not withdraw her hand.

'So am I,' he said gently, 'but there is nothing whatever that we can do about it.'

Even the ancient taxi she picked up at South Kensington failed to jolt her into any sense of reality. All the way to Campden Hill she sat with the immediate effect of his words continuing – not ending and beginning again in her mind, but continuing at the same pitch; without allowing her to draw the breath of memory, without her being aware even of time rushing past her, or streets accumulating behind her; making some distance between the moment when she had heard him speak, and now, when she remembered what he had said.

Her taxi drew up behind Julian's car: she paid her fare and let herself into the house. There was a letter from her husband on the ebony table. As she slit open the envelope, Julian and Dorothy appeared on the stairs above and below her. Julian said:

'Awfully sorry, Mamma, but something's cropped up. I've told Dorothy. I say, what's the matter? You look *awful*!' Then he saw Dorothy, and added: 'I shan't be late. See you later, perhaps,' and almost ran out of the house.

Dorothy, who was brandishing a blue envelope, said: 'Dinner is ready, but I'll give you a few minutes. Miss Deirdre came round and left this. She asked me to tell you that she's gone away to the country for a few days – to *think*, she said.' Dorothy frequently made it clear how much she disapproved of both practices, and now lingered, ready to discourse on her aversion from the country, and her contempt of thought – Deirdre's coupling of the two providing her with an unique opportunity, but Mrs Fleming simply plodded silently upstairs, a letter in each hand.

She read her husband's letter in her bedroom, sitting in front of her looking-glass. He said nothing of his intentions about Julian's wedding, but simply asked her to lunch with him at what she recognized to be his dreariest and least frequented club. She put the letter back in its envelope. 'You look *awful*!' Julian had said. She remembered, suddenly, Tolstoy's remark about Karenin being 'offensively, disgustingly' unhappy; smelling to heaven in his grief at Anna's departure. This must be true, and not simply of Karenin, or that man (even now she did not know his name) would not have said what he had said at the end of Leila's party. It must be true of her, for all her age, her experience, her life behind her. She was a positive freak of unhappiness – indecent, and absurd – she should not be seen: it forced people either to conceal their discomfort, or it exposed her to the humiliation of their pity which they must feel that she did not really deserve. Dependence is not pretty after twenty. Crustacean self-containment was the order of her years: a self-containment, progressing until the passing dignity of death had been accomplished. At over forty one was no longer lightly accorded excuses for grief, for illness, for any frightened demands one might attempt of other people. One was supposed to have found a place in the world, and if one had not, the world ignored one's failure, and put one into what it regarded as one's place. Even when she was being most hysterically unhappy, Deirdre contrived to appear attractive: her beauty mysteriously justifying the pity and protection she evoked. (Have I appeared as I did just now to Julian—*all day*?)

Her eyes strained at her eyes in the glass; in this light they seemed to have died, were almost without colour; and they had once looked the imperishable origin, the very height, the immortality, of blue. She had learned – years ago now – to continue looking at people after she had spoken to them; thus she had been able to say the simplest things and invest them with a beauty, significance, or a wit, which everyone had been eager to believe. She had been able, as the books say, 'to shun admiration', because she had been so sure of it that she was enabled to select. The intricate, the elaborate, homage given to a fascinating and intelligent woman had been hers; and she seemed now to herself never to have enjoyed it, to have been barely conscious of it.

And now, even such private ruminations were despicable; she found them not even pathetic; to have lived her life on the timbre of her voice or the colour of her eyes seemed commonplace extravagance, deserving nothing. Many people had to live without such ephemeral qualities. (But they were not the whole reason for my existence – at no time in my life were they that: they were simply – attributes – which I did not waste. *He* did not marry me for my eyes or my voice – although perhaps without their attractions he would not have observed me. I was provided with greater choice, and so there is now perhaps less excuse for my having chosen wrongly. Or more excuse?)

Dorothy was ringing the little clamorous handbell which Julian had brought her from Geneva. Mrs Fleming rose from her dressing-table, and the blue envelope fell to the floor.

Deirdre's writing sprawled reproachfully at her: wearily, she opened it.

Darling Mummy,

I am just off to the country. Miles is taking me to somewhere called Burford where we can stay for a bit and I can think things over. I've told him everything and he wants to marry me immediately – but of course I must think seriously before doing that – so we are going to stay away a week while I think. Miles is really *frightfully* kind which is much more important than a good many things, and he's terribly understanding about the whole thing. Of course it will mean starting one's life again – completely washing out everything that has ever happened to me, but I do feel safe with Miles and I shall have the baby. I'm sorry about missing Julian's wedding but June seems to me so *enfantile* that honestly I can't see why he's doing it and this does seem more important. I'll send him a telegram. She doesn't like me anyway and I'm sure Miles would *loathe* her – he likes people to be more interesting than him which is rather sweet of him. Miles said that he wants to meet you when we come back. Don't be put off if he doesn't say a *word* – he's frightfully shy about meeting people – it really is an ordeal for him and he loathes it. He never talks much anyway. Thank you a million times for trying to help.

Love,
DEIRDRE

Don't tell Papa, but his birthday cheque will be madly useful for shapeless garments for me! Now I must fly to start my new life.

The letter was dated '4 p.m.'. She put it back in its envelope. Nothing now was needed to endorse her sense of futility and failure. She knew dimly – dumbly – that she would try to prevent Deirdre leaping into this fresh classical disaster, and knew also that she would fail. The blackmail of the alternative was too strong – the lure of a 'new life' too potent.

The war-time, music hall, American phrase (she did not know its origin) 'Where do we go from here?' slipped neatly into her mind like a coin into a slot machine which was empty, for she had no answer. The desire to go backwards, to retire into her life she knew, was very strong. But she was living; and so unable to escape from the passionate gravity of the present, which physically, is always now.

So, she went downstairs to dine alone.

If she had known then, however, how to find the man who had so frightened her at Leila's party, she would then have gone to him. But she did not know.

Dorothy had cleared the second place from the table.

My new life, she thought, and sat down to it.

PART TWO

1942

1

'The situation is perfectly simple. All you have to do is to meet me from the 7.38 at Euston.'

Thus Mr Fleming on a trunk call from the previous night from goodness knows where. Indeed, put like that, what could be simpler? With the world at war, meticulously grinding vast cities exceeding small; with such catastrophes as Singapore and Dunkirk behind one; with such feats of administration and of the spirit as the fifth column in France or the battle of the RAF over Britain; with the ubiquitous removal of men, women, and children into more or less danger as the immense situation demanded; with the value of lives rocketing up and down like shares on a crazy stock market – the mere meeting of a train seemed almost inanely simple. Mrs Fleming slung her gas-mask over her shoulder, delved in her bag for her torch, and went to meet the 7.38.

She picked up a taxi in Holland Park. Of course he had meant her to meet him in the car, but he did not realize that the petrol ration would not begin to last for the journey up from Kent and back. He would be annoyed about it, and he would be exasperated at the explanation. He would, she reflected, almost prefer the car to have blown up than to have run out of petrol. The worst of her (very representative) war-time existence was that it did not efficiently provide for even such a small emergency as a trunk call from her husband. Their house near Tenterden now contained Deirdre, and the little girl who was parked on them for the war; three convalescent naval officers, one badly shell-shocked; a bombed-out mother and her terrified and dirty family of three; and Dorothy, to whom even a succession of invalid young men did not compensate for the horror of living in the country. There was also a glamorous, sulky, and altogether improbable Land Girl. Each of these ill-assorted, more or less unhappy people constituted an emergency of one kind or another; and while it is generally agreed that a crisis often brings out the best in people, and in particular, the British Press constantly averred, of the British people, the crisis was usually assumed to be of a few hours', or perhaps days', duration. The duration of the war, however, already an immense quantity of time, yawned and stretched before Mrs Fleming now as drearily as old age and death; and everybody in her household (with the possible exception of the children) had long ceased to live up to their new-found national characteristic of being magnificent in a crisis.

Mrs Fawcett *might*, she supposed, have been magnificent the night her house was bombed; indeed, poor woman, she was reputed, though garrulous, to have behaved with a presence of mind, which had had, none the less, the elements of courage: but now, deprived of her home and neighbouring enemies, whose reputations she could only continue to impair in retrospect, and her husband, who for years had been the chief inspiration of her invective and contempt ('a few more like *'im* in the Army and we shan't win the war, they must be daft!'); all remnants of her glory had vanished – the village had run its gamut of admiration and envy at her bomb story, and she was reduced to falling (in every possible direction) upon her three unfortunate children, whose fear of their mother far exceeded any they had experienced in a blitz. She quarrelled with Dorothy and the Land Girl, and hit her children continuously with a kind of expert wildness, which, practised though they were, they hardly ever managed to evade. She refused to clean her part of the house, and swapped her children's rations for cigarettes. This was her third billet 'and here they tell me I've got to stay whatever it's like which won't be much as I can see', she had remarked on arrival.

Dorothy lived a life dominated by Hitler, and reinforced by the wireless. So far as she was concerned England had no government: everything was badly organized and therefore

Hitler was personally responsible for it. The blackout, the rations, the shortage of soap, of petrol, of fuel for the boiler, of knitting wool – everything – was contrived with fiendish ingenuity by Hitler. She was convinced that nothing but the murder of him would end the war; and as she imagined him sleeping in bullet-proof pyjamas at least forty feet below ground, attended only by satellites who were drugged into agreeing with him, her ruminations about his possible death were consistently gloomy. Sometimes, Mrs Fleming thought, she was even beginning to doubt his mortality. She listened incessantly to the wireless, and proclaimed her utter incredulity of everything it told her. She worked from morning till night, and adored the naval officers and children between whom she made no distinctions at all. They were all untidy, all careless, and they all liked chocolate semolina, which she made them with persistent devotion.

Mrs Fleming regarded the Land Girl with urban apprehension, feeling that the girl's proximity to Nature could only result in natural but (for Mrs Fleming) embarrassing consequences. She exuded sex; spent all her spare time in the house on her appearance; and concentrated exclusively on men, with a single-minded candour that evoked terror in the debilitated convalescents. The only point on which both Dorothy and Mrs Fawcett were agreed was on disliking Thelma. In spite of the fact that Thelma had to get up at six in the morning in order to bicycle to her farm, she was frequently out all night. The other Land Girls did not like her. Mrs Fleming had great difficulty in liking anyone so unaccountable and unresponsive. She sighed. Leaving such a household, even for one night, filled her with experienced misgiving. Getting away was like beginning to thaw one's frost-bitten mind to the point where one began to perceive its degree of paralysis – and then returning to the frost.

Euston Station in the dark concentrated for its effect almost entirely upon smell: fish, smoke, lavatories, coal dust, sweat, oil, newsprint, cheap scent (carnation or violet), animals, disinfectant, and furniture polish. The immediate effect, as Mrs

Fleming got out of the taxi, was so overpowering as to be almost tangible. Like a curtain of fog, she felt one could stretch out a hand to touch it, and if the sudden flash of a torch illuminated her hand, it would be mysteriously and deeply ingrained with soot.

The taxi refused to wait, and she went in search of her husband's train. Inside the station, she became aware of its noise: a vast conglomeration of harsh and dissonant sounds – an orchestration of finality, of departure (for at first she was unable to discover any indication of an arrival); doors slamming, whistles blowing, shouting, platform gates clanging, opening for a power-driven luggage truck, and clanging again – an endless train moving endlessly away out of the bleary undertow of light into the dark; leaving behind it a disembodied suburban voice intoning its destination through a faulty microphone.

She discovered the board indicating arrivals, and found that her husband's train was well outside London and already forty minutes late on schedule. The taxi would never have stood for that. She went in search of coffee.

The buffet was very full. She stood at the marble-topped counter which glistened with innumerable liquid or sticky circles where wet glasses had stood, waiting for the coffee which she knew would be undrinkable. Beside her was a silver three-tier food stand covered with a glass dome. She was asked whether she wanted anything to eat. Beetroot sandwiches, and structural pieces of pastry shaped like bombs (Cornish pasties), reposed on charming paper lace mats. The beetroot gleamed between thick bread with the dull resentment of alligators' eyes. She did not want anything to eat.

Anyway, she reflected, keeping the house in Kent had provided a reasonably safe home for Deirdre, and Julian in his holidays. Her husband had wanted to send them to America or Canada, had, indeed, made all the arrangements, and then faced her with them; and she, guilty in her need of her children's company, had nearly succumbed to this opportunity for them to be safe, properly fed, kindly cared for, and travelled.

But she had chanced, the week before, to go with a friend who was seeing her children off to Canada, and the experience had been painfully unforgettable, fragments of it returning to her whenever she went to a railway station . . . Parents coaxing their children on to the train: one little boy had asked:

'Will it be a *long* time?'

'Oh, no, a *very* little while.'

'Until Christmas?'

'We'll see, but it won't be very long.'

'You'll love it anyway,' his father had said; and suddenly the child had known that they were lying, and that the time was utterly beyond all three of them: he had not cried, but had stared silently at them with a kind of helpless grief and resentment until the train had left.

One child had had to be torn from her mother by an escort, and carried into the corridor crying out the bitter discovery of her homesickness.

'She *said* she'd like it. She *said* she *wanted* to go,' her mother repeated over and over again. People kept telling her that the child would forget; would be all right even by the time they reached Liverpool – and meanwhile it screamed and screamed that it wanted to go home – it *didn't* want – it *didn't* want . . .

When the train had disappeared, its mother leaned over a luggage truck and was violently sick.

Then there were the ones who had been toughened – who had been told that they were not to be afraid of school, of the dark; that they must not cry. They said their farewells, and climbed into the train like disciplined little troops, feeling furtively for their handkerchiefs, or holding very tightly to their bears and dolls. And many of course found it gay and exciting. It was *their* parents who collapsed afterwards, or who walked away telling each other the same lies that other parents had told their children. It wouldn't be for long. It was much better really . . .

Anyway, she had Deirdre. Julian had had to continue at his prep school, which he finished at Christmas. She had him in the holidays. The framework provided by school terms and holidays was curiously comforting to her in her present life. It helped to justify the monotony of petty day-to-day anxieties (What on earth can we have for lunch? Why does the Petroleum Board never answer letters? etc.): it comforted her in the gradual loss of that other framework: the tenuous but uneasy relationship she had had in London with her husband, which now seemed perceptibly to be draining away. She saw less and less of him, and consequently he seemed at short irregular meetings such as the one she now awaited both strange and familiar in entirely the wrong proportions. He refused to talk about his work, which was clearly very exhausting and moved him constantly all over the country. She knew dimly that he did trips in bombers and a wide assortment of naval craft, but she did not know why, and he refused to tell her. Occasionally, he rang her up to tell her that he was back, or all right; which simply confirmed her fears without informing them. Whatever he did occupied his mind entirely, as on the rare occasions when he came down to Kent, he was either preoccupied or bored. But above all, the children, and particularly Deirdre, enabled her (sometimes, at least) to see her life as dull, but not meaningless: the selfish private panic that she sometimes felt about being nearly forty dissolved a little as she watched Deirdre growing up. After all, what was one supposed to be doing with one's life at thirty-five? Indeed, if it were not for the war, what *would* she be doing? This, in the middle of Euston Station surrounded by khaki, by uniform of every description, was beyond her imaginative powers: indeed, she found it as difficult even to remember what her own life had been like in 1939, as to strip all the people in the buffet of their war clothes and dress them for peace. That pre-war life, by the very phrase, now seemed a frivolous inconsequent dream, of which leisure and pleasure had been natural phenomena. She stopped pretending that she was going to drink her coffee, and decided that if she could find somewhere to sit, she would abandon herself to nostalgia.

It was very cold outside the buffet, and suddenly she began to dread meeting her husband; the absence of a waiting taxi;

their strained and inadequate conversation while they waited for one; and their return to the desolate half-shut house. Now, she almost wished that she had accepted Richard's offer to accompany her, although she had refused it for what still seemed excellent reasons. Her husband resented the convalescents *en bloc*, and ignored her argument that the alternative was more Mrs Fawcetts, as a piece of feminine unreason.

She went to look at the indicator board, from which, she discovered, her particular train seemed to have disappeared. An ancient dyspeptic-looking man whose job it was to alter the details on the board, met all her enquiries with a sardonic smile, which only enraged her because it was obvious that he could hear what she asked, and knew the answer. Eventually, an equally ancient fat porter took pity on her, and told her that the train had come in a few minutes ago. 'Platform 18, you ought to find it over there,' implying that she would be very lucky if she did. She ran for the train with the indicating ancient glaring malevolently after her.

He was at the barrier when she arrived. He had given up his ticket, and stood motionless in his black velvet-collared overcoat, which always looked too big for him, clutching what she knew would be an exceptionally heavy small suitcase. He did not seem to see her as she approached him, and when she called his name he shook himself and blinked.

'Ah,' he said.

She explained about the indicating board, and as she did so, she knew that the explanation was unnecessary, and sounded foolish and pointless. She interrupted herself by saying it didn't matter and realized that she would have to tell him that she had been unable to bring the car.

They were still standing where they had met, with the end of the crowd off his train filtering past the ticket barrier into the dark. She said:

'Sorry I couldn't bring the car. We'll have to try and get a taxi.'

'Not if we have to try very hard. I'll ring up for a car.'

She turned to him in surprise, but he was searching in his

pockets for change. He pulled out a bundle of five-pound notes, and she knew that mysteriously, as usual, he would possess no other money.

'I've got it,' she said, praying that she had – that that much of their life would be smoothed for them by her possessing twopence.

He took her arm, and propelled her towards the call boxes.

She *had* twopence, and he went into a box with it, leaving his case with her.

'Ten minutes,' he said, when he joined her. 'What about food?'

'There is a meal at home.'

'Any meat?'

'Bacon. And eggs.'

'I need meat,' he observed. 'We'll pick some up on the way back.'

She followed him outside the station feeling unaccountably depressed. The feeling of dread at meeting him had not disappeared, had, on the contrary, increased. Three times already she had felt ineffective and improvident, and as though she was old enough to know better.

Eventually, a car appeared which he said would be theirs, and it was. He packed her in, and said something to the driver, who covered her knees with a rug which felt dirty even in the dark. They drove off.

'Where on earth are you going to get meat?' she asked, but he touched her sharply through the rug, and his reproachful pale blue eyes gleamed with mocking conspiracy.

'Tell me how it is with you,' he said a moment later.

'It is all exactly the same, which I suppose is a good thing. And you?'

'It is all exactly different.'

'Another job?'

'Possibly. It will not affect *your* life in any way,' he added. He did not in the least mean to console her, and a little angry, she retorted:

'But yours? It must affect *your* life.'

She felt him grin suddenly in the dark, and then stop grinning. Then he said: 'Oh yes, it might radically affect *my* life.'

She knew immediately that he was thinking about death, and the incompatibility of her present continuing existence, and his possibly mysterious death, jolted about her mind in passionate disagreement, preventing even such conversation from continuing. This vast graveyard of private relations she thought, and wished suddenly for the day to have ended – for sleep to conceal her solitude. She glanced at him. His head was sunk into the collar of his coat, and it was too dark to see his face. She roused herself to continue being the right kind of wrong companion.

'Deirdre is still convinced that you are really a spy.'

He was silent.

'It is all the Buchan she has been reading.'

'I am glad that she can read,' he answered politely.

'Oh Conrad, don't be so ridiculous: of course she can read. She is ten.'

The car was stopping – she thought they were in Soho, but she was not sure. They were stopped, and she was sure it was not Soho. He got out of the car and knocked and rang at a narrow little door. After a long wait, he was admitted, and the door shut. She became ridiculously afraid that she would have to make conversation to the chauffeur of the car. But he sat, immobile and silent, and seemed to expect nothing. It was very cold. She realized that she had had nothing to eat since a sandwich at the National Gallery after a lunch-time concert with Richard. And when we get back, she thought, the kitchen will be freezing cold, and I shall be so hungry that I shall not even want meat – but surely he won't be able to get *meat*.

The narrow door opened; he appeared, and for a moment she saw silhouetted behind him the figure of a very pregnant woman in an overall, who was either laughing or coughing convulsively – she could not determine which: and then the door was shut, and he had returned to her.

'Now home,' he said: and put a parcel on the floor of the car.

'I do try to live up to my daughter's literature,' he added a moment later, and she knew that he was trying again. Then he touched her, and wrote something on the window with his little finger. The word was 'Stake'. They had always had a private convention of misspelling single simple words (she could not remember how it had started), but he had not employed it now for a very long time. She wrote: 'Good: I love Staik' (the word was always endowed with a capital letter). He watched her write, read it with intense gravity, and then wrote as quick as lightning: 'Steyk is good for you'. Then the windows were used up.

The silence back to Campden Hill thereafter was an easier one.

2

THE kitchen was dankly cold. The fire had gone out. Most of the cupboards and shelves were bare of stores and utensils, making the low stone-floored room more largely unattractive. The wooden shutters over the windows did not seem to quench the raw draughts, and the harsh ceiling lights with white china shades did not cheer the room – seemed merely and heartlessly to show it up in all its uninhabited discomfort. A calendar for 1939 hung on the wall: the days had been torn off it until September – a piece of ostentatiously subtle detail which was like the cinema.

She began cooking their meal. She was neither an experienced nor a natural cook; her husband minded very much what he ate, and she was now extremely tired. She had brought vegetables from the country that morning, and had prepared them in the afternoon. She unwrapped the steak. It was a very large steak; she had no onions, and the lack of them seemed suddenly all-important. If she did not warn her husband that there were no onions, everything would be spoiled. She went to the foot of the basement stairs and listened for him. Whenever he returned to either of his homes, he immediately prowled, like an animal, all over them – he did not unpack his luggage, or go to his study, or read his letters, he simply occupied the entire house, and then took up his life in it exactly where he had left off. Oh dear, she had not told him about Richard coming up for the night. Richard was out, but his things must be somewhere; Conrad would come upon them, and then she would feel she ought to have told him first. Such was the state of her mind racing about in the bottom gear of anxiety, when her husband reappeared.

'Oh Conrad, there are no onions and the fire is out. I am sorry.'

He looked at her carefully.

'You are grossly overtired. Go and change.'

'I cannot change *and* cook dinner!'

'If you think you are presenting me with that alternative, I would infinitely prefer you to change. If you stand about you will feel much worse. Where is the food? Ah!' He seized a large knife. 'You are alone in a basement threatened by a comparative stranger with a murderous weapon. What choice have you?'

'None at all,' she answered gratefully and retired.

She heard him drop the knife as she climbed the stairs.

In her room she found her corduroy long coat for dining laid out on her bed, and the electric fire switched on. She knew then that although he had never done so before, he would cook the meal and relight the kitchen fire, and that she was not meant to feel merely ineffective and improvident. She changed with the utmost attention to detail (he always maintained that living consisted of no fundamentals, outlines, basic truths, or principles, even for one person, let alone society, but simply a vast quantity of detail, endlessly variable and utterly unrelated). His most satisfactory and astonishing aspect was his capacity to astonish her.

She discovered strands of his dry brown hair in her comb – even his hair was unexpected. She wished suddenly that she could change her appearance – that she could join him unrecognizably different. But she did not possess that talent, as some women possessed it – the mysterious ability to recast the shape of their heads, or emphasize a new aspect of their faces – to seem what hitherto they had never seemed – her extreme simplicity of appearance permitted almost no variation that did not fall below her standard.

At the end of her changing, she stepped back from the long mirror to look at herself with the kind of professionally objective scrutiny that she had evolved from years of this ritual. The tall thin creature in peacock blue that the ribbed velvet rendered almost black, stared back at her with a solemn and minute curiosity; observed dark hair impeccably drawn away from the face; collected for a second the startling eyes; paused at the pale velvet shadows thrown on to the crest of the cheekbone; hesitated as the earrings of cut steel swayed faintly; considered seriously the redness of the mouth; then travelled swiftly down the long dark lines from which the narrow white nervous wrists shot out like pieces of separate life. She was ready.

She had recently read in a magazine an article called 'Be Forty and Enjoy It'. She had read it carefully, wondering why the fact of being forty constituted such a menace to enjoyment. The article evidently thought so; but all she could glean was that the unfortunate women of forty should try very hard to look thirty-five, and not think about it. She *was* thirty-five; if it had not been for Richard, she would not have thought about her age at all, and when she did, it seemed merely a statement of fact like the date, by itself, and meaningless by itself. She went downstairs to join her husband.

He had relighted the fire which now blazed, and he was seated in one of Dorothy's old basket chairs, with a glass on the table beside him. As she entered the room, she knew that he had been asleep, but he slept and woke with such lightning facility, that only she would have known it.

'Now,' he said, 'have a large glass of duty-free gin.'

His suitcase, she noticed, was on the kitchen dresser.

'What about our dinner?'

'You must first drink enough to stop worrying about things that don't matter. I have cooked us the most delicious meal.'

'You are a very gifted man,' she said, subsiding into the other basket chair with the glass he gave her.

'I have bushels of lights,' he replied. It was the kind of remark that really amused her, without making her laugh.

'I shall never do it again,' he added a moment later.

He had been watching her with a detached gravity which she knew was the token of his approval. And I must make no move, she thought, not thank him for choosing my clothes, or warming the room; I must remain apparently calm and indifferent to anything he does, and everything will be all right.

'I want to shop tomorrow morning. What would you like?'

'I should like some earrings,' she said at once. He liked her to have some requirement immediately available – he liked to gratify some wish of hers that had lain for a while on the surface of her mind – he did not like her to be detached from material longings – from a kind of childlike greedy acquisitiveness – although there were, of course, infinitely secret rules to this live-and-let-give aspect of them both. She must want something in which he was interested – and it must be something which he could possibly give her. She knew that the ear-rings would be beautiful, and would become her.

'And a penknife?' she asked. He loved penknives, and possessed an enormous collection that she was not allowed to touch.

'Why do you want a penknife?'

'It would be very useful,' she said with the weakness of truth, and knew that she had lost all chance of getting a penknife.

He snorted, and finished his gin. He had a theatrical snort.

'Does anything matter now?'

'Absolutely nothing. I have a lovely hot corkscrew going down my throat. I haven't had gin for weeks.'

He was getting dishes out of the oven.

'You have worked hard,' she said, watching him.

'I have,' he agreed. 'But then it is much more exhausting seducing somebody one has known for a long time.'

The corkscrew, burning, shot suddenly down to the end of her spine. She said: 'What made you think of wrapping the steak in paper?'

'Hot *buttered* paper. It would have dried up if I hadn't. That unpleasant little spilt-milk quality – common sense. Come and eat.' The remarkable meal was on their plates.

She asked what he had done with the potatoes – they were brilliant, and there was no milk.

'I can't remember. I expect I used alcohol of some kind. As I shall never mash potatoes again they had to be brilliant.'

'You are a valedictory cook.'

He laid down his knife and fork. 'But *think*,' he said, gazing at her with an earnestness in which she was not intended to believe. 'Understand how fortunate you are to be present on such occasions. Supposing I was a dogged, far less talented little man, trying something new, but determined to get the hang of it, think of the potato you would have to endure – and how little it would matter to you in the end that I had got the hang of it. One should do everything not wisely, but a little too well.'

'With such consequences?' She was half laughing, half perplexed.

'Of course. Then one need never do it again.'

'I entirely disagree with you, and I do not at all see how the world would go round.'

He stretched his hand palm upwards towards her across the table.

'My dear,' he said, 'the world will continue to rotate whatever you do. It has its own axis to grind. You and I have no hand in it at all.' His fingers curled into his palm and straightened again.

'Do not identify yourself with this business. You have nothing to do with it. It is not, even indirectly, your guilt. I will fight because I hate, and because I choose to fight, not because I feel that I could have prevented the war. I will buy you ear-rings, but not a knife.'

She gave him her hand. She felt then distinctly that she was a part of him, not, perhaps, the part she would have chosen, but then perhaps it was not a question of choice. The notion (it seemed extraordinary because it had never struck her before), that perhaps *he* could not really choose the part she played for him, occurred to balance their uneven intimacy.

'I shall buy myself a knife,' she said.

He smiled seraphically.

'You'll choose one which is perfectly useless.'

And as she was allowing him to get away with that, the front door slammed. Oh Lord, I never told him about Richard, she thought. Oh damn, why did I forget? Aloud, she said:

'It's Richard Corthine, he came up for the night. Sorry darling, I forgot to tell you.'

He withdrew his hand. The footsteps, heavily hesitant, sounded above them.

'He'll probably go straight to bed.'

The footsteps had reached the head of the basement stairs: she was wrong. She looked at him – his face was already devoid of any expression.

When Richard Corthine came into the kitchen they were looking at the food on their plates but not eating. He had intended simply to say good night, but the air of tension was so apparent to him, that he determined not to leave her alone in it.

'I just looked in to say good evening. Good evening, sir. I imagine your train must have been madly late.'

'Madly.' Mr Fleming's lips hardly moved.

'You are back very early, Richard. Have you dined?'

'Oh yes, thank you. The other chaps wanted to go to a cinema afterwards so I came home.'

'Do you dislike the cinema?' Mr Fleming enquired.

'No, I don't dislike it, but it's not much good to me at present I'm afraid.'

A shadow crossed his lean unshadowed face, and he moved with deliberate cheerfulness to the fire. 'You've no idea how cold it is out.'

'Richard came up for them to see how his eyes are getting on.'

'How *are* they getting on?'

There was a short silence and Mrs Fleming looked at Richard.

'Sorry, I thought you were asking your wife. Oh, they don't say anything, you know. They never really tell one anything. I tried to get a chap to gang up with me on the tests, but he wasn't in favour. They said if they (my eyes I mean),' he screwed them up apologetically, 'if my eyes improve over the next few months they might give me a shore job.' He cleared his throat. 'In fact they'll probably sling me out at the end of the war. It's their usual form.'

'And how is the rest of you?' It was impossible to ignore the malice so barely concealed in this question, but Richard had good manners which he used even when they were not required.

'It *was* only my eyes, sir. My eyes and these headaches,' he answered, with a steadiness which somehow increased the malice of the enquiry.

'Of course. It is sometimes a little difficult for me to keep track of my wife's invalids.' He was working his way through his steak and did not look at either of them.

Richard thought: God, she looks wonderful in that dress: bloody little man; if we have coffee I can stay awake until we're all so tired she won't have much of him to put up with.

Aloud, he said: 'Are you back for long, sir? Have they given you a proper leave?'

'My dear Corthine, I am not a Naval Officer – I don't get leave, definite or indefinite.'

Mrs Fleming said abruptly: 'What about some coffee? Shall I make it?'

'You have not finished your steak.'

'It was delicious, Conrad, but I can't eat any more.'

Richard said: 'One never wants food one has cooked oneself.'

'Ah, but she *didn't* cook it. *I* did. I hope you are confounded?'

Richard said that of course he was, and then Mr Fleming continued gently: 'You know, I don't believe I would have *trusted* her with a steak.'

'Well, whether you trust me or not, I am going to make coffee.'

'Have a bit of Icelandic cheese?' He seemed to produce it from nowhere. She shook her head, and went to light the gas under the kettle.

Richard thought: Good, she wants coffee too. I wish I'd never come downstairs – no, I don't, that's selfish – she ought to have let me come to the station with her – she was tired out before she went, and obviously dinner wasn't going with a swing. What shall I talk about? What's a nice uncontroversial subject, although *he'll* argue about anything if he's in the mood: better if he argues with me, then she can have her coffee in peace. Funny how living in a house with a woman gives one insight. A year ago I'd have had no *idea* what was going on. He said:

'Were you in Reykjavik, sir?'

But Fleming, at precisely the same moment suddenly shot at him: 'You must be extraordinarily tidy!'

'Oh?' Richard was immediately and unreasonably defensive. (What the hell is he after now?)

'I do not recall any trace of you about the house. Is that the result of Dartmouth? Has the habit been instilled in you since you were thirteen – everything shipshape and above or below board as the occasion demands?'

Mrs Fleming said: 'One doesn't necessarily have to go to Dartmouth to be tidy. You look tired, Richard. Do you want to wait for coffee, or would you rather go to bed?'

'I'd love some coffee.' Damn, now I can't even take my dope with it, although she always knows when the pain starts. He had a headache which reminded him always of making fishbones of a chestnut leaf: every time he moved, another strip of leaf was torn out from behind his ears up to the sides of his forehead. The uneven tearing pain was so sharp that if he was thinking at all, he always felt at those times that he was able to think with unusual clarity. But perhaps it is simply that *she* has taught me to be discerning. Whenever he had this kind of headache (there were two other kinds, one not so bad, and one infinitely worse), he imagined himself remaining in the Navy, rising to great heights solely on account of his integrity with people.

Mrs Fleming, with an attempt at lightness, said, 'Oh this watched pot business. It *won't* boil.'

Richard thought: Yes, he's watching me, but I won't boil either – that'll fox him. He made one more effort – this time selecting the degree of stability which an old destroyer mounted with a number of new guns might be expected to have in the North Atlantic – a subject about which he suspected that Fleming knew a good deal. He was eager, he was genuinely interested, he was even tolerably informed – when he had served in the particular class in question there had clearly not been enough armament – on the other hand he knew somebody who had recently been in an old ship when she had rolled ninety degrees with a heavy sea running – he had not heard the results of the subsequent enquiry into the efficacy of existing stability tests – perhaps Mr Fleming . . . ? But he got nowhere. Fleming remarked that one could not indefinitely continue putting new guns into old destroyers. Then they both realized that the coffee was made. A relief, thought Richard, and then felt that no, of course it wasn't a relief, because here they all were sitting round the table again.

She said: 'I wish we had some brandy.'

'Have we none?'

'We moved what there was to the country. You remember.'

'An extremely foolish move. What have you *done* to this coffee?'

She made a little gesture of weariness, but her hair was still perfectly neat. 'The usual things. Do you dislike it very much?'

He drained his cup. 'Very much. It was revolting.'

She tried hers. 'It is so hot that I cannot taste it.'

'Well, drink it quickly before you can.'

Richard drank some and scalded his tongue.

'It seems very good coffee to me,' he said.

The sharp smaller pain of the scald was a relief from the uneven strip tearing in his head. The evening is nearly over, he thought, and, in spite of trying, I don't seem to have done much good.

The evening was over. On the stairs, Fleming halted, looked down on the others and said: 'Does Richard know where he is sleeping?'

'Of course he knows.'

'I'm on the top floor.'

'Go right down if there is a raid.' When she said that, he knew that she knew about his headache, and a wave of the comfort and security which her knowledge and solicitude always engendered in him, stopped him, while the others had continued to climb.

They were waiting for him on the landing outside their bedroom.

He said good night, and climbed the last flight alone to the attic floor where the children had slept. There is nothing I would not do for her, he thought, wanting to do everything. He did not realize at all that he could do nothing.

3

MRS FLEMING sank on to the stool before her dressing-table. She was speechless with apprehension and fatigue. There was no point in being angry, either with Richard or with Conrad: each saw the other strictly in their own terms, in relation to themselves in relation to her. She had become used to beginning and ending her day alone, and the knowledge that she was now trapped with the remnants of the evening until sleep released one or both of them (and sleep, she well knew, was not easily achieved in such conditions), added to her nervous agitation. She resolved to work her way through it all with amiable bravado; she knew from long experience that it could not be ignored, and she did not choose to postpone it until they were embarked upon the eternity after the lights were out. But he forestalled her.

'How very much I dislike the young. Their complacent certainty that their infantile dependence will be met. Their utter lack of self-containment. Their determination to be compensated for the disastrous consequences of their casual curiosity. Their greed for indiscriminate approval – their lack of technique – their senseless demands – they will pick endless watches to pieces and expect others to mend or replace them – their inability to profit by the experience of others and their refusal to experience anything for themselves. Their contempt of reserve – their ceaseless searching for somebody before whom they can swagger and be saved – their brash resolve that each time they are burned is the first – their ridiculous belief that they are Adam – the first new specimen of their species, magnificently unique, when they are only one more pathetically identical detail turned off the bench. Their faith in their own indispensability – their tiny wisdom and their colossal impatience —' He had stopped.

'Yes?' she said. 'Go on.'

'There is no point: I have undressed. I do not like that young man.'

'And there is now no point in my saying that after all he is only young.'

'None whatever. There is no point in your saying anything. What, or should I say who, has possessed you to design anything so badly?'

She said: 'I did not design it.'

He seized his bottle of hair lotion and shook it furiously.

'I will not spend my evenings with you in an atmosphere of

Freudian night nursery. I will not play down to that adolescent's Italian comic opera. Give me gout and a little more money, and a few more doors to the kitchen and we should have been complete.'

She had unpinned her hair, and now, laying her ear-rings in their niche of bruised velvet, considered the tiresome necessity of taking off her clothes. She hated undressing in these conditions; becoming, she felt, more and more vulnerable and literally thin-skinned, while he always managed to follow the most commonplace ritual – even absurd little things like rubbing lotion into his hair, without losing control of any situation he was making at the time.

'You should be more discriminating in the flattery you require. Or if that is beyond you, more selective as to time.'

She heard herself saying: 'I thought Richard had gone out for the evening. What *does* it matter anyway!'

'You spend ninety per cent of your time with children, invalids, fools, and animals. What a mind will yours become!'

'I thought that was the company approved for women by most men!'

'You are so intent on becoming most women that you forget who I am. If you had sent the children away as arranged you could now be living an intelligent life.'

'I thought you said that I must not identify myself with the war!' Almost afraid that she had scored, she swung round on her stool and said: 'Conrad: I am disliking this so much. It is not simply this evening that exasperates you – what is it?'

'These young men with their persistent nagging devotion, constantly presenting you to me in a light which I find unattractive. If they had reached an age where they were capable of discovering romantic inspiration in someone more than their mother or their nurse I should bear with them.'

'If they were encouraged to see me in any other light, the position in Kent would become impossible.'

'Exactly. That is what comes of burying yourself in Kent. You should travel for your affairs. Look at Marseille.'

'What about Marseille?'

She felt all the blood in her halt, and then jerk forward again to catch up: then she repeated: 'What about Marseille?'

He was brushing his hair now, but he stopped to say pensively: 'Isn't it odd that while affairs are on, there is everything in the world to say about them, and one can't; and when they are off, it doesn't matter saying anything in the world, and one doesn't.'

Glad of this generalization she said: 'There is always poetry.'

'Poetry?'

'People write it when they are in love.'

'My dear, what *years* since you were in love. They use the telephone. Or does that young man write poetry to you?'

'He writes poetry. I've never seen it. No, I expect it's all about the sea.'

'I'm damn sure it isn't. Does he do *everything* badly?'

'You sneer so much, like someone perpetually exhaling. You never absorb a breath of anybody. It is so – so *dull* of you!'

She had managed to undress, and now she went into their bathroom and shut the door. He had the capacity to make her incurably angry, with herself and with him. Why had she told him that Richard wrote poetry? Why give him that handle? Poor Richard – whose life was the Navy, which was in all probability going to divest him of his life. She knew that Richard regarded his future with a kind of panic: he simply saw all his competence, his knowledge, and his status removed from him, and he could imagine nothing in their place. When she had once inveighed against a Service that could act so harshly, he had immediately contradicted her, upholding any decision they might see fit to make. 'You see,' he had said earnestly, 'that is their strength. Never to have men who are anything less than I was. That was what made one – oh, proud, you know.' He had frequent nightmares of his trying unsuccessfully to sell vacuum cleaners or washing machines, and sometimes, he said, the object he was trying to sell got smaller and smaller each time that he failed, so that the failure was smaller too, but felt worse because it ought to be easier to sell something small. He had been told what to do all his life; the very channels for his initiative had been charted: he might perhaps have questioned decisions made for him to act upon, but he would follow them at all costs with an impersonal loyalty which required no recompense, not even any acknowledgement but permission to continue his service. She remembered one of his fellow officers who came to see him in Kent saying that when, after hours of searching, they had found Richard and dragged him out of the water, frozen and unable to see because at that point he was blind, they had asked him how he was and he had said, 'I'm in it up to the eyes,' and laughed. Everybody had laughed, and it wasn't until they handed him a flask of whisky that they realized he couldn't see it. Well, he could see again; and perhaps he wouldn't get chucked out. She made a little prayer to the Royal Navy to allow him to continue risking his life in their employ, and went back into the bedroom.

Her husband was in bed, reading Donne.

'You need more scent,' he observed.

She glanced at the bottle: it was half full.

'I mean, now.'

She sat obstinately on the bed, her dressing-gown round her shoulders. He threw his book aside, fetched the scent and stood over her.

'I am too tired to care.'

'I will care for you,' he said, immediately: 'lie down.' His hands were comforting contrast to his eyes now fixed on her with soothing, faintly satirical, detachment.

'You are like a gardener spraying his favourite rose bush.'

'A good gardener sprays *all* his rose bushes,' he replied, and then added, 'few people can avoid a gallantry as I can. I am saving my breath to warm your ardour you see.'

'I see,' she said, but she did not feel anything.

He put a little scent on the corner of her pillow, and returned the bottle. 'There. I like you to enjoy the good things of your life. Now you will have some faint echo of your smell.'

'I suppose there are rows and rows of bushes,' she said

drowsily. She did not very much care. He had an hypnotic effect upon her: when he intended her to feel soothed, almost immediately she was. 'Perhaps that is because you do it so seldom,' she said aloud, and realized that he would not know what she meant. 'The contrast,' she added as though that explained it. She heard him laugh a little as he turned off a light, and with a flicker of curiosity she asked him why he laughed.

'I was remembering you climbing into bed reeking sweetly of toothpaste. A long time ago.'

'Was that absurd?'

'It was simply charming. How little you knew! How little you cared! I don't know which charmed me most.'

He was lying beside her, and now he leaned over her, reaching for the other light. When he found the switch, he paused, looking down at her with a serious, almost fanatical, expression.

'I was extraordinarily in love with you – once.'

'A long time ago.'

She thought she was smiling, but she was not.

'I remember it more completely in the dark,' he said, and made the room dark.

He did not speak to her, which rendered their anonymity complete; except that she recognized his hands breaking down the familiar resistance of her mind, until the moment, when, without knowing it, without love or affection, she kissed him. The kiss was not returned – she would have cried out or died for it, but there was suddenly no time to lose or spend: her mouth was covered and she was not alone.

The tide, which for so many hours had been making, eddying, creeping up to its height – struggled with all its irresolute strength; and then violently turned – sweeping her out in hurrying darkness to the wide estuary where separate bodies lie in an accomplished silence.

Out of that silence she thought he said:

'I shall never do that again, either.'

But she had already drifted too far from him in sleep.

PART THREE

1937

1

The situation had been growing steadily worse for days. The facts that they had achieved the journey from England in a heat wave, with both children, their nurse, and a very great deal of luggage, to a villa which with the Talbots they had rented blind; that the villa had surprisingly displayed almost all the assets of beauty and comfort passionately listed in a series of letters which its agent had mistakenly written in English; that the children had suffered the minimum of sickness, heat spots, and diarrhoea, and their nurse had so far only managed to work in one of her customary bilious attacks; that they had not quarrelled with the Talbots, and that they were all agreed about the desirability of St Tropez, were beginning to count for nothing. Like the sun which shone with gentle tireless determination, drenching the sea with its brilliant glancing power: drying their hair, soaking into their bodies, glinting, gilding, bleaching, burning, permeating, strengthening the light and heating the atmosphere; dominating colour and smell and almost all sound but the cicadas, who seemed the very tick, the frantic mechanism of heat: like this sovereign element they had come so far to seek, Mr Fleming's boredom which they had come so far to avoid, pervaded the whole party, beginning to touch and to cling to everything they touched. They were not all aware of it, of course, but to Mrs Fleming it was so urgently alive, it was growing so fast that she felt it must destroy all of them in the end. There were another ten days of the holiday to run; fourteen of them had already been spent. Certain people literally spend holidays, she thought, and he is one.

At first it had not been so bad. He had been very tired

when they arrived, and the combination of his fatigue and the change of environment had entirely occupied his mind with his body. But he had slept so furiously, had bathed and eaten and drunk with such scientific attention to his own rehabilitation, that now he was spoiling for some stimulating experience. He was bored by Leila's husband; Leila, who sometimes amused him, was pregnant; he was (naturally) bored by her, and the children had always bored him, he said, since nine months before they were born. He was now engaged upon becoming bored with St Tropez: using up the beaches, eating steadily through the repertoire of cooking, drinking so much of the delicious *vin du pays* that any moment he would, she knew, morosely take to boiled water; methodically exhausting every topic of conversation; declaring that it was unfair of green Penguins to be identical within as without; even quarrelling with the sun, which, he had begun to claim, over-simplified everything. He did not quarrel with her, or with any of them. He merely defied them to amuse him, at the same time making it clear that it was essential he be amused.

She supposed it was all her fault; by which she meant that she was responsible for their being in St Tropez with their children and the Talbots. The holiday had been planned months before: she had wanted to take the children abroad, the Talbots fell in gratefully with a plan which did not involve their being alone together, and at first she had not minded very much whether Conrad accompanied them.

But the last three months had been very difficult; and under the unexpected strain of violent and internally uncontrollable jealousy, she had succumbed to the pallid pleasure of dominating external events: she had got him to say that he would join them, and she had made it impossible for him honourably to evade his promise. She was consequently very unhappy; and the discovery that it had taken her thirty years thoroughly to understand that nothing is worth having if one schemes, if one dislocates the character one hair's breadth by imposition or manipulation, haunted her in this full sunlight as relentlessly as that other discovery had haunted her during the dusty summer evenings in London.

She had known, of course, that he was not faithful to her; but previously she had thought his attentions had been so casual and diffused that they had not seriously interrupted her life with him. Now, she was bitterly uncertain. She reflected that usually in the summer when she retired to Kent for the children's holidays, he appeared at odd intervals, and that her decision to remain in London this year while electric light was installed in the country house had irritated him profoundly. He had at once proceeded to be out or away: she knew that his work was exhausting him to a point where he always behaved badly, but almost immediately she behaved so badly herself that she could not forgive him for being responsible. She had taken to going alone to the opera, where, one evening, she had seen him in a box with a ravishing young woman. She had waited in her drawing-room for him until past two in the morning, and inspired him by her evening dress, her tears, and the hour to lose his temper with her. He had begun calmly by saying that the whole scene was horribly dated, and that were she to attend the opera more often she would learn that such behaviour as hers invariably led to disastrous consequences; but when these remarks merely elicited from her a flood of ill-considered and conventional allegations he became dangerous: wholeheartedly agreed with her, ignored her tears, and left her on the discouraging note that there were only two kinds of people – those who live different lives with the same partners, and those who live the same life with different partners; a remark, he said, to which she could not possibly object, since she had so perfectly created the situation which provoked it.

She was left feeling that she had had just enough reason for behaving badly to make her having done so intolerable. During the ensuing week's silence she ceased going to the opera. When, after the week had elapsed, he returned to Campden Hill Square, she asked no questions and he told her no truths: they did not try to approach one another, and she worried frantically about whether, at thirty, she had ceased to be attractive. At a dinner given by the Talbots to discuss the holiday, she had contrived to make him tacitly agree to joining them, and now here they all were . . .

It was the middle of the afternoon, and she lay naked between sheets, awake, and very much alone. The shutters were closed and she lay in the dark. She disliked using a lamp, and when earlier, as she always did, she opened the shutters, the burning light almost struck her as it always seemed to do, and the room immediately became stifling.

They had bathed and sunbathed all the morning and now they were all supposed to sleep: 'To have a good old siesta', as Don Talbot said every day. He slept with the Continental *Daily Mail* over his face on the terrace, and Leila lay stupefied for hours in their bedroom. The children slept like exhausted puppies, while their nurse covered pages of violet-coloured paper with a post office pen (what did she find to say, Mrs Fleming wondered: her description of anything being usually confined to its being 'nice', or 'not nice', and to people 'kind', or 'unkind'?).

And he, what was he doing? Often he chose these burning hours to sunbathe alone in the garden or on the beach, returning at five for a shower: apparently refreshed, recharged by the sun and the silence. After the shower he would drink quantities of the local absinthe or pastis, stuff which in this native state was so potent that she dared not drink it at all; and as his eyes sharpened under its influence, he became incredibly amusing, in a manner so far over the Talbots' heads that she was constantly and helplessly divided between her amusement and their exclusion. All the time, of course, this intellectual clowning was a show: with the Talbots she was nearer to him – or at least as near as the front row of an appreciative audience; but when they were alone together, the show ceased, all the lights went out, and she did not know where she was. She tried to be calm and patient, but their leisure and the climate were not conducive to either intention. Tempers would rage here, she thought, turning to find a cool patch of sheet in her bed, as violent and meaningless as the local thunderstorms. Very often, at least twice a day, she resolved to talk to him, but she was so afraid that she would perpetrate any of her desperate folly in London that she dared not try. Each day, and particularly each afternoon, she thought that if he made love to her they might be able to talk; but as each night and particularly each afternoon drifted by and he did not, she imagined herself resisting him more and more completely, until to achieve her, he would have entirely to want her. Thus the mirage of his desire for her shimmered in her mind, vanishing each night with the sun, returning each day in the desert of these long, solitary afternoons, when her body lay stretched on her bed, and her mind was stretched over those interminable sun-baked hours until he came in for his shower. Then it was that she suffered defeat; day after day as he entered the room she knew that the situation was unchanged, and was therefore, illogically, worse. Sometimes, she thought that she hated him: sometimes, that she loved him so much that she would wither and die from the private shock of his indifference. Always she clung to him and to herself; she was unable to face the abstract of their emotions; of love, desire, or indifference – they could not be translated into any other terms – as though in banishing her jealous imagery of the girl at the opera, she had banished the whole world of possibilities, leaving them with nothing but each other. She built this stockade against the attacks of humiliation, and each day as she made the same discovery afresh, the attacks and her defence developed with a frightful equal efficiency, like weapons of war designed to combat one another.

Each day, after the discovery, and while he had his shower, she would get up and dress for the evening with a passionate, an almost fanatical, care. She washed her long thick hair free from salt every day; her skin was becoming an even gold which darkened smoothly, enabling her to wear paler and paler colours, until at any moment now she would be able to reach the final contrast of white. That was the kind of decorative timing which he had taught her – not to wear white until her skin was of a colour perfectly designed to carry it.

She looked at her watch, faintly luminous in the gloom. It was twenty minutes to five. She was listlessly considering the possibility of leaving her hot bed and having a shower, when she heard a door below shut with a distant decisive click. She leapt out of bed and opened one shutter. She did not want to feign sleep, but she could not bear the thought of his coming into the room and finding her awake in the dark.

When he entered the room she was brushing her hair, holding her head over the side of the bed in order to get a satisfactory sweep.

He watched her for a moment, and then said:

'The Egyptians polished theirs with silk.'

'They had Egyptians to polish it then,' she replied, continuing to brush. She waited for him to introduce some fantastic thesis on hair – he seemed in the mood for it, but now he proceeded to fill his fountain pen without saying anything. The strain of having minded being alone, frayed and snapped gently in her – she felt wonderfully, suddenly peaceful watching his deliberate neatness with his pen. She put down the brush in order that she might touch her hair, so that if in a minute he touched it, she would know how it felt to his hand.

He said: 'Do you want a shower?'

'I might this evening. Eventually.' She stretched in the bed until the well-being reached down her body to her feet. 'You are taking a long time with your pen.' It was the nearest she ever got to inviting his attention.

'All three pens,' he said, 'and then I'll come and talk to you.'

She seized the hairbrush, and resumed her brushing. But he began to talk where he was.

'Either one marries a woman who gradually sharpens, intensifies, exaggerates herself, to the essence of her original appearance – or a woman brimful of a kind of beauty that runs over and dissipates – that blurs and diffuses until there is no constant picture of her at any one time, but simply a vast series of impressions – even asleep, she is not a picture of herself, but of someone who *was* like her, asleep. The first is intellectually aesthetically desirable: her men can watch her becoming more what at the beginning they hoped she would be; only that was at the beginning and in the end they no longer want it. The second is always elusive, always disappointing, fascinating because there is no contrast, maddening because nothing is ever attained. There is merely a choice between the woman with a bone structure, a core, an architectural personality that will wear; and a creature of light and colour and shadow who requires all the senses to enjoy her; whose character is so freckled with feminine possibility that it can never be defined; who will shame the intellect, and outface the desire for beauty – but who will always unconsciously accentuate the difference between the men she attracts and herself – a most comforting charm, since it provides a structure for social and erotic behaviour. One need never pretend to treat her as one would another man. She has nothing to preserve since she cannot preserve her youth; she can stand up to being courted and married and raped as she would never clearly envisage an alternative. She would not torture herself with the rigorous standards of intellectual romanticism – she would not relate any one thing to another except when she indulged in such orgies of inconsequence that it was amusing. On seeing her for the first time ten years after marriage people would ask why on earth did he marry her —'

'With the other kind of woman people say meaningly that they quite understand why he *married* her.'

He looked up. 'That is what they say.'

'But do you really think that there are only two kinds of women?'

'Only two kinds that I should marry. I always talk about myself. Other people's opinions are so dull that I am never sufficiently informed to discourse upon them.' He put his pens on the dressing-table. 'You see, you have not asked which kind of woman you are.'

'I have not asked because I know.'

'You have not asked because you want me to tell you. The second kind of woman would have asked because she thought I wanted to tell her.'

He leaned out of the window to fasten back the shutter which had been slowly closing, and said: 'I am going to Paris tomorrow. By air from Marseille.'

She checked the little cry of astonishment and despair. She picked up her comb and said: 'It was silly to fill all your pens. They will flood in the aeroplane.'

'I thought perhaps you might drive me there.'

She made a minute gesture of indifference and examined her comb.

'There is a plane leaving Marignane at about seven o'clock. You will have to stay the night in Marseille. Would you mind that? Because if you would, I'll drive myself, and send someone back with the car.'

His solicitude about her minding the drive hardened her artificial indifference. She said:

'Surely Nice is nearer? Why don't you go from there?'

'I prefer Marseille. I prefer the drive.'

'Are you coming back?'

'No.' He sat on the end of her bed. 'I didn't want to come here at all. You know that. The thought of even one more evening with the Talbots appals me. I am prepared to work in tedious conditions, but I will not attempt to play in them. You presumably like it, or you would not have elected to come here with them in the first place. I shall see you in London in – how long is it – ten days' time.'

'And supposing I said that I wanted to come with you!'

'It wouldn't be true.'

'How on earth do *you* know?'

'You have made it perfectly clear that you want me to stay here with you. I have now made it perfectly clear that I want to go to Paris. I have not invited you to come with me for two reasons. One, I want to be by myself, and two, you are responsible for the children who have still ten days of their holiday to go.'

She put down the comb and hid her shaking hands under the sheet.

'My dear, very often two people want two different things that cannot be reconciled. You must accept that, because I won't have a lot of sandy compromise thrown in my eyes. It doesn't suit either of us. Do you understand that?'

'It is all unanswerable.' Her mouth felt so dry and rigid that she could hardly speak. She wished desperately that he would go out of the room, but she felt with the insanity of pride that she would never ask him to do anything again – not even to go out of the room. If she said anything at all, some of the shocked, pent up, blistering, miserable emotions would spill out and flood them – he would suddenly see her as she really was, and she would be over this crumbling precipice.

He was looking away from her out of the window during this silence; now he got up from the bed.

'You make such intolerable alternatives for yourself. It would probably be better to cry.' And then he did leave her.

On the terrace before dinner she said: 'Conrad has to leave us tomorrow: isn't it sickening?'

The Talbots agreed that it was absolutely *sickening*. They did not really feel it was.

After dinner when she said good night to the children, she told them that he was going, and they immediately asked whether she was going too. When she replied that she was not, Julian said: 'Well, that's all right then,' but Deirdre, balked of the drama of her mother suddenly leaving her, cried: 'But you said he would go dark black here, and now he won't have time!' and burst into tears. 'Don't be silly,' said her brother severely, 'he's going to Paris – well, that's French – he can get black there,' and Deirdre was instantly consoled.

Much later, when they were in their room again, she broke the exquisite pain of their silence by saying:

'I – will drive you to Marseille – if you like.'

It did not sound at all like a concession, but an appeal.

She was sitting on the edge of her bed, barefoot, twisting her hair out of the way for the night.

He picked one of her hands from her hair, and stared down at her. He looked suddenly, hopelessly, sad.

'Good,' he said, and put her hand back, on to her lap.

The next morning she bathed before coffee. There was a little beach near the villa, and good for early swimming, although too small to be much use later in the day, when even half a dozen people made it seem crowded. This morning she shared it with a large black Labrador, an expert swimmer, and very friendly.

It was very early and beautiful. There was a self-assurance about this climate, she thought – it had none of the pale trembling transitory quality of an English summer morning – a beauty that would take the breath and vanish with the dew, would dissolve, as like as not, into any one of a variety of undistinguished days. Days here began like Juliet; with a bewitching blend of freshness and maturity. It was cool, but the faint throb of heat left from the evening before had not stopped: colours were throaty, full pitched, and perfectly balanced – they did not seem to experiment with one another – there was none of the secret glancing uncertainty of early morning light in England.

She swam in the small lagoon, and then lay on a flat rock over which the sea washed with irregular lazy afterthoughts.

She had not really accepted the fact that Conrad was going to Paris. Ever since he had told her, she had recoiled from the shock – since she had first checked her initial cry of despair – since after that she had not wept, or implored – she had strung herself along from one event to another – telling the Talbots – telling the children – the servants – and finally the offer to drive him to Marseille: this last because she knew that he loathed driving himself, and because it prolonged the time before he had really gone – and because she had wanted to break the intolerable silence and unbalance of feeling between them. (But he had come exactly half way towards her mind – which is never far enough – touched her hand and retreated again) – and now she was strung up for the drive, she was thinking in terms of Michelin, of petrol, and where they would stop for lunch. She carefully did not consider the long drive back alone, or her return in St Tropez for ten days without him. In the night, while she had not slept, while she had lain deliberately still because she had not wanted him to know that she was awake – she had struggled with what she recognized to be childish illusions about this holiday – she had tried not to separate it from the rest of her life but to see it in proportion – three weeks out of ten years with Conrad: out of – what was it – twenty years before him. Put like that – three weeks were nothing. It was foolish to indulge in elaborate preconceptions: anticipation was a featherweight, doomed to compete with the inevitable, convincing bulk of reality. The trouble was that one had to face reality without knowing beforehand precisely what it was to be. One had somehow to discover and tread the hard, between the sloughs of fearing the worst and hoping for the best. Anything more complex and one fell into the trap laid for imagination – anything simpler and one existed in a kind of vacuum of mediocrity, where one refused to play the game at all in case one lost . . .

When, at a quarter to eight, her husband joined her on the terrace for coffee, she had washed out her hair, and packed. She was wearing a white silk shirt that had belonged to him and a coarse black linen skirt. Her damp hair was tied to the back of her head with a scarlet sash. He remarked upon her simple magnificence, and she, drawing out the flat gold watch which she wore round her neck on an exquisite chain he had given her, replied evenly that he had better say goodbye to the children as they ought to leave in six minutes.

Five minutes later, as he handed her into the driving seat, he laughed, and said, 'Yes?'

'I was wondering whether a woman could *ever* continue to be mistress of herself, a man, *and* a situation.'

'Only, I think, when either the man or the situation are not worth having. Now N98 to Toulon. Then, I thought the coast, in case we want to bathe, and because of Cassis.'

'Let us do whatever you would most enjoy.'

This made them both actually laugh; it was his age-long preface to doing exactly what he would most enjoy.

2

THEY reached Marseille a little before five. Exactly twenty-four hours, she thought. They were driving down the wide dusty road edged with exhausted plane trees which, pollarded, and clipped into a jaunty shape, looked none the less dirty and fatigued – by the dust from bicycles, from the gigantic lorries, from the little rattling battering trams that journeyed ceaselessly out from Marseille to Mazargues, and back. The road, like all main roads into any big city, achieved a kind of vast squalid importance – everyone travelling upon it was either hurrying to get into the city or out – it was a life line with a low opinion of life. The petrol stations, the huge crude advertisements, the little cafés right on the road, the crowd of factory workers pouring out of irrelevantly elegant iron gates, the scattering of large French mongrels – everything seemed designed to be seen at the rate of forty-five kilometres an hour – it being a point of honour with all traffic to exceed the speed limit by a minimum of five kilometres.

They were approaching the square where the trams stopped.

'Air terminus?'

'We have an hour. Let us get you fixed up at an hotel,' he answered.

'I will do the fixing,' he added a moment later. 'Then we'll have a drink.'

It was very hot, and with the car stopped, almost intolerable. Their bathe in Cassis seemed fantastically long ago, and she began to regret her decision to stay even one night in Marseille. Well, in an hour he would be gone, and she could do anything she liked. And I shall do *anything* I like, she thought, without any clear idea of what she would like to do.

He emerged from the hotel looking so actively, so intensely, impassive, that she knew he had achieved something.

'They showed me a cupboard looking on to an open sewer which I have naturally refused. I have secured you instead an enormous double room looking on to the harbour– Come and see.'

'But I don't need a double room!' she said, as the small lift gave a deep gasping sigh and moved slowly upwards.

'What a ridiculous thing to say. If you lived your life on the principle of only having what you strictly needed, you wouldn't enjoy a moment of it. By eleven o'clock tonight you may be very glad that you have a room large enough' – he glanced at the lift boy whose face was ominously inexpressive – 'to watch a thunder-storm from with somebody to stop you being frightened.'

'One has to marry to ensure an irregular sex life,' he hissed in her ear, as they walked down a dark corridor behind the boy.

The room, which faced south-west, was, of course, dark. The boy turned a switch, and the room flickered with a tinselly Victorian light, which suited the heavy white bedspread and the damp smell of clean laundry.

'It is now the same price as the cupboard. I don't suppose the taps work. No. Cold from the hot, and nothing from the cold. Now. You wash, and then we can have a drink outside.'

He opened a shutter, and went out on to the blazing balcony.

Her mind had reached a state of immediacy when looking for her soap entirely occupied it. When she had washed, and done her hair, she turned this full shallow attention to the drink they were to have.

'Half an hour,' he said, as they settled themselves at a table below her room, and looking straight on to the harbour.

She looked at him vaguely.

'I shall have to go in half an hour.'

'Oh! Oh yes.'

'What will you drink?'

'A *fine*.' She looked as though she was watching the people who surged and lounged, and spat, and stared, and skulked on the road and the quay before them, but she did not see them. She was suddenly, and with bitter sharpness, remembering Paris with Conrad: she realized that he was leaving her, and going – to Paris of all places – and a wave of jealousy submerged her, so violent that she could neither see nor speak. Through the sick faint haze she heard him say, 'There's Thompson!' and by the time she had regained control of herself, another man was sitting at their table with them. She realized that she had been introduced to him, and smiled. Her brandy had arrived; she drank it and leaned weakly back in the cane chair.

'. . . only arrived this afternoon,' the man was saying.

'By air? And what will you drink?'

'What I should really like is a whisky and soda. And your lady would like some cognac or whatever it was.'

He extracted a battered packet of Gold Flake from the breast pocket of his shirt and handed it politely to her.

'Do you use these things?'

'No, thank you.' (Boring little man: where on earth did Conrad pick him up?)

While they waited for the drinks, he scratched the back of his neck and then wiped it carefully with a dirty silk handkerchief covered with anchors.

'I've been bringing a boat down for somebody,' he said, stuffing the handkerchief into a trouser pocket. 'Warm here, isn't it?' He selected a limp cigarette and looked enquiringly round. 'I wonder if I could trouble you for a light?'

'What sort of boat?' asked Fleming instantly: he seemed really interested, she noticed with resentment.

'Converted Brixham trawler – and how. Skinned her, they must have – teak throughout, fancy aluminium mainmast –

two new suits of sails, a blooming great engine fitted this spring – a *bath* – about eleven burgees and a monkey. Took a year to refit her, and now her own builder wouldn't know her – she's such a fancy job. Businessmen playing sailors. He's only had one game, and then he got stuck on the Brambles. He'd have had the crew playing football round her if they could have got a side to play against.'

The cigarette, which had hung unlit from his mouth throughout this speech, now dropped limply on to the table. He picked it up, pulled out a few straggling wisps of tobacco and flattened the end with his thumb.

'Are you leaving her here?' Fleming asked.

'Nope. Cannes is my terminus. But I'm ahead of schedule. Thought I'd look round here for a couple of days. Buy some bananas for the monkey.' He looked over the back of his chair and said: 'Pouvez-vous m'obliger avec une lumière?' The Frenchman smiled with weary scorn, and gave him a box of matches. 'Merci beaucoup. Years since I've tried to speak this. But I can always get m'self around.' At last he lit the cigarette: it ceased to be the uniquely squalid object that had begun to obsess Mrs Fleming. He was rather like a monkey himself, she thought, an English monkey – if that was not too great a contradiction in terms. He had small unselfconscious animal movements; he concentrated extremely on the cigarette, and the box of matches, and wiping the sweat from the back of his neck with his handkerchief. He said what came into his head the moment it arrived, and when he had nothing to say, he watched them with a calmly childish curiosity which seemed entirely physical – 'What colours are you wearing? Are you as hot as I am?' – nothing more complicated than that. For the rest he was small and very brown and gave the impression of being furry.

He had thought of something else.

'Tell you what,' he said, 'why don't you come and see my boat?'

'Unfortunately I'm leaving almost at once.'

'He has an aeroplane to catch,' she said, trying to be nice

about it. She had drunk her second *fine* and felt much better.

'What a shame!' He seemed really deflated. He finished his drink carefully and then turned to her: 'I suppose you wouldn't care to come and see her? She really is a lovely boat—' he added with a kind of eager friendliness – as though, if she had not been such a lovely boat, he would not have dreamed of asking her.

She looked up, hesitating – she did not at all want to see the little man's boat – and caught her husband's eye snapping with satirical amusement – waiting to see how she would get out of that one – and determined not to help her. She pulled her watch out of her shirt and looked at it.

'First I must see that Conrad catches his plane.'

'My wife would have made an admirable secretary.' He hitched his chair nearer Thompson. 'Isn't it fascinating that all wives resent being told that, and all secretaries resent being told that they would have made admirable wives.'

'It's the past tense that does it,' said Thompson calmly. 'No woman would like being told what she was, or would have been. They like the future – the future and the present.' And he smiled suddenly at her showing most perfectly dazzling teeth.

'Whereas for a man, without a past you have no future at all.' Conrad seemed to have forgotten about his aeroplane – he did not seem surprised at Thompson's (to her) unexpectedly penetrating remark – and he was savouring what he had himself just said in the leisured considerate manner which, she knew, prefaced hours of conversation. For a minute she thought of letting him miss his plane: but then he will catch another later on, and by then I shall cease to feel strung up, and simply be muddy and bad-tempered about his going. She rose from the table.

'I am going to make sure they haven't taken your bags out of the car. Three minutes?' she said, and then to Thompson, 'Do keep him up to it, I've driven him miles to get him here in time.'

Oh dear, even that sounded faintly hysterical, she thought,

walking through the hotel. She had begun to feel acutely self-conscious – as though she was too tall, and her arms hung in a curious manner, and her eyes could look at nothing easily: as though she was walking too loudly fast, hearing her footsteps pounding so hideously out of time with her heart. 'Too full of herself,' she remembered a nurse saying of her when she was a child, and she thought now, what an agonizing thing to be, and how she would give any of herself away, in order that there might not be so much – but nobody would take it – she finished, fumbling in her bag with cold clumsy fingers for the key of the car.

Her husband appeared, minutes later, and with Thompson. In spite of knowing that it was a good thing not to be alone with Conrad, she resented his bringing Thompson, as she would have resented any third person. The car had stood in the shade and she had become unreasonably cold sitting in it. Fleming hesitated outside, until Thompson said, 'No, you go in front': a harmless remark that she knew ought not to exasperate her.

'Make up your mind anyhow,' she said, 'or you'll miss the wretched bus.'

They got in.

They had missed the bus. They saw the end of it disappearing up the hill as they reached the terminus.

'Thompson will drive me,' said Fleming.

She ignored this, and proceeded to drive unnecessarily fast to Marignane.

Fleming talked to Thompson all the way: she noticed that he answered monosyllabically, and wondered what on earth he must think – but then there wasn't anything for him to think, and he didn't think anyway.

In spite of her driving, the bus beat them to it – largely because she was unable to pass its formidable lurching bulk – and they arrived almost together. They all got out, and Thompson brought the bags and put them on to a waiting truck. They were all standing outside the door through which the passengers from the bus were hurling themselves.

'Let them go,' said Thompson. 'They all travel like that.'

They waited until the (presumably weakest) last had sulkily jostled through, and the doorway was empty. An aeroplane was coming in to land. When it had roared over their heads, Fleming turned to Thompson and shook him warmly by the hand.

'I'm delighted to have met you again. Come and see us in London. My wife will tell you where. Look after her for me. I'm sure you could if you tried.'

And Thompson shook his hand and said: 'Have a good trip.' Fleming turned to her, and put his hand on her shoulder. She, stupidly thinking that he meant to kiss her, lifted her face. But he said simply: 'Enjoy yourself,' dropped his hand, and went through the door.

He had gone. Deeply mortified, she turned to Thompson: he was staring at the aeroplane which had just landed on the runway to their right. She knew he had seen her expect to be kissed, and scalding tears of humiliation burned her eyes.

It was too much to be left like that, and with this odd little man there to see. She pretended to watch the aeroplane – and heard him walking the little way back to the car – she could not really see the aeroplane – the worst of ridiculous or shameful behaviour was stopping it – the mere stopping accentuated it for anyone else to see – even that little Thompson man.

She walked slowly back to the car trying to adjust her mind.

He was leaning against the car grinding something into the ground with his foot. He wore espadrilles that had faded from dark blue to streaky mauve.

'Want to move?'

'I don't think there is much point in staying here,' she replied, and heard her voice stiff with the effort not to tremble. (Damn; take another turn on the screw.)

'Do you want to drive or shall I?'

'I should think I'd better.'

He gave her a friendly, speculative look, and opened the door for her.

When they were both in the car, he said:

'Do you mind if I smoke?'

She shook her head.

He extracted the battered packet again.

'Is there a match in this motor?'

'Try the front pocket.'

He pulled the knob, and it fell off.

'Sorry about that. It *was* loose, you know.'

He picked it off the floor of the car and looked at it critically. 'A botched job. I could do it better myself.'

'You can still open the pocket with it if you're careful.'

'Yep: I know. But it beats me how they've the face to make anything so badly.'

'It doesn't matter,' she said. 'You light your cigarette. I'll have it mended some time.'

He looked at her hands lying slack on the wheel. She had not attempted to start the car.

'Shall we find somewhere and have a drink?'

One of her hands shot out suddenly for the knob which he was slowly sliding back into its socket. She pressed and turned, the pocket opened, and the knob fell out again.

'There,' she said. But there were no matches. The pocket was empty. After he had looked, he looked at her.

'You do feel awful, don't you?' he said.

She did not move or reply. He touched her arm and said:

'You let me drive. You've had enough of it.'

The moment that he touched her, tears streamed from her eyes – she resolved before him without a word.

She put back her head as though to stop the tears from running out of her eyes, and her hands suddenly tightened on the steering wheel with the same effort. He waited a moment; then carefully loosened her fingers and held them. He did not speak to her. He merely soothed her hands as though she was some nervous animal that had taken fright – he did not treat her as a complex sophisticated woman whom he did not know, and whose tears would be an impossible embarrassment – but simply as he would treat any distraught creature, with a natural, physical kindness which was instinct in him.

Gradually, as the first shock of tears ceased, and the remaining few slipped more slowly, still silently, away, she moved her head and shook it as though finally to release herself. He put her hands one upon the other, and that was, she found, a comforting thing.

'Sorry about that.'

'So am I.' And he got out of the car for her to move into his place. In the driving seat he leaned across her, picked up the knob from the floor, and stuffed it in his pocket.

'I'll mend that later on,' he said, and started the engine.

'Plugs need cleaning,' he said, later, 'another little job for me.'

'Do you *like* cleaning plugs and so on?' she asked.

'I like an engine to run sweet. She can't if she's not serviced. I like to do that myself, because then I know it's done right. Shall we find ourselves somewhere for a drink? Then you can have a bit of sleep.'

'How do you know I want to sleep?'

'Because if you have a drink and a little sleep you'll feel like a proper meal,' he replied seriously.

She nearly laughed.

'Would that be such a good thing?'

'Would what be such a good thing?'

'My drinking and sleeping in order that I should want to eat.'

'Of course it would. You must take my word for that. You see I'm not an intellectual type at all – not highly strung or what have you, so naturally I think about eating and drinking and sleeping a lot of the time.'

'You like people to run properly, like engines.'

'That's it.'

He drove the car well. Perhaps she ought to make some more conversation between them.

'Do you find it tiresome remembering to drive on the right?'

'Nope. Roads are easy. England and Scandinavia on the left – everywhere else on the right. Rivers are much worse – you get whopping big tankers bearing down on you for a joke if they think you don't know the passing rule – heading straight for you – then if you're in a small craft you get the wash.'

'Are boats your profession?'

'No. I haven't got one. I just do what comes to hand. We could drink here. Looks all right, don't you think?'

It was a small café with a *terrasse* covered with wide trellis and creeper.

They drank Cinzano and cognac. The tablecloths were grass-green check and on one table crouched a thin wild-looking cat. 'Il a peur – toujours peur,' said the girl who served them, when they remarked on its glaring abstract terror. 'C'est affreux,' she added indifferently as after she tried to touch it, it drew back almost snarling with frightened dislike.

Thompson snapped his fingers at it – casually once – but he had been watching it, and it turned to look at him. Now it leapt off its table, walked slowly to his feet, and looked carefully up at him with unblinking yellow-glass eyes. Then, neatly and perfectly, it jumped on to him, settled, and folded its paws with its head pressed against his shirt.

She watched his hand stroking its bony back, and the cat seemingly soothed and reassured, fluffed its meagre fur and tried to look luxuriant.

'Doesn't look as though it has much of a life, does it?' he said.

'Is it an intellectual cat?' she asked.

He looked uncomprehending. 'How do you mean?'

'I've never drunk brandy with Cinzano before.' She felt suddenly self-conscious and also relieved because she felt that with him there was no need to feel self-conscious.

'I think it's a good drink,' he said. 'Do you want another?'

'Yes please.'

While they were waiting for it, she made up her mouth,

and he watched her with the same friendly interest and curiosity she had first observed in him. With most people she would not openly have painted her mouth; but he was different – so easy it didn't matter – he was not the kind of man to regard it either as an intimate gesture, or simply as bad taste. Nevertheless, when she had finished, she gave him a little worldly smile, admitting the necessity but faintly deprecating what she had done, and he smiled back.

'That's fine now,' he said.

'You'd better buy some matches,' she said a minute later, trying to identify herself with his requirements as she felt he had tried with hers.

He paid for the drinks and his matches in his atrocious French. He put the cat gently on to their table, and they returned to the car.

'What time is it?'

She looked, and told him.

'I must get back to my boat. I'll drop you first at the hotel for your sleep.'

'I thought I was supposed to inspect your boat.' She discovered suddenly that she did not want to be abandoned.

'You can see her tomorrow if you like. If I take you there tonight with no warning, the crew I've left on board will take all their clothes off, and I shan't be able to show you anything.'

'Why will they do that?'

'It's just one of the things they do if they are faced suddenly with a woman on board when they haven't had notice to clean up. I gave half of them shore leave tonight – I've got to see they haven't all gone off – taken French leave I suppose one might call it.'

He laughed and she began to find his continuing practical enjoyment of everything he did restful and endearing. She did not want to dine alone.

'If I go to sleep now I shall never wake up for dinner.'

'No, you probably wouldn't, left to yourself. But I thought I'd slip back to the boat, see to the crew, collect some tools for your repairs, and wake you when you've had an hour. Then we'll go and find some good sea food. Does that suit you?'

'Yes,' she said simply, because really it was exactly what she wanted. His face had screwed up more like a monkey than ever in the effort to make all those plans. When she agreed, he turned to her and smiled, his polite friendly smile – his eyes, she noticed, were like small warm brown chestnuts.

'Hooray,' he said, and it did not sound a silly thing for him to say.

3

BACK in her large room, she had a shower, undressed her hair and opened the shutters. The sun had gone; the grey airy twilight slid into the room, and almost at once, began perceptibly to darken and retreat. She wrapped herself in the spare white peignoir and lay on the bed to sleep.

She woke very slowly – aware of the distant tinselly light by the basin – of the sharper sounds of night begun in Marseille coming up from the street – of the windows framing a soft dark sky, now hectic with lightning, silent, without thunder – and then of Thompson standing beside her bed.

'Don't hurry,' he was saying, 'it's awful waking up.'

But she stretched and enjoyed the return of her senses gradually until she was wholly awake.

'I've brought you something to drink.'

He had poured it out, whatever it was, and handed her a glass.

As she sat up, she saw dimly reflected in the mirror across the room and facing her bed, a figure, golden brown – almost naked except for the gleaming white wrap round one shoulder and dark hair streaming into shadow. Had it not been for the gold watch slung round her neck, and the arm stretched out for the glass, she would not immediately have recognized herself, so unexpected was the reflection, so marvellously unlike her idea of herself did she seem. The blacks and the brown and the richness of the white – even the attitude of this savage, beautiful reflection, filled her with a sudden ravishing conceit.

And there was Thompson, holding out the glass to her. She pulled the wrap round her and took the glass. He did not say anything, and as the blush which seemed to begin in her mind came out all over her skin, she thought thank goodness it was only he, and not anyone else. The thought, like the rest of her, was utterly confused.

They drank, and then, while she dressed, he sat on the balcony smoking, and telling her what he could see. 'A black man selling tortoises – he's got them all on top of one another in an orange box – poor devils.' And, 'Two children doing conjuring tricks – they aren't much good though.'

'Is it still warm?'

'Balmy. You won't be cold.'

Really, she might have known him for years. She took a great deal of trouble over her appearance – the vision in the looking-glass, which it seemed to her on closer examination she did not in the least resemble, prompted her, none the less, to compete in some measure with its exotic improbability.

He came in from the balcony just as she was screwing silver rings on to her ears.

'I've found out where to eat. Are your ears pierced?'

'No. Ought they to be?'

'*I* don't know. But I'll do them if you want them done.'

'Oh really, Thompson! Did you fetch tools for that from your boat?'

'I've done it before,' he said.

'Then you'd have to alter all my earrings. Twenty-four pairs.'

'I could only manage the ones without enamel. Enamel flies if you fire it,' he said. He was perfectly serious.

'I'll tell you if I ever change my mind.' She was not sure whether she had hurt his feelings.

'What a lot of things you can do,' she added, as they left the room.

'I have my uses, you know.' He had her white peignoir over his arm.

'Why?'

'That has its uses too.'

They ate: they talked. Their conversation was easy – almost desultory – the food was very good. They did not argue or discuss, or tell one another the story, or any story, of their lives. He was neither very amusing nor dull. He did not, she felt, expect, or even want to be amused. They concentrated on their dinner – not with the ferocious apathy of the French couples round them, but with the greedy enjoyment of people who do not customarily eat either so well or together.

They reached the end of their meal, and she said she wanted a very sticky liqueur, knowing that he would neither blench nor treat her as a tasteless cretin. They had two each, and then he bought a bottle of cognac.

'I would like a French cigarette,' she said suddenly.

When the girl brought some packets on a plate she picked out a blue one, and looked at him enquiringly.

'Very strong those,' he said, 'have the yellow. Unless you want them extra strong,' he added.

'I liked the colour of blue.' But she took a yellow packet. He lit her cigarette for her and watched her enjoy the beginning of it.

'You don't smoke much, do you?'

'I used to smoke far too much, so now I don't smoke at all.'

She smiled at him and thought: How odd, what ought to seem too intimate is easy between us; but that conventional disclosure seems very intimate. She had forgotten these minute inversions of feeling, that with certain kinds of experience shift all the contours of any settled view.

He asked for the bill, and she began to worry about the amount of money she was costing him, and, rather diffidently, she said so. But he pulled out his dirty battered note-case stuffed with dirty battered money, and said: 'Don't. I was paid an advance on this trip and this is how I like to spend it.'

'Yes, but you are spending it twice as fast.'

'Oh no, I don't think so,' he answered carelessly, and then added, 'I'd probably be drinking it if I was by myself.'

'But you wouldn't be,' she said, discovering this.

He smiled the same ingenuous amicable smile.

'Not if I could help it.'

Outside, in the air which was like warm velvet, they hesitated. The sky, now phrenetic with stars, was not entirely dark; the people in the street were substantial shadows – their talk, clear but unintelligible, the echo of daylight talk.

They were immediately absorbed into this atmosphere and appearance of blood heat, and got silently into the car.

'Would you like to drive out somewhere? I thought we might swim.'

She nodded, and then realized that he probably couldn't see her and said yes.

'Do you know where to drive?'

'I think so. I had a good look at a map while you were sleeping. Anyway I can usually feel my way about.'

'I'll get you back all right,' he said a minute later; 'I can always find my way back.'

'Like a cat, or a pigeon,' she murmured. 'I wasn't worrying about it.'

'I drove in on this road today,' she said some time afterwards. It was the only reference she had made to anything that had happened to her before she met him.

By the time he had found them a little bay, the moon, very late and lovely, had appeared. The rocks on either side of them curved sharply round, making a small lagoon, and the water ended in warm white sand.

'All right?'

'Incredible. Of course in a way one gets used to it.'

'To what?'

'Oh it being like – oh – *Coral Island* or *Adrift in the Pacific.*'

'Those are books, aren't they?'

'Children's books. But there isn't a grown-up equivalent for them except fragments like the beginning of *Erewhon.*'

'You like reading then,' he said. It was not the envious accusation of the illiterate – simply a statement.

'Yes. It creates new requirements: and sometimes the very good books fulfil them.'

They had been picking their way down the path from the road, and now their feet sank soundlessly into the sand. There were no other people in the bay.

'I was apprenticed to a firm of boiler-makers once,' he said. 'I had to read then. Awfully dull stuff with diagrams.'

'And before that?'

'We read a play at school. I can't remember much, except that it started with a shipwreck. Funny thing; trying to start a play like that, don't you think?'

'Very difficult.' Dear Thompson, she thought: he hasn't got another name – dear Thompson. Now he was pleased because he had found a comfortable rock: he arranged her peignoir, his towel, and the brandy, and invited her to climb up to it.

'Might have been hewn out for me.'

'Are you going to smoke another of your cigarettes?' He felt in his pockets for her Gauloises, and the silk handkerchief covered with anchors appeared. She eyed it with affection.

'Thompson, it is a wonderful handkerchief. Where did you get it?'

He was still searching for her cigarettes. 'I put them in the pocket of the car, I'll get them.'

'I don't really want one at all.' She was watching the sea. She felt him preparing to disbelieve her and repeated: 'Really I don't want one.'

'I mended that knob,' he said. He had lit a Gold Flake.

The sea seemed varnished with silver oil which stretched thinly and broke to black water before and after each rhythmic, vastly gentle, undulation. Further out, these dark ribs narrowed and seemed less restless, until right out, up to the horizon, it was a sheet of stern unmoving silver.

'Good,' she said. She roused herself, and put her hands behind her head. 'I mean, thank you, of course.' She wanted suddenly to be out in the silver, beyond the restless ribs, right out to the streak below the sky. She rose to her feet.

'I want to bathe.' She jumped down the seaward side of their rock. The water was only a few yards away, but the sand was dry. Her desire to be in the sea was so urgent that she heard her shirt tear a little as she wrenched it over her head. When she was free of her few clothes, she remembered the watch round her neck, and with a little choking sigh of impatience she felt for the clasp on the chain. She put the watch in the pocket of her shirt, kicked off her shoes, and ran into the water. When it reached her knees she could not run – she took several long, dragging steps, and looked down at her body – it had gone white with the moon, and the water was half way up her thighs. The beads of splashed water stood silver on her skin. She looked once more at the beautiful distance, and flung herself towards it.

He joined her, very soon, or a long time after, and swam beside but not near her, but he left her the silence. Each time she looked ahead, the silver edge of the sea seemed as distinct, as remotely perfect as it had seemed from the shore. But later, when she looked again, the edge had narrowed, and then suddenly it was not there; the waters had darkened to an infinity of black, and there was no horizon. She cried out, and turned in the water – a soft black wave washed over her head; after the wave, she had no sense of direction or desire for it – she knew only that she must breathe air and that breathing involved continuous, difficult movement.

When he reached her, she was treading water, and the waves, broadside on, were slapping her hair down over her face. She felt his hands under the pit of her arms holding her up. 'The moon went out!' her voice was pierced with distress. 'It was all the same – all dark.'

'Not too dark,' he replied. He pushed her hair to the back

of her neck and turned her round. 'Land,' he said: 'can you manage it, or shall I do it for you?'

She did not say anything, but obediently began swimming as he directed. The waves were running behind her now, washing through her with a kind of spectral ease, and then riding away into the dark; each wave losing identity just before it was replaced by the new, soft, hurrying bulk of another. He swam with her – holding back her streaming hair – she was moving slowly – very tired now, he thought.

After a while he said: 'Rest for a bit?'

'How far is it?'

'Not much further.' They had been a long way out, but surely it couldn't be much further.

She made some small, inarticulate sound, and continued. His arm ached with the effort of holding back her hair, and for a moment he wondered whether they were, in fact, making any headway, or whether they were being swept out or very much to one side by a current.

The shore happened suddenly – there seemed nothing but sea ahead – and then, suddenly – only a few yards away there was shore. They both saw it at the same moment – the uneven end of the sea and the stillness of the faintly white sand. He wanted to try the depth, but he felt her weakly increased effort and did not halt her. She swam into the shallows until her head and shoulders and her arms were out of the water. He got to his feet, and stretched out a hand to help her, but she lay still, almost on her face, with her arms thrown out on the sand above her head, and the sea swaying gently up and down over her back. He looked for their rocks: they were an indeterminate distance to the left. He bent over her; she was shuddering faintly; he thought that perhaps she was crying; but when he told her the rocks were near and tried to help her to her feet, she turned to him with the small supplicating smile of utter exhaustion.

As he carried her slowly across the bay, the moon began to reappear, and by the time he laid her down on their rock the sea was again like marcasite, and her body drenched in the cold light. He covered her with the peignoir and started looking for the brandy. He was beginning to feel very cold; he wrapped himself in his towel, found his knife, and got the cork out of the brandy bottle.

She lay propped against the rock, exactly as he had left her. Her eyes were closed. He put an arm round her and raised her head.

'Come on. Brandy.'

She opened her eyes, drank a little, and choked. He waited a moment, and then tried again, but she turned her head away.

'I knew I'd choke.'

'I'll clear the bottle a bit for you.' He drank, and felt the liquid searing down his throat, and some cold brandy dripping down his neck.

She had begun to shiver violently; her whole body shook, and her teeth chattered against the glass rim of the bottle – he poured a certain amount of brandy down her, spilling at least as much as she drank in his desperate attempt to stop the paroxysms. Her shivering frightened him as nothing else had done: he felt that she would shake to pieces. He put down the bottle, and began rubbing her furiously. After a moment she sat with her head resting on drawn-up knees, and he worked hardly, methodically, up her back, until he gradually felt the lassitude of their mutual returning warmth.

'Drink some more, and I'll get your clothes.'

When he came back to her she was leaning against the rock again, and immediately she offered him the brandy. He put the clothes beside her and took the bottle.

She said: 'Thank you for holding back my hair.' She spoke calmly, but her eyes were trembling with some entreaty which, because he did not thoroughly understand it, he decided entirely to misunderstand.

'Have a Gold Flake?'

'You have one. I should think you need it.'

He smoked a cigarette and dressed. They each drank some more, and she tried to comb her hair.

'I should leave your hair for the moment.' He looked at her clothes and then enquiringly at her, and with an immediacy that he found deeply touching, she put down her comb, pulled her wrap from her shoulders, and began weakly searching among the small heap beside her. Her nakedness and her fatigue seemed to him almost unbearable, and, without a word, he began carefully putting on her clothes.

When he had dressed her, he kissed her.

She drew a little away from him.

'I wasn't trying to – anything – when I went out into the sea—' Her eyes were filled with anxiety.

'I knew you weren't.'

'All the time?'

'People walk when they do that: they don't run.'

She gave a little sigh of recovery and acceptance.

'We live on this, don't we?' She indicated the bottle.

'It's all we've got. Are you hungry?' She doesn't want to talk about it, he thought, give her a free rein.

'No, I simply feel deliciously, noticeably warm. You treated me like a horse. Have you looked after horses too?' He's so simple – he's easy to deflect, she thought, he won't think of asking me about the sea now.

'I was brought up with them. I think I'll groom your hair next, or you won't go on feeling warm: it doesn't last, you know.'

'My mane.' She inclined her head.

'I'll rough dry it, and then we must go.'

'Must we?'

'I thought it would be more comfortable if we did,' he said simply.

She remembered that after the salt and brandy, he had tasted unexpectedly, wonderfully sweet – something between honey and nuts, and she shivered once.

'You'll lose your pretty watch,' he said. He felt in the pocket of her shirt for it, and fastened the chain round her neck. She looked down at his hands. Hands were never simply one thing

– she discovered, looking at his – never simply practical, or sensitive, or sensual . . . He was tucking the watch into her shirt, and, involuntarily, she shivered again.

He got up and held out a hand to her.

'I'm not really cold,' she said as she stood up.

'You are not in the least *cold*,' he said, 'but if we don't go now, I shall kiss you till you won't be able to stand.'

She turned to him, and he was smiling the same polite friendly smile that was her first recollection of him. Heavens, she thought, I know nothing; nothing at all.

He collected their things, and they walked slowly back to the car.

He drove, and she slept. He drove fast because by then he wanted her very badly indeed.

Back in the bedroom with the tinsel light, they surveyed one another. In their clothes they felt as many people do for the first time together without them – a self-conscious apprehension, a kind of mutually nervous appraisal, as each private anticipation meets with reality, recoiling or adapting, justifying or delighting.

'I think I shall wash the salt off me,' she said uncertainly. She wanted a separate reason for getting out of her clothes.

'No need,' he said. He said it carefully: he felt the situation getting out of hand.

She moved restlessly to the dressing-table and started brushing out her hair. She was beginning to feel unaccountably angry.

'Anyhow I must dry this out a bit.'

He did not answer, and, when she looked in the glass for him, she saw that he was methodically undressing, folding things and putting them on a chair in the corner of the room. Sure of himself, she thought – but then I want him to be that – but not so sure of me. Perhaps by now he can't separate us.

'I don't know your name,' she said coldly across the room.

'It's Thompson, T-H-O-M-P-S-O-N, and the sooner you get out of your clothes the better.'

There was silence after that; she was both angry and frightened at feeling so miserably self-conscious – of the distance between her and the bed – of his being now naked and she not – of her inability to associate him with the desire she had felt earlier – of exasperation with him for not bridging these distances, and anger that she should need him to do so – and finally fear that her desire had entirely escaped her and vanished. She heard him go to the bed.

'You get in,' she said, 'I'll join you.' (That is sufficiently, clearly, squalid: I don't care any more, so it's easy. You cannot lead a man to expect this of you and then fail him.)

She got up from the dressing-table and went quickly into the room or cupboard containing the shower.

When, washed of salt and wrapped in the second peignoir, she emerged, ready to be calm and deliberate, and, she told herself defiantly, experienced; she found him lying on his face on the bed: pretending to be asleep – trying to save her, she thought, more of this disgusting embarrassment. She walked over to the bed, but he seemed really asleep. He lay uncovered, with his head on one arm, and the other stretched out across the bed. He had a wiry elegant body – small and tough – the limbs well turned at wrist and knee and ankle. She stared down at him – her hostility and her defences evaporating – the sight of him gave her a feeling of peaceful affectionate pleasure. She slipped out of the peignoir and lifted his arm carefully so that she could lie down in the bed where it had lain. She hardly remembered pulling the sheet over them before she slept.

He woke her very slowly in the night to make love to her. She discovered then the ecstasy which lies far beyond any false summit of delight: he guided her throughout the difficult ascent; waiting for her, honouring her with his absolute attention and care, until when the final moment came, his entire body had communicated itself to hers – the journey had ended, and they met perfectly as lovers.

4

LIKE a dream the hours came and were there and went, totally disregarding the time they were supposed to represent. She discovered, much later (she discovered much else at the time), that any emotion, if it be sufficiently strong, is elusive, not accurately memorable – that only the small practical fringe – the attendant commonplaces remain vividly in the mind – and that the memory of them only serves to conceal the core or essence of violently felt experience.

So, for a short while she could remember lying as it were on the summit of their mountain; the mists lifted from a vast panorama below, which displayed itself to them as endless, as beautifully comprehensible – a magnificence which they alone were seeing together – and then, very soon, they were left remembering that they had seen it. For longer, she could clearly remember waking, in streaming sunlight, with such a sense of her own comfort and peace, such well-being and delight in herself, that the fleeting revelation of this being the first time she had ever woken thus was almost impersonal – seemed remote and insignificant; she did not stop to question it, although she remembered turning to him, finding him awake and saying: 'I feel like – exactly as though—' and his replying: 'I can see, but you feel much much better than that.'

She could always remember the point-to-point obstructions – telephoning Leila and saying that there was something wrong with the car and she would be stuck for another day or two – was that all right? Leila (she sounded more depressed than incredulous) saying but wasn't it ghastly in Marseille in the heat? No, no, she had found some people Conrad knew with a boat who were being very kind to her. Well, do come back soon: Don's awfully bored without you. —She asked about the children. —*What* about them? —Were they all right, was Nanny being good? —The children were divine: Leila simply never saw them, but oh, my dear, *pregnancy* – you simply feel as though you're never alone, not a minute to oneself, and it's no good my telling Don that he's getting just as fat but in different places – he comes out in a sort of prickly heat with rage – and I've lost my passport so I suppose I'll be stuck here till the baby's old enough to let me travel on *its* – no, darling, the children are at the beach or somewhere, but I'll tell Nanny about your wretched car. Don't worry about us, we're perfectly all *right*; weren't French telephones *awful*? Did Conrad catch his plane? she added, and do be careful of the *sailors* in the boat. Sailors were devastating, especially in foreign parts. Esmé, she knew who Leila meant, had had the most extraordinary time in Tenerife, *quite* extraordinary – if Esmé hadn't kept her head she would have lost everything else – not, darling, that Leila thought *you* need worry – you're far too sensible, but still, all alone – but, of course, you aren't alone, are you . . . ?

At this point, she had had enough, and stemming what was clearly the consequence of Leila being denied an English telephone for a fortnight, cut herself off.

After that the day was hers – or theirs.

'Do I look too sensible for sailors to devastate?' she asked Thompson much later.

'Do you what?'

'Look as though I wouldn't – you know perfectly well what I mean.'

'Nobody looks sensible all the time.'

She watched his face after he said that, and recollected the same expression, as when, with Conrad, he had made the remark about women liking the present and the future – after which he had smiled at her. He smiled now in exactly the same way, and she shivered. Instantly he was solicitous. He observed, and seemed fascinated by, her slightest physical reaction.

'Are you cold? Do you want my arms round you?'

She shook her head: 'A goose walked over our bed.'

He did not understand what she meant.

She never saw his boat. There was the afternoon: there was the night. She had never before felt so refreshed, and so exhausted.

The next day she said she must go. He asked her to stay, and she explained about the children.

'I'll drive back with you then,' he said.

'How will *you* get back?'

'I'll get back.'

They started from Marseille at about four in the afternoon. The gap in time between this drive and the drive with her husband seemed so enormous, that she was surprised she could remember the first drive at all.

When they were nearly arrived, he said:

'This hasn't been very long, has it?'

'Let's go up to Gassin.'

'Where's that?'

'It's a village on a hill. There's a road up to it somewhere along here on the right. We could drink up there.'

'That's what I like about this country,' he said, 'you can drink anywhere.'

This was the first time she remembered Leila's telephone conversation, and her remark about telephones, and *that* also seemed weeks away in time. Marseille had begun to slip into the past. The present trembled on the brink of unreality; and the future – she could not think beyond the week ahead at St Tropez – but she knew that she dreaded it.

They found the road, which climbed with a steepness only made possible by its tortuous method. The sun was subsiding into the wooded hill as they climbed; the atmosphere was neutral. The village, perched extremely on the summit, and held there by the confidence of time, and a small parapet, seemed at first to be very quiet, to be almost deserted. But when they had stopped the car, and started to walk up the narrow cobbled slopes through the little bunch of leaning yellow-grey houses, they became aware first of the animals, and afterwards of the people. Tortoiseshell and tabby cats regarded them with inscrutable indifference; a number of dogs all clearly related, but otherwise unlike any known breed of dog, followed them a few snuffling steps; there were chickens sententiously picking their way from grain to grain; goats were picketed outside open doorways, and there was a wild fox on a chain running up four steps and down three – up three steps and down four, with a kind of frenzied perpetual motion: it did not seem to look where it was going because it miserably knew – always it moved a little too far in each direction, so that the chain choked it back. 'I hate that,' Thompson remarked without heat, and they saw a very old woman with a face like a walnut watching them watch the fox. She nodded and called something unintelligible, but she had no teeth and her voice seemed to crack out of her face. When she saw that they did not understand her, she nodded again with courteous resignation, and pulling her black shawl round her shoulders, resumed her unimpassioned study of the fox.

On the south-east side of the village was a wide terrace, flanked by the parapet, below which the hill dropped sharply away. There was the smooth glinting gulf: across it, the lights in Ste Maxime flitted uncertainly, and below the terrace heavy woods bloomed with dusk. They sat on the parapet and drank a bottle of wine. It was then that they had their only conversation.

It began because she was so possessed with a panic of unreality, that she thought the sound of their voices would help. And so, without real curiosity, she said:

'You said you just do what comes to hand. Does that mean that you do *anything* – that you don't care what it is?'

'I choose, you know. I can choose because I don't mind doing nothing – unless I'm cleaned out for money.'

'Then you have to take any job?'

'Well, I can't afford to be so choosey then –'

'But what are you *really* interested in?' she persisted.

His face screwed up in the effort of consideration.

'My main interest. Oh, women. Women, every time.' He

drained his glass and leaned towards her with the bottle. He was smiling – defensively – ('I wouldn't have told you that, but you asked for it').

'Crowds and crowds of different women?'

'I expect so. I don't think of them like that.'

'Simultaneously? Or consecutively?'

'What do you mean?'

'I mean, do you like several women at once, or one at a time?'

'Oh, I see. Oh, one at a time – of course.' He looked shocked. 'Have some more wine?'

'Please. And each woman imagines herself the glorious exception?'

He smiled again, unhappily: 'That's right. Of course, she is, in a way.'

'But not in the way she thinks.'

'I don't know what she thinks, you see,' he answered. He was now harassed into his original politeness.

Still cut off from being herself, she said:

'Is it vulgar of me to ask you all these things?' And he answered simply:

'I don't know the meaning of that word.'

She had never felt so vulgar in her life.

Later, he said: 'It doesn't make you happy, though, does it?'

'It doesn't make me anything.' Then she added with a rush: 'I'm sorry. I don't feel real. Everything seems a long way ahead or a long way behind, and I seem in the very middle of a vast vacuous interim. Do you understand that?'

He shook his head. 'Never mind. What do you do in London?'

'Why?'

'I just wondered what you did.'

She took a deep breath. 'I run one house in London and another in the country.'

'What country?'

'Kent.'

There was a pause while she waited for him to say something about Kent; but he said nothing, and she continued faster and more defensively: 'I look after my children. Julian's at his prep school and Deirdre goes to a day school near London. I—'

'So they are away or out all day,' he interrupted.

'Yes. That's what all children do at that age. Many children,' she corrected herself – obviously he had not done it. 'Then we entertain a good deal. Conrad likes streams of people.'

'So you have a lot of cooking.'

'I don't do the *cooking*. I couldn't possibly cook well enough for Conrad. I do the arranging of it. There *is* a lot of arranging, you know. I read, and look at pictures, and garden, and listen to music – and Conrad minds awfully about clothes so I spend a certain amount of time on them—' She stopped: she knew dimly how it all sounded to him and she knew dimly what it was all like – equally and differently unsatisfactory and incomprehensible to them both, and her talking only made it more irreconcilable.

'I suppose I'm a sort of scene shifter for Conrad,' she finished. 'He likes an elaborate setting, and he likes it to vary. I try to do that for him.'

'I'm sure you're very good at whatever you try to do,' he said; and they surveyed one another worlds apart across the small table. Anyway, I can leave him, she thought; it will not be difficult at all, and years hence it will simply be a surprising and friendly thing to remember. We have nothing in common, she thought, and if we go on now, I shall be back before the children are asleep.

They had paid for the wine, it was drunk; and they got up to go.

'Let's go back that way,' he said.

At the end of the terrace they found a narrow archway – a covered alley. It was very dark, and she slipped on the uneven stone. He put out his hand, holding her elbow to steady her: his hand felt like a distant memory, until he said:

'Shall I see you in London then?'

The blazing present flashed upon her; she came back to her senses, and in the illumination of being herself, she saw him again quite clearly – him and herself and nothing else at all.

She faced him without answering and kissed him with all the violence of their lives suddenly returned to her.

'Still want to go back tonight?'

'I must go back.'

They walked in silence to the car.

They drove in silence almost to the villa. Then she said:

'Isn't this a foolish place to drop you? How will you get back from here, it isn't a main road.'

'I shall have a meal somewhere, and look round. Get a lorry tonight, or early in the morning.'

'But you'll have to get back to the cross-roads for a lorry.'

'Don't worry about me, I'm an old hand at this.'

She stopped the car.

'Shall you go tonight or tomorrow morning?'

'Depends: don't worry about me,' he repeated.

She wanted badly to know whether he would go from St Tropez that night or in the morning, but knowing that such a requirement would seem inexplicable to him, she resigned herself to the extreme discomfort of uncertainty.

'I won't worry,' she said.

He got out of the car, and then, with a natural unconsidered grace, picked up first one of her hands and then the other and kissed them. The gesture reminded her suddenly of a longshoreman on the Thames, who, standing in the stern of his craft, and propelling himself down the river with a single scull, had looked up at her just as he was about to shoot the bridge from which she watched him, and, with inimitable gallantry and timing, had taken off his large black hat, flourished it, and bowed.

Now – Thompson.

He said: 'Goodbye, and thank you.'

'Thank you,' she said, 'for having me.' And he answered with unexpected urbanity:

'A delight which I hope to repeat in London.' He gave one of her hands a little shake. 'Bless you,' he said: 'I'm gone.'

She did not watch him go. He had contrived his departure too well for anything but a disconsolate little drag of the heart back into neutral – a blank screen in the mind's eye, and an imperceptible evaporation of the spirit.

From a standing position the car did not pull well up the hill.

Leila said she was looking quite marvellous. Don Talbot looked curiously at her and said nothing.

'Are you glad I'm back?' she asked her children – hearing herself courting their approbation, and Deirdre, flinging herself on to her mother, cried:

'Oh yes, I am! I *am*! I *am*! Darling darling Mummy – ages and ages – I *am*! I *am*!'

But Julian, hunting in his bed for a spare piece of Meccano, simply said: 'I knew you'd be back.'

5

DURING the hectic uneasy week that he spent in Paris, Fleming had conscientiously tried to get rid of his desire for Imogen Stanford. He employed all the usual methods, but they proved unusually unsuccessful. He tried not to think about her, and found it as breathlessly difficult as the amateur's effort entirely to empty the mind. He embarked on a heavy programme of intellectual amusements, but whenever he thought that he had successfully distracted himself, some exasperatingly irrelevant thought of her sprang into his mind, and when, as he often did, he failed to distract himself, he thought about her anyway. He tried analysing his feelings about her to the point of their elimination, but the analysis was protectively dishonest, and availed him nothing. He tried to exhaust his thoughts of her by deliberately and exclusively considering her for an hour at a time. In desperation, he selected an attractive antithesis to her, but he found, and not soon enough to avoid considerable embarrassment, that he did not in the least want her. After this last experiment, which was both expensive and humiliating, he gave up, and returned to London.

In the aeroplane, he bolstered his defeat by such thoughts as her extreme youth – she was only twenty – and youth was resilient; that she was unlike many young women, in that she had a career to think about (she was learning to paint), and therefore was unlikely to become obsessed by him; and that in any case all young women were flattered by and attracted to any personable man considerably older than themselves who took trouble over them. Her vanity was amused and soothed, and her heart untouched: that he had always been honest with her – by which he meant that he told her only such truths as he thought she could take – and that he had already taught her a great deal. Gone was her contentment with dirndl skirts and ill-fitting trousers; her predilection for sweet white wine and sandals and ridiculous scent smelling of nearly dead flowers; her tendency to lose or forget telephone numbers, cheque books, latch-keys, and lighted cigarettes; her dangerous habits of impartial truthfulness, consistent inaccuracy, and utter unconsciousness of her own beauty. But when this last word came to his mind, he was shamed from thinking about her with such devilish selection.

All those aspects of her, he knew, were both true and absurd, because they might easily apply to any young girl of twenty, but he also knew, with the integrity born of experience and interest, that she was by no means any young girl of twenty. Apart from her startling, dazzling appearance, she had the innate quality of something beautifully made. Hers was not merely the resilience of youth. She had selected him (he was her first lover), from a mass of opportunities – wealth, he reflected, was hardly in this context, the word, as an attractive woman will automatically collect a plethora of men whose perceptions are sharp enough to perceive only her most obvious attractions, and who have not, consequently, very much to offer in return. Probably she thought she was seriously in love with him, and of this she must be most gently disabused. For the rest, he reflected, she had learned not always to say what she thought, and the larger business of teaching her to think what she said, could belong to the next man to whom she belonged.

He filled his ears with cotton wool as the aeroplane began its descent, concluding in his mind that he was simply a pleasantly instructive incident in the beginning of Imogen's life – neither significant nor damaging – that the situation was therefore well under control . . .

When he telephoned her, Imogen, wearing out a dirndl skirt and a blouse with a great deal of unfortunate embroidery upon it, was making an elaborate soup. She thought she was thinking what she was doing: Conrad had once said that he was exceedingly fond of good soup, and so every day since he had been away she had made soup – thick soup and thin soup, and soup with bits in it and sieved things in it, hot and cold, brown and white and pale green and pink – she had not known before that there were so many kinds. There had been a heat wave, and neither she nor the girl with whom she shared the studio liked soup; but she told herself that it was a useful accomplishment, and she thought about Conrad as much while she made it as she thought about him at any other time – at her art school – in her bath – while she was talking to other people – while she bought paper, or charcoal, or bones for more stock – when she saw somebody who was not like him in the street – and when the telephone rang and it could not possibly be he, because he was in France.

It was he, and he was not in France. He was at the airport, what was she doing? Well, he would be with her in two hours.

Two hours. She wound up the clock and looked at the hands. They stood at twenty minutes past eleven, but they could not be altered because the screw was broken. She wrote '11.20' on her drawing block, and propped it up on the table. She had time to look carefully round the studio and decide that it was fairly tidy (Mrs Green had been that morning), before she had to dash into the bathroom to be sick.

When she emerged green and shivering, she found Iris back, lying on the sofa, smoking.

'I thought you were out. My dear!'

'I wasn't out, I was being sick – awful waste – I've only got two hours.'

'You look frightful. I'll get you some brandy.' She rose neatly from the sofa and went in search of a glass.

'Conrad's back! He's come back five days early. He's coming here.'

'I gathered that,' said Iris dryly. 'Here you are –'

'Is it all right to drink brandy just before a bath?'

'It's always all right to drink brandy. Sit down to drink it.'

Imogen regarded her anxiously over the rim of the glass. 'I've got to wash my hair.'

'You washed it two days ago.' Iris looked at her – still palely green, but even in those pretentiously awful clothes, still tremblingly, absurdly beautiful, and forbore to add: 'Don't be ridiculous.' Instead she said: 'Wash it if you want to, and I'll trim the back for you first if you like. Where did you put the good scissors?'

'They're either in my dressing-gown pocket, or else they're in the bread-bin. The bread-bin,' she corroborated after thinking about it. Since Conrad had explained how wasteful and tiresome it was to lose things, she had taken to putting everything into what she described as a safe place. When Iris pointed out that this often made it difficult for her, Imogen replied reassuringly that it was much better because now she could find things for them both, whereas before nobody could find anything.

'He likes it to be cut down to a sharp point,' she said

minutes later. She sat on a kitchen chair with a bath towel tied round her neck, and her hair so faintly gold that it was almost silver falling straight down to her shoulders. She looked up at Iris to strengthen this statement. She never had any colour in her face, but she had ceased to look green.

'Keep still. Have a cigarette. Calm down.'

'Have to scrub my hands. Conrad says if I held them properly the nicotine wouldn't go all over my fingers. Thank you. Good thing I've saved my decent clothes.'

'You would have.'

'I mightn't.'

'Look at all that disgusting soup we've nearly drowned in.'

She looked up again. 'Don't tell him about the soup.'

'I won't tell him anything, but I'll tell you.'

'What?'

'Just that you mustn't be so single-minded about all this. You mustn't let your life revolve round him.'

'But why not?'

There was something about her eyes – a simplicity, a kind of stark innocence which Iris found unanswerable.

Perhaps it is better to look like me, she thought afterwards, you don't get hurt so ingeniously.

When she went into the bathroom, Imogen, looking like a carved angel whose hair has been washed away, said:

'He must love me or he wouldn't have come back early.'

'He may have had to come back.'

'Why are you against him, Iris? Do you dislike him?'

'Would it make any difference to you if I did?'

'No – but I can see that it's a bore for you to have the flat upset because of someone you don't like.'

'That's all right: he's your man. Anyway it is you who upset the flat and I must be devoted to you even to consider sharing a house with you. Hurry up, or your hair won't be dry. And for goodness' sake open the window when you've finished or you'll have the paper off the walls.'

'I haven't had that sort of bath.'

While she quietly emptied pans of unfinished soup, cleared

the kitchen, and changed her clothes, Iris, witnessing the extravagant attention, the infinite care about detail, the mounting delight in her achievement that Imogen employed, said nothing. The discrepancy between the preparations, which were unexpectedly, even shatteringly, sophisticated, and the pure unadulterated passion of joy with which they were carried out, disturbed and paralysed her judgment. Only when, at the end of the two hours she went into the studio, and found Imogen standing by the window that looked on to the street, and Imogen turned to her and really wanting to know, asked: 'Please: do I look all right?' she answered inadequately: 'You look all right,' and then, quickly: 'Enjoy yourself. Make the most of it.'

'I do. I shall. He – Conrad – says that before he never knew the meaning of the word. Iris — You *don't* dislike him, do you?'

'No, no, of course I don't dislike him. Stopped feeling sick?'

'Completely. I feel ready for – oh – anything!'

He had brought her a dress from Paris of a grey which, he said, would help him during the next week to determine about her eyes. Was there, then, a *week*? Well, five days. But her eyes were so dark with delight that he found only their shape – the clear downward curves at the ends of the heavy eyelids were memorable, and they would always be so, giving her face a quality almost pagan, older than any angel; no kind of morality, he thought, could attach to eyes set as hers.

During the spending of those five days, while he watched her making the universal, privately miraculous discoveries about love, he, walking and talking and watching and loving and sleeping, discovered that he loved her. Since, of all primary emotions, love is perhaps the least blind, he made a myriad quantity of discoveries about her, charming, alarming, breath taking, admirable, and fearful. He found her intense immediate capacity for enjoyment both entrancing and infectious. He forced her to show him her drawing and painting and discovered that it was simply a temporary translation of her creative impulse with people. She had a good, though undeveloped, sense of colour, and she could not draw at all. She had simply needed to make something of things, because she had not, until now, known how to make anything with people. But her beauty, now that all the lovely aspects of her interlocked with her happiness, glowed and glittered and shone – overrunning all the bounds of his imagination: it was there in a room after she had left it; she lent it to anything that she wore or touched; it lighted the faces of people who looked at her; it so charged anything they heard of, saw, or experienced together, that, to him, at least, she seemed its essence; there seemed no beauty in anything that did not originate from her. He observed how, in five days (they had not, until now, spent more than a few hours together) her feminine mind, the small darting intuitions that before had occasionally startled his admiration, became steadier and more confident; how with her concern for his pleasure and peace, she collected and guessed and protected and felt her way with him: how quickly she learned to embroider his wit, to rest on his silence, to entertain his interests, and respect his reservations.

Her only reservation with him had been her attempt to conceal any of her work from him. At first he had thought that this was because she thought that she was good, and that he would not recognize her ability: after he had seen it, he knew that it was because she knew she wasn't, and was afraid that he would confirm her knowledge. He tried to be encouraging about the drawings, but it was she who pronounced their death sentence.

'Anyway,' she said, 'I don't care about them any more.'

He looked down at her sharply: she was sitting on the floor, her head bent over the folder. One of the black tapes had knotted, and after trying for a minute to unpick it, she broke it off and shoved the folder out of sight under the sofa. When she looked up, she caught the end of his expression, and said:

'Were they very awful?'

'I've told you about them.'

'Unlike Ophelia, I was not deceived.'

'What *do* you care about?'

Her long delicate mouth slowly smiled.

'Oh you, my darling love – you.' She moved towards his chair, and put her hands on his. 'I love you as though you were God and had created me, and then as though you said, "Look, there is light, there are trees and stars, and days and nights, and this is life and this is rest, and I am always with you." Only,' she finished, 'sometimes, of course, I can't see you.'

In the short silence that followed, and long before the implications of her confession had begun to dam up his mind, his love and his fear were conceived.

6

ON the sixth day, in the evening of which he expected his wife's return from France, he went back to work. He found himself as unable to tell Imogen that he loved her, as he found himself incapable of trying to diminish her love for him. While he was with her, these impulses, equally strong, effectively cancelled one another out, and as he could see no alternative while he remained with her but their strengthening with relentless impartiality, he escaped to the professional problems, which would, he knew, have accumulated during three weeks away from his work. He sent Imogen back to her art school, and Iris a tremendous bunch of the flowers of her name, with a note thanking her for her tactful accommodation. That day, with the desperate strength of a man who has at last uncovered his own weakness, he took decision after decision with the brilliant ease and force of indifference; straightened out what promised to be a major feud between two of his partners; prevented a maniacal architect from making the offices uninhabitable; interviewed five potential receptionists, turned them down, and procured a suitable sixth, wrote twenty-three letters and signed forty cheques; lunched with a kleptomaniac millionaire who divested him of all three of his fountain pens, but was otherwise amenable; and obtained counsel's opinion on a right of way recently discovered in Kent to run with admirable precision down the centre of his tennis court. On his way home, he collected three dozen oysters from Bentley's, and his luggage from his club.

They were back: she was back. As he let himself in, he heard sounds of the children bathing at the top of the house, of activity in the basement below. He faintly smelled her scent – saw that her pile of letters on the hall table had been examined – that she had put flowers in the dining-room – and knew that she would be upstairs unpacking and changing her clothes. He stood there for a moment, trying to meet her in his mind's eye, distilling her personality – trying to make her more like a well-remembered character in a book – collecting and reminding himself of her idiom, of how, chapters away, they had behaved on meeting after a separation: but there had not before been a separation like this, where skins of another life must be cast and cast until there seemed to be no skin left . . . Absurd: she would be glad to see him, and he had brought home oysters. He shrugged his shoulders at the image he had made of her, and took the oysters down to the kitchen.

She was lying on the Regency day-bed in their bedroom. He had bought it years ago, because, he had said, it was a piece of furniture perfectly designed for her, but although she had seemed delighted at the time, he had never before seen her lie on it. Strewn over her and the bed were samples of wallpaper; she dropped a piece as he entered the room: but she turned her head to greet him, ignoring the paper. He was unprepared at a distance of ten days and an immense quantity of feeling, for her burnished elegance. He picked up one of her hands to kiss it, but she withdrew it, saying:

'I don't think my nails are dry.' They were lacquered white. She met his eye almost timidly: he thought she wanted approval for her hands and said:

'They are fascinating, but if you do that to them, you will have to keep them perfectly.'

'I know they are rather borderline,' she answered.

'How was the trip back?'

'Oh – hot, and considering the children, and Leila as she is at present, uneventful. Very smooth, really.'

'They are a couple with whom familiarity is breeding something pretty contemptible.' Then, he added: 'I'm sorry I find them so dull.'

It was most unlike him to say that. There was a silence while both of them wondered why he had said it.

'I find him dull,' she said at last. She was collecting together the pieces of wallpaper.

He said: 'You have got down to work very quickly,' and she answered with the quickness of faint irritation:

'It isn't work. It's only choosing.'

'It is choice that distinguishes the *artiste* from the common woman —' he began, but she interrupted:

'But I am not an artist either!'

'Oh darling! Are you obsessed with a need to be something?'

She looked up: 'Am I? I mean, is it an obsession?'

Of course, she's tired, he thought. Aloud he said: 'My dear, if I had been the kind of little boy who kept beetles in a match box, stamps in an album, or bricks in the brick sack, I might have grown up into the kind of man who wanted to keep a woman in a house. But I was always racing my beetles till they escaped, swopping and losing stamps, and building something with the bricks. The beetles weren't fast enough, the stamps were too often fakes, and there were never, by any chance, enough bricks. So you see, you may do what you like.'

'As long as I no more than like it.'

He was combing his hair with her comb.

After a silence during which she could hear the comb in his hair, she asked: 'Have you seen the children?'

'I laid oysters at Dorothy's feet, and came straight to you.'

She rose from the day-bed.

'I'll say good night to them, and join you downstairs.'

He stood still when she had gone, and then went to wash.

The thought of the children suddenly crowded his whole day upon him: he realized that he was very tired, and wished that he had organized people for dinner as well as food. Early bed, he thought, turning off the taps, and remembered her behaviour in St Tropez. 'Early bed,' he repeated almost viciously to himself, surmounting a wave of angry guilt, and went down to the drawing-room.

He asked her that first evening when she was going to Kent, and she replied that she was sending the children, but that she was not going down immediately. There were a number of things she wanted to do, she added quickly: she seemed to expect his resistance to this plan. He answered urbanely that she should, of course, do exactly as she pleased. He thought she intended watching him, and was secretly angry and alarmed at the prospect. She knew he was angry, and at the thought of his guessing the reason for her wanting to stay in London, a spasm of terror fled over her face, which she afterwards feared he had seen. But she caught no breath of his alarm, and he had not seen her face. They both found it difficult, if not impossible, to look at one another. They finished the evening with mutual exclamations of exhaustion; with that faint over-emphasis of commiseration, the one for the other, which is designed more to underline than to comfort fatigue. She fell asleep at once, as all day she had determined to do; but he, overtired, and baffled by her behaviour, which had given him no chance to unwind – lay for hours with circular aching thoughts. He resolved not to see Imogen the following evening (in the small hours even this temporary negation of his desire seemed heroic), and finally having decided at once to transfuse some people into the flagging bloodstream of his private life, he slept.

That evening was representative of many days and evenings after it. They were like two people standing on distantly removed rocks in the sea, each of them holding the end of a heavy cable which was their only means of contact. If the cable was slack, it was heavy in their hands, and communication was impossible; if either of them tried to haul in their end, the weight became untenable and they trembled from the trembling tension. In the days that followed, the cable either dragged, while they stood hopelessly isolated – or shortened and shivered, burning their separate hands – precipitating the moment when one of them must cross the perilously taut line to the other.

When he returned one evening to dress for a theatre party, he found her asleep and unchanged, in the drawing-room. In the moments before she woke, to present him with her face but not her eyes, he made the terrible discovery inevitably experienced sooner or later by men who marry beautiful women: that her beauty, set in its immobile continuity of sleep, brought him to a sudden emotional standstill – he saw, perhaps more clearly than he had ever seen, that she was admirably beautiful, but he saw it with an utterly disinterested appreciation – he had no desire to identify himself with it. Afterwards he was always to have this curiously complete picture of her, annihilating desire, undoing love, jamming any movement of feeling, because in his mind she was always lying there, as complete, as still, and beautiful as death.

The notion that perhaps she was dead occurred to him in a sudden violently unreal crossing of his mind: dead, and finished for herself as well as for him. The perfect ending . . . To know all may be to forgive as much, he thought, but to see everything is to care nothing.

The telephone rang. Before he had moved, she was alive again and had reached it. He watched her, surprised at her urgent immediate interest in an instrument she so much disliked. It was clearly a call of no consequence. When she put back the receiver, she said with the faintly timid smile that prefaced much she now said to him:

'Wilfrid – Papa – is very ill. I thought it might be about him.'

'It wasn't.'

'No – it wasn't anything.' She turned from the telephone with the weariness of an impatience that has persisted too long. 'Shall we have a drink here before we change?'

'If you like.' Fatigue, he thought objectively, becomes her. She is reduced by it to an absolute of distinction. 'Sherry?'

'Brandy.' She perched unrestfully on the arm of a chair, and pulled out her watch. 'How long have we got?'

'Long enough to drink in. What is the matter with Wilfrid?'

'Something inside. They aren't sure, but his heart is bad and it's complicating their investigations. He looks dreadful.'

'You've seen him?'

'I was there this afternoon. He's in St Mary's, you know.' She spoke defensively – as though she thought he didn't believe her. She took the glass from him. 'Of course he's been feeling ill for months without seeing anybody. He didn't want to go to hospital. He hates it. I think he thinks he's going to die.' She drank some brandy, and her voice rose a little. 'He'd much rather die in his own house.'

He was silent; he knew how she suffered from the illness of other people. Even if she knew them very little, her imagination made no allowances for her ignorance; she did everything possible to alleviate their miseries, but under the agonizing pressure of her distress for them, she never believed that she did anything; her pity never retreated before the advance of any achievement, until the illness was resolved one way or another. She would have made a wonderful nurse, people said, watching her in one of those situations, and perhaps only he knew that she would never have survived six months of such a career.

He picked up a box of cigarettes and offered them to her.

Her fingers felt in the box while she looked at him.

'That is a Turkish cigarette which you detest. Have this one.'

She looked down. 'It's a French cigarette!'

'You used to like them.' He picked up a match. How odd that fear should always make women look ten years younger. But he was prevented from considering what it did to men by her saying:

'I'd rather have Turkish.'

He lit it for her, and did not move away in case she wanted to touch him for knowing that she wanted to smoke. Women's affections operate like insects – with tiny significant gestures: then he remembered Imogen putting her hands on his and dropping her heart at his feet – the gesture to end all others, he thought – and wished desperately that it did.

She had finished her brandy and was off the chair, stubbing out her cigarette.

'They are not habit-forming, at least,' she said.

'Do you very much not want to go to this theatre?' he asked her upstairs, and she answered with unconvincing vigour:

'Of course I want to, of course.'

'You are a very bad liar.'

'No.'

'Well, you have never managed to deceive me for a moment.'

'And you? Are you such a good one?' she said, after a fractional hesitation.

'My dear, I have passionately wanted to go to this play since five o'clock this afternoon. Can you imagine my feelings now?'

'Absolute indifference. Let's go then.'

7

HE had not seen Imogen for several days, and when he arrived, she did not expect him. She had been bathing, and wore a robe of rough blue towelling.

'I was drying slowly inside it, but I haven't got very far.' Her confusion at seeing him always made her talk as though he had been away only five minutes. She threw open the studio door for him, and waited, poised to disappear.

'Come and talk to me while you dry.' He did not want

to be in her surroundings without her animation. 'Where is Iris?'

'She's away for a week. She's inspecting things in the Midlands.'

'So you've been alone?'

'I've been thinking,' she answered gravely.

'Let us find something to drink, and tell me your conclusions.'

'Touch me first.' She smiled, to lighten the request, and held out her hand. He shook it carefully.

'I am delighted to see you,' she began carefully, but it did not stop tears from slipping down her face. 'Oh – really: they don't matter.'

'Imogen, I believe you capable of fainting for joy. Have you ever done that?'

'No: I simply get sick.' The tears made no difference to her eyes. 'We could drink Dubonnet. I'll get it. You sit down somewhere. Are you very tired?' she called from the kitchen.

'You should never ask men whether they are tired. You should simply treat them as though they were, and then evince ravished astonishment later on when either you find that they are, or that they aren't.'

'Impartially?'

'Oh yes. Their vanity is easily whipped.'

'I don't need to know about men.'

'That is both arrogant and short-sighted of you.'

'I'm not arrogant,' she said anxiously – showing that she was used to the accusation.

'Aren't you? Well, you should be.' She was standing still in the kitchen door, with a lemon in one hand, and a knife in the other. He looked at her without seeing her, and then again observantly – but it was all right – he could make no picture of her: he found that he was relating to her lack of colour, the differently entrancing textures of her skin: there was no photograph, he discovered, when all the senses were employed.

When she saw him watching her so intently, she looked quickly down at herself as though she felt there must be something wrong. She has no vanity, he thought – I really must teach her a little conceit.

'At least nobody can say that last week they saw somebody rather like you in the street.'

'If they did, it would have been me they'd seen,' she said simply, and went to get glasses.

The flowers he had sent to Iris were nearly over. Bad shop, he thought, they ought to last a week, and then counted up the days that they had lasted. Until now, he had always liked to live in as many different environments as he could either afford or contrive, but now, it was beginning to be disquieting. When he was at Campden Hill Square, he found himself wondering how life was being spent in this studio – whether there were wild student parties with night-lights in saucers and Spanish music on the portable gramophone, and Imogen dancing by herself – parties with black coffee and wine and very little to eat – or whether Imogen sat on the large yellow cushion which she dragged about the floor and on which she always sat, eating Bath Oliver biscuits and reading plays aloud to herself. He always thought of her by herself – even in a party.

And then, when he was here with her, he discovered that the moment she was out of the room, he was thinking about his wife and their house – enduring now the thought of her father's illness – enduring thoughts about him of which he was dreadfully ignorant: sitting alone with a tray of food in the drawing-room (she had sent the children to Kent in order that she might devote more time to her father). She would go to the hospital and read to him until his drug worked and he slept for a few hours, poor devil. Then she would go home and try to read herself to sleep, but she did not use drugs, and he knew that she was sleeping very badly.

He was about to switch his mind on to his work as a relief, when he realized that Imogen had returned with the Dubonnet and glasses, and was sitting quietly on the floor beside him.

'What an unobtrusive creature you can be!'

'I thought you were either thinking, or asleep.'

'I might have been both. Intellectual people are so used to thinking that, naturally, they do it in their sleep as well.'

She looked up, smiling. She was beginning to feel happy about his being there. 'Pour it out.'

'I'm not an intellectual, anyway,' she added, taking her glass.

'No? Nor am I then.'

'What *is* an intellectual?' She had a charming habit of tilting her head at the end of a question, really wanting the answer.

'Intellectuals are the intelligent theorists who are sneered at by the clever administrators. It is because of them that the world goes round the wrong way far too slowly.'

'Because of the intellectuals?'

'Yes – the administrators reverse their theories, you see.'

'Which *are* you?' she persisted.

'I'm a diabolically clever administrator. I make pounds out of the intellectuals, but I'm much kinder to them than most of my contemporaries.'

'But then, you are exceedingly kind,' she said.

He denied it – he resolved to be kinder – he wondered whether he had ever been kind before. Aloud, he said: 'Here I am kindly talking nonsense when you have conclusions to divulge. What are they? No, wait a minute. I will administrate the evening, or three hours hence, we shall still be sitting here and you will be quite dry but very, very hungry. Put some clothes on, and we'll have dinner while you tell me.'

'All right.' She stood up.

'Take that off first, would you?'

She made a small, self-conscious gesture with her hands, and the blue robe slipped to her feet. He tried to look at her carefully, but in the entirety of nakedness she was dazzling – it was not possible to look at her for long. I need her, he thought savagely – and if she loves me – why not?

'Go and get dressed.'

She picked up the robe, frowning a little.

'Conrad.' He saw that she was trembling. 'I don't understand you.'

'What don't you understand?'

'I was going to ask you whether you loved me.'

'You've picked a very bad moment.' He got up from his chair, and walked to the window. 'Go and get dressed.'

He heard the murmuring rub of her robe trailing from her hand on to the floor, and the door shut with a dejected quiet.

In the taxi, when his desire had subsided, he said:

'Of course I love you.'

Upstairs in their restaurant they were alone, and he chose their dinner and gave her a glass of vodka.

'I've never had it.' She drank, and said: 'You have to drink it in the present.'

'Now then.' He was beginning to feel curious to the point of apprehension.

'It was about my future.'

'Yes?'

'Well, you've made me see one thing very clearly.'

He was silent.

'You've made me realize,' she repeated steadily, 'that there is no point in my trying to paint.' She was staring at her empty glass – twisting it round and round in her fingers.

'Are you sure of that?'

'I am sure. I mind rather, at the moment.' Her voice had become less steady – she shook it together with a little laugh. 'I expect I'll get over it quite soon.'

'You may not be a painter, but there are innumerable decorative possibilities.'

She relinquished her glass. 'I don't think of it like that. Either painting, or myself.'

'Designing, advertising, and so forth,' he persisted.

'Oh – clothes, and material and wallpaper. I shouldn't care twopence about any of that. So there would be no point in my trying to do it.'

'What are you going to do instead?'

She turned to him: she had an unusually intricate pattern of lines on her forehead. 'That is what I don't know. What could I do?'

There was a short silence while they both thought; then she continued: 'I never thought of not being able to paint. For years I was told that when I had finished my education I could come to London and go to an art school, and, of course, I always wanted to. It always seemed so far away, that I never thought beyond it. Stupid of me. None of it has turned out at all how I imagined.'

'Why don't you try to do it for a little longer?'

'I can't let my family go on paying for a training which I know is no use. You know what Tonks said to the student about knitting. Well, it seems to me that I'd better learn to type or something.' She gave him a bewildered meaningless smile, and began to eat her smoked trout.

'Good: well, now I know, I'll think about it.'

She turned to him. His face was closed and utterly unresponsive. She had thought that he would immediately produce a host of possibilities, and recoiled against what she felt was his reduction of the problem.

'You need more horseradish sauce,' he said.

After all, it is my whole future, she thought, watching his expert dissection of his fish. She remained wrapped in this thought for the rest of dinner, and asked him small dangerous questions such as why did they not go to the opera any more, and why had he not told her that he would be free that evening.

Afterwards, they walked slowly, until they were nearer one another. The hot dusty streets were smelling of horsemeat and garlic and cheap cooking oil; spattered with a few limp scurrying leaves; lined with the motor cars belonging to the theatre crowds; and cornered with women wearing thin black silk stockings and high-heeled dirty white sandals – with hair imitating Ginger Rogers and tied back with pieces of limp white chiffon. The sky above them reflected the neon lighting as the colour of a black grape skin against light. A noble looking tramp was settling on a bench at St Giles-in-the-Fields for the night. His hair and beard hung nearly to his waist in luxurious ringlets and curls the faintly greenish black of a bad black dye. He wore a bowler hat and two overcoats, with a paper carnation pinned to the outer lapel. He had taken off his boots, and his toe nails – immensely long – gleamed like the black talons of some bird. He was eating soft bread which seemed ferociously white against his beard. When he observed them, he gave them a courtly, sardonic smile, and with a neat animal movement of his shoulders, turned his back on them.

'Did he mind our looking at him?'

'Shouldn't think so. I was wondering what the statistics were for men as opposed to women living that life.'

'I should hate it,' she began, and he interrupted with a stab of irritation:

'Oh – you would. The life is far too self-contained for most women.'

'*You* wouldn't like it either.'

He hailed a taxi without answering her, and thought: How continuously personal women are. They apply everything to themselves, or someone near them: they are incapable of general application. The effect of what she had said in the restaurant about painting and her future was beginning to knock about in his mind, hitting blindly at any blind or tender spot, piling up his resentment against her, and making him very angry that at his age he should have propelled himself into such a mess. She sat, miserably attendant upon his mood, her hands in her lap, her head a little bent, waiting for him to speak, even to be angry aloud (for his anger filled the cab and was stifling).

When they arrived at her flat, she slid from her seat and out of the door like a child imitating a lizard. He remained.

'Tell him to go to Campden Hill Square.'

'Will you please go to Campden Hill Square?'

She did not look at him, and she had moved to the door of her house before the cab moved.

He tried to settle down with his anger: he had meant to hurt her, and he had succeeded: by how much, he wondered; was she crying – had she flung herself upstairs into some dark corner to cry? Or was she angry – was she standing in a blaze of light, blazing and trembling with rage? Or perhaps neither; perhaps she had wanted him to go on, and had been simply tired and bored. Damn all emotions; they preclude any sort of planned existence; they are worth next to nothing afterwards, and provoke childish excesses of anticipation. In a minute he knew he would stop the cab, but in an ecstasy of self-destruction he allowed it to continue while he derided himself for what he knew he was going to do. Well, there was to be no sentimental reconciliation like anybody in a film. She had wanted to talk about her future: right: they would talk about it, and she should be made to see exactly how responsible she was for herself – the weapons of tears or sex should only be allowed a single, physical, edge, and if it became clear that she needed a few corners rubbed off her heart in order that she might in future live down to the accepted standards of being in love, tonight was the night for rubbing. This cauterizing philosophy of being kinder to her in the long run had the advantage of complying with his immediate need to cry down and depreciate. He stopped the cab. One could spend one's life, he thought, fumbling for silver which he had not got, being kinder to a number of different people in the long run. It was the neatest preclusion of kindness imaginable.

There was light in her windows. He rang the bell, and waited for what seemed to him an unnecessarily long time before she answered it. Her hair was untidy, but she had not undressed, and she looked at him with a curious blankness.

'May I come and talk to you?'

She moved aside for him, shut the door, and followed him up the unkempt stairs that belonged to no one living anywhere in the house.

The studio stove was lit, and the deathly smell of burning paper filled the air.

'What are you burning?'

'Paper,' she answered, and her voice was as blank as her face. He saw an empty drawing folder lying open on the floor by the stove.

'My dear, you aren't burning up all your drawings at this hour of the night?'

She moved to the stove and shut it. 'I don't suppose I shall manage all of them tonight – it takes much longer than I thought.'

He sat down: 'Well, I must say, it's intensely dramatic of you.'

She did not reply. He watched her moving about the room for a minute, and then said: 'I suppose it is all my fault that you are burning them?'

She was kneeling by the stove again unpicking the tapes on another folder. She flushed a little: 'It isn't your fault that I am unable to draw.' The drawings had to be torn before they would go into the stove.

'You know perfectly well what I mean. You could hardly have contrived anything more aggressively destructive.'

'I had no idea that you were coming back.' She did not look at the drawings before she tore them. There was something hard and elusive about her which he had not encountered before. She is older than I have ever seen her, he thought, although her head is still the head of an ancient young angel.

'But you would have taken care that you told me all about it afterwards.'

She turned her head, and answered honestly: 'Perhaps. I don't know. What was it that you wanted to talk about?'

'I can't talk with all this destruction going on. Come over here, and have a cigarette.'

'You want to be the centre of destruction.' It was the kind of remark that he had taught her to make, and he found himself bitterly surprised that she had learned so fast.

She took a cigarette, but remained standing in front of him, and looking up at her, he suddenly realized that she was intolerably unhappy: that she was so consumed by the overwhelming ache and burn of this discovery which she was attempting to conceal, that it was frightening her – she moved and spoke alternately with the quickness or deliberation of panic.

'Imogen,' he said her name almost as though he was afraid of waking her; 'if you don't tell me, I shan't know.'

She did not move. 'All one's life,' she said painfully; 'there is this little path, and that little path – hedges, I suppose, on either side – one can't see very much, just a narrow alternative from time to time, until quite suddenly – at least, *I* didn't expect it – one comes to the end of the path, one can see everything – an endless desert of possibilities. I suppose – everyone feels that?'

He said, as though it was a reassurance: 'I don't know. Some time in their lives, perhaps.'

'It is most solitary and blinding.' He could hardly hear her.

'It is a predicament of the courageous imagination,' he added.

'Is it?' He felt her seize upon this.

'I think so. Either people don't look, or they won't admit to what they see.'

'That isn't anything to do with imagination.'

'It is all part of the mind. Do you think that the imagination is always employed with the fantastic, the falsehood, the distortion, the wishful improbability? It is the single most powerful weapon for discovering a truth. A lot of nonsense is talked about the imagination, because, like most powerful implements, it is dangerous.'

She was regaining her balance. To give her more time he continued: 'When imagination is successful, it is called vision, and when it is abused or a failure, it is called morbid or worse. God has a hand in it when it is good, and the psychiatrists when it isn't. Don't,' he added, 'believe exactly what I say. I am approximating, or marking time, or something like that.' He smiled at her, and she began to smile back; stopped anxiously, and said:

'What was it you came back to talk about?'

'Oh, you, of course. The most fascinating subject in the world, excepting me. But I was forestalled by this – conflagration.'

She glanced at the stove.

'Sit down. It is much harder to be anything sitting down.'

'All right. I didn't do that on purpose to annoy you.'

'I see that now. But I am naturally so bloody-minded that

I always expect other people to be the same. Why did you do it?'

'I wrote to my family about it last night. When I told you this evening, I thought – I thought that –'

'You thought that I would help, and I didn't.'

'A bit. I thought you would know exactly what it felt like. I see that that is silly, because nobody can know exactly what someone else feels like about anything.' There was a pause while she digested this discovery: then she said: 'And I suppose I thought that you would think of something else.'

'Yes?'

'Well then, as you didn't, I felt when I was alone here that I had better really burn my boats while I had enough courage to do it. I was afraid of waking up in the morning all soothing and dishonest with myself about it. If I burned everything, I thought I wouldn't, at least, be able to pick over my work and find excuses for it.' She looked at him, and her face was not blank any more, she was talking again as though she could see him. 'The trouble is that I don't see what to do at all.' She added violently: 'I don't want to exist and drift and make nothing. I would rather not be alive than do that.'

'You've had the idea of painting for a long time. You cannot expect immediately to be presented with an equally significant alternative. It takes time, but you will find one.'

'But *what* might I *find*?' she persisted like a child.

'I don't know yet. It will be your discovery, if you look.'

She looked so disappointed that he added unwisely: 'Anyway, you will marry and have children.'

'You? Could I possibly marry you, do you think?' Her face was lit with intention: so ingenuously without design, so passionately certain of her love, that his heart moved. He said: 'I didn't mean that. I am married, already.'

He saw her immediate acceptance: that he did not want her, or want her enough – the sudden death of that brilliant hope sinking to the bottom of her heart. She tried to smile and answered: 'I didn't really think I could, of course,' and folded her hands, one upon the other in her lap.

He wanted then desperately to protect her pride which was not vanity – to comfort and reassure her, but he could find nothing entirely safe to say or do.

She unclasped her hands, stared at the palms, and put them flat on the floor.

'It's probably very late,' she said at last. 'You'd better go.'

'I don't want to go.'

'Then, don't go. Stay – if you like.'

Shutting away the memory of that inflexion, he knelt beside her.

8

HE went home early in the morning before anyone was up. On the hall table was one of Dorothy's notes: 'Madam Mr Tomson rang will ring again.' It was not until he was half way upstairs that the name clicked, and he remembered Marseille. Why on earth should – but there was only one reason why Thompson rang up any woman. She, and Thompson! No, but really, she would be little Thompson's Waterloo – must already have been, as Thompson was not the man to waste time . . . then why was he telephoning now? He shrugged and gave it up.

The bedroom was empty; she had not spent the night in it. He pulled off his clothes and fell asleep trying to imagine his wife calling Thompson by his perfectly ghastly Christian name; but he couldn't even remember the name, only howling with laughter when he had heard it first, and advising Thompson never to use it. 'It was my mother,' Thompson had said. 'She was very interested in the East at the time.'

He was half way through breakfast when his wife came into the room, wearing a coat and carrying her morning letters. She sank wearily into her chair without a word. He rose to get her coffee. 'Black, please, Conrad.' After he had put the cup before her and she had sat in silence warming her hands round it – the situation seeming impersonally tense – the product of their separate fatigues – she said:

'I suppose I ought to have told you. They rang up and said that they were operating suddenly, so I went to the hospital to be there afterwards when he came round in case he wanted anyone, and by the time I realized I'd be there all night, it seemed too late to ring you up.'

'Is he all right?'

'I don't think he knows much about it.' She drank some coffee, and repeated: 'I don't think he knows much.'

Her face was absolutely worn by fatigue – expressionless, familiar, enclosed – he remembered that she had looked like that after her first child, and how difficult he had found it then to make contact with her. Now he said:

'But do they regard the operation as successful?'

She was stirring more sugar into her coffee. 'How can one tell? He is not dead, and they say he is doing as well as can be expected. They haven't dared say that he is perfectly comfortable, because it is obvious to the meanest intelligence that he is not.'

'You saw him?'

'Yes.' There was a pause, and then she said: 'Isn't it extraordinary how everything shrinks about people in pain except their eyes. But perhaps it isn't just pain.'

'Well,' he said sharply, 'what is it?'

She stared at her cup. 'Oh – agony of mind as well. That is what one cannot bear to —'

'You torture yourself,' he interrupted. 'You were not so devoted to your father. Be simpler – more subjective. Bear those ills you know.'

She said nothing, and he fell back to the position of practical concern. 'Are you going to sleep today? Dorothy can answer the telephone. She'll give you any important messages.'

The faint animation of some new anxiety crossed her face. She looked up. 'I can put the telephone by my bed.' She gathered up her letters. 'I might want to talk to them myself.'

When he left to go to the office, he glanced at the ebony table. The message written by Dorothy was not there.

The atmosphere of impending crisis enveloped him until he was not rid of it even in his office, nor walking about the streets, nor in his club. Certainly it was at its worst in Campden Hill Square. There, he felt the drag of a death struggle which his father-in-law illustrated, and which, he felt, was repeated in his association with his wife. He was unable to approach her: he had not with her been used to that effort; for many years she had come to him and been delighted to find him at the end of her journey; but now she was distant, and he knew only that she was distraught: her heart and mind were set entirely apart from him, her consideration the mechanical forethoughts of routine. Sometimes, he thought, she seemed almost glad to have him out of the house . . .

With Imogen, the situation was more transparently uncertain. She had stopped going to her art school, and although she did not discuss any alternative, he felt that she was obscurely, and perhaps unconsciously, dependent upon him. Since the evening when she had so simply asked whether she might marry him, he had laboured to devolve his emotional responsibility for her on to the practical. He tried to be commanding and kind, and watched her accept what he was determined to give, refusing in his turn to take anything from her until he had established it either as commonplace, or as an indulgence of her generosity. She was unhappy; he perceived this, and straightway canalized her unhappiness; imposed upon her the conflict of alternative careers – discussed her future with exhaustive enthusiasm, enclosed her heart and hedged his own with an ugly evergreen caution which preserved the immobility of balance between them; so that she wept alone, and he thought alone, and their love lay untouched, extant, but deeply frozen.

Alone, he probed and analysed, threw away excuse after excuse, and then anything which resembled an excuse, made up the separate parts of his mind, discovered that they did not fit, and tore them to pieces again. He tried seeing his wife as sentimentally bound up in dependants, her children, her father, as tediously, omnipotently maternal – as dependent upon him only for an environment where she might employ these instincts. He tried seeing Imogen as an infatuated adolescent, as a tentative young whore, as an imperfect schemer after destruction. He had only to be with either of them for these simplifying phantasies to resolve into a vortex of anxiety and ignorance – and worse, for the two women to dissolve into one another, until they were baffling and inseparable – a composite picture in his mind.

He worked feverishly these days. Long afterwards, he was to remember strafing a young office clerk for muddled thinking. 'I was in two minds about it at the time, sir.' (There were nearly tears in his eyes, he was so desperate to hold down his job.) 'It won't never happen again, sir.' Poor devil, thought Conrad, so uncharacteristically, that he was provoked into saying:

'Two minds are all very well, Blackburn. But never let your right mind know what your left mind is doing.'

'No, sir.'

'All right, Blackburn.' And the boy went, his escape as much a mystery to him as his muddle had been.

That evening, he went on an impulse of admiration for his wife to St Mary's Hospital, intending to collect her and at least see that she had a reasonable meal. She was not there, they said, she had left the hospital at five thirty – they did not know when she would return. Mr Vaughan was quite comfortable. He left the entrance to the private wing which was impregnated with the odours of ether and floor polish and carnations, which echoed with the starched shuffle of the night nurses going down to their first meal; stood outside in the weary little road which led nowhere but to the hospital, and then went home. But she was not there, either. She had gone out, reiterated Dorothy unnecessarily. He went to his club and dined alone, drank a glass of port with one of his oldest enemies, and went home to prowl aimlessly about his house.

She came in at eleven o'clock, into the bedroom as though she had not expected to find him there, for she halted at the door a moment before walking across the room to her dressing-table.

'I am not staying. I have to go back.'

'Back?' He watched her mercilessly until she was forced by the pressure of his eyes to look at him. He propped himself up in bed. 'You look as though you have a fever,' he observed. He had not forgiven her for the scene about Imogen before they went to France.

She flushed, and dropped her eyes, made the little nervous gesture with her hand across her hair, and said: 'Do I? I am just tired.'

'I should think you are utterly exhausted.' At that moment he was hating her; for deceiving him, for deceiving him so badly – she had positively forced his commiseration for her father – for sheltering beneath such an unassailable alibi. She had her back to him, she was searching for something in a drawer, and as he acknowledged his actually murderous instincts, he realized how deep, and he had thought impregnable, his regard for her had been. He had never, until now, questioned his admiration of her character; that she was neither dishonest, nor stupid, nor indifferent; that she had possessed the courage of her emotions, which, in his opinion, was the most to be expected of any woman. Now the whole structure slid like so much shale down a mountain, changing the face of his concept with a frightful, sudden, indifference. There was the frightful complete silence which follows such avalanches; then he asked:

'Are you going to be out all night?'

'I don't know. Perhaps only an hour.'

'Would it not be simpler to ring up the hospital first, and find out how he is?'

'I know how he is, far better than they will tell me.'

'Nonsense. There is no point in dashing about like this if it is to no purpose. He was quite comfortable when I left.'

'*You* left? When were you there?'

She had been tucking a scarf into the neck of her shirt, but now she turned her head, so that with the looking-glass he could see her three times.

'Earlier,' he replied after a pause: he was almost enjoying the simplicity of his hatred.

'I must have been dining,' she murmured; she seemed confused – aware that something was wrong, and afraid of knowing more. She pulled out the scarf impatiently, and started to tie it in a bow. 'Was he really all right when you were there? Did you see him?'

'I took their word for it. You must have had a remarkable dinner, if you have only just finished.'

He was still watching her: he saw her eyes cloud suddenly with something like fear, or pain. Then she said distantly: 'I dined – oh – ages ago. I have been walking. I have walked about for hours.'

He put down his book, and got up.

'I am not playing this game any more. Do you understand? I am out of it from this moment. You may do as you like, and I shall not care whether I like what you do. Your only ingenuity has been in landing me with a great deal of unnecessary guilt . . .' God knows what else he might have said, but the telephone rang, and she flew out of her frozen silence to answer it. The conversation was brief: there was not time for the haze of anger to clear – he had not known what he was going to say – and he found he was unable even to see her until she said: 'I have to go immediately. Conrad. Do you hear me? I *must* go.' She stared at him with a kind of urgent misery, and then ran out of the room, the rush of air from her departure stirring the pages of his open book.

Watching the pages hesitate and settle, he felt nothing but a sick astonishment.

9

'WHAT is the matter? Please tell me.'

'Nothing to do with you.'

Imogen laughed, and he said: 'Why?'

'I never thought that one could say "Nothing to do with you" like that. I thought it was always cross.'

'Have you *always* thought the same things about the same things?' he enquired irritably, and she answered humbly:

'I suppose I have.' Then she added: 'But would it help to tell me what is the matter?'

'My father-in-law was very ill. I began last night to say unforgivable things to my wife, in the middle of which the telephone rang and she rushed to his side arriving just in time to see him die.'

'Yes?'

'That's all.'

'Oh. Of course, I don't know what it was like before.'

'No, of course you don't. The trouble is that I don't either.'

'You must know whether you love her.'

'I am not a woman, so I don't know anything of the kind. Responsibility succeeds desire – some men enjoy one, and some the other – that's all.'

'Don't you see it in *any* other terms?'

'There have been seconds when I have seen it in other, indefinable, terms.'

'Which do you enjoy – the desire, or the responsibility?'

'Both; provided I may engineer their proportions.'

'But you *are* attached to her,' she persisted.

'Clearly. She is my wife.'

'Is *she* unhappy?'

'You don't imagine that being married to me is fun, do you?'

She turned her head away.

'I don't imagine anything at all.'

At home he discovered his wife stamping letters, while her young cousin (in London on his way up to Cambridge) discoursed to her upon his future.

'. . . what one really *craves* is some quite useless work for which one is grossly overpaid, and where one has all the time in the world for one's *interests* – mocking up a really brilliant biography of one of these dictators or someone – proving they're madly aristocratic, or it's all adrenalin for instance – only one knows people who are doing that – or one could simply found a bureau for giving people bad advice; make them pay like anything and then they'd do the opposite and it would all end happily ever after . . .' He had to breathe occasionally, and in the pause, when Mrs Fleming was about to say, 'Nonsense, Roland,' encouragingly, she saw her husband, checked herself, and gave him a little formal smile.

'Oh, good evening,' said Roland; 'I was worrying about the future.'

'Generally or specifically?'

'Oh, generally, with specific relation to me.'

Mrs Fleming threw away an empty stamp book and said: '*Is* there any other way of worrying about it?'

There was a pause, and then she said mildly: 'I had no idea that I should stop everyone talking. I shall post these while you decide what film you want to see.'

'She says she has to be taken to a film,' said Roland.

Fleming suddenly suggested: 'Why don't you post her letters for her?'

Roland looked faintly surprised, and began uncoiling the weedy waste of his legs, but she interrupted: 'No – I should like the air': and then as though she was afraid of what she had said, she held out the letters to her husband and added: 'Unless *you* want to post them?' In spite of the faint emphasis, she did not meet his eye. He shook his head, and, when she had gone, tried desperately to remember exactly what he had said last night.

They travelled across the desert evening – eating, talking, watching the Marx Brothers – after which Roland thanked them politely, said that he thought he would have a Turkish bath, and lounged off into the night, 'As casually,' she remarked, 'as he arrived.'

Alone together, she was so self-possessed, that he began to feel frightened for her. He asked her about her father, and without any emotion she told him the arrangements she had made. She did not take long to tell them, and at the end they both wished that there was more to say: but there seemed nothing for it but to drive silently home. They got out of the car and she said: 'Oh – I could put it away tonight.'

'Don't bother.'

The monotony of agitation, he thought, trudging upstairs. Dorothy had left sandwiches in the drawing-room.

'Do you want any?'

'Why not?' She started to eat one as though it was filled with sand.

'Are you going to join the children?' he asked.

'I expect so: should I?'

'Wouldn't it be a good thing?'

She put the sandwich on a plate. 'If you want me to go.'

'I don't mind whether you go — ' he began, and stopped, as she interrupted: 'I know.'

There was a silence. Then she said: 'Their terms start in about a week anyway.'

We had better talk, he thought wearily – talk it all out somehow – women usually respond to such a method, even if it results in pushing the balance further in either direction than they anticipate. Perhaps we ought to have Imogen here as well, and do the thing thoroughly – but Imogen wouldn't understand her: she would not see anything in our relationship. Perhaps that is because it seems entirely composed of a kind of middle distance memory – one cannot pretend that one doesn't remember, and one cannot pretend that one remembers clearly.

'Do you think that we had better try and talk to one another?'

She had been lying back in an armchair with her eyes shut; now, without any other movement, she opened her eyes and said: 'I don't think so, Conrad. At the moment I should be no good at talking. I don't care enough about anything at all.'

When the distant memory had faintly died, he said: 'Do you know that that was the first thing you ever said to me?'

'I don't remember. How odd that you should.' But she did not ask the circumstances of her not caring.

'Possibly indifference is useful for this sort of talk.'

'For men. Not for women. Women are quite useless for anything when they are indifferent.'

He looked at her thrown back in her chair; her feet and her hands lying elegantly useless, her attitude the epitome of indifference, as though she had finished everything in her life, and could not imagine why she was not dead. I used to be fascinated by her indifference, he thought, but then it had not the same quality about it – she was only lying in wait for something which it enchanted me to discover for her. Now, she seems disenchanted; I should have to think very hard before I loved her, and neither of us seems to care enough for the subtle sensitive effort which we should both have to make. But we cannot go on like this . . .

She sat up in her chair.

'I shall probably go to Kent, before the weekend. Make your plans as though I was going, anyway. That was what you wanted to know, wasn't it? But I am not going to bed yet. I still have a great many letters.'

He finished his drink. 'Don't stay up all night.' He got up, feeling strangely awkward.

'I won't. I shall feel much better when the letters are off my mind.' She felt his awkwardness, but she was unable even to make that the last straw. She gave him a social unconvincing smile on which she intended him to leave the room.

'Don't imagine anything at all if you can help it at the moment,' he said, and she answered with lightning clarity:

'I sometimes think that the only imagination we have is in thinking that we have it.'

She is not dead, he thought to himself; just badly shocked; she'll recover somehow and recognize herself again, but what the *hell* do I *do*?

He threw off his clothes, to indulge in the immediate escape of sleep, but he dreamed and dreamed, and woke sweating from elusive fears to sleep and dream again of the same unidentifiable anxiety and grief. When, eventually, he looked at his watch, it was after four, and she had not come upstairs. He was strung up to the point when her not being there disturbed him. All the evening he had dreaded the end of their day together, but now, at this hour, the suspense had degenerated to an almost physical alarm, when he knew that he must find out where she was.

She lay huddled at one end of the sofa. There was a lamp lit by her desk which made very little light in the room. She wore her coat, and there was a handkerchief clenched in her hand. Her face, touched by shadows and marked with the tears which had died on it, was the colour only of shadow and light, and absolutely still: her head propped in the extreme corner of the sofa seemed unnaturally disposed for such stillness. He stood, remembering the last time that he had found her asleep there, and how remotely, perfectly beautiful she had seemed – the picture presented itself and then faded before the reality of her now. Now she was not beautiful, she had no appearance for him; he felt only a confusion of gentle recollections – of when she had been vulnerable: afraid, or ill, or tired, or sad – of times when, afterwards, he had wondered what she would have done without him – to ease her safety, to free her from fears, and enclose her with affections. The price of sustaining their marriage at so high a tension of reality and love had been those casual infidelities which, from time to time, he had needed for the satisfaction of that aspect of him which dictated no fair bargain, but a simple gain – the something-for-virtually-nothing, assurance-of-vanity requirement: an instinct common to all men, and too often disastrously fulfilled in their wives or sublimated in their work. 'What you do every day must be better done,' his father had once said to him, advising him against what he precociously outlined to his father as a five-year plan; 'therefore, be cautious of routine: employ it only so much as you can live up to it. Let your second-rate behaviour be as random as your mistakes are various. Do not join that insufferable body who remain constant to their disabilities.' His father had been the only man with whom he had felt any affinity. He remembered how, when his father had died, old, impoverished, and sanguine, 'I have drawn the distinction between life and death: I have been a noble grasshopper!' he had actually wept, and turned blindly to his wife. Now her father had died, and she had not been able to turn to him because Imogen had not been, was not, a casual infidelity. With the heart you have no choice about chastity, he thought; it is not a question of morality: it just won't split. I love her, he thought, thinking of Imogen, and walked slowly towards his wife.

She stirred as he leaned over her; her hands shot upwards with a convulsive gesture as though to protect herself; a frown fled across her forehead with the curious lilting speed of a sharp breeze across water – her eyelids trembled – she woke with a hard desolate little cry, and shrank away from him as though he was some blinding light. Staring at him, she began weeping: even before she was awake her tears streamed uncontrollably – she put her fingers under her eyes to break the rush of tears, and as he knelt by her he thought she made some faint incoherent negation of something that was not to be said or done. He heard himself asking the gentle foolish questions that are asked of children or animals – meaningless words that discover nothing; a helpless attempt at comfort since there is never any reply – but she seemed beyond comfort. He saw her cast wildly round the room for escape, and then back to him immediately before her.

He stood up, and told her carefully what he was going to

do; but when he bent over her she resisted him with a kind of weak frenzy, until she was in his arms, sobbing bitterly now as he carried her upstairs.

He laid her on the bed, and, shutting the door, watched her a moment before getting sodium amythal from their bathroom; but when he returned with the capsules and a glass of water, she lay as he had left her, her hands clenched by her sides, weeping, but more quietly. He offered her the capsules and she frowned twice and shook her head; he propped her up and told her to take them – she gave a deep sigh and did as she was told.

Swallowing the water helped her to some control of herself, and she asked for a handkerchief. When he came towards her with it, she said: 'Please don't ask me: please don't speak to me.' He shook his head, gave her the handkerchief, and began to take off her clothes. When he had found her nightgown and pulled it over her head, he collected the pins out of her hair until it was also undressed. He pushed her hair back from her face – she seemed much calmer – and thinking that she had reached that need, he kissed her forehead – but she twisted away from him with a small heart-broken sound. Better trust the drug and let her finish, he thought; it isn't a bitter sound any more; but what have I, or anyone else, done to her? I've never seen her break like this – she is far beyond anything I've ever known about her. Hysteria . . . but then if one thoroughly understood the reasons for anybody's hysteria, one would be hysterical oneself. He had continued rhythmically to stroke her head. He felt that she was very near sleep; her eyes were closed and she was quiet. He was just moving to switch out one of the lamps, when she whispered: 'Conrad. I haven't got my watch.'

'Do you want it?'

She nodded.

'Downstairs?'

There was a pause, and then she said slowly: 'I put it in the fireplace. I so much hated the time.'

He found the watch lying in a corner of the hearth where

she must have thrown it, as the glass was shattered, and the lovely enamel back badly cracked. He pulled out the remaining splinters of glass and took it up to her.

'Is it broken?'

'It doesn't go, but you'd better wear it.' He fastened it round her neck, and as she looked at him with infinitely grateful calm before her eyelids closed again like heavy books, he said: 'I don't suppose it is irreparable. At any rate, I will try and get it mended.'

'*You* will,' she murmured, with content.

'Yes,' he answered. '*I* will.'

10

'WHAT is the matter?'

'Nothing.' She went on studiously arranging the flowers he had brought her with unnatural finnicking concentration.

'That, my very dear Imogen, is just a time-wasting reply.'

She looked at him over the roses with defensive hostility. 'It is what you often say to me.'

'And then you ask me again because you really want to know.'

She took a rose out of the bowl, and broke the stalk. 'You ought to know without being told.'

'Is it because I cannot stay to dinner?' He knew that it was, but he felt too weary for an argument.

'Because you won't stay. Oh – not really even that. Because you don't want to stay. You say your wife will be alone if you do, and I shall be alone if you don't.'

'You must accept that. I told you on the telephone this morning.'

'I know. I do accept it – I try,' she corrected herself, 'but I can't help minding.'

'It is only one evening, and anyway, here I am now.'

'You mean I see so little of you, I should make the most of it?'

What an interminable brink, he thought; each thing we say, or rather I say to either of them; lines of it, days, weeks . . . to either of them . . .

She swept the broken stalks off the table into a waste paper basket. 'Down on my knees, and thank God gorging for a bad man's love?' She was trying to play his game, and smiled unhappily.

'Where did you get that from?'

'Out of *The Taming of the Shrew* and out of my head.'

'Well! Does that mean that you are a shrew and I am a bad man?'

'Poor Conrad. You do look dreadfully tired.' She ran to get glasses. How few women run prettily indoors, he thought. With any luck we shall be all right in a minute.

When she had given him a drink, she dragged her yellow cushion up to him and they sat in an abstracted but amiable silence, until she said: 'I think really I meant that you are trying not to be a bad man, and I am trying not to be a shrew.' Then she looked up at him solicitously, and added: 'I'm sorry if I am one.'

He laughed, disarmed, and kissed her: and throwing her arms round his neck she clung to him, without speaking, or kissing him.

'I shall have to get rid of my glass if that's how you feel.'

But she slid away from him on to the floor again, and said hurriedly: 'Will it be like this for long?'

'Our being in love?'

'No – your worrying about her. Is she very unhappy about her father?'

'She is very unhappy, anyway, not entirely about her father.'

'Will it be like this for long?' she repeated.

'I don't know, darling. I'd tell you if I knew anything.'

She sat silent for a moment, picking the fringe of her cushion, and he felt her struggling to control herself, and knew that she could not, long before she cried out: 'I'm jealous of her! I've tried and tried not to be – it is the worst feeling I've ever had, and I don't understand it at all. I am so miserably awfully jealous I feel sick with it, and the rest of the time I am so ashamed. I thought if one was so dreadfully ashamed of a feeling one could get rid of it. It isn't hating *her*, really, I don't even know her – it is your house, and your furniture, and what the rooms look like that I've never seen which all belong with her; and your friends, and all the years and hours you've spent like that; making plans at breakfast, and then if you've planned that I should see you, you can't, because your life with her streams steadily on, and with me there are just isolated flashes.' She looked at him with miserable honesty. 'I don't expect you to understand about being jealous. *You* don't feel it, but with me it goes on and on however hard I try, until I can only try not to think about you at all, or I spoil you in my thoughts. I don't expect you to say anything, but I am so dreadfully ashamed, I thought you ought to know.'

'Why do you think that?'

'It wouldn't be fair,' she answered simply: 'you might be imagining me better than I am.'

There was a pause, and then she said carefully: 'Please could I have a cigarette?'

When he had lit one for each of them, he said: 'Have you thought at all why people fall in love or love one another?'

'I have thought, but I don't know.' She spread her fingers with a little movement of denial. 'I don't think I know anything.'

'It seems to me quite simple. It is always based upon some mutual requirement, or complementary need. The point is to concentrate on what you have got with anyone, and not on what you haven't.'

'Well?'

'Well? You work that out.'

'I know you want me,' she said, after thinking a moment, 'you find me attractive, and you need someone for that.'

'There have been moments when I thought that feeling was reciprocal.'

'Yes, but—' She frowned with the desire to make herself understood. 'I can't concentrate all my – my feeling into simply going to bed with somebody. It isn't all I want.'

'Then don't. Don't try to concentrate it. Split it up among more people.'

'That's what I can't do!'

'You want to spend all your time with one person, being everything to them.'

'No.' She was nearly angry. 'You are sophisticating the argument. Of course I don't want that. I just can't divide my heart, that's all. Perhaps you can, I can't. Perhaps men always can, or perhaps their hearts don't run over into all their life. I told you, I don't understand anything, I'm trying to find out because of what I told you just now.'

'You thought if you knew more, you would not feel jealous?'

'I thought it might help me not to,' she answered.

'There isn't time to talk now, but you are wrong about my being simply attracted to you. You really know that, but perhaps it needs saying.' He got up and smiled at her. 'I need you in more ways than one. We are not really so dangerously different. I am simply older, and consequently more dishonest. Don't be infected by me. I must go.'

She walked downstairs with him to the door. At the door, she touched his arm timidly: 'Conrad. Does *she* need – does she love you – do you think?'

'She – no – I don't think she really loves me.'

How curious, he thought, walking away from her, how curious that it should be so much easier to betray someone if you kiss them.

He walked, past the taxi rank, half way up the wide dreary road to the park, and then stopped; neither wanting to go back to the rank, nor to finish the dreary road. There was nowhere to sit – he was forced, in this case, to employ an alternative. Then he saw a telephone box, and felt hopefully in his pockets for pennies, but there were none. I will put twopence into each suit, he thought, and was flattered by even so small a resolution.

He pressed button B in the box and twopence jostled forth. He began dialling Imogen's exchange— Really, the whole business is becoming positively Freudian, he thought, as he started again. He wanted to evade dinner at home with his wife, and he succeeded with unexpected ease. She answered; his brother Joseph had turned up, and invited himself to dinner. He asked whether he might return in time to drink brandy with them, and added on an impulse of candour: 'I have something to think out, and want to dine alone.' Afterwards, he wondered whether he had been foolish to say that: perhaps she would not believe him. He did not usually give such weak reasons for his absences. But the truth *is* weak, and very, very, flexible, he thought in his taxi, extraordinarily hard to break, however improbable.

All the time in the taxi, the crisis gained momentum, although he refused to acknowledge it until he was actually dining.

He chose his food and wine with great care, almost with the deliberation of a man for whom it was to be the last meal. He had not, he supposed, the Embankment mentality; in trouble, he was more of an Algernon.

He looked round the small restaurant: it was half full, and he had easily secured a corner. He was the only man dining alone; although often before he had observed somebody doing exactly what he was doing, and had wondered idly why they did it. Boredom and greed he had usually concluded. Perhaps he had been wrong. Perhaps they, too, had been unable to nerve themselves on to the merry-go-round without the support of good food and wine. He took a last look at the couples round him, decided that the best things in life were very, very expensive, and plunged into his private vortex.

He began with the premise that his behaviour was inexcusable: there could be no excuse for making two people who loved him continually uncertain of his affection or interest, and therefore extremely unhappy; but if the situation continued, this was inevitable.

If, as Imogen had confirmed, the heart could not be divided, why did they require the heart? Why could not his wife be content with his children, their houses, the certainty that he would not socially compromise her, and the knowledge that if she kept her head they would be old together? And Imogen . . . why could not she settle for his desire, the more exotic amusements, and spasmodic, but fairly regular attention? They might, of course, either or both of them, be induced to accept their portions, but, he realized, only at the expense of those virtues which made them in any way desirable. They were not naturally promiscuous, and therefore any attempt at imposing promiscuity upon them was bound to lead to disaster. On the other hand, he could hardly expect his wife indefinitely to lead a celibate life (he remembered Marseille, and her misery the previous night, and began to understand that situation) . . . nor could he expect a young and beautiful creature, designed for love, to live undamaged by his partial return. She would grow older – she would rationalize her real needs by something less attractive. She would, she must, to some degree become capricious and demanding, dishonest and resentful, as his wife must become dulled by their mutual deceit, and both discover that there is no humiliation so entire as not being quite good enough. If their lives continued like this, there was a far greater chance of Imogen being unfaithful to him. He realized with some shock that even the thought was intolerable. 'I don't expect *you* to understand about being jealous,' she had said: and then remembered what he had felt about his wife the night her father had died. He had then, he supposed, felt jealousy, of a sort, although it seemed odd, and really rather unpleasant to be jealous about somebody whom one did not want. Did he then, perhaps, want and need both of them, and was it simply their whole-hearted temperaments which made the business so exhausting? It was not until then that he understood their likeness to one another: Imogen was potentially his wife; his wife had been an Imogen. His reason snapped under the weight of this discovery, the clarity of his mind gave way to a mist of memories . . . of his wife when he had first seen her – so lovely, so young, so despairing of life . . .

Before he had spoken to her, before he had even known her name, he had wanted to be responsible for her peace and pleasure; he had known that her despair was deeply attractive to him (it had none of the second-hand chronic quality he usually associated with the word) and he had been certain of success for the simple (and, now, he thought, astonishing) reason that he had never wanted anyone so much. He had pursued her through her indifference, her almost savage shyness, her countless unpredictable fears, her secret prejudiced intelligence – she had succeeded, he found, in concealing from her family both her heart and her mind, they having vitiated her beauty for her by so constantly denying it, that when he had first told her she was beautiful she had lunged out at him wildly and cried that she knew what she looked like – he need not look at her. When, as a result both of his perseverance and his extravagant imagination, she had finally consented to marry him, he instantly removed her from her family – he remembered stopping the car, rushing into a chemist, and flinging a toothbrush into her lap 'for your new life'. That had been the beginning. That was years ago, and he did not want now to recall the landmarks which pointed their descent.

Imogen, however, had not been complicated by a singularly destructive family and that other misfortune (he did not choose to think of that now); she surely was not therefore so vulnerable? But he knew that she was as likely to be hurt by him as his wife had been hurt by anyone else: as he might now hurt his wife. I've simply picked the wrong characters for this situation, he thought, or at least, one wrong character, but when I picked the other kinds there wasn't a situation, because I didn't care in the least. But to manage *this* efficiently, I've got to care so much that I shall be good for nothing else, and I'd give a good deal to be clean out of it. He began to imagine himself clean out of it –

champagne. They didn't drink anything else, you see, so that was bound to do for them.'

'What happened to it?'

'That was the terrible thing. They did it – as a farce – instead of a pantomime, at Christmas. They let Elsie play the part I'd written for her; they paid me twenty pounds and I was so excited I didn't realize what was going on. I went out and bought a string of pink pearls for Elsie – she loved pink – they were in a box lined with pink velveteen, and I planned to give them to her with a card on the first night. It was she who had given me her bottle of green ink she hardly ever used for writing letters, and her box of notepaper to write the play. They were shifty about letting me see rehearsals, but they were all laughing and saying how good it was – except Elsie, who just kept saying get on with starting another play, and just before they went up on the first night she called me and said she was very proud of me, and if the play didn't go as I expected I must not fret but see it was all for the best and everybody had to get started somehow.'

He stopped, and said: 'I haven't thought about all this for years, and this is the third time today that I've remembered about it.'

'Go on: what happened?'

'They put me in front, in a box all by myself, and for about ten minutes, until the house lights went, I felt no end of a nob. I saw myself wearing a top hat and owning theatres, with Julia Neilson, Lewis Waller, Playfair, Dion Boucicault and others all on their knees to me imploring me for plays. I don't suppose those names mean anything to you, but they meant a lot then – they were the epitome of heroic glamour – thousands of people adored them and collected postcards of them in their famous parts just as avidly as they collect pin-ups today. I'd just got as far as postcards of me, when the house lights went. From the moment the curtain went up, I knew something was wrong; and when I saw the pink flannel shrimps, the size of bananas, and the house laughed at them, my heart dropped like a small burning coal into my boots, where it remained for the whole performance, while I struggled with my feelings. My feelings!' he laughed: 'you've no idea what they were like – resentment, shame, rage, self-pity, sheer, obstinate refusal to accept the situation – shame and rage again. They went round and round, accompanied by a full house in holiday mood, roaring with laughter at what I considered to be my most heartrending speeches, agonizing situations, and beautiful moments. When Elsie came on in a white nightgown several sizes too large for *her*, and a long wig of golden hair streaming down her back, I nearly burst. The conflict was so awful, you see: a bit of me thought she looked wonderful; and a bit wanted to laugh, because she was somehow a caricature of herself, and there was everybody shouting with mirth, and her entrance was one of my beautiful moments – well, I sat there seething until – I don't remember what made me – but I laughed – by mistake, of course: it made me furious; I was crying as well, without any noise – with tears on my scalding face like spit on an iron. And I thought if they could see me now – the author looking like this, they'd laugh more than ever: they were the world, you see, and it would be my fault if I gave them another chance to laugh at me. So I watched the rest of the play with a kind of glassy calm – if I was a failure I was going to be dignified about it. And so I bolstered myself until my nose cleared, and I imagined myself facing the company afterwards, with worldly indifference. I hadn't bargained for the end, at all, when they clapped and the cast started to cry for author; Edward Burton – he was the actor manager – sent for me and they hauled me on to the stage and I found myself standing between him and Elsie, unable to look at either of them, as the bitterness of my failure rolled over me all over again. I had set out to do one thing, and the fact that it had turned out to be something quite different, escaped me. I could only see what I'd failed to do.'

He became aware, as he stopped again, of how much he had been talking; he had talked and talked, and she had finished the kitchen. He made a small conclusive gesture with his hands. 'Well: that was that. But it was the classic example of things not turning out as I had meant them to.' He looked round for a cigarette, and she pushed the packet across the table to him.

'You were fourteen when all this happened?'

'Don't you feel I ever could have been?'

'It just seems so young to write a play and have all that happen, and very hard to bear at fourteen. What did Elsie say to you?'

'Oh, she saved my bacon – or sense of proportion – as usual. She talked to me nearly all night till she was dropping, bless her. Had I realized that lots of people wrote plays who never had them performed at all? Of course I hadn't. Did I realize how much easier it would now be to get another play put on? Of course I didn't. I explained that I wanted to write about life, and she said there was nothing to stop me but I'd have to learn something about it. The best thing she said was that one wasn't born knowing things, but one had a chance to find out what one wanted to know. She – do you *want* to hear all about this?'

'Yes, I do.'

'She said that as I wasn't living in castles with a whole lot of earls, it would be difficult to write a serious play about them and that I'd written a play out of other plays, and not out of what I saw or knew. Then she said: look at her: could I imagine her behaving like Lady Geraldine FitzAbbot? Not her – she wouldn't be so silly: she wasn't pure and high born – she was fat and rather common; she liked her stout and a good laugh and she dyed her hair and she loved Teddy Burton and there was nothing pure or noble about her – but at least I *knew* her. Then I began to see what she meant, and felt so much better that although it was three in the morning, I gave her the pink pearls and asked her to marry me, and she was sweet about it all – the pearls and the proposal.'

'Did you really want to marry her?'

'It may seem absurd to you, but yes – I did, then. She

seemed to me so *good* – such a good, kind creature, and I found that such an attractive quality – I wanted to stay with it. I still feel like that, sometimes.'

'You mean, you still sometimes wish you had married her?'

'Yes – no, that's not what I meant.'

There was a silence, and then she coloured, and said: 'I'm so sorry. Of course that's not what you meant.' She was thinking of Lillian, and her possible implication of disloyalty.

He put his hand on her shoulder – let it rest – and took it away. 'I know it's not what you meant, either.' He understood her – that she didn't know he had not been thinking of Lillian.

In the taxi, driving across town to the piers to meet Lillian, he thought of Alberta arranging flowers and unpacking in the apartment she had so neatly made habitable, and Lillian in the boat locking and unlocking pieces of hand luggage, and worrying about whether he had remembered to meet her. Out of her country family life, Alberta – in the middle of New York – could do what was required of her: she could adapt what she had been bred and brought up to be, because something else in her was steady – was not rocked by outward changes. But if Lillian made physical gestures her body broke down, and he did not think that she recognized any other kind now: her courage was therefore constantly misspent, and sinking into the parched field of her activities. She was as pinned by this fixed image of herself and her desperate efforts to serve it, as Alberta was free to be served by her own imagination. That, he supposed, was the difference – and he hovered above it, uncertain where he should stand . . .

2

LILLIAN

THE restlessness started the night before we were supposed to dock. Up until then, it hadn't entered my head – I don't know why not. Jimmy had been his sweetest – really I'd enjoyed the trip – even when he got seasick, which he always does, poor thing, he was so pathetic and good-tempered about it, and so grateful for being looked after that somehow even his being prostrate for two days hadn't spoiled the journey. I read to him – he still likes C. S. Forester and almost any poetry I choose best, and we had delicious little picnic meals in his cabin although the poor creature couldn't eat much. But he adored being looked after – I think that's never having had parents or a proper home – and it was heavenly to be the nurse for a change. He said I was good at it, and he meant that, which was so warming. He told me about his life in orphans' homes which he's never talked about before, and it sounded awful – much worse than he realized. The sense of being a collection – of everything being based on justice rather than feeling; everybody dressed the same, having the same, acting the same, and knowing everything about each other. He told me that he was sent a tin motor car anonymously for Christmas, and he kept it buried in the garden so that the others couldn't share it and told everybody it was lost and dug it up to touch and look at it by himself. Of course it got all rusted and fell to bits, but he said it was worth it to have a secret. It was the only secret he managed to have, he said, the others all got found out in spite of telling lies. He said that even at the time he felt disconnected from his life – as though he was watching somebody else go through the motions of it. I understand that: that's why he is so useful to Em and adores him so, and I really must ***not*** be jealous of that. But the night before we were supposed to dock there was fog and we reduced speed and everybody was talking at dinner about how late the fog might make us. It was then: it came over me just like the beginning of a disease or fever that perhaps in a week Em had become attracted to her and seduced her because that would be the easiest thing in the world to do. And immediately I thought what nonsense – think of her – she's just a dull little schoolgirl, and if he wants to seduce somebody, he can do better than that. Then I thought of that horrible Gloria Williams – mincing lethargic creature with those hideous legs – a genteel martyr if ever there was one – if he could get off with *her* he might do anything. The vulgarity of my thoughts about him sometimes appals me, *and* the language in which they are couched, which, of course, is in keeping. After all, *I* picked her, and God knows I have learned to consider this squalid little possibility. After dinner, I asked Jimmy to walk on the boat deck with me, and while he was getting our coats I resisted the urge to confide in him – to share this apprehension: I don't want Jimmy to discover that Em talks to him more than he talks to me, and so I have always pretended to Jimmy that I know everything, and understand, or don't care. But while we were pacing up and down in that curiously heavy, billowing air, I asked him what Em had had to do all the week in New York, and when he told me, I felt much better, because really there would hardly be time to start a new affair as well. Only I do hope we don't get delayed too much by this weather, and nobody will say anything definite about that. After a bit, Jimmy said would I like to go to the movies – they were showing *The African Queen*, which we'd both seen, but it is Jimmy's beloved Forester, and I adore Katharine Hepburn, so we went. Afterwards, Jimmy had a drink and we talked a bit about where we would be in the summer, and I said I wanted to go to Greece, which shook him, but it's quite true – I do, and Em has promised me for years. Jimmy looked miserable, and said he loathed sightseeing, and wouldn't it be too hot, and I explained about my idea of living on an island, and having a really simple life. I also told him that I thought that an island would be a good place for Em to write and be away from the theatre or contacts with it. I begged him not to put Em off, and he looked shocked, and said of course he wouldn't dream of it. Then, suddenly, we had nothing more to say and he suggested going to bed. I couldn't sleep. I read and read: in the end I took a pill, and it was like falling slowly into a heavy warm sea – silent and colourless; dark and empty and immeasurable. At the very beginning of my waking, I dreamed of meeting Em. I could float, which made my movements most gentle, and he was standing on a very small island, with one tree beside him. I felt my hair shining, my skin moist as I rose out of the water and turned to him, nearer and nearer, until our eyes were almost fused in our meeting. Then I saw that his island was floating also – away from me – and that I was not to reach it – that I had come up out of the sea on to my separate island, but with no tree, and I sank on to the pale sand which darkened as the sun went slowly in and I woke. It was late – if there had not been fog we should have docked by now. I rang Jimmy, and he'd had breakfast and knew that we should dock at six. At least we knew. In eight hours I should see him – *if* he was there to meet me – *if* the fog did not get worse – *if* he had news of the time that we were to dock. Jimmy came and talked while I had breakfast and was very calm and stern, and said I was working myself up, and he'd call Em's hotel and make sure that he knew we were due at six. He tried to make the call while I thought how funny it was that I couldn't even *enjoy* being excited any more. The call was no good: everybody was making them, and by the time we were through the delay, Em had checked out – which at least means the apartment is on. I wondered what on earth he and the girl were doing, and started to feel bad about her again. Perhaps I get excited by the wrong things – or perhaps excitement is no good anyway. Really I would like to meet him much more like the first half of my dream – with a kind of beautiful, calm confidence – and very quietly. As it is, I can't keep still: can't eat lunch; get more and more breathless, and a pain inside ticks over like an engine ready to start; the palms of my hands sweat, and I keep thinking that I've forgotten to pack something. And yet, whenever I feel like this – right up to whatever is going to happen – the event seems, as it were, to start without me: I am not in it – all my imagination of it is dislocated and there seems nothing to take its place. Once, I remember him meeting me (also in New York), and within a few minutes, we were having an argument about some dreary people we hardly knew, and I told him how excited I'd been about meeting him, and he said: 'In order to talk about the Smithsons?' And then I remembered thinking that excitement was useless. That's the trouble with me: I hardly have any real feelings – just awful substitutes – intellectual imaginings, and physical anti-climaxes. Yes, but how does one *have* real feelings, and how can I have them about Em if he doesn't have them too? I *did* have them about Sarah. Oh! Sometimes I wish she had lived a little longer so that I would have more of her to remember now; her two years seem so short that I've nearly lost the taste of them: all my memories are coloured with the pain of losing her. Surely that was real – that wrenching, aching loss? Afterwards Em once said to me: 'Only joy is unmistakable: remember your joy in her.' He said it in the kind of way that made me feel it was true, but I couldn't understand him; I didn't accept what he said, because not having been allowed to suffer instead of Sarah, I refused not to suffer as well as she. It's very odd: I think so much about these things – but I hardly ever think about them in this way: it is something to do with the ship being late, and these eight hours being slipped into my life – not how I expected or meant. I understand what people mean when they say: 'I would die for her'; in certain circumstances, not being able to becomes a kind of outrage. There is something weak and dangerous about making a person the centre of your life: people are damaged and die too easily – but *where* is anything indestructible? My chief feeling about Em is fear that I may lose him, and as I've never really had him, this is absurd. It is funny, the way I'm always trying to give things I haven't got, and am terrified of losing something I've never had, but I don't seem to laugh at it enough to do any good. I think it was sometime after lunch, when Jimmy had gone off to tip our stewards and people, that I made a solemn promise to myself that I would honestly try to be kind and generous to Alberta – try to understand and make the best of her; and having made this promise, something of the calm – the dream-like calm was there, and it didn't even seem difficult to do. When Jimmy came back, he went on treating me as though I was terribly strung up – he didn't see any difference: it made me angry that he couldn't see – and that's how I lost my short-lived calm. We had already made the arrangements – I was to go straight off the ship with my dressing case and meet Em, and Jimmy was to wait behind, see all our luggage through the Customs, and follow us – but we made them again. Jimmy said why didn't I have a rest, but I couldn't. In the end, I decided to change; I had a new suit of very pale blue silky tweed which I'd never worn, and a dark blue silk jersey, and some shoes which were very plain, but exactly the same colour. I sent Jimmy away, and he said he was going up to look down on the sea, and he'd meet me at five.

I spun it all out as long as possible: had a bath, painted my nails, massaged my hair – but even so, I wondered how countless women manage to keep quantities of men waiting while they bath and change. Perhaps their minds aren't on it like mine seems to be: as some women are about houses, so am I about my body. It is my house, and I enjoy cleaning and grooming and decorating it; and to do it in an orderly, thorough – almost detached – manner, is pleasant exercise . . .

Time: it fidgeted and jerked; it clung drowning to the last straw of each second; it hung, breathlessly, over my smallest movement. I thought of railway station clocks that move every minute with a comforting convulsion – of slow-motion films, of speedometers, of sand running through an hour glass, of my hair growing, of the sundial at Wilde whose shadow never seemed to move when I watched it, of the only time I saw the Derby, of my forty-five years (I am more than forty-five!), of the way Em can give the illusion of a whole afternoon and evening in a forty minute act, of the seventeen hours with Sara . . . the whole business seemed inexorably elastic.

I tried to read. I thought of all the people in the ship who had expected to arrive this morning – the atmosphere of impatience and frustration had been noticeable at lunch – I thought of the extra drinks that were being consumed to fill in time, of the patient crew answering the same questions for hours, of the New York skyline, the Statue of Liberty, and the number of people who had never seen it before . . . From my porthole, I could see that there was much more wind – the fog had almost cleared, but I would need a scarf for my hair – a white one, if I could find it . . .

The time had its life – somehow – it seemed to me always to have been dead, but in the end, it had to make way for more of itself that had been waiting and that I had waited for. There is the curious sensation in a large ship: when she is moving, her engines, however discreet, pulse like the circulation of blood in a body, and all the people in her seem to move over her with the scurrying, soundless activity of ants – they seem nothing to her mainstream of life and movement: but when she is stopped, these activities break into sounds, she becomes simply a hive for people and their noises; cabin doors, luggage shifted, voices, breaking glass and changing money, greetings and farewells, footsteps going down to collect trunks, and up to the sea gulls. She is no longer moving in the moving water; it heaves and slaps against her with time to repeat itself; the air moves round her with a kind of intricate liberty which was not apparent during her journey.

As I was walking off the boat – leaving the concentrated turmoil of crowded passages and doorways for the spread-out confusion below on the quay, I suddenly saw myself, as though it was the beginning of a film. A tall well-dressed woman picking her way down the gangplank – what is going to happen to her? Is she going to meet somebody, and who will they be? She looks apprehensive, and either she is rich, or it is a very bad film, because she has a mink coat slung over her arm. The camera looks for a moment with her eyes at the scene before her – a casual sweep, and then more searchingly. As it is a film, she is looking for a man: and she is either desperately afraid of him, or desperately in love. There he is – the picture hovers at its distance, and then approaches him; he was in the background, and he does not know we have seen him. He is standing with his weight on one leg, staring at the ship. He is a small man; hatless, wearing a blue muffler, and the breeze is raking up his thick, dark hair. His eyes, screwed up a little against the cold air, are not characteristic like that: they should be still, and very bright, but he does not know he has been seen. The woman – we go back to her – has smiled, and perhaps it is a better film than we thought, because it is not possible to tell from her smile whether she is afraid or in love. Supposing, at this point, as much were to happen to me as must happen to the woman at the beginning of a film; some great change, some violent alteration which illuminates the purpose of itself, so that at the end of it I can see where I am placed . . . While I was waiting for the Customs to clear me, and Em was out of sight, I wondered what change there could be. In a film the change could only fall into one of two categories: the external, and some engagement of the heart or body. I didn't want my externals changed, I suddenly realized, excepting my wretched health – and that would not be merely a change – it would be miraculous. With the help of that miracle, I might even have another child. And yet what were miracles? They seemed generally to be events which the people who benefited from them totally failed to understand. If my health were now suddenly to improve, I should not understand why; I should only know just enough about it not to be able to attribute it to some new drug, because I know that there are no new drugs for me. It was then that I discovered that I had lived all my life on the supposition, the hope, that things would be different; that I lived inside as though I was the person meant for these changes, and was waiting to live in them – in fact, as though I was someone else.

'Have you anything to declare?'

I felt my suspicion reflected in his eyes. He held out his hand for my passport, and I resisted the melodramatic impulse to say: 'I have these papers, but I do not know who I am, except that I am not what I seem: isn't that a declaration?' But he pushed them back into my hand and said: 'You've come to the wrong place, lady. This is for American citizens.'

Still wondering who I was, I asked him where I should go.

'You're an *alien*,' he said, as though that answered everything.

So it was a long time before they let me through to find Em with a taxi, and by the time I did find him, his familiarity was so welcome that I actually ran to him.

'There, darling,' he said, 'there,' and I clung to him knowing all the clothes he was wearing and the smell of his skin, and wanting that moment to tell him everything that I had been feeling and had discovered.

'I wish we ran into each other like two drops of water.'

'Then you wouldn't be able to tell me anything: I'd know it already – you wouldn't like that.'

'Perhaps you do know.'

He signed my face with his finger: he was smiling faintly. 'Is Jimmy going to bring the rest of the luggage on?'

'Yes.' We moved towards the taxi – he was holding my shoulders, and I said: 'Admire my suit.'

'It's charming – I have been.' I looked down myself with him to my shoes. 'They are pretty, too. And you've washed your hair, and look at your hands. You take so much trouble, my darling, do you know why?'

I wanted to tell him, but I couldn't, because I also wanted to surprise him with my answer. Instead, when we were in the taxi, I said: 'Jimmy was terribly sick – for two days.'

He laughed; 'You sound so proud of it. Of course, *you* weren't.'

'Of course not. I looked after him, extremely well. We both enjoyed it.'

He looked pleased. 'I hope he's recovered: he's going to have to go to work here.'

'Have you found anyone for your play?'

'No one. The only possible is tied up with a film contract – she can't leave for long enough.'

'How is Miss Young?'

'I left her covered with dirt. The poor girl has had to clear up the apartment. They'd lent it to some people for a party, and it was a shambles. It's a good thing you didn't come at ten – she's been at it all day.'

'What have you been doing?'

'Oh – buying flowers and things – and walking about.'

'And thinking?'

He looked suddenly guarded, and I added: 'Not about my arrival – I didn't mean that.'

He said: 'I never know what quality one has to reach in one's thoughts to constitute thinking. I have been remembering – do you count that?'

'I do it all the time.' I felt a fleeting contradiction in him, although he had not moved: then he took my hand gently, and said: 'Perhaps "remembering" is the wrong word. I don't mean that I have been recalling exactly what happened: I mean that I have been reminiscing with a selection of events and my impressions of them.'

'Why?'

'I've been trying to find something. The curious thing is that one doesn't just start with revolt – one has a clear, innocent reason for it. At the beginning, something seems valuable: one desires it; it seems necessary and possible and worth fighting for. Then the whole plot of this thickens, and by then one has the experience of activity and struggle and one forgets what the whole thing was for.' He was silent.

'Have you forgotten?'

'Very nearly all the time, but I remembered a little this morning.'

We were both very quiet: then, it costing me, I said: 'Em, I'm not sure that I ever knew.'

He turned to me as though I had said something marvellous, kissed me – and at that moment I could remember his earliest attention and care – 'Yes, you did once; everybody does a little, but they don't make it last, and I don't think I've helped you.'

'It wasn't *you*.'

'It was nobody else,' he said sharply, and Sarah flared up and began to die painfully, as he dismissed her. He took my hand again, and my fingers felt stiff against his. 'Lillian: don't cast yourself on that reef any more. Remember you are here, with me, and that there is more to come. Move in your time: feel what it is – now. You will be so unbearably alone if you live in that other time.'

'I *won't* forget! I don't want to.'

'I'm not asking you to forget anything – only to remember more.'

'Tell me something to remember, then.'

He thought for a moment, put one of his large handkerchiefs into my hands, and said: 'I will tell you. When you were a child – I think you were about ten – you had your tonsils out. Afterwards, your parents sent you away with your nurse for a holiday, and as your nurse came from one of the Scilly Islands, that is where you went. The first evening that you arrived, you were put straight to bed. You were very tired from the longest journey you had ever done – a train from your home to London; from London to Cornwall; a boat to the main island; and finally, a little boat run by your nurse's uncle to the small island which was her home. You didn't notice anything that night: but next morning you woke very early with sun filling the small whitewashed bedroom. You found yourself in a feather bed, which had a kind of bulky, silky softness, and that was as strange as it was charming. You put on your clothes, lifted the squeaking latch as quietly as you could, and went out, because you couldn't wait to start being on the island. Your house was on high ground, and you could see everything. It was rocky, with green turf – like bice, you said, in your paintbox – and gorse, and slender strips of land brilliant with flowers: you had never seen whole fields of flowers growing in your life. The sky was blue, and the sea streamed and creamed round the edges of the island which had rocks and little shell-shaped bays of shining sand. There were no roads, and this made you feel wonderfully free, but not lonely, because there were a few other clusters of cottages and the air above them had delicate veins of chimney smoke. You walked where you liked, up the hill until you came to a smooth grey rock shouldering out of the ground. And there you found a little hollowed place in it, filled with slate-coloured water. You sat down on your heels beside it . . .' He stopped. 'Wait a minute – yes, and put your hands face downwards on the rock. You'd never left England before, and you thought of this island having been here all the time of your life – which seemed a very long time – rooted in the sea, rising up to the sun, complete and the perfect size for an island, and you had never known about it until now. The air smelled of salt and honey: the little basin of water shivered from invisible winds, and you were singing inside as though you had several voices. You looked into the little basin – it was glittering – just containing your face, and you felt so new on the island that you decided to christen yourself. You said your name aloud, and marked the water on to your forehead, and it was softer, and colder, than snow. Later in the day, when you were out with your nurse, you came upon another rock, and it also had a little basin, but with hardly any water, and your nurse said that these rocks were the first places on the island to be touched by the sun, and that the bowls had been made a long time ago for sacrifices. You didn't tell her, or anyone else about your rock, until you told me.' He waited a moment, and then, still in the same, quiet story-telling voice, he said: 'There you are. I remember so well your telling me that, you see, and when you told me I think you meant to share it, but perhaps you gave it to me by mistake.'

'You've kept it very well.' Indeed, he had: the morning

which I had not remembered for years was back with me in its true language – fresh and unfaded, as when I had told him first, as when I had felt it. The taxi stopped: he said: 'We have arrived. Have you arrived, darling?' Before I could reply, the porter had opened the taxi door.

'You read that notice on his cage. So I give him four bananas and what does he do? He *eats* them! He peels them like he's tired and his mind's on something else, but he eats them so quick and hands the skins out to me that in a few minutes it's like there never were any bananas at all, and he's back to his staring at me like I was illiterate. He *dominates* me.'

Em finished paying the taxi and took my arm. The porter followed us to the lift, and asked if I wanted a monkey. Em pinched me and said: 'My wife is allergic to monkeys.'

'I adore them,' I said, 'but they give me a rash. Lobsters and monkeys.'

The porter said forget it – he'd still got twenty-three apartments to call.

In the lift Em said: 'He isn't absolutely crazy. He really got landed with a monkey that doesn't seem to belong to anyone, and, as you see, it's preying on his mind.'

I think I smiled at him, but I was in full possession of the peace he had given me in the taxi, and so warm with it that I would have smiled at anything he said. He was saying something else.

'. . . worked to get the apartment straight for you – ever since ten this morning. Will you say something nice to her about it?'

I remembered then that in a moment we would not be alone together, and had to use some of my precious warmth to say: 'Of course I will.' But I had the warmth – and at least I could say it.

3

ALBERTA

New York

My dear Uncle Vin,

I am answering your letter at once, because I feel you are worried, and also because I find the nature of your anxiety distressing – this last, I do promise you, not on my account. You have so often said to me that a great deal of gossip goes on in the theatre, and that if people took less notice of it they would be much happier. I have now spent a week here alone with him – Mrs Joyce arrived this evening – and I don't think anyone could have been kinder, more considerate, or more interesting – in fact the things you say sound incredible. Apart from his charming behaviour to me, you seem to have left out the fact that he is married, and from the trouble that he took today it is clear that he is devoted to Mrs Joyce. He spent hours – while I was tidying up this flat in which we are all to stay – buying her favourite flowers, and champagne, and a box of something called Marrons Glacés (chestnuts in sugar) which she fell upon when she arrived, and said were her favourite sweets. He went to meet her himself, and when they came back, they both looked happy and as though they'd achieved something. I would also like to point out to you, Uncle Vin, that he is sixty-one, and could therefore quite easily be my father, and if it wasn't for Papa I wish he was. I hope it is clear that I like and respect him very much, and that is why I hate your believing those horrible idle rumours about him. As for me, you know I have never been in love in my life, and cannot easily imagine what that would be like, but at least I do know that the kind of vulgar intrigue which you imply has nothing to do with love, and cannot start at all unless both people are disposed towards it. When Papa said to me, 'It doesn't matter what you do, as long as you are thoroughly aware that you are doing it,' I think

I understood him. How could I – even supposing it crossed his mind which I am certain it never would – how *could* I encourage him to make poor Mrs Joyce unhappy when she is ill, and has already had so much unhappiness? If I did, it would not be what Papa meant at *all*, and what good could come out of such idiotic irresponsibility? I am sorry to employ this vehemence, but I do feel so angry and sad that people like him should be subjected to such gossip, and although I know that this is nearly always so of remarkable people, the gap between theory and my experience of it is a very large one. So please, Uncle Vin, if you hear anything more of this kind, say that you know better from first-hand evidence.

Now I've read this to see if I've said what I meant, and realize that I haven't once thanked you for worrying about me, which I know you have done with the best reasons. Please don't worry Papa with any of this, though. I'm writing this in bed: the others have gone out to dinner, including Jimmy Sullivan, who had to wait to get all their luggage through the Customs, and didn't arrive here until half past eight. They asked me if I wanted to go with them, and I said no, because I thought Mrs Joyce would like to have dinner alone with him, but then in the end Jimmy went too so it wouldn't have made any difference. This is a beautiful flat and I have a room with so many cupboards that my clothes get lost in them. Mrs Joyce has two *enormous* trunks full of clothes, apart from suitcases. She is very glamorous, in an interesting way – you feel she really *is* – not that she can sometimes manage to be. I am going to help her unpack tomorrow. Finally, to put your mind thoroughly at rest, I may as well tell you that I am not alone in this room, but am sharing it with an unusually gloomy little monkey. He somehow came up in the lift with Jimmy by mistake, and he glares at me all the time in a moping sort of way. I've given him some grapes, and he ate them as though they were wasting his time, and spitting the pips out over his left shoulder, and now he's bored to death and is sitting in a kind of hunched up elegant heap – although Jimmy said all he needed was company, which clearly I'm not managing to be. He shows one quite simply that material comfort is ***not enough***, which is interesting, because it's much harder to see about people. Mrs Joyce wanted to let him out, and she did – in the sitting room. He broke a lamp, upset three vases of flowers, tore some curtains and made four messes; he did all this frightfully quickly and then ran up the curtains and it took ages to catch him, and even Mrs Joyce said that perhaps he was better off in his cage. It's a pity monkeys can't read, because they look as though they can, much more than a lot of people who actually do. Oh well. Much love, darling Uncle Vin – and please don't worry about me – and I promise I'll tell you if I have any difficulties or get ill or *anything*.

SARAH

4

JIMMY

LOOKING back, at the end of it, on that first week, I realize that we didn't come to what seemed a crazy decision at any one point of it. I say we, because I'm not even sure now who had the idea, I only know that neither of us would have dreamed of it at the beginning of the week. I didn't have a chance to talk to Emmanuel until the morning after we arrived, because the evening was devoted to Lillian, and somehow everything goes wrong if we talk theatre in front of her, and she'd been so excited at meeting Emmanuel that I'd been afraid of her having another attack – I still was – all evening. She was really lit up – not with drink – pure gaiety, and he was responding. He seemed much better than he was in London: less tired and edgy – serene somehow. I guessed he'd been writing, but I didn't ask, and then when she did, he said yes, and I knew he was lying – so it wasn't that. But at least he seemed to be over Gloria, and I'd been afraid we'd have the dregs of her with us for weeks. The new girl – she really is the new girl personified – seems to have done her job well. He doesn't seem to have broken any dates, got drunk, or trodden on anybody's toes; he's managed to make the apartment *and* the ship on time, and I haven't seen him so smooth with Lillian for years.

I left them after dinner; they wanted to go home, and I wanted to walk the streets a bit and show myself the town. It was too late to go to a theatre, and I walked around looking for a movie, and wondering why, whenever I come back here, I always feel like this. I mean, I know the feeling so well, you wouldn't think I'd have it any more. It's all right in England: I tell myself I'm travelling – I'm a foreigner, and I don't even have to tell myself that in France: but here, I look forward to coming back, and then have a kind of resentment that it isn't my home: I feel it ought to be – it's just that most of the ingredients are missing. Twice a year they send a letter from the home where I wasn't born: they ask for news I don't want to give, and give a whole lot of news I don't want. I had a drink on the way back to the apartment and tried not to feel resentful about not being able to spend the evening with Emmanuel, which would have made everything OK. What was it Annie had said in London? The Father Figure, and I was so nuts about him, transferred, I think she said – she was showing off her Freud – that I'd never have a satisfactory affair with a woman. I don't suppose I shall; it seems to me a dreary, interim arrangement. I'd rather lay a woman and never see her again, or be in love with her. I had another Scotch, and started trying to imagine the kind of girl I could be in love with. Slender, but not too tall, with beautiful hair and a low voice – gentle and ready to trust me; someone to whom I could show the world in exchange for her showing me herself. I looked round the bar and imagined myself waiting for her to walk into it: in a sense, I suppose, I *was* waiting for her – and then I thought of the number they'd written into Emmanuel's musical: 'Fate Made a

Date with You and Me' which they'd scored now to merge into the big first act finale number – a waltz: 'The Time and the Place and the Loved One'. Emmanuel had said it was very good and looked like being a hit number. Well, she hadn't turned up, my girl, whoever she was; no sense in looking for her (after all, most of the time I didn't need anyone else in my life), but one thing I knew, and that was she only had to walk into the bar – any bar where I was, and I'd know it was she. It was a little like finding the perfect actress for a part, which perhaps Emmanuel and I would be doing together tomorrow . . .

The first thing we did when we got shot of the apartment was to go to the drugstore we always went to when we wanted to think aloud together with no chance of being interrupted. There was nothing unusual about it except that we always went to it. We got coffee and I bought a pack of Luckies, and we sat and looked at each other. Then he said: 'Well, Jimmy, it's just as difficult as we thought. Neither of the ones we wanted is available. There are about six whom various people want to star in something – I've seen four of them and they're no good: two to go. And of course they've put us through a lot of the routine stuff – agents who want to give a girl the impression they're working for her – or want her to have the experience of an audition.'

'Have you tried Alex?'

Emmanuel smiled. 'I didn't have to try. He was round at George's office like a flash with what he described as his greatest discovery in years.'

'Was she?'

'Her appearance was memorable. There turned out to be only two small snags. She hadn't one word of English, and she'd done no acting in any language whatever.'

'She must have been some eyeful.'

Emmanuel said impassively: 'It was extremely difficult to look at her for long.'

'What does Mick say?'

'He's sympathetic, but he feels I can't have written a play

with a girl who doesn't exist. He's beginning to take it as a slight on America that I can't pick anyone. He has a new agent on the coast who he says will turn up something if we give him time. The point is this, Jimmy. I like actresses who know their job. I like them professional, at least, with a pinch of dedication about them. But if we can't find one of them who would be right – and with Luise and Katie out of it, we look like not finding one, then I like the field wider open than these people – Mick and George and so on – are prepared to open it. The bunch of models, call girls, and bit-part kids is the wrong kind of wide. I'd rather pick a girl off the street who looked right, and have you teach her to act.'

'Yeah, but we're supposed to open this fall, and I can't teach anyone what they need to know in three months.' I thought a minute, and then added: 'Unless they were exceptional, of course.'

He looked at me, his heavy eyelids belying the amusement in his eyes. 'Well, Jimmy – then they've got to be exceptional.'

I got up to pay our check. I knew better than to argue with him then.

That was our first conversation about it.

We spent the rest of the morning seeing George's two girls – the last of the six that he'd got together. We let the first one do the whole scene. She was tall, with what Emmanuel described as a voraciously wistful expression, but she had a good voice with a lot of colour in it. Then when we got to the bit where she goes around taking the pictures off the walls, he said: 'There's a bird that walks like that – a large bird.' So it was for me to get her a nice bucket of clean sand and hold her head in it; she was out, thanking me in anticipation.

Mick was there, and I could feel the whole situation getting on his nerves. Nobody likes to get into real casting trouble, and Mick likes to do everything fast and brilliantly: if personalities advertised, he'd be the done-overnight, solved-while-you-wait problem man. There was a break after the first girl left, because the second girl hadn't shown up. The actor who had been reading for us lit a cigarette, and finally went to sleep on three chairs which he arranged in a row for the purpose. Mick came over to where we were sitting, and did some sales talk on me, and Emmanuel stared at the top of the proscenium arch where a batten wasn't properly masked, and except that he wasn't listening I didn't know what went on in his mind.

Mick's parents had been Polish, and I think he still thought in that language. He had a head like a bullet, a crew cut, a merry sly smile and he loved you to agree with him, but it brought on such bouts of gaiety and energetic appreciation of you that you couldn't stand it for long. If you didn't agree with him, he sulked, and his enterprise in that direction was such that in the end you were responsible for his never having seen Poland which was palpably killing him. But he was a good fixer if he could fix fast, and the set-up that employed him worked on the principle that almost everything could be decided fast if the right man was taking the decisions. Like almost everyone else in the business, Mick resented Emmanuel's control over his plays, and the fact that by sheer weight and merit he could uphold them. Mick knew that experienced and prolific playwrights don't grow on trees, but just now he was kicking up. Emmanuel, having borne with it for some time, stopped looking at the corner of the proscenium arch, and speaking under Mick, but distinctly, said: 'Jimmy, take him away and talk to him, he's beginning to take my mind off something else.'

'Mick?'

'Sure, sure I'll talk to you. Let's go.'

We went to a small room that he used as an office, and he let go. He'd been fifteen years in the business – he'd worked with some difficult people; he named them and there was hardly anyone left when he was through; but he'd never had trouble like this. He'd read the play – it was just great, but what had got into *Mister* Joyce that he couldn't seem to visualize anybody in what was after all a straight lead? What was so out of this world about it that he hadn't already catered for? Sure, he understood about quality – if I liked he would agree that Mister

Joyce was a genius – the play was a work of genius – *I* was a genius – so what? Weren't there, wasn't there one single *female* genius who could just play one itsy-bitsy part in one goddam play, or must we all kow-tow to genius Joyce as though he'd written the Bible and nothing less than Sarah Bernhardt would do? Mister Joyce gave him the feeling that we were all wasting time, and whereas it would make him happy – it would make him *delirious* to go on providing Mister Joyce with an endless succession of beautiful girls to look at day after day if it gave his power complex a kick, there was just one little thing that world genius Joyce was not taking into account, and that was that his, Mick's, time *was* money. The stark revelation of this final statement seemed to strike him afresh as he said it, and he had to take in some breath. Then he said there was just one more thing that he wanted to know. Would I just tell him how we had found somebody in London for the part who didn't make Mister Joyce sick in his stomach?

'We didn't,' I said. 'The girl we wanted went sick, and we had to make out with somebody who's upset the whole balance of the play. That's why he's so anxious to have the right girl here. He knows what he wants, and he's quite right.'

'Yeah – with one detail hardly worth mentioning – she just don't happen to *exist*!'

'Snap out of it; you've only been on it a week.'

'A week!' He looked as though he was going to burst. 'He thinks I've been on it just a *week*! I tell you something else. It'll end up by his picking some little girl with no sex appeal, no box office, no record, no nothing. And I'll have to try to sell her to MCA – she's spiritual – Mister Joyce is in love with her – we *all* love her – little Miss Wide Open Spaces 1958 – do you think they'll buy it? I can tell you now what they'll tell me to tell you to tell Mister Joyce to do with her and that won't make a news story, and while he's living happily ever after for five minutes, they'll withdraw and he'll be landed with the play *and* the girl . . .'

'Mick, you're making me tired.' He really was: I could feel

the pricking at the back of my neck which is the beginning of getting angry. 'He can always find backing for a new play and you know it. Don't get too big for other people's boots. Be your age and keep your job.'

They called through to say that Miss Harper had arrived. I slapped him as hard as I could on the back and as he fell against the filing cabinet I grinned at him. 'Maybe this is it.'

Of course it wasn't. She was a nice girl, but dumb as they come – she didn't know what she was doing – she just looked good.

We had a weary lunch with Mick and George. It was agreed that everybody perfectly understood everybody else, and was hopping with confidence over everyone else's ability. George gave Mick the job of lining up a whole lot of screen tests to be run through for us; Mick cheered up quite horribly and started loving us all again, and I watched Emmanuel staring at things and not eating his lunch and going blue under the eyes and I thought goddammit do they *really* think he's in it for his power complex? He was just trying to finish a good job, that's all. When we got to coffee, there was a call through for him: I went to take it, and it was Alberta with a message from Lillian to say that she'd fixed the evening for all of us with the Westinghouses – so would we be back not later than seven? I asked if Lillian was there, but she wasn't – she was out lunching with some Russian princess who knew a lot about herbs – and that meant we'd have to go to the Westinghouses'. Then Alberta said she was sorry if she'd distressed me and rang off. She has a sweet voice, but she says some funny things with it. I told Emmanuel about the Westinghouses and he screwed up his eyes and then said unexpectedly: 'She has a pretty voice – that girl,' and George and Mick became galvanized and said which one, and when he said it was his secretary they lost interest.

After lunch, Emmanuel said: 'I have an overpowering desire to sleep. Where can I go?'

He said it to me and very quietly, so I knew he wanted to get away from George. Then he got up from the table, nodded amiably to Mick and George and walked out. I didn't take time to care for the check, I got up to follow him: 'He'll jay walk himself into hospital,' I said. Mick smiled slyly; George said: 'Or revwire.' I grabbed our coats and caught up with him a few yards down on the sidewalk. 'Lillian's out.'

He looked at me expressionlessly: 'Let's go home.'

In the cab, he said: 'Do you know that girl found what was wrong with Clemency?'

'What girl?'

'My secretary.' He still looked like nothing.

A bit later he said: 'I've a damn good mind to chuck the whole business.'

'Not put the play on at all?'

'Not put any play on.'

'What for?'

He looked at me then, and suddenly smiled. 'That's just it, Jimmy. There has to be a reason one way or another. I haven't found it.' He yawned. 'On with the play.'

I didn't answer. He always started a depression this way: wanting to sleep all the time, and making elliptical damaging little stabs at any project in hand, and if you took him up withdrawing to somewhere you couldn't reach him. But I knew then that something would have to be decided somehow, and thought that I would put a call through to Katie and see if there was no way of hooking her.

When we got to the apartment, he waited while I found a key, and opened the door, and at once Alberta came out of the living room. Emmanuel walked firmly up to her and took her by the arm. 'I want you to do something for me. Would you take the calls, Jimmy? Now – where can we go?' He pushed her gently into the kitchen, and turned back to me. 'I want to try something. Stop Lillian from stopping me, will you?'

I nodded, and went into the living room. A minute later, Alberta came in, picked something off a table and went. I shut the door, and put the call through to Katie in California. The time was half past three. While I was waiting for the first call to come through, I made a list of all the others that could be any use, and wondered how that kid had managed to upset him about Clemency. Of course, she wouldn't have meant to – the people who did, moved him not at all. But this kind of thing had happened before: somebody, something, had shifted his view of a completed work, and then there was the devil to pay until he got it back to his satisfaction. Once or twice he hadn't, and they were the worst times of all. That was when I earned my salary: when he lost money, made enemies, and really got down to influencing people. Then it had to be a case of my country right or wrong, and I had the curious sensation of what it cost to believe in anybody. Then I not only had to stand people calling him a fool – a swollen-headed bum perfectionist – a capitalist who didn't care about the security of the workers in the theatre – a sadist who liked to use his power to revenge himself upon some producer or star he'd fallen out with – I had to stand him agreeing with them. 'Why not?' he once said: 'There is no doubt that I have been a fool: that's a useful word; it will cover almost anything. They are quite rightly worrying about the consequences, as I, too late, concern myself with the cause. A fool is somebody who will not keep still, but cannot possibly be responsible for his actions. I am a fool.'

Oh well – it hadn't come to that.

The call to Katie came through at last. At the end of two minutes she had really convinced me that she was tied up, and after that she was free-wheeling on her reasons. Her studio had suspended her a few weeks back: she was scheduled to make two big pictures: she was suing her third husband for failure to pay alimony, and anyway she couldn't leave her hypnotist who was trying to stop her taking sleeping pills. This took another eighteen minutes of her beautiful voice. She couldn't, she said, even work Las Vegas for a week on account of her studio, when God knew she needed the money, and life was twice as expensive as it had been what with lawyers and the hypnotist who hadn't managed to stop her taking sleeping pills yet so any minute she might be suspended again – for good. We exchanged a lot of abstract emotions and hung up. She was an actress, though: she had the lot: and I knew it, even while I caught myself wondering how on earth we ever thought she could play Clemency. I was just starting to call a couple of people I just liked, and thought I'd call, when I heard Lillian, and put the receiver back just as she came into the room. She was not alone.

'Hi, Jimmy. This is Princess Murmansk – you've met, haven't you, Della?'

'Why yes – we certainly have. How are you?'

The Princess – I didn't remember her – had an accent straight from New Orleans where she must have been some landmark – she was well over six feet tall.

'The Princess has been explaining to me how you can do absolutely everything with herbs.'

The Princess smiled, exposing a large quantity of well-kept teeth. Only Cinerama, I thought, would do justice to her. They exchanged herbal cigarettes, and we all sat down.

'You look at a loose end, Jimmy: where's Em?'

'In the kitchen.'

'What on earth is he doing?'

'He's working with Alberta.'

'Why in the kitchen? Why not here?'

'Because he doesn't want to be interrupted.'

'What's he *doing*?'

'Search me. Working.'

Lillian gave an angry little laugh. 'How extraordinary. Well, Della's dying to meet him, and anyway we came back to make some of her marvellous tea.'

'He specially asked me to take all calls and see that he wasn't interrupted,' I said, and noticed that we had both instinctively got to our feet. I tried to smile. 'Don't say I didn't warn you.'

She went. The Princess stretched out a yard or two of leg and said: 'Does it get to be part of your reflexes protecting the great man?'

'It gets to be.'

Lillian came back followed by Emmanuel: I took one look at him and wished I was somewhere else. Lillian said: 'I've got our secretary to boil water and get a tray together, but the actual *skill* will have to be you, Della. My husband – Princess Murmansk.'

'I'm so happy to meet you.' She extended a hand and Emmanuel shook it.

'I do hope I haven't disturbed your inspiration.'

'I have never been fortunate enough to have any. If I had, neither you nor anyone else would be able to disturb it.'

Lillian said: 'Really Em, that's rude of you.'

'Not rude – just hypothetical.'

I couldn't take it. I went to see how Alberta was making out with the tea. She looked flushed, and when I came in she gave me a quick little smile as though if she didn't smile she'd cry.

'Can I help any?' I said: she was putting cups on a tray.

'I just have to wait until the kettle boils: thank you, Jimmy.'

'I'll stay and watch it with you.' I felt suddenly that she was getting the rough end of something she knew nothing about. She looked at the two chairs where they must have been sitting, and pushed her hair back from her forehead.

'Has he been working you hard?'

She looked bewildered. 'Not working *me*, exactly. He's been making me read to him. He said he wanted to hear something.'

'Yeah – he does that. Has he found it?'

'Some of it, I think – but of course, I haven't asked.' She waited a moment, and then said: 'Mrs Joyce was angry when she came in and then he was very angry.' Her voice was very low. 'I don't understand.'

'He didn't say anything, did he?'

'No – but that made it worse. Jimmy – do you mind me asking you something?'

'Go ahead.'

'Who am I working for?'

'You're working for him, and sometimes that means working for her. Sometimes it doesn't.'

'It isn't that I mind doing *anything*. But if they tell me to do something, and it makes the other angry that I do it . . .'

'Like this?' I indicated the tea tray, and she nodded. 'Forget it. Listen: they're not beautiful simple people, so they make difficulties from time to time: just don't get involved – it irons out – but whatever they do, you keep it small. OK?'

'OK,' she said carefully. 'Thank you, Jimmy. I expect it sounds stupid to you, but my experience of married people is unfortunately superficial.'

'What about your parents?'

'My mother died when I was nine. The kettle's boiling. Do we take it in, do you think?'

'I'll find out where her highness wants it.'

I strode into an atmosphere you could cut with a knife and said: 'Alberta wants to know where you want the boiling water?'

'Tell her to bring it in here with the tray.'

Well, we had tea – if you can call the sickly bitter stuff that woman made, tea. Lillian chattered – the princess answered questions about her herbal rest home; and Emmanuel sat almost silent, and fidgeting, until he suddenly smiled at her with great charm and said he had to go.

'Darling – you can't go out now. The Westinghouses!'

'Tell them I'll be late.' He'd gone.

Lillian looked desperately at me. 'Jimmy – do explain to him, the party's being given for him. He *can't* be late.' As I left the room, I heard her saying: 'He's always like this when he's working on a new play; I do hope you'll forgive him, and understand.'

I caught Emmanuel waiting for the elevator: without looking at me, he said: 'One shouldn't meet that woman indoors: she's too big.'

We both got into the elevator. I said: 'I couldn't have stopped that.'

He gave me a bleak smile. 'I could.' He shrugged. 'Well – it's done now. And the only thing that would put it right again, I can't do.'

I was silent.

'I did it last night. It takes a kind of energy I don't seem to keep for long. Or can't afford. Or won't. I have something else to do.'

Then he said angrily: 'It's like marking *sand*. The tide comes in, and you might never have done it.'

'Are you going to show up at this party?' I asked desperately. I didn't want to ask, but I had to.

'You take her to it. If I'm not coming, I'll call them. I promise.'

I put their number on a piece of paper and put it in his pocket.

'I've lost my temper. It's like getting drunk: you know it's going to poison you, and you don't stop. Freedom! We all talk about it, and don't know the meaning of the word!'

The elevator, which had reached the ground floor some time back, suddenly started up again. He laughed.

'You see, Jimmy? It's just like this. We go up and down, up and down, without the slightest control. Where's the break? What the hell can we *do* about anything at all?'

He spread out his hands – they were shaking – small, nervous, blotched on their backs with large freckles. 'See? I haven't the control of a *cat*!'

'They have a lot,' I said.

The elevator stopped, and a wooden-faced couple got in. Their collective gaze shifted over us and the floor and the walls. They only knew how not to look at each other. I pressed the button for our apartment floor, and said: 'Well, I'll take them both to the party, and hope to see you there. And I'll fix somewhere good to work tomorrow.'

He looked at me, and his look went to my heart. 'Bless you, Jimmy.'

I gave Lillian his message dead pan, and went to my room. Alberta had already gone to hers like a sensible girl. But I knew that Lillian would get rid of her lady friend and come after me. She did.

'What do you mean, Jimmy, he'll call if he's not coming?'

'I don't mean anything at all. It's what he said.' I was lying on my bed with the beginnings of a headache and closed my eyes, but she closed the door and went on: 'Does that mean he *isn't* coming, do you think? Because if so, I must call the Westinghouses . . .'

'He said he'd call: I should leave it to him if I were you.'

'If you were me, of course you wouldn't have interrupted him in the first place when he was "working". And if I were you I wouldn't have interrupted him either.'

'That's true,' I agreed amiably, but that only made her dangerous.

'Doesn't it strike you as odd that I'm the only person who's *capable* of interrupting him?'

'Perhaps you're the only one he cares for.'

She didn't know how to take this. Then she said: 'He wasn't working, anyway. He was just listening to the girl reading.'

She wasn't that stupid – surely? But I looked at her, and saw that the only bit of her that was working at the moment was. I decided to have one real try, and then give up.

'Lillian – honey – you're wrong there. If Emmanuel says he doesn't want to be disturbed that's good enough: we don't decide whether he's working or not – *he* does. It made him mad today because he's got something on his mind, but he'll come back all right if you don't grow the whole thing up meanwhile. Be sweet to him – apologize.'

She looked at me, and I saw she was finding it tough. With an effort, she said: 'I'll think about it.' Then she gave herself a little shake, and said: 'I don't blame you for talking to me as though I was a child: the whole thing has become such a storm in a teacup. I want to leave at seven fifteen.'

'Does Alberta know?'

'She ought to. I told her the arrangements this morning.'

Well – that was not the end of it. I went to tell Alberta: she was sitting on her bed writing in a big book, and she just nodded, and went on writing. I wondered what – and guessed it was a novel. Young girls write novels nowadays like they used to press flowers or make candy. At seven, Emmanuel came back. At eight, we left, in an atmosphere nobody could want to call their own. The party was some blocks down on Park Avenue, and except for Lillian saying how dirty the cab was nobody said anything.

The Westinghouses were a nice couple – around their fifties – with a son in the business and several other grown-up children who usually showed up at parties. He was a good-looking man – always sunburned – with an appearance of nobility that had somehow never got around to attaching itself to anything. The prototype for heroic theory, Emmanuel had once said: but Emmanuel was fond of him – they even went once on a disastrous fishing trip together – Emmanuel was nearly drowned, and the rest of the time so bored that he got drunk and stayed that way for nearly two weeks. Debbie Westinghouse was one of those women you only see here – half doll, half little girl – she'd never had a thought in her head, and that went for the nasty ones too – she was crisp, and silly, and sweet and simple, and so clean you could have eaten off her. She loved her family; the room was littered with snaps of her grandchildren, and she understood that books were for other people. She cried very easily, but not for long, and she told everybody that Emmanuel was a genius with the kind of gasping credulity of a child talking about a magician. Van Westinghouse was always very kind to her, and she certainly made him feel a man.

They had collected about thirty people to meet Emmanuel, and they must have known why they were invited, as nearly all of them turned to look at him when we came in. I knew Van Westinghouse would take care of Lillian – he had a lot of old-world charm for other people's wives – and Emmanuel would be swamped, but the poor kid, Alberta, looked out of it all: she had on a dark blue dress that wasn't right for her or the party, and she looked as though she knew it. There was nothing I could do about it: we were plunged into large scale and paralysingly efficient introductions. A collection of well-groomed, intelligent, successful people – for some reason they made me think of a whole lot of shiny new automobiles – powerful, well serviced, fitted inside with all kinds of modern gadgets – like insomnia, contraceptives, equality, and fright. Emmanuel once said that no talk was too small for opinions, they were only the suburbia of intercourse, and cocktail parties were their rush hour, and I was in a mood this evening for that kind of remark to stick in my mind. I had two drinks rather fast and listened to three people – Debbie Westinghouse admiring Lillian's dreamy clothes, an intense young woman who'd written a book all about emotional freedom, and an old, rather nice guy who seemed stuck on English furniture. Usually at these parties, I do at least get myself an attractive girl, at least to drink with, but tonight there seemed two good reasons why that would not make a gay evening. One was Alberta, for whom I felt kind of responsible, and the other was Emmanuel. Alberta was answering questions about England, and looking like a schoolgirl up for an examination, and Emmanuel was listening to a journalist who'd just been on a three weeks trip to India, and who was telling him what an opportunity the British getting out was for the Indian people. What the hell was a party *for*, I wondered. Van Westinghouse was bringing out a cheap edition of Emmanuel's plays – Johnnie, his son, came over to tell me about it: three volumes to start with, with three plays in each: they had galleys, but they were still waiting for a preface and could I turn on some heat to get it? Not tonight, I said. Who was the girl we'd brought – was she an attachment of mine? For some reason this irritated me: I think because I knew Johnnie thought she looked odd, and because I agreed with him. I explained why she was here, and Johnnie said OK, OK, he'd only been asking and got his sister Sally from across the room. She came over, smiling, and looking so good that I felt better just looking. She'd become a model since last time I'd seen her, and she'd changed. I told her she looked wonderful, and she smiled her wide smile and said clothes certainly did something for a girl. Johnnie said: 'Oh, come on, Sal. Tell him you're in love!' 'He's a photographer – I certainly am. He's a genius!' She said it just like her mother. She gave her glass to Johnnie, and smiled again at me and asked me who was the girl I'd brought. Somehow she didn't irritate me asking – so I told her about Alberta and said she was a sweet kid, and was just going to add how young she was, when I remembered that Alberta was at least a year older than Sally. 'She hasn't been around very much – lived in the country,' I said instead – and wondered why everything I said about Alberta seemed wrong or patronizing. That was just when Johnnie knocked against a bottle which fell over Alberta's dress. Sally saw it, and gave a little throaty gasp and went to the rescue. She took Alberta away at once – Johnnie made me an apologetic face – but at the far end of the room, I caught sight of Emmanuel. A good many people had gone, and I could hear that all was not well. He was leaning against the piano, and I didn't like the easy, angry look on his face. I went over '. . . this *extraordinary* illusion you have that we all know what we are doing?' he finished, and as an afterthought emptied his half-full glass of what looked like Scotch.

The intense dame who'd written the book about emotional freedom gave him a winning, intellectual smile, and said soothingly: 'But surely, Mr Joyce, it is the duty of the more knowledgeable person to inform and guide the common man.'

'If you deal in such an inflated view of humanity, possibly it is. Personally, I have never met anyone in the least knowledgeable, and I don't think I'd recognize the common man if I stumbled up against him in the street where I believe he lives. I think society is made up of cranks and morons.' He smiled pleasantly round the room, embracing us all, and somehow managed to get Johnnie to fill his glass again without a word. There was an indiscriminate outcry – of people claiming to be common etc., out of which the man – whom I recognized as the journalist – said: 'You'll be telling me next that you don't believe in progress!'

Emmanuel smiled brightly: 'That's what I'll tell you next. But *you* think information is progress. You think a lot of cranks telling a lot of morons what they ought to think constitutes education. There are a few little worms turning in England, but that is only because they want even their emotional lives for free – they can't even face paying for *that* – they want it on the basis of free milk and public lavatories and they simply illustrate the rot of private irresponsibility – this is what makes most of us cowards . . .'

The journalist was high anyway, and he lost his temper. 'Is this a social message out of one of your plays?'

'I don't write plays with social messages. It is a misuse of the theatre.'

'But surely, Mr Joyce, you consider yourself knowledgeable?' Emmanuel didn't reply, and the journalist said again: 'I repeat – surely you're under the impression that you're knowledgeable?'

Emmanuel said: 'I am attached to the notion that if one is below an impression, it is a false one.'

'You see? You're just evading my point: you damned artists, you think you can run the world. You just think you know everything – for God's sake. Give me the days when the artist was a workman with a job to do and knew his place in society.'

Emmanuel said smoothly: 'I am sure that we all wish that you had lived two hundred years ago,' somebody laughed, and Emmanuel held out his glass to Johnnie.

At this moment – mercifully – Alberta returned to us: Emmanuel saw her first, and although his face did not seem to change, I knew there was a reason for looking, and turned my head. I don't think I'd ever looked at her before – at any rate, now I hardly knew her. She was wearing a black dress with a high Chinese collar, and very short, tight sleeves; her hair was sleeked back – smooth and shining – and her skin made the other women in the room look as though they'd never been in the air on a fine morning. Even Sally, beside her, looked as though she'd lived it up a bit. Emmanuel said: 'Here, at last, is somebody who will answer your question.' He held out his hand with the glass in it, she hesitated, and came over to us.

'Do you consider that I am a wise man?'

She looked at him with unselfconscious steadiness, and said: 'No I do not.' Then she added gently: 'But I think such men are very rare: it has not been my fortune to meet one.'

Emmanuel smiled and inclined his head to her, and there was something like a triumphant recognition about his face and the movement. The sour smell of calamity seemed to have gone: the journalist offered Emmanuel a cigarette, and Johnnie rushed to get Alberta a drink. Sally winked at me and murmured: 'Clothes certainly make a difference to a man about a girl, anyway' – and then I saw Lillian, with an expression on her face like a stubbed-out cigarette. Whatever Lillian may be, she certainly *isn't* supporting cast. Johnnie had given Emmanuel another slug, and he was reciting something to his host and hostess: Debbie was taking it seriously, and Van looked uneasy. I caught Van's eye, and after exactly the right interval, he moved casually over to me.

'I hate to say it, Van, but do you have any further plans for this evening?'

He looked around. 'When the numbers got to around ten, Debbie wanted us to go some place to eat.'

'They're around that now.'

He made a count, during which I noticed that the journalist had got hold of Lillian and was pouring his opinions over her like a bucket of sand on to a chemical fire.

'If you could include Lillian in your care, and your literary pals, perhaps Johnnie could bring the rest of us in due course.'

'Fine.' He went to tell Johnnie: he knew quite a lot about Emmanuel.

Well – the first part of the arrangement worked. Lillian went quietly – she'd decided to behave well about it all, to invest her anger for private distribution I guessed. But when it came to moving Emmanuel everything broke down. When I got back from seeing the others into the elevator, I found him sitting on the floor, making Sally and Alberta compare their childhoods: they became like a couple of kids telling him, and Johnnie was listening and watching Emmanuel's face respectfully – he was a kid with an eye for memories. As soon as there was a chance, I said: how about moving?

Emmanuel said: 'Where?'

'Johnnie's driving us to Patrick's for dinner. We're joining the others there.'

'Well, at least we know where they *are*.' He turned back to Alberta: 'Have you changed your clothes recently?'

'Yes. This dress belongs to Miss Westinghouse. Mine had an accident.'

Emmanuel looked approvingly at Sally and then at Alberta. Johnnie stood around waiting to go, but nobody seemed to take any notice of him, and then Emmanuel started to tell a story about a dress his mother had told him she wanted, and how it had seemed to cost so much money that he imagined it had been made for Queen Alexandra. 'Of course, she never got it,' he finished, and watched pity bloom on the girls' faces like the moon coming out. But Johnnie began feeling the strap of his wrist watch and looking nervous, so I said again that we should be going.

'Where?'

We went through it all again.

'Call them, and say I'm terribly drunk and it's delaying us. If you point out what an embarrassing evening they would have with me – shouting and spilling my food and breaking things, they might not want us at all.'

When Johnnie and I went to make the call, he said: 'I don't know what Dad will say. He doesn't *seem* drunk, at all.'

'He isn't, but if we join them he'll arrive high without drinking another drop. Put the call through and I'll talk to your father.'

'Gee – if he was really like he said at Patrick's, it sure would be exciting.'

'Just dull,' I said: 'Those evenings are all the same – it's just the audience that changes.'

I told Van Westinghouse that we wouldn't be joining them,

and said to tell Lillian I was sorry but things weren't working out that way. Would he look after Lillian, and I'd call him in the morning? He would. He was, as Emmanuel once remarked, in that minority who were at least wiser after other people's events. I turned to Johnnie, who had the look of an expectant schoolboy about to break bounds.

'No more Scotch for anyone – and some small place to eat.'

And that was it. We did go out and eat at Giovanni's, and it was a good evening. All the strain and tensions seemed to have dropped from Emmanuel and he charmed us all – making Sally tell stories and asking Alberta what she thought of them, improvising a preface for Johnnie in the language of a well-known American weekly: 'Slum-born mongrel-playwright Emmanuel Orchid Race Joyce stabs at self-analytical artistic processes as taking people out of themselves and putting them back wrong' etc. But mostly he listened: every now and then he told a story – something very small, but the way he told them they were irresistibly fascinating, and we sat like a bunch of kids, round-eyed, begging for more.

It was not until after the zabaglione, when we were all drinking coffee, that Sally began asking about the new play. Emmanuel answered her, and I had the feeling that he was having a final conversation with himself, and also with me about it. He told her very simply the kind of play that it was; the difficulty about Clemency – what we had done and how we had failed to find her: Johnnie and Alberta were listening too, but the collective attention seemed not to interfere with our privacy. Johnnie, very diffidently, suggested Katie for the part, and I said yes, but she couldn't do it – I'd tried her again that afternoon. Emmanuel was looking at me now, and I knew the feeling – of private summing up, of conclusion – was true. It came into my mind that he was going to scrap the play; that he'd found the reason for doing so which he had said was necessary, and I blotted up this inky fear until I must have changed colour with it . . .

'. . . and so, I have decided to make an experiment, if the

victim is willing,' and both he and I turned instinctively to Alberta, who had been very still, whose eyes, clear and astonished, were the only sign she gave of this news. There was a long, full silence; then she said: 'You know that I know nothing at all about acting.'

'Jimmy will teach you all you need to know.'

She looked at me: I was seeing her for the second time, and entirely different again.

'I'll teach you,' I said, 'if you're willing to learn.'

'Are you willing?'

She put out her hand, as though she was in a dream, and must touch somebody, and Emmanuel and I both put our hands on the table.

'I will try to learn,' she said. Emmanuel touched her then, and she smiled.

And that was the end – or the beginning – of that.

CHAPTER IV

1

ALBERTA

My dearest Aunt Topsy,

This letter is partly for Papa, because it seems that the moment one is in a position interesting enough to warrant writing letters, one has very little time for them. You are the *most* reliable correspondent, and keep me thoroughly in touch, although I'm sorry to hear about Jemima Facks – I must say I should have thought it was extremely difficult to fall down a well *head* first – I mean one would have to be so neat about it: but then I suppose falling runs in the Facks family, and she has had a good deal of experience. Anyway, it's a good thing she had such presence of mind and thick pigtails.

We have just moved into an apartment and I have spent this morning helping Mrs Joyce who has just gone out to luncheon with a Russian Princess (not a real one – she just married a Russian Prince). You asked me to describe Mrs J., and I'll try, appearance first, because I've seen more of it. She is very tall and thin and extremely *elegant* – with rather knobbly bones and thin blue veins which show out of the sides of her forehead and on the backs of her hands (like Lady Gorge, only not so useful-looking – prettier). She has very fine hair which is a mixture of yellow and white – grey, I suppose, but again, pretty, cut short and waving carelessly about in what turns out to be a very expensive manner, and huge rather pale blue eyes with black pupils. Her skin is very white and looks thinner than most people's – almost papery, and her mouth droops slightly downwards but is a beautiful shape. Her hands and feet are what Clem would call pre-Raphaelite – very long and faint-looking, and altogether, if she had long hair one could imagine her in a garden of carnations, or sitting in some banqueting hall; she is very much like a heroine – someone to be rescued or saved. She is extremely delicate, as she has something wrong with her heart, and she had a daughter who died – it is still all very sad. I had to do her unpacking – goodness! – she has two cabin trunks with hangers for dresses down one side and drawers for clothes down the other – apart from countless suitcases. She also travels with her pictures, drawings and paintings – nearly all portraits, I wondered if any of them were of her daughter, but naturally didn't ask. Most of the morning she was in bed talking to people on the telephone, while I put things away until there wasn't any more room to put them. I suppose they are all the consequence of a glittering life, but it must be rather sad not to have anywhere permanent to keep them. Mrs Joyce said I must buy some clothes here because pretty ones are so cheap. I have got one or two things . . . Then she suddenly *gave* me a summer coat: it is a lemon colour, and a little too long for me, but it is beautifully cut – it is loose and absolutely simple and she said it was a French one but she had cut out the label. This evening we are all going to Mr Joyce's publishers who are giving a party for him. I don't think I could possibly have been more lucky in getting this position. The work is not hard, varied, and nearly always interesting, and the Joyces are so very kind about including me in all the things they do. They seem used to doing things with Jimmy Sullivan, and I just get added on; this is a great help against homesickness, which I'm afraid assails me from time to time. Please tell Mary that I am writing my diary as much as I possibly can, and that I look forward to hers also.

I do not know how long we are to remain in New York – it depends upon the casting of Mr J.'s new play which proves a difficult matter. When that is settled, we are to go somewhere to the country, as Mrs J. wants a holiday and Mr J. has to write

– but no certain plans are made. Tell Papa that I quite agree about experiences knowing their place if only one will let them, and that I am trying to remember this. I must add that I find the vast luxury in which I am now living enjoyable; it is rather like *being* a parrot, instead of just looking at one – but perhaps you don't think parrots are luxurious birds? Humphrey says my taste in birds is vulgar – but I suppose one's taste in anything is conditioned in part by one's curiosity about it, and I have never managed to care for little brown birds one can hardly see. I am saving half my salary: this can be certain, the rest is a constant battle between what I need and what I want. You would not like the food here at all. It is either foreign and tastes like it (which I like) or else it looks like ours, only larger, and does not taste at all, so that you have a kind of dream of what you're eating. It is no good my trying to describe New York as I did in my first letter. It would get dull, because I don't know where to begin or what needs describing and what doesn't. I shouldn't worry too much about Serena wanting to be a doctor – it takes such ages she'll probably end up by being a nurse – think of Florence Nightingale – you wouldn't mind that, and you *have* brought us all up awfully well, and, as Papa says, once we're up there isn't much you can do about it. I do hope your hay fever hasn't started: give my love to everybody – including Napoleon and Ticky, but most of all to you and Papa and Mary and Serena and the boys.

Your loving SARAH

This is after tea, and there is such a feeling of tension, that I have escaped to write this in peace. Even the monkey has gone: his owner has turned up at last, and I am quite alone for a bit, which one certainly couldn't be with him. I don't understand people at all well: or just when I think I'm beginning to, they change into someone else. Or do I change? Everybody has turned out unexpectedly today – so perhaps I have too. Take Papa: anybody who really wanted to meet him could do so, and at the worst he's simply shades of himself: one might say: 'He's rather pale today', but he would still be a recognizable colour. I think this is unusual though – there are fewer people like Papa even than I thought. This morning, helping Mrs J., the thread that seemed to run through her morning was her feeling for him. She asked me endless questions about what he had been doing all the week, and whether I had been with him or not, and when I told her about all the shopping he'd done before her arrival she seemed pleased. (I didn't tell her about his buying me clothes – even when she asked me whether I'd got any new ones. This is another piece of deceit, which begins to sit on me rather too often, I think.) But then, when she came into the kitchen, and I was reading to him, she seemed an entirely different person who neither loved nor cared about him – and he was different as well; I didn't know either of them, and had a miserably insular feeling that I wasn't used to people treating each other like that. I was making tea with these bleak thoughts, when Jimmy came in, and *he* was different too: I suddenly felt I could tell him about it, and did, and he made it all the right size with a flick of consideration. He seems to be both experienced and kind, and I do admire him for that. The pear blossom will be out at home, and the magnolia will be right out. They will be having tea in the dining room with drops of water on the pound of butter and white crystals on Aunt T.'s blackcurrant jam, and Ticky on the picture rail shrilling for sugar. But of course, it isn't the same time at home as it is here. That is a curious separation – the hours as well as the miles. This morning Mrs J. asked me whether I'd ever been to Greece in exactly the same voice as she had asked me earlier whether I had been to Saks – a shop on Fifth Avenue – I haven't been to either. Jimmy has just come in to tell me the time of the party tonight. I have never met a publisher. I did ask Mr J. about them, and he said that nearly all publishers hovered uneasily between a business and a profession, that they suffered from the most unpredictable raw material, and that most writers were like a zoo masquerading as a circus with one or two societies for the prevention of cruelty to authors. Then he laughed and said he was a member of the zoo; but none of this – although memorable – is really illuminating. I have no suitable dress for this party and this makes me wish that I was not going to it. It was so odd, reading the play today, to reach that scene that I have heard so many people read. It made me see how, in a well-made play, everything depends on something else. We got a little way into the third act before we were interrupted – I'd stopped feeling nervous ages before, and when we stopped I realized that my throat was aching, which I hadn't noticed at the time, at all. I have never known *anything like* his attention: it is as though he is listening, seeing, almost breathing in the play – as though the words as I read them were falling into his body, and as though everything outside the play had been turned off and didn't exist. Somehow it is impossible not to be drawn into this attention – not as a person – but as a path between it and him. Sometimes I seemed to be nearer the play, and sometimes nearer his attention to it. He hardly spoke at all: once or twice he repeated a line after me, and I realized that I'd got some of the words wrong – even one word – but he always knew and always repeated them right. Ordinarily, I think I'd have felt confused at being corrected – would have wanted to interrupt with apologies, but as the play grew, these personal feelings diminished, until afterwards I wondered whether all apologies weren't simply to oneself for failing to be the marvellous creature one wanted to appear. It is so much more interesting to be a vehicle – transporting something – because one seems to have a place in relation to so much else, instead of being a tiny over-emphatic full stop. Mary will not understand this, but whom does one write a diary for? I think to save oneself a few conversations with oneself. I do hope he finds the right Clemency. I almost feel that I'd know her now just by looking. I think Jimmy feels this: the best part of Jimmy is his recognition, and that is not a small thing to say of anybody. Must go and put on boring dress for glamorous party.

*

This is twenty past two – too late for opinions or fears, but they want me to be Clemency for the play. They know that I know nothing. I have undertaken to try and learn.

2

EMMANUEL

HE woke in the night – eyes burning, hands clenched – as though he'd been fighting with himself to stay asleep, and lost. I drank a good deal, he thought, as another part of his mind started to fidget and jeer. 'No sooner said than done!' it began; 'now we'll see the result of all that grandiose simplicity!' His body seemed to be stretched, strained out, weightlessly over the bed. Now, if only he knew exactly what to do, he would leap out of bed and it would be done. It was a quarter to five. 'Just think what you can't do at a quarter to five – or a quarter to anything come to that.' By eight o'clock he would be wrapped in lead, his head throbbing like an electric pump, his eyes little pinpoints of self-pity: but now some feverish energy remained from the evening and the decision he had taken in it; now he could tackle Mick, even Lillian – work through the traffic of their reactions to the business of getting the girl right on a large enough scale. In practice that would be Jimmy's job, although he'd keep an eye on it: he wasn't sure whether Jimmy had seen what he saw in Alberta. We can't stay in New York once the news has been broken to Mick and the boys, he thought – they'll scare the lights out of her: that means finding somewhere quiet for a month or two – where Jimmy can work with her, and I can work, and Lillian can – somewhere that Lillian wants to go. That is all that has to be *done*, he reflected irritably; but he wanted the whole thing settled now, while he lay there – to be handed a little public peace so that he could afford some private excitement. I'm getting old, he thought, to need favourable conditions for everything. It's time we lived somewhere: travel as well, of course, but have some point of departure, some deeper shades to our behaviour – a home for Jimmy, some possible responsibilities for Lillian, and a key to his own cage for himself. This idea – suddenly presenting itself from above and beyond any immediate action – coloured his bleak and crowded mind, softening considerations, lighting necessities, touching up his distant, fleeting pleasures; and like magic slides, pictures of Lillian in an element he could provide – hedged in with roses, aired with music, with her own library, with parks and trees and far-off animals – soundlessly, speechlessly – jerked and slipped to his attention and out of it . . . He leapt out of bed.

Her room was grey and cold and smelled faintly of lemons, and he heard her make the small undergrowth movement of someone caught awake in the dark who means to be woken. If she had been very angry, she would have sat up, switched on the light and stared at him until he was breathless . . . Patiently, he roused her.

'What is it?'

He sat on the bed shivering.

'I have a plan. You must hear it now.'

She switched on the light. One thing that always surprised him was how she looked in the morning – fresh and gentle, and years younger than her age. Now, any resentment for his abandoning her at the Westinghouses' was neutralized by her curiosity – her hair was ruffled like silky waves in a primitive picture, and her eyes, shining, were waiting, poised for him to begin.

'We are to live in a house: I have been thinking what we need, and the first thing is for some external structure which does not change. It would give us better chances, and provide us with the necessary sense of commitment. We are living like twentieth-century savages in hotels and boats and aeroplanes. It is bad for your health, and my work, and does not give us any sense of adventure or freedom any more. You are deprived of many things that you love. You could have a garden, and animals, collect your books and gramophone records. I have been thinking most carefully about all this,' he added, and the second time it really felt as though he had, and as though he had never thought of it before.

She laid her hands one upon the other and leaned a little towards him: 'I could have a walled garden.'

'If you like.'

'And a wilderness, and grapes and nectarines – and a proper herb garden and those charming cows with bruised faces . . .'

'You could have anything you like.'

'I think they are Guernseys: and you could have a beautiful room to work in – Oh! what about Jimmy? He hates fresh air.'

'He loves the sun. He'd come and go.'

'He wouldn't count English sun.'

'Are we to live in England?'

'Where else do you want to live?'

He felt her reach the edge of her pleasure and look down. He said: 'I hadn't really thought about that. But I'd thought we might as well pick a good climate.'

'Where had you thought of?'

He said again: 'I hadn't thought of anywhere really. I mean I hadn't even considered whether it should be here or somewhere in Europe.'

'Only not in England?'

'My experience of English country has been as limited as it has been unfortunate. Skies like saucepans and a smell of gumboots and damp tweed. Don't you remember staying with the Maudes and your hot water bottle steaming in the sheets?'

'It doesn't have to be like that – truly.'

'And tremendous damp dogs smelling of haddock, and all the food served at blood heat and mice trying to keep up their circulation at night. Don't you remember that frightful mouse that was running to and fro simply to keep warm?'

profoundly engaged with her sleep. He touched her: her eyes opened immediately and shut again.

'Antonia.'

She opened her eyes.

'Coffee, Antonia.'

She stretched slowly, and then lay perfectly still, looking at him. She seemed then to him incredibly, frighteningly beautiful.

'Is it very late?'

'Fairly late. Time for coffee.'

'I thought it was late,' she murmured, and sat up.

She was warm and naked: he saw her breasts start a little with the cold air, as he gave her her dressing-gown. He was pouring her coffee when she said:

'Conrad!'

The dressing-gown lay loosely round her shoulders: she took a quick little breath, and turned her face up to him.

When he had kissed her, she said:

'Lighting me for the day – as though I was a fire,' and then looked at him with a kind of nervous affection.

'Put your arms in – you are still half asleep.'

But she answered: 'Oh no – I am perfectly awake now.'

It was her first experiment in loving him.

The tempo of their life changed – became less designed, less charted with organized amusement. They spent hours walking slowly about the streets; hours sitting outside cafés with what Antonia described as 'practice drinks' (she was working her way through the vast repertoire of everything that could be drunk in a café or bistro) – days of idle discovery – outwardly exploring Paris, but, as he once remarked when they were hesitating over which street to take: 'Our destination is really one another' and when she asked:

'Haven't we arrived?' he said at once:

'Oh – we shall travel all of our lives: there is no arrival.'

They talked – and they were silent. There was privacy for

intimate detail – there was leisure in which to mark time. Once – very late in the evening they were sitting inside a café; she was drinking her first Pernod – and he was watching her, concealing the amusement which her dogged and impartial experiments aroused in him. She put down her glass with a startled sigh, and said: 'I had imagined it clear – and bright green.'

'Are you disappointed?'

'Oh no. But now I have two ideas about Pernod.' She thought for a moment, and then added: 'Like Paris.'

'Have you two visions of Paris? You'd better drink some more of that or you'll never get used to it.'

She nodded and then said: 'I nearly always do – about everything. It's odd: but the actual experience of something never seems to interfere with the imagination of it beforehand. It just means that one has two of everything. Do you think when I'm ninety, I shan't remember which is which?'

'We shall have to wait and see.'

'How did you imagine Paris?' he asked a few minutes later.

She thought for a moment. 'All the trees pale green, or with flowers on them. The buildings like slices of one enormous castle. Women wearing high heels and pink hats – very tidy animals with ribbon round their necks. The men with beards, and rather dark and boneless, and the children with long hair and white dresses and black stockings playing on neat bright green grass. Round tables out of doors with wine on all of them, and baskets made of plaited sugar with sweets made to look like something else. Fountains about everywhere, and sunlight with dust in it. At night, hundreds of lights in the streets – no curtains and the windows glowing: and steamers on the river with music coming from them. People going to the opera with monocles or black velvet round their necks. Large black pots with just water and carrots and things in them, but steaming deliciously – and butter made into swans and roses. Scent, of course, wrapped in beautiful little boxes, and people spending the whole day choosing a really pretty paper-weight . . .' She stopped for a moment, and then said: 'Of course, I'd never been here.'

He looked at her with such grave affection that she took the plunge.

'What I can't imagine properly,' she said at last, 'is our life in London – I mean about your work and everything.'

'Let's dispose of that quickly. What do you want to know?'

'Well – what kind of lawyer are you?'

'Company law – very lucrative and interesting. I've got another man to work with. You won't have to be nice to him – he is without exception the dullest man I've ever met in my life, but he's exceedingly good at his job. You needn't work up a wifely enthusiasm for my career: I am by no means dedicated to it and don't want it overlapping with our life.'

'I thought that all good lawyers took it very seriously!'

'I'm probably a very bad one. A real menace to society. If I turn out like that I shall have to think of something else to do, shan't I?'

She stared at him, perplexed by these uneasy proportions of mockery and truth.

He took her hand. 'Your first concern, my darling, is our house.'

5

BACK in London, he showed her their house. The first time she saw it, it was empty and very dirty, and during their visit there was a thunder-storm. When they arrived, the house seemed filled with dusty sunlight, which rose politely from wherever it had been resting on floors and window-sills, and then hung motionless and golden in the air until they moved to another room. But before she had seen the whole house, the sky had begun to darken, to behave like all the romantic pictures of storms: the flowering trees in the square were swaying – their leaves suddenly distorted by gusts of panic – a crescendo of movement before the first explosion of the clouds. The explosion – the violent implacable rain. As she turned to him he put his hand on hers.

'Does it frighten you?'

She nodded. She wanted, as suddenly as the storm had started, to be lying in his arms – to be entirely surrounded by him. This desire occurred with such furious single-mindedness that she clung blindly to him – until his arms went round her.

'Not fright,' he said, and there was just time before she kissed him to hear his amusement.

A minute later he said:

'What a mistake it is to take a *totally* unfurnished house.'

She did not reply. She was exhausted.

'Shall we go?'

She looked at the streaming beaten windows.

'Well, we shall just have to get wet. Do you mind very much?'

She shook her head, and they started down the steep dark stairs.

He said: 'You mustn't tell me you are frightened when you aren't – or I may not believe you when you are.'

When she remained silent, he put a hand on her shoulder.

'Antonia!' He felt her shiver. She looked up at him quickly, and away again.

'I won't then.'

'Shall we come back tomorrow?'

'Yes.'

As they slammed the front door, there was a clap of thunder immediately over their heads. She looked so white that he began again to think that it had frightened her, or, at least, that she very much disliked it.

'Take my hand and we'll run to the bottom of the hill.'

She took his hand, looked at him again with a kind of astonishment, and said faintly: 'I love you.' She felt so shaken by the violence of her discovery that it seemed hopeless to say any more. She dropped his hand, and they ran steadily separate down the hill to Holland Park.

They were staying in a small hotel in Kensington. It was what most of its inhabitants called quiet, which meant that it combined an air of restrained discomfort with bad food, and the apparently everlasting boredom of both the staff and the guests. It smelled faintly of Madeira cake. 'Contrast, my darling. It enables us to concentrate on one another and our house. And of course we provide a delightful contrast for them,' he had added. That had been yesterday, and today she considered the prospect of their rooms, decorated in shades of saxe blue and mud, with a contentment that flowered now in the taxi almost to ecstasy.

'You must have a hot bath,' he said, and she noticed they were both soaked.

'Both of us.'

'All right. Then an extra large Ark Tea.'

They had discovered that tea in the hotel was graded in three stages of daintiness, but whatever its size, there was always a pair of everything they ordered.

By the time they had arrived, and paid off the taxi, she was beginning to feel cold: but her hair lying dankly on her head, the little icy shocks that seemed to originate from her throat or her wrists or her ankles, were all overlaid by a kind of joyful certainty – of ease and of excitement.

They walked out of the rain and into the warm brown afternoon paralysis of the Tea Lounge, and while he collected their key, and ordered tea to be sent to their room, she collected the battery of dull cardiganed curiosity which concentrated upon them. On the stairs she laughed and said: 'They always feed the animals half an hour earlier than one thinks. There were two llamas in the lounge.'

'Llamas will eat anything. Tea-cake, loose covers, paper napkins.'

'Serviettes! They've got bluebells round the edge.'

Their sitting-room seemed dark and cold.

'Now. We'll draw all the curtains, and light all the lights and the fires. I will. You get out of that ridiculous coat.'

But when, a few minutes later he joined her in the bedroom, she was still standing just as he had left her, and with a little sigh – half sensual, half despairing – she threw herself into his arms . . .

After that, he was easily able to dissuade her from wearing innocent, sensible night-gowns. 'You really cannot wear wool next to my skin.'

In the weeks that followed, before they moved into Campden Hill, he concentrated upon the house, and she upon him. She spent most of the days with him, and for those hours when she was alone (and without him, she seemed to herself to be alone) she thought, with a curious limited intensity, about Conrad, about her love for him, and about love. In love, she fell, as though in a dream, an incalculable distance – from a height where she had scarcely breathed, to the brilliant warm air of affection, down to an earth which was only inhabited by Conrad. Looking into water or a glass, her image seemed to be Conrad's, and she fell further, drowning in the composite reflection. She discovered that this delight of loving did not dissolve her perceptions into some shadowy amalgam of his own; nor did it dull the activities of her private mind (which before loving him had been her only resort to pleasure); but found herself living at a sharpened pitch, where her intellect was more alert, her judgment more apt, and her ability to express what she thought, and felt, and saw, and heard, was enhanced by this new passionate devotion. Her senses seemed now to be suspended at a level which, in fact, he had determined, just as her choice of colours or furniture for their house was set in his key; but from that level and in that key she became original.

The days were spent in choosing and buying: in taking things to be altered, or cleaned, or painted, or recovered, or sprung, or mended, or made into something else: in harrying the chimney-sweep, the plumbers, the builders, the house-painters and the various domestic agencies. In the evenings they would bath and change and escape from their hotel to the theatre or cinema or a restaurant. He did not suggest other people to her, and it did not then even occur to her that except for a nod, or his particular way of raising his hand across a room or a foyer, they never met any. She was utterly absorbed in him and in their house. At the end of each day she was physically tired, but she was so happy, that even her fatigue was a new kind of delicious contentment.

They had decided to furnish only their drawing-room, dining-room and bedroom, leaving the top floor of the house untouched. Their dining-room became green, their drawing-room white and yellow, and their bedroom (she wanted a wallpaper, but was imperceptibly overruled) a Venetian red with white furniture. Three times she endured the fearful ritual of interviewing a servant, unsuccessfully, and on the brink of a fourth attempt she lost her voice. 'I didn't know you disliked it as much as that,' he said; 'I'll do it.' She gazed at him gratefully uncomprehending.

'Got her,' he announced on his return. 'Not the one they sent. *She* was just another anaemic harlot with a squint.'

'Who *did* you get?'

'A nice young round one. She says she can cook, and she looks capable and greedy.'

'Where did you find her?'

'Coming out of the Agency, on her way to interview someone else. Her name is Dorothy,' he added.

'Dorothy what?'

'I haven't the slightest idea. We shall have to wait until somebody writes her a letter.'

6

HE took her, without warning, one day to see his father, who lived in a little villa in Maida Vale, near the canal.

'Does he know we are coming to see him?'

'No, he dislikes plans.'

'How do you know he will be there?'

'He always reads in the afternoons.'

She noticed that he was almost snapping with irritation. He pulled the bell, and pieces of plaster fell off from round the knob. It was the first time that she had observed his nervousness. Before the watery jangle had died away, they heard a heavy uneven tread, and saw, through the blurred glass panes of the door, the dark stooping figure of a man. She touched his arm. 'Your father?'

'No, no. George. Good afternoon, George. Is my father at home?'

'Oh yes, Mr Conrad, 'e's *in*.'

'This is my wife.'

George finished shutting the door, and turned deliberately to face her. She held out her hand. 'How do you do?'

He looked doubtfully at her hand, and then shook it. 'How do *you* do?' He managed to make it sound like a shaky retort. She noticed Conrad prowling restlessly away from her, and followed him.

Conrad's father lay in a huge basket garden chair on a wrought iron veranda so small that his chair occupied all of it. He was almost entirely covered by a paisley blanket, and was reading a small but she thought unusually heavy book; his hands shook so much with the effort of holding it that she wondered how he managed to read.

He put down his book and looked up at them as they stood in the tall narrow frames of the french windows: he looked quickly at his son, with a curious, almost photographic glance, embracing him in that short exposure of time – and then slowly at her – his eyes, she now saw, were as clear, as simply inquisitive, as the eyes of a child.

'Madam, you have bereft me of all words. Unfortunately, I am, for extraneous reasons, transfixed.'

She said nothing: she felt unaccountably shy – afraid of moving or speaking (moving forward was, in any case, virtually impossible).

'A triptych, Conrad, I have no doubt, but move me in, and get that lazy old devil to give us some tea.'

George immediately appeared out of the dusky room, and she retired into it while the two men carried the basket chair back into the house.

'Well – and how do you like Conrad?' he asked – but he asked with a kind of innocent malice, which was more endearing than offensive.

'Very much.' She looked up, and caught the crescendo of a gleam, before he turned to Conrad and said:

'I think that shows good taste – a trifle esoteric, perhaps. It is an extraordinary pity, considering the selection one is supposed to employ over all sorts of trivia, that one should be so powerless in respect of ready-made sons. I have no daughters, as you know, and I do not imagine that you expect me to make some queasy sub-sentimental remark about having gained one now. But I am delighted to see you, as indeed, anyone would be. I am ravished by this lovely appearance you have made.'

His voice was very like Conrad's, she observed – gentle, a little pedantic in pronunciation; but he spoke with an effortless flow, unusual, she felt, in someone of his age (his appearance was formidably ancient).

'I did not attend your wedding because I no longer go out – the conduct of my mobility is now so elaborate – such a precarious business, that I have ceased to feel it worth while. The hills remain green for too long nowadays to sustain my interest in their metamorphosis. And George,' he raised his voice as George trembled into the room with a gigantic tea tray, 'George has always been a man of inaction – a creature whose mind vacillates and whose body is unaccountably frail.'

'I'm not tied to me chair 'aving to read books all day.'

'He is deaf also,' said Mr Fleming sadly.

'We're none of us what we were.' She watched George rearrange the paisley blanket with shaky care. 'And you'll strain yourself insulting me one fine day. Water off a duck's back – shall I pour out?'

'Madam will pour out,' said Mr Fleming instantly.

'Arf a cup for 'im, or it'll be slop slop all over the blanket.' George grinned with sudden malice, revealing a set of startling aluminium teeth, and then, content with his last word, shambled out of the room.

She looked at the two men – at Conrad sprawling in his chair, uncharacteristically silent – at his father smiling faintly down on to his uncontrollably shaking hands.

'Antonia,' Conrad indicated the tray.

She asked hesitantly: 'Do you really want half a cup?'

'Oh yes. He's perfectly right: since my last stroke I produce a storm at once in a full tea-cup. Why were you called Antonia? I imagine your parents were expecting a boy.'

'Yes.' She began handing him his tea, but Conrad intercepted it. Mr Fleming continued gently: 'You must have been a most marvellous shock to them.'

She noticed Conrad arranging a bed table which he seemed to have procured from nowhere; as he put down the cup, the old man looked at him with a sudden, agonizing gratitude. She felt Conrad as suddenly withdraw; with a denial in him so violent that she thought he must have moved or spoken, but she could see that he had done neither. She remained frozen with concern upon the crest of a situation which she did not understand, until she felt her hand burning against the tea-pot and heard Mr Fleming's unexpectedly tranquil voice: '. . . and bramble jelly. I shall only want one, so I should like it exquisitely spread.'

The business of eating and drinking was painfully precarious for him, but he carried the situation with a courteous serenity – talking all the while – saying, not the first thing which came into his head – his mind seemed so freakishly packed that she could not imagine there being room for any casual thought – but freeing from his imagination a cloud of ideas which circled about the dingy over-furnished room like exotic birds. He did not ask them any questions, but she found herself telling him about Paris; discovering, as she told him, that she was also telling Conrad: and that the implications of her memory and her delight gave him pleasure. Fleming was attentive; Conrad seemed more at ease, and she was filled with grateful relief at finding herself so charmed and apparently so charming. Eventually, when she had reached the point of their new house, she stopped suddenly feeling that she had talked too long, and asked Mr Fleming whether he would come and see them there.

'Ah: that I might do.' Then, turning to his son, he said: 'Those houses are surely rather large. Are you going to keep great state, or are you merely providing for a host of healthy intelligent little sensualists?'

Conrad shrugged his shoulders, but she saw his face close up to a lack of expression so complete that for a moment she was afraid, but Mr Fleming, who could not have observed this, continued: 'Conrad, unfortunately, does not like children. I fear that this is the natural result of years spent with Joseph – and really he can hardly be blamed. Nor can I. Joseph would undoubtedly have been a suitable son for someone – even, indeed, an admirable brother – but from the earliest moment it was clear to me that that inability to select one's children would in the case of Joseph prove disastrous. You know how all babies have an ineluctable dignity which enables them to survive any quantity of humiliating circumstances? Joseph was the only baby I have ever seen without it. Now, of course, he has contrived a good deal of pomp with no circumstance whatever. But perhaps, on the whole, I have still been more fortunate than most parents.'

At the end of this speech, he turned affectionately to his

son: she watched his expression – his older-relation-of-Conrad's face – close, like Conrad's, to a deadness which made them, for a moment, identical.

The crack of silence, like all terrible silences, came to an end – in reality, perhaps, almost at once, but in her frightened feverish ignorance its end seemed later than she could bear. During it, Conrad had got up and walked to the fire-place, his father had struggled with the last of his tea, and she had sat with her mind racing from one blank wall to the other. (Children? But why should he feel so passionately about them?)

'I want to give Antonia a present. Conrad: the object which is, I think, on the extreme right of the looking-glass.'

That was the breaking of the silence. Conrad picked it up and presented it to her. 'A present from my father.'

It was a snowstorm. She suddenly remembered having one as a child, and wondered where it had gone, even when it had vanished. Hers had been a small thatched cottage with two pine trees; this was a lighthouse on a rocky point surrounded by raging sea.

'You must shake it,' said Mr Fleming, and she felt him watching her intently while she shook it, and the little globe gently seethed with snow. She held it so that he could see. He watched it to the very end, and then murmured: 'The best illustration of casting bread upon the waters. Do you want it?'

'Yes, please. I used to have one, but I lost it,' she said to strengthen her desire for his present in his mind.

'Well, don't lose that one. I often fear that they will cease making them.'

'I won't lose it. Thank you very much.'

'I haven't much nowadays, to give,' he said: he looked suddenly very tired. Then he raised himself in his chair: 'He often comes to see me – you don't mind that, do you?' He shot this out with a kind of querulous anxiety – damn her if she stopped it, but he did hope that she wouldn't.

She said: 'Of course not. I should hate you to be wasted,' and wondered whether that meant anything to him. But he collapsed again in his chair and muttered: 'Every other day, you know. I read, and digest the matter, and then I am able to tell him a number of things which he probably does not want to know.' He looked up. 'At least he allows me to fulfil the function I have invented for myself. Divide your life so that you take longer over living than you take over dying: that's the ticket.'

Conrad nodded at her, and she rose to her feet.

'May I also come and see you again?'

'My dear, I should be desolate if you didn't.' He held out a shaking hand: she thought that she was meant to take it, and then realized that he was trying to point at something.

'That picture. I want to load you with presents. Go and detach it.'

It was a small upright panel; like no picture that she had ever seen. It presented a vast, pale coil of smoke rising upwards, into which were woven four figures. At the top and the bottom appeared a spirit, each holding by the hand a small child: but the children were being separated – their arms were stretched out to one another – their faces touched by an anguish of parting, as the spirits, the one with an inexorable serenity, the other with as inexorable evil, seemed, with soft silent motion, to be dragging one child up and the other down. All colour was subdued to the fantastic design, and the implacable contrasts of the four faces. Her attention at this moment was distracted by Mr Fleming's voice:

'It is a panel eighteen inches by ten, painted in tempera by William Blake. I want you to have it.'

'The man who wrote the poetry?'

'The man who wrote the poetry.'

She looked quickly from Conrad to his father.

'Oh! Thank you for it! It is the first picture that I have ever been given.'

'It is the last picture that I shall give.'

'For both of us?' She felt in some way that Conrad had detached himself from the present.

'No, no. I never give a present to more than one person. Diffuse giving in that manner and it becomes a public-spirited affair – generally vulgar and heartless.'

'I see.' She was thinking about it; delighted, and also a little anxious – that she should be given such a picture – that Conrad, obscurely, did not want her to have it.

'Like people, it is capable of many interpretations.'

Before she had thought, she answered aloud: 'And one at a time will never be enough.'

He raised his eyebrows. 'One person?'

'I meant one interpretation.' Again she looked at Conrad, and got nothing back.

'Now you must go.'

She put the picture on her chair, and moved nearer him, with some idea of taking his hand. 'Goodbye. I do thank you for both my presents.'

But it was he who took her hand in both of his, so that she felt their trembling on the palm and on the back.

'It is curious that once I thought I had married you. It took me so much time to discover that I hadn't.' There was a short silence while he gazed at her in a manner both penetrating and gentle; then he added: 'You see, I have *always known* what I have been missing.' He gave her hand a little shake. 'That is why I have given you my picture. Away you go.'

They left the house, and she had not forgotten the snowstorm.

7

SHE broke their silence in the taxi by saying:

'I *do* like your father,' and he answered politely:

'He, as you saw, liked you.'

In the minutes which followed this exchange, she discovered that words break only the crust of a silence, and that uneasy silence is fraught with unspoken words. She wondered why on earth she had not discovered these sad familiarities before.

'I don't know anything,' she said aloud.

'What is it that you want to know?'

She turned to him. 'I don't think you can tell me.' For a moment she saw him respond with a flicker of amusement at her surprise, then, as she added: 'I shall have to find out for myself,' his face clouded again to this new passivity which she did not understand.

After a long pause, he asked: 'Is it your intention to have a large number of children?'

This question, both bleak and blank, warned her that she was very near an edge, but she did not know how near, or how dangerous: in an attempt to shift her ground, she said: 'Do you dislike the picture? Why are you angry?'

Without looking at it, he replied: 'It is a good picture. I detest it. I detest it,' he repeated, as though that ended the matter.

'But, Conrad, *why*?'

He was silent.

'You haven't answered my question.'

He looked at her, she felt now, with deliberate hostility. '*You* have not answered mine.'

She realized suddenly that the taxi was grinding up the steep hill to their house. At the same moment, he said: 'We move in tonight. A surprise for you,' and she felt her heart drop down out of her throat.

When they stopped, she leaned towards the picture that had been propped on the floor of the cab.

'Give me your snowstorm,' he said, and took it, and shook it gently. 'Now that I *do* like. That is a present which I thoroughly approve your having.'

The way in which he said this angered her, and she retorted: 'Yes: because it is suitable for a child! I have been moved in here like a child. I do not want this kind of childish surprise.'

Instantly she felt his fingers murderously separate on her wrist – she thought that he was going to say something violent – that some fury of abuse must break from him, but he remained silent, and after he had dropped her wrist she became suddenly afraid of what he had not said.

They entered their house without a word, and he led the way upstairs to the drawing-room. Everything was completely arranged – there was even a bowl of wallflowers burnishing the air with their brown velvet scent. She stood uncertainly in the middle of the room.

'Our unpacking has not been done,' he said; 'I thought we might do that now before dinner.'

She turned obediently towards the door. The room did not feel like her room. The contrast between his fingers on her wrist and his voice now frightened her again, and, for the first time with him, she felt alone and without him.

'I am going down in search of drink.'

She nodded: she could think of nothing to say.

Their luggage lay neatly stacked in the middle of the bedroom, which, orderly and exquisite, seemed, with a kind of superior detachment, to be waiting any attempts she might make to untidy it. In spite of her having chosen with Conrad how it should look, its finished appearance now defeated her: the white carpet and the red walls – even the simple white painted furniture seemed to her intolerably sophisticated: the white muslin curtains blowing gently from the open sash-windows seemed to arch their backs with a delicate indifference: the smooth coverlet on the bed made it look like a stage bed. The fire basket was carefully laid with clean paper, the twigs and small pieces of coal – to light it, she felt, would be a violation of its elegance. She remembered moving to the house in Sussex when she was a child – the disorder, the first picnic meal eaten in the kitchen with packing-cases and tools strewn all over the floor: the smoking oil-lamp, and the candles stuck on to saucers which everybody had had to carry about the half-furnished rooms – the sense of adventure which had pervaded her first night there – she had slept on a sofa wrapped in her father's old army sleeping-bag. In the morning they had boiled fresh eggs in the tea-kettle because the saucepans were not unpacked, and all the water had had to be pumped by hand from the well by the kitchen door. She had enjoyed those first days more than any other time there.

Now – this was her house – her home. I may live here for ever, she thought, and was suddenly, irrationally homesick for the mud-coloured room in the Kensington hotel. I *have* to live here now: I am married. I have to live in this house with him; even now, when I do not understand him and there is nobody I can ask. 'What is the longest river in the world, Miss Dawson?' 'The Amazon, my dear.' But she was no longer a child. She had graduated from these matters of fact to questions like the moral worth of such people as Napoleon and Henry VIII – problems whose solution she had early recognized were dependent upon the ethical views of first Miss Dawson, and later herself. These earliest discoveries of different points of view had been alarming, but they had also enchanted her. People did not resemble one another, and their differences were deeply and delightfully engrained beyond their physical appearance. Now, however, one could not run away and play with Napoleon's possible states of mind. She was no longer playing, and she certainly could not run away. She must unpack all those clothes which he had given her, but she stood looking at the trunks without touching them. They contained nothing, she then realized, that had belonged to her before she had married. She felt suddenly and utterly without refuge – like a child who has been sent to stay with people, and has not even its own railway ticket as means to escape. He was angry with her, and she did not know why – she did not even know why his anger frightened her so much – but she could neither avoid nor ignore it. 'If you are unsure of anything, dear, ask me.' Dear Miss Dawson; she had never thought uncertainty necessary. Perhaps it wasn't. Perhaps she had only to ask Conrad why even the thought of children drove him to such a distance of hostility . . . Did that mean that they would never *have* children? She most passionately did not want to consider this – she knew that that was why she had not answered his question in the taxi. Surely it was a situation which must simply arrive – by which she recognized that possibly she meant him to design it – but not, but *not*, a clash now about what were, after all, only potential requirements? He had precipitated the conflict; she did not know why, and not knowing that, she felt she knew nothing.

She heard him coming upstairs, and looked again at all their luggage marked with Paris labels. This seemed to collect all her experience of him: she added it rather defiantly to her courage, and turned to face him.

He came into the room carrying a tray of bottles – smiling – not to her, but rather as a part of his general appearance. For the first time since they had been married, she badly wanted a cigarette.

'You don't seem to have got very far.' He put the tray on her empty dressing-table.

She shrugged her shoulders. 'I wanted a drink first. It *is* rather formidable, isn't it?'

She felt him turn sharply to look at her: at least, she thought with a surge of arrogance, none of her behaviour was lost on him.

'Some of them are simply books, you know. They can be left.' He sounded matter of fact, almost soothing, but there was still something wrong about the way he said it.

She walked to a window, and looked out on to the square. There would not be a single cigarette in the house, and absurd though it seemed, she could not go out and buy any.

'What are you thinking about?'

She answered stiffly: 'I'm waiting for my drink.' He should not, she felt wildly, pursue and trap her thoughts – but as he handed her a glass, she heard herself asking: 'I suppose there isn't a cigarette anywhere about?'

Instantly he drew from his coat pocket her small silver case and handed it to her.

'I didn't know that you had that!'

'All the time. You have been admirably good about it.'

She answered honestly: 'It has not been difficult. I haven't wanted to smoke.'

'Until now.'

He did not produce a match for her, and she looked about the room.

'Over there,' he said: he did not move.

She walked with her drink to the fire-place, and picked up the box of matches. The obscure sensation of being 'handled' again struck and humiliated her: again she felt cornered by him; now with this petty habit of smoking which he had decreed bad for her palate and unsuited to her personality. In so short a time he had so much altered her that she felt lost, panic-stricken, almost unrecognizable to herself. Her fingers, shaking, broke the first match in striking it, and she felt suddenly, intolerably, self-conscious as the creature he had made of her – someone who was frightened and ashamed of lighting a cigarette.

'I left my picture downstairs. I want to hang it.'

He walked to the stool in front of her dressing-table and sat down. He said nothing.

'I want to hang it in here. There are no pictures in this room. It is unbearably bare.' Her ill-chosen words to describe the room made her angrier: she repeated: 'I left the picture downstairs.'

'If you want a picture in here, I will give you a picture.'

'I've already been given one. I don't want you to give me a picture – I want the Blake.'

He swung round on the stool to face her. Then he said deliberately: 'I have put that picture away. I do not want it hung in my house. I have told you, I detest it.'

'I thought this was also my house!'

'Don't you think that on so important a point as a picture we should agree?'

'Agree with *you* – I can see that you mean that. I see now that this is to be your house in which I am to live, and that I –'

He interrupted smoothly: 'This is my house, and you are my wife.' But behind his apparent urbanity, she felt that he was angry and involved.

'So that I am your property, and anything belonging to me is really yours!'

'The legal aspects of that situation are no longer what they were. I am not prepared to discuss this any more. I am sorry that I dislike your picture, but my feeling against it cannot be changed, and I will not have it hung in this house.'

There was a short silence. Then she said:

'We had better return it to your father, then, and you can explain why.' But he answered immediately:

'We must not do that! It would hurt him – it would hurt his feelings – and I won't have that.'

She turned on him to cry '*His* feelings!' but his face, lit by a look of profound humility and determination, stopped her: she said nothing, and in the silence that followed her anger drained heavily, reluctantly away.

When she tried to open her trunk, she found it locked, and from where he was sitting, he threw her the ring of keys. She had thought that the scene, or quarrel, or whatever it was drearily called, had finished; but with this gesture she knew at once that it had not. When she had opened her trunk, he began:

'I asked you a question in the taxi: you didn't answer it.'

'Conrad, wouldn't it be better to unpack now, and talk about that later?'

'Why?'

'All right: now, then.' She sat back on her heels – her heart had started again to thump. She added faintly: 'I can't really remember what it was you asked me,' and knew that he didn't believe her.

'I asked you whether it was your intention to have a large number of children?'

'Surely that isn't an intention which there would be any point in my having by myself?'

'You are again evading the question. Why can't you be honest about it?'

'Honestly, I haven't thought seriously about it at all. Yes, I suppose so. Not a large number – but I think I always imagined that I should have some children.'

'And it had not entered your head to say one word about it until now?'

'I tell you, I haven't been thinking about it. It was you who started it. It seems to be you who feel strongly about children. Why haven't *you* talked about it?'

She had left the matches by the fire-place, and got, with some difficulty, to her feet. As she struck her match, he asked:

'Do you feel, then, that without children, you will not be "fulfilling yourself" – whatever that may mean?'

She threw the match away into the beautiful fire-place. 'Oh do stop asking these – venomous questions! I tell you, I don't *know*! Why does it suddenly matter so much? Either we shall have children, or we shan't. I mean —' she felt colour flooding her face: 'I mean – if we decide to have them, of course.'

'Exactly. If we decide.'

She walked shakily back to her place on the floor. 'Well – couldn't we decide that later?'

'You thoroughly misunderstand me. I am talking about the principle – not some idiotic feminine time-table.'

'*Talk* about it, then! Stop *asking me*, and talk about it!'

This retort, reasonable and collected, actually broke from her because, while it no longer seemed to matter what she said, she could think of nothing else to say. But it *was* reasonable, she thought, forcing herself to continue looking at him (if his eyes were really made of glass, he wouldn't be able to see me). She felt with a kind of terror his anger distilling to hatred, and looked down away from him at the little white hairs from the new carpet which had come off on her skirt. ('Is there *no end* to what people can feel for one another?')

'Please – do – talk about it.'

At the very end of her asking him, the intricate balance of

power and pain seemed suddenly to equate, to assume those half-hidden but familiar proportions which enabled them to communicate with one another.

'Yes. I will talk about it.' He got up and moved intently, silently, about the room, stopping when he began to speak.

'People generally get married for extraordinarily few reasons. Legalized sex; economic security; somebody to die with. Children seem to me simply an ingenious reinforcement of these arguments. But supposing that one married for none of these reasons. Supposing that you take one desirable woman as you find her – and loving what you have found, you marry her. From the moment of your finding her she is not the same – nor is she ever from that time on in any sense *fait accompli*, unless you choose, because it is easier, to recede to elementary behaviour with someone else – or, unless you so charge your life with activity extraneous to her that she is forced into isolation – or, unless you jam her intentions towards you with a whole lot of new intentions towards other people. Marriage could be the fascinating, difficult experience of living in two bodies instead of one – it matters far less than people think which alternative body they select – it matters far more than they imagine how they inhabit it thereafter.' He stopped abruptly as though he was considering what he had said. 'There, under the cover of these vast generalizations, you know what I believe about marriage.' He waited a moment, but she said nothing. 'The particular and the general provide endless refuge for one another. I was not beginning to talk about women. Only men – only myself.' He stared at her as though he was expecting her to question him, but she did not. 'And you? Women? They are a different mechanism. I don't think that anything of the kind – living in two bodies and so forth – applies to them. The most mysterious, intricate point about women is that they require someone else to teach them to live in their own body. Without that, they are lost, because they are never discovered.'

'And when they have learned?'

He seemed astonished. 'They have never learned, because

they are always changing – always requiring something different. There is no end to the business – no end at all.'

'Don't men change also?'

He answered with the careless immediacy of irritation: 'But, of course, everybody changes all the time. The point with two people is that they should change at approximately the same speed in approximately the same direction.'

'I meant, don't the women teach the men *anything*? Is the whole thing really so unbalanced? Are women so passive – lying in wait for something they don't understand . . . how do the men know, anyway?' – interrupting herself – 'who teaches *them*?'

'My dear, I was not generalizing. Most people, men or women, know nothing, and, as they say, care less. I was talking about us. You ought to understand that: you are a woman.'

'But I *don't* understand! If you are going to have this – vast continuous effect on me, what am I going to do?'

He sat on the end of the bed, facing her.

'Be my wife.'

'That is another thing'; she was now too alarmed and distracted to be careful. 'If you think that children are such a frightful mistake, why did you marry me? Why marry, at all?'

He leaned suddenly towards her: she heard him draw breath with a little scorching hiss, and there was just time for the shock of knowing that now they were over the edge before he began:

'So you *did* determine on children when you married – if not before – you see? It was always your real intention behind this profound dishonesty – that *I* should be merely a means to an end – that you should order, and dominate and control . . .' He was pouring out words with a deadly facility again – as though he had trapped her, she felt frantically – only I can't be trapped; I haven't been dishonest – I wasn't lying – it is he making me feel like that. This is simply ridiculous – she thought uncertainly – but it wasn't – all these weeks we've been living on this edge, and I never knew. She realized with a shock that she had actually not heard the words which were streaming from him – felt only the waves of anger surging towards her, breaking over her with such painful violence that the whole room seemed to be rocking as they broke.

'. . . your attention distracted – your mind retarded by their ceaseless infantile demands – and for *what*? They will grow up *as I did*, to see us destroying one another in the illusion that we are preserving them.'

He stopped suddenly; and as suddenly she could not see him for the curious black mist that seemed to emanate from his silence. She put out her hands to tear the mist apart, but it was too far away from her hands – she could not touch it. After some immeasurable time, she heard her voice, distinct and calm: 'Let us – not – have – children.' She saw him through the mist for a moment as she said it – sitting on the bed, a long way away – a mere speck in the distance of conclusion. Words, love, reason, we don't need them any more: there has been an accident between us. It would be better to keep quite, quite still, or I shall discover how much I have been hurt. It is over now – the damage has been done – there can be no – more – damage. What relief – that it was over, and one didn't know beforehand what it would really be like: living in the future in such a protective dreamlike affair . . . I love my house. Soon, we shall actually move in, and be living there. I can still, *still* remember exactly how I imagined it would be . . .

She put her hands up to her eyes to press out this liquid memory of her imagination; but it still swam with a magnified distortion behind her fingers. She heard his voice again – saying something now about unpacking – about drink – and took away her hands to see whether he had resumed his ordinary proportions: but her hands were wringing wet, and she could not see him. She wrung her hands (that is why people say in books 'she wrung her hands'), smiled feverishly in his direction (princesses in fairy-stories 'weeping bitterly and wringing their hands') and suddenly he was beside her, his eyes enormous – too near – enormously concerned . . . He was touching her – repeating her name again and again – looming over her until she lay shrinking in his arms – protected, trapped by his comfort (*you* cannot comfort *me*: you are the last person to do it!). She tried to say that, turning her head away from him, but there was such bitter weeping that she did not think he could possibly hear. *He* would surely have comforted her – who was he – Geoffrey? – no, she had discovered him: after discovery, people were neither kind nor comforting – never confess your love; never, never come near anyone – the further you venture with them, the longer the way back by yourself . . . don't think of it – don't remember it – don't weep for it . . . 'I can do without you!' and flung herself hard into Conrad's arms.

As she said this, the weeping halted, and as her tears began, she understood that all the weeping had been hers.

He held her patiently – until she fell into the rhythm of his comforting – until he had entirely ceased to be her fear, her enemy, and become her refuge – from what? She lifted her head to ask, but she was stupefied by her returning ease: there seemed no need to ask, and no need to know. She pulled his handkerchief out of his pocket, and they wiped her eyes.

'There,' he said: 'Shall we unpack your clothes now, or would you like another drink, or shall we go down to dinner?'

She shook her head: she could not bear to think what to do.

'You choose,' he said. 'This is our first night here.'

'Don't let us stay here tonight!' She barely saw his look of astonished concern before her eyes clouded again with new scalding tears. 'I don't want to! I want to go back – to go back to where we were before – not like this –'

'To go back where? How far back do you want to go?'

She shook her head speechlessly: the places flicked backwards in her mind like the pages of a book – rootless, restless, incomprehensible – not a time nor a place occurred now as desirable, because her experience of them now was tainted with her knowledge of their future. This had always been waiting to confound and confine her: there were to be no children. Pictures of children – dazzling, unrecognizable illustrations –

flickered instantly in this lightning sheaf; back, and back, and further back to the beginning of the book until she was a child herself. Bewildered and diminished far beyond choice, she said:

'I don't want to choose.'

'I have done too much to you! You need not choose.' He lifted her up and laid her on the bed. 'You don't weigh enough.'

'I hate milk.'

'Then you shan't have milk. But it can be made to taste quite unmilky, you know.'

'But all the time there is the *feeling* that it is milk.'

'Well, then, not milk. Other things. Now I'm going to run you a hot bath. You shall christen the bathroom.'

'Where are we going to have dinner?'

'Up here. You're going to have it in bed. I'm going to light the fire.'

'Oh no!'

'Darling, why not? It is getting cold.'

'It's too beautiful to light.'

'It can be made beautiful again tomorrow. Just the same.' He picked the box of matches off the floor by her trunk.

She put her arms behind her head and watched him touch the clean paper in three places with a match.

'Conrad!'

'Antonia?'

'I don't want you to make love to me.'

He put the matches on the mantelpiece and returned to her. 'I know that. I am not simply the person who does that to you, you know.'

'*I* know that.'

He pushed her hair back from her forehead, pressing it gently with his fingers. 'Now: your bath.'

While he was in the bathroom, she said: 'Really, you are the person who does everything to me.'

'I'm sorry: I didn't hear that.' He stood in the doorway, anxious, attentive. 'Is there anything you want?'

'Nothing. Only to go back *to* you. I want to go back *with* you – not by myself.'

'You will not be by yourself. I shall see to it that you are never alone. I love you, you see.'

'I see.' She knew now that now he was again protecting her, she was safe from him.

PART FIVE

1926

1

Their situation was beautiful. The house, lying half way up the incline of a small valley – like something poised on the shallow palm of an elegant hand – was fringed at the back with the fingers of pine and larch trees: before it was lawn and rough grass descending to the wrist of the valley where a concord of little dark streams met, and separated, and vanished into a cuff of willow and alder. Up the other side were fields casually picked out with single perfect oaks, beeches and Spanish chestnuts – and just below the skyline the branch railway track was laid – straight, like a ruler – with a small black train puffing across the backcloth twice a day; from right to left, and, in the evening, from left to right.

The house, secure and content in its position, presented a simple, good-tempered face – brick of an amiable complexion – widely spaced features of white windows and a comfortable door, the folly of its porch overwhelmed with clematis, honeysuckle and wisteria. Behind its façade, however, it rambled, changing its mind and its nature; no architect's dream – having slipped a hundred years before out of its corseted design into a comfortable spread of wasted space – of rooms which were not personally related to one another, and which seemed not to have been built for any particular purpose. At the back was a quantity of outbuildings: stables, sheds, greenhouses, and a garage, and, behind them, a tall tightly packed wood.

The place was really too large for them, Antonia's parents had said over and over again: but they had bought it, because it was cheap, because they had been unable to agree upon an alternative, because his health required him to leave London, and because, faced with the country, she was determined upon

Sussex. The space had its advantages; she wanted a house large enough for weekend parties, and he wanted the room to escape her friends. For Antonia, the change had been miraculous. Her childhood had been spent almost entirely in London with occasional visits to the sea, until her mother had rented a cottage for weekends (a form of restlessness in which she excelled). Then Antonia had experienced the violent delight of pining not for 'the country', but for one particular bit of it – her distant London imagination made intimate as, season by season, she slowly learned their immediate landscape.

The final move from London had coincided with the end of her education, and the joy of her undivided country life outweighed even the exquisite shock of arriving as they had used to do at the cottage on a Friday evening in summer, and finding the orchard, which the last time had been frozen turf, so thickly grassed, so richly flowered, that there seemed not an empty pore in the earth. Even this kind of minutely finished splendour was not, she discovered, more marvellous than its barely perceptible appearance.

The earliest recollection Antonia had of her parents was people saying that her father had a very good brain, and that her mother was fearfully, divinely, attractive. As she grew up, she might have observed the subtle change in these generally idle opinions: her father became someone who knew a very great deal about something – an authority – and her mother someone possessing a tremendous zest, a gusto, a *joie de vivre*: but at seventeen, or even eighteen and nineteen, Antonia had not encountered the experience to conclude anything from the gradual devastation of her father's mind and her mother's appearance. A day school sandwiched between years of governesses had produced no lasting friends of her own age, and she accepted the friends of her parents without any great curiosity or interest. Her father had one or two people with whom he exchanged abstruse technical pieces of information; her mother had a floating crowd with whom she played games in and out of doors, went to parties, and used the telephone. As a family, they had no mutual interests, and virtually no conversation.

The house embraced them all, and Antonia, at least, had been unconscious of their extremely separate lives in it. For nearly three years she had gardened, walked, and ridden, and (after emerging from the stupefied indigestion of her parents' library) read with increasing discrimination. She also made constant attempts to write down what she saw and heard and smelled – efforts which were remarkably free from self-consciousness, since she was simply interested in the subject of her writing, and not in its effect upon herself. She tried to draw; she tried to make her clothes; she tried to teach herself Russian; she collected books, and postcard reproductions of pictures; she made a garden entirely of wild flowers and herbs; she tried to cook from various ancient and exotic recipes – all these pursuits she followed entirely alone with an enquiring content. She associated more nearly with the people out of her favourite books than with her parents or their friends. With the last she was neither communicative nor shy: she cleaned tennis balls, arranged flowers in their bedrooms, fetched the trays of lemonade and gin, made up a fourth at bridge, tidied the Mah Jong, and wound up the gramophone: went because she was asked and not particularly wanted, because she was asked and did not care whether she went, on the excursions to other people's houses, where different sets of people played the same games and drank the same drinks – all with a docility which was both indifferent and self-contained. When her mother unfavourably compared with other girls Antonia's ability to 'join in the fun' she was embarrassed: when (more and more frequently) her mother attempted with public ridicule and private interference to invade the rest of her daughter's life she was unhappy. Dimly she felt that from her mother's point of view she was not a success. Then she would make further, conscientious efforts at weekends, but this only seemed to shift the ground of her mother's criticism. She was, her mother said, too tall and far too thin; her hair, although positively dark, was too fine to be manageable and she had almost no colour. Her eyes were her only good feature, said her mother, and proceeded to dress her in every shade of inferior blue which detracted from them. Her mother, to whom colours were merely light or dark, put down the unsatisfactory results to Antonia's innate obstinacy and indifference, and Antonia, when her attention was thus drawn to it, was unhappily overwhelmed at being unable, as her mother said 'even to look nice'.

Her mother also frequently told her that her father had wanted a son, and Antonia, who naturally saw intellectual achievement in her father's terms – the masculine scholar and recluse – accepted his disappointment, and even occasionally, on his behalf, wished that she had been a man. She supposed, quite simply, that had she been one she would have provided her father with the mind and company suited to him. She had tried to read his works – his books, his published lectures and articles – but although she generally managed to get to the end of them, and even at the time to understand what they meant, a week later the information she had absorbed dropped out of her mind like so much dead wood.

She grew up, therefore, feeling, not precisely a failure so much as an unnecessary appendage. Any brief, hesitant trials she had made with people had not in fact either rewarded or touched her. She had remained isolated; unaware that any ecstasy, despair, or pleasure could be a mutual business. Antonia – until she was nineteen . . .

Then, into this piece of elaborate, sensitive still life – dropped Geoffrey Curran. His entrance was inevitably simple. He was just one more friend of her mother's friends. He arrived, as they usually did, on a Friday evening; at the end of a day that for Antonia was so fraught with the restless anticipatory ritual to which her mother subjected the whole household on Fridays, that afterwards it was difficult to remember exactly how she first met him. It was he who told her about it, and then, of course, she could remember it perfectly. 'It was just before dinner, and you were the last to come into the drawing-room. You wore a blue silk dress and a wide silver bracelet on your delicate arm. Your mother introduced you, and you nodded your head carefully to each person's name. Then we all sat down again, and you sat with a quick little movement, holding the sides of the seat of your chair with your hands. The bracelet slipped down to your fingers, and you had to shake it back.' Then she could remember. She had been afraid of being late. She had been fetching drinking water from the spring down the road, and she had stayed too long turning her pony out afterwards. Then she had changed hurriedly, knowing by the silence upstairs that everyone else had gone down. It was an early summer evening – the sun had just set, and the air was fraught with the gently evening grumble of birds. Bats leered about with amazing silence; and when she opened her window, she let in an indiscriminate flitter of moths. Daisies lay faintly on the lawn, still staring upwards to the end of the light – floating on the dark turf – extinguished, drowned, out, one by one, as the mushroom shadows grew mounting out of the ground. It was the last time alone in her life.

Downstairs, she hesitated a moment by the drawing-room door, examining the clasp of her bracelet, trying to remember how many of this weekend's guests she had met before and should identify. They were so very much alike, she thought, and it was bad manners not to know who was who.

Her mother was wearing cream-coloured lace and had a long ivory cigarette holder. Four men got to their feet as she entered the room: her father was patiently mixing drinks.

'This is my huge daughter Toni. Enid and Bobby you know, Margot Trefusis, Geoffrey Curran, Alistair you met at the Framptons, and George Warrender. There! Now we can all sit down. Want a drink, darling?'

And she remembered, in that confusion of eyes, the second of blinding illumination when she looked at Geoffrey Curran (he looks as though he can *see*!) before she subsided, abruptly forgetting that she had thought anything so odd.

During dinner she discovered that he was Irish, that he took horses, and poetry, and people whom he did not know, easily in his stride: that he talked with abandon, and listened with care. They did not talk to one another – only, every now and then, if he was telling a story, he would collect her into his audience with a separate, charming, attention – his eyes inquiring, admiring, amused, holding hers until her interest was secure . . .

Back in her room, instead of immediately resuming her private life she found herself considering the evening and the guests; all of them – those she had met before, and those who were new to her. That her mind came to rest for the night upon Geoffrey Curran did not prevent her sleeping; she was subject to no disturbing thoughts – no intolerable curiosity: the aching uncertainty of loving secretly and in ignorance had not yet begun, and she knew nothing of it. She thought him interesting; his conversation had not been confined to gossip, or to games as he played them: she particularly enjoyed his voice and his range of description, which compared with the few imperative, over-worked adjectives employed by the others, enriched his quietest, most commonplace remark. He was old, of course, he must be well over thirty, and perhaps his talking as he did was a result of his having led a long interesting life. Or perhaps because he is Irish, she thought. She fell deeply into sleep on the edge of the conclusion that she had never known anyone whom she had known was Irish, and perhaps that accounted for him.

2

SATURDAY was a very fine day. At breakfast, eaten in the small sunny morning-room, everybody remarked on it; the first really beautiful day of the summer. The tennis in the afternoon was safe – and the Framptons' cocktail party afterwards would take place out of doors. Antonia's mother was dynamic with last-minute plans for the success of these arrangements. There was to be one expedition to Battle for fish and various other provisions, and another to Hastings to collect two racquets that had been restrung, some drink, and a new housemaid who was arriving from London that morning. Somebody must roll and mark the court.

'Ooh! Let me be the marker!' cried Enid. Her voice was so high-pitched that it had become husky with the strain. 'Bobby can roll: good for his figure. I've always *longed* to mark a court all by my small self. Absolute heaven: Minty, darling, I'll be dreadfully careful.'

'Do you mind rolling, Bobby, dee-ar?' Antonia's mother switched her personality like an arc lamp on to Enid's husband.

Bobby made a good-tempered but hideous face. 'I can see I'll be doing it all right. I *always* do it – it's my broad shoulders or something. The moment people see me they think – there's someone to roll the lawn.'

'It's your *shape*, darling. Like horsy people ending up by looking like them.'

Curran turned to Antonia. 'Do we look like horses, would you say?'

She regarded him gravely. '*You* don't.'

'And what about yourself?' he teased. 'You keep a horse, don't you?'

'A pony. A large pony – I suppose she's nearly a horse. She's just over fifteen hands.'

'Oh goodness! No horsy talk *now*, Toni, dee-ar! We must get started. George! You are my chauffeur for the morning. You're coming to Hastings to collect the new maid. Just your line, darling. You can sit holding hands with her all the way home.'

'Tricky – if I'm driving.' (George Warrender was a huge square man who laughed indiscriminately to be on the safe side.)

'It's your marvellous, marvellous company I want, not your marvellous driving. Alistair, will you terribly *sweetly* take Margot and Geoffrey into Battle and be an angel about the fish and things? Wonderful. Then Wilfrid can have a heavenly peaceful morning.' She got up from the table, and ruffled what remained of her husband's hair. 'Just what you'd like, Wilfrid, dear. You don't want a hot journey in a car, do you?'

And he replied obediently: 'I do not.'

'There! Everybody happy? Now I must go and do a teeny bit of housekeeping, and then we can all start. Twenty minutes, George?'

'Whatever you say.'

Araminta swept out, and Wilfrid smoothed his hair.

Margot said: 'Isn't Minty *marvellous*! The *amount* she manages to get through!' (Margot was one of those young women whose social reputation rested upon her public approval of everyone surrounding her.)

Curran said to Antonia: 'And what will you be doing with yourself this lovely morning?' She looked startled, he observed, as though she was unused to any enquiry or interest about her movements.

'Oh – things in the house. We're a bit short-handed until the new maid arrives. And I shall probably put up the hammocks. And pick the asparagus for dinner. Things like that.'

Her father said: 'Antonia, will you ask Araminta to come and see me before she goes to Hastings? I should very much like some books I have ordered collected from the library. If she has time.' He retired with the *Morning Post* under his arm, and his going made no difference to the room.

The morning, which earlier had been tentatively decorated by sun, became slowly charged with a dazzling, beating heat. As the haze was stripped and scorched away, the garden colours feverishly heightened; the pulsing dynamo of insects quickened; the hot air was loaded with lavender and sweet briar.

Antonia, her housework over, went slowly out to pick the asparagus. Enid and Bobby were quarrelling on the tennis-court. She slipped by without them seeing her, wondering whether they ever noticed the kind of day it was. She passed her father's study, and saw him chewing his pipe over a book. *He* didn't notice either. She went to the greenhouse to collect her trug, and urged a frantic, boiling bird to freedom. Thomas the gardener was fiddling with his precious sweet peas. She waved to him (he was stone deaf and it was too hot to shout) and followed the narrow cinder path past the buddleia which was already a riot of butterflies to the kitchen garden. Here was the smell of warm twine from the fruit nets mixed with the faint purposeful aroma of slowly ripening fruit. There were patches of marigolds and pinks and sweet williams, and the expanse of strawberries lying on their fresh golden bed. The marrows were flowering like pale paper hats out of crackers. One or two of the smallest tomatoes were ripe – little hot red and yellow buttons – she ate some: the skins were tough, but they were incredibly sweet. The rows of asparagus fern looked effeminate and cool, like people at the beginning of a garden party. She picked a cabbage leaf so vast that it covered the bottom of her trug, and carefully cut her asparagus. Thomas, after three years, trusted her, but she knew that he watched all her picking with a sternly critical eye, and once or twice he had spoken to her – gently, repetitively – more resigned than angry at her folly, but at the end of those half-hours she had felt like an indiscriminate thief. Thomas was a very beautiful man, she thought; it was curious how gardeners nearly always looked very bad-tempered or beautiful. Thomas had an expression of gentle nobility which lightened only when he smiled, when complimented or congratulated upon some prize he had won. Then he contrived to look angelically malicious; translating what was an innocent triumph of skill into terms of immense secret cunning. He approves of me, thought Antonia, he simply tolerates my mother and Wilfrid because they live in the house belonging to his garden, but I think he even likes me sometimes, because I like the garden so much. Curious: she had never bothered before whether Thomas liked or disapproved of her . . .

By the time she had taken the asparagus to the kitchen, she was too hot to want anything but to lie in the garden with the end of *Northanger Abbey*. There were the hammocks, however, which had not been up this year. She sighed: something always went wrong the first time one tried to hang them; however carefully one rolled them up, they rotted malevolently in the garden room all the winter. 'At *least* you might put up the hammocks,' her mother had said. Anyway, she would not have to play tennis in the afternoon. There were already too many people; and she, an unenthusiastic and poor player, need not be called upon to make up a single set.

Everybody was exhausted by luncheon time. The court was rolled and marked, but Enid and Bobby were not on speaking terms. Only Araminta and George seemed gay. They were late for luncheon; they had stopped at a pub for a tiny drink: the maid had felt sick in the car, and they had had to stop anyway. Margot said that she had a headache, and Alistair said that Battle was far too crowded on a Saturday. Wilfrid hardly ever contributed to general conversation: he discovered that Araminta had forgotten his book, and settled into resigned silence. Curran was the one who tried to talk to him, Antonia observed during the meal; she watched her father gradually drawn into explaining the purpose of his present book, and then watched Curran listening with every appearance of intelligent interest. She began by thinking that Curran was simply employing his manners, but by the end of luncheon she was half-convinced that he really cared about sixteenth-century social customs. She wanted suddenly to ask him, but did not dare.

At three o'clock they began playing tennis – all the party assembled to watch, excepting Margot, who had retired to her room. The court was laid at the bottom of a steep bank of rough grass, on which lay those of the audience who could bear the sun. The sun blazed. Antonia began by pretending to watch, and reading her book, and ended by pretending to read, and sleeping.

She was woken by her mother's voice, and someone tickling her arm with a dandelion.

'. . . on to the court with you,' Curran was saying. He was smiling down at her, and it was he who held the dandelion. 'Your mother wants you to make up a four.'

She sat up, dazzled with waking.

'Margot's with us again. We want a women's doubles. Bobby and George are exhausted.'

'All the men will watch from the bank.'

'I'm umpire,' said George Warrender. Everybody seemed to be talking to her. An infinity of time seemed to have passed while she had slept.

'Hurry *up*, Toni. That child's capacity for *sleep*!' her mother again.

She looked round helplessly. 'Must I? You know I'm no good. Won't somebody else . . . ?' But her father and Alistair had disappeared, and the women were standing about the court in various attitudes of impatience. As she got to her feet, she became aware of her throbbing head. Curran smiled encouragingly and said: 'Go on. I'll watch your every stroke, and, when you win, I'll strike the skin off me hands with delight.'

Suddenly, she wanted more than anything in the world not to have to play bad tennis in front of Geoffrey Curran. Discovering that she was to partner her mother seemed only the last part of some plot to expose her incompetence. Her head ached: the sun seemed to explode in her eyes, and press itself together again at the back of her head. After the tossing for sides, she walked to her place facing the sun feeling sharply, freshly, self-conscious; with that terrible sensation of having lent her own critical eyes to someone else for the single purpose of watching the worst of her.

The set opened with her mother's service, which went smoothly enough. Her mother was the best player, and with George and Curran applauding her, she won the game easily, without Antonia being required for a single stroke; but while she collected balls, and kept out of the way, her nervousness unbearably increased. After this game, I shall *have* to play – eventually, I shall have to serve, and I *can't*: they all go into the net or miles outside the lines. And it was all worse than she had imagined. To begin with George said: 'Bad *luck*!' every time she lost them a point, and with a dry mouth she apologized to her mother, but in the end he stopped saying anything, and she did not dare to apologize. She lost count of the points or even the games. After she had completely failed to serve a single ball in, her mother suggested she serve underarm for the rest of the afternoon: the suggestion, made overtly in tones of good-tempered resignation, masked, she knew, such anger and dislike, that her eyes burned with unshed tears, and she could not see any of the white lines. She no longer looked at her mother, and never in the direction of Curran. She knew that the game could not go on for ever, but her anguish of humiliation seemed unending – the escape that would have to be made – the lawn that must be crossed, towards Curran, there being no other reasonable exit – the eyes – the talk – the hearty commiseration concealing the profound contempt . . . 'I have a headache – I am so sorry to have let you all down – to have let myself down . . . I have only just discovered that I cannot bear being watched doing anything so badly . . .'

It was over: nearly a love set. She walked slowly towards the grass bank, her legs shaking: she apologized, and felt their eyes turned upon her – 'It didn't matter a *bit*: it was only a game . . .' With trembling shreds of dignity she did not offer them her headache. Half way up the steps she turned as her mother called to her, and saw the corners of her book warping in the sun where it lay beside Curran.

'Toni! Your petticoat is nearly an inch down below your skirt – *do* try and hoist it up somehow, it looks definitely odd like that.'

She left her poor book to its fate: left them all having looked at her petticoat, and then immediately, at anything else.

In her room, she bathed her face, and then went to the bathroom for drinking water. The bathroom looked out on to the little back lawn where tea was laid, and the window was open.

'. . . *I* don't know,' her mother was saying. 'Of course, I should understand if she was simply bad at games – if she had any other interests! Wilfrid says she doesn't really know a thing in spite of years of governesses, and she hasn't the sort of brain to do much good at a university – although heaven knows a blue-stocking daughter would be a ghastly enough prospect – even *that* would be better than this total lack of interest in anything. Nobody has ever *noticed* her, if you know what I mean – and personally, I don't blame them. Her appearance – you'd think the average girl would mind frightfully about that, but *she* doesn't. When I think of myself at that age! The fun I used to have! It's shattering! Of course I was a perfectly ordinary young girl . . .'

Through the clamour of interruption – of gallant denials, she heard Curran's voice – startling; incisive; calm: 'She has the most remarkable eyes I've ever seen in my life.'

She heard no more. Looking suddenly up to her reflection, she saw her own eyes, hurt, astonished, before the tears ran out of them, and she fled to her room.

It was like being born a second time: this violent picture – this seeing of her own appearance through other people's eyes. Unable to think, she wept, huddled in the hideous leather armchair in which she had spent so many hours reading about imaginary people, until the instinctive reasons for crying incoherently occurred . . . She *was* bad at games – but she was not interested in games – it was not that she didn't care about anything: she simply cared about different things, and that hadn't seemed to matter until her mother had drawn everybody's attention to her – to her dullness, lack of interests, and generally unattractive appearance. She hadn't *wanted* to be noticed at all, and to be unfavourably noticed in this way made the prospect of seeing any more of the house party intolerable.

Curran's remark about her eyes only filled her with the terror of unbalance – seemed only an unwelcome confusion, interrupting the accepted view of her otherwise complete insignificance. She felt then that it would be somehow easier to be considered entirely unremarkable – that a single grace would neither save nor console her; and the thought of a single person defending her, simply prevented her from sinking into the camouflage of her background. Her eyes would give her away. He was probably being polite, she thought, and then, because he had not known that she would hear him, she wanted to look for herself. But her eyes looked now merely blurred and dark; staring back at her with solemn, searching anxiety, and just as she turned away from the glass with a wavering disapproval: 'My mother is perfectly right.'

When, an hour later, her mother came to chivvy her to the Framptons, she found Antonia curled up in the leather armchair as easily and deeply asleep, in spite of her tortuous position, as a young animal. She had not changed, her mother told the others, and if they waited for her, they would be late. So of course they did not wait.

She woke to the empty pleasure of the house – the sunlit evening after a hot day. While she had slept, the roses in the bowl beside her had yawned so widely that they had shed their outside petals in an ecstasy of exhaustion: the room was cooler, and outside there was a soothingly distant cuckoo – saying it again and again, and then a pause – assuming for her the responsibility of sound and silence.

She woke refreshed, and with a violent curiosity; as though, asleep, she had been presented with some tremendously exciting discovery, which awake, she was to discover and pursue. She stretched herself out of her chair, and looked at her watch, but watches galloped on her wrist with such extraordinary disregard for their function that she had no idea of the time. She was reflecting contentedly that they must all have gone to the party – that she had, at least, escaped them for a bit – when there was a knock on her door. It was the new maid, who had been sent to tell her that her mother and everyone was staying on at their party, and would not be back for dinner. Her father wished dinner half an hour earlier than had been arranged, and did this suit Miss Antonia? While she delivered this message, her eyes roved round the room, nervously, with a kind of inexpert collection of the scene. Her eyes were red, Antonia noticed, her face was puffed and a dull pink – her apron looked paper stiff and new, and the absurd frill round her damp straw-coloured hair seemed pathetically incongruous. As she observed this, and discovered that it was about seven – but the maid would go and make sure if Miss Antonia wished – she realized that she knew nothing at all about the new maid excepting what she had just noticed.

'I don't know your name, I'm afraid.'

'Dorcas, miss.' She stared at the floor.

Antonia asked awkwardly: 'Are you all right? Have you got what you need?'

'It's a bit strange at first. I've to find my way about. I've not been away in service before. Ever.' This confidence seemed nearly too much for her; she glanced hurriedly at Antonia with the shadowy attempt at a smile, and began screwing the corner of her apron with soft pink fingers.

'Are you homesick?'

But Dorcas stared at her with a kind of dogged incomprehension, and answered: 'It's strange, at first, but I'll manage, miss,' and Antonia was left feeling clumsily curious, which was not at all what she had felt when she had asked the question.

'I'm sure you will.' She smiled, but the little maid was staring at the floor again, and she did not dare ask her any more. 'Dinner at half-past seven, then?'

'Yes, miss.'

'Thank you, Dorcas.'

'Thank you, miss.' And she went, shutting the door with such nervous caution that it sprang open. They both arrived face to face to shut it. 'I'm sorry, miss.' Antonia saw a large pear-shaped tear rolling across her face, but this time they managed to smile at one another – a tentative acknowledgement of the door . . .

As she dressed for dinner she began to imagine the evening: sitting opposite her father with the green glass bowl filled with polyanthus between them – their appearance for one another across the table – the possibility that alone together they might embark upon the great unknown areas of communication that she felt now must exist between sixteenth-century social customs and what her mother and George Warrender had done that morning in Hastings – that he might christen her curiosity with his personal experience: as she knew nothing about him, so she felt that there must be everything to know . . . Her father – Papa – his name was Wilfrid . . .

He put down his book with an obvious reluctance when

she came into the room, and as she walked over to him, feeling almost as though she was meeting him for the first time, she saw his eyes flicker a second from her and back to the book with a glancing regret which she now realized was so habitual that he had ceased to conceal it.

He said: 'Shall I get you a glass of sherry?' His manner with anyone but another enthusiast upon his subject was uniform: she might have been someone he was meeting for the first time.

'I'll get it.' When she had poured it out, she perched on the arm of the sofa, and said: 'Supposing that we had never met?'

She saw him screw up his eyes – adjusting himself to this complicated, unimportant idea: then he said: 'I think I should still have offered you a glass of sherry wine.'

'That's what I thought.' She looked at him expectantly, but he did not turn this particular pebble, so she continued: 'And then what would you do? What would you talk about with me at dinner?'

He looked at her with wary resignation. 'There would probably be other people there. I don't expect that I should talk to you much.' He made his little dry unnecessary cough. 'My small talk is rather limited you know.'

'But would it have to be small? I mean if there weren't other people there, of course. Wouldn't you want – ' she hesitated, trying to discover exactly what she meant – 'Wouldn't you want us to find out what we were like?'

'Really, my dear Antonia, I don't know.' She felt the sliding edge of alarm in his voice. 'In any case, this is an absurd hypothesis. We have known one another for years.'

'I don't think I know anything about you.'

He coughed again. 'There is remarkably little to know.' He finished his sherry with a conclusive gesture. 'In any case, families don't pioneer with one another much, you know. They seek fresh fields to conquer. One can only occupy oneself with research upon one's family, and I don't think yours is a mind which could easily apply itself to research. Shall we go into dinner? It was waiting for us before you came down.'

'I am so sorry!' She looked despairingly at her watch. 'I set it a little while ago. It doesn't stop – it simply doesn't go at the right speed. You should have told me.'

He picked up their glasses and put them carefully on the tray of drinks, saying: 'It doesn't matter. The meal is cold.'

His voice, she thought, was exactly like the meal.

They ate their cold tongue by the light of six candles – she had remembered that there would be polyanthus, but not their deep-set appearance by candlelight – this piece of slipshod imagination lying diagonally across her mind in the way of her perfect attention to the present – while he filled her few startling gaps of clarity, the moments when she could have recorded, or observed, or anticipated, with the landscape clutter of words; mechanically, carelessly spoken – laid like the familiar objects strewn in familiar disorder upon a dressing-table. So, they ate their tongue: but during the silence while their plates were being changed, she looked carefully at him – he had the appearance of an indifferent portrait, consistent and incomprehensible – and resolved to try again to break through this palisade of filial platitudes . . .

'What do you think I ought to do?'

Distrusting action of any kind, he simply said: 'I don't understand you.'

'Well, then, what do you think I am like? How do I seem to you?'

'You must remember that I am not acquainted with many, indeed any young women of your age. I have therefore no standard of comparison.'

'Do you need one? Can't you just consider me – and – tell me? I do want to know,' she added.

He looked at her steadily for a moment. He was perfectly still, and there was something about his rigid, humourless expression which she found both pathetic, and a little frightening.

'Women are invariably concerned with the appearance of things. Generally, I think, with the effect of their own appearance upon other people. I expect you want me to tell you that you are pretty – although I should have thought that there were enough young men incessantly in and out of this house to inform your conceit without my doing it – but yes, you seem to me suitably equipped to make a number of men unhappy, if that is an object. You will doubtless marry one of them one day, and as you have not shown any particular interest or ability in any other direction, I assume that, in common with most young women with an attractive appearance and a commonplace mind, marriage, and all that goes with it, is to be your metier.'

There was a dead silence. Then he said: 'Wasn't that what you wanted to know?' The edge had gone from his voice, but she was too much distressed to notice.

'I am not an authority upon appearances. I may be wrong. But you have every opportunity to find out.'

She could not reply. His indictment of her mind (*he*, of all people, must be an authority upon the *mind*!) struck her with the dreadful accuracy of a truth: no shallow injustice, no glancing indifference, but straight and deeply to the heart. She said nothing. He finished his asparagus, and thought deeply about something else.

Outside the dining-room, he suddenly remembered her again, and said: 'Come to my study. I have something for you.'

Her warped copy of *Northanger Abbey* lay upon the foolscap on his desk. He picked it up and gave it to her.

'Your book. Geoffrey Curran brought it into the house. He said that you had left it in the sun on the tennis court this afternoon. Nobody, I think, who really cared for books could treat even a novel in this fashion. Now I shall work. Good night, my dear.'

3

THE next morning there was no sun, but a grey, heavy, almost tangible, heat. Everybody agreed that there was to be a thunderstorm, and spent the morning in listless disagreement about everything else. Antonia breakfasted early to avoid the others, and then went out to garden. 'I'll weed for at least two hours, and then I'll read a book, not a novel, but something really serious.' Thus did she plan the aimless isolation which she had suddenly discovered to be surrounding her; but alone in her garden, she thought all the time about it, and afterwards, alone with her book (she did not choose one which presented her with any company) she began to find the precision of the little sledge-hammer question 'But what shall I *do* about it all?' both painful and frightening. By the end of the morning she was almost grateful for the ordeal of luncheon.

At luncheon, even before she had had the time to live through her first self-conscious moments with the house party, the storm began. Then, as the first crash of thunder echoed heavily away, Curran leant across the table to her and said: 'When this is all over, and the country is fresh and sweet, would you consider taking me with you for a ride?'

She sat facing the window, and he saw the lightning reflected in her eyes as she looked suddenly to him to say: 'Yes!'

Later on during the meal he noticed that without lightning, her eyes had still the appearance of astonishment and joy.

It was about five in the evening when they set out – he on the stout grey which her father occasionally rode, she on her neat, pretty, little liver-chestnut. She had asked him whether he wanted to go anywhere in particular, and he had said that he knew nowhere, and left it entirely to her. They had time, picking their way down the steep hill to the spring, to notice and approve one another. He sat as though he had grown up on a horse, and she, he thought, with a kind of graceful tension which physically became her. They rode in silence, past the spring where the full chuckling gutters emptied into the stream, past a hop field, rampant and dripping, to the corner where there was a disused mill. Its pond had silted into a swamp – there was the custard smell of marsh mallow, and she saw one or two delirious dragon-flies. As they turned off the road down a bridle path, the little church clock struck five in its usual, childishly abrupt manner. The evening sun was out, lighting the dandelions in the damp misty grass, giving to the tall hedges on either side of them a fresh glinting golden haze: cobwebs clinging to their wild rose and blackberry were so encrusted with seed pearl drops that they hung in broken glittering swags – the delicate mist on the fields beyond lay softly, like shallow smoke – and the sky, washed clean and calm of its cloud, mounted this quantity of brilliant detail with a vast, blank serenity. She looked down from looking up at the sky, and felt him, watching her.

'There's a good gallop later on,' she said; 'I was just looking at things while we walked.'

'So was I. I was discovering the meaning of seeing through someone else's eyes.'

'Were you?' she said awkwardly: she did not like his saying that. Immediately, he withdrew from this stock personal position. She doesn't like it! he thought — She's different; very young – and shy, I do believe. Aloud, he said: 'Even more than anything to be seen, I adore the multi-coloured smell – so violently fresh. Do you notice that, also?'

'Fresh and sweet, you said before.'

'Did I? And when did I say that?'

'At luncheon,' she replied diffidently.

'Isn't your memory the tall book!'

But she gave him a solemn glance, and said: 'My father says that my memory is practically non-existent.'

They were approaching a wood: their path was edged now with young bracken, the fronds were tightly curled, as though snarling from the damp. She started a gentle jog-trot, and he followed. Her mare began to get competitive, edging ahead, laying and pricking her ears, tossing her head so that the rings of her running martingale creaked against the leather, and her neck started to darken with sweat. Curran dropped back to watch Antonia. In spite of her tension, her hands were quiet, good hands, he thought, with professional approval.

They were in the wood now; and the trees met over their heads, making an exotic light of lush gloom and slippery sun. She was bareheaded, and the noisy drops from the trees made darker streaks on her dark hair, and soaking circles on her thin white shirt. The rich brown mud splashed up their horses' legs, and Antonia said: 'I'm afraid I'm splashing you. We shall be out of the wood soon, and she knows she can gallop. She always starts this sort of thing exactly here.'

'You don't really need that martingale, do you?'

'It's supposed to help a bit. It's when she's jumping. She gets so excited – up goes her head, and I can't collect her.'

'Then you need a proper one. Those contraptions just give an animal an idea of its own importance.'

She liked the way he said 'contraption', and looked back at him, laughing. 'Is it because you are Irish that you know about horses?'

'It could only be that, now, couldn't it? I was born with a silver bit between my teeth.'

'You wouldn't have been *born* with teeth, you know.'

'Oh, but I was. I was the little ready-made article. My mother had scarcely thrown away her orange blossom before I made my appearance – complete with hair, and nails, and one or two teeth.'

'By the skin of your teeth,' she said, and blushed.

He smiled, delighted with her. 'That's right. You see, our priest was a very powerful man. My father stood six feet in his stockings, but Father O'Rorke had the breadth on him. "You should marry Patsy Gallagher now, considering the way you've persuaded her." "I will not!" said my father. "Consider the shocking shame you'll be bringing on her and your own damnation into the bargain," said Father O'Rorke, gripping me father's jacket with a hand like a spade. It was no good. My father stuck to it that he had no mind for the business. "Then

God is witness of my awful unwillingness, but I'm compelled to lay me hands on you. Unhitch your jacket, my son – you'll be imploring me to marry you in it." Well, he pounded me poor father to a pulp, extracted the promise from him, blessed him as he lay in the mud, and was on his way. He married them three weeks later.'

When he told the story, his brogue became rich and pronounced – the rest of the time his voice had only the faintest suggestion of accent and inflexion. He had told it with such a lively unselfconscious pleasure that, fascinated, she had forgotten that the story was about his parents. Now she remembered, and asked:

'And were they happy?'

The question did not seem to be one that he had considered, and he thought a moment before replying: 'Where they were matched they were happy. My father had a terrible temper on him, but my mother was a creature of such elegant pride that she was entirely fearless. It was she read up such quantities of poetry, and French books in the language – she could gallop through those faster than my father could read a horse's pedigree. But she was always expecting something wonderful to happen to her – up to the very day that she died, she believed that. She married beneath her, you see,' he concluded, as though he had explained everything.

'Oh.' It was all beyond her horizon, and there was nothing she dared to say.

'And now, tell me about yourself.' They had unconsciously slowed to a walk while he had been talking, but now they were coming to the gate at the end of the wood.

'This is where we can gallop,' she said, and trotted ahead to open the gate.

'After our gallop, then. You lead, to keep your little mare happy.'

Their ride was round two sides of a large corn field, over a small stile, past a field of clover – it would be flowering now, she thought, and then they were off, and she thought of nothing – feeling only the air on her skin, and the hard quickening rhythm of the mare's shoulders beneath her. Curran kept up with her until they came to the stile, when he checked, to let her over first. Her mare jumped it big and carelessly, fumbling a little the other side. He's right about getting a standing martingale, she thought. The scent of the clover mingling with the delicious heat of her animal – her short hair blowing across her eyes – it was getting too long – and then out of them again – the air – the everlasting joy of it – and then they were slowing for the sloping track down to the lane. She turned to him, flushed with excitement.

'I must have done that dozens of times, but it is always wonderful.'

'Yes?' For a moment their eyes met, and the moment was so violently charged that anything he might have said would have diminished it. But he had an instinct for timing a silence, and exactly at the height of her confusion, he said: 'Now, you were going to tell me about yourself. Come now – use up this dreary lane so determined to make us pay for our gallop. Embroider it with the story of your life. All I know about you is your ravishing face – your pretty voice – and that you ride far and away better than you play tennis.'

She said stiffly: 'My mother feels that my appearance leaves a great deal to be desired.'

He whistled, and then looked carefully at her. 'Does she now?' he said slowly. 'And would you be regarding *her* as the last word on the subject?'

'There – there haven't been any other words.'

'The first word, then. That's a different matter – entirely. I wouldn't go placing your whole heart on her judgment. She's a very attractive woman herself – one might say.'

'I know,' she answered quickly, 'of course I don't.'

'Women are sharp at discovering each other's little faults. It's the men who can tell you what you look like. You'll find that's the way of it.'

She considered this inversion of her experience for a

moment, and then said, hesitantly: 'Don't – doesn't anybody ever do both? I mean, notice one's appearance *and* one's character?'

'Now you're going too fast. That is the fairy story. The princess who was as good as she was beautiful.'

'Of course. I suppose that people are *never* as good as they are beautiful: usually the more they are one – the less they are the other.'

'I wouldn't be too sure of that. It is all, as the damned scientists would say, a question of degree, and the story-tellers like extremes. The ugly wicked witch, and the good beautiful princess. People are more beautiful if they are admired, more lovable if they are loved.'

'Oh yes!' She suddenly discovered this.

'Look at yourself. Getting more heart-breakingly attractive throughout this ride, all because I've been admiring you from the second we started.' He said this with such wicked determination to confuse her again, that she determined to outface him.

'And *then* what happens?'

But he was not in the least outfaced. 'Oh – after a while of it, you would begin to see how perceptive I was – how clever to see you in such a beautiful light.'

'And then?'

'Then, because you observed it in me, I should become fifty times more perceptive – I should see you through a rose-coloured veil, but it would not in the least obscure you – it would suit you more than anything you could contrive for yourself, I should be a better man in your eyes, and therefore a better man in my own. So would your beauty and my character develop in these magnificent strides of our imagination.'

'Then?'

'Then we should fall madly in love, and live happily ever after,' he finished gaily.

They were almost home. They rode up the drive in a silence swollen with secret, dissimilar delights.

*

After dinner, somebody asked whether he had enjoyed his ride, and Curran said: 'A dream of a ride. When I do eventually start my riding school, I shall ask Toni to be my riding mistress.

'Indeed, yes – it's all planned,' he added, as he saw her look of astonished pride.

The dream had begun.

After dinner, they all danced to the gramophone, and, of course, he danced with her. He had the kind of face which went with dark colouring; incisive, sensual, animate – but he was fair. He danced with enjoyment of the music, and attention to the other couples – sometimes he spoke to them, and they nearly always laughed. Whenever he looked down at her and saw her change from rapt contentment to the little serious smile she offered him when she felt his eyes on her face, his heart turned over with a remembered, tilting excitement. Once, her mother brushed past them, saw Antonia, and cried: 'Wake *up*, Toni! The child looks as though she's sleepwalking – in a trance!' Then he saw her, utterly unprepared, painfully wake from her enchantment, and assume an expression of careful neutrality – an attempt to feel nothing at all – which made him more sharply aware of the contrast – which uncomfortably touched him.

He danced with everyone else, and twice with his hostess. He wanted to be asked again, and he had a general, instinctive desire to please. The second time that he danced with Araminta, she said:

'You have been an angel, bringing my Toni out of her shell. She is just terribly young for her age – of course, she *is* terribly young, I suppose.'

The answer to that was easy. 'And *you* are terribly young to have even a young grown-up daughter.'

She settled into the crook of his arm (she was half a head shorter than Antonia), and murmured: '*You* are an absolutely *divine* dancer. You must come and stay with us again.'

'I'd love that.' He smiled down into her prettily shaped eyes, and noticed how when they did not appear shrewd, they were vacant.

When, a little later, he looked round for Antonia, she had disappeared.

'Toni's gone to bed,' said Enid, 'aren't you *heartbroken*?'

He had known Enid for years, so he simply seized her round the waist, saying: 'It was *you* I was looking for, my darling.'

She gave her husky incredulous laugh. 'There's nothing like a good roll over the haystack to find the needle, as hardly anybody I know knows better than you.'

'Talking of needles, what about that gramophone?'

They went to its rescue.

Antonia had not gone to sleep. For a while she had watched him dancing with the others – they all, she felt, danced better than she – and she did not anyway want to dance with anyone else, so she said good night to the nearest couple, and slipped away.

In her room she undressed as quickly as possible, put out her lamp, and drew back the curtains. The moonlight crept coldly over the room with a soft secret silence. Images, steeped in this silver light, shifted about in her mind – idle, disordered, repetitive: her face burned with a fever of recollections, and she lay perfectly still. She suffered no anxiety then about the future. She did not need or imagine any return – and, she thought, simply, that he need not know.

4

HE went away the next morning when the house party broke up, and she felt calm, and curiously relieved that he had gone. She had only a continuous, almost insupportable need to be alone; but on Mondays the clearing up after weekends made privacy impossible: her mother skimmed the house of flowers, gramophone records, bedside books and biscuit tins, cigarette boxes and house linen, and distributed a fresh supply. It was on Mondays that her mother suddenly decided to rearrange a room, or to move a piece of furniture from one end of the house to the other. These activities were usually accompanied by a post-mortem upon Antonia's weekend behaviour which always made her more or less unhappy, but on this Monday she was struck with a sudden indifference to everything her mother said, and instead of miserable silence while she searched for an apology or an excuse, she found herself replying with an immediate, agreeable equanimity. Yes, her clothes *were* awful – she was going to do something about them. It was no good expecting her to play tennis well, she didn't enjoy it and had decided to give it up. She hadn't particularly wanted to go to the Framptons, and it seemed to her almost rude to one's hosts to go unwillingly to their parties. When, somewhat baffled, her mother set about Antonia's inability to make small-talk, Antonia retorted: 'Nor can my father make small-talk. Unfortunately, unlike him, I also have, he says, a commonplace mind. You had much better stop worrying about me. I am perfectly happy.'

During the hot empty summer week, however, her happiness became less perfect – became tinged and tainted with the fear that perhaps she might never see him again – not once more in her whole life.

Araminta often went to London for Wednesday or Thursday night, and this week, Antonia suddenly asked whether she might go with her. This did not suit Araminta. Why did she want to go? To buy two lengths of linen for summer dresses. 'Oh, I'll get *them* for you. You want blue, I suppose.' 'No. I'll mix the colours on to a piece of paper, and I shall want them exactly like that.'

She mixed for a whole afternoon, and produced a deep sage green, and a daffodil yellow.

'They'll be too dreadfully difficult. Greens are always tricky, and yellow is practically impossible. I shouldn't have thought either of them were *you* – but I'll do my best.' And Antonia knew that she would, because in small matters her mother was extremely conscientious.

Her mother (and George Warrender) returned on Friday morning, with a perfect green, a paler version of the right yellow, and a deep terracotta dress, also linen, with a plain top, and a pleated skirt. 'You can't possibly manage with two. I don't suppose for a moment it will fit, but Miss Hilder can come up and alter it.' But it did fit, perfectly.

'Oh, thank you! It does fit – it's perfect, and I'd forgotten this colour.'

'That's marvellous, darling. It looks marvellous on you. Doesn't it look marvellous on her, George?'

'Marvellous,' said George, and laughed admiringly.

Antonia felt suddenly that her mother was very much kinder than she had realized, and kissed her. Araminta looked pleased, and, to hide her confusion and surprise, lifted her arm which was weighed down by a bracelet strident with lucky charms, and said: 'And look what that *angel* George gave me. This sweet little platinum fiddle. Isn't it a dream?'

And Antonia, while she dutifully admired the platinum fiddle, thought how much prettier her mother looked when she was being kind.

The weekend guests arrived – and apart from George Warrender they were all different from the weekend before: another man sat opposite her in the dining-room. She watched (as she must have watched so many times, only before she seemed not to have noticed it) various guests making dabs and stabs at conversation with her father, and remembered exactly a week ago (no, it had been Saturday luncheon) that Curran had engaged him in easy, animated discourse. She sat longing for the evening to be over, so that she might escape to the understandable loneliness of being by herself . . .

But alone, her happiness, the extraordinary peace of mind which had been hers when he had gone, seemed now to have dwindled to a little painful pin point of anxiety to which, however restless her mind, she seemed fastened. No thought matched with any other: she felt bereft, and she did not know why; she felt sadly isolated from everybody else in the house, and yet she did not want to be with any of them; she wanted this long, empty day to be finished, but had no desire for the next one; she could no longer bear to remember minutely the evening ride after the storm, and yet she was terrified of forgetting any moment of it. She felt exhausted – wasted, and sleep seemed not only more exhaustion, further waste, but impossible. Burning, shivering, from these irreconcilable longings and rejections of longings she lay, until, just before her thoughts ran down to sleep, she wondered how all the countless people who must have felt as she was now feeling had managed to bear it.

On Saturday, she decided that she must accept the likelihood of never seeing him again, and on the strength of this strength, the day spent itself for her in a consciously usual manner.

On Sunday afternoon, without any kind of warning, he arrived. The house party were playing tennis, and Antonia was preparing strawberries for the cook to make jam. She had collected the trug, a vast pan, and a basin for the stalks, and settled herself on the front lawn. The strawberries, beautifully piled, completely filling the trug, smelled warm and delicious: the distant sounds of tennis were soothing, even enjoyable, she decided, and began to feel familiar solitary happiness flowing steadily back into her – the pleasures of the sun hot on her hair, of twisting each stalk and its white conical root out of each strawberry, of her fingers becoming transparent pink, and tasting sweet, but more sophisticated than sugar. She could almost, she thought, experiment with those mysterious, curiously unsatisfying sensations which had so much possessed her – that tide was now so far out that she could hardly imagine when it had been in, concealing the pleasant, empty wastes which before had always contented her. 'You want to be the only pebble on the beach,' a governess had often said. This did not seem to her now to be a question of desire or choice, but simply of acceptance.

Then she heard a car in the drive, and the tide gave a little lurch towards her, so that she could see it quite clearly. More people to play tennis, of course.

She heard the gate open and shut, and saw him. Her heart gave one violent leap, and then settled into an entirely different position. He had seen her, and came quickly across the lawn – without speaking, but smiling with a kind of conspiratorial friendliness.

'I've just sneaked over. I've no invitation to come. Do you think that will cause a rumpus?' He was exactly as though he had not been away at all.

'No – no, I'm sure it won't.' She felt as though he had been away for a year.

'I like you with all the strawberries round you. I can't tell you how delighted I am to set eyes on you. May I eat one?'

'Of course.'

'Choose it for me. Won't you?' he added, as he saw her fingers hesitate over the pile.

'I was choosing a good one. They are only jam strawberries, you know. Some of them are rather squashed.' She held one out, and had, for the first time, to look at him.

'Perfect,' he said, and ate it watching her.

'You look hot, and a little sad,' he observed, his eyes still on her.

She began twisting stalks out of strawberries again. It was surely not charming to look hot, and sadness was out of the question. But he persisted.

'Have you had secret troubles, then, my poor Toni?'

'If I had, they would, as you say, be secret.'

'Ah, but one has to tell secrets to *someone*. That is what friends are for.'

'They are the people to whom one betrays secrets?'

'To whom one betrays oneself. "I love you: I wish I saw more of you" people say: they don't necessarily mean more *time*, you know – they nearly always mean more of *you*.'

'So time doesn't count very much? I mean – how long one

has known somebody – or how much time one has spent knowing them?'

He smiled gently at her. 'With you and me it doesn't count at all.'

She felt the blood rushing over her face, and realized that that was why, a few minutes ago, he had said she looked hot. 'Anyway, I haven't any secret troubles.'

Then her mother appeared: saw them, and came straight over – calling – shouting, and then talking – swinging her racquet against her neat, childish knees.

'. . . how lovely to *see* you! Where *have* you sprung from? George will have a spare pair of flannels. Toni, you juggins, why didn't you come and *tell* me?'

She was up to them. Curran was on his feet – explaining that he was weekending with the Leggatts, and, discovering how near they were to one another, had got them to drop him here for the afternoon – he couldn't resist seeing them – he did hope that was all right?

'It's marvellous! Algie's turned his ankle, and we're desperate for a really reliable man. You must stay to dinner. George will drive you back. It's only Robertsbridge, isn't it? It's the Edmund Leggatts, isn't it? I've met her at a party somewhere, but I can't remember a *thing* about her, except that she had a madly attractive husband who she was meanly incarcerating at home with malaria. *Is* he madly attractive? But of course you wouldn't know – men are absolutely hopeless about that sort of thing. Come into the house and find clothes for tennis. You don't want to play, Toni, do you? She's given it up – isn't it *middle-aged* of her!'

He was swept into the house, and she was left, alone with her strawberries, and the tide – a spring tide – approaching, galloping in – overwhelming her peace.

He stayed to dinner, and talked charmingly to her father. After dinner, Araminta was insistent that everybody dance, so of course they danced, and he danced with Araminta. (George Warrender said that actually he preferred to work the gramophone.)

When, much later in the evening, he came up to her and collected her for a record which they had danced before, she felt a wild release of happiness: although, not alone with him, hardly speaking to him, she had felt happy all the evening.

After a minute, he said: 'Tell you something.'

She looked up.

'You don't look sad any more.'

And she answered joyfully: 'I'm not sad, at all.'

But after that record, Araminta said that George must drive him home.

'I'll come with you, George, darling – to cheer your lonely return.'

George, as usual, laughed, but he looked much more cheerful than when he had been changing the records.

When Curran said goodbye to her, he touched her hand, and said: 'It was you I came to see. You have eyes like stars in the sky at night. It was you I came to see.' Then they were both overwhelmed by the communal leave-taking, and breaking up of the evening.

So – the point of no return: the last moment before a distant approaching figure is recognizable and can be identified – has seen and been seen; before there is no turning back, and they must be met, suffered, or enjoyed, or a mutual indifference underlined. He had come to see *her*, and at the instant of their parting in the crowded room, they met.

In the night she woke, and all the time of her life seemed concentrated on the moment of waking, and all the meaning of her existence on her being deeply, irrevocably, in love.

5

A FORTNIGHT later, he was invited to stay with them for ten days. He arrived with everyone else on a Friday; she heard them arrive, and for nearly an hour afterwards, she could not bring herself to go down: the joy of knowing that he was in the house was so great, that she was afraid that she could not meet him calmly. Her fear that anyone – particularly her mother – should guess or know anything at all about it filled her with sickening terror, and she wondered whether he would understand her need for absolute secrecy. She did not know.

His manner, when she walked into the drawing-room, was impeccably casual; indeed at first he seemed really not to notice her, and her pendulum of anxiety swung to the end of his indifference, but later, as she drank sherry and listened to an argument about whether hard or grass courts were the most fun, he was suddenly at her side, muttering:

'I have a curious feeling that *I* shall turn me ankle tomorrow, so that I shan't be able to *move* except on a horse.'

Which was how they came to have their second ride.

They went out for the day, taking sandwiches with them. Araminta, initially exasperated by Curran's unfortunate accident with his ankle, seemed uninterested in any other plan for him, and when Antonia suggested taking him to see the famous Battle Great Wood, her mother immediately agreed in the way that she always did when she wasn't even listening.

As soon as they were a few hundred yards up the lane, Curran leapt off his horse, and undid the long crêpe bandage which he had wound round his ankle.

'Remind me to put it back,' he said, and stuffed it into the pocket of his old riding jacket.

'There really is nothing wrong with you?'

Even now, she hardly believed him, he had been so convincing earlier in the morning: so courageous, and distressed, and apparently so crippled. But he laughed his curious glancing laugh that without him she could not precisely remember, and said: 'Play acting – the whole affair. Did I take *you* in as well? I must have surpassed myself.'

'I think I am easily deceived. At least I was sorry for you.'

'Bless your gentle heart. Now – tell me about this wood of yours.'

'It is called Battle Great Wood. It isn't as great as it used to be – although people can still get lost in it.'

'Have *you* ever got lost in it?'

'Oh no! I think one would have to be on foot and very stupid. I just ride there sometimes.'

'Would this be good country to start a riding school, do you think?'

Without answering, she asked eagerly: 'Are you really going to start one?'

'Would you really help me if I did?'

'Oh, I should *love* it! But I thought you were going to have the school in London.'

'It's the obvious place. There's a little more money in it there, I'm afraid.'

'I don't like London,' she said, suddenly remembering her dislike of it.

'Then it can't be in London. What country shall it be – you choose.'

'I like woods –' she began, and then said: 'Do you mean what *kind* of country, or simply *which* country?'

'I meant which kind,' he replied, watching her. 'How old are you, Toni? Seventeen?'

'Nineteen,' she said, shocked at the amount he was wrong. She waited a moment, and then, elaborately casual, asked: 'Do I seem to you to be only seventeen?'

'Well, yes, I think you did. Does that offend your dignity?'

'Of course not.' She sounded so deeply offended that he laughed outright.

'Oh dear! Toni, *don't* be cross with me. Many women, you know, like to be thought younger than they are.'

'I know that, of course.' She had begun to trot ahead of

him on the verge at the side of the road. 'Anyway, you can't just tell people what you think they would like to hear.'

'But if you like people you want them to like what you tell them.'

'Flattery,' she said, without looking back. The simplicity of her contempt both annoyed and fascinated him, and he rode level with her, but, to his consternation, her eyes were filled with tears.

'Toni?' When she did not reply, he asked gently: 'What have I done to you?'

There was a short silence, and then she said:

'You are not to say things to me which you do not mean. I won't have it,' she added stiffly.

'But I've never done anything of the kind!' he cried, wondering what on earth he had said to her.

'Do you *promise* you haven't?'

(Heavens, she was young!) 'Toni, why should I flatter you? I've meant every single word I've ever said to you. Will you do me the honour of believing that?'

'Of course; if you ask me to.' Then she smiled at him, her immediate acceptance startling him as much as had the appearance of her tears. (Heavens, he thought again, she is *young*!)

'We go to the right in a minute, and then we are nearly there.'

'We have good weather for our expeditions,' he said, following suit.

She looked about her. 'Yes, but it isn't drawing *attention* to itself, like it was the other evening after the storm.'

They turned to the right of the road, into a narrow sunken lane, its high banks covered with wild strawberries and dog violets. On their right, the wood had now mysteriously begun.

'The thing about the wood,' she said, 'is that when you are well into it, there doesn't seem to be any weather, or time.' She looked to see if he had understood her, but he was attentively at a loss, so she went on: 'I mean, whatever the weather, or whenever one is there, it seems as though it is always like that. No evening, or night, or rain, or darkness – it seems complete, and separate, and permanently the same.' She stopped, and then added thoughtfully: 'Of course, it is different every time one goes there.'

'Is that how you think to yourself?'

'Only sometimes: only about some things. It's odd: it seems perfectly clear when I'm thinking it, and absolutely stupid when I try to talk.'

'Always?' he asked, and she answered at once as he expected.

'I've never tried before.'

(The sky above the heavy tapestry of the wood was a piercingly tender blue.)

'I *like* flattery,' he said unexpectedly.

She turned to him.

'You see, I'm flattered that you haven't tried to talk to anyone else.'

'But that is true!'

'Yes, but you might not have bothered to tell me.'

'You asked me, so of course I did.'

He groaned aloud. 'Toni, you frighten me! Do you not allow yourself any comforting deceptions with people or yourself?'

She considered, and he noticed that she was faintly blushing.

'I don't know. I don't think I know exactly what you mean. I think I am absolutely ignorant. Have you noticed how, if they *are* that, people nearly always sound priggish? I didn't mean to be.'

He thought – There is a difference between ignorance and innocence. Aloud he said: 'I know you aren't a prig. Well, if I promise never to flatter you, and you promise constantly to flatter me, we shall be happy for ever.'

She turned to him, laughing – but her eyes were really like stars – he thought – she'll break my heart with eyes like that.

She said: 'Here we are. Here we go into the wood.'

The entrance to the wood seemed casual enough, but in a few minutes they might have been in the middle. It was laced by endless paths and tracks, flecked with glades where timber had died or been cut for fencing – presenting enormous proportions of contrast: of heat from the strips of sky above the sun – baked tracks; of cold from its infinite shades and greens: of immense silence and the miniature orchestration of insects – of no colour – the trunks of the big oak and Spanish chestnut trees were simply lighter or darker, like shadows – the ground a rich texture of dust – the old, odd, dead leaves the mere bones of their bronze – the snapped-off twigs like silver ghosts, as though they had once been drowned in moonlight; and then the pink-purples of loosestrife and foxgloves, the warm yellow of toadflax, the cold yellow of celandine, and the greens of moss, of lords and ladies, of wood anemone, of bracken, and of oak leaf – rich, glossy, delicate, luxuriant and simple.

'Where are we going to eat our lunch?'

'Why? Are you hungry? Do you want to stop now?'

'No – I was just wondering whether you knew your way, or had some mysterious plan.'

'I was going to take you to the only stream that I've found. It isn't very far, and then the horses can have a drink. Are you afraid of being lost?'

'I am sure that *you* won't get lost. I am only afraid of losing *you*.'

'I won't let you get lost,' she replied.

However, after another half an hour's riding he decided that, without her, he would undoubtedly have been lost. They had changed their track so many times, that with the sun at its midday height above them, he had no longer any sense of direction.

'Nearly there. In the spring you hear the stream before you see it. But now it is far too languid to make a sound.'

They came out into a clearing in one corner of which was a vast oak, and on the far side of it a bank down to the stream. She jumped off her horse and looked round with a proprietary triumph which he found endearing.

'Don't you think it is a good place for a picnic?'

'Perfect,' he agreed. Watching her, he had forgotten to dismount.

'That is what you said about the strawberry.'

Perhaps she is not so unselfconscious after all, he thought, as he led his animal to the stake where she was tying hers. She has an infallible instinct for timing these memories of hers. Women nearly always know what is in the wind, after all . . .

She was scrambling over the bank to the stream.

'There is a deepish place where I thought we'd put the cider. At least it might cool the bottle a bit.'

He followed her. She had jumped down from the bank on to a small triangular island, so small that there was scarcely room for her and the hopeful little oak tree which grew at one end of it. On one side was a broad gravel bed over which the water lay as shallow as a biscuit, on the other a narrow swooping channel, dark green with the weed washed like long hair by the rush of water.

'I deepened it a bit, once,' she said, and wedged the bottle under a root.

'Do you want a hand up?' he asked, but she pushed her hair back from her face with wet fingers, and said carelessly:

'Oh no – I can easily manage.'

They tried watering the horses, who sniffed the stream slowly, with a delicate, contemptuous indifference.

'Proverbial horses,' she said, and they tied them up again.

They settled under the oak tree for their lunch. She unpacked the canvas bag, while he fetched the cider.

'Don't spoil my oak tree,' she called.

'Why? Did you plant it?'

'Oh no. It did it, itself. But I like it there.'

As soon as they were still, with their food unpacked, the insects seemed to gather in ceremonious clouds.

'It might help if we smoked.'

'You smoke. I don't. At least, I never have.'

'Have one now? They're gaspers, I warn you.'

She looked doubtfully at the packet.

'Gaspers? Are they nice? Honestly, I really haven't ever smoked.'

'People always smoke their first cigarette in a wood. It's traditional.' She took one, and he lit it for her. 'You draw on it and puff.'

She answered stiffly: 'I know how people do it, of course.'

He watched her, puffing jerkily with a carefully composed expression.

'All right?'

She nodded, and some smoke got into her eyes.

He poured out the cider and said:

'Nobody ever smokes *all* of their first cigarette, you know.'

'Don't they?'

'No. That's traditional, too.'

'I did like it,' she said, and stubbed it out very carefully.

They ate their lunch – talking very little – contented by the heat and the leisure of being alone with no possibility of interruption. For her this meant simply the perfect delight of a lazy summer day spent privately with him: for him the delicious mounting certainty that with all this time he would (in some sort) be able to make love to her. He was discovering the difference between her unselfconsciousness – the confiding ease which she displayed towards him, and her sudden, abrupt withdrawals into a confusion, an extreme shyness, and this was to him as fascinating as it was unaccountable.

They had drunk all the cider, which, she said, made her almost want to sleep, and now she lay on her back against the gently sloping bank, with her hands clasped behind her head, and her eyes shut. She had refused a second cigarette, but when she heard the match strike for his, her eyes opened for an instant, and she smiled: 'Wake me up, if I *do* go to sleep.'

He nodded, and settled himself against the oak tree with the appearance of drowsing over his cigarette, in case she should feel that he wanted to look at her.

The heat, and the silence which was disturbed only by the

sensual conglomeration of insects, sharpened his senses to the point when he wanted nothing but to watch her, until simply watching her should become unbearable. Her position, her stillness, was in itself attractive – lying still, he thought, she was attractive almost to the height of beauty – and there was at last time now for him to enjoy all the details of her attraction. Her head, turned a little to one side, showed the long line of her neck, from the purely white skin down to the small hollow of her throat faintly powdered with gold from the sun. Her shoulders under the white shirt seemed almost childishly boned – no smooth, secretive flesh rounding their shape – giving to her arms the appearance of being not straight – not curved – but of some third elusive linear distinction. He imagined her breasts – small and white, they would grow with a different whiteness, enhanced by their delicate decoration. After them, the long hesitant lines resolved, slipped away to her waist into which the shirt was neatly tucked. She seemed to be all length and qualities of whiteness: no colour but her hair and her startling eyes – Irish colouring – but she had told him that she was a part Welsh, and not Irish at all. He remembered her pretty hands, which were now hidden by her head: a short strand of hair lay with a sharper dark across her forehead, and he imagined her wet fingers, or the sweat of a hot day. She slept now, he was almost sure of it: that curious composition of a vulnerable repose was hers: the soft even breathing, and her eyelashes with the instant's poise of a butterfly . . . He remembered her asleep on the grass bank by the tennis court; how he had observed then how gracefully she slept, how he had been struck by the sudden, violent colour of her eyes when he had woken her . . .

'This is the second time of waking.'

She opened her eyes slowly: she had been fast asleep.

'No dandelion, this time.'

She stared at him – waking – beginning to smile: he saw the second's alarm in her eyes as he bent over her – then felt the smile dissolve under his mouth as he kissed her. Her hands, locked behind her head, were suddenly crushed by the weight;

he stopped kissing her for a moment to free them, and she flung her arms round his neck. He held her head a little away from his to ask: 'Has anyone ever kissed you before?'

When she shook her head, a passionate tenderness overwhelmed his desire for her; he pushed the strand of hair back from her forehead with the absolute gentleness of possession. 'You'll never be able to say that again.'

They looked at one another in silence, she with astonishment, he with delight. Then he said: 'You are so *lovely*! I've never seen anyone *like* you! This is the beginning of your life, and it's I who have the fantastic luck to be there! Toni, Toni *darling*, sweet creature, say you love me a little!'

'Do you love me?'

'I'm mad about you! I adore you – I've never felt like this in my life before!'

He lifted her into his arms, and she, touching his face with her fingers, started to say: 'I *do* love you,' before he began kissing her again – touching, exciting, overwhelming her with their senses. Loving him, she startled him with her response, until he wanted her so urgently that he had forgotten that it was she he wanted. When the confusion of love and desire between them was at its height, he laid her breathless and trembling on the ground, and began wrenching undone the buttons of her shirt. Her hands flew up instinctively, and he said: 'Yes, you undo them: you'll be much quicker than I.'

She sat up.

'Don't stare at me – don't waste a second. Take off all your clothes.'

She was still dazed, but somewhere a distant pounding terror had begun.

'My clothes?'

'I want to make love to you – because I want you. Oh, Toni, don't pretend you don't know what I want *now* – after that.'

She looked wildly round at her sunlit wood: something had gone incomprehensibly, terribly wrong. 'I – I *can't*!' The pounding came from her heart. 'I – *can't*! I *can't*.'

His hands, which had been heavily on her shoulders, pushed her heavily away. 'Do you mean to say that you can behave like that, kiss me as you did just now, and then calmly stop when it suits you, like any little cold-blooded bitch? I'm not so likely now to believe the tale that you've never been kissed.' He was so furiously frustrated, that he hardly knew what he was saying. 'You make me mad with wanting you, and then, with your clothes half off your body you say that you can't!' There was an angry silence, until the palpable injustice of this last remark pulled him up, and for the first time since he had laid her on the ground, he looked at her – pulling her shirt together, staring speechlessly at him – with an appearance so stricken, so utterly at a loss, that he was seized suddenly with an uneasy, exasperated remorse.

'It was my fault, really: I'm sorry. I was carried away.' It was intolerable, he felt bitterly – she said nothing; she looked so dead white; he wished she would *say* something. He tried to smile at her. 'It's all right – I know you didn't understand.' Then, in spite of himself, he added: 'I thought you loved me,' and felt the instant quickening of response, before, in a very low voice, she said:

'I *do* love you. I've never loved anyone else, and I love you with all my heart. I – I wouldn't have – kissed you, otherwise. I'm very sorry. I didn't know that it was a bad thing to do.'

'Poor little Toni – you don't have to say that, when I'm the one who has made such a mess for you: forgive me, darling, for upsetting you so badly – will you do that now?'

She nodded; but when he took her hand, she made a little, painfully resistant sound, and twisted away from him face downward on to the ground.

Now he did not hesitate: her saying that she loved him had restored all his confidence and kindness – he picked her up and held her in his arms, stroking her hair, and comforting her as though she was a child. She *isn't* much more than a child, after all, he thought; I've never made such a mess of anything in my life.

When she was nearly calmed, he felt in his pockets for a handkerchief, and out came the crêpe bandage.

'Will this do, do you think?'

She nodded, and the last tears spurted out of her eyes. He mopped her face carefully, and kissed it; and then, feeling her stiffen, he said: 'That's just kiss and be friends, like the children. You don't have to worry about it.'

She smiled, and it seemed then a minute adventure in her face. Nearly home now, he thought, if I'm careful. Aloud, he said: 'I think the time has come for me to indulge myself with a cigarette.'

She slipped instantly out of his arms.

'Would you like to try again?'

She turned to him, and for some reason – inexplicable to him – blushed scarlet pink.

'Oh no! Thank you.'

She began packing up the remains of their lunch with careful neatness.

'I wish we hadn't drunk all the cider – ' he began, but she interrupted him:

'Geoffrey!'

'Toni!'

'There is one thing I have to ask you.' She was sitting back on her heels, not looking at him.

'Ask me anything you like.'

'No – but it isn't easy,' she cried, and then stopped completely.

Filled with an apprehensive curiosity, he urged her on, until, eventually, she said.

'It may sound absurd to you – but I would be terribly grateful if you wouldn't tell my mother anything about me. I simply couldn't *bear* her to know. I – *couldn't* – *bear* – it,' she repeated.

No request of hers could possibly have startled him more. The idea that he would tell her mother, or, indeed, *any* mother, that he had attempted, and failed, to seduce her daughter, seemed to him so incredible that he looked searchingly at her, but her expression of nervous anxiety remained. At last, he said slowly:

'Of course, I wouldn't dream of telling your mother. It shall be just between our two selves. Yes?'

'Yes,' she said, with such deep gratitude, that he could no longer doubt her sincerity. There was a slight pause, and then she went on: 'She might suspect, you see – but if she asked me, I should *lie* to her!' She looked so passionately determined, that he found himself nodding gravely, as she finished half to herself: 'For the first time.'

'Well, but if I promise that, will you promise to come riding with me sometimes?'

She looked up, and he saw that her eyes were alive again.

'Do you *want* me to?'

'Of course I do! We'll make elaborate plans to fox your mother, hey?'

She smiled with a charming secret delight, and they went to untie their patient fly-ridden horses.

Perhaps everything will be all right, after all, he thought, in spite of getting away to such a bad start.

She rode, light-headed, with an exhaustion of which she was hardly aware. He knows that I love him, and he understands about not telling my mother, she thought again and again. He knows, and he entirely understands.

The journey out of the wood and home, therefore, was easy and peaceful.

When they had returned, and joined the others, she was amazed at the ease with which she felt able to behave as though nothing had happened.

He, however, still feeling guilty, felt that her studied calm was extraordinarily unconvincing, and wondered whether, with her mother at any rate, she would get away with it. He devoted himself to Araminta for the rest of the day, observing George Warrender's helpless discomfiture with a streak of cynical malice.

Antonia thought that she had successfully avoided any conversation with her mother, but when she was undressing, Araminta tapped lightly on her door and opened it immediately before there was time for a reply. Antonia, who was brushing her hair, stopped with the brush defensively poised.

'Don't look so startled. It's only me, popping in to say good night.'

There was a slight pause, during which Antonia put down the brush, and Araminta skimmed restlessly round the room, eventually pouncing on the terra cotta dress which Antonia had just taken off.

'Darling, you really *should* hang your things *up*! How can you *expect* anything to stay wearable if you don't?'

'I was going to hang it up. I've only just taken it off.'

Araminta's light, incredulous laugh sharpened her weariness to the pitch of nervous action. Her mother never came to say good night to her – she had obviously come for something. She swung round on her stool.

'What is it?'

Her mother was stooping to the glass on the dressing-table, patting her shingled waves into shape, and Antonia saw her second's anger at being attacked, before, with deliberate good temper, she said:

'Well, darling – far be it from me to criticize, but I think you were really a teeny bit rude to poor George this evening: he had nobody to talk to, and you simply read a book! Of course, nobody could be more delighted than I that you have at last found somebody you like – but you must try not to – well – *throw* yourself at somebody's head at everybody else's expense – if you see what I mean.'

There was a silence, during which Antonia thought of so many things to say that she could (fortunately) say none of them. Eventually, as she felt that this was simply provoking her mother's remorseless curiosity, she said flatly: 'I see— Was that all?'

Her mother had retreated to the door. 'That was all, darling. For goodness sake don't sulk about it, it was entirely well meant – for goodness sake don't take everything so *to heart*.'

She was gone, and at last, it was the very end of the day.

6

THE rest of Curran's visit was conducted with perfect summer weather, and a faint but unmistakable tension, of which, in some degree, everybody was aware. Antonia, who was perhaps most aware of it, probably understood it least. She thought, simply, that every shade and degree of all her senses, which seemed to her exquisitely, unpeacefully heightened, were because she was in love: but she did not exist in a private world which contained only herself and Curran. Now, when she saw the little train from the morning-room window at breakfast, she felt that she could exactly smell its blue-puffed smoke: when her father arrived late for luncheon she felt that she could tell whether his morning's work had pleased him: she was sharply aware that George Warrender's behaviour was not, as her mother said, merely liver, but unhappiness of some kind; felt sorry for him – and tried, hesitantly, to take his mind off whatever it was. She knew that her mother was mysteriously, deeply angry with her, and tried, without any success, to annul the anger: but she was protected from understanding any of this by the screen, the filter, the instinctive relation that everything now had for her to Curran. So sudden had been this process of relating everything to her love, and then so continuous and complete, that almost immediately after acknowledging the change, she became unconscious of it. She was entirely possessed by her new and perfect pitch of happiness: entirely sensitive – entirely subjective – without even her earlier capacity to compare or analyse or understand the implications – like being suddenly able to read a set of foreign languages without translating a word of any of them.

The scene in the wood seemed miraculously not to have wrecked the situation; after a day or two not even to have altered it, and she was unquestioningly grateful to him for that. She was content to be very seldom alone with him, and his discovery that she neither sought nor avoided his company seemed to him as extraordinary as it was intriguing. If she loved him surely she would attempt some sort of private plan; if she did not, surely she would prevent any effort he made? But she seemed not calm, but passive about arrangements, although she responded eagerly to affectionate teasing, and easy, intimate, small-talk, whenever they were alone. For a few days he established this relationship with her, finding that her silence with the others was not so much colourless, as watchful and acutely observant – afterwards she would tell him what she had been thinking; they would continue the conversation from wherever it had been carelessly dropped – and he noticed with amusement her honest memory, her breathless care in reconstructing the scene. For the rest of his visit, he listened and argued and encouraged her to talk about herself – to tell him what she thought and felt – exploring the length and breadth of her inexperience, but finding, also, that there was nothing stale in her mind.

Once, when they were picking raspberries, she asked him about himself, and he laughed and turned easily aside from her question – a bird was caught in the nets, and they freed it together; she held the creature, breathing like a mill race, its beak wide with terror, while he carefully cut the twine from its little cold feet, until with a single, silently explosive jerk it was entirely gone – and she had forgotten the question.

The evening before he left he kissed her again. They were sitting on a stile at the end of the spinney behind the house. At their back the wood was unevenly dusk and dark – in front the end of the sunlight lay on the thick summer grass.

'It is rather like sitting in the front row of a theatre.'

'Have you been to many theatres?' he asked, watching her.

'Not very many. I've never sat in the front row.' She seemed to feel that this was an admission. 'But it is what I imagined the front row would feel like.'

'Will you come to a theatre with me? We'll sit bang in front if that would please you.'

'Would that be a good thing?' She did not really want to see him in London, but did not like to say so. There was a little silence, and then she asked: 'What about your riding school?'

'Oh, that will progress, I have no doubt, but I've yet to meet the man with more money than I to start it, and I have to go home first.'

'Home?' She stared at him – she hadn't thought of him having a home.

'To Ireland,' he said; 'that is my home, you know.'

'Oh, yes.'

'I shall be back, though. I shall come back to see you.'

'And to start your school,' she said, and he smiled, liking and knowing that she was not being prim, or coy, but simply, anxiously, accurate. He said: 'I shall miss you.'

She turned suddenly to him, and he felt that it had been both an inadequate and a stupid thing to say.

'Will you jump down, and let me kiss you?' She hesitated, and her colour slowly vanished.

'This is a different wood: it won't be at all the same.' He saw her fingers tighten on the top bar of the stile before she jumped.

This time, knowing now how to assail her confidence, he told her that he loved her.

He went, and the sharp shock of his absence – even after she had imagined and dreaded it – astonished her.

A day or two after his departure, her mother had a letter from him at breakfast.

'Geoffrey's b. and b.,' she said, having flipped through it. Her husband looked up from his catalogue enquiringly.

'Geoffrey *Curran*,' she said impatiently. 'He seems to have enjoyed himself, and he sends his love. He's off to Ireland some time or other – awful writing – the kind one simply can't be bothered to read.' There was a pause, and then she continued: 'That wretch, Thomas, wants dozens of wilting little bundles of damp moss fetched from Battle station. Anybody want to go to Battle?'

Her husband shook his head: Antonia, trying not to stare at the letter, said nothing.

Araminta, who hated silence, said: 'You never want to go *anywhere*, Wilfrid,' as though Battle was a great opportunity lost. 'I suppose, as usual, it will be poor little me.'

'I'll go on the bus, if you like.'

'I do wish you'd learn to drive the car, Toni. No, I'll do it. The Parkers are down, I'll drop in and see if they'd like a spot of bridge sometime.'

There was another silence: Araminta sighed restlessly, and flicked Curran's envelope across the table. Wilfrid made a note on his catalogue and asked: 'Are you going to London this week, Araminta?'

She shook her head. She seemed more than usually wrought up.

'There's no point in this heat. Nothing to do when I get there. Goodness! I wish we were all *abroad*, or something!'

'Well, my dear, *you* could go, and take Toni with you, if you like. I shall be perfectly all right by myself.'

Antonia got up from the table and went to the window.

'I often think you're *better* by yourself! What on earth do you think would be the fun for either of us trailing about the Riviera with Toni? I *do wish* that sometimes – *only sometimes* – you would occasionally do what somebody else wanted for a change. You think you make it perfectly all right by telling *me* to do whatever it is by myself – you think that lets you out of any effort – it doesn't occur to you that I don't *want* to do everything alone —'

He interrupted: 'I wouldn't have described you as a solitary creature. You have an enormous quantity of friends . . .'

But she retorted: 'What on earth should I do if I hadn't?

We can't all spend our lives musting over books while everything else is being done for us, you know.'

'It is not a ubiquitous pursuit,' he agreed mildly.

She stared angrily at him.

'You are absolutely *extraordinary*! It doesn't matter what anyone says – you don't seem in the least hurt – you don't even seem to care!'

Antonia turned round to them, wanting desperately to cry: 'You can't *do* this – *I'm* here. Stop it!' Pointless, illogical – far too late.

Her father was looking steadily across the table with no trace of expression.

'Do you *want* me to be hurt?'

Her mother stared defiantly back. 'Yes! I do! Yes!'

He got heavily to his feet, and went to the door.

'It would be too difficult for me to know where to begin.'

He was gone. Her mother gave a little sharp gasping cry, and burst into tears.

Panic – agony – somebody was awfully hurt – so awfully, that she could hardly bear to touch them. She went to her mother, and stood with her arm round the shaking shoulders. Her mother suddenly and wildly clung to her. 'I didn't mean it. Can't bear people who don't *feel* anything. That's why I say such awful things – it was only because of *books* he asked whether I was going to London – I can't bear being lonely—' Tears were pouring down her face: her long beautifully kept nails dug into Antonia's arm. 'I didn't mean to be a cad about France with you, darling – of *course* you shall go to France, to Paris, perhaps, by yourself for a bit – but two women careering about France – mother and daughter *en pension*—' she tried to laugh— 'It isn't as though I'd *choose* to live here – I'm sorry, darling – I've run clean out of sleeping pills – always makes me feel like hell – it's only if one felt he cared in the *least* – that's what makes me so bad-tempered . . . Have you got a hanky – can't seem to find one. Oh, darling! I've hurt your *arm*! How did I – the grip of emotion – I'm terribly sorry – darling, how dreadful it *looks*! I must look a sight too – I can feel my mascara running for dear life – it doesn't hurt too terribly, your arm, does it?'

'You do love him really, don't you?'

Her mother looked up – the crisp black of her eyelashes had dissolved to soft colourless fringes round her streaming eyes. 'My dear, you don't know the first *thing* about love! Poor little baby – those dreadful marks I've made, and you were being so sweet.' She blew her nose and picked up Curran's letter. 'I tell you what we'll do. We'll *both* go to Battle and fetch the plants, but we'll go to the Gateway first and gorge on coffee and cakes. Then the plants, and the Parkers on the way home. How's that?'

She had folded the letter so that Antonia could see the blue scrawl 'Geoffrey' upside down. Looking at her daughter's drawn face, she laughed, and patted her arm.

'Of course I love him. Why do you think I put up with living in this backwater? Ring for Dorcas to clear, darling. I'll be ready in a jiffy.'

She went, and Antonia was left standing by her empty chair. In a little while she would be going to Battle with her poor mother. She thought of the Gateway, with its warm smell of home-made cakes, and felt a little sick. She rang the bell for Dorcas, and then went back to the breakfast table, picked up Curran's envelope, and, ashamed of feeling so rich in comparison to either of her parents, went upstairs with it.

7

HE did not write to her. July burned – the sun rose, glinted, yawned in the wide sky, and reluctantly, voluptuously, sank spreading colours of a dying violence each night. They sat on the front lawn after dinner and watched the sky carelessly, delicately, brushed of cloud. They did not talk very much:

Antonia thought that one should be able to have wonderful conversations in the dusk – but nobody seemed to want them. She was discovering that it was better if her parents did not talk about anything in particular, and also that there was nothing which she could say collectively to her parents. So she sank into the mysterious frenzy of her private mind – half resting upon his return, half living with him as though he had never gone away. She had tried to imagine him in Ireland, 'the Emerald Isle', his 'home': it became a magically small island – very green, with wild horses and gentle rain – and no other people, except, she once supposed, their children; one house for them – no roads, and round them, lurching, lasting out for ever, the climate-coloured sea. He had said that he loved her – as the weeks went by she returned more and more easily to the exact intonation of his voice – to the moments before and after his saying it, until it was the single dazzling speck of memory set in the centre of her imagination.

She did not expect him to write to her.

July—August. The usual guests at weekends (excepting George Warrender who had gone abroad) – the same country summer life. Her father worked with his study window open; the smoke from his pipe exactly matched the lavender hedge beneath his window. Her mother changed her clothes to play games, and then changed her clothes because she had been playing them. Her arms became thickly powdered with freckles, her hair bleached by the sun: she was thinner, Antonia noticed – why, she is even thinner than I am! She seemed to play all these games more intensely – several times, Antonia observed, palpably minding if she lost. She had one habit of laughing so wildly at something anybody said at a party that everybody had to hear her repeat it: and another of asking Wilfrid in an intentionally childish voice whether she might do a number of foolish things which Antonia knew he could not possibly prevent, and about which in most cases he was too uninterested to have an opinion. 'Wilfrid, shall I grow my hair and wear it in two plaits like a little German girl?' 'I'd adore to see their faces if I rode through Battle on a bicycle in my bathing-dress.

Wilfrid, *may* I?' 'I wonder whether rolling *stark* naked in the dew before breakfast *is* good for the skin? Wilfrid, would you mind too terribly if I tried – just once, Wilfrid?' – and so on. But perhaps, Antonia thought, she has always done that kind of thing and I simply haven't noticed it before. Underneath all her mother's behaviour she sensed the swift undercurrent of unhappiness which checked the shaming, flaming anger that she sometimes felt on her father's behalf, and left her questioning and afraid. Nobody, surely, would say those things if they were happy, and if people were unhappy, one was instinctively sorry for them. It seemed such bad luck – and so extraordinary. It wasn't exactly her father's fault, although she didn't think that he tried: he seemed to continue his life – mildly, indifferently – very seldom stabbed by her mother into some sort of temporary bewildered resentment, which dissolved as soon as he could disassociate himself again, and which left no emotional residue for his wife at all. Either, Antonia thought, one had to be self-contained like her father, or contained in another person, like herself.

August – soon it would be September. A wonderful summer, people said; but the shock of his going had had time now to change. For a long while she had been not unhappily resigned; then, suddenly, and for no apparent reason, she began to regret his absence – no more, she thought, than that; but the regret grated and burned – spread over all the hours when she was alone, until it coloured and corrupted all the times when she was not. It was like home-sickness, she thought, only not for one's home. If only he would write to her – a few lines, simply saying when he would be back – she would be able to bear it more easily; she would be able to sleep. For sleep, which had always been a simple, unconscious business, played with her now each night, like a cat with a mouse, pouncing upon her at the last point of her fatigue and resistance – knocking her out for the few remaining hours before it was breakfast. She woke slowly – the morning post urged her downstairs, and the small expected stab of disappointment of no letter from him, started day after day.

Eventually, even Araminta noticed that she was not looking well. They were having tea in the garden after a bathing party to Cooden Beach. Araminta looked up from the match that had lit her cigarette, and saw her daughter's strained and listless inattention – for a second Toni looked exactly like Wilfrid – which made Araminta say:

'Toni, darling – what on earth is the matter? You look absolutely *rotten*, darling; are you feeling ill?'

To her consternation, Antonia's eyes filled suddenly with tears – she sat rigid and still for a moment without speaking, and then, with a clumsy movement, got to her feet and ran into the house.

The guests drank some more tea, fingered their coloured necklaces or their old school ties, and cast desperately about for some means to escape the incident. Too much sun on the beach, someone said with a burst of social inspiration: but Araminta was concerned – she hadn't meant to upset poor little Toni like that. Perhaps she *was* ill. When, however, she followed Toni into the house, she could not find her anywhere.

Antonia had used the last vestiges of self-control to hide herself in an attic where the apples were stored. This was impossible; she must pull herself together – she *must*! Either she must endure the situation or she must find a way of ending it: she stopped crying, and thought carefully . . .

At dinner her mother explained that they were right about the sun, and that Toni had retired for the evening with a headache.

A few days later, when plans were being made for forthcoming weekends, Antonia said:

'What about asking that man, Geoffrey Curran, some time?'

Her mother stopped sorting bridge pencils. 'Isn't he in Ireland or Scotland, or somewhere? Sharpen the blue stripey one, darling, it looks all right, but the lead has broken inside.'

'Wouldn't Enid know whether he was back?'

'She might. I shall see her on Thursday. I'll ask. You rather adored him, didn't you, darling? Thoroughly unsuitable, but, I must admit, fascinating. Why *do* people always pull the tassel off the *yellow* pencil – extraordinary – I must have mended it at least three times. You'd adore *anyone* who adored horses, you juggins – I suppose one day you'll grow out of it.'

She was silent – laughing secretly at the idea of such general adoration – and because she was suddenly sure now that he would return – even finding it pleasant to be so thoroughly misunderstood.

On Friday her mother announced that he *was* back, and was coming to stay the next weekend.

No sudden shock this time – but a whole week in which to collect her imagination and fear and delight. The time spent itself with unbearable slowness – reluctant to drip from one minute to the next – almost as though it was running out. In a sense, she thought, it was the end of time: these were the dregs of suspense – after Friday it would be new again – at a starting-point.

The days grew longer – seemed more and more drawn out with trivial incident: her mother loaded her with the minutiae of weekend preparations, and found her unusually acquiescent, but as she never bothered to account for her daughter's behaviour unless she was being a bore socially, Araminta observed nothing.

On Tuesday and Wednesday it rained: a series of heavy gusty showers. Unripe fruit was beaten off the trees, flowers were sodden of colour, high wet branches in the copse creaked hysterically. The tennis lawn grew green again – but Araminta bewailed the weather. The least it could do in the country was to keep fine. Antonia, who had decided to take Geoffrey to Bodiam, realized suddenly how much every private plan with him was dependent upon its being fine, and dutifully echoed her mother's complaints.

On Wednesday night the wind got up: on Thursday there was nearly half a gale blowing all day: a young cat belonging to the cook went mad chasing leaves and twigs and minute imaginary terrors, and the morning-room fire smoked everybody out of the room at breakfast.

Antonia spent the day cleaning tennis balls for her mother

and taking the horses to Battle to be reshod. She had saved the shoeing until Thursday because she enjoyed it, and because it took up a whole afternoon. The blacksmith hardly ever spoke. He had a deceptively savage appearance, with a huge black beard, and his forearms heavily tattooed: he muttered and slapped his horses over – working with incredible speed. There was always a crowd of children who hopped in and out of his way, like sparrows, telling him all about their lives. Horses and children relied upon him, his appearance and taciturnity were just what they wanted – and even that day, Antonia found his skill and his few grunts soothing. At half-past three his sister brought him his blue enamel mug of tea – they lived together in a tiny white cottage at the back of the smithy, and she kept poultry. She was small and dark and wiry, and talked all the time; like the children, she told him everything that had happened to her since their dinner: he grunted without looking up, and went on paring the mare's hooves with gentle dexterity. The children fell silent while she was there – she asked one of them about its mammy, but it subsided into an agony of reserve, and so, with a remark to Antonia about the terrible wind, she went.

When the job was done, and Antonia had paid him – he fetched the change out of an old tobacco tin – they led the horses outside, and Antonia mounted.

'Do you think it will rain again?'

He handed her the leading rein and looked at the sky. He had brown gentle eyes.

'Blow out, I reckon.' He ran his hand down the grey's neck and added warningly: 'Termorrer, though.'

The air was cold after the warmth and sizzling smell of the forge. There was a cart-horse waiting inside. She asked anxiously:

'You mean it'll rain tomorrow?'

'No – it'll blow out – twenty-four hours, I reckon – round about.' He wet a black splayed thumb. 'Don't fret,' he said, and wiped his thumb on his leather apron.

She thanked him, he touched his forehead, and turned back

to the forge. As she adjusted her leathers, she heard one of the children: 'Teacher asked Ireen what she had in her mouth, but she swallowed it so then it was quite fair for her to say "Nothin", Mr Jarvis, wasn't it?'

It was the longest conversation she had ever had with him, Antonia reflected, as she jogged home. She stopped fretting about the weather.

Thursday evening – she would never have believed in the length and breadth of such an evening. They dined early – she and her father and mother. The meal seemed endless, but it was barely a quarter to nine when they had finished, and were back in the drawing-room with their coffee. A state of amiable indifference prevailed: her parents were not exasperating one another, and in her anxiety to conceal her private tension, Antonia was being exactly what they expected her to be. She even told them about the blacksmith, which ordinarily she would never have done – and her father listened politely. Her mother laughed and said: 'I bet he has a terrific past. Those strong silent men . . .'

Antonia looked up, and saw her mother's eyes seriously imagining this. Perhaps she *does* care about other people, she thought, and said quickly aloud: 'He doesn't seem at all unhappy, though.'

Her mother laughed again – shortly. 'Unhappy? I shouldn't think so. I must pop upstairs for a spot of telephoning. I want to remind Bobby about the peach bitters – he's got a head like a sieve, poor lamb.'

She was alone with her father, and it was far too early to go to bed. Unexpectedly, he saved her from this predicament, by asking her to play chess – a game which neither of them enjoyed, but which was recognized as something they did together.

When Araminta returned, she found them sitting on low chairs opposite one another, their heads bent over the pretty board. Wilfrid had his back to her, but Antonia looked up and smiled. She's really turning out quite attractive, thought her mother with a little two-way stab of triumph and envy: she would not have wanted a really *plain* child. Anyway she is dark, and I'm fair, so we couldn't be less alike. Of course, she is really like Wilfrid— She was far more like Wilfrid, but what with him added up to a general weakness of appearance was translated to a certain delicacy in his daughter.

Her father won the game. It was just after ten: Antonia said that she was tired, and escaped, but even that was not the end of the evening. Alone, her mind bounded with relief, that she need not any longer conceal her exquisite impatience, but there were, she discovered, many variations upon this theme. Apprehension: that something would prevent his coming; that he had not intended coming at all; that in all this time her appearance had mysteriously changed to disappoint him; she tried to determine whether this was so by looking carefully at herself, but it was very difficult because she did not really know how she had looked in the first place. He had not written to her; he had not even sent her a message in his letter to her mother. Perhaps, in spite of what he had said, he did not love her. She tried to remember his saying it, and immediately could not. She had flung herself on to her bed, but the angry uneven gale was tearing at her half-open window – and now she was cold and afraid. She pushed the window open before shutting it, and leaned out. Instantly, the wind seemed softer, wider – no less urgent – it was travelling too fast to smell of a summer night – but below its racking of the sleepless trees – beneath these irregular peaks of force – there was a steady barrier of such violent air that she could hardly collect breath from it. The trees tossed and creaked and shifted; branches strained, sprained, out of position – pitched against one another in agony – screeched, wrestled, and were shudderingly free until the next assault.

When, at last, she shut the window, and turned to the calm air of her room, her fears had blown out into the night, and she could remember perfectly what he had said.

On Friday, the wind still blew, suiting the tempo of the day, which, unlike the others before it, rushed to its conclusion.

At six Araminta went to the station to meet Bobby's train. 'Bobby who?' her father had enquired.

'Bobby *Rawlings*, darling. The Brewers are bringing Geoffrey Curran down with them. It's only Bobby to be met. For goodness sake, don't go *off* somewhere, Toni; show them their rooms and give them a drink if they arrive before I'm back.'

Her father went back to his study, remarking mildly that a great many people were called Bobby nowadays.

She dressed – in the terracotta linen – and prayed that the Brewers would arrive before her mother got back. She brushed her hair until tears came to her eyes – excitement – she was shivering with excitement, and the minutes running out. She had only one very unobtrusive lipstick, too pale to accentuate her dress, but she dared not go to her mother's room to steal another, in case she missed the car in the drive. If the first car was her mother, she would go and get it, she would not go down without it. If the first car was Geoffrey, she would go down wearing the pale lipstick. This foolish little bargain became terribly important as the minutes dropped one by one into the back of the week, and neither car arrived.

All her jewellery was oxidized silver and semi-precious stones. She had never thought about it much before, but now it seemed wrong – both clumsy, and muted. She put it on, and took it off again – tried to look at herself without it – but her mind's eye was too crowded, overwhelming, blotting out her finished appearance. Half-past six: there was a sulky, fitful sun, but the wind was dropping: the sky was streaked with furious blue. She opened her window, and heard a car turning into the drive. She stayed long enough to see, and there were the Brewers waving at her, and a third person in the back of the car. Shutting the window, she ran – her blush subsiding with her down the staircase.

Going to the car, greeting them, explaining about her mother, carrying Alison Brewer's hand luggage into the house, she was conscious of his eyes upon her, although she did not meet them. Would they like a drink immediately, or would they like to see their rooms first, and wash? Alison, immaculate and brittle as a biscuit, said she was simply filthy, and could they go up first?

So she led them upstairs, the Brewers down one passage to the Strawberry Room (he came, too, because the Brewers had so much luggage), and then back down the passage and round the corner to the small room in which he had slept the last time he had stayed. It faced south, and the transparent red curtains were drawn as Dorcas had once been told to do when it was hot. She crossed the room to draw them apart, and heard him put down his case. She pulled one curtain – in a minute she would have to turn round – he did not speak, and her heart was too high in her throat to say anything. The second curtain was sticky – she tugged it, and it flew suddenly right off the end of its rod. She turned to him then, to laugh, to apologize – but he was standing perfectly still, watching her – very near her – and she could do neither. He suddenly, simply, held out his arms – she took one hesitant step, and he was kissing her.

'May I put my hand on your heart and say you love me?'

He said it so softly, that for a second there was a confusion of hearts: he knew this, and said: 'You know me. *I* haven't changed: at all,' and saw her uncertainty resolve again to delight.

A car door slammed faintly, and she started from him. He nodded, the small conspiratorial smile which she remembered came and went on his face, and they moved together to the half-open door.

'You go down first. Just a minute.' He took her head in his hands, and kissed her quickly. 'Sweeting.'

The evening was very gay. They drank, and had dinner, and then they played vingt-et-un. At dinner he sat next to Araminta, who asked him in a perfunctory manner about Ireland. He had bought a couple of horses, he said, and, gradually collecting his audience – he gave such an account of his buying them, that everybody was listening and watching him, and Antonia was able to watch him as well – to relate her memory of him to his actual presence. He was thinner – no, browner, and that made him seem thinner, but otherwise exactly the same – not precisely the man she had imagined all these weeks, but the man who had stayed here all those weeks ago. The two pictures of him became one . . .

The story took up a whole course of dinner.

'Oh, I'd give *anything* to imitate people!' cried Araminta, dabbing below her eyes with her table napkin. 'But anything! Wouldn't you, Bobby – or *can* you, secretly?'

Bobby began to say that he couldn't begin –

'It doesn't matter, darling – one can't have everything . . .'

Curran leaned across the table to Antonia, and asked after her horses.

'She took them to be shod yesterday, especially for you, Geoffrey. She's dying to take you riding, aren't you, darling?'

Curran said quickly: 'I'm dying to be taken. Where shall we go?'

She saw his eyes, encouraging, protecting her – and filled with a new assurance, she began: 'I thought you might like to see Bodiam –' but her mother interrupted gaily:

'You know perfectly well that you don't care a hoot for Bodiam, Toni, my sweet. It's any excuse for a long ride. Anyway, not tomorrow. Tomorrow, we're going to have a positive tournament – Bobby and I were planning it in the car.'

'Bodiam Castle,' began her father mildly to Curran, 'is of considerable interest for more than one reason . . .'

(Safe. It isn't as difficult as I thought, but I can't do it for very long.) But the rest of the evening was much easier. Everybody was in a good humour – particularly Araminta, who felt that her house party was being a success. When Noel Brewer suggested vingt-et-un, 'He simply adores gambling – any form of it,' Alison assured everybody – everybody fell in with the suggestion. While the others collected drinks, Antonia and Curran counted chips together, and she had her first conversation that everybody else could hear, but which nobody else could understand. She was so lit with love – so much seething and glittering with it, that all her movements, her sorting and counting of the coloured chips, were neatly deliberate, and her voice carefully self-contained: only every now and then, when his fingers touched, brushed hers, or he made her look at him by a persistent question, the memory of him in the little room blazed up in her – his holding out his arms – his putting his hand on her violent heart – and she burned with joy.

Noel Brewer won steadily. Curran was the first to go bankrupt – although Wilfrid retired early from the game leaving him his pile – Curran went through it with a careless abandon. He was such a good loser that everyone wanted him to take longer over losing: his reckless misfortune quickly became a focal point of the game.

'Shall I lend you some?' She had not thought before she said this, and felt the blood running into her face.

'You'll have to give it to me – I've small chance of returning it – quicksilver is all it is for me tonight.'

Antonia began counting some of her chips, but her mother cried:

'Oh, *Toni*! You're so careful! What's a chip between friends?' and pushed half her pile over to Geoffrey.

Antonia looked mortified: 'I wanted to give him exactly half.'

'It doesn't matter, darling. My wretched husband'll win it all. It's devastating! He's like some awful professional!' A remark which, from the way in which he denied it, seemed to please Noel Brewer.

'Give me one for luck,' said Curran, and Antonia put a white chip into his hand.

But he lost, and retired with unruffled good temper. The game, somehow, had no impetus after that, and so, with much frenzied calculation, Noel was paid. Everybody talked about bed for five or ten minutes, and the evening was over.

It was a clear, calm night – the sky flooded with stars. She thought that she would never sleep, but she had scarcely time to think it before she slept.

*

Saturday was fine. She spent the day in an ecstasy of frustration. The good weather meant tennis – nearly all day, and he played his fair share of the tournament. Antonia comforted herself with the possibility of their riding before dinner; but at luncheon, it became clear that Araminta had got him to ring up the Leggatts at Robertsbridge (she had determined to meet the fascinating Edmund Leggatt) and they immediately issued a general invitation to the whole party to drinks either before or after dinner.

'Oh – after – please Geoffrey darling – who knows when we shall finish the tennis?' and Curran returned to the telephone.

'They want us to change, and dance,' he announced, when he came back. Araminta gave a little yelp of delight.

'Goody goody! *What* nice accommodating friends you have, Geoffrey!'

That means ironing my long frock, and I hate it, it's much too young for me, thought Antonia miserably. She had refused to play tennis, and was suffering a general reaction from the evening before.

At tea-time she took the horrible blue organdie dress to the pantry to iron it. A small barred window looked on to the drive. She noticed suddenly that it was darker, looked up, and there he was, holding the bars with his hands, and smiling at her.

'Is that your pretty dress for tonight?'

'It isn't pretty – I hate it, but I haven't got another one.' Her face had lighted up when she saw him, and then quickly clouded again.

'What is it, darling Toni? Drop your iron and come and tell me.'

She hesitated, looked at him; then put down her iron. He seized her hand through the bars.

'Secrecy looks like neglect – is that it?'

'It's just that— Oh you are much *better* at this than I am! Or perhaps you don't—'

'Oh, but I *do*! I do all the time. I couldn't sleep last night for thinking of you.'

'I went to sleep at once!' she said, just discovering this.

He dropped her hand. 'You see? I have just as much reason as you to feel in the cold, but I won't. You have such a delectable candour – that's what it is. Give me your hand again: no, give me your little face – your eyes are too wide apart for the bars, but I can just manage to kiss you.'

The bars pressed, hard and cool, down the sides of her face. A bluebottle droned breathlessly about the room.

'It's hurting you, this prison,' he whispered, 'I'll have to get you out of it.'

She stroked his hair with her fingers.

'I'd like to take you away with me now. Carry you off! I will, too.' He gave a little triumphant laugh.

'Where?'

'To Bodiam Castle – tomorrow.' Then he saw her eyes, and said: 'Or further afield?'

'Anywhere,' she answered simply.

'Don't look at me like that when we dance tonight – I shan't be able to bear it,' he said, at last. 'Damn this contraption.' He shook the bars between them.

She laughed then with pleasure at the way he said that word. 'At other people? Am I to look like that to them?'

'You are *not*! You are entirely mine – you don't belong to *anybody* else. Is that crystal clear to you now?'

She shut her eyes for an instant, and repeated: 'I am entirely yours,' so low that he scarcely heard her. It seemed to her the most solemn moment of her life.

Then they called him, and he went. She heard him shouting cheerful, unimportant lies, and thought that she would never be able to match the courageous presence of his mind.

The rest of the day, which ended with the evening at the Leggatts, swirled round her, slipped past her – like a long dream. Afterwards, her recollections of it were a confusion – a haze of time and people, without the sense of time or proportion. It might have been a minute, or a whole life – but it seemed neither her minute, nor her life; as though she was enchanted from it.

She remembered, at some point, coming slowly down a beautiful staircase – the steps were of stone, and so shallow that she seemed hardly to descend, to a crowd of people: not until she saw him standing by a window, aware that she had been seeking her love, although when she reached the window, he had gone . . .

She remembered a wide grass path set between borders of sweet-smelling herbs – the scent of verbena crushed in her fingers – and beyond, the luminous glow of pale roses. Someone was with her then, but it was nearly dark, and she was almost alone . . .

Somebody played the piano, and dancing with him she did not know whether they talked or looked at one another at all . . .

A piece of lemon drifting in her wine cup – the rind beaded with silver, the fruit magnified by the glass which he had given her . . .

The thought occurring that she was invisible, that she made no sound: that her senses were lost to him: she was some ghost, some rich shadow of what she had been: that only he could see or touch her – without him she did not exist.

A clock striking one – an isolated marking of the time. 'Late,' she heard them cry: and later: 'Here's Toni's wrap – Where is Toni?' He took the wrap and put it round her. Her mother's voice: 'You look tired, my pet.' They could see her now that she was wearing the wrap, and she was suddenly very tired. White mist on the lawn – a clamour of headlights. He put her into the back of a car, and got in beside her.

'Home,' they said. She put her face against him and slept, her fingers clutching his sleeve . . .

8

'I CARRIED you out of the car and up to your bed. When I laid you down, you opened your eyes, sat up, and said: "Don't leave me: if you go, I shall vanish again." I promised I'd come back, and then your mother came in, and I went.'

'What did she think?'

'She just thought you'd drunk a little too much wine. *She* didn't mind.'

'I *hadn't*!'

'I know that, but it was wiser to agree with her, and – anyway – I wanted to see your room.'

'*Did* you come back?'

They were actually on their way to Bodiam: he rode for a moment without replying.

'I tried, once,' he said at last: 'but your mother was still flitting about the passages – so I had to retreat.'

'What on earth was she doing?'

He looked at her curiously, and then looked away. 'Seeing to you, I expect.'

She frowned. 'It sounds exactly as though I *was* drunk. Horrible! I *know* I wasn't.'

'You wouldn't look like you do this morning if you had been. How do you feel?'

She turned to him, checked herself, and said instead: 'Thank you for carrying me.'

'I adored carrying you. You must promise not to throw your weight about in any other direction.'

'I did promise that – yesterday.'

They were picking their way uphill – diagonally across a large field.

'Beware of rabbit holes,' she said. 'I came down badly once because of one. But it's better riding than the road.'

'Can we keep right off the road?'

'Not all the way. It depends on farmer to farmer. Most of

them don't mind now – they know I shut gates and ride round things. What is the time?'

'Just after half-past eleven.'

'Is that all? Have we really got the whole day? Was it easy to arrange?' She had been late for breakfast, and, when she had come down, had found her anxious plan miraculously ready-made.

'It wasn't difficult. Your father had fortunately interested me so much yesterday in the castle – that the whole thing went like clockwork. So here we are, for the whole day.'

'The whole *day*,' she repeated, and they smiled at one another.

It was fine, with the promise of heat, and they rode for some time without talking. At the top of the hill they could see more country – shimmering in the haze – like someone holding their breath, to keep absolutely still, she thought. They were skirting a small wood, and the flies came out of it in hordes. He warned her before slapping a horse-fly off her mare's quarters – but otherwise there began to be the faint tension of silence between them.

'A bit of road in a minute, I'm afraid,' she said, but he simply nodded – he did not answer.

When they were through the gate, and walking on the broad grass verge by the road, she began asking him about his riding school. He had found some possible stables, he said, off Knightsbridge – they were cheap, but in a bad state of repair – it would take time to put them right.

'You have decided on London?'

He heard the faint disappointment in her voice, and said:

'I'd no real choice in the matter. Will you mind that very much? I can charge people more for the hour, and perhaps keep one or two private horses at livery. It's handy in several ways.'

She remembered saying 'Anywhere' to him, and thought, no – of course, she could not mind.

'After all,' he said, sensing her acceptance: 'if I come to Bodiam, you will have to come to London.'

'How much does it cost people to ride in London?'

'Five shillings an hour – sometimes seven and six. A special rate for *you*, of course.'

'For me?'

'Oh yes,' he said gravely. 'Everybody has to pay to ride in London, you know.'

'But I thought I was going to *help* with the school!'

'Darling! So grave and gullible – you'll never know how much I love to tease you! Of course you are. But I shall have to speak to your parents first, before they're likely to trust their only daughter to my wild life.'

'Will you *really*? Will you . . .' She was overwhelmed – unable to speak at the prospect so suddenly before her – her whole life coming out like the sun – dazzling, immediate – it was far too much to bear . . .

'Dear, *dear* little Toni: don't mind everything so much. It's *easy*, most things are no trouble at *all*, unless you make them troublesome.' He seized her reins and stopped their horses. 'Of *course* I'll talk to them. You've been too much alone in your life – you take it all too seriously, and it's all a wonderful business.' He smoothed her hair back from her eyes. 'It should be more wonderful for you than anyone I've ever met, if you don't shy at every new prospect. Look, when do we get off this devil of a road?'

She pointed ahead. 'Just beyond that white house. Why?'

'So that we can get off these damned animals, and I can give you a serious talking to about not taking everything so seriously. This is too narrow for the pair of us. You lead – and away with you!' He hit her mare with his hand; she snorted, and broke into a resentful hand canter ahead of him.

'You can take two things seriously, if you've a mind to,' he called, a few minutes later.

She turned her head; she was laughing now.

'What?'

'Your own health – and money.'

But when they did get off the road, and had tied their horses to a bit of hedge, he did not talk seriously to her at all –

the tension had exploded, and there seemed no need. They must move, if they were ever to get to Bodiam, she said for the third time, slipped from him and was on her mare before he could stop her.

The rest of the journey they spent partly on an amiable argument about why he thought that health and money were the only things to take seriously – she did not agree with him, but did not know why not – and partly on the pleasure of their ride. It grew hotter: white convolvulus wilted in the hedges – the road when they encountered it was like blue steel, and patched with mirages – the animal smell of cow parsley, and the caramel scent of drying hay filled the warm air. She noticed these things from private habit, thinking about him with a kind of private experiment – she was not used to this minute impassioned consideration, any more than she was used to her own feelings swinging so far from the end of anxiety to such a certainty of peace. The thought that he would have to go away tomorrow occurred, but did not interrupt her pleasure. She said something about it to him: he said that he could stay any time he liked with the Leggatts, and the answer seemed perfectly good to her. Buttercups glistened in the sun – the wild roses paled from the heat . . .

They were nearing Bodiam: the hop fields stretched across the valley before them, and he told her about the River Liffey, and how its water made the best stout in the world. Could they drink some, she asked. It was a very hot day for stout, he said. Oh, *please*, she wanted to – she didn't mind about the heat. She was like a child, he thought – she would eat ice cream before breakfast in a snowstorm if she wanted it. She was wearing a lemon-coloured shirt with her sleeves rolled up— Oh, all right, but not until they reached Bodiam. She wouldn't like the stout, he added: she said she *would*, and he saw her resolving to like it.

The hops, an aromatic sea, were on either side of them: showing alternately the dense green embroidered poles, and a bare narrow vista with geometric precision; but alternating with a slight jerk, like lantern slides, as they passed. Had he ever had a hop pillow, she asked. No – he slept too well – he had never needed one. Had she? No – she had smelled one – delicious – but she slept well too – usually – and briefly she remembered, and he wondered, when she had not.

Then they were over the last rise, and the castle was before them: thrush coloured, and surrounded by very green turf. It was placed half way up the rise, commanding a view of the little river. It looked very simple, and apparently complete. Antonia stopped to look at it.

'At this distance people might be living there. It was the last fortified castle to be built in England.' Then she added: 'We can go up one of the towers.'

He stared painstakingly at it. He was not very interested in castles – but the mixture of love, information, and adventure with which she presented it to him, touched some secret spring – of compassion – tenderness – concern for her separate happiness, which he had never felt in his life before. The moment, with its responsibility and regret, passed – and he said:

'It doesn't look as though it was built there – but as though some giant set it down complete.'

'And then scooped his finger round it to make a moat. Yes! Are there castles like this in Ireland?'

'There are castles. I don't know. You see, I've never really looked at them.'

They started to pick their way down the hill.

'You don't tell me very much about Ireland,' she said.

'I'll tell you anything you want to know.'

'But I don't *know* what I want to know! I want to be told.'

'Do you want your glass of stout before we see the castle?'

'Yes please. We can eat our sandwiches inside. There is a grass courtyard. We'll have to tie the horses somewhere, though.'

She was easily deflected.

'How do we get across the moat? Or is it dry?'

'It's not *dry*!' she said, shocked. 'It has a lot of water, and water lilies. But they built a causeway on the north side – oh – years ago.'

At the pub he ordered her stout, and beer for himself. 'You *won't* like it, and then I shall have to drink it for you.'

'I shall! I know I shall!'

But she didn't, and in the end he poured it into a bed of phlox that grew by the door of the pub.

'I don't suppose they've ever drunk it before, either, but they'll love it,' he said. '*Now* what would you like, Miss Vaughan, crème-de-menthe?'

'Ginger beer,' she said meekly.

The village was very quiet. There had been one or two fishermen by the bridge, but no one came in or out of the gate which led to the castle.

'If we go soon, we shall have it to ourselves. A bus arrives some time in the early afternoon, and then there are always people. We can ride in the first gate, and leave the horses up by the man's little cottage.'

'What man?'

'The man who looks after the castle. He has a lot of rusty nails and things that they found in the moat. We have to pay him. Shall we go now?'

She wiped her mare's eyes clean with a wisp of grass, and it whinnied softly, thrusting its nose into her neck.

'We must find them some shade. There are a lot of oak trees round the castle.'

'They've got a pair of good tails. They'll help each other out.'

'I should think so! I wouldn't dream of having an animal docked!'

'Oh,' he said, half laughing. 'It's all very well to say that you yourself wouldn't dock an animal – but you can't deny your loving care to a poor beast just because somebody else has docked it – is that fair now?'

'I hadn't thought of that.'

'Domestic creatures never have any choice, you see – not like the wild ones.'

'You could divide people up like that, couldn't you? Wild, or domestic?'

'I don't know. I wasn't being serious. Could you?'

'But you *could*,' she persisted eagerly, and then stopped. 'I believe you are laughing at me.'

And he answered solemnly: 'I believe I am.'

They were waiting for some bicycles to pass before crossing the road.

'Health and money,' she muttered furiously, but she was not at all cross.

'*Your* health – *your* money. Don't make abstractions.'

'I'll *make* you care.' She was struggling to unlatch the gate that led into the castle grounds. 'I'll make you care about horses that aren't yours, and people, and –'

'I care about you – my darling love, and you aren't mine – entirely – yet.'

She said nothing, but he saw a faint tremor run down from the back of her head like wind on a field of grass. He shut the gate, and she gave him a quick nervous smile which melted to a look of such radiance that his heart turned over.

They rode, past the tiltyard and up the slope to the castle. As they drew nearer, it became a little more of a ruin. Tufts of grass and ragwort grew on the battlements, or simply out of cracks in the walls where the mortar had decayed: greasy black rooks flew heavily backwards and forwards from the tops of the towers to the tops of trees; their ceaseless cries sounding like the end of a fractious, inconclusive argument: but from the smooth round towers, the dark slit windows – no sign of life. The moat was still – like thick glass, perfectly reflecting the walls, except where there were great pads of water lilies in full flower. They rode slowly round to the north side where there was the cottage of the man who kept the rusty nails.

'There are yellow iris down by the river,' she said suddenly.

'How deep is the moat?' he asked, without thinking much – he was as absorbed in her, as she in her castle.

'Deeper than people, of course,' she said, after thinking about it. 'I don't know how deep. Are you hungry? Shall we go in and have lunch there?'

'Let's do that.'

They found a suitable place for the horses, bought their tickets, and walked across the causeway. When they reached the portcullis, she looked up at it to show him, and he put his hand on the back of her neck.

'When you shiver – you start there.'

'Geoffrey – I don't believe you are noticing the castle at *all*!'

'I am! I am!' he said – with no intention that she should believe him.

'It's my kind of building. I don't really like churches much.'

'Just castles. Or just this castle?'

'I haven't seen another castle as beautiful as this. I like houses too. I like places made for people to live in.'

Through the great gateway, there was a large courtyard, covered with short green turf, and, round its edges, foundations and bits of castle – the neat grass contriving to make these pieces of ruin very suave in their appearance.

She said that she was too hot, and could they eat first, and look properly at the castle afterwards? So they had lunch on the site of the Lady's Bower – leaning comfortably against the smooth masonry, with small birds hopping round them for crumbs. When they had eaten, he offered her a cigarette, but she smiled and shook her head. His pale blue smoke drifted, the hot moments spun out on the golden air – even the rooks' argument seemed desultory . . . She pressed the back of her head against the stone, and felt its warmth penetrating her hair. Life seemed endlessly beautiful – even the rooks, she thought, were hardly bothering now to make the worst of it. She looked up at the cream blue sky and opened her eyes to the sun: an immediate burning flurry clutched at her nose, and she sneezed. Emerging from the sneeze, she felt his hands holding the top of her shoulders – his presence blocking the sun and the sky: he kissed her – and at once she was carried out of her depths.

'When I kiss you, you cling to me as though you were drowning. Did you know that?'

She shook her head, and his face was in focus again.

He pulled her closer to him.

'Hay – clover hay – and new potatoes, and your hair a little sweeter.'

'What?' She was whispering – so urgent seemed their privacy.

'How you smell, my darling love. I adore it so. Promise me something, darling – will you do that now? Wait one moment before you do.'

But they were interrupted by a batch of sightseers, and he exclaimed violently under his breath: 'Damn!' They broke apart and looked at one another, his eyes subsiding to a humorous despair – her alarm to confusion.

The sightseers trickled heavily through the gate – glanced casually at them, and then looked again; their general curiosity which they had expected to be leashed to the castle – enlivened, diverted by the spectacle of two lovers. Somebody said something – they looked again – somebody else laughed. Antonia, her face burning, started to pack lunch.

'Let's go,' he said; 'I don't want to see the castle with them.'

She nodded gratefully, and thought: How exactly we know one another's mind.

And so they rode away almost in silence; only when they reached the last point on the road from which the castle could be seen, she stopped, looked back and said:

'The people don't really matter at *all*. They don't make the slightest difference to it.' Then she thought for a moment: 'Of course, *we* don't, either: but you would have liked the castle without them,' and made a little gesture of dismissal with her hand.

'I'm very glad to have seen it.'

She looked at him sharply, not believing this, and he said: 'With you. It's you – not the castle – you know that,' and she was so sure that he loved her that she simply thought: Well, at least he's *honest* about the castle.

Much later, past the windmill at Staplecross, she broke the long silence by saying: 'There is a different way home,' and they turned to the right off the road on to a track. Here were a few straggling cottages in front of which were tiny gardens, crowded with honeysuckle, roses, beehives and hens, fuchsia and sweet briar hedges, and a smell of moss, and phlox and warm cabbage leaves and cinder paths. The track ended with a jerky gate: a small empty field and then woods stretched before them. She remembered the next bit of the ride for the rest of her life.

They rode slowly across the small field to the entrance of the woods – a bridle path roundly vaulted by trees. It was dark after the baking field with a chequered streaking light – the sensation of the hazy golden air had resolved to a frantic exchange of sun and shade. There was the slippery uncertain movement of the sun between the branches – slanting, shifting across her mare's neck on to the ground, against the larger rhythm of their progress: and her mind possessed by the starting darting uncertainties of loving him (what was she to promise?) against the vast certainty of love itself. For she felt now that each movement, each moment, was propelling them towards some mysterious ecstasy of accomplishment, and she was poised within herself for it; her senses confined to each step along their dark streaking path, and therefore sharply aware of each step. Sometimes the path lightened to a patch of clear yellow sunlight – then she looked up, and there was a patch of sky like a deep blue pool above them. Height, depths, distance – the yellow patch balanced the blue: she wondered whether love matched so easily, and it occurred to her with a discovering thrill made up of arrogance and humility, that if he loved her as she loved him, there could be no end to the beautiful distance of their lives. She turned to look at him, and at once his eyes met hers – urging her on without a word.

'There is a little meadow a bit further on.'

He put out his hand as though he was going to touch her, and changed his mind.

It was hardly a meadow, simply a narrow slip of open land, dotted with ancient molehills, and covered with very short fine turf. The sun lay over it like a fine golden film, and leaning against the edge of the wood were bramble bushes winking with black and red fruit.

'Beware of rabbit holes,' she said, and remembered the hours ago when she had last said that.

'This is the place,' he said.

'For me to make my promise?'

'Your promise?'

'You asked me to promise you something – just before the people came.'

They had stopped.

'Yes, yes, so I did.' He dismounted, and stood beside her. 'Jump now – with all your might. I want all your weight hurled down on to me.'

But she sprang lightly down into his arms, and laughed. 'I promised *that* this morning.'

'What?'

'You don't remember *anything*! Not to throw my weight about in any other direction.'

'You promised that yesterday.' And, reassured by his memory, she leaned forward to kiss him, but he said: 'Let's tie these animals out of the way first. Give me your beast.'

She sat quietly, hugging her knees, while he tied the horses to the edge of the wood behind her, thinking slowly: I am so happy. Whatever happens, I shall never, never be happier than now. But even such a thought seemed only to salt her content to an extremity of happiness, and she flung herself down, wanting suddenly to feel the turf like short green fur against her face – imagining the whole world – and touching this particular piece of earth's surface to exchange and share her life with it.

When he returned to her, and saw her face pressed against the ground, he thought that perhaps she was crying, and remembering that he had got very near her when she had last done that, he flung himself down beside her, prepared to be sensually comforting.

'What is it, darling love?'

And she answered solemnly: 'I am so beautifully happy.'

He took her into his arms, and then sighed, so that she, in her turn, asked: 'What is it?'

'I am so beautifully *un*happy. There's the difference.'

'Why, darling – *why* are you?'

He pulled her lemon shirt away from her neck to kiss it.

'I don't want to tell you now.' His hand slid round to the back of her neck. 'I *must* kiss you. You *must* kiss me. Now.'

His breath was like smoke on her face – his eyes near, nearer still – grey, with black pools – then all black . . . She kissed him passionately because he had said that he was unhappy; then because she loved him and he was kissing her, and then there ceased to be any reason. Her head lay hard against the palm of his hand; his other hand stroking her skin with quick, nervous, possessive movements, until it enclosed her breast – she gave a little fainting cry of astonished ecstasy as her heart leapt under his hand, and her mouth had suddenly a furious sweetness. At the height, on the brink of this torrent, he stopped, and said roughly:

'Now you see why I'm "beautifully" unhappy. I want you – I want you entirely – want, want, *want*! You're beginning to understand what that means, now, aren't you? Wait a few minutes more.'

There was no chance to reply; she heard her shirt tearing a little, but the sound seemed to come from a distance: it was as though they were galloping – their bodies racing one another; the only near things were his mouth and his requiring hands.

When, at last, he released her, she was aware of nothing but the loss of him – that the race was not over, but stopped, and a sense of intolerable anguish that was almost anger assailed her at his abandonment. Bruised and breathless, she saw him staring down at her – searchingly – and then with a little, hard, triumphant smile at what he saw: her eyes dark, and filled with tears of desire; her mouth printed the shape that he had left it. She felt his fingers tighten on her bare shoulder as he bent over her and whispered:

'You understand now, don't you? You want *me* now, don't you?'

And she repeated, 'I want you,' like the echo of his whisper.

His expression changed – and still whispering, she said:

'Will you speak to them tonight?'

'Who?'

'My parents.' Her eyes shone with a suppressed and delicious excitement. 'As soon as we get home?'

He frowned, in a genuine effort to understand what she meant, and seeing her face cloud, he felt suddenly tender towards her: 'Oh darling, don't start to be sad! The least little thing upsets you — ' but she interrupted:

'I don't call our marriage "the least little thing"!'

'Our – *what*?'

'You said this morning that you would have to speak to my parents first.'

'Oh! Yes, so I did, but that was about the riding school. I didn't say anything about marriage!'

Some instinct made her prop herself up. 'But I thought you meant – don't you *want* us to be married?'

He turned sharply towards her, and then looked away.

'It wouldn't be any good if I did. I am married already.'

The silence was as though he had suddenly flung something down a deep well, and they were both intently waiting to hear it touch the bottom, as, after the time which was a little too long, they both stirred at exactly the same moment.

'You – are married – to someone else.'

She put her hand over her forehead, as though she was brushing something away.

'Yes.'

'In Ireland.' She thought of his saying he must go home, and the island that she had made.

'Yes,' he said again, and looked at her. She had gone very white, but she seemed perfectly calm. There was another silence while she stared at his hands, and watched him nervously picking the skin from the sides of his fingers.

'I don't love her, you see,' he said at last. 'We were married when I was too young to know my mind, but of course she's Catholic, and wouldn't hear of a divorce. I'm very unhappy with her.'

'But you go back to see her sometimes?'

'To see her – and the children.'

'Are there a lot of children?'

'Two – and the baby.'

'The baby,' she repeated, and then asked: 'What is *her* name?'

'Ellen. But, Toni, it's you that I love! You must believe that. You must know that I love you.'

She put her hand up to her forehead again, and then said almost confidingly: 'You must think I'm an awful fool, but I still don't understand why you didn't tell me this.'

He thought for a moment. 'I would have, of course, in the end. I didn't immediately, *because* I love you, can't you see that?'

She shook her head, and said simply: 'No.' She was still staring at his hands.

'I had no idea – I didn't know that there was such a – such a misunderstanding about everything.'

She tried to look at him then, but felt suddenly so sick that she did not dare move at all – even her head. She shut her eyes, dug her fingers into the ground, and the sickness lurched heavily away.

At the end of its going, she heard him say: 'I'm sorry if it was such a shock to you.'

Misunderstanding – shock – the words thudded distantly at the bottom of the well. She opened her eyes, and it was then that she discovered her shirt, hopelessly torn off one shoulder. She picked at the frayed cotton ends, to pull the pieces over her breast, and heard herself say: 'It must have been a very old one.' The pieces would not stay unless she held them there. 'How do I get home with a shirt torn like this?' She repeated the thought aloud, because it seemed so worrying.

'I may have a pin,' he said surprisingly. He had. 'It isn't a safety pin, so mind you don't get hurt.'

She took the pin clumsily, and stared at it.

'Better let me,' he said uncertainly.

She was so passive, so still, while he pinned the shirt that he thought that perhaps after all – all was not lost – although it seemed odd that she wasn't crying. He was just going to put his arm round her, when she said:

'Why – why don't you live with her? If you have all those children – and a baby?'

'She bores me. I'm bored to death there after a week.' There was a pause, and then he added desperately: 'And if it's the baby you're worrying about, I may as well tell you that she just likes having children. *She's* got the wherewithal to look after them, and it keeps her quiet. She won't be coming to London, you know.'

'I wasn't worrying about the baby.' She said it politely, almost as though she was afraid of having embarrassed him. She looked down at her shirt – it covered her breast, but the top of her shoulder was still bare.

'I'm sorry, darling. I'm afraid I've done it all very badly.'

She shrugged her shoulders experimentally.

'It's all right. It will last until I get home, but—' He thought that she meant to misunderstand him, and was immediately angry.

'Am I to understand that you don't want me to speak to your parents about the riding school?'

He saw her face contract for a second, and she put her hand up to her forehead again, almost as though she thought he was going to hit her. Then she said:

'Please don't speak to them. I'm sorry I misunderstood you. I would like to go back now.'

'Sorry,' he muttered, as they went to their horses. He felt drearily ashamed. Obviously, he had hurt her – he'd made an awful mess of everything. He had no idea that she was so over-sensitive. Her innocence! he thought with a kind of horror – really one ought to be warned about people like that. No good thinking about it – he'd concentrate on trying to be nice to her. He went to help her on to her horse, but she had climbed up before he got there.

'Toni – I am sorry. That was a beastly thing to say. Will you forgive me now?'

But she answered in an unnaturally high clear voice:

'Oh no! It wasn't beastly at all! Come on.'

Sh rode ahead of him, and she rode hard. The horses were soon in a muck sweat, but still the way back seemed long. Whenever the tension of silence seemed to him to have become intolerable, she made some commonplace remark for which he was disproportionately grateful. For what seemed hours they rode through the rest of the woods, across a road, and then endless fields – she opened gates and waited for him to shut them. He said once that they would have to cool the horses off when they got back, and she said that she would do it; 'You can play tennis.'

They were trotting along a stretch of road, and he had ridden level with her: he looked at her as she said this, hoping to detect something in her face that he could understand – some trace of emotion – pique, anger, spite – he felt that almost anything would do, but nothing seemed to be there, and she added in the same closed voice: 'Not if you don't want to, of course.'

When, eventually, they reached the drive, she slowed down and said:

'I'll drop you at the garden gate, and take them round the back.'

'Toni, are you very angry with me?'

She shook her head, and rode a little faster.

'Well, let me come and cool off my animal with you. Don't let's have an uncomfortable situation, darling – there wouldn't be any sense in that, would there?'

'Toni! I *am* sorry – cross my heart. I'd no idea –' He wanted to say that he'd no idea about her, but somehow he couldn't quite say that. She took the reins without a word – in spite of the heat she was still very pale. He watched her ride away very straight on her horse: he had no idea that the moment her back was turned, the tears streamed out of her eyes until she was entirely blinded.

Afterwards, she could never clearly remember the rest of the day. Walking the horses round and round the big meadow by the side of the copse until long after they were cooled – faint with pain – the same phrases recurring in her mind with the corners of the meadow – saying to him: 'I am entirely yours'; his saying, 'I must go home first'; and her imagination of the 'Emerald Isle': 'I must speak to your parents first before they trust you to my wild life'; 'Two – and the baby'; 'I want you'; 'Misunderstanding – shock – ' when she had said that she was entirely his! He asked me to say that. Misunderstanding! The sickness lurched back at the word, so that she had to stop to endure it – clinging to the pommel of her saddle. The island was full of other children, and a baby that he had had with Ellen. She said that name aloud, and thought how familiar a sound it must always have been to him: and still her own island hovered resolutely before her – and her mother's streaming protective contempt when she had said: 'My dear, you don't know the first *thing* about love!' the morning that his letter had arrived. She didn't know anything, because he had not told her that he was married. He said he loved me. Had everyone else known? Enid? Her mother? Had the – misunderstanding – been entirely her own? Sickness again invaded the pain. Her father's indictment of her mind made an ugly rush at her; only stupid people had misunderstandings (she was desperately trying to adapt herself to the squalor of that word, because it was the word that he had used). Then her mother fidgeting about her bedroom saying that one mustn't throw oneself at somebody's head at everybody else's expense. This now made agonizing shame, as she thought how desperately she had wanted him to think that she was pretty, to love her, to go out riding with her, to make plans to be alone with her, to write to her (which he had never done), to make plans for the future – she dropped her head into her hands – scalding, blistering shame – she did not know how to bear it.

The sunlight on the oak trees was very thin, very yellow, and the horses' sweat had dried, roughly matting their coats. Time to move – to do the next thing – but she did not know how to begin. The field had been a kind of suspension: the house would be full of people who had spent the day differently – and he would be there. Her tears occurred, dispersed, recurred, and she seemed to have no control over them – she was terrified by their treacherous command.

In her room, she unpinned the lemon shirt and took it off.

It took her a long time to dress; she kept crossing the room and forgetting what she was looking for; dropping things and looking at them for a long time before she picked them up. She wasn't aware of thinking about anything at all, until she saw a bumble bee trapped in the sashes of her window, and went instinctively to let it out. Here, again, she was clumsy – the bee escaped, but she pinched her finger; and then, with no very clear idea or reason, put the injured hand on the ledge of the sill and with her free hand dropped the sash on to it. That hurt very much, and it took her an agonizing second to lift the sash again. The skin was broken; she watched the separate dots of blood appear, until they got larger and ran into one another. Her hand throbbed with an irregular kick – she had bruised it badly – possibly cracked or broken a bone. She clutched her left wrist tightly with her right hand to stay the pain, and felt the tears pricking again in her eyes. But she was one up on her tears now. She had provided their reason – for the evening if necessary – and the moment that she thought this – they unreasonably stopped.

Going downstairs; entering the drawing-room – the sun blazing on her face as she opened the door so that at first she could see nobody; collecting a drink; her mother exclaiming about her hand which she had clumsily bandaged – and everybody looking at her hand: his eyes on her – looking up, meeting his faint conspiratorial smile (exactly as though nothing had changed!) and knowing suddenly that he didn't believe that she had hurt it, that it was another ruse like his sprained ankle: wanting him so desperately to believe her that she stared stiffly beyond his head, until she heard herself saying that she had only bruised it, and she didn't care any more.

At dinner – after the soup – picking up her fork her hand snarling, shooting with pain, so suddenly that she dropped the fork with a clatter on to the table and everybody looked up. Somebody boned her fish for her then, and her father was asking him about Bodiam. She heard him talking easily, volubly, but she didn't listen. Eating seemed difficult, and half way through she managed to think: It's fish. I don't really like fish, and stopped trying to eat it. She smiled a great deal; if anyone spoke to her, or when anyone said anything. Occasionally, he said something to her, and then she found that she couldn't smile; she felt that he was watching her, and she said something without really looking at him.

Dinner over: getting stiffly out of her chair, thinking then for the first time in her life: I am so tired: I'm very, very tired; and following the women into the drawing-room – the curtains were drawn now, and there was no sun. Holding her wrist again while they poured coffee – Alison Brewer saying: 'Have you put anything *on* that hand?' and her mother mentioning Friar's Balsam and Pomade Divine in the bath-room cupboard. She could escape on that. No, she hadn't really put anything on it, if nobody minded she would do so, and go to bed. Nobody minded the teeniest, weeniest bit.

In the bath-room cupboard she found some of her mother's sleeping pills. She took one out of the bottle, but somehow, when she got back to her room she couldn't find it. She put the lemon-coloured shirt into the waste paper basket. The sleeping pill didn't seem to matter – she ached just to be lying absolutely still in the dark: if she kept still enough she wouldn't disturb her mind . . .

In the same dark she woke violently: crying with terror at some unendurable anguish, some dreadful secret violence that had disappeared with her waking, had slipped below the surface of a dream – leaving only a panic of confusion and pain. As the pain in her hand touched her senses, she wept more quietly –

more and more, and quietly, until, in a tremulous, irregular silence, she slept.

9

SHE had never been unhappy before, and there was nobody to whom she could talk; and so, lacking the equipment of experience or sympathy, she travelled painfully through the weeks, with the kind of stolid courage often seen in unhappy children, and with a pride which was her own. Her pride was like some kind of brace; it was always uncomfortable, and sometimes agonizing, but it held her upright: it staunched the curious internal drip from her heart; it concealed her weakness, and supported her against the sudden recurring shocks of misery that slammed at her without warning round the corner of a calm and dull day. Particularly it enabled her to conceal everything from her mother.

'You never said goodbye to Geoffrey,' she had said the next morning, and Antonia had immediately replied:

'Oh dear, how awful of me! Well, I don't expect he minded too dreadfully. I think I'd better go and see Dr Atkins about this hand – it's swollen up like anything.'

Interminable weeks later, her mother returned from one of her London trips unusually good-tempered and gay, and after dinner said:

'Oh! I met Geoffrey – *riding in Knightsbridge* – just as I was coming out of the hairdresser's – too romantic!'

'Is he – have you asked him down?'

'I *did*, but he can't, poor lamb. He's up to his eyes in his school. I'm lunching with him next week. He sent his love to you.'

It took her some time to throw his love (casual, meaningless, untrue – exactly, she thought, what Miss Austen meant about people sending their love) over her shoulder. 'Give my love to Toni,' he must have said, and she could imagine the expression on his face when he said it: or, perhaps – 'Give my love to everybody.' That would be better – but that involved her father and she realized with a pang of dismay that there was nobody who would ever send even casual love to her father.

Her mother seemed to go away more frequently, or for longer – either two separate nights a week, or two or three days on end, and Antonia spent most of those evenings alone with her father. They took to doing the daily crossword puzzle together: he was much better at them than she, but politely preserved the myth each time that she might possess the necessary knowledge or ingenuity to manage what he could not. She was grateful to him for this, and longed to please and dazzle him with achievement, but on the rare occasions when she got something right, he merely wrote in the word in his painstaking script and turned to the next clue – he did not seem particularly surprised or pleased.

Frost – mushrooms – the swallows gone – berries violently cheerful in the hedges – the trees stripping gracefully, the patient evergreens becoming smug – coming into their own like an Æsop's fable – outdated butterflies and roses frozen crisp – the smoke and romance of autumn turning into the brisk settlement of winter. The horses had to come in for the nights – she did not ride them.

One day her father asked her whether she was going to Hastings – which meant that he wished she would. He wanted some books, and she went on the afternoon bus, glad of an errand.

It was a raw slate-coloured day, and she walked straight on to the sea front. Hastings was empty. A few old gentlemen, immutably wrapped and muffled, were being pushed in Bath chairs by gaunt women wearing sensible shoes and ugly gloves; one or two ill-chosen persons were being forced to chase the magically absurd movement of their blown-off hats; the people who are always leaning over railings and staring at the sea were there; a child was being bludgeoned into bowling its hoop. But the whooping, yelping peach-coloured crowds were gone: the shingle over which they had sprawled for their tightly packed picnics – bald head and bathing cap almost touching sandalled, sandy feet – was dry and bright: even the orange peel, the chocolate papers, the paper bags, the newspapers, were gone; and overhead, aimless, ravenous gulls played with details of the wind.

She walked towards the cliffs and the fishermen's harbour; the damp salty air stiffened with tarred hemp and fish. The boats were in, lolling and beached; the cork brown nets hung from poles between the tall black pitched huts. The seagulls were more strident here. She stood to watch the sea, running grey and heavy – plunging dispassionately against the harbour wall, breaking from grey to a shower of white drops and oily bubbles – and swooning out again under the next sleek diagonal wall of water. Watching the sea, she could think about anything – it provided that mysterious repetition of movement which made rhythm. She seemed then to herself to have been walking for weeks down a long narrow passage, with all the doors on either side shut, and her thoughts were like the carpet: she trod on them, but their pattern repeated itself, so that again and again, like the waves of water breaking on the harbour wall, the same memory recurred to be shattered – to swoon away under her feet. The passage seemed endless, and in spite of her movement in it, she seemed imprisoned. It's just the passage of time, she thought sadly, and began a cautious wondering about the doors. People? Opportunities? People to whom she could not talk, things she did not want to do? Shut, or actually locked? I can't talk to my mother, and I can't bear to ride. What a shattering situation! she jeered, and watched the tight-lipped jeering horizon below the chalky sky. I ought, she thought solemnly, to think more about other people, and less about myself – and remembered writing this sentiment in her diary when she had been fourteen, and it had been very new. Then, the mere writing of things had disposed of them – a welter of priggish little dictates, written out and forgotten until now – rose in her mind, and settled uneasily again like hot ash: she had not known what she was writing about. People, then – but she was tired of the passage analogy – her father – the people who came for weekends – but her father was very much alone, and now she knew that the only time she had tried to talk to him had been when she had wanted him to talk about her. I must get his books, she thought, that's what he wants, and it's what I came for, after all.

Walking away from it, she wondered if that was why there were always people leaning on railings and watching the sea.

That evening, she asked her father whether there was anything that she could do to help with his book. On the whole he thought not, he said, after thinking scrupulously of the whole. Was there not *anything*? Some donkey work that didn't involve intelligence but that had to be done?

She was sitting with her feet tucked up under her in the large chair in his study (they did not use the drawing-room when they were alone) and her face tilted towards him. Something of her eager humility reached him – he had the scholar's profound respect for humility – and he smiled suddenly at the pleasure of understanding it.

'There is, of course, the Index.'

She was attentively silent.

'A tedious business – it will contain many cross-references – and when it is done it would have to be carefully checked before the amended version is begun upon.'

She said: 'Yes,' and waited, until he added sternly:

'There must be nothing slipshod about the Index to this book, or what little use it might ever become would be dissipated.'

'Do you think you could teach me to do it?'

'There is nothing *difficult* about it. It is entirely a question of patience and concentration.' He looked doubtfully at her.

'I promise you that I will concentrate,' she said.

So he taught her, and for hours a day she laboured at a task which was by no means entirely dependent upon patience and concentration for its success. Her father, she discovered, had such an intimate, detailed grasp of his subject, that he assumed a knowledge of it in her which she was far from possessing. Her mother laughed at her – carelessly, and then with a hint of something nearer jealousy or alarm (surely Toni wasn't turning into a dreary *bookworm*?), but it did not interfere with *her* life, and Toni seemed now to fit in with people at weekends much more easily than before, so apart from inciting a little general mirth at dinner on Saturday nights about Toni's occupation, she left it at that.

Then, one day, she said:

'Really, I must do something about my figure this winter. The summer's all right, with all the tennis, but in winter one simply eats like a *hog* – I'm getting fatter every single minute, and it just won't do.'

Antonia looked at her. She had put on a little, a very little weight, but it suited her – she looked much better and more contented, Antonia thought. Aloud, she said:

'You were a little too thin before. Now, you're just right.'

Her mother laughed nervously.

'It's sweet of you, darling: I don't want actually to *lose* weight – only to stay exactly as I am. I thought I'd take up riding again.'

Antonia was really startled. 'I thought you *hated* it!'

'Not if I've somebody amusing to ride with.'

There was a pause, as awkward as it was brief, while they both wondered separately why on earth she had used the word 'amusing'; then her mother said:

'I thought we might ride in the afternoons. Then I can do my little domestic chores in the morning while you're being madly intellectual with Wilfrid. How's that?'

'I have to work in the afternoons as well, or I won't get it done in time.'

'But, darling, you must have *some* fresh air!'

'I do. I go for walks, apart from gardening.' She said this very sulkily, because she could see what was coming, and was frightened by it.

'But don't you *ride* any more? I thought your whole life revolved round horses!'

'Well, it doesn't. In fact I'm bored with riding. I shan't do it any more.'

'Really, Toni, your whole life seems to consist of giving things up! First tennis, and now riding!'

Antonia said nothing. Araminta lit a cigarette angrily, inhaled, and said: 'It isn't good for you, you know. At your age, you ought to be *adding* to your interests, not simply giving everything up all over the place. You've got frightfully washed-out looking again, all pale and bony, and honestly, darling, it doesn't suit you.'

But Antonia cried:

'If riding is going to make you thinner, I don't see how it can make me fatter, and anyway, I've told you, I don't want to!'

Araminta looked at her daughter. She was trembling – well, shaking, actually – and a little pulse was beating in her face (just like Wilfrid, on the few, now happily distant, occasions when he went round the bend about something), and all about *riding*! But something quite different started to run into this – a fleeting, uneasy, intuition . . . She put her hand uncomfortably on Antonia's arm.

'Darling – I'm sorry to have been a bore about it. You do *exactly* what you *like*. Just tell me some good rides, and I'll see whether I can rake Wilfrid out. He never walks a step, and he certainly doesn't do a thing about the garden.' She smiled, to put paid to the whole tiresome business, and escaped. She did not at all want to pursue her intuition . . .

When she had gone, Antonia, still trembling, reached out for her mother's packet of cigarettes, lit one, and inhaled as she had seen her mother do. A comforting dizziness blacked out the trembling, and at the end of it she felt better – indeed, she felt nothing at all.

Winter was no longer a brisk business, of frost and clear crisp light; of sudden sounds and sharp branches. Now, sometimes, the days began with a cold milky quiet, and the sun, enormous and unwinking, hung in the sky like a tinned fruit, giving everything a dirty varnished appearance: the birds looked dusty – the sky was oil. Now, sometimes, the sea mists rolled in, white in the distances, but with you, their sensation changed to a raw freezing dampness, and distance was concealed: trees, bushes, hair, were encrusted with tiny iced beads – newspapers were limp and silent to read, and the roads were slippery. Then, sometimes, it rained all day – noisily, quietly, sadly, angrily – in chuckling life-size drops that slammed and bounced, or with a thin driving spite that dissolved into an icy slush – and the sky was tumbled and smothering – like old bedclothes.

Araminta said she *loathed* November, and went to London more than ever.

December: snow, and berries, and silence: the birds dark and lumpy with the cold; the sky loaded, stiff, weighty, with yet more snow, which slipping, drifting down, fell to cover each ledge and crack of the country, making neatness of disorder, and disorder of what had been neat. At night, it froze, and snowed again – the trees shook it like fruit from their overladen branches; all tracks, stolid and pattering, were smoothly covered, but the flower beds became untidy heaps of sugar, and the poor rabbits had no life at all. Icicles, and little streams of warm air breathed out; sharp violet shadows like the lids of dazzling eyes – water glazed, corseted, frowning with ice: sparks from logs on the fire, from brushed-out hair, and in the sky at night from the smallest whimpering stars. In the mornings, the sun staggered out, suffused and ineffective, like a drunk in *Punch*.

Then, one Friday afternoon, Antonia, going to Hastings, met Dorcas on the cook's bicycle in the drive. She was clearly unmoved by the weather, for she was wearing a shirt with rolled-up sleeves. It was only after their greeting – Dorcas seemed more than usually embarrassed, blushing and swerving on her bicycle before riding ahead – that Antonia recognized the lemon shirt she had thrown into the waste paper basket so many weeks ago. It had been carefully mended. I don't suppose she has many clothes, she thought. It cost her no more than a pang of recognition. I'm better, she thought; I hardly care at all, if I'm careful. But, somehow, she lingered at Hastings – she did not want to go home, so that when she did get back on a later bus, her mother's weekend party had already arrived. All she knew about the guests was that she did not know them: a couple, she believed, and an unknown young man. She was late changing because she had to wait for her bath, and, from the noise in the drawing-room, she guessed that she was the last down. She walked into the room, prepared to be apologetic, docile and helpful with the cocktails, prepared to be observant and more interested in other people than herself . . . utterly unprepared to meet Geoffrey Curran.

He had his back to her, but her mother had not.

'Here's my huge daughter, at *last*! Toni, this is Muriel and David Morrow – and – Bobby Dermot couldn't come – he's got a hideous cold, poor lamb – so I persuaded Geoffrey instead – whom you *do* know.'

It was just the shock, she told herself, drinking the sherry which he had handed her, just the having no warning – being ambushed when she least expected it. She had not dared to light a cigarette because of her hands, but now David Morrow offered her one, and she took it. It was over, she kept repeating – he had said something, and she had replied – but the ice round her heart was broken. He had seemed uneasy – for once uncertain of himself – he had not met her eye – and she had seemed – what? Collected? Calm? At the moment, the presence of her mind was more than she could bear.

At dinner, they talked about horses (excepting, of course, her father) and she said very little. The four of them, the Morrows, her mother, and he, seemed very used to one another's company: their efforts to include her father or her were perfunctory; explaining something at which they had all laughed so that it was not in the least funny or even comprehensible; referring to a host of unknown people and places: whoever was speaking said 'we'. He did not ignore her – but his manner, though apparently easy, was odd – both bluff and patronizing. He's treating me like a child! she realized. Not even like someone who he thought was seventeen, but really like a child! Perhaps, she thought, her mother had forced him to come down, and he was miserably embarrassed, and having thought this, it was easy to detect embarrassment in him.

Araminta was on the extreme edge of gaiety, her attention fully taken up with the two men. To Antonia, however, she was alternately maternal and conciliatory – 'the child smokes like a *chimney*, it isn't good for her'; and: 'Toni knows every inch of the riding country round here, don't you, darling?'

The thought that it was odd how well her mother seemed to know him, considering that she had said nothing since announcing their meeting at Knightsbridge, crossed the confusion of her mind, but she reflected that her mother hadn't mentioned the Morrows at *all*, and she seemed to know them equally well. Weekend people were always like that: but not knowing what it was that she was trying to reassure herself about, she did not feel reassured. She turned her attention rather desperately to Muriel Morrow who sat opposite her. Hair of an indeterminate red – an expanse of face too large for unhappily delicate features: minutely thin pale eyebrows, small blue eyes, a child's nose, and a tiny mouth; so that her expression was constantly like somebody trying to have a large party in a room with inadequate furniture – her gaiety uncomfortable, her enjoyment anxious – her refuge the constant assertion of what fun she was having. She had an attractive clear little voice, like a bell, and pretty, helpless hands. Antonia, having got so far, tried to consider Muriel in relation to the others, but her own feelings were so negatively jammed, that they did not seem to move in any direction at all.

After dinner, the women sat in the drawing-room, and conversation dropped like the wind. Araminta powdered her face for a long time with critical care, because she had nothing much to say to the other two. Muriel, who had dabbed furtively at her nose and made no impression on it, started all over again, coating her face with broad despairing sweeps. Antonia sat still, smoking. There was a long silence, except for the fire, and the ceaseless tinkle of Araminta's charm bracelet. Antonia thought: Soon they will come in, and I'm frightened; I don't know why, but I *am* frightened.

Eventually, Muriel put her powder away with a small sigh, leaned forward to Araminta and said:

'*Do* let me see it!'

'What?' Araminta shook her arm. 'Oh that. It *is* fun, isn't it?' She unclasped the bracelet, and threw it, so that it fell noisily into Muriel's lap.

Muriel, desperately anxious to please, said: 'It's absolutely *marvellous*! You've got so many things! Has it taken ages to collect them?' But Araminta merely said:

'I've been given nearly everything.'

But Muriel, clinging to the conversation, began dropping the bracelet from the palm of one hand to the other, saying: 'It's frightfully heavy: I shouldn't think you've room for any more things,' and like a child she began counting the charms aloud, and exclaiming over them. 'I *adore* the monkey with ruby eyes. That's sweet – *that's* rather sinister – oh dear, I wish I had one of those! Oh look at the little fiddle!' Then after more counting: 'Do you know, you've got *seventeen*? What's that, an old seal, or something?'

'Wilfrid gave me that years ago. Put another log on, Toni. It doesn't go with the others, but I can't hurt his feelings.'

And Muriel said admiringly: 'Of *course*, you can't. It's rather a funny colour, isn't it? Don't *you* think so, Toni?'

And Antonia, wrapped in her insensate fear, agreed without thinking that it was, and then loyalty to her father made her add: 'It's probably a pretty design. You could try it with sealing wax.'

One of the others said, yes, you could, without much interest, and then, as they heard sounds of the men joining them, and Antonia was steeling herself to being in the same room with him again – to his moving about the room – talking – talking sometimes to her, with everything dead and gone between them – Muriel suddenly cried:

'I *knew* there was something missing! Where's the little silver riding crop that Geoffrey gave you?'

They were opening the drawing-room door: Araminta simply said:

'I haven't put it on, yet,' but Antonia looked at her, and then could not look away – her senses suddenly sharpened to a pitch of feverish discovery – her mother was furiously angry! She almost snatched the bracelet from Muriel, who, her attention diverted by the men's return, had not noticed – had possibly not even heard Araminta's reply, for she babbled on:

'Oh, *Geoffrey*! Minty hasn't even bothered to put your dear little riding crop on to her bracelet! There's ingratitude for you!'

There was only a fractional pause, but tension infected the room. Then Curran said easily:

'Do you mean the one you asked me to buy for you? The little *silver* crop?' and Araminta replied:

'Yes. I'm not sure if I like it yet, but you must remind me to pay you back.'

They did not look at one another, and it was then, that, as certainly as she knew that they were lying – Antonia knew that he was in love with her mother.

Afterwards, it seemed as strange to her that she had not known this before, as it seemed strange that she should know at that moment. At the time, however, recoiling violently from this, terribly certain, intuition – she told herself that she had no proof of it – that she did not really know. But that was no good: all the evening she had been drifting with her fears – now, without warning, she was suddenly hit, cast, thrown up by a vast wave of emotion, on to some bleak shore of a reality – and for a while she lay where she had been thrown, winded, gasping for reason. No time for reason – the next wave assaulted her, she was dragged out by another murderous sea clutching the straw of his having loved her (but love, for him, meant only want – he must now want her mother) – and then she was beached again with the certainty that her mother was his mistress.

Her father had disappeared: they were going to play bridge, and she picked up the newspaper and pretended to do the crossword puzzle. She heard her voice telling her mother that she would be quite happy doing this. *Her* mother! *His* eyes, his hands, his voice saying: 'I want you entirely. Want, want, want! You're beginning to understand what that means now, aren't you? Wait a few minutes more!' She waited, enduring everything that she had most passionately tried to shut out of her memory; until there was nothing left that he had said or done to her, and she was forced on to the present; the reasons against his saying or doing those things to her mother coming and going – more straws that would not bear the weight of her panic. People who were married did not do this! But he was married, and he did. But not her *mother*! Surely, surely not her mother! Then her mother suddenly wanting to ride again, with somebody 'amusing' – the little silver riding crop for the bracelet – the sweet little platinum fiddle that George Warrender had given her . . . she was sucked out from her beach and drowning again – her mother had been given everything on the bracelet . . . she was thrown back this time high and dry of emotion – beyond the reach of another wave. Still, somehow, she could not leave the room: it did not occur to her that she was able to move, although her mind was working perfectly now, and with a kind of logical skill and speed which it had never done before – remembering, selecting, adding and subtracting – arriving always at the same answers.

At the end of some unknown time, the bridge party broke up, and she got stiffly to her feet with the others. At the head of the stairs everybody said good night, and Araminta warned them not to wake Wilfrid: 'He'll have gone to bed hours ago, and there's no light from his room, so he's asleep, poor old poppet.'

Antonia, sleepless, with no light from her room, lay rigid in the dark: the capacity to think had left her the moment that she was alone, and only the edge of a kind of animal instinct remained. At some point far on in the night, she thought she heard footsteps, and, at the moment when she was deciding that they were too quiet to be more than a shadow of her imagination, a door closed – too quietly – clicked back, and shut again less quietly. She turned then, on to her face, and wept with a most sudden bitterness, for her father.

10

THE next morning, when she got down to breakfast, she found that her mother and Curran had already gone riding, leaving the Morrows and her father almost paralysed with uncongeniality, amid the wreckage of the breakfast table. The Morrows seized upon her eagerly – Araminta had said that Toni would take them somewhere – where should it be? Only for the morning – the others would be back for a late lunch, and there was some vague scheme for the afternoon, but David didn't know what it was. Come on – entertain us – they said. We aren't fussy about how it is done, but we must be entertained somehow. Her father slipped thankfully from the room with his newspaper. 'What about the Professor?' Muriel asked, almost before he had closed the door. 'Do we take him too?' He would be working, Antonia replied, and reflected wearily that this was her father's house, and that he, more than she, must object to his being treated in it as he was.

All through the morning, while she entertained the Morrows for her mother, she suffered from the incessant, frightful outrage which it seemed then to her they were all practising upon her father: for now, suddenly, everything that Araminta and her guests had ever said or not said, done, or omitted to do, took on a new, and horrible significance. Now their attitude to her father – which before had seemed to be largely composed of embarrassment and indifference (Muriel's remark about the Professor was typical) – meant very much more: the indifference was insulting, the embarrassment guilty – calling him 'Professor' which he was not, but which they often did – seemed to her insufferably patronizing. Bad manners, and it taking all sorts to make a world no longer seemed to apply and with a deadly facility were replaced by squalid little phrases like: 'under his nose', or 'behind his back': this last, because having stumbled upon something which so much shocked and revolted her (and part of the shock was the amount of time that she had not known it), she felt that everybody else must always have known – everyone, of course, excepting her father . . . *He* was so calm, so quiet! He disassociated himself from them with such an unassuming dignity; and his manner, untouched by theirs to him, was invariably courteous and serene. The Morrows, she decided, simply neither knew nor cared what they were doing – but Curran! He could have picked anyone else . . . and then, because all her sensibilities had shifted from him and herself to her father, and she could therefore observe Curran with an entirely new detachment, she realized that he *might* have picked anybody, but that, in fact, her mother had picked *him*: and he had simply responded. Her mother, then, on top of her careless indifference, her sledgehammer preoccupation with her own interests, was practising a deceit on her father, a continuous accumulating treachery the discovery of which, Antonia felt, might very well kill him. For he, of all people, seemed to her not made for this: he knows nothing about *people*, really, she thought; even I know more than he does about them. His potential bewilderment, shock and destruction haunted her, all the time that she was driving about the country with the Morrows. The thought that Araminta might really love Curran did once enter her mind, but the string of his predecessors dismissed it. Her mother's fitful interest in a particular game attached now to whatever man had been most frequently to stay at the time that she was playing it: her visits to London, her spells of hysterical restlessness and discontent with her surroundings – everything that had packed Antonia's mind while she had been ostensibly doing the crossword puzzle – returned now to confirm and enlarge her anxiety.

Now that *I* know, I suppose that I am deceiving him too, she thought. But I couldn't tell him – I couldn't bear to see his face – and I wouldn't dare even to try and comfort him – poor, poor papa. And I suppose when they are in London, they all laugh about it, and say what a bore he is, and how easy it is to deceive him. They don't realize how simple it is to tell lies to trusting people. And it was then that some dim but passionate idea of protecting him came into her mind.

When Curran and her mother returned, Araminta sped upstairs for a bath before lunch, which was already late, and the Morrows, placated with strong cocktails, asked him how he had enjoyed his ride.

'I adored every minute of it.' Then, defensively aware of Antonia, he added: 'But then, I always enjoy riding. I wish you'd been out with us.'

Araminta shrieked down the stairs for Muriel to be a *lamb* and bring her a drink in the bathroom. When she had gone, Curran offered Antonia a cigarette.

'No, thank you.'

He raised his eyebrows. 'Minty says you smoke all day and all night.'

'It's too near luncheon.'

'She says you've given up riding since the summer. She's worried about you, Toni.' He dropped his voice – glancing at David Morrow who was immersed in a newspaper. 'I'd hate to think that I was to blame in any way.'

She said nothing.

'Look, why don't we go for a short ride this afternoon? It's all right, your mother suggested it,' he added, seeing, and misinterpreting the expression on her face.

She faced him coolly – her heart hammering with anger and contempt.

'I'm working this afternoon with my father, and anyway, I can't imagine anything that would bore me more.'

That touched him – she saw him flinch, and then the anger before he said: 'Still a child! Won't anything make you grow up?'

She answered steadily: 'Some things do.'

And after that, he left her alone.

All the afternoon she worked in her father's study with him. She had looked forward to being safe and alone with him, but she was exhausted from lack of sleep and the grinding confusion of her morning with the Morrows, and now she found that she could not concentrate on her work or her private anxiety. Again and again she found herself staring at her father staring out of his window, his face screwed to a tension of thought – at the same time withdrawn and exposed. It's a good thing he is concentrating on *sixteenth*-century social customs, she thought with bitter protectiveness: whatever he finds out about them can't destroy his life. For the first time she was looking at him with an outside eye: her anxiety for him and her fatigue equated their difference in age – seemed almost to invert their relationship: he looked spent, he did not look well, he added up to a general impression of weakness. He wasn't a very *strong* man, she began to think, and remembered quickly that he had been badly gassed in the war – he certainly did not look like somebody who could survive any more shocks. Then she realized that he was looking at *her* – noticing only that she wasn't concentrating upon her work, and she smiled at him with a deliberately guilty air – as though her attention had merely wandered to something frivolous. It occurred to her then that perhaps the only certain way of protecting him was to take him away from the house – leaving her mother with a clear field to do what she pleased in it; but she was at the stage of fatigue when although once she had had this idea, it persistently recurred, she could not think how to achieve it.

The day dragged through: ending with all the ritual – now ghastly – gaiety of a Saturday evening. Curran talked to her father at dinner, but now she hated him doing it, and interrupted him more than once with a savage assurance: whatever anybody did about her father seemed impossible to her now. If they spoke to him, she imagined their tongues in their cheeks; if they ignored him, their rudeness accumulated in her mind. She watched him with a jealous and despairing concern; observing for the first time a dozen details of his behaviour: the neat and orderly way in which he ate his food; how, with a minute adjustment of surprise, he always blinked and screwed up his face when he was spoken to; his deprecating little cough before he disagreed with anybody; his fingers stained with ink and nicotine; the sleeves of his coat shiny at wrist and elbow, and his sparse soft grey hair straggling hopelessly over his rather ragged collar. He had a dry toneless voice which tailed off into a barely audible quiet at the end of a sentence – as though he never expected anybody to wait for the end of what he had to say. All these things now seemed to her unbearably, dreadfully, pathetic, just as his painstaking quantity of knowledge inspired her utmost respect: and because she was so much on edge, she felt all the time that if for one terrible second, he applied the force of his mind to the situation round him, he would immediately understand it, and as suddenly, be destroyed. All the evening, until he retired to his study, she imagined that the others were propelling him inexorably towards this precipice of worldly knowledge, and that she stood by herself between him and them, pushing him back to safety. And that is only one evening, she thought, there is tomorrow, and all the other weekends of our lives; and, strained and drained by the last twenty-four hours as she was then, she could not bear to think of the prospect.

She lay awake for hours trying to think how she could get her father away; where they should go, and what reason she could give for their going – arriving at no solution: and woke from a sleep which was full of her mother – telling her mother frantically over and over again that she must *stop*, and her mother, who was dressed as a doll, opening her china eyes and saying: 'Stop what?' 'You know what I mean! You are a – a –' but then she couldn't find the word she meant, and her mother laughed, twitched her frilly skirts, and cried: 'You poor baby – you don't know the *first* thing about what you mean!' and she was crying with anger because she *knew* that she knew, only she could not bear to think of the word. 'Won't anything make you grow up?' he had said; and she thought that she had grown up so fast that she seemed to be looking from a great height at what she had been, and had so suddenly got so far away that she could see nothing at all. But I can't talk to *her*! she thought, as the dream surged back: I'm simply not brave enough: I don't know what to say, and wept then, at her own lack of courage: weakness of any kind was not going to protect her father.

Sunday seemed indistinguishable from Saturday, except that more snow fell. She spent nearly all of it with her father, and in avoiding one second alone with Araminta. When they were all together, however, she continually found herself watching her mother – having thought that she could never again bear to look at her, she now had difficulty in looking at anyone else. Her language, her laughter, the way that she threw herself into a chair, the mock intensity of her undivided attention, the apparently careless but ruthlessly competent way in which she swept everybody up into any one of her immediate plans; her extraordinary energy about each separate part of the day, the particular covert impression of herself that she was making for Curran – all of this fascinated and repelled Antonia, almost to the point of hypnosis. Her own self-possession with the Morrows and Curran, however, astonished her – it seemed in those two days, to have become unpainful and complete. In the evening she even played card and paper games with them, as though she had always known all about them, or, alternatively, still knew nothing.

On Monday morning, the Morrows left before breakfast in their car, because David had to get to work. Araminta had said, that if he liked, she would take Curran to a train at a more civilized hour – for some reason she was determined upon this plan, and so, naturally, it became the plan.

Antonia overslept, and hurried anxiously down with the picture of a trio at breakfast accusingly in her mind, to find that her father had already eaten and disappeared into his study: Curran and Araminta were alone. Her self-possession shrivelled at the sight of them, their heads bent over a newspaper together: they were not reading it – she had the impression that they were arguing about plans – that they had expected, but did not want her. They both looked up, an expression of good-humoured blankness replacing their intimate discontent, and Araminta said:

'Well! I was beginning to wonder what on earth had happened to you! I suppose it would be tactless to ask you whether you've slept well?'

Antonia said: 'Terribly tactless,' and poured herself coffee.

Curran observed: 'When I was Toni's age, I could sleep the clock round,' which made Araminta say immediately:

'I *can* sleep for ages and *ages*, but it seems such a sickening waste of time. Anyway, you'll be nice and fresh for the party tonight, darling – I've been trying to persuade Geoffrey to stay down for it, but he's too sickening – he won't.'

'What party?'

'Oh, Toni! *Really!* The *Leggatts*!' *Don't* try to tell me that you've forgotten, or I shall scream.'

'I'm afraid I had.' She had, completely.

Araminta let out a neat little practised scream, like an engine, and turned laughing, to Geoffrey: 'You see what I mean? The child's hopeless! The next line will be: "I don't want to go, and anyway, I've got nothing to wear." The answer to that is that you said you'd go when they asked you, I've accepted for us, and you've got your white dress, which is perfectly ravishing if only you'll bother to put it on properly.'

Antonia, who was coldly angry, said: 'This picture of me as an absent-minded tomboy is so convincing that you must long for it to be true.'

Curran raised his eyebrows; Araminta, really startled, stared, laughed nervously, and said: 'You juggins! I was only teasing you. I'd forgotten you'd only just woken up. Geoffrey, *what* about changing your mind? Edmund will be delighted – he so adores you.'

'Edmund must languish. No, Minty, I must get back. I've had my holiday.'

'Well, when are you coming again?'

'As soon as you ask me.'

'Really – you are impossible! You know perfectly well that that's utterly untrue. Well – I shall hold you to one weekend in three, if that's all you allow yourself. Now we must *fly* for that train. Toni, do you know where Wilfrid has got to?'

'In his study, I expect.'

Araminta leapt to her feet. 'Come on, Geoffrey – you've just got time to say goodbye to him – after all, he *is* your host.' Geoffrey opened the door for her. 'You'd better say goodbye to Toni now, because we shall have to fly as it is.'

Antonia looked up from her paper.

'Goodbye.'

'Au revoir, Toni. I hope I shall be seeing you soon.'

She said nothing to that, and through the closed door she heard her mother's voice . . .

'Really, my family . . . I must apologize . . . their heads in the clouds or buried in books . . .'

Alone, Antonia drank some of her coffee, and lit a cigarette. One weekend in three! And he would come down to them because her mother wanted him to: she would only stop wanting him when she found somebody else who might be far more available – might, like George Warrender, or the young man called Bobby, come every weekend. This future was too much for her – there was nothing now that she could do about it – but, she suddenly realized that if she could prevent Curran coming down every third weekend, her mother would simply spend more of each week in London: it would serve the double purpose of protecting her father, and lessening the time she would have to spend alone with her mother. The remains of her anger at her mother's treatment of her during breakfast flared again – they had clearly discussed her, and she could easily imagine the dishonesty of the terms they had employed. She would prevent his coming – she was no child, but somebody as ingenious and determined as they. She lit another cigarette: she would go to her father. She knew that on occasions as rare as they were surprising, her father became absolutely, immovably obstinate, that having made up his mind about something, nothing or nobody could change it. She remembered her mother wanting to lay the tennis court outside his study window; wanting on another occasion to keep a Bedlington; wanting to give a fancy dress party in London years ago; wanting to send Antonia to school in Switzerland (she remembered the last with shuddering clarity because she had been so terrified by the prospect); she remembered the arguments, the scenes between them, and her mother sulking for days, but whenever he had opposed this minute proportion of her requirements, having to give way to him in the end. She must therefore get her father to be against having Curran to stay. Put as simply as that, the problem actually seemed simple: she did not doubt or question how to set about it – she was strung to a point where any action seemed easier than none. She had heard the others leave in the car, and knew that her father would be in his study finishing the newspaper before he started work . . .

Outside his door, she thought: I haven't thought properly what to say; and then thought that if she had given herself time to think her courage might have failed.

He was sitting exactly as she expected, with his feet on a small stool, smoking his pipe and reading the *Morning Post*. He looked up as she came in, and smiled absently at her.

'You're early, Antonia.'

She noticed with gratitude that he always used her proper name, and felt a rush of affection for him: he was returning to his paper, so she said quickly:

'I wanted to ask you something.'

'Yes, my dear?' He lowered the paper, but did not put it down.

She sat opposite him in silence – her heart was beginning to thump a little: it would be easy once she had started, but it was difficult to start.

'Papa – this may not seem serious to you – but it is serious to me.'

'Serious,' he repeated, and put down his paper. There was a second's silence, and then she said:

'Please don't have Geoffrey Curran to stay any more!'

He waited a moment, and then said: 'My dear, that's nothing to do with *me*. You must ask your mother.'

'No! I'm asking you, instead.'

He looked at her – he was beginning to screw up his face, and then without any real curiosity, asked: 'Why don't you want him to stay?'

'I don't like him.' She searched for a word that would impress him. 'I dislike him profoundly.'

He remained mildly uninterested. 'That does not seem to me adequate reason. He doesn't come here very often, does he? I don't seem to remember his being here for some time.'

'No – he hasn't. But he's been asked again, quite soon, and I know he'll come.'

'Well – when the occasion arises, can you not detach yourself and control this unfortunate opinion?'

'Papa – you don't *understand*! It's not just what I think about him, it's what he is – what he *does*,' she corrected herself.

His pipe had gone out: he lit it carefully before asking with resignation: 'What does he do?'

'He rides the horses into a muck sweat and doesn't cool them off properly'; she was getting desperate; 'and he drinks far too much, and won't play games except for money. He marks books by folding down the pages and shutting them,' she added – perhaps *that* would touch him – but then she could see that it hadn't.

'Well, my dear Antonia, the horses are, of course, your province, and you must see to it that he does not endanger their health. I cannot recollect having seen him the worse for drink, and your mother enjoys a little mild gambling. What was your other objection?'

'The books,' she said hopelessly.

'Ah yes. I agree that that is a lamentable habit, but as all the books of any value or interest are in this room, I think I can protect them. You must exercise tolerance, my dear. It was not so very long ago that your own treatment of books was open to question. I cannot share your dislike of Mr Curran: he seems to me to have wider interests than many of our guests. Now. Let us stop worrying, and settle to a little work,' and he shifted his chair up to his large desk.

It was over, she thought, wildly, and she had got nowhere – had accomplished nothing. Her reasons had not been good enough – he simply thought that she was indulging in some feminine freak, or a childish whim. She looked at him bent over his papers, which he was methodically laying out all over his desk. He was probably quite happy, had already dismissed the subject from his mind; was safely concentrated upon – what was he immersed in? – midwifery; in a moment he would be unfavourably comparing Victorian methods with those of his beloved epoch, and she was the only person who knew and cared that he was *not* safe. She knew now why she had not dared to consider what she would say to him. The only convincing reason that she could give to prevent Curran coming, with its ingenious humiliating distortion, was one which filled her with nauseating fright.

She looked once more at her father. I do love him, she thought; one should be able to do anything for somebody one loves.

'I said that this might not seem serious to you, but that it is serious to me.'

'What, my dear?'

'About Geoffrey Curran.' She was patient now, with fear and courage. 'Papa – *please*! I didn't give you the real reason just now for not wanting him to stay.'

'I didn't think that you had.'

'Didn't you?' She clutched this straw of his perspicacity eagerly.

He smiled his humourless smile. 'Women are devious creatures. It would have surprised me if you had been direct.'

'I'm sorry.' She was blushing now – feeling that he could never know how much she deserved this stricture on her honesty.

'But if I am – if I do give you the real reason, I'm sure that you will understand.'

There was a silence, and then, staring on the ground, she said: 'He pursues me all the time. Of course, he *says* he's in love with me, but he isn't. He's tried to seduce me – he's married already – to somebody in Ireland – but that doesn't stop him in the least. He's always getting me alone somewhere, and trying to – trying –'

'To seduce you?'

She nodded. 'I hate him, but that doesn't seem to make the slightest difference. I hate him,' she repeated with relief at finding this to be true.

'Do you?'

Something about the way he asked – something cynical and controlled – made her retort: 'Of *course* I do! Don't you believe that?'

There was a dreadful little pause, which afterwards she was always to remember, before he said:

'I believe none of it.'

'Why – why do you think that I'm asking you to stop his coming here, then?'

'Oh – I believe that you don't want him here. But the reasons you give – particularly the last one – seem to me – shall we say, an ingenious distortion of the truth?'

She could say absolutely nothing.

He gave her a moment, and then continued relentlessly: 'You say, eventually, that you don't want this young man here because he pursues you, tries to seduce you, and is constantly getting you alone for this purpose. How does he manage to do that, unless you are, to say the least, acquiescent? This house is full of people, and on the occasions when he has been here, you are under no obligation to remain one minute alone with him. I suggest that you have done so, because your feelings about him are, to put it mildly, ambivalent.'

With difficulty, she said: 'If all that is true, why do I want him to stop coming here?'

'That, as I said, is a separate business. If it is true that he is married, you *might* want to escape from the possibility of conflict.' Again there was the cynical emphasis on the word 'might'.

She said slowly, dully: 'I don't know what you mean.' All she did understand was his unaccountable, startling hostility.

He made an impatient, waspish movement with his right hand, and leaned suddenly towards her over the desk.

'I am not *blind*. You have come to the wrong person with this story, which convinces me of nothing but how much a woman you are. All these excuses, rationalizations, distortions entirely feminine in their concept – always blackguarding the wretched man – concealing any real motive you have, because you know very well how unattractive the motive is – does not all this excite *some* shame in you? Or are you so much a woman now that you do not understand the meaning of that word?'

'I can't tell you the real reason!' Tears were running down her face – he was attacking her, and she didn't understand a single word. 'I can't! You *must* believe me – ' *she* had come to protect *him*: 'I can't tell you the real reason!'

He looked at her – his more savage anger draining away until, almost kindly, he said: 'If you had told me in the first place that you were simply, intolerably, jealous – I should have understood you.'

She stared at him – trying to see his face clearly.

'Jealous? Of whom?'

'Of your mother, of course.'

'My *mother*?'

He looked out of the window, and then at her: the cynical unpleasant control was back in his eyes and his voice. 'Who else?'

It was like being plunged into the dark, with somewhere, anywhere, an open pit – a matter of seconds, but after one foot was in the pit, no time at all. She must have repeated: 'My *mother*?' because he cried:

'I am not deceived by this melodramatic reiteration! Not in the least! You are no Emilia – I know that you are not so innocent as you pretend, and as for me, I have known it, lived with it so long, that it has ceased to be a matter even of the smallest importance – only I am not prepared to be hood-winked or pitied or drawn into any aspect of the squalid intrigues that seem to revolve round these situations! I have told you that Mr Curran seemed to me a little better than the usual run . . .'

She slipped violently into the pit – bottomless, nowhere for her feet, and blinded by its blackness – recovered to hear his voice rasping above her; '. . . at least I am not *blind*,' and realized that one foot was pressing hard upon the other, the pain mounting to an exquisite relief. His face was twitching on one side below his cheek-bone; she put her hand up to her face, and then her head to adjust the extraordinary dead weight of her mind. The usual run . . .

He had always known; *he* was not blind – she thought he was angry at *her* blindness – she could not then begin to think that he had ever cared.

She nodded silently, almost solemnly, as though they had reached some momentous agreement, and left him.

In the evening, as she was driving the two of them to the Leggatts'; Araminta said:

'Really, Toni, you must try not to be so devastatingly *rude* to me in front of other people. I mean, I'm sorry if I irritated you this morning, but you really must control yourself.' She laughed, and added: 'It's so *embarrassing*!'

Antonia said: 'I'm sorry.'

'Now you're sulking, darling, which is worse.'

'I don't think that I am.'

'Well, you might at least say you're sorry as though you cared!'

And Antonia replied: 'I don't care, in the least.'

It seemed suddenly to her the formula, the solution – one didn't care about anything. All day she had accepted, felt distantly that she had knowledge now of people and life – and kept the knowledge distant because it seemed to her not power, but the machinery of terror. Now, in the dark, feeling her mother's irritation, and finding herself unmoved by it, her indifference spread and stiffened, poured slowly over everything like lava down a mountain, obliterating all terror and concern and affection, until there was nothing left in sight. Emotionally, she thought, it must be rather like lying down in the snow to sleep – and didn't care about that, either.

The car was draughty, and it was very cold. Araminta, after a little gusty sigh of pure anger, had subsided – had dramatically resolved not to say another word all the way to Robertsbridge. So they drove through the frosty winter silence – Araminta sinking from anger at Toni into the hectic sentiment which invariably occupied her private mind – Antonia entrenching in her new overwhelming conviction.

They drove slowly round the large lawn in front of the Leggatts' house, looking for somewhere to park: and she remembered leaving the party there in the summer.

They walked in silence from the car. Inside the Victorian porch, with glass doors, the warm scented house was like the centre of some dazzling flower. Edmund Leggatt stood inside the second door, beside an enormous steaming punch bowl.

'Drink!' he shouted cheerfully, managing to make a personal greeting of the word: 'nobody is allowed one step further without they warm their vitals. Araminta, my dear, how mysterious you look – up to the ears in fur – cold, and mysterious, and very, very seductive.' He slopped some punch with a silver ladle into a small green glass and handed it to her. '*And* Toni. I can see how lovely you're going to look under that red shawl. Drink!'

'Edmund, darling, how delicious! Wilfrid's awfully sorry, but he couldn't get away.'

'Wilfrid?' For a moment, Edmund looked blank, but his face cleared. 'What a shame! Here are the frozen fragments of the fjords. Drink!' and he began again.

Antonia drank her punch quickly – her mother was already engaged upon the party – was not even going upstairs to take off her coat – a young man was removing it for her. The punch burned with delightful power, and she felt immediately and thoroughly warm. She seemed almost to float up the shallow stairs to the warm bedroom to take off her wraps. The room was dim – splashed with little dull pools of light, and their watery reflections in the many glasses hung about the walls. It smelled of freesias and face powders, and it was empty. Somebody had left three-quarters of their punch on the dressing-table; the delicate steam was misting the mirror. When she had taken off her coat and shawl, she sat down in front of the misted glass, drank the punch and looked at herself. Her appearance was blurred, and even when she wiped the mist away, it did not seem as clear-cut, as decisive as her mind: 'Women are chiefly concerned with the appearance of things', her father had said – but now, she was not concerned about anything at all. To see that the intricacies of her dress were properly fastened – to comb back her hair so that the line on her forehead was smooth – to note that the indeterminate shifting shadows on the bones of her face were not smudges, but only shadows – was, she supposed, no more now than habit, since she did all these things as a piece of unemotional ritual – the reasons for it lost and gone. Only, perhaps, her appearance was not quite right for the state of her mind; she did not look as old as she felt, and the second glass of punch seemed merely to continue her warmth without adding to it.

At the top of the staircase she paused to look down at the heads and hands and shoulders of the throng below her. Their voices, their laughter seemed to run up to the tremendously high encrusted ceiling, and stick there – an inversion of gravity, she thought – and started down the gentle stairs. At the turn of the staircase she could not, in the distance, see over all the heads – there were too many of them packed right up to the large window, where, in the summer, she had seen Curran standing. Now he was not there – was replaced by an anonymous crowd – and she was simply relieved that he was not there: perhaps not even relieved – merely indifferent, not caring about anything.

On the last step of the staircase, somebody took her hand.

'Were you looking for someone?'

She shook her head.

'You had an expression of searching.'

She looked at him.

'As though you were concerned about something.'

'I couldn't have. I don't care about anything at all.'

She looked at him calmly – wondering why she had actually said that, and they stood silent for a moment.

'Do you know anybody at this party?'

She withdrew her hand. 'My mother is here.'

'I don't suppose you know her very well.'

'Well enough to know that she will stay to the very end.'

'And you wish that it was the end now?'

She made a small, instinctively escaping movement of her head.

He said gently: 'This isn't the end: it may very well be the beginning': and picked up her hand again as though it was a piece of essential equipment without which neither of them could begin to move from the end of the staircase.

The Sea Change

This book is in good memory of
David Liddon Howard
my father

INTRODUCTION

WHEN it was first published over two decades ago, *The Sea Change* was saluted by the critics of the day as what it is, a beautiful and unusual novel. It is also one of the most *interesting* novels I have ever read.

The theme, indicated by the title, can be seen as stated – glancingly though with startling rightness – in the words of a principal character. It is towards the very end of the book: he is standing in the sun at Athens airport, he has been watching the take-off bearing away two people close to each other and himself; now their aircraft is up 'glinting and small' in the sky. 'Now, although they would be unstrapping themselves from their seats, they could not leave the aircraft':

> they could make what they wanted of the journey, but they could not escape it. The balance of what was inevitable, and what could be changed occurred again to him now as he tried to see his own framework . . .

This balance of what is inevitable and what can be changed – the theme then is the possibility of moral change: change in perception, feeling, subsequent behaviour. In *The Sea Change* a man and a woman are able to achieve, at some catalytic points, a measure of such change against – and with – the odds of the given framework of their natures, antecedents, past events. The theme of choice, of limited free will, a theme that can never be quite absent in any novel of enduring stature; here it is treated very subtly and with utmost realism. Which includes hope. Plausible, realistic hope that lightens the burden of individual tragedies, inadequacy and muddle. Elizabeth Jane Howard's talent is as complex as it is original. I would call her a romantic realist of immense literary intelligence and range of insight (psychological, without taint of jargon or received ideas), who exercises classical disciplines – form, elegance, concision, wit – in the language and construction of her work.

The action of *The Sea Change* takes place in a spring and summer of the late 1950s, moving after a few days in London to New York, to Athens and to Hydra, the Greek island. These changes of scene and the transitions that affect them, the night flight to America, the boat trips to and from the island, are intrinsically linked to the flow and development of the narrative. There are four protagonists, two men and two women; their story is deployed turn by turn and turn again by themselves. Four people – four voices: living and reflecting on what is happening to them at that hour, on that day, each according to her or his modes of thought, feeling and expression. (A narrative device Miss Howard also uses in her novel *After Julius*, and which is tricky to bring off; in her hands it works: the symmetricality conveys the variations, pace and flexibility of musical composition.) To begin with we are concerned with three characters – Emmanuel Joyce, a playwright, 'and a good one', in his early sixties; his wife, Lillian, some twenty years younger; Jimmy Sullivan, Emmanuel's disciple, manager, dog's body, who shares the Joyces' life and home (except that they have no home; they live at Claridge's, in rented flats, in houses in the country lent to them so that Emmanuel 'can work', out of suitcases which with Lillian means numbers of large trunks: at every move Jimmy spends hours at the airport getting them through customs). The focus of attention appears to be Emmanuel, a man half Irish, half Jewish, who escaped from a desperately poor and brutal childhood by his talent (the word genius is used by entourage and public) and is now a public figure engulfed by fame, money, adulation, and by the demands of fame, money, adulation and an artist's work. The most constant and wearing demands on him though are made by his wife. Emmanuel is not seen in his best light at once. The book opens with a squalid melodramatic episode for which he must be held responsible. Within pages we find him making amends with gentleness and imagination; we begin to see him as the man he is, tender, tender-nerved, irascible, living on the brink of emotional exhaustion, controlled if not always, generous, open to temptations, snatching at escapes: a man held by his conscience; a good man, like and not like a Graham Greene character, a man moved unbearably at times by pity.

He has been married for some twenty years; she fell in love with him, had artistic longings, was getting bored, stifled by her world (country gentry, philistine, well-connected, parents dead, childhood home, a beloved house, sold, gone, pulled down by the developers, the loss resented for ever). For him, she was a beauty, a token of the barriers he had crossed – a feather in his cap. They had one child, a girl. She died at the age of two in hideous agony from meningitis. Lillian, who has a serious heart disease, can never have another child. Such a death is one of the hardest things to accept: it remains, after those long years, a lingering sadness for the man; for the woman it is a tragedy in the present. She has *not* accepted it. Her loss, plus her precarious health (when her heart acts up, she might in fact die at any moment), have been forged into a perpetual claim on her husband's attention and love, a rival to his work and fame. He has responded with years of steady care, infusing her with life and the courage to live it, a task punctuated for him by almost hourly apprehension (her moods, her heart, her tears), by irritation and his concealed disappointment in what she has become; punctuated also by his frequent infidelities, rarely serious, never lasting, always bringing some degree of disaster to all concerned (Jimmy picking up the pieces, as he puts it). Lillian has remained the priority. At the time we enter the story, Emmanuel's stamina and patience have worn thin; he is uncertain whether he can or even wants to write another play. We feel the weight of his tiredness and strain dragging through the pages.

In Lillian, Miss Howard has faced us with a dilemma. There

she is, nursing her grief (the dead child's photograph goes on every journey, is stood on every dressing-table) with her chic, the care for her clothes and looks, the devouring self-regard, her need to be soothed or entertained or both at every minute. One could kick her; then one remembers. *Also* – she *is* beautiful (those large eyes . . .), and intelligent, and she can be nice, and is sensitive about at least some aspects of the outer world – landscapes, good food, flowers, paintings. She is articulate; nor is she devoid of self-knowledge. It is the application of it that falls short.

Jimmy is of an entirely different breed – born in an English slum, orphaned, transplanted to America by emigrating relatives, abandoned to be raised in a dim, bureaucratically benevolent institution against which he tries not to nurse too big a chip, he's been helped in this by Emmanuel whom he loves and sees plain. Jimmy is a stray; he has served with the US Army, speaks 'with a kind of American accent' but clings to his English birth as one thing of his own. He is a very nice young man – sometimes a little stern: he has principles – stage-struck, perfect at his job of assistant director, mediator, peace-maker, indispensable to Emmanuel who is the centre of his life – Jimmy has none of his own, except for the occasional, quickly discarded, girlfriend – he is often furious with Lillian (when he sees her effect on Emmanuel and his work), but also often charmed; he looks after her too. These three are a family.

Now comes the fourth character, the outsider, the catalyst. She comes by way of a suddenly required new secretary – the Joyces are about to leave for New York to cast a play – a clergyman's daughter fresh from Dorset, new to life, in a shapeless camel-hair coat with a copy of *Middlemarch* in her pocket, all of nineteen years old, Alberta, as original and enchanting a creation as one may ever hope to find. I will not spoil her impact by giving anything more away.

In Elizabeth Jane Howard's novels her men and women have always been equally convincing. With Emmanuel here she has brought off a rare double, a man and a credible first-rate artist; with Alberta, a girl who is spun out of goodness, truth and fun, and a brand-new child-clear intelligence, she has wrought a literary miracle.

That is the cast; the story must be left intact for the reader to approach in the intricately structured order built for it by the author. *The Sea Change* is a long book but there is nothing in it that is garnish or indulgence. Every dazzling detail – conversations, encounters, flashes of wit, an angle of stage-craft, the colour of sea and skies – is related and relevant to the deployment of the whole. The control throughout never fails. We enjoy the parts as the whole becomes revealed as the complex, entertaining and at the end deeply moving tale of four people's lives. We have been made to feel as well as see.

One cannot write about Elizabeth Jane Howard without saying something about that *seeing*, about her extraordinary power of description, her sense of place, of the look, the sensuous feel of landscapes, animals, objects, houses; how *much* she has seen and how exquisitely she evokes it with appropriate magic or precision. She can make us see anything from a goat to a table laid for dinner by the sea, the expression on a face to an ashtray the morning after. She *has* the Flaubertian eye.

I must mention the existence at least of assistant characters as the book is alive with them. Some are off-scene like Alberta's saintly and eccentric father, and the poignant Friedmanns (E.J.H. has a way of getting to a core through grotesque exteriors); we have – on-scene – the small boy on Hydra, an infant prodigy, who speaks of himself as a critical statistician, walks about with H. G. Wells's huge *Outline of History*, and does not wish to meet Emmanuel Joyce because 'the Greeks wrote far the best plays and it might hurt his feelings if this fact were to emerge'. And we have the Greek kitten . . .

The Sea Change is a novel that can be read all too easily at an expectant gallop; there is ever more when one reads it, and rereads it, with slow alert attention. Let me end by quoting a few lines here and there almost at random. At a London party of the well-known and successful,

> They had certainly made the most – and in some cases too much – of themselves.

> A fragment of a night on Hydra.

> They walked behind the mule to the port, facing a young moon that lay couched in little clouds like a young beauty on a bed of feathers.

An expression of man's fatal ability of living beyond the present. Alberta is facing an impending ordeal, and the dread of it 'keeps bouncing towards me and away again – it has just come back like a tiresome ball that seems both unerring and silly;'

> there is a considerable difference between knowing what to do and actually doing it, I suppose one spends most of one's life in this gap?

And when the sea change comes it is precarious . . . There is no facile optimism in that hope. The resolution is 'like a new-laid fire with the paper burning before the paper becomes black ash and the fire has to live on its own'.

> How rare it is to live any promise out; how hard to keep every minute of any decision; how painful to reach even to the height of one's own nature . . .

Sybille Bedford, 1986

CONTENTS

CHAPTER FIVE · HYDRA

CHAPTER SIX · HYDRA

CHAPTER SEVEN · HYDRA

CHAPTER EIGHT · ATHENS

CHAPTER I

1

JIMMY

IT might have happened anywhere, at any time, and it could certainly have been a good deal worse. Paris, for instance, or even New York, before an opening; with Lillian's heart giving us all a bad time, Emmanuel on his first-night strike, and I bouncing from one emotional situation to another, picking up the pieces and giving them back to the wrong people. In fact, it happened in London, two weeks after the play opened, at approximately twenty past twelve last night in the bathroom of the furnished house in Bedford Gardens. It might have been an hotel – it might have been a block of flats – in fact it might have been far worse. Far worse: she might actually have been dead. Sticking to facts, however, Emmanuel had put off sacking her for days: I think he'd even let her think she was coming to New York with us. We always do travel with a secretary, so it would have been quite reasonable if she'd thought that. Yesterday morning, when I tackled him about her, he tried to get me to do it – he even produced the gag about his being paid to be responsible for other people's emotional problems, so why should he face his own? But I knew then that he would do it. She cried a lot; poor Gloria, she's given to tears. He was very gentle to her all day; Lillian was persuaded to keep out of her way, which was the kindest thing *she* could do, and I did my best. She brought Emmanuel his letters just before we went to drink with Cromer before going to see a girl in a play whom Emmanuel thought he wanted for the New York production. Emmanuel offered her a glass of sherry, and we all had a sticky drink together: she seemed all right then – a bit quiet, and puffy round the eyes, poor thing – but on the whole I thought she was being very controlled. In the taxi Emmanuel suddenly said: 'What a pity that girls don't look beautiful, like country, after rain!', so I knew he was feeling bad about her. Then Lillian said: 'I look marvellous after I've been crying – easily my best,' which was clever of her, because she made him laugh and it's true.

The girl in the play looked right, but she wasn't – Emmanuel said her voice depressed him, and of course Lillian thought she'd be perfect, so what with the argument and dinner we weren't back until after twelve. We had a drink and Lillian started again about the girl: it's funny how people who love arguing are nearly always bad at it. To change the subject Emmanuel wondered why all the lights were on. They were: in the sitting room when we got back, and all the way up the stairs. Most people can get depressed or agitated out of their observation, but Emmanuel doesn't: he never stops noticing things, but he only mentions them when he's bored. Lillian said 'How extraordinary!' and dashed upstairs saying something about burglars. We sat on the arms of the armchairs, and Emmanuel looked at me over his lime juice, raised his eyebrows, dropped them with a twitch and said: 'Jimmy. Here we sit on other people's chairs, drinking out of their glasses. I'd like to be at least one of the three bears: I prefer an hotel to borrowing everything.'

'In three weeks you'll be snug at the New Weston,' I said.

He raised his glass. 'I can hardly wait.'

He'd gone blue under the eyes; whenever I most want to comfort him I seem to underline his despair – well, perhaps it isn't despair, but it is so quiet and continuous and often makes him look so sad that I can't think of another word for it. And then, whenever I feel like that about him he always makes me laugh. Now, his eyes snapping with the kind of amusement that people who don't know him think is malicious, he said: 'If we *have* burglars upstairs, Lillian is getting on with them rather too . . .'

And then from upstairs she screamed – if you can call it that – the most dreadful sound: I can't describe it – a scream, a howl, a wail of terror with a train of shock in its wake – a thud, and silence. Emmanuel's face had closed on the instant to such a breathless frozen acceptance of disaster that I thought he wouldn't be able to move, but he was ahead of me up the stairs.

Lillian was out on the bathroom floor: the door was open, the lights were on, and we could see her as we rushed up the stairs. Emmanuel was on his knees by her: 'She's fainted: look in the bath.' But he didn't need to tell me. In the bath was Gloria Williams. Her shoes were arranged neatly beside it as though she'd gone to bed, but she was still wearing her horrible mauve jersey and her tight black skirt, and she looked exactly like the jacket of a crime story. For a moment I thought she was dead.

'She's not dead, is she?' said Emmanuel. He was hardly asking and he didn't look up. Then I realized that the heavy, groaning breaths were not Lillian's but Gloria's. 'No.'

I felt for her heart in an amateurish sort of way: there was a reluctant, irregular bumping. There was no water in the bath.

'Help me to get Lillian on to her bed, and call a doctor.'

We did that. Emmanuel put a handkerchief soaked with something out of a bottle from the dressing table on to Lillian's forehead while I was talking to the doctor's wife. By the time I'd finished the air reeked of eau de Cologne, and Emmanuel had gone.

In the bathroom he was kneeling by the bath, slopping cold water on Gloria's face and slapping her hands, and he didn't seem to be doing much good.

'Phenobarbitone,' he said; 'and God knows how much sherry. *Sherry!*' he repeated with a kind of wondering disgust. 'Doctor coming?'

'About five minutes. I told his wife about the breathing while he was dressing. Lucky we know a good doctor.'

'We *always* know a good doctor,' he said.

'How much stuff has she had?'

'The bottle's empty, but I don't know how much was left in it. Let's get her on to the dressing-room bed.' She was much smaller than Lillian, but unexpectedly heavy, and her breathing was beginning to frighten me.

'I'm sure we ought to prop her up.' We did this: her head rolled to one side and I heard a little click in her neck.

'Black coffee?' I said tentatively. 'I mean – isn't the thing to wake her up?'

'The thing is to get the dope out of her, and I defy you to do that. How *do* you make somebody sick if they're unconscious?'

'She's not absolutely unconscious – look.'

Gloria had half opened her eyes, but only the whites showed which made her look worse. They flickered heavily and shut. Emmanuel said: 'Lillian!' as though even the idea of her was his fault, and vanished.

I tried to prop Gloria's head up more steadily, but it resolutely drooped: ashamed and inefficient, I pushed her dry wispy hair off her forehead, and wondered why the hell she'd had to go to these lengths. Love for Emmanuel? Despair? Spite? Sheer bloody-mindedness? Or six vital months spent with one of our leading dramatists? I was just thinking how awful it was that I couldn't feel sorrier for her when the bell rang, and I heard Emmanuel go down. The doctor was coming – and immediately I started to feel sorry for her. Poor Gloria; she was an awful colour: her face looked as though it had been made up over nothing . . .

The doctor looked tired and reliable; Emmanuel followed him into the room and then said: 'Keep an eye on Lillian for me, would you, Jimmy? She's rather confused.'

Lillian was lying on the bed with her eyes closed. She had then, and always has what would once have been described as 'a striking pallor'. Emmanuel had put her mink over her which somehow made her look even more weighted down and fragile – because although she is tall, she is extremely thin. She has ash blonde hair like shot silk, and is not at all like poor Gloria. Asleep, she looked gentle and delicate: she wasn't asleep – her eyes opened smoothly like a piece of exquisite machinery and she nearly smiled at me.

'Shock,' she said. 'Light me one of my cigarettes, Jimmy, like a lamb.'

Her bag was on the stool in front of her dressing table, and in the triple glass I could see her watching me. She has one of those faces that are all eyes and mouth and white complexion – very attractive at a distance.

'The doctor's here,' I said. I gave her a cigarette and struck a match. The huge black pupils of her eyes contracted from the flame: eau de Cologne and the herbal cigarette were horrible together. Her face clouded.

'Why hasn't he come in then?'

'He's seeing to Gloria. She's not very well,' I added carefully.

Her long thin fingers clutched my sleeve, and painfully, a bit of my arm. 'Gloria! Oh! Is she—? Has she—? Oh, what on earth has Em done now?'

'He's helping the doctor, I think.' I was determined not to understand her, and she knew it, because she wouldn't let go of my sleeve. 'If you're all right, I think I'd better go and see if I can do anything.'

'Jimmy – I got such a dreadful shock – I can hardly remember a *thing*. You know my heart stuff in the bathroom? If you're going to leave me, I think you'd better get it. Don't worry anybody – just fetch the stuff.'

I got it. In the bathroom I saw the decanter with 'Sherry' on a silver vine leaf slung round its neck. It was almost empty. Somewhere in the house a clock struck one. I met Emmanuel on the stairs looking brisk and very sick.

'He's telephoned for an ambulance. How's Lillian?'

Then he saw the bottle in my hand, and the much-worn mechanism of concern marked his face.

'She's OK. She's smoking. Is Gloria going to hospital?'

He nodded. 'But the doctor says she's all right. She'll live to regret it.'

'Is he going with her?'

'He wants to talk to us first.' He looked suddenly bitter, and good tempered. 'You'll have to do the talking, Jimmy.'

I gave Lillian her stuff, and she said that if someone brought her some brandy, she thought that she could get up.

'You're much better off in bed,' I said truthfully. 'And you'd better lay off the brandy until the doctor's seen you.' I escaped downstairs on that. At that moment, the last thing I could bear was Lillian: the same old Lillian, only this time it would probably be worse, because although several of Emmanuel's secretaries have fallen in love with him, none of them has ever done anything like this. 'I happen to love my husband so much,' it began, 'that I would do *anything* for him. Naturally he needs outside interests, and who am I, constantly ill (etc. etc.) to stand in his way? I know they are not *serious*: his only serious interest now is writing plays – but all artists need a sense of freedom and every kind of opportunity . . .' and so on: whitewashing anything is a messy business. 'He knows if ever there is any trouble, I am always there . . .' was the end of it. He did, indeed. Hell, even if I did think she was a bitch, I was being worse about her than that. She's had her share of disaster – the trouble was that none of us ever forgot it – and her active ambivalence about Emmanuel's work nearly drove him crazy at times . . .

The doors of the ambulance slammed outside, and I opened up to the men before they'd managed to ring the bell. They tramped carefully up the stairs with a stretcher, and carefully down again with Gloria, extraordinarily diminished, upon it. Emmanuel and the doctor followed. The doctor went out with the stretcher, and Emmanuel, looking guilty, said where was the brandy, Lillian had got to have some before she would face the doctor. I poured out a small glass, and to my dismay, he drank it – as quick as a flash – and held out the glass again.

'Lillian, this time,' I said. I couldn't bear his mournful brown eyes asking for trouble.

'Lillian this time.' He took the glass and went.

The doctor shut the front door, pulled the curtain across it and walked towards me (the door opens straight into the sitting room which has always seemed to me to be carrying the English system of draughts about as far as it can go).

'Would you like a drink?' I was nervous: I knew he was going to ask questions, and I felt that some of them might be rather awkward to answer. He said he'd like a small whisky, and I set about it. I was just about to ask him if Gloria was all right, or something silly like that, when he said: 'You are another secretary of Mr Joyce's?'

'Well, in a way. I manage things for him: business, and travelling, and if he directs his plays I act as a kind of assistant.'

'Miss Williams is his secretary?'

'She was.' I handed him his drink, and he nodded sharply at me.

'What do you mean, "was"?'

'She has been for the last six months. We're leaving for New York in a week or two, and he wasn't taking her there.' I felt a kind of nervous patience in my voice; this was like the police, and, if I wasn't very careful, the newspapers. Before he could say it, I said: 'Look – I fully realize that this is a serious matter – we're all most upset by it. Apart from anything else, it was a frightful shock. I'm afraid I don't know what happens about these things, but if you'll tell me how I can help – anything you want to know – ' I heard myself make an unconvincing noise – 'naturally I'll do my best.'

He sat turning his glass round and round in his hands, looking at me tiredly and not saying anything. I ploughed on. 'Mr Joyce told her this morning that she couldn't come to New York. She was terribly disappointed and so on. I suppose that is why she took the phenobarbitone.'

'How do you know that she took it?'

I think that gave me the worst shock of the evening. 'She *must* have! She was all alone . . .' The icy trickle reached the middle of my spine – 'I *don't*, I suppose.'

He smiled then, in a finished sort of way which made him look incongruously pathetic. 'Oh, I think she did take it. I wondered why you thought so.'

'She *is* going to be all right, isn't she?'

'She should be all right. They'll be pumping it all out of her now, and then I shall go and have another look at her. The point is, Mr . . .'

'Sullivan.'

'Sullivan, that people don't do that sort of thing without what seems to them, at least, good reason. And, as you know, whatever the reason, it is an offence to do that sort of thing. Is there any chance that she can have taken it by mistake?'

'I don't know. She *could* have, I suppose – ' I left that straw in the air where it belonged.

'Was she attached to Mr Joyce?'

'Well – I think she admired him. You know, he always seems a glamorous employer – the theatre, and so on, and all the publicity . . .' I took the plunge – 'and while we're on that subject, it may seem callous to you, but it's part of my job to stop anything like this getting a press. Not that anything like this has ever happened before, of course.'

'Of course,' he agreed. He almost seemed faintly, not unkindly, amused. 'Who found her, and when?'

'Mrs Joyce. It must have been about five minutes before we called you.'

'About twenty past twelve. Where did Mrs Joyce find her?'

'Upstairs. She went up to her bedroom because the lights were on, and that's when she found her.'

'On the bed?'

For some idiotic reason, I just nodded.

'What about her relatives? Have you got their names and addresses? The hospital will want them, tonight, if possible.'

'She lives with a sister. I can find the address.'

I had just done this, when Emmanuel came into the room. He walked straight over to the drinks table, poured and drank another brandy. Then he turned and faced us: his eyes were bright, and he looked unnaturally fresh.

'Give Doctor Gordon another drink, Jimmy.' He looked amiably at us, but there was a kind of defiance about him which I knew and distrusted. 'Well, now, where have we got to? Have you got Gloria out of the bath yet?'

He noted the doctor and me – he positively revelled in our reactions before, in an intentionally flat voice, he said: 'I'm sure that Jimmy hasn't made the situation clear to you, doctor. He is under the impression that he has to protect me – annihilate at least one dimension of mine. We found this young woman in the bath having taken all the available sherry and phenobarbitone, because she fancied herself – and very possibly she was – madly in love with me, and having had an affair with her as short as it was unsatisfactory, I was abandoning her. I was not, you see, at any time in love with her. These discrepancies occur – particularly if one is irresponsible and unscrupulous; they are probably inevitable, but one doesn't anticipate them. If anticipation is the thief of experience, every now and then one needs an experience – even if one is just ticking over because of the repetition.'

I knew it all. The way that he could be explicit and pompous, give anybody the other side of the picture with such a devastating honesty that it was the only side they would see. They would end up hating him with all the good reasons for doing so that he had handed them on a plate. He was making for the drink again.

'Emmanuel: you're drunk now, and you'll be hell if you drink any more. We're not amused: have some nice lime juice and lay off talking for a while.'

He stood where I had stopped him, clapping his hands gently together: the doctor, who at least had a kind of hardy convention which was soothing, made a dry noise in his throat and suggested visiting Mrs Joyce upstairs.

'I am sure she would be enchanted to see you,' said Emmanuel graciously.

I started up with the doctor (I was fairly certain that even if it occurred to him, Emmanuel would not make it), and by the time I got down again, he had pinched another drink.

'I was wondering where your courage' – his voice rose – 'your fidelity . . . Jimmy, why don't you find me sooner and tell me to stop whatever it is . . .'

'Drinking?'

He made a shambling, helpless gesture with his hand. 'Further back.'

'I wasn't born far enough back.'

'My fault again.' He leaned forward. 'Jimmy – don't you ever want a life of your own?'

'No,' I said. 'I've thought about it, and I don't.'

There was an unpeaceful silence edged by the rise and fall of Lillian's voice upstairs.

'Do you know how old I am?'

'Yes,' I said, 'you're sixty-one.'

'Sixty-two, sixty-two,' he reiterated more easily.

'According to the files, you won't be sixty-two until the nineteenth of September.'

He glared at me. 'I'm like a century. I like to think ahead.'

The doctor came down, said that Mrs Joyce was all right; he'd given her a sedative and she was going to sleep. He'd ring up in the morning and he'd be getting along now.

When he'd gone, Emmanuel looked up hopefully and said: 'Jimmy. Let's go *out* to drink. Let's find a nice bar where our feet don't reach the ground from the start, and everybody but us is drunk.'

'You can't,' I said; 'wrong country; you can't drink all night here. Let's get some sleep.'

He took no notice of this. 'Why *don't* you want a life of your own? A private life? You're young enough.'

'I have yours,' I said gently: he was beginning to look as though he was made of glass, or paper.

'She was so beautiful. She wore a blue cotton dress: it was old, and it had faded on the tops of her shoulders in the sun.

Her hair was a real brown, and her skin smelled of fruit and the tops of her arms were round. We lay in a chalk hollow on the Downs by the sea, and the air was streaming with poppies over our heads, and the blue air was brittle with larks. I asked her questions and she answered – she never told me anything more than I asked. She filled me to the brim and never slopped anything over. She had the most complete smile I've ever seen in my life. That was one fine day.'

He took his head out of his hands and said: 'Jimmy: now I must have one more drink.'

'We'll have one each.' I got up to get them and he said: 'I've told you all that before, haven't I? It is one of the things I tell you, isn't it?'

'Yes; you've told me before.' The odd thing was that in one sense he'd never told me. The feeling was the same; but the settings, and even, perhaps, the girl, would be different each time. I'd heard about it in a pub – all plush and frosted glass, and they were sharing a bag of hot potato chips with a fog outside; another one was on top of an open tram with a tearing sky above them; she was wearing his raincoat and the wind made her hair come down. No – the girl wasn't different, I suppose: he'd simply pick out different aspects of her – her fingers eating the chips – her eyes looking up at the sky – her neck before her hair came down over it. Once it had been a snowy morning at the Zoo, and once a lake and a rowing boat on a September afternoon, with leaves dropping silently on to the water round them burying her reflection. I knew it was the same time in his life: and the more times that he told me, the more sure I was that there had only been one time. There was a kind of pure joy about the way he remembered her, and a kind of pure grief at the end of his memory. If I'd asked her name, he would have given her a dozen names, but it was the same girl, and each time he told me he added another occasion to that one time. He only told me when he was drunk, anyway, and I don't think he told anyone else.

On the stairs he stumbled, and clutched my arm to steady

himself. He stood for a moment clutching me, and then said – much too loudly:

> 'There once was a bastard called Joyce
> Whose shoes on the stairs made a noyce . . .'

He'd gone a bit green by then.

'We mustn't wake Lillian,' I said hopelessly, and he earnestly agreed.

At the bathroom he looked at me as though I hardly knew him and said: 'Jimmy, if you want the bathroom, use it now, because I shall have to be sick.' He gave me the harassed embarrassed smile he usually reserves for actresses he can't remember, and added: 'My heart always goes to my stomach.'

Later, after I had made sure that he finally got to bed, I fell on to my own, but I couldn't relax. The others could sleep one way or another; it was I who was left twisting and turning over the practical problems – soothing myself with the might have been much worse formula. But if I thought much about that, it stopped me cold. Supposing she *had* been given the phenobarbitone by somebody? Not by Emmanuel; he might hit anyone if he got angry fast enough, but he'd never poison them. Not by me – I was all for a quiet life. That left Lillian. She was mad about drugs; she'd probably think that phenobarbitone was a nice quiet death for Gloria. Of course, she *hadn't* had anything to do with it, but I was tired enough, and resentful enough and sorry for myself – all the usual reactionary crap – to consider the responsibility with brutal calmness. It was I, after all, who would have to pack up this particular set of Emmanuel's troubles – all he had to do was to smile; and Lillian could lie on her back racked with nostalgia and the mitral valve in her heart . . .

2

LILLIAN

I HAVE woken up in so many bedrooms that now I concentrate upon the shape of my body before the shape of the room. There are three kinds of waking for me. One is like being cast from some smooth deep water on to a rocky shore; I am aground and wake with the same shock – the day is hard and slippery under my eyelids and my bones ache from years of wrecking. There is a kind when I move like a ship mooring so unobtrusively to the day that memory of my last dream is not crushed; I come so meekly alongside reality that I can scarcely believe that I have arrived. And there is a third kind – when I seem slowly, imperceptibly to discover myself lying in warm sand, and the water is creeping down my body, leaving it bleached in a delicious lassitude. This last kind is the best, but I only have it now after sleeping-pills, and they won't always let me have them. This is the time when I am devoted to myself; before I have made any false move of the day: when I can imagine actually wanting to eat breakfast; and then dressing – putting on for the first time a pair of simple, but exquisitely made shoes, and a scarf of some ravishing colour that I've never worn: spending the morning with somebody younger, not very happy, who really needs me to be gay and gentle with them; having an exciting lunch with somebody I have never met before; in the afternoon buying wonderful shirts for Em, and some windcheater or windjammer or whatever they're called, for Jimmy (he adores tough sporting clothes although he'd never see the daylight if he could help it); racing back to give everything to them while we have heavenly English tea; Em asking me about some character in his play – the one he hasn't even started writing yet – but he and Jimmy look so kind and secretive that I know that something lovely is going to happen to me, and when they can't bear it any longer they – no Jimmy

– goes and gets it, and gives it to Em to give to me . . . a wicker basket and inside it is a golden labrador puppy that I have wanted more than anything else and that Em has never let me have because of the quarantine and he gets asthma with dogs – but he's changed about it entirely, and he chose this puppy especially for me . . .

I am back where I seemed to have begun; the last time that I had a puppy – on my fourteenth birthday, at Wilde, in 1925. That was my last real bedroom and I can remember it best with my eyes shut. I can remember all of that day with its currents of pleasure, its peaks of excitement: I think that it is the only day that I remember which has nothing in it that I want to forget or have forgotten. It was the first time that I had ever had an animal entirely of my own; it was the last birthday before I was ill; it was the first time that I stayed up to dinner (bronze silk stockings and my christening present jewellery – changed like the grown-ups); it was the last autumn we spent at Wilde, and the whole day had a most lingering beauty which I didn't know that I noticed at the time, but now I can't say the word autumn without remembering it; it was the first time that I thought about the future – 'for ever and ever' – 'the rest of my life'; it was the last time that I accepted my parents as the puppy accepted me. After that day, everything seemed to swoop and pounce and happen too fast; as though I was running breathlessly behind my life – shrieking with the need to choose – out of earshot – in a frantic slipstream of the events which rocketed on before me; a paper chase of examination papers I couldn't pass, prescriptions to stop a pain I couldn't describe, the death certificates of my father and mother – in the same boat for the first time in their lives, and drowned, the catalogue of books and furniture, of pictures, of silver and glass and the auction of Wilde; a picture lying on a railway carriage seat – Em looking intelligent and disastrous and so fascinating that although someone had wrapped a sandwich in the newspaper, I picked it up and remembered how horrible my family had always been about Jews . . . Marrying Em – papers, papers, papers. I nearly caught up with the chase then; seemed to reach something, but he only stopped a little while to admire the view of me, and then flew on: my heart was affected – I couldn't keep up – I gasped and pounded and had always the weak angry sensation that he could fly; for him, at least, there was no uneven ground. He streamed away, above and ahead of me, scattering a new trail of paper – of plays, opinions, letters, cuttings, invitations, and tickets, tickets – for theatres, for boats, for trains and aeroplanes; 'I'll go on ahead by plane; you follow by boat in comfort.' In comfort! I seemed always to be in mid-ocean, in the dark, cut off – from the remains of my family who never approved of my marriage, the combination of somebody who was half Jewish and wholly an artist exceeding the wildest bounds of their worst imagination (they concentrated as hopelessly on his origins as I on his destinations) – cut off from Em to the point where I seemed only to discover him through secondhand sources; through reading his plays – through the people he worked with and swung towards with the sudden irascible illumination of a lighthouse – through the newspapers who fired rumours and accounts of his more violent, scandalous doings which lit up his behaviour to me like starshell. And then, for two years, Sarah – but she dies – in such hideous evil agony that I wanted to kill her. I sat with her for seventeen hours, until her small mechanical shrieks ran out and her head was still: then there were telegrams. Hatred; murder; and a great fear of God: I wanted the doctor's children to be like Sarah; I wanted everyone I knew to suffer for her – to nail them to her pain which they would not stop: I wanted to brand them with the senseless wicked cruelty which had been done to my little, beautiful, dear Sarah. I had been weeping – imploring them to do something – to stop it, and when they had done nothing and it was stopped, I tried to kill one of the nurses. At least I struck out at her and wanted her to be dead. Then Em took me away for nearly a year. We travelled, but he was with me all the time – with such patience for my bitterness that in the end my heart, which seemed so hard and intolerably heavy, suddenly opened, and a great weight of grief gushed out: the exquisite relief, the weakness; the sinking into a single merciful sorrow – that Sarah was dead – it was almost like bleeding to death. It was then that Em gave me transfusion after transfusion of his love; seemed to pour all his life into me – all his creation into my comfort – gave me every breath of his compassion. At first I couldn't say anything about her; then from the morning when he held my head and for the first time since before she died I could weep and say again and again 'I'm so sorry that Sarah is dead: I'm so sorry that she is dead', I couldn't stop talking about her. Then he mourned with me, and gradually he made of it a natural grief – not monstrous, but life-size – until he had taught me to live with her death. He said that her dying was an innocent business: that there was nobody to hate or to forgive for her death – that it had not the terror and dirt about it which there must always be when people were responsible to one another for such things . . .

These are the things that seep through my mind on the mornings when I have the third and best kind of waking – all past and done with – but in them I have a memory of life, a distant gratitude for gesture, for that committed animation from which I seemed to have died. Out of Em came Sarah; out of Sarah came Em; but I also had something to do with it, and I want so much to have something to do with somebody.

The daily maid who brought my breakfast said that Mr Joyce had overslept, that he was finishing his coffee and letters, before he came up. There was only one letter for me, and it is curious that only when I picked it up did I remember the extraordinary shock of seeing that woman in the bath the night before . . .

Dear Mrs Joyce,

I wonder if you have any idea of the misery you have caused me during the last few weeks? But I imagine that you are so completely wrapped up in yourself that it has hardly occurred to you that I existed (by the time you receive this I shan't exist any more). All this time – the only time in my life that has mattered to me – I have been watching *you* – wondering why he ever married you – whether he ever felt anything but pity for your weakness which you have made so dull and dangerous for him. *You* thought that I was just another secretary – there must have been so many I can see that now – you never realized I was different because I had a heart. I may not have your background, or your looks, but in the end, you know, that doesn't make any difference to what one feels inside. All I asked was to be with him, I recognize his loyalty to you. He'll never leave you, however much he wants to, but you couldn't even let me have that. You have to hang on to both these men – being as bad a mother as you are a wife because that's all that Jimmy wants from *you*. I could have borne anything if only I could go on being with him, but suddenly, for some mysterious reason I am not to go to New York. I am to be sacked as though I was anybody. *He* would never have done that by himself – not to me – so that in my sanest moments it is hard for me not to guess who arranged that I should be left. Let me tell you that you will do this sort of thing once too often, and then God help you. He must be on somebody's side though apparently not on mine. It's odd that most people are sorry for you because of your past, and the only shred of pity I can work up for you is about your future. Well – thanks to you, I have none, but at least I had a present, once, which is more than you ever had.

GLORIA WILLIAMS

There was something about those pages being impeccably typed that made them worse – something striking and venomous and machine-made: only the signature was written – sprawling in green ink, like somebody suddenly revealed in the wrong coloured underclothes. I was still staring at it when Em came in. He walked straight over to the window and stood with his back to the light, but even then I could see that he looked dreadful, and I felt suddenly angry that he, out of all this, should look ill.

'How are you?'

I didn't reply; just looked at him as though I couldn't understand what he meant by such a question. I was thinking of Gloria's shapeless silken knees tilted in the bath; sick that he had touched her, angry that I had no longer an innocent anger with him – that I knew so much that I couldn't understand. He was picking a matchbox to pieces – seemingly intent – but I knew he was watching me with the acute delicacy of somebody in a fight waiting for an opening to knock me out with pity – to leave me defenceless and protective towards him.

'How is Miss Williams?'

'Not dead. All right,' he added.

I wanted to smoke; my hands were shaking too: I had no matchbox, and instantly he was lighting my cigarette: he looked pathetic and intent doing it, and my anger rose again.

'As far as I can remember, it is approximately eighteen months since you last achieved anything like this.'

'My dear Lillian – nobody has ever been found in the *bath* before.' But his eyes filled with tears, and he sat down on the bed suddenly.

'Well, if you wanted first-hand evidence of a young woman literally dying of love for you . . .'

'I don't want any of it: no part of any of it.' He reached for one of my cigarettes, put it back, and started fumbling for one of his own.

'She *might* have been dead, and I might have died discovering her. What does that make you? Lucky? Apart from being damned irresponsible, of course. But perhaps you think it's *bad* luck. A clean sweep and you could have started making all the nice familiar mistakes, with nobody to watch you. Except Jimmy, of course – he's a real audience – numb, dumb and devoted . . .' Suddenly I heard this thin and savage voice; I had never heard it before – hearing it twisted everything round so that what I was saying sounded reasonable – a better life for him if I had died and only Jimmy was left to care for him. This was extraordinary: I stopped, and thoughts streamed back in the silence. 'I can't admire you.'

'No,' he said at last. 'I don't see how you can.'

'And I don't seem able to help you.'

'Are those the reasons?' He looked sad and enquiring – and intolerably like Sarah, and he was going to twist about like some intellectual fish: I had to make him laugh, or I'd lose him.

'All I ask is that they shouldn't end up in baths. It's so bad for my heart.'

'You can ask more than that.' He spread out his hand, and I pulled the bedclothes round me.

'If I did, you'd say I was blaming you. "Let there be no deserts," you said.'

'Now I say – mind on your own count. Don't fabricate a climate for concern.'

'Do you remember when you said "Let there be no deserts"?'

'Cherry said it in *The Orchid Race*. Just before she goes back on her street.' He sounded preoccupied, which he always does when he's trying to evade me.

'*You* said it after Sarah died. In Florida on the beach in the dark. You simply put it in a play afterwards – like everything else.' The familiar sweet aching was there when I said her name to him. Miss Williams, or anybody else, couldn't destroy that, and with the life of this feeling I burst into tears. 'You wouldn't have done these things if she hadn't died. If there had been another child! You would have had some difference between real life and what you write – it would not have all been the same. She would have been sixteen – I can't ***bear how far*** I have to imagine her now. You wouldn't have wanted ***her*** to have that kind of shock – you'd have conducted your life with more taste – more discrimination – I wish you'd stop worrying about humanity and live more like . . . like . . .'

'A gentleman? Or other people?' But neither of us even tried to laugh. He picked up the napkin from my breakfast tray.

'Darling, don't distress yourself. Have a quiet morning in

bed. Don't race so much.' He was mopping my face, and I didn't mind his touching me now.

'What are *you* going to do?'

'Jimmy has organized the morning to the brim. I've got to lunch with Sol Black, and there's this party at the Fairbrothers', but you can cut that.'

'What are you doing in the afternoon?'

I saw him square himself to be elusive.

'Going to work a little.'

'Here?'

'No – out. Lillian, you know I can't work here.'

'I won't disturb you. I'll take the receiver off. I'll only warn you in time for the party.'

'I've told you a hundred times I cannot work in the house: I must be alone.' He managed to look both angry and patient.

'I'm coming to the Fairbrothers' – I want to.' It would be the only time of the day with him. 'And you needn't think I'm going to lie about in bed all day. I've got a lot to do before we go to America.'

'Rest in the afternoon before the party. How *are* you feeling, really?'

'Perfectly marvellous.'

'Jimmy said don't answer the telephone today – he'll do it.'

'Don't start telling me how wonderful Jimmy is.'

He didn't.

'Perhaps *I'd* better engage the next secretary. At least we might have a lady, while we're at it: they're no more expensive and at least they won't wear such awful stockings.'

'Were Gloria's stockings so awful?'

'All greasy and stretched; panic-stricken stockings.' I felt better that he hadn't noticed. He smiled faintly when I said 'panic-stricken'. 'All I ask is that we don't have another neurotic virgin. All their imagination's gone the wrong way.'

He laughed suddenly.

'What?'

'I was thinking how *very* little that had to do with "being a lady".'

'Em; you know perfectly well what I mean.'

'You mean somebody not brought up in a slum as I was.'

'Now you're just being difficult. You're different because you're an artist.'

'That's like the countless dear people who've said to me: "I don't usually like Jews but you're different."'

'There's no point in getting angry with *me*: *I've* never said that.'

He threw the napkin on to the floor. His hands still shook. 'Imagine Lillian – imagine meeting an elephant, and presuming so far. Different from what? From whom? How many elephants have you met? Are you sure that what you met was an elephant? What kind of palsied constricted vulgarity are you employing now? If I am the exception, then I am interested in the rule. You are so much the rule that you can't stand an exception. You're only nourished by being able to take things for granted, and the only things we can take for granted are either not pretty, or totally unreal. Honest intentions, I tell you, are the fertile ground: they edge their way out and make cracks in society . . .'

Jimmy came in.

'I did knock. Some society in Bradford want to know whether you'll waive the royalty on *Our Little Life*.'

'That awful play. Why do they keep doing it?'

'Seven women, two men, and one set.' There was nothing Jimmy didn't remember about Em's plays. 'They call themselves the Mad Hatters,' he added morosely. He looked ill too.

'What are they doing it for?'

Jimmy picked up my telephone.

'Mr Joyce would like to know why you are putting on the play,' and Em snarled silently at the instrument.

'They say it's to raise money to build a swimming pool for their Club premises.'

'No. Tell them I haven't got a swimming pool. Parochial bastards.'

'Mr Joyce is very sorry, but he only waives royalties for international charities.'

When Jimmy had finished, Em said peevishly:

'That play's like a double-bed eiderdown in a cheap hotel. It gets thinner and thinner, but it still slips all over the place. I thought we didn't allow ourselves to be besieged on the telephone anyway.'

'We don't, usually. It's my fault. I just can't help being unnaturally polite this morning. It's my weak character. How are you, Lillian?'

'Displaced. Em's been bullying me about class structure.'

Em got up from my bed. Jimmy said: 'Emmanuel, you'll have to shave before lunch today. Don't you think so, Lillian? He can't go out to lunch like that, he looks like a charcoal biscuit.'

Before I could agree, the telephone rang, and Jimmy was caught between blocks of interminable listening and short bursts of disagreement. Em lit another cigarette and wandered to the window. It was raining: it would probably rain most of the day, with cold, gusty sunshine – like somebody who does not know how to laugh. Suddenly, because I knew then that I could not laugh either, I had a picture of the three of us – back this morning where we started, to our shallow centre made up of ritual allowances for one another, traditional misunderstanding and a kind of idiomatic discomfort. Em turned towards me, and for a moment I wondered whether we were both thinking the same thing, and whether he knew it.

'But those are *twenty-four*-foot flats,' Jimmy was saying: 'you might as well put them in Piccadilly Circus – you *can't*: you'll have to border them till the whole thing looks like the wrong end of a telescope.'

He was tapping his cigarette with his forefinger – not listening to Jimmy – preparing to go. If only Jimmy wasn't on the telephone I might have caught him: we could have talked about telescopes – which *was* the right end, or were they just an instrumental admission of failure, only resorted to when one could not really see anything at all . . . He left the room and my mind reeled after him: I hadn't even shown him the letter – but weeks later I'd say something about it as though I'd said it by mistake. This kind of restraint would impress him: his face would light on me – already I could feel a warmth like the instant's burning of the piece of paper on which Miss Williams had written her letter . . .

When Jimmy had finished, I asked him to have lunch with me. He couldn't, he said. He'd got to have a drink with the girl we'd seen last night to tell her that she wasn't right for Clemency in New York. There was a call for understudies at two – he didn't think he'd get lunch at all. He turned all these reasons into excuses with his face. That's when I know about people – with the most bitter, exacting certainty. 'See you at the Fairbrothers'?' he finished hopefully.

'My dear Jimmy, I'm not going to the Fairbrothers' to see *you*.'

'No chance,' he said, and contrived to look defeated. When he had gone, I squeezed the letter into my hand against the sick burning jolt of being humoured. I hate it: I hate that kind of shallow understanding – the allowances made for me and the person who allows himself to make them. I'll make my own allowances for myself: I'd rather he'd taken the trouble to say I was a bitch. But although he thinks in those terms, he'd never call me that. It doesn't go with my liking poetry and Sicilian jewellery and English country life. And after all, I am Em's wife: a kind of holy relic. I looked at the letter, crushed up into exactly what it was worth. Em didn't care about *her*; probably was bored by and disliked her; might even have swung into a violent distaste – so active with him that he would actually have wished her dead . . . But this suddenly frightened me, fitting too easily into my second picture of Em – not the majestic migratory bird, but the little figure with mournful eyes – on a platform by himself, in the dock; against the party, the crowd, the law, who hate him and do not know why he is here, and he does not hate them but does not know why either. I am the only one who knows, and they cannot hear me, and he won't understand because he is fixed upon the crowd with a kind of reckless grief – indifferent to their judgment. My head has started to ache, and it is raining hard now. The only kind of day that I could have by myself would sound like a schoolgirl's diary. 'In the morning, head ached – am I in love? In the afternoon bought gramophone records.' And then some extraordinary little clutch at a cultivated comparison: Satie with Seurat; Renoir with Roussel – the self-conscious yardstick of appreciation so pathetically employed by the young; such intellectual bathos in the old. I shall stay in bed until I am better, or it is time to go to the party. If I could tell them that simply to know something was only like having keys that will unlock anything but one's private house, they would not write about Satie in their diaries: but Sarah did not even have time to write her name: she just liked colours, and any noise designed to charm her. Remembering her little starting shout of laughter is as sharp as Em's sudden blaze of anger – it seems so extraordinary to be left simply with the anger, and that it should be his . . .

3

EMMANUEL

He left the house with the spurious sensation of freedom that he had come to associate with leaving any place where he had slept. There was no sense of accomplishment – no movement in a better direction; simply an opening, with the streets and the daylight before him. His day had been arranged for him by Jimmy and Lillian – on the usual basis of ought and not. Lunch with Sol Black and another possible Clemency – early, because he had said that he wanted to work all the afternoon. That meant going to the dreary little top floor room in Shepherd Market that Jimmy had hired for him. He had spent a week actually trying to write in it, but had been defeated by its impersonal cosiness – its almost furtive air of artistic information. With its divan, its cheap bookshelves packed with the sine qua non of the last thirty years – its postcard reproductions of Etruscan art and its chipped pottery ash trays, it had seemed to him the place to be poor and young, silly and serious, and desperately in love. He was sixty-odd; his income bounded precariously ahead of his enormous income tax; he was no longer silly without an effort, and hardly at all serious, and he had the greatest difficulty in remembering what it was like to be in love. In fact, the room seemed to underline to him everything that he had lost; and so he had used it off and on, but not for writing. Anyway, did he want to write another play? *Poor Man's Friend* looked like running here for a year, at least, and the Broadway production was assured – it only remained to find a girl for Clemency. Somebody of nineteen – like Betty Field; but there wasn't anybody like her. The young actresses today couldn't kick up their heels any more – there were no pretty clowns whom you fell in love with while they were laughing at themselves. Nowadays they were all stern and intelligent about it, and talked about timing – somehow they'd forgotten their bodies: it was like meeting a kitten who turned out to be a ballet dancer. No good talking like that, and worse to think so: nostalgia was a dangerous drug – one developed such toleration to it that even deadly doses failed to stimulate the imagination which ended by living on its own fat with no hunting summer ahead . . .

He was on a bus – he did not know where he was going – but he bought, as usual, a sixpenny ticket, and allowed himself to be swept, with good-tempered surges and patient moments, down Bayswater Road. It was raining quite hard now, and the park looked its worst. Enormous trees, their new green lumpy and sodden; the grass, soured by soot and frost, had no sense of direction, and all this endured under a sky both dirty and hopeless. There had been some streaks of blue – Lillian's favourite colour – when he had looked out of her window earlier. Poor Lillian. He wished that he either wanted to write another play, or, at least, didn't want *not* to write one. But what on earth was he to do this summer if he didn't write? His inability to think with any hope or confidence so far ahead jolted up more recent events: the last few weeks; last night. Lillian, who might really have had a bad heart attack: Gloria, who might really have killed herself: Jimmy, who might easily have lost his head or washed his hands at the unnecessary shock and squalor of the whole business . . . But when he came to himself in all this, he was assailed by exactly the pattern of panic that made him have a drink (he'd even got the first drink out of Jimmy by a trick) – such horror of being himself, of consequences spreading like ink on to other people that he had to desert, to abandon himself, to go out of his mind which so disgusted him, and become a man who would naturally do such things. He was feeling sick again – must get off the bus; must stop drinking; must stop seducing secretaries; must stop upsetting Lillian . . . He got off the bus, took a taxi (he always took them if he knew where he wanted to go), and went to the theatre to find Jimmy. In the taxi he felt such profound, humble gratitude to Jimmy that he wasn't at all sure he could bear to meet him. He had had it before – several times now – and once when Jimmy had actually been there he had said: 'I don't know why you do it. You're worth six of me.' And Jimmy had looked at him – soft and cynical and said: 'Yeah, but there *aren't* six of you, Emmanuel; thank the Lord for that, whichever way you like to look at it.'

He found Jimmy with a photographer arguing about stills. They were both leaning with their hands on a large desk over which the glossy plates were strewn. The photographer was sulking, and Jimmy was discarding plate after plate with a kind of professional petulance. They both looked up when he came in – the photographer assumed good humour and Jimmy winked. 'Don't think that you haven't done a wonderful job, Lionel, in the ***main***, it's just that, particularly with Miss Cockeral – I'm looking for a different quality; a kind of . . .' he paused with two fingers held an inch and a half apart; 'you know what I mean?'

The photographer, let loose like a horse in new pastures, tossed his head, snuffed this meaningless air, and seemed soothed.

'It's elusive, but if anyone can get it, you can.' Jimmy began blocking up the plates. He had metaphorically shut the gate and was talking over it – finishing the job. 'Now look, Lionel. She's filming for the rest of the week as we all know to our cost – she won't be in the mood to co-operate in the way you ***need***. I'll talk to her, and fix something for next week, and then I *know* you'll get some wonderful pictures for me. How's that? By the way, have you met Mr Joyce?'

The photographer held out a hand like a fish slice.

'I'll show him the pictures,' said Jimmy, still soothing.

The photographer whinnied, released Emmanuel's hand, and looked reproachfully at the plates.

'He'll understand about them being roughs,' said Jimmy smoothly. 'Be seeing you, Lionel,' he added as an afterthought.

Emmanuel smiled – really with pleasure at being able to see Jimmy so easily: the photographer gave him a yearning, dazzled look, and went.

'He wants to do you, of course.' Jimmy lit a cigarette. 'My God. What's he *done* to Elspeth though? She's a nice, sexy girl, and he's made her look like she's been underground all her life resisting something.' He shoved the plates into a drawer. 'You haven't forgotten your lunch, have you?'

'No.'

'Got the key to your room?'

He began feeling absently in his pockets for the key, but before Jimmy could say, 'It's OK, I've got the duplicate here,' he said: 'I don't know that I want to write another play, Jimmy.'

'Why not?'

'"Why not?" That's not how to do it. I've no statement to make.' He touched the desk – pressed it with his fingers. 'Out of touch: equal proportions of feeling helpless and detached.'

There was a silence during which he knew exactly what Jimmy was not saying. 'Have you got Gloria's home address?'

'She's still in hospital.'

'I want to see her sister.' He waited a moment, and then said: 'I must.'

When Jimmy had given it to him, he said: 'You know anything about this girl Sol's bringing to lunch?'

'Only what Sol said: nothing. She's had no experience to speak of. Of course Sol says she's out of this world.'

'I don't blame her: it's not a very nice world.'

'You come along with me and get fixed up at the chemist's.'

'I'll have to do something, or Sol'll talk me into engaging her blind. Why can't you come?'

'I've got to tell Annie it's no go, and there's a two o'clock call.'

'Annie?'

'You saw her last night. Her voice depressed you.'

'Yes, it did. Didn't it you?'

Jimmy looked embarrassed. 'She's depressed me in other ways.' Then he said almost angrily: 'Pay no regard. I shan't lose any more sleep over *her*. She wouldn't be right for Clemency – I always told her that, but she wanted me to get you to see her.'

'Well, I may have to get you to see Sol's girl. I don't suppose she'll be right, either.'

'If we ever find any who is, I'll fall for her. I *love* Clemency. Come on; drug store?'

'Chemist,' said Emmanuel gently. At that moment he loved Jimmy.

Sol Black, who had chosen the restaurant, met him in the padded draught which was its entrance. After they had stood there for a few minutes exchanging greetings and being hit and trampled on by waiters and other clients (they were neither of them large men), Sol indicated a very small, low table jammed in a corner near the bar between two groups of drinkers. Their chairs, higher than the table, were wedged behind it, but with some skill Sol levered them into position and they sat – the table rocking, and Emmanuel brushing potato crisps off his knees. It was almost dark, but otherwise the general impression was red: the air impregnated with scent, French dressing, and damp suits (it still rained). Sol talked, but it was difficult to hear what he said: ice shakers (or bracelets?), women laughing who had no business to do so in public, and the heavy murmur – like distant surf – of men boasting about money, made anything but an exchange of platitudes almost impossible. The air-conditioning operated just above Emmanuel's right ear and he tried to shift himself a fraction towards Sol's white shining face.

'Of course! You want a drink,' Sol said instantly: he had a capacity for looking tragic over imaginary shortcomings. 'Hey! We'll get one ready for Martha, too.'

Emmanuel said he didn't drink at lunch time.

'You don't say! God! How I admire you people. Sure you won't break the rule – just this once?'

'Tomato juice.' His voice sounded useless – it sank into the padded walls anonymously – without a murmur.

Sol ordered two Bloody Marys and a tomato juice for Mr Joyce, and the waiter moved off like a knight on a chessboard with the order.

'. . . As I was . . . saying – about this girl – Martha – she's not the usual run – you must believe me. She looks good, of course, not conventional, mind you, but is that girl intelligent! She's read everything! And she really understands your work: she's said things about it which really made me sit up. Little things, mind you. And you know all those Russians? Well, she's read *them*! Not just the dialogue – the whole works . . .' his face glistened, his voice broke: 'and music,' he said hoarsely, 'boy!

has she come out the other side of that!' Their drinks arrived and he waved the bill away.

'Has she done any acting, Sol?' Emmanuel asked gently.

'Well now you're asking. Cheers! Yeah, she's been in Rep: wanted to do it the hard way – she's *cultivated* . . .' He took a deep drink. 'She's twenty, you know – just a kid really – she couldn't have done much of anything. I want to bring her in on the top, because I *know* she's got what it takes – I'm a *hard* man,' he added appealingly: 'Look at me!' he gazed at Emmanuel with liquid eyes; 'Broadway, London, Hollywood, I've been everywhere – they're all the same to me. You can't tell me any more about human nature, and if I tell you this girl's got what the public wants and a great future ahead of her – she's *got* a great future, period.'

'Have you seen the play, Sol?'

'Took Martha last night. It's great: she's wild about it – just crazy about that girl Vlem – Clem . . .'

'All right, stop selling her, Sol. I'd like to see her.'

'Well, now: here she comes!'

He tried to get up, and Emmanuel clutched the table. A tall girl in a dark blue suit was weaving her way over to them. The skirt was tight, the jacket was loose on her shoulders; her dark brown hair was neatly scraped back from her face, which was big and well proportioned. Sol introduced her; everybody smiled, and she sat down on a third chair which seemed to grow up out of the floor. She was wearing a white shirt, very open at the neck, and as she sat down Emmanuel realized that she had the most beautiful breasts that he'd ever seen in his life. This made him laugh aloud which he seldom did: the others looked at him enquiringly, but at that moment, the head waiter, a man with a diabolic expression and shoulders like a grand piano, loomed over them and laid a menu about twice the size of the small table upon it. They protected their drinks like guilty secrets between knees numb with cramp and screwed their eyes in the appropriate directions. The menu was in mauve handwriting hectographed on to rough grey paper; it was written in food French, and Emmanuel couldn't be bothered with it. He watched the others: Sol expansive, generous – struggling with greed and his waistline; the girl – Martha Curling she was called – trying to choose what was expected of her; the head waiter whose features had settled to an untrustworthy co-operation – and then back to Miss Curling's breasts. He had never seen anything like them – he wanted to congratulate her, to laugh again – to celebrate such a delightful phenomenon. He ordered oysters in their honour, and tried to take a more general interest in the proceedings.

'. . . you dig your knife in and all the butter runs out,' Sol was saying.

The girl was fingering one of the buttons that were not done up on her shirt: she had large irresponsible hands, and Emmanuel wished she'd take them away; 'but then I suppose she has to eat with them,' he thought.

'Is it a Russian dish?' she was asking him: 'I mean, Kiev?' she added intelligently. Emmanuel smiled charmingly at her and didn't reply: he never answered a question that bored him. She decided to leave the button alone, and have steak. The waiter went, and Emmanuel realized that unpleasant though he was, he nevertheless created an area of calm.

Eventually they were herded to a table which was not unlike a roundabout on the Great West Road, only smaller, and unless they actually sat on the table, much less safe. It was a good table anyway, said Sol, with satisfaction. He loved people, but they made him sweat – and already he had exerted himself until he looked like a melting candle. They all had lunch: but the girl had a kind of inert self-confidence that Emmanuel found dispiriting. She tried to fix him with her large pale blue eyes, which seemed somehow to reflect great wastes of her character: she worked her way perseveringly through his career – comparing his plays with one another – broadcasting her innocuous opinions like weed killer on a well kept lawn, with Sol behind her rolling the mixture in. Emmanuel ate his oysters and tried not to feel predatory or exasperated. The other two drank a wine foisted on them with expert contempt by the wine waiter: the girl unfortunately added bravado to her repertoire and Sol gleamed phosphorescently in the gloom. She was practically asking for the job now, and Sol was heading her off – he had finesse if you looked at things large enough – by asking about Lillian and Jimmy.

'Your children?' She was deflected: her face composed to that indulgent lack of curiosity which by now he related to that question.

'My wife and Jimmy Sullivan: he directs for me – manages everything.'

'Do you mean to say you haven't *got* any children?'

'We had one: she died of meningitis. My wife is not allowed to have another; she has kidney trouble and something wrong with her heart – it was very dangerous for her to have a child at all – so no – I haven't.' He said this quite mercilessly – to the girl and to himself – so that the girl would never again ask anybody those questions, and so that it sounded to him as though he was talking about somebody else.

The girl looked stunned: then Sol leant forward and said: 'Will you tell Lillian I saw her at the opening Tuesday looking so beautiful I meant to send her flowers for it? *Honest!*' His eyes were like deep velvet; his great soft heart, like a cushion, plumped up to receive them.

They were drinking bitter, boiled coffee. Emmanuel said: 'I'll tell her, Sol, but she won't believe *me*.'

'Then I'll *send* the flowers!' His smile was like an advertising sign. 'What does she like?' He started unpacking his breast pocket – a flurry of leather wallets and books and cases fell out.

'Something blue that smells.'

'Blue that smells,' he wrote laboriously in a tiny book. 'Say, what would that be? Heellio . . . Higher—'

'Hyacinths,' said Martha. 'It's not too late for them, is it?'

'Not too late,' said Emmanuel, and smiled at her. He had noticed with his sharpest detachment that he had only upset her about herself and not in the least about him.

He escaped in the end – recapturing his coat for a small consideration – and set off for Finchley Road where Gloria and her sister lived and ran a small typing bureau. His progress was erratic: as usual, he started by taking a bus whose intentions he did not discover, but he did not notice this for about half an hour because, in order not to consider immediate events, he was engrossed with the past, trying to unwrap the layers of choice and responsibility and get to his intentions . . .

Once, at their beginning, they had hardly seemed wrapped at all: the tissue of poverty, gigantic hunger, and being always cold or sweating from enclosure had covered his life, he had shivered and panted his way through it – his private self fortified by the permanent self-appointed post of Prime Minister which he enriched by incidents like the King sending for him: 'Never, in all my career as King, have I known a Prime Minister of nine. There are no lengths to which you won't go, my boy, if you keep this up.' He kept it up and there seemed no need for ambition in terms of life at 492 Napoleon Road. He could even watch the spectacle of his parents tearing each other to pieces with a kind of unquestioning detachment. His father, a small man, strong as a cat; his eyes blazing with abstract convictions: a disposition both fiery and shiftless – mostly out of work, and often mysteriously drunk even then: his mother, soft, and pale and dark, with her lacerating silences – her grief-stricken sense of commitment: she had defied her orthodox family in marrying an Irish Roman Catholic, and so burned her courage down that her spirit guttered like a candle for the rest of her life. He could not remember ever thinking of them as anything but not the same – different – elementally irreconcilable like fire and water. But the night his intentions were born was a memory distinct as the smell of frying sprats which accompanied it, and the heat of his mother's face charged with waiting. She was wearing an overall patterned with flowers too large for her, and her shoes, which she only wore out of doors or on fine occasions. That evening was one of them; the anniversary of his parents' wedding, and, as usual, they were waiting for his father – had been waiting with the sprats unfried, for nearly four hours. His mother had once wept in that time, as her fragile idea of pleasure broke to despair – and he, what he had gone through about those sprats! When the waters of his mouth had given out, he had magnified them, had made each one the size of a whale, big enough to carry him on their backs, big enough to swallow whole somebody he disliked. He had become a sprat himself for a while, surrounded by gleaming friends with fat economical bodies – then he got desperate and tried to count them, to work out what would be his share . . . Meanwhile the air trawled from the hot dirty street, and netted in their small room by the lace curtains, seemed to get heavier – to press upon them like a weight of clouded water – as hopes silted up from expecting something good to waiting for something bad. After his mother had wept, which she did with lamentable discretion – one little cry of sound and a few cold tears – he knew that the evening was spoiled, that the sprats meant nothing to her and that if he was not careful they would be forgotten. He became inspired – adding up suddenly that his mother responded only to two things: sickness or bullying. Sickness was out of the question if a single sprat was to pass his lips: he got the whip hand of the situation and bullied her. Shaking her head, faintly blushing, smiling at he knew not what family resemblance, she fried the whole lot. He watched the silver fishes swoon in the clear fat (she used a special kind), jig a little as they stiffened, lost their beauty and became crumbly and confiding. She had just put a plate with seven fishes on it – five large, two small – in front of him when his father arrived.

Emmanuel, years later, was to divide second-rate actors into those who could make exits and those who could make entrances. His father was essentially a man who made entrances. He had flung open the door so that it hung gaping on its hinges, and now he leaned diagonal and dramatic in its narrow opening: breathing heavily and with a piece of blood by his left eye. Below this eye, and the other one which shone with a purer rage, he was smiling. He paused long enough for this awful incongruity to sink in but not long enough for them to get used to it before he began: 'I've been out after me sense of proportion: I have to remove myself from life to get anything out of it – if I stayed here I'd be the size of a fly on a dusty lump of sugar – that's you my *darling* – sweet and dusty – giving me such a thirst for distance that I can glory in a street corner – anything outside this rotten little hole – have you thought that if we were all dead we'd take up much the same room lying down? Isn't that a damned thought? But as you lay down when you married me and never got up perhaps it's another of the billion trillion things you don't notice . . .' And on and on. He could not remember all of it. His mother was crying, and as his father lurched past him to her he suddenly thought of his one visit to a circus – the best day in his life – because his father smelt of lions, a hot, tawny, meaty, sawdust smell. 'If you were as far away as the stars I might miss you – but not much, because you wouldn't gleam – you wouldn't twinkle a mile away. You're the kind of woman one bumps up against in a foggy life and spends the rest of it apologizing. I come back from me great thoughts of the utter ruin of this country to the smell of fish, and you snivelling – what's that but a stinking little beano? If you're a poor man your possessions cost money – for me that's you and that little toad – I could keep myself one way or the other when I was knee-high to him. You may be all I have in the world but *by God*, I could do without you! I was worn out with family life before I'd taken a girl round the corner. And what 'ave I got? That mooney young savage – that chewed and spewed out little piece of rope heading for damnation as sure as an egg comes out of a hen – a little knocked-up piece of work without blood or brains; with a future the length of his own nose, and eyes like some lady's dog . . .'

Emmanuel had never felt so important. He tried to see the end of his own nose – a squint at the future – but he was already so drunk with language that it made him dizzy. His mother had subsided on to the only chair with arms to it: his father swaying perilously over her – pieces of his overcrowded mind breaking up like a wreck, as below him she shuddered like the sea.

'. . . I'm like a man with a great weight on his back – but it's no river I'm crossing – no holy child to bless *me*, and no bank in sight: I might be carrying the river itself, you're so like a weight of water, Leah. I could be in America by now, giving meself a fine time of it, but ever since you married me the corners of me life have turned down – there's no smile in it – you're so set on concocting a tragedy out of a chance. I can walk the streets with me head in the air at the stars – all over the sky all over the world – that's a spectacle with some size to it, but I come back here to you jammed in this little trap of a room, chock-a-block with a thimbleful of grief – making the worst of me all the time I'm away. One day the balloon will go up and by God I'll be in it. Is it my fault your family are like stones to you? Is it my dreadful sin I'm not a Jew? Have you thought of my poor mother negotiating the saints about this little heathen?'

His mother uttered one loud wailing cry at this, threw her apron over her head, and there was a savage silence. He could not remember now how the scene between them ended: they went into the other room where they slept, and he was left alone. Words, words, words: he did not consider their meaning – his heart was so packed with their power. There was a kind of force about them that stretched his little, open mind (for the first time he thought of its size, and knew that it was small because he felt it growing with an irregular surging excitement). It hurt him, and he did not know why; he remembered looking at his arms and legs for some mark, while pieces of his father's language rocketed in his head with explosions of colour and sound. He seemed to be as big as the room now – if he moved his hand the walls would fall down: his eyes were already outside them, and some other part of him was further than that – higher and further than his eyes. He tried to catch this piece by pinning it down. America? The stars? Negotiating the saints with his unknown grandmother? But this piece was gigantically obliging – if he said America, it was there, and rushed to supply him with detailed evidence: cowboys eating golden ice cream galloped over him; rivers spiked with Indian canoes poured towards him; mountains, cactus, animals, seeded like magic. The stars were not made of gold: they were silver – crisp and pointed, so that if you pulled them together with your fingers, they fitted in one piece of patched and dazzling beauty, and the dark air round them was warm, like feathers to his skin. His grandmother – wearing a white dress because she was dead – carrying an umbrella like a dame in the pantomime he had seen at Drury Lane, was jabbing it at a circle of saints – all men, with golden beards, bare feet, and heavy holy eyelids, and he laughed because she could not break the circle with her umbrella . . . This piece of him could go anywhere; indeed, he could not stop it – it was like a marvellous machine to him. Did his father, using all those angry, travelling words also have such a machine? He decided not: his father was too angry and despairing: but perhaps his machine had broken down, or perhaps he made it run the wrong way. This was an easy, but frightening thought: if the machine was so very obliging and one went the wrong way with it, anything could happen . . . Oily black underground rivers crept up with a horrible silent speed, so that his feet hugged the legs of the chair: the sun was an enormous red angry stare, and he could hear the blood behind his ears like thunder – he was the size of a drop or a grain – drowning, scorched – he threw all his remaining weight against the machine – it gave a convulsive shudder and was stopped, and the words lay scattered about like broken pieces of it. They had to be used right: had to be put together, and then they could reach, could cover, anything. He looked down at his hands lying each side of the plate of fish, and saw them, and saw the difference in his sight. His hands were soft, grey, boneless, small, calm, and rather dirty; but they were simply waiting to do what he wanted; he could move a finger, turn a wrist, have any power with them – they were another kind of this astonishing machinery. He felt so wonderfully made that he was easily contained in the small greasy room; he felt now that he was a right and powerful size in it. He looked at his hands again and thought: 'I shall write the words. I'll use them like that,' and a burning shot up in his heart until he felt his eyes alight with it. He went to the small stove on which his mother had cooked the sprats, and opened the fire box. It was nearly out – one layer of red, and below it a powdery bed of grey. The pan of sprats lay on the top; he touched one and it was almost cold. He lifted the pan carefully and tipped the fish on to the fire; it gave a creak of amazement, and rustled to life. New clear flames with unexpected streaks of an unearthly blue slipped up and down over the fish. The blaze suited him, and when it began to die down, he fetched his own plate and fed the fishes one by one to the fire. He waited until the very end: then pulled out the bottom drawer of the dresser, which was his bed, turned out the gas, and plunged into sleep.

Here, he was woken up: the bus had reached its terminus, and, as the conductor pointed out, he was not now much nearer Finchley Road than he had been when he boarded the bus. He became quite passionate about Emmanuel's poor sense of direction: reproached him bitterly for not stating his destination; explained to him three or four ways by which he could have reached Finchley Road by public transport; and made it very clear to Emmanuel that his concern was the more justified as the situation meant nothing personally to *him*.

Emmanuel apologized, which had a calming effect, and the conductor asked whether he was a foreigner. He could not really say that he was. That was funny, because the conductor felt that he'd seen his face somewhere.

'I do go abroad a great deal.'

'Oh well, that must be it, then. You'll have to take a taxi,' he added pityingly.

They lurched down the stairs together, and the conductor, with an obvious effort of generosity, remarked: 'Mind you, I can see the funny side of it.'

*

Gloria and her sister lived in part of a neo-Tudor gem set well back from the Finchley Road. He had never been there before, and he had never seen Gloria's sister, who was older than Gloria and called Beryl. He waited for her in a small bleak room which had been furnished for the purpose: instinct, which had driven him here, seemed to have abandoned him, and he was now trapped with a blank and nervous mind.

She came in dressed as a professional woman of twenty years ago: the classical navy blue coat and skirt which were supposed never to date and did, as indubitably as people's faces. The white shirt with a bow at the neck – stud pearl earrings, as far removed from their function as tinned fruit: hair contorted with the same rigid gaiety as a municipal garden, and a face whose energy had all been put into withstanding the unexpected. Her expression now, covering what seemed to be curiosity and resentment, was one of breezy caution.

'It's Mr Joyce, isn't it? I had no idea you were coming.'

'I came to ask you whether you had seen your sister?'

'She was sleeping this morning – so I'm going this evening after work. She's quite comfortable, they say.'

There was a short silence and then she said: 'It was a terrible shock, of course.' She said it not looking at him and as though there was no other kind.

'I wonder whether you could spare me a few minutes to talk about Gloria?'

Her expression deepened. 'Of course. Won't you sit down? I'll just tell my girl to take the telephone.'

As she went out he realized that she was really wearing the same clothes as the girl with whom he had lunched – with a difference which somehow touched him. He sat on one of the uncomfortable chairs and stared at a water colour of some angry-looking jonquils in a gilt basket until she came back. She sat in the other chair and they looked at each other.

'I wanted to tell you,' he began carefully, 'that I had absolutely no idea that Gloria would even attempt to kill herself. I am going to New York in a week or two, and yesterday I had to tell her that I could not take her with me – with us. I hadn't even realized that she had thought she was going until my manager – Mr Sullivan – told me he thought so. I had absolutely no idea that my telling her would have this effect.'

She said nothing, so he asked: 'Did *you* know that she was expecting to go to New York?'

'I knew she wanted to go, naturally.' There was a pause, and she added suddenly: 'You must have had *some* idea of it. You must have known she thought she was in love with you.'

Taken off his guard, he said: 'Thought?'

'People can think about love the same as they think about anything else, can't they? And if you think all the time about that sort of thing you get narrow-minded. Gloria's romantic, of course.' She said this last with a mixture of pride and resentment. 'Mind you,' she added, 'I don't think you've helped much.'

'I think I've done very badly indeed.'

She did not confirm or deny this, but he felt her open a little to the confession. She was thinking. Then she said: 'I suppose you'd give her a good reference?'

'Yes – of course. She's a very good secretary.'

'I usually send her out for the interesting temporary jobs, but there doesn't happen to be one just now. She gets fed up sitting here all day typing manuscripts. If *you* gave her a very good reference, I might be able to find her something to take her mind off everything.'

'Oughtn't she to have a holiday first?'

A complex of emotions came and went on her face: she gave an unnecessary cough and said: 'I don't think that could be managed at present. We're a very small business, you know – just us and a girl, and she's only training. As soon as they're any good, they go, because I can't afford to pay them enough. Gloria does get a holiday,' she added hastily; 'it's just that it has to be fitted in when we're slack.'

'Do you have one?'

'I usually take a week at Christmas. We go down to my

brother at Eastbourne: he's married, and I always say Christmas isn't Christmas without children. But Gloria goes in the summer as well.'

'I was wondering,' he said, not looking at her, 'whether you'd let me arrange a holiday for both of you now – any kind of holiday . . .' he searched for what they might like; 'a cruise, or something like that. To Madeira or Greece – or anywhere you like.'

He heard her give a little gasp; saw her hands clench together in her lap; her neck, her face painfully coloured a dark pink, and her eyes filled with tears. She was withstanding nothing at all, and plainly exposed she lifted the whole situation from the cheap embarrassment he had felt in offering to pay for his behaviour, to a most gentle pleasure at being able to afford her delight. He went on explaining that he would help for somebody to run her bureau while she was away, and ended by saying that nothing could happen to it in six weeks or so.

'Six weeks!' She searched for and discovered an inadequate handkerchief. He gave her his; she took it without noticing – crying and trying to explain to him. She'd always wanted to go abroad, but Mother had only died last year, and had been too poorly for thirteen years before that; Mother simply couldn't bear to go away, even for the week at Christmas. She'd started the typing bureau because she'd had to work at home. She'd been engaged for nearly four years but he wouldn't have Mother to live with them, and you couldn't blame him – Mother didn't like him, and Gloria – she was only seventeen at the time – said she'd die if she was left alone with Mother. You couldn't blame Gloria – she and Mother had never really got on. In the end he'd got fed up and gone off, and you couldn't blame him really. She was forty now – no chicken, ten years older than Gloria – so she felt responsible for her in a way, and she'd been trying to save a bit for a rainy day – her heart wasn't what it was – and she hadn't felt justified in taking a holiday – let alone going abroad . . . 'Abroad!' she repeated, cramming his handkerchief from one hand to the other with shiny, nervous fingers.

He said he would have some itineraries of cruises sent to her to choose from, and that apart from making her choice, she was not to worry about any of the arrangements. He must go: he got to his feet – she sprang to hers like a clumsy young girl, and his handkerchief fell to the ground.

'Oh!' It was the first time that she was aware of it.

As he returned it to her, she said: 'It's *ever* so good of you to do this – and to think of me. I hadn't thought – I think I'd better talk to Gloria first: she might prefer to go alone. She might feel that you were *her* friend, and that I had no business taking so much from you. Besides, she might feel she'd have more fun on her own.'

'She has to be looked after,' he said firmly; 'she's been ill. Either you go with her, or she doesn't go.'

Her face lightened and she followed him meekly to the door.

'And if I were you,' he ended, 'I should not tell Gloria that I had anything to do with this trip. I would much prefer that you didn't, and I think it will be more of a success if there is an element of mystery about it. Didn't you say she was romantic?' He was smiling at her now, and afterwards – for the rest of her life – this precise and delicate goodness was her secret blessing.

In the taxi he lay back; his body relaxed, and his mind drifting towards the moments that he recognized but could never invite. He felt calm and alert, and he knew he was waiting for something. Somewhere, at an extremity, he was touching it: as though he was adrift in an ocean with his fingers on a raft: the swell was moving him and the raft in its different way, and the difference was at the end of his fingers . . . Her neck and her face suffusing that painful pink; her clumsy movement to her feet; her acceptance of his handkerchief . . . the machinery of money – use it, abuse it, it was still the same stuff – people only generalized about anything out of a personal lack of grip . . . 'Her heart was not what it was.' He wondered if she had ever known what it had been. He started to imagine her heart: raw – touched by the man she didn't marry – grabbed by Gloria – squeezed to its death by her mother; the substitutions encouraged, bolstered by provocative whining: 'Beryl's the one with a head on her shoulders: Beryl's strong – she's a good worker': and beneath that we've all got bodies that must be warm and clothed and fed: the rainy days are always with us: where would we be without Beryl – without her heart she won't be able to consider where she might be without us . . . and Beryl 'settling down' to earning her bread and spreading it on both sides for Mother and Gloria – always goaded into her place by the unwinking certainty that she was a substitute – doing for them the least that a man might have done on top of the housekeeping-nursing which was her mother's idea of companionship: pinched by circumstances which she had not made but was constantly expected to improve – expected also to be in four places at once, and to 'lose herself' in the process. The outlets: the week at Eastbourne in December; an unmarried sister-in-law exhausted with the maintenance of chronic illness and romanticism, picking gratefully at the crumbs of goodwill that her brother and his wife had to spare. 'It was only for a *week*; it was *Christmas*, after all.' During that week, the continual nag of Mother hating her to be away; of her and Gloria not getting on; of the knowledge that even in a week they could accumulate a bulk of resentment and self-pity that it would take her fifty-one weeks to redeem. The mother had died: Gloria, if the slightest chance offered, would abandon her, and she would be left to her own resources, having served their purposes, and never her own. The spark he had touched in her – its endurance, its dignity in surviving at all – blazed now in retrospect, and illuminated elements with no limit – no horizon but a deeper blue – a rounding off of such distance that the eye could not carry it.

At this moment, like the faint movement of air before a warm wind, the shut red knowledge of sun through the eyelids, like the sudden stroking of a shadow, this kaleidoscopic collection of fact, invention, instinct, and heart, shivered, shook itself, and fell into a beautiful pattern which filled and spread to the edges of his mind. Not to touch or test it – not to move any of his formidable machinery near it – but simply to let it lie there printing itself was like the motionless effort of a time exposure, and at the end of it he was matchwood and water. He got out of the taxi shaking, and so cold that it took him minutes to find the change.

Even if they rented houses, he thought, they never managed to live in them. The sitting room had the watchful, uninhabited air that made him feel rootless and apologetic about it. Upstairs, he heard the petulant sound of drawers being opened and closed – felt steam creep out of the bathroom as he passed its open door – smelled face powder and scent on the wing. Lillian would have dressed for the party, and he was probably late.

She had been to the hairdresser: her head was shining – stern and casual – an expensive business. She was wearing a dress which in a dishonest and conciliating moment he had once said that he liked. It was a floral silk – predominantly blue – with a skirt tightly swathed over her hips, and a low square neck that showed all her delicately prominent bones. It emphasized all her angles without giving an impression of her shape as a whole, and he did not like it. She was adding a pair of diamond clips, diamond and pearl earrings, and a pearl collar with a diamond clasp. He was late and she did not like it; she was dressed and he did not like it: she would want to know exactly how he had spent the day and he did not want to tell her; she would want to tell him exactly how she had spent hers, and he did not want to know. This is where we start from, he thought; do I want to make anything of it? He said: 'Sol Black said how beautiful you looked on Tuesday and sent his love. He was really struck: I think you'll get flowers.'

Her face assumed the expression of indulgent scorn that a compliment she wanted from a man she despised always engendered. 'He's so effulgent!' She sighed, and started to fill her Fabergé box with herbal cigarettes.

'Did you rest?'

She shook her head. 'I don't like being alone here now. Did you work?'

'A bit.' The pattern shimmered in his mind like a heat haze; resolutely he kept it out of focus.

'Em – you're developing a nervous tic. You keep screwing up your eyes. Don't you think you ought to see an oculist? Although I can't see why *writing* should strain your eyes.'

'Nor can I.'

'It worries me,' she said, and looked up at him for approbation.

'Don't worry. You'll upset your head, and it looks very pretty. I've only got to change my shirt: won't be a minute.'

But she followed him into the dressing room where first Gloria and then he had lain on the bed.

'Where have you got to?'

'Got to?'

'In your new play. How far have you got?'

'Not very far . . .' His temper loomed and changed into an ugly shape before he could stop it.

'Darling, it's not an unreasonable question. People keep asking me, and I feel such a fool not knowing the first thing about it.'

'Well, you can tell them not very far.' He ripped out his cuff links savagely, and started hunting for a clean shirt.

She said something – he knew what the sense of it would be and didn't listen to the words – by now he had split into three worthless pieces: with an appearance of anger, he was dressing; with an appearance of patience, he was flowing into her gaps of silence; with (was it an appearance of?) despair, he was running over his pattern of deceit with her; his barren periods – of months – when he pretended that he was working; his moments of being part of some truth which he kept inviolate from her; his weeks of writing – hanging on by the skin of his skill to the memory of those moments – endured privately without her knowledge or consent; and the payment for all this. When the work was whole and out of him, he let her read it before anyone else – let her pat and prick it and mark it with L: let her argue and discuss and find the faults which she felt were her contribution – thereby losing to her all the fine flush of a piece of work finished. Because of her, play after play slipped from the heart where it had been building and was cast upon his waters of Lethe – all over, bar the cheering, and there wasn't any of that . . .

She was almost in tears – he must have lost his temper. He started to lie to her and she looked relieved. As they left the house, she left her centre long enough to say: 'Poor Em. You should have told me you had to re-write the whole act: it must have been awful for you.'

In the taxi she said: 'Well, the least I can do is to find you a new secretary.' And he took her blue-gloved hand feeling deeply ashamed at the appearance of nobility – brittle and blistering on her face.

The day had worn itself into something of a calm – the sky skim milk, the river watered half-ripe wheat; the plane trees along the Embankment whose new leaves had been washed and tossed all the day were fresh and still and golden green – and the starlings like clouds of black ash – fled to their noisy and uncomfortable night in Trafalgar Square. The Fairbrothers gave their party three floors up in a suite looking on to these sights, but the suite was so packed with the blurring agitation of social intercourse that they might not have been there. The party was about show business: almost everyone there had something to do with it, and he thought that this would be apparent to any odd member of an audience. The women were better dressed – on the whole – than the average English party. They had certainly made the most – and in some cases too much – of themselves; their eyes and mouths designed to be seen at a distance, their hair and their hands well groomed, their feet beautifully shod: they wore real scent and a lot of it; artificial jewellery and a lot of that: ingeniously cut brassieres or none at all. A few of them had poodles, which, like their handbags, were either very large or very small, and their voices, at whatever volume, were meant to be heard. The men might have been more difficult to place. Sick men, prosperous men, crafty men, nervous men; men who looked as though they ate too much; men who looked as though they never slept; men who kept and understood their bodies like a well-tuned car. Men who hoped they were somebody else; men who wished they were not: men looking for an opportunity; men escaping from responsibility. Men who made things; men who took things; men who broke things. Men who had nothing to gain; and men who had nothing to lose. Their difference from other groups of men was the immediate and thorough knowledge that they had about each other's careers. Success or failure could not be concealed from one another, or, indeed, from anybody else: they had almost all had their bad luck, bad taste, or bad judgment confirmed in public: some of them had been on a financial switchback for years; many of them had some startling ability, and there were a few artists.

Lillian was soon swallowed up, and he stood repeatedly refusing a drink and exchanging minima with the immediate throng. The room had a feeling of pressure about it – apart from scents it smelled mysteriously of cold summer food, although he could not see any: there was the usual methylated haze of smoke above the hats and heads, and there was noise spilling, cramming, flooding the room with the windows open like sluices to let some of it out. His hostess had given him some soft drink – the glass was cold and sticky in his hands – she was asking about Lillian, and he looked distractedly round for Lillian to come and give an account of herself. She was talking to a man whose face he knew and a girl whom he didn't. The girl was certainly an odd member of the audience: very young; listening, wearing a cotton dress and a white cardigan and noticeably out of place. Lillian had caught his eye – he indicated her position in the room to Mamie Fairbrother, and they moved towards it. Arriving, he remembered that the man's name was George (George *what*?) and exchanged a cautious greeting with him. Lillian and Mamie were well away, and as he turned from them he caught the girl looking at him with an expression of such solemn, open enquiry that he nearly smiled. Then Lillian said: 'This is Miss Young. She wants to be somebody's secretary, so I've told her to come and see you tomorrow morning.'

4

ALBERTA

TOMORROW morning I am going to be interviewed by Emmanuel Joyce. He is a playwright, and I met his wife at a party last night – on my second day in London. He wants a secretary to go to New York and Mrs Joyce seemed to think I might be suitable. She was awfully nice to me, and I saw him for a moment: I was wondering what on earth I had expected a playwright to look like, and he noticed me and nearly laughed . . . It would be a wonderful chance – travelling and meeting interesting people, if only Papa won't be nervous about it. He gets nervous at such extraordinary points – he says himself that there's nothing reliable about his fears. But Aunt Topsy'll want me to go (after all it was her idea that I should do a secretarial course) and we shall play at me being Emma, and she being Miss Taylor, and Papa, whether he likes it or not, will be Mr Woodhouse. In the end he'll laugh and agree, and then he won't say anything more – just leave anxious notes in my bedroom: 'Wash grapes before eating them.' 'Do not look at Goya's war drawings alone: they may make you too sad.' That was when darling Uncle Vin took me to Paris. Papa doesn't mind me going about with him in spite of his being an actor (apart from being his brother anyway) because he always plays clergymen (although he sometimes plays wicked men dressed *up* as clergymen in spy films which Papa doesn't see because he hates the cinema and there isn't one nearer than Dorchester) and Papa simply says that clergymen in plays help to make the Church an integral part of people's lives so Uncle Vin is helping quite as much, and more interestingly, than *he* is preaching to about forty people. I can't think what he'll say about New York or Mr and Mrs Joyce. But perhaps when they know that this would be my first job they won't take me. Uncle Vin says there is an awful lot of never jam today in the theatre. I must go to sleep. We had the most lovely morning shopping, and I bought all my presents for home. A scarf for Aunt Topsy, and six butterflies from a shop in the Strand for Clem, and a magnifying glass for Humphrey, and a false beard for Serena because she hates being a girl (Uncle Vin was terribly helpful about that), and a diary for Mary because she's got to the copying stage and wants to imitate me, and a marble egg to keep his hands cold for Papa. Then Uncle Vin gave me a marvellous lunch in a restaurant (hors d'oeuvres, lobster, and Camembert cheese) and let me choose a gramophone record for a late birthday present. I chose Sir Thomas Beecham conducting the fortieth symphony of Mozart – the other side is the Jupiter – and Uncle Vin said jolly good choice. Then he took me out to a huge party at the Savoy Hotel, and that's where I met the Joyces. (The party was simply filled with famous people, but unfortunately I didn't know who most of them were.) Now I must wash my cardigan for tomorrow.

Wednesday. Uncle Vin offered to take me, and I said I didn't want the Joyces to think I was a child, and he drew in his chin and went away without a word. In the end I went to his room. He was in his dressing gown playing 'If You Were the Only Girl in the World' on the piano with a cigarette drooping out of his mouth. I apologized handsomely (he said that) and we arranged to meet at a place called Notting Hill Gate which he said was near the Joyces' house. Well – then I went. I wore my tidy skirt and the white shirt that Aunt T. made for Mary and didn't fit her. Uncle Vin explained about buses and waved me off with his fingers crossed.

A man opened the door: he seemed surprised to see me, but I told him why I'd come, and then he asked me to wait in the drawing room (which we walked straight into) and he went upstairs. It was a long narrow room, very smart and full of precious things that matched each other – not at all like home or Uncle Vin's. I got rather nervous, and after a bit Mr Joyce came down. He is a little man, not much taller than me, and he looked tired, I thought, and if he wasn't so famous I would have thought he was embarrassed. I had been sitting down, we both stood and then we both sat and nobody said anything. Then, instead of asking the questions which I had expected, he said: 'A good secretary has to have a sense of proportion for somebody else. Have you got one for yourself?' Then he smiled, and said: 'Don't bother to answer; it's my business to decide that about you. Tell me why you want to be a secretary.'

So I told him about Papa, and Clem not getting a scholarship, and Humphrey wanting to go to Oxford and Aunt Topsy having used her money up on Serena going to Switzerland for her wretched chest, and Mary being what Papa calls an unknown quantity and Papa not being allowed a cheque book by Aunt Topsy because of inflation which she says he doesn't understand, and Aunt Topsy giving me a course in shorthand and typing. I'd thought then that I'd help Papa, but he'd said that although as a daughter I had become a necessity, that he constantly appreciated, as his secretary I would be a luxury that he could not afford. So I'd come to London to look for a job. That made it clear that I hadn't had one before.

'You are the eldest?'

I told him my age, and it didn't seem to surprise him which was a comfort. He asked me if I had had anything to do with the theatre, and I told him about Uncle Vin. Then he asked me if I'd been abroad, and I told him about Paris and Uncle Vin again. Then the man who had opened the front door came downstairs, and said that someone called Sol wanted a word with him. He went, telling the man to tell me about the job. He seemed rather shy and took a long time telling me, and he was so vague I didn't understand him much. In the middle Mr Joyce came back and listened for a bit, and then interrupted saying that he'd like me to work for him so never mind, Jimmy, tell her later. They both smiled and I did too, because I liked how they were. Then Mr Joyce was staring at me and asked my Christian name. I told him. There was an odd silence as though I'd said something wrong – then he asked me if I had any other names and I told him the other one, and said I absolutely refused to be called it. They both smiled, and Mr Joyce said out of the question, he wouldn't even call a hen that, but would I mind if he thought of a name for me and they all called me by it, but I would have the right to veto. I thanked him and tried to remember exactly what veto meant, but then Mrs Joyce came in and the subject was changed because she hadn't got money to pay for her taxi. The man Jimmy asked for my address and telephone number and I gave him Uncle Vin's and left. Mr Joyce shook hands with me and called me Miss Young and then Mrs Joyce did the same: she was wearing beautiful gloves but her rings hurt through them.

Dearest Papa,

This is a very important letter so will you and Aunt Topsy both read it and give it your most serious but open-minded consideration?

I have been offered the most wonderful job by some people known to Uncle Vin, as a private secretary. They want me to go to New York with them, but only for about three months, and then I should be back in England. The salary is enormous, for someone of my age, and it works out at more than £500 a year here, but different in New York and even more. Also they pay my expenses of travelling and where I live – probably with them, so you will see that it is a princely sum which would make all the difference to Clem and Humphrey. Also the experience which is of a very good kind would be invaluable to me, and will probably change my whole life. Mr Joyce is a playwright, but a very good one and if you had met him I'm sure you would agree that he is mercifully unlike what you, Papa, might call to mind if you envisaged such a person. Aunt Topsy has probably heard of him as he is quite old and has written so many plays – Emmanuel Joyce is his name, and he has a very nice wife who is rather ill and it was her idea that I should work for them as the other secretary has had to go to hospital. Then there is a nice quiet man called Mr Sullivan who is a manager and who will tell me what to do. He has a kind of American accent, but he is very shy. This letter is becoming ill-expressed, but you can imagine my heart-felt excitement at the prospect very possibly before me if you, dear Papa, will consent to it without too much private anxiety. Uncle Vin says it would be madness to refuse this offer, and although he rolled his eyes, he really meant it. He says that it is time I saw something of the world, and that most people have to pay to do that, and I am so lucky I don't have to pay anything at all. The only thing is that *if* you agree, will you please do so with as little delay as possible? The Joyces go to New York at the end of this month and want to make their arrangements as soon as possible. Of *course* I should come home to say goodbye to you all and pack my clothes, and write to you frequently all the time I am away. Uncle Vin has read this and says that no time must be lost, and did you see him in *Death Takes a Dance* which of course you didn't but he is trying to shame you into more interest in his career. Give my love to Clem and Humphrey and Serena and Mary and Mrs Facks and Napoleon and Ticky – and of course, Aunt Topsy.

Your loving SARAH.

CHAPTER II

1

LILLIAN

I NEVER feel more alone than on the day that I leave a country. I should like to leave lacerated by my departure from one place, and throbbing with the adventure of discovery or return to another. I should like the last day to be spent with all those people who haven't seen enough of me while I'm here recognizing their regret – ringing up, trying to have lunch with me, and in the end sitting on my bed while I finish packing – filled with affectionate, envious speculation about where I am going. I would like more friends to come down to the airport with us and we would all be very gay with champagne to conceal our feelings: they would wave to me at take-off – people *do* do that for personal reasons with just a bit of waving to the aeroplane thrown in – and I would not simply be part of the aeroplane, but Lillian Joyce waving back to particular people and then settling in my seat, unstrapping my belt and looking forward to my welcome at the other end of the journey. I have been on so many journeys: I must have watched hundreds of greetings that I would have liked: faces like a sunburst; two people literally running into one; the kind where they walk off together asking questions and squeezing arms, stop for a moment, and laugh before they walk on. Em once met me like that – in Geneva: I was over half way having Sarah, and we were going to see a doctor because my back which ached all the time I was pregnant got so much worse, and he was supposed to be a great authority on kidneys. Em had been on an exhausting journey for the opening of one of his plays in

Denmark, and then came straight to Geneva to meet me. Aeroplanes made me feel as though I was having jaundice then, and what with the sickness and my back I got off the plane feeling like a queasy barrel. Somehow, he managed to join me in the Customs. He came straight over and put his arms round me and his hands on the small of my back, and as he touched me the pain melted so suddenly that I thought I was going to float from the ground, and Sarah gave a little leap on the instant: he felt it, and said: 'What a welcome – like meeting Elizabeth.' That was such a meeting that I didn't care when the doctor looked gloomy and said the same things as all the other doctors: that I shouldn't be having a child; that I must expect to feel more and more sick, and my back to feel like breaking in two – a long list of things I mustn't eat and the usual injunctions about leading a very quiet life. He couldn't know that compared to now I'd never led a life at all; that I didn't care what I felt like so long as the machinery of my body was working and Sarah was being made. The thought of her life was such a centre of strength that I never cared – even during the last long weeks – about the continuous sickness and pain and my possible – I told Em afterwards, probable – death. I lived that time: in the beginning as months; then weeks, and in the end I was aware of an hour in my life, but it was all without impatience or fear.

Now, since there is no chance of his meeting me like that, I have insisted on flying with Em and the others going on a separate flight. But that hasn't altered the desolate day of departure: I'm leaving nothing here that matters and there is nothing in New York that I want. The worst of it is that I am taking so little with me – am travelling so light – it is such a spectral business. Everything is done: the packing – the arrangements – the agents have looked over the house; Jimmy's girl has made a scene on the telephone which shocked poor little Miss Young; Em disappeared for nearly the whole of yesterday and nobody knew where he was which always frightens me so much that I'm horrible to him when he comes back, and some people we hardly know have been badgering us to have a drink with them some time before we leave this evening. And that is exactly how it is when we leave anywhere. The only new ingredient is the girl: she's been with us a week now, and they say she does letters well and seems intelligent. I suppose New York will grow her up a bit, but at the moment the poor thing looks like a typical little English frump. Anyway it's better than a plastic blonde, or some ghastly would-be actress trying to get at Em. I gave her an old jersey I hadn't got room for yesterday, and she was really sweet about it – as though I'd given her a marvellous present – I must say she has nice manners.

And now I've got the whole day to fill in, until the car comes for us at six o'clock. Em likes going for walks on these days, and Jimmy – if he hasn't any work to do – goes to films, and I oscillate between fiddling with my appearance and fidgeting round picture galleries, or bookshops to find something to read for the journey. At least I suppose we might all have lunch and spin that out for an hour or two: Miss Young – Alberta is her extraordinary name – has the day off: she really doesn't look as though she's called Alberta, but except for plays people are seldom right for their names . . . Anyway we wouldn't have to have her, which is a relief, because she shows signs of being starry-eyed about the journey and that's very difficult to take if one is as bored as I am.

2

JIMMY

'MAKE it fun for her, Jimmy,' he said this morning: 'She's never done it before – make it an occasion.' It was almost as though he wished he was flying with her himself, and, considering his alternative, one can't blame him. Madam's luggage! I've never known a woman with so many impersonal possessions; she even travels with her private picture gallery, which is why we always have to be at airports early – to get through all the Customs forms and excess baggage. I spent the afternoon with her to give Emmanuel a rest because she's always jumpy before a journey. We met at Wilton's for lunch and she was late which was the best way round. She'd got us a table at the back, and I could tell by the way she came in that she wanted to enjoy herself . . . a smile of conspiratorial exhaustion, followed by a little sigh of potential gaiety – '*What* a morning!' and left it to my imagination. 'Let's have a *delicious* lunch.' We did: Lillian has always had a fine feeling for food and loves ordering it, so I let her choose for me as well. We talked of this and that, and then she suddenly shot at me: 'Jimmy! what do *you* think of Em's play?'

I knew what she meant, but I said: 'You know, Lillian. I think it's a honey – the only problem is finding a girl who can do that kind of thing.'

'You know I don't mean that one. I mean the new one.'

I didn't say anything – so she repeated: 'The new one. The one he's had to re-write a whole act of.'

'I didn't even know that about it.'

'*Didn't* you?' She sounded incredulous, but a little pleased as well. 'I thought that if things were going badly, you'd be the first person he'd tell.'

'Well, he hasn't. I haven't seen it, he hasn't discussed it, and I don't even know what it's about.' I managed to sound resentful (Lillian is an authority on resentment); it covered my embarrassment about a play which, so far as I knew, he hadn't even begun.

She raised her eyebrows in a commiserating manner and was silent for a minute before saying: 'I wish he *would* talk about it – to one of us – before it's too late.'

The waiter brought our sole, and I didn't reply, ostensibly until he had served the fish, hoping really that I needn't say anything; but she adores intimate criticism – she doesn't see it as destructive gossip, more as a means of measuring her intelligence by the yardstick of her inside information.

'I mean that the whole idea of that play is fantastically difficult for anyone to do – the inversion of a Cinderella with the girl getting plainer and poorer all through the play. No amount of spiritual growth is going to compensate for that with an audience – they can't *see* it, unless you make her some sort of a saint, and he won't do that. I told him all this the first time I read it.'

It's no good: I can't keep out of it. In that much time she'd swept me along her current – past the danger notices – the drum of my own temper roared ahead and I hadn't the strength to get back. I'd had to deal with Emmanuel the night after she'd read the play, and at the memory of him then my detachment snapped.

'In the first place the girl does grow inside – in exact proportion to her external changes. In the second place, I don't know what you mean by some sort of saint, but he's made her a significant force on the credit side, I should have said, if you think of the last act. In the third . . .'

'You *do* know what I mean. People don't laugh at saints; you can't make them ridiculous – the girl's almost a clown.'

'In the third place I don't even agree about her getting plainer or poorer. It simply depends what you mean by those words.'

'I mean what everybody means. I *don't* mean Hollywood stuff – wearing well-cut rags and all that glossy simplicity racket. Really, Em's plays are above that.'

'He doesn't mean that either. He means a different kind of beauty, a different kind of richness—' I realized suddenly how loud my voice was by the expression on her face, felt even angrier, and dropped it. 'The right actress can convey these things – it's all written for her.'

'Exactly! The *right* actress, but he hasn't found one. The girl here plays for laughs all the time, and now we're going to New York for endless auditions, and you know as well as I do that there isn't anyone there young enough who can do it: it's crazy!'

We were right on the edge; she was breathless, and her hands were shaking. It was Emmanuel who was flying with her, and I was supposed to be giving her a pleasant run. I started to hand us back along the banks.

'I agree that the girl here isn't right. She's been a great disappointment.'

'But it was obvious from the start that she never would be.'

'Well – we hoped. I know you realized that before we did.' I was sweating now with the effort, and shame that I had made it necessary. I tried to smile and leaned towards her.

'Please eat your fish. Emmanuel would be furious if he knew I'd taken you out to lunch and then argued with you so that you couldn't eat it.'

'But we're not arguing,' she said, and slit her fish from the bone. 'You agree with me really.' She looked quite gay again, and poured us both more wine. 'There isn't anybody to play Clemency, and if Em had talked about the play before he wrote it, we might have got him to see that.'

We were going her way somehow or other. I had rejected violence – had dragged us into calm water, and now she tied me up and let us both down quietly until we emerged at the level she had determined. The only way that I could defend Emmanuel was to agree with her. By the time I had agreed with her that one could tell Emmanuel how to write plays if only he would listen to what she said, we had finished our pineapple, and she proposed that we drink some kirsch by itself. It was too late to go to a picture, and I had a desire to sleep which nearly overwhelmed me, but she looked wonderful. Warmth and enjoyment always brought the faintest, most delicate pink to her cheekbones; her eyes, which were chiefly remarkable for their size, sparkled with an affectionate ease – she liked being with me and visibly it did her good to like anything.

I'd forgotten her question in the sudden memory of the first time I had seen her – been struck by her, you might say – for she was a dramatic and beautiful sight. It was just after I came out of the Army, in America: Emmanuel had offered me my job and asked me to weekend with them in Connecticut – they'd rented a house for the summer. I'd changed and gone down to the sitting room. It was a hot June night – *Aida* was pouring out of the radiogram, and the windows were open on to the garden, but the room was empty. It was a large, pleasant, quite ordinary room – books, low tables, and well-shaded lamps scattered about, and an enormous fireplace for burning logs; but it was the first private house I had been to since my discharge, and it had a kind of haze of luxury and civilization over its comfort. There was a tray with bourbon and orange, cherries and ice, etc., to mix an Old Fashioned, and I was just wondering whether I dared to start on one – when something made me turn round to face the window.

She was wearing a long dress of some finely pleated material – a very dark blue – bare on one shoulder and caught on the other by a swag of wonderful pearls. She was facing me; her arms were lifted to draw the curtains behind her, her face and all her skin had the most astonishing radiance and her hair looked as though there was moonlight on it. She smiled, and said: 'I'm Lillian Joyce,' and at that moment something strange happened to me. All through the war, in various Godforsaken places, I'd listened to men talking about what they'd left and what they were going back to. Women; their wives, their mothers, their jobs, their homes, or just women – women they'd slept with, women they'd never even seen – the usual reminiscence of sentiment, sex, swagger, and plain homesickness; and I'd mostly listened because I'd never had a home or family and (although I never told them) hadn't even had a woman. They called me Orphan Annie – I was Annie for years – and I didn't want to add to that. I'd listened because I always hoped I'd understand why we were fighting the war, but I never did understand for myself – although sometimes I thought I could see why they thought they were. But when I saw Lillian like that and she smiled, I suddenly knew. I wasn't in love with her; I didn't even want her, but I was struck by a kind of adoration. I'd have done anything to keep her as she was then: there was nobody like her, but at the same time she was every woman. I felt that all these years I'd been helping to preserve her, and my whole war seemed natural in that moment.

The waiter was standing over us with the kirsch, and I asked for coffee.

'What was it, Jimmy?' she was asking.

I wondered whether to tell her.

'You looked so sad and tender. Were you thinking of Annie?'

How the hell did she know about Annie – a secret I had made sure died with Private Sullivan?

'Don't worry about her. She was only making the stock scene; she'll get over it.'

'Oh – that one. I'm not worried about her.'

'Well – what was it?' She was asking in the best kind of way: gentle, and flatteringly curious.

'Do you remember when I met you?'

She shut her eyes and opened them again. 'In America, after the war. Do you know, Jimmy, I don't exactly. In New York, was it?'

'No – in Connecticut: that house you had for the summer – in 1946.'

'I remember. That was the summer they stopped me bathing. My God, there didn't seem to be anything left that they'd let me do.' She lit a cigarette, and then asked: 'Why – do you remember it especially well?'

There was no point in telling her something that happened to me; she would only see it as something much smaller which she had not noticed happening to her. I finished my coffee and smiled: 'How could I forget such an occasion?'

Dimly, she seemed to sense a loss – that she had missed – a compliment? An effect that she had made? She asked for more coffee, and while it was being poured into her cup said: 'Well,

I'm glad it's not Annie anyway. She simply wanted that part, I'm afraid, Jimmy – she's hell-bent on her career.'

'Yeah: I know. After nine years, I should know.'

There was a short silence, and then she asked me whether I thought the flight with Alberta was going to be trying at the same time as I asked her whether she minded leaving England. Then we both smiled and disclaimed any concern on either count. After a moment I repeated that I wasn't going to stay awake all night whatever Alberta might do, but that I didn't think she'd be any trouble and I liked her. 'She's very conscientious – a funny little thing – very English with all that prim enthusiasm.'

'Like me? You once said how English I was.'

'You are – but it's different,' I said lamely. It was difficult to attribute enthusiasm to Lillian, and primness didn't seem to apply either.

We had an argument about paying for lunch which somehow felt so meaningless that I said so.

'Nor do I. It's because we're leaving the country tonight,' she answered. 'I'm only determined to pay because I want you to do something for me, so don't thank me: try to feel a little in my debt.'

Outside, she said that she particularly wanted to go to a certain picture gallery where there was a private collection of French pictures being sold – the owner having died. She knew pictures bored me, but she asked very nicely, and I felt she really wanted to go. We walked there slowly: it was fine for a wonder, sunlight, and in St James's Square the traffic sounded like a dusky murmur of summer. I knew she was thinking of Emmanuel before she said: 'He chooses such funny bits of London to walk in!'

When I took her arm to cross a road she said casually: 'I don't really mind leaving this country in the least because there is nothing in it now that I really care about available for me, and I'm far too feminine to care without that. You know the people who bought Wilde were really building contractors in disguise? Well, they pulled it down for the materials, and so far as what remains of my family are concerned, I might as well be dead.'

I went on holding her arm when we were on the sidewalk, with the pangs of being too hard about her on my conscience. Whenever I spent a few hours alone with her I felt something like this: she was no more entirely composed of affectation than most people; she was simply somehow out of her element, and if one can't throw a fish back into the water one gets a kind of guilty irritation when it doesn't keep still. I made a resolve to try and like her pictures – at least to take an interest in them.

Well – I tried. I told Lillian to go ahead at her own speed, and I would take one or two pictures slowly and see if I could get something out of them. The first was called *Lundi Matin*, and was of two women sorting laundry in a rather foggy looking room. They wore drab Victorian clothes and had untidy buns and rather blotchy faces. The whole thing had a dusty shut-up appearance: then I discovered that it was done in those dusty chalks that come off on everything, and supposed the poor man couldn't afford paints. The next one was very small and macabre – a row of gentlemen in dress clothes in a theatre box – all laughing. If you got too far away from it, their faces looked like a set of false teeth, but even close to they looked a nasty lot. Then there was an extraordinary picture of what looked like a huge wooden tiger in an overgrown field. Everything was very carefully, and I thought badly, painted in this one, including the tiger who had a kind of glassy squint, but at least the colours were a bit brighter. I'd just reached a huge picture of hardly any pears on a red table with a green background, when Lillian joined me. She looked dreadful – there was no pretence about that: I put my hands under her arms – they slipped trying to grasp her through her fur – and practically lifted her on to a seat. Her handbag fell off her wrist as she sat down, I seized it and struggled with the clasp. 'Push, Jimmy,' she said. I could only see salts in her bag, unscrewed the stopper and gave them to her while I hunted for a capsule. She made a small choking cough which meant things were better, but meanwhile the gallery owner was standing over us, spinelessly concerned.

'Would you get a cab?'

'Shall I ring for one?'

'Any way you like.'

Some people who had been looking at pictures were turned now with far more interest, to us, except one – a woman – who was quietly engrossed.

'I'm afraid they're engaged.' He shook the telephone and looked hopelessly about him.

Lillian had leaned her head against the wall: she was still a bad colour, and she was trembling, but I think the pain was dying down. I looked hard at the woman's profile and said: 'I wonder whether you'd be so kind as to get hold of a taxi?'

She turned round, saw Lillian, nodded, and went out of the gallery.

'Shall I try to get hold of a doctor for Mrs Joyce?'

This increased the crowd interest; an expression of distaste crossed Lillian's face and she murmured: 'No – home.'

The gallery owner's secretary appeared with a thick white cup of water which I gave to Lillian. She couldn't hold the cup, but she drank some. The woman came back.

'The taxi is outside.' She had a foreign accent.

I looked at Lillian; she smiled faintly and nodded.

The gallery owner hovered: 'Is there anything else I can do?'

I thrust the cup of water into his hands. 'Do you want to walk it?'

She did; but when, with the woman on one side, we got her to her feet, I felt her legs giving way; picked her up and carried her out to the taxi. The woman opened its door. Lillian, with a tremendous effort, said: 'Thank you so much.'

'Where to?'

I gave the Bedford Gardens address, and we were off, but Lillian, looking suddenly very frightened, said: 'I'm perfectly all right; I just want to go home.'

'That's it. We're on our way now.'

We rattled and swayed along in silence until we came out of the maelstrom of Hyde Park Corner, when, as though she'd been considering it all the time, she said: 'Isn't it funny that all I want is to go home, and you understand that, and we haven't really got one?'

I said: 'Yes,' and she went on:

'Poor Jimmy, you've never had one, and mine is demolished; I don't know which is worse. It's a bit underprivileged of us, isn't it?'

'Don't worry about it: collect your strength.'

She gave a little laugh and said: 'It takes some looking for.'

I put my arm round her, and she looked pleased. A little later she said: 'You ought to get married, Jimmy – then you'd have a home – and it's very kind of me to say that, because I'd miss you.'

Because I was loving her courage, I said: 'You are kind, Lillian. You're one of the kindest people I know.'

By the time we got back to the house she was OK – a bit blue under the eyes, but relaxed, with that kind of quiet elation she has when she gets through one of these things.

Emmanuel wasn't back, so I put her to bed, and turned on her electric blanket and fire for her. She lay down without a murmur, but I saw her eyeing the open suitcases which were all over the room, and I said: 'Sure you want to go tonight?'

She gleamed at me. 'Why not?'

I bent down and kissed her forehead, and she made a little settling of contentment into her pillow.

'I'm all right, Jimmy, I promise you – there won't be any more troubles. Thank you so much.'

It was what she'd said to the foreign woman, but she was saying it quite differently.

'I'll be downstairs if you want anything. Wake you at five thirty? Yes?'

'Yes please.'

As I went out she called: 'At least we managed to keep off Miss Williams.'

'That was quite something.' I shut her door and went down to wait for Emmanuel, hoping he'd get back before I had to wake her up.

He did – looking so pleased with himself that I wondered where he'd been. I told him quickly about Lillian because I had to, and I was accurate about it because I knew that as usual he would have to make a decision – or try to make one if Lillian would let him. He stood motionless while I told him – Emmanuel's full attention is of a kind that I've never had from anyone else – and when I'd finished, he held out his hand for a cigarette.

'She ought not to go, of course.' He thought for a moment, then added: 'You remember when I stopped her?'

'I do.'

'Do you think I could persuade her to follow us by boat?'

'No – I think she's had that one.'

'Even if we left Alberta to travel with her?'

'She's not a trained nurse; she's just a kid – it's not fair on her.'

'Well then, I must do it, and you'll have to start the Clemency hunt.' He saw my face and said: 'Come on, Jimmy: ring up our friend in Cunard, and see what there is – tomorrow if possible. No – I'll do it. Is the telephone switched on downstairs?'

'As far as I know.' Then I felt ashamed, and said: 'I'll get through for you.' He loathed telephones, and he didn't want to travel by boat.

While I was working my way through the switchboard to his secretary to the man, I was feverishly assembling my objections to Emmanuel arriving six days late in New York: at least six days – it might be more. There might not be a sailing, or they'd be booked up – but if there *was* a sailing, I knew he'd get a passage. Emmanuel always got everything he didn't particularly want. It wasn't just the auditions. He had a television appearance on the series of authors introducing their own plays: there were two public dinners being given for him and the people who were giving them, at least, thought they were important, and there was a first night of the big musical of one of his earliest plays – all this within the next week – he *had* to be there . . . I was through; he was at my elbow, and I left him to it. It was a quarter past five, and as I went upstairs it occurred to me that I could wake Lillian early, and get her to insist on flying as arranged – and then what? She might be very ill on the plane – she might even die, and then how would I feel? An interfering lunatic, and not having a life of my own didn't give me the right to interfere with other people's. It wasn't even fair on the airline: I'd got morose by now about the whole thing. The door bell rang: it was Alberta back – with her luggage. I helped her in with it, and noticed irritably that she was wearing a completely shapeless camel hair coat, and looked as though she had been crying. I told her briefly what was going on, and she said: 'Would you like me to cancel their aeroplane?'

'It's probably too late, and Mr Joyce is calling someone anyway.'

'Mrs Joyce likes very weak tea. Shall I make her some?'

'Yes, do.' I tried to sound pleasant, but I wasn't. I was mad, because I knew what I had to do, and I did *not* want to do it.

Emmanuel came back. 'All fixed: we're lucky. The *Mary*: sailing the day after tomorrow. They had one spare, and they've had a cancellation of another – double state rooms. I'd better go and tell Lillian. Will you call Claridge's – we're supposed to be out of this house this evening?'

'Wait a minute.' I told him he'd got to go that night, and why, and then I said I'd stay and go with Lillian if she really felt she didn't want to fly. He looked impatient – almost angry – when I said that, and interrupted: 'It's not a question of what Lillian feels. It's what has to be done.'

'Well, I'm telling you – I'm prepared to do it!'

He looked at me coldly. 'The way you are at the moment, I wouldn't want to go to Hatch End with you – let alone New York. Nor, I should think, would Lillian.'

His loyalty was engaged, he would be immovable, and it was all my fault.

'I'm sorry. It's just that I don't take kindly to sudden changes. We had a very good lunch together, and I'll make it a good trip if you'll let me. Could I tell her about it?'

He looked sweetly at me then, and I felt good again. Then Alberta came up with the tray.

'You take it, I'll be up in a minute. And don't argue with her.'

I left him giving Alberta instructions about calling Claridge's and the airport.

Well – that's how it was in the end. The funny thing was that we *all* drove to the airport: there was an argument about it, and I suppose all you can say is that some natures are more human than others – in this case Lillian's; she flatly refused to be left behind. We drove in a huge Daimler – a ponderous, calm journey. Emmanuel reminded Lillian from time to time of other journeys they had taken, and got the minimum response: Alberta sat staring out of the windows at the Minibricks houses and coy flowering trees, but she didn't say anything, and I sat trying to remember what I'd forgotten. I'd given her Emmanuel's engagement book, and told her that she must get him to everything on time. I told her this in front of him; she looked nervous and impressed, and she smiled and said wasn't it extraordinary about time – the only moments when it was important one didn't notice it. We were past the last Tudor pub – the last cheery injunction to eat, smoke, or drink alarmingly cheap, quick, nourishing commodities, and into the tunnel on the airport road. I did remember something, and gave Alberta a ten-dollar bill – she hadn't a dime – and she put it away in her bag saying in a nervous practical voice that she'd remember how much it was. Poor kid; she looked terrified – or maybe just excited – but ever since she'd been told that she was flying with Emmanuel she'd been speechless.

The bonus about London Airport is that they're all as nice

to you as people are before you have an operation, and as you aren't going to have one, it makes you feel good. They met us with the information that the tourist seats for Alberta and me had been rebooked. The press also met us and took some pictures of Emmanuel and Lillian getting out of the car. We weighed in the luggage and the press took some pictures of Emmanuel and Lillian waiting while it was being weighed in. The tickets were checked and we all went up the escalator, and the press came too. They wanted farewell pictures, and as we were drinking, a picture of Lillian drinking to Emmanuel. She was the only one who wasn't drinking, but she seized a glass of water and smiled at him with the right kind of gay devotion. They asked who Alberta was, and we looked round for her, but she'd left us and was talking to a man in an overcoat with a mothy fur collar who looked a typical English heavy. Lillian raised her eyebrows, and Emmanuel said: 'Her Uncle Vincent. Let her say goodbye to him in peace,' and then we got rid of everybody and sat down to wait. Lillian was being alternately gay and querulous: Emmanuel was abstracted, and I was just wishing like hell that we were all going. The thought of going back – of Claridge's – of the train to Southampton – the whole measured business filled me with impatience and despair. Years ago, when I began living with them, Emmanuel had said to me: 'Three is not an easy number for people, so don't try to do anything in that context unless you are able.' I'd said OK and put on my most successful expression of obedient comprehension, and now I was just beginning to see what he'd meant.

Lillian was saying '. . . really – it's ridiculous. I could perfectly well be flying. I do *wish* that you wouldn't all make plans behind my back – it's much more nerve-racking in the end.'

Emmanuel was stubbing out half-smoked cigarettes and smiling at her, when a boy came up with a Cellophane box of flowers.

'Mrs Joyce?'

She looked at Emmanuel, and opened the box, and I gave

the boy a shilling. It was a spray of bright mauve orchids and they came from Sol Black. Lillian looked at them with exaggerated horror.

'My God. They might be all right forty feet up a tree in Brazil, but can you *imagine* pinning them on to your dearest enemy?'

Emmanuel said: 'He just knows you like flowers.' He was beginning to look hurt; as though he'd given them to her.

'But these *aren't* flowers: they're some other diabolical form of life masquerading as flowers to lull everyone's suspicions. I wouldn't be seen dead with them.' She turned to Emmanuel. 'For goodness sake see to it that I'm *not* seen dead with them.'

He took the box from her without a word, and mercifully, at that moment his flight was called. We all got to our feet, and looked round again for Alberta, who advanced from the other end of the hall rather shyly – with uncle.

I saw the expression on Lillian's face, but Emmanuel must have felt it, as he put the orchids on the table and walked forward to meet them. They talked for a moment or two, and Emmanuel shook hands with the uncle and then turned back to us: the other passengers were through the door by now. He kissed Lillian with such kindness that there was something compassionate about it; nodded to me, and stood aside for Alberta, who had hugged her uncle and now said in her rather high clear voice: 'Goodbye, Mrs Joyce. I do hope you have a good voyage.'

Lillian was staring at Emmanuel, but she said: 'Thank you so much.'

Then Alberta said goodbye to me and went through the door, and before Lillian could say anything, Emmanuel had nodded to both of us and followed her.

I took her arm and we walked back past the table with the orchids on it to the escalator, down and out to the car. The driver wrapped a rug round our knees: I told him to pick up the luggage at Bedford Gardens, and we were off. As soon as the car started to move, Lillian broke into a flood of tears. I leaned forward and closed the limousine glass, and, as I did this, I realized that Alberta's uncle had vanished at the barrier, and we hadn't had to offer him a lift. Lillian had thrown herself rigidly against the seat – she was crying with her hands clenched to her sides. I found a handkerchief and put it on her lap, and waited. Overhead I heard a plane, and wondered whether it was his – it was funny what a curious sense of loss I had when he went somewhere without me.

Lillian was subsiding. I pulled her head against my shoulder and said: 'Poor sweetheart. You have had a day of it. What would you *like* to do now?'

She'd stopped crying – she must have been exhausted, and now as though she was half asleep, she said: 'I should like to be a round little woman with healthy pink cheeks and no figure, with three children and a husband whom nobody thought was wonderful but me. I'd like to live in one of those little houses and go to the seaside with the family once a year, and have a mongrel dog who was very faithful, and be very good at making cakes and knitting patterns like the magazines say. I should like a cast-iron routine with me being the variant – instead of endless variations with me being the routine.' She stopped a moment and then said: 'Of course I only want that sometimes – or with part of me.'

'You aren't a routine, Lillian: you're full of surprises.'

'Like my behaviour about poor old Sol's orchids. I recognize that: I call it routine. Did you know I hoped Em had sent them?'

'No.'

'It doesn't excuse me in the least though. I didn't even think of giving them to Alberta. She might have liked them.'

'Oh come,' I said – groping for a lighter note: 'poor Alberta; you said you wouldn't even pin them on your dearest enemy.'

She moved her head so that she could see me: she looked suddenly worn to her age.

'When I saw her going through that door with Em following

her, I did hate her: I'd been dreading that moment, and I hated her.'

3

EMMANUEL

SHE chose her sweet off the tray with care, and, on impulse, he took another of the same kind and gave it to her. She was still wearing her bulky coat, and her seat belt would hardly go round her, but the stewardess, with a kind, professional smile, had seen that it was fastened, and now she would have to stay hot and uncomfortable until they were up. They had taxied to the end of the runway, and the engines were being run up, one by one – he had explained this to her with the first of them – and now she sat tense and expectant, staring out of the window at this roaring dusk. After a moment she unwrapped a sweet and ate it thoughtfully. The engines were collected together; with a small shudder of release they were moving into the short race for speed to become airborne. He felt her attention to the ground; her second's astonishment when she realized that imperceptibly they had left it; her amazement at the dwindling houses dropped like pebbles into the bottom of the air. They made a circuit, and below them were houses no longer, but lights marking the earth with intricate chains and swags, and an occasional rolling glint of water like sheet iron. They were climbing – up into a melting sky cropped with milky hesitant stars, and the sun gone – leaving a flush upon the air like the scent of heat. The cloud was as distant as mountains in an allegory: the sensation of speed settled to movement with the lack of comparison: they were in the air, and then, as with the crackle like a mechanical clearing of the throat it announced its course, height, and cruising speed, they were in the aircraft. Belts were unfastened; cigarettes were lit.

'Would you like to take off your coat now?'

She nodded: she was calm again, but her eyes shone and there was something friendly about her excitement. Her coat was taken away, but not before she had extracted a battered book from one of its pockets. She was wearing a white cardigan over a blue and white checked shirt, and her absolutely straight hair was smoothed back from her ears by a black velvet snood. He looked at the book in her lap: it was a Victorian copy of *Middlemarch*.

'Is that a good book?'

And she answered briefly: 'Marvellous!' Then she added: 'but I don't think I can read it now,' and put it into the rack in front of her.

'No – you can't. You'll be very busy for the next hour or two.' Drinks and hors d'oeuvres were being handed and wheeled about, and now approached them. She said: 'I'm very inexperienced about drink: my opportunity for it has been rather limited.'

So he chose some sherry for her, and had a glass himself. He watched her choosing hors d'oeuvres until he said gently: 'Of course you can have as much of this as you like, but there is a seven-course dinner coming later.'

Her hand shot back into her lap and she went very pink.

'I didn't know. Goodness! I thought this was dinner. Thank you for telling me.' She took one canapé off her plate and handed the rest back to the stewardess. 'I'm so sorry. Is that all right?'

'Does your father disapprove of drink?'

'Oh no. But we don't have it very much at home because he gives it to everybody who comes to the house and it's gone in a trice. My aunt says that he does not discriminate about his generosity. Do you know that all my brothers' clothes have to be locked up to stop him giving them to people? And Papa's clothes are very clearly marked because my aunt says that this discourages people as it is known that he only has two suits left.'

'And what about your aunt's clothes – or yours, or your sisters'?'

'Well, he only asks for them. He never routs about in our rooms. It's only the boys who are in constant danger.'

'What else does he give away?'

'Oh – food, and books and furniture, but he's got down to the big pieces now, so we tend to hear him at it. But once he gave all our winter blankets away in the autumn before we'd started using them. It depends what people ask for. Hardly anybody *asks* for a dining room table. But fruit and vegetables! We've simply had to give them up.'

'People must impose on him.'

'They do, of course. But he says it is much better to be a fool than to miss somebody who really needs something.'

'There might be something between the two extremes.'

'There is: but my aunt advises us not to argue with him. He gets deeply distressed.' Her face changed at the thought: 'You see, to agree with us about that would mean altering his principles, and he feels that one should determine these as early in life as possible and then act on them. If one kept altering one's principles, one would be acting from expediency or chance, and he says that one is short-sighted and the other of incalculable distance. What do *you* think about that?'

'I think that relatively few people have principles. They can be expensive to maintain, and most people aren't prepared to pay enough for them.'

'Papa says that the great examples help in forming them – and after that he says that appreciation is a very good thing.'

'*Does* he!'

She looked at him and went pink again. 'I'm sorry. It's probably rather dull hearing what somebody else thinks when you haven't even met them.'

'It is not in the least dull. Your father sounds the most interesting man I haven't met for years. I should like him very much.'

'Oh – everybody *does*; they almost love him – well, a few really do and the rest think so. Even the gypsies round us do. They used to steal the most enormous goose or turkey to give him for Christmas every year. This worried Papa because naturally he accepted it, and he couldn't always find where they stole it from to give it back. He said Caesar seemed to live further away each year. So in the end he went to see the wife of the head gypsy and told her all about his rheumatism and she said that she would cure it, and he asked her to do it instead of a goose which anybody could give him but nobody could cure his rheumatism. So now he gets a jar of greenish brown paste to rub on or drink with hot water.'

'Does it cure him?'

'Well, it makes him much better; I don't think it actually cures him.' She looked suddenly round her: people were being served with dinner. 'It seems so *odd* to be talking about him here. He says that only the great man or the bore are totally unaffected by their environment . . .'

'It depends which environment: one would not say you had been unaffected by yours.'

She flushed again. 'Wouldn't one?' and he realized that it was with pleasure.

They had dinner, which took a long time, as Alberta was deeply impressed by it and ate everything. During it, she asked him about New York and the work she was to do, and he explained that they were going first to an hotel and afterwards, possibly, to an apartment which friends often lent them; and as soon as they had cast Clemency, to the country somewhere. In New York she would do all his letters, make the appointments, and accompany him to auditions – at least until Jimmy arrived. Then his wife might want various things done for her – shopping commissions, telephoning, and letters. 'But you'll have some time to yourself,' he finished; 'there is a great deal to see there, and the shops are irresistible to women. There are two warnings: you told me that you're inexperienced about drink: a little drink goes a long way in New York until you're used to it. Secondly, a number of people will want to play Clemency and will stop at nothing to get an audition or to see me at the hotel; and still more people will want to know who *is* going to play her, or even looks like doing so. You must never let either of us be bounced by surprise tactics – especially out of working hours, and you must never know anything about what is being decided.'

She listened so solemnly that he said: 'That sounds pompous, but it is not meant to be more than necessary instruction: the American theatre doesn't work quite like ours.'

'I'll do my best. If I get stuck, may I ask you?'

'Me or Jimmy. Don't worry Mrs Joyce with anything unnecessary. We have to look after her: she has a heart trouble.'

She looked at him and her face changed again, as it had for her father. Her face, which was very young but not remarkable, was sometimes unexpectedly beautiful because of the simplicity of expressions upon it. Whatever she was feeling was occasionally to be seen – fresh, and entire – like the difference between looking at clear or muddy water.

Their tables had been removed, and now she was fishing in a battered handbag for a handkerchief, and he noticed punctures on the leather flap where there had been initials.

'We must get you a new bag,' he said gently: he was touched by her thinking of this detail in connection with changing her name.

She pushed it under her seat again. 'It is worn out really – I've had it since I was fifteen: I would have got a new one anyway.'

Passengers were being offered brandy etc., and he asked her if she wanted any.

'No thank you. But I enjoyed the wine enormously; more than any I've ever had.'

'Jimmy told you why we wanted to change your name, didn't he?'

'Yes.' She was silent a moment, and then said: 'I suppose that must be one of the hardest things to accept.'

In spite of himself, he said sharply: 'She hasn't accepted it. That's the trouble.' This was the trap of travelling: the surge of illogical, unreasoning intimacy: to spread it, he asked unseriously: 'What would your father say about that, do you think?'

She thought for a time without answering. 'I don't know. He says that experience is like food, and if one's system is working properly it uses some kinds for nourishing and others should just be eliminated. He says that the most unhappy people are the ones who can't get rid of the useless experience.'

He was past the small personal confidence, and interested again.

'Perhaps good experience – like food – can go bad on one.'

She laughed and said: 'Yes – one mustn't blame the experience too much: it doesn't make itself.' She was silent again; then she said diffidently: 'Do you know what I think?'

He leaned back in his seat thinking: it's infectious – my fault, I asked for it – let's have it. 'No,' he said.

'The whole of life – for people – is like an enormous unfinished carpet with loose ends hanging out, and some people spin a few more inches of a strand, and some weave in one of the existing strands, and very occasionally somebody does both those things: that makes a piece of new pattern in the design which goes on and on. And other people spend their lives trying to see the whole roll of carpet that has been made in order to see what must be done to finish it.'

He was caught by this: laughing at himself for his shady little fears and delighted with her. '*Do* they see it all? Those last people?'

She hesitated: 'I'm not sure. If they do, they can go on to something else: they don't have to be carpet makers any more.'

'You've left out the unpickers. They are often sadly diligent.'

'I have: indeed, they are.'

'Then you could have some who are like moths: they simply eat carpet. It is amazing that any carpet gets made at all.'

'It should be amazing,' she said seriously. He looked at her; recognized the amazement, and there was no more to be said.

Lights were being dimmed in the aeroplane; chairs were being flattened; people were settling for the night, and she went to wash. How she avoided the little mantraps of personal remark and confidence, he thought: she had made the climate for their conversation – he had simply responded, because for once, and unusually, he had felt in good company.

She came back with freshly brushed hair, washed face and shining eyes. 'Goodness! Isn't it all beautiful – neat luxury – like an egg!'

When she was sitting in it, he said: 'Now: this thing is called a Slumberette; they will bring bits to fit on to it for our feet, and the rest of it subsides under one until one is helplessly comfortable. You press this and lean back.'

She pressed the knob and shot backwards with a startled gasp, but 'they' were instantly on the spot – rescued her, and packed her with blankets into a comfortable mummy.

'Do you want to read for a bit?'

She shook her head, so he turned out her light, and adjusted her air conditioning so that it did not ruffle her hair.

'If you can't sleep, there is your reading light.'

'Thank you so much. Are you going to sleep?'

'After a little neat luxury.'

When he returned, she was already asleep, and he felt suddenly alone, and crowded by the thoughts he had by himself. This was the time, he knew, to make the adjustment that this kind of travel hardly allowed: of time, and place, of work, people, incident, and country. The end of a day which one has physically left behind one is a different end. Poor Lillian: she had made the worst of his departure, and she would be suffering for it, and, possibly, making Jimmy suffer with her. The confounding thing about Jimmy was that just when one was getting irritated by his creed of vicarious living, and watching his comfortable selections from one's life with mounting resentment, he engaged himself for one so thoroughly that one was touched all over again. He didn't like boats; he was raging to find a Clemency in New York, he was worrying about the TV performance of *The Molehill*, and he found days and days of Lillian's company difficult. Well – by the time they arrived he might have fixed up the apartment; that would be better for Lillian – for all of them. Alberta was too young in some ways to manage hotel life by herself, and Jimmy always lived with them wherever they went. Then they would find somewhere in the country for a few weeks: not by the sea because it made Lillian miserable not being able to bathe, but in good, deep country – Massachusetts, for instance, would be about right: then he would be able to get down to New York from time to time if necessary. Then, for a few weeks, they would have what the Friedmanns at lunch today had called 'a lovely home'. It gave him pleasure to think about the Friedmanns – partly because they knew so clearly what they wanted – partly because he had been able to give some of it to them. He had enjoyed his lunch today more than usual – although he always found it interesting, but, possibly because he had not on this occasion seen them for nearly a year, the effects of their continuity and change had impressed him more than before. The house was the same: comfortable, beautifully kept, and furnished more heavily than ever with a kind of imaginative vulgarity. Thus, to strike a match you went through some mechanical whimsy; to sit down you removed one of the flouncy dolls who used to sit on beds in the Twenties pretending to be Gertie Lawrence at the Chelsea Arts Ball; to turn on a light you approached an Elizabethan manuscript in full sail; the lavatory paper was concealed in a musical box which lashed out Swiss banalities at you; the sitting room had the bursting flaccid appearance of an overripe plum.

Mrs Friedmann had received him: she had put on weight, and was generally glowing with maternal wealth. She had such a sense of occasion that she invariably dressed for it to be on the safe side. Today she was dressed in lavender marocain, with a good deal of angular expensive modern jewellery at key points like road signs, and shoes whose burning discomfort had only to be glanced at to be believed. She was corseted from just below her neck to just above her knees, which streamlined her imposing bulk, and she was heavily made up with blue eyelashes and a purple mouth, but this did not detract from her habitual expression of active delight.

'Come in, come *in*! When we heard you were to come we were so happy. Hans is getting some wine to be prepared, and the children are not yet from school here. But please, please come in.'

In the sitting room they both sat down: Mrs Friedmann, however, never wasted preliminaries.

'I have been so anxious for you to see our children – they have so much changed in the last year. But first I must again thank you and assure you that I love them all the time as my own, but sometimes I think *more* than that because I have had time to know what the loss is of no children, and these two are so remarkable that it is my honour to care for them.'

'You've thanked me quite enough before, Mrs Friedmann, and really for very little. It is the children who are lucky . . .'

'Children should be above luck! But I know that I can never repay you, but I am happy to owe you so much.'

Here there were sounds of children in the hall and her husband arrived.

'Mr Joyce, I am delighted to see you here. Berta, you will perhaps now go to the kitchen, my darling angel, and finish that our meal may be soon? I have sent Matthias and Becky to wash their hands again.'

She went at once, and he looked admiringly after her.

'My wife is as good as she is beautiful.' He got some sherry and poured it out. 'Mr Joyce: since I do not wish to mix business with family matters I will try to put the business in a nutshell. As you know, at the time that you so kindly approached us with the children, I had no work, no money –

nothing. If Berta had been able to have a child I should have been overjoyed, but I should also have been desperate. It is only because of your great generosity that we were able to take Matthias and Becky and do for them all that we could wish. Our happiness is extremely good, and Berta has been a different woman with her life so rightly filled. But now is different: I prosper each year and have now twenty-five men working for me and three delivery vans and all premises convenient. I can now afford to educate the children and buy for them everything that they need.' He raised a hand as Emmanuel was about to speak. 'Only for one thing. Money of yours has been saved now for nearly a year: if more of it might be saved I would buy Matthias a good instrument. I have heard of a Gagliano going very cheap, and it is a very fine instrument. I have a friend who knows of these things, and he has tried it and says that it is worth what they ask. When we have bought it for the boy we do not need any more money. Some money I have already put down for the Gagliano to secure it for him but he does not know. Berta wishes to put ribbon round it and make a surprise.'

Mr Friedmann took nothing for granted. Emmanuel could not remember any conversation they had had which did not, so to speak, start at the beginning: each time his situation after the war and his subsequent gratitude was faithfully and persuasively outlined before he arrived at present affairs. Emmanuel also knew by now that it would not do to agree immediately about the money: that he was meant to consider Friedmann's proposals at least during lunch – if not longer. He therefore replied with weighty caution, and Friedmann was delighted.

'Of course! You must have all the thought you could wish,' he said, his eyes blazing with innocent conspiracy.

Lunch – and the children. The girl had grown since he last saw her and was something of a beauty, with a very white skin and enormous slanting eyes. She gazed at him solemnly throughout the meal, but whenever he looked directly at her, she hung her head, her black hair flopped each side of her face and she gave him a rich slow smile. The boy – he was older –

was awkward and very shy: with his gentle, protuberant eyes, elaborate nostrils, and small delicate mouth, he reminded Emmanuel of a young hare – since he seemed quiveringly poised for some convulsive movement which would defy pursuit. Both children spoke German and English indiscriminately, but a guest was clearly an unusual event, and they did not speak unless they were asked to do so. As soon as they had finished they kissed their parents and left the room. Friedmann told Becky to fetch her drawings and Matthias to tune his violin. Mrs Friedmann served coffee, and Emmanuel congratulated them both on the children. Mrs Friedmann glowed.

'They are different. Just has Matthias grown out of sleeping with the piece of bread in his hand. All these years he has needed it, not to eat, but to know that it was there, but lately he has been collecting pictures of composers and musicians – newspapers, postcards, anything – and sticking them to the wall round his bed, and every night my husband goes to see him and they talk about one of the people in the pictures. My husband knows a very great deal which Matthias wishes to know. They were talking about – Schumann, was it, Hans?'

'Schubert, my darling, Schubert.'

'Ja, ja. I know nothing at all! Of course Schubert who was so poor, and after as Hans was to go Matthias held out the bread and said: "I don't need bread at night." And since then no more bread.'

The girl, they said, was an easy child. After all, she had only been a baby when she left the camp – a few months old, with nothing, or very little, to remember.

'But the boy does remember, too much.'

'What does he remember?'

'He will not say. He will never talk about it. I know, only from the questions he asks me now – difficult questions with some knowledge behind them.'

Mrs Friedmann interrupted: 'Yes. And you know we gave them days of birthday as they had none and we did not know how to find them? Well, last June, when Matthias was to be thirteen, on his day he said: "This is not my birthday: then it was cold."'

'Sometimes I cannot *answer* him, Mr Joyce,' said Friedmann. 'I have no good answer for Buchenwald – perhaps I do not wish to find one. He ask why, why, all the time. Why this for one because he is such and such, and that for another. I say to him: "You are a boy; Becky is a girl: you are not the same. You are a Jew, and your friend" – he has one friend from school – "Martin is a Gentile. You have music, Martin wishes astronomy, Becky likes to draw. You are not born the same, and therefore injustice is nonsense." He is passionately concerned with justice: everybody must have the same, but I think when the mind is very young there is a confusion between having and being. But I think also he will learn because he wishes to know.'

'And Hans will tell him,' Mrs Friedmann looked at her husband with a certainty that went to Emmanuel's heart: 'because he is knowing so much of everything.'

Friedmann smiled at her, but said nothing until she had gone ahead of them to the sitting room, when he smiled again at Emmanuel and said: 'As you see, Mr Joyce, the philosophical responsibilities of this great household are entirely mine.'

In the sitting room Matthias stood by the piano with his fiddle, and Becky lay on the floor with a drawing block. They had hardly sat down before Matthias said 'Bach', and began to play.

It was a long time since he had heard any unaccompanied Bach, and the sound was a royal shock to him; waking suddenly some part of the heart that keeps awe and adoration locked: charging and changing his body with a stream of joy. Then he looked to see it coming from the boy, but the boy had changed too: he was no longer shy or awkward; he had now a kind of gallant stability – he was struggling with music too difficult for him and an indifferent instrument, but his eyes were luminous with intention, his mouth still, his whole face and body serving one purpose. He was too young to conciliate or to compromise with his instrument: he treated it sternly as though it was the best, and made his own whole in spite of it. Afterwards, nobody said anything, until Becky looked up from her drawing, and said: 'Well done, Matthias, you can very nearly play that piece now.'

He had left soon after that, but as he sat now in the aircraft the boy's playing occurred all over again and shed light on his memory either side of it. He had promised the Gagliano, and said that he would write about the rest of the business from New York: but in the taxi he had had other thoughts – of regret, envy, and confusion. These were the children who were connected to his worst mistake with Lillian: so sure had he been that she would want and love them that he had gone far in the arrangements before he told her, and when he did they had both suffered a bad shock – as they fought their way through layers of dishonest objection and justification to the raw bone of his wanting to pay for the war which he had not fought, to her wanting nothing but their child. To wanting Sarah back, in fact, or another Sarah. He looked at the girl sleeping beside him, and for a moment, imagined that she might be his daughter. He would only have had to marry Lillian three years earlier . . . But Lillian's daughter had died, and so had the parents of Matthias and the parents of Becky – if this girl had been his daughter she would be dead now – if he had been the father of either Matthias or Becky he would be dead now. These were matters of fact – of accident? Where would little Alberta put that in her carpet? When he had left the Friedmanns he had said to them that he did not think the children could possibly be in better hands, and meant it, and Mrs Friedmann's blue-fringed eyes had filled as she said: 'We *love* them: but Hans will see that it is wisely.' What he had really meant, he discovered, was that he and Lillian would not have done so well even if she had wanted them. 'We're really not fit for it,' he had thought, churning along in his taxi, and then the boy's music had come back – he had accepted his unfitness, and wondered whether when one thanked God for Bach, one did not also thank Bach for God. Compassion for Lillian filled him, because she did not see their unfitness, and he made a promise to look after her well on the journey. And then, accident, which trod softly on anyone's dreams with the confident deliberation of a cat, had prevented Lillian and substituted Alberta, and it was he who had been looked after in the end. Interesting – that the best parts of the day had been the boy and this girl beside him. Two children . . .

He was tired, and empty now of reminiscence – the small domestic lights of his day went singly out, and thoughts recurred in faster and more distant fragments, until – mere pinpoints of light – they too were gone, and blankness rolled slowly over his senses like a blind. But when the darkness seemed complete – just above the reach of his daily mind there was a light – more clearly to be seen as it shone alone: he knew he must turn towards it and climb until he touched it in order to work again, and it was then that he began the slow ascent.

4

ALBERTA

New York

Darling Uncle Vin,

This won't be a long letter, because in spite of there being so much to say, I seem awfully tired, and I haven't even written to Papa yet. There is one trouble. It is about my flying here with Mr Joyce. As you know, this was a last-minute plan because poor Mrs Joyce was ill, and I asked you at the airport not to say anything to Papa about it, as I know it would worry him and I am too far away to put him at his ease about it. I suppose if I wasn't so far away, he wouldn't worry, but I am, and he would, and so I have decided to deceive him. This is wrong, but to tell him now seems wronger. Isn't that odd? I don't think I've ever been in this position before. Please write to me about it and write to me anyway. We had the most enormous and grand dinner on the aeroplane you can imagine: hors d'oeuvres, cold soup, salmon, chicken, ice cream and little chocolate things, cheese, fruit and coffee and a pale yellow wine (not champagne but still delicious) and sherry first, and brandy afterwards but I didn't. Mr Joyce is very interesting to talk to. He listens, for one thing – that was when I told him about Papa – and he sticks to the subject so that one doesn't just stop at the beginning things people usually seem to say. He told me a bit about what it would be like here, but it is too soon to tell you how accurately. But he made it all sound much easier than I had been feeling it would be, and he was charming about Papa, and said he would like him. Quite soon after dinner I went to sleep like a hedgehog I was so full of food. You sit in wonderful chairs that fall over backwards to make you comfortable, but I woke up very early because I was cold and rather stiff, and Mr Joyce got my coat and most kindly wrapped it over my blanket. He looked awfully tired – as though he hadn't slept at all, but he said he had a little. It was light again: the sky is quite different when you are looking out into it and not simply up – you can love it instead of just admiring it. It was misty below, so I couldn't see America even when it was beneath us, but Mr Joyce said we don't come over New York – just a rather dull beach. We had coffee and orange juice – a whole glass full – and then we started to come down, which hurt my ears in spite of swallowing and blowing my nose. Suddenly through the mist I saw land quite near, and the airport buildings slanting up at us. When we came down the rubber tyres *smoked* as they touched the ground, and in the end there was a kind of ticking noise when we stopped. It was seven in the morning (quite different for you Uncle Vin) and there was a feeling of us all starting a new life. The airport didn't seem very different except for people's voices. Mr Joyce was photographed getting out of the aeroplane, and it took us ages to get through the Customs, but then we had a car to drive us into New York. Enormous advertisements – really as big as houses – and the most beautiful bridges and sometimes the traffic goes at different levels so you can't work out where you are going to be, and the sun had come out so that from a distance New York looked like a bunch of upright needles glinting, and the newborn feeling went on when one looked at them. All the traffic seemed deliberate and silky, but Mr Joyce says it isn't in the city. When we got there it was like being in a ravine sometimes, but with sky at the end as well as above, and that somehow makes one feel more on the surface of the earth and very small. At the hotel the girl in the lift was a terribly pretty black girl, and everybody says 'You're welcome' when you thank them for anything. We are on the sixteenth floor. I have a small room with a bathroom and shower and telephones. I've unpacked and had a bath and some breakfast – America is a land swimming in orange juice – and I have to go to Mr Joyce's room when he telephones me. I'm writing to you because unpacking made me feel too far away from home to write to them just yet. I think aeroplanes are rather breathless. I looked at *Middlemarch* to see if it had stayed the same; Mr Casaubon's begun to be ill and without wanting to I'm sorry for him. Do you think some people are *meant* to be ill? I wasn't thinking of poor Mrs Joyce: she looked dreadfully unhappy at being left behind, but as though she often has bad luck of that kind. Oh what I most wanted to say: it was so sweet and good of you to come all the way to the airport – I was missing you dreadfully in the car on the way there – and it was much better seeing you again without *soaking* your rheumatic joints through your clothes, darling Uncle Vin I must say you do take family relationships with all your heart, and the least Papa can do is go to *Death for Breakfast* when it comes to Dorchester. I'll write to them tonight – the telephone – I must go.

Your loving SARAH.

20th May, New York.

I have written to Papa, at last. So much has happened, that it was quite easy – I simply said 'we' all the time, and it is only five days now until the others arrive here. It is curious, though, what an oblique difference deception makes: it made me write all the time about events and not my feeling about them. I tried to describe New York but did not succeed at all well. I think this is partly because apart from being here for the first time, everything that I am doing here is new as well – so I haven't had a chance yet to see more than the obvious differences. I've met so many people in such a short time (counted it up – it's thirty-six hours – far more than one new person an hour) and they are all kinds of people I haven't met before, so that now I've reached a point where I can hardly understand what they say. Our life has been like a very crowded map, and we have had to go to all the places as quickly as possible. I don't know how Mr J. stands it – except that he's not as old as I thought – he's four years younger than Papa – and I suppose he's used to it, but on the other hand he's had far more to do than I have. So far we've spent two hours on the letters that were waiting here – goodness! the people who write to him! – and three hours on auditions for the girl called Clemency in his play, which I haven't had time to read yet, although now I nearly know one scene by heart, we've watched it so many times. None of the auditions were any good, but it was very interesting to watch. One poor girl was so frightened that she sat looking at her script and not saying anything until she burst into tears, and Mr J. was very nice to her and asked her to come back, although he said afterwards that she was much too tall anyway. He is an extremely kind man. Then we had an extraordinary picnic lunch in an office with two men who had been at the auditions. They just ate yoghourt because they were dieting, but they talked about what they would have liked for lunch all the time we were eating ours, until I must say it got quite difficult and hard-hearted to go on eating it. They asked me if this was my first time in America, but otherwise they talked to Mr J. about the play. Then we went to Rockefeller Center which is just like a whole town going on in one building with lifts – no, *elevators* – being the transport, like trains. Mr J. had to rehearse his introduction to another play of his they are doing on television. That is a whole other life too, and fearfully complicated. Mr J. only had to sit in a chair and talk, but it had to be the right amount of time, and they wouldn't let him read from the piece he'd dictated to me in London. So that took much longer than it was meant to, and we didn't get away until half past six, and he sent me to telephone some people to put off a drinks engagement, and that's when I realized to my horror that he was taking me with him to the public dinner at eight thirty that evening. It was evening dress, and I haven't got one because the green net that Aunt T. made two years ago was really too childish to bring. I felt so miserable about this, that I didn't dare say anything until we were outside Rockefeller Center, waiting for a cab. I didn't want to go to the dinner in the least and I was feeling awfully tired, but I knew he didn't want to go either – and not having Mrs Joyce must be making it far worse. The trouble is that none of my clothes seem right somehow. I've got my silk dress here, but honestly it's the kind of dress that secretaries seem to wear after breakfast – it no longer seems to have an element of festivity about it. Well, I told him in the end: I was afraid he'd be angry, but I explained that I would let him down even more if I went in my dress. I always gabble when I'm nervous – and I went on explaining about my dress sense being unformed, and the dress only just not having puff sleeves because Aunt T. finds them easiest to do, and all the time he was looking at me and I had no idea what he was thinking. (Partly I think that's the heavy lids to his eyes.) Then he said: 'Good. You've provided a perfect opportunity for both of us. We'll go and buy you a dress and a bag and things this minute. I refuse to go to the dinner by myself, and secretaries aren't expected to have evening dresses as a rule, so don't blame yourself. Here's a cab, come on, let's enjoy ourselves.' In the cab he asked the driver what big store would be open late, and the cab man said it depended what our requirements were, and when he was told he thought most seriously and then said he recommended Bloomingdales. (He turned out to be a man who thought seriously about everything.) It was open late that night and he could recommend it personally because his daughter bought her best things there and looked like a million dollars. Mr J. said fine, and thanked him. The driver said we were welcome – Lexington and 60th, and we set off. Somehow Mr J. had stopped me wanting to cry, and both of us feeling tired, and now he smiled at me and said he'd always wanted to do this. The driver said he strongly advised me to make a list of what I wanted to save time. Mr J. began to make a list: he put down a dress and a bag and shoes, and then said what about stockings? The cab driver said that was no way to make a list if one was dressing a lady: we should start scientifically from the skin up – if one was organizing a project one must use plain English and that meant girdle, bra, and panties. Mr J. said he was quite right. The driver said it beat him how some people administrated their simple everyday lives. We got wars, and psychiatrists, and traffic jams just because none of us stopped to check the efficiency of our motivation – he'd been saying this to people for years now and it was surprising how little difference it made, and did we know why? Mr J. said no, why? Human nature, said the cab driver. He didn't speak for a moment and then he sighed and swerved the taxi away from a woman who was trying to cross the road with a dog. It wasn't that human nature ever changed, he'd concluded, there was just too damn much of it. Take atomic energy. That was quite predictable if one was an educated guy, but you could go through every college in the world and still not get the other side of human nature. This was why he had no regret about not going to college although he'd sent his daughter; not that he guessed it would make much difference. Mr J. said it probably wouldn't. Then he got more cheerful, and said well, how was the list? I said we hadn't been doing it because we were so interested, but that was no good. Did we realize, he said, that Mozart could write down a whole symphony of classical music and play a game of chess simultaneously? So couldn't we even fix a shopping list and *talk*? So far as he could remember, we'd omitted perfume, make-up – there was a new non-greasy clingstick foundation selling in five shades in two sizes – jewellery, Bloomingdales were running a line in charm bracelets just now and his daughter had gotten one with miniature bottles of deadly poisons all round it which seemed to him cute and by the way, what was my name? They sold handkerchiefs on which they would instantly print your name or nickname, but perhaps the British weren't so hot on nicknames – anyway, here we were. I said my name was Alberta and he said it was a swell name. Then as Mr J. paid him, he said have a good time mister and he sure hoped I'd be a social credit to him. Then he hooted with laughter, and said forget it – just a political sally, and drove off.

We bought a terribly pretty dress. It was a heavy corded cotton, pale mushroom colour with a little apricot velvet on it. It wasn't the kind of dress I'd even imagined, but it was the only one I tried on; we both thought it was the prettiest, and suited me. We bought a stiff petticoat for it covered with roses and very pretty too, and shoes that matched and *four pairs* of stockings (I've never had so many good ones before) and then two bags. A gold one for the dress, and a black one for day with A.Y. on it in gold. Then Mr J. said what about an evening coat – even the cab driver had forgotten that – and we went to the coat department – up again – and he found a peacock blue velvet coat which he said would be good with my dress. Then we went down again and bought gloves for the coat. Then last of all, he bought me a white handkerchief with strawberries (white ones) embroidered all over it and a bottle of scent which he said he liked and I must trust. It was terribly hot in the store and we both had to carry our overcoats. All our parcels were being packed together: he said that he would go and collect them and then he suddenly thrust some money at me and told me to go and buy underclothes while he got the parcels, and meet him at the entrance we had come in by. 'You must have everything new at once for once. Just spend that, and get as much as you can.' It was a fifty-dollar bill. It seemed a lovely meaningless amount – I realized then that dollars weren't being money to me at all, and we'd bought so many things so quickly that the whole expedition seemed a mixture between an adventure and a game. I spent all the money except for a few small coins, and got the most lovely things I've ever seen in my life. It wasn't until we were in a cab, and I saw the great pile of parcels, and remembered Jimmy giving me a ten-dollar bill yesterday in London, and my saying that I'd keep careful account of it that I suddenly realized that all these things must have cost a great deal of money – much more than I was earning, and anyway I'd planned to keep that for Humphrey and Clem. I don't think I've ever felt so suddenly and completely dreadful – so burning, and ashamed, and caught out by myself. I couldn't say anything – and there seemed nothing that I could do – except wear the things, and thank him for taking so much trouble, and pay him back for them by degrees. He was smoking quietly, and then, as though I had been thinking aloud, he leaned towards me and said: 'Don't worry so much. This was my idea, my responsibility, my pleasure. I am not in the habit of doing it, but it was necessary this evening. It has nothing to do either with conventional scruples or your salary, and if I have overdone it, it is a reflection upon my character, and not yours. Will you please remember what you told me about your father giving away clothes to people who needed them?' I said people didn't need evening dresses, and he said I shouldn't be too sure of that. Then he said: 'Because Mrs Joyce isn't here, I am asking you to do far more than either of us expected of you. This' – he indicated the parcels – 'is all part of that. Do you understand now?' I think I do. At least I felt very much better – as suddenly as I had felt worse. At the hotel, he said we had only got three-quarters of an hour to change, and would I come to his suite as soon as I was ready, because he was a quick changer? So I put on all the wonderful new clothes, and powder and lipstick and my locket, and brushed my hair a lot, and scratched the soles of my shoes and put the ten-dollar bill in my new golden bag, and some scent behind my ears. Aunt T. says that ladies should only wear a touch of scent, but although it smelled delicious in the bottle, I couldn't smell a touch on me at all – so I put on a whole lot more until I could smell myself quite easily.

He was quite ready and standing by the window. He said: 'Take off your coat: I want to inspect you.' He looked at me with careful kindness – very like Papa. 'Well, I must say, I think we both have excellent taste.' He touched my locket with his finger. 'What is that? Topaz?' I explained that it was my mother's and Papa had given it to me for the journey here, and that there was a beautiful ring as well, but that Papa was keeping that for me until I was married, and he asked immediately: 'Are you going to be married?' I said I didn't know, but that if I didn't, Mary or Serena would, and that there was only one ring. 'You have no plans about it then. It is a distant point.' I said it was out of my sight, and he put on my coat, smiled, and said: 'You like the scent.' I said yes, and explained that I had only Aunt T.'s hearsay to go on about the right amount, and that I hadn't agreed with her. I asked him if he could smell me properly, and he said: 'Distinctly,' so that was all right. When we got to the lift, I thanked him for all the beautiful clothes and everything: he looked very pleased and said that he was enjoying them just as much as I. As we went down in the lift, it felt as though we had been doing that for weeks, and not at all since this morning, and I asked him whether he found the measurement of time more of a convenience than not. He was feeling in his pockets for something, and asked the lift girl (another one, not nearly so pretty, and they are called coloured, not black) to go back as he'd forgotten something. 'Notes,' he said: 'I've got to make a speech.' I keep forgetting that he's the kind of man who has to make speeches and gets photographed. While he was away, the girl asked me if it was my first time over, and I said yes, and she said she hoped I was enjoying it and I said yes. When he came back he said he found measuring time more *in*convenient than not – that it was a scourge for writing plays, and either dull, or nerve-racking in the rest of his life. 'Like this evening – you'll see,' he said, and looked somehow bitter, and friendly at the same time.

I did see. I can hardly write about it – it was so terribly dull. Boiling hot – and so much to eat that I couldn't taste anything after a bit, and people who seemed to have known each other for years not at all well. He was very kind, and kept introducing me to people, but they only asked me if I was an actress, and if it was my first time over and whether I was enjoying it. In the end I wished I *was* an actress, just to make a change in the conversation. There were a lot of cinema men and their wives and the whole thing was in aid of something, but I couldn't see how we could be helping anyone by having a huge, dull dinner. I couldn't even sit next to him at dinner, because he was the guest of honour and I was fearfully dull for the men sitting on either side of me. I asked one of them if they had read *Middlemarch*, but he said he hadn't – he hadn't even time to get through *Reader's Digest* so a book would be out of the question. He must be dreadfully busy, because even Mr Asquith, when he was Prime Minister, had time to read at least fifty pages of a new book every day. He asked me what my ambitions were about two courses later, which seemed a funny way to put it, and I said I wanted to be a good woman, and he stared as though I'd said something rude, and then said I sure looked good to him, so I suppose he misunderstood me and thought I meant good in his moral sense and not in the Christian one at all. So then I tried the other man, who looked older and asked him what interested him most and he said golf, but his heart had packed up and he'd had to fall back on painting. I said what an interesting and lucky way round, and then I realized that I was being narrow-minded about golf: conversation is much more difficult than I thought. I've hardly ever talked to people I haven't known in some sort, excepting Mr J. and of course he is different. He smiled at me twice during dinner, and that was much more like speaking than anything else. After dinner, there were two speeches before his, and I felt awfully sleepy, and couldn't understand what they were talking about – they seemed to veer without any warning from vast generalizations to something that happened to them last week, with people fidgeting or laughing so that one couldn't hear. Mr J. was the best: he didn't talk for very long, but he was much easier to understand. Then there was another long time after the speeches, and then I had to queue to collect my coat and had to get change for the ten dollars to give something to the woman, and didn't know what to give her. I gave her a dollar in the end (this was too much) and then we got into a car which was waiting for us and my head ached. Without meaning to, I went to sleep in the car, and Mr J. woke me up when we got back to the hotel. Well – I *have* written about it. But it's clear that there isn't going to be time here to write the kind of diary that Mary and I write at home. I shall have to try and select the salient points – if I understand which they are in time. Mary will be disappointed, because she will be writing hers (she was terribly pleased with the one I gave her) and we were going to have a tremendous read to each other when I go home. It has taken me all the afternoon to write to Papa and write this. One thing is clear. I am very lucky to be working for Mr. J. because he is the most considerate and kind man. He has given me the afternoon off to rest before we go to the opening tonight of the musical version of his play called *The Orchid Race*. Extraordinary name – what can it be about? I have never been to a first night in my life – and to go in these rarefied circumstances will certainly rank high in my experience of the world. But then, my dear Sarah, your experience is laughably little. I feel like Celia: can it be possible on such a sudden, I can fall into so great an experience? My goodness, I couldn't have managed without my lovely new dress. I've just thought: accounts of places are not very interesting, unless one has some idea of the writer's feelings about them – or their feelings generally. There seem to be two kinds of life going on, then, and when very little seems to be happening is when one has a busier life inside. So much seems to happen here to everybody, that I wonder how they manage the inside part. It seems to have got the wrong way round somehow – it is the skyscrapers who seem so calm and immovable and they are filled with scurrying people, instead of the people being calm and scurrying inside. Scurrying is the wrong word: I must say I'm glad I'm not a writer. What am I? Somebody on a brink, I should say – like thousands of people – so is the brink private, or universal? I think the *idea* of a brink is universal, and the actual brink is always a private one. Clem would say this is half-baked philosophy – but I don't think I can manage yet with ready cooked.

CHAPTER III

1

EMMANUEL

On the morning of the day that Lillian and Jimmy were to arrive he went for a walk. He went early – because he was sleeping badly: the ship was due to dock at half past ten, and he needed refreshment for the day. He started uptown, along Madison Avenue, with no particular sense of direction; but the faint, elusive liberty which always stirred when he left a night stretched now in the early air and encouraged him simply to go on. He had left a message for Alberta that he would breakfast with her at 9.30 before they went to meet the travellers. In a sense, he was meeting them now: apportioning appropriate pieces of himself to the cut-up artificial day which lay ahead. Their arrival, which ought to be a beginning, was seeming, somehow, an end. Had he enjoyed Alberta's company so much? It was hard to say. He had liked the alternating solitude and company of somebody undemanding, eager, and new to the offerings of his daily life. He had enjoyed being kind, because his kindness had been so simply enjoyed. I am not so kind as she thinks me, he thought – yes, to her I am that: and she is one of the very few people who accept what I am to her uncharged by what I am to anything else. She had made an ordinary, tiring week interesting and worth the candle at both ends. Or perhaps he simply enjoyed the freedom from intimate routine difficulties. No Clemency: Lillian loathing hotels except when they were on holiday – the hunted expense of privacy . . . Supposing one bought one's oxygen for the day every day – that would be a nice direct way of paying for existence, instead of having it clothed in State taxes, with privacy like mink; a luxury to be flaunted by people who didn't know what to do with it. But perhaps there were animals – like the mink – who could wear privacy for free. The trouble was not so much that one was trying to avoid paying for things, it was trying to find out how to pay. When you buy something – on the whole you choose neither the price nor the currency. Some people seemed to spend their whole lives trying to pay for one thing without knowing how to do it – and probably I am one of them. If they know, of course, there is an element of dedication – there is more height and light about it – a little dignity and the possibility of something more than mere behaviour. The passionate interest now commonly displayed in the sub-conscious was probably due to the fact that hardly anybody's behaviour rose above that point. It was therefore natural that they should pay large sums to see anybody who had achieved even partial control of their bodies – let alone anything else. Am I, in any sense, a dedicated man, he wondered? Jimmy would say that I was dedicated to the theatre – to writing plays. Lillian would say that I ought to be dedicated to making a life with her. I don't think either of them would stop to consider these purposes: why should they – they are supposed to be my purposes, and I haven't stopped to think about them much. He stopped now in the street to consider them, but arresting his body, he lost his mind: it noted that he was on the corner of East 57th – it reminded him that this was Lillian's favourite street because of the picture galleries, and then it asked him why he had stopped at all. At that he went on; observing the morning and the scene set in it – the sky a startling blue – air like soda – the light freshly minted by sun – the streets clean and almost empty – too early yet even for people walking their dogs – the scene not yet swelling with its crowds: an empty city has an innocence which country, inhabited on a much larger scale, has not, he thought. He was back to how they were to inhabit this city that day – the four of them. After Lillian and Jimmy had arrived they would go straight to the apartment on

Park Avenue. Lillian would start to unpack – would say she couldn't possibly face it, and that she wanted her favourite morning drink of champagne and orange juice – and then they would all sit in the sitting room exchanging little canapés of news until it was time to decide where they should lunch, which meal would compromise between a festivity for Lillian and a businesslike snack for Jimmy. Then he and Jimmy would go off on the audition racket, and Alberta would help Lillian unpack and hang her pictures. Once he and Jimmy were in a cab and on their way to the west side, Jimmy would relax and ask him all about the week. He'd ask about *The Molehill* and what cuts they'd made; he'd ask about *The Orchid Race* (it looked like a smash hit and he'd enjoyed it in a detached sort of way); and of course he'd ask what the Clemencys had been like. Then he might ask if the new play was shaping, and he would answer no, it wasn't. Finally he'd ask how Alberta had made out. And he would tell Jimmy that she had done very well considering that she hadn't known her way around at all: that she was conscientious and enduring and good company. Then he'd tell Jimmy about the expressions on the faces of Messrs Rheinberger and Schwartz sitting each side of her at the dinner, and leave it at that. They'd go back about six and he'd see Lillian who would have been resting and she'd have an 'at last' expression and ask him all about the week. He'd tell her who had called them up, and what places they'd been offered in Connecticut and Massachusetts, and explain about not going south because they had to be near New York until they'd achieved Clemency. And then she would want to know how Alberta was getting on, and he would tell her that she was very clever to have found Alberta, who was quiet and nice and had very good manners. Then she'd ask if he was getting on with the new play and he'd say yes, he was; that was why he wanted to move out of New York as soon as possible. Here, he broke down: he was cutting a poor pair of figures out of this – the only difference between him and a chameleon was that the creature had real reasons for its behaviour, and he hadn't. He could not say that this flickering dishonesty and failing in either saved his life or earned him his bread – so why do it? Because, of course, they were not the only real reasons for doing anything. Right: if he was not, as a medical friend of Lillian's had once said, an integrated personality, he could at least indulge in a really personal argument – Joyce v. Joyce – or perhaps it was Emmanuel v. Joyce. Very soon after his first success he had discovered that women who were certain of seducing him nearly always said how marvellous it must be to be Irish and Jewish if you were a playwright, and the ones who wanted to seduce him but lacked self-confidence always asked him if it wasn't very difficult for a playwright having so many points of view – sympathy, in fact, was a more tentative approach. This was more than thirty years ago – in England, when class consciousness was more or less confined to the upper and upper middle classes, and had not spread democratically to all 'income groups'. (How the Indians would howl with laughter at this childish equation of money with caste.) The point had been that, with success, he had met a lot of people who didn't want to sound rude or patronizing about his background, were incapable of being anything else, and therefore picked on his mongrel blood as a safer alternative. He hadn't minded; he hadn't wanted to talk about his background either – he had discovered at one attempt a number of shocking platitudes. If your parents had been well off, or even comfortable, it was quite in order to hate them; but if they had been damned poor, and you'd been brought up in what they called a 'distressed area' – the thought of their two rooms and 'area' still made him smile – any breath of criticism was disloyalty and being stuck-up: your parents became characters and you were expected to have a character attitude towards them. So he had never told anybody but one how much he had hated his father in the end . . . by the time he had outgrown the dresser drawer and had to sleep always on his back in it – in winter with his knees drawn high up – in summer with his legs lolling over the end so that the wood bit into the soft place under his knees – he used to lie there and imagine his father dead: in winter of pneumonia – in summer of prickly heat which he had read about and sounded awful enough to kill anyone. But his father lurched and jabbered on; charged with disastrous vitality – bored by everything but his own imagination of himself and haunted by all the chances he might have had. By the time he was eleven, he had been earning more regularly, at least, than his father: by the time he was twelve he had caught his father pinching these wages out of his mother's pocket and had knocked him against a gas bracket which had knocked him out. This random shot – which had astonished Emmanuel – had terrified his mother and produced a kind of angry respect in his father for a day or two, but when this was succeeded by a menacing swagger, he felt it was time to leave . . . That was one morning he would never forget – November; raw and foggy; six o'clock, the time when every other morning for months he had lit a candle, wriggled out of his drawer, pulled on a jersey over his shirt (he slept in all his clothes but his jersey in winter), eaten the piece of bread and dripping left out for him overnight, and trudged off to the stables where he worked. Fifteen milk ponies: they all got a small feed before being harnessed for their rounds, and he used to pinch a pocketful of oats to eat while he fed them. The stables were dark but comforting after home; he liked the warm smell of manure and the ancient smells of dirty harness and dried sweat, and the animals welcomed him with confidential nickers as they stood in their line in patient cynical attitudes awaiting the day's work. Daisy, Bluebell, Captain, Lilly, Brownie, and Rose, Twinkle, Major, Melba, and Blackie – good Lord, he couldn't remember all of them now – he would feed them – mostly bran and chaff and a few precious oats, and then start lifting their heavy collars down from the pegs on the white-washed wall, and hoisting them on to their shoulders. He was tortured by chilblains in those days; the icy slush of the walk cooled his feet, but his hands were chapped and swollen so that he could hardly grasp the collars, and the men arrived long before he was through. But the morning that he left home he woke even earlier than six, and lay in the dark collecting his final impression of it. Except for the cheap clock with its weary hysterical tick there was silence – darkness, and smells: of distant cabbage; of partially washed clothes – his mother took in washing then, and there was a tub in the corner with garments soaking that these mornings was covered with thin grey ice – the curiously angry smell of mice, like sweated cheese; the little peevish draughts of leaking gas; his father's clay pipe – a blackened greasy odour that was in the imagination until one touched it; the rotting plaster of the walls like damp, sleepy pears; a sour damp rot smell from the floor; the purple Church smell of the book his mother had won at school as a prize; the tea leaves which she kept for the small mat in her bedroom; the faint wafts of urine from the yard . . . he collected it all, and the wanting to pack himself with bread and dripping till the yawning grave inside him was filled. If he had the luck to be shipwrecked on an island in the Pacific, like those holy little nippers he'd read about – if he ever had the chance to go on a crusade, or the King wanted anywhere discovered for England, by God he'd remember this – because whatever his luck or chance, he was making a change for himself. First he was going to earn a lot of money and then he was going to build a huge house and put his mother in it. She was going to have a fur coat – several of them – and nothing to do ever, and the house would be boiling hot and full of Jews because she liked them best. He'd come for her one day in a carriage and four horses and silk handkerchiefs for her tears, and just take her and her book and leave the rotten rest . . .

Some of this blind vehemence overran him even after fifty years, and he bumped heavily into a stranger: they recoiled with dazed aggression and apology, and he was back in New York, shivering from the jolt and needing coffee. He looked round him, having no idea how far he had walked, and made for the nearest drug store across the street. It was while he was waiting for the coffee to cool that he saw a headline in the paper lying on the counter: ATLANTIC STORM: TANKER COLLISION OFF CAPE COD. 'QUEEN MARY' DELAYED.

The whole day changed: he had been certain of it and shivering in the heartless spring air of the street – the sunlight cold and dazzling – the angles of the shadows sharp and deep and crazy and turned at their centre to cavernous draughts: he had felt heavy and cold and old; hemmed in by foregone conclusions, imprisoned by mechanical experience, actually 'doing time' with this day: but now, sitting up by the soda fountain with bars of dusty sunlight round him, his hands warm round the coffee cup and the newspaper spread like a proclamation of chance before him, these little currents of warmth and light and uncertainty brought him to life; the atoms of dust were distinct in the sun – each particle seeming to have a gentle mysterious purpose – so that it was like looking at a magnified bloodstream. I am sitting on this stool, a small and ageing man, and at this moment anonymous to everybody but myself – there's balance for you – that's the right way round for once. I have a power, a little beyond me, to design a certain kind of communication for people who have not got this power. I can show them a certain sense of proportion – give them some balance – which is all that design is for – to put something in its right place in relation to whatever lies on either side of it. Proportion is always beautiful: beauty is always significant; therefore design is always necessary, and I am one of the thousands of designers. He felt an impersonal joy about all this, and looked again at the slow unearthly movement of the dust in the bar of sunlight. He was warm and smiling from the centre of his heart and he kept his head very still until the glow had spread to it, as he had learned long ago not to fly to a piece of paper with the first little vestige of an idea, which merely blunts the memory and renders it indiscriminate. He remembered an argument with Jimmy about this, because not immediately recording them meant that one forgot some of the ideas, and Jimmy had thought this lazy and wasteful. He couldn't make Jimmy understand that it wasn't: that it was wasteful and lazy not to make one's memory work for one; it had to select what was worth remembering and then wait for it – instead of premature explosions on paper – like a bird breaking open an egg she has just laid.

He saw the boy who had served his coffee eyeing him with a kind of apathetic curiosity: nothing would surprise *him*, unfortunately. He asked for his check, what the time was, and what street he was on, and the boy provided this dull information as though his customer was drunk.

As he walked back to his hotel he reflected that usually at this point of his walks – on his return – he was consciously bracing himself, storing up his private life to last for the day when he did not expect to have any, and focusing his patience and attention: but that now patience did not seem to be called for, and his attention was not straining after any particular direction but at ease, and therefore ready.

'. . . and so,' he finished, 'I thought that as I had nothing worse to do, you and I would spend the day.'

She sneezed and continued to look at him expectantly.

'Until the boat arrives at six o'clock. Or do you want a day off to yourself?'

She shook her head. They were breakfasting in his sitting room: she was eating waffles with maple syrup, and he was drinking coffee.

'What would you like to do, Alberta?'

'Tell me what there is.'

He told her all the things he could think of – the sightseeing – going to the top of the Empire State Building, or Radio City – the Frick Collection, the Bronx Zoo, Greenwich Village, shopping – having a Chinese lunch, etc. etc. – and she listened with the impassive but acute attention of a child. When he had run out of what he could immediately think of – and it was surprisingly little – she sneezed again, and he said severely: 'But if you're getting a cold we shan't do any of it.'

'I'm not, I'm not.'

'Well, hay fever. You're probably allergic to maple syrup.'

'I'm not allergic to *anything!*' she said and scraped her plate defiantly, but she had gone pink, and presently she added: 'I'm sorry, but excitement makes me sneeze. I've been sneezing ever since we got here, but naturally I have tried to be unobtrusive about it.'

'You've succeeded,' he said solemnly.

'I expect to outgrow it, of course.'

'Excitement, or sneezing?'

'Sneezing first.'

'Do you mean that you *want* to outgrow excitement?'

'I – no, I don't mean that. I mean that I'd like to be much *more* excited about fewer things. Perhaps even one thing in the end. May I say what I think about the day now? I wish to change the subject.'

'I think we should do what we have to do first, and then see what happens.'

'Move the luggage to the apartment?'

'Yes, and see if the woman did come and clean it, and everything is ready for Mrs Joyce. Perhaps she has had a horrid time in the ship if there was a storm.'

'You are quite right. Let's go.'

'I'd better see if the letters have come.' She went to the telephone, and looked at him questioningly. He nodded. She was wearing a sweater which he recognized as Lillian's – a very pale fawn which she had said didn't suit her skin in winter. With it she wore a dark grey flannel skirt, very old, but well polished English brogues and the stockings he had given her. He longed suddenly to take her out and buy her everything she could possibly want – then he remembered Lillian's remark about Gloria Williams' stockings – and a whole set of extremes reared protectively in his mind, hedging any past from this present – forcing all comparisons to such a background that they were barely distinguishable.

She was asking for the bill to be sent up with the letters. Her high, clear little voice had a command about it which was, or seemed to be, unconscious, and therefore agreeable. She projects herself, he thought, thinking of the exhausting hours he and Jimmy had spent trying to get various people to do this in a theatre. The letters arrived, and there were two from England for her. She asked if she might open them, and watching her pleasure in the contents of the first one, he realized that he couldn't remember when he had last had a letter which he was eager to open.

'Are your family well?' he asked when she had finished reading.

She nodded: she seemed so full of their news that he said: 'I like hearing about your family – do tell me.'

'Serena and Mary both have colds which they say they caught by accident, but Aunt Topsy doesn't believe that illness is accidental, so they are in bad odour. Napoleon has had five more children, but we were expecting her to: she is a cat; she was called Napoleon before we realized who she was. Mrs Facks says the world is coming to an end on November 11th and Papa does not agree with her, but he says that the employment of reason would be cruel as she has so little security. Mrs Facks works for us – off and on – because she has so many children. They live on chips and tomatoes, and Aunt Topsy says she keeps them under a paving stone – they are a very queer colour for people – but they are awfully strong really, because they're always having mumps and things and it doesn't seem to impair their strength. Serena has decided to be a doctor for her career, which is much more suitable than her previous choice.'

'What was that?'

'An admiral,' she replied briefly, and folded the letter.

'What about your brothers?'

'Humphrey is at school, and Clem is still down from Oxford, but staying with an extremely rich friend in Yorkshire which worries Papa, as he says it is healthy to have ideas above your station, but useless to get ideas which aren't your station at all, and he's afraid Clem may with his friend.'

'And how is your papa?'

'Well. This is my aunt's letter, he has simply put a postscript saying mind the traffic being different in America and his blessing. The other one is from my uncle, and I'm going to save it up for a bit.'

'Well, I – we – are going to save all mine,' he said, and stuffed them into his pocket.

Outside, there was far more wind than there had been on his early walk: the sky was hurried by clouds – the streets glittered – and there had been a shower. When they had visited the apartment earlier in the week they had discovered it all shrouded in darkness by curtains and blinds. It had been hot, as the heating was full on; it smelled of stale cigarettes, and when they had turned on some of the lights they were presented with luxury smitten by contemporary squalor. Full ash trays, innumerable dirty glasses of every description, coffee cups, a great bowl of dead dogwood, nuts all over the floor: in the bed rooms, unmade beds, tissue paper, crumpled Kleenex, and dirty cotton wool: the bathrooms were full of used bathtowels and razor blades, the tiles smeared with toothpaste, and in one a stack of newspapers had been put in the bath on to which the shower – which could not be thoroughly turned off – had dripped. The kitchen was spattered with dirty crockery, cartons of half-eaten food, and open tins whose oil or syrup seemed to have reached every available surface. Over everything there was dust, and above the dust a layer of irresponsibility which was somehow disgusting. 'Really, it's as though they were rich monkeys,' Alberta had said when they had surveyed it. 'I mean not quite sure what anything is for,' she had added. They had seen the porter, who assured them that a woman came every day to clean up, and that all would certainly be well by the time they wanted the apartment. Alberta was quite right: they ought to make sure of everything – see that the right beds were made up, and get coffee and flowers and things like that . . .

The porter was a different one: he produced a key, put them into the lift with their luggage, and vanished. Alberta opened the door: it was dark; it was hot; it smelled the same. In silence, they switched on the lights: the dogwood was a little deader, and the odour of its decay was the only addition to a scene otherwise unchanged. He felt suddenly, furiously angry. But for the merest chance, he might have brought Lillian back – to this. He walked to the main window in the living room – he was so angry that his feet hurt on the ground – jerked up the blind, and wrenched open a window. That was not enough: he seized the dogwood and flung it out of the window, and turned round for the bowl which had contained it, but it had fallen to the ground and a sticky green stream oozed from it. That was the last straw. He picked up the bowl, and hurled it into the fireplace where it broke with a cheap dry crash. Alberta said: 'I know exactly how you feel, but this is all my fault, so please don't break any more.'

'That bloody woman – that damn porter – what do you mean, *your* fault?'

'I should have seen whether she came before today. It may not be the woman's fault: she may be ill, and the porter has changed. Anyway, I'm your secretary, it's my responsibility and I'm very sorry. Now we'd better clear it up.'

'I won't have you clearing up this disgusting shambles. I'll call the porter. He can damn well get someone to do it.'

'All right.'

'Well – what are you doing then?' He stared at her aggressively, while he jogged the telephone.

'Opening a few windows: I don't know how else to stop central heating.'

There was no reply from the porter and he went down in search of him. The situation was not Alberta's fault: it was he who had been so confident and airy about the arrangements. His temper cooled in the lift, and by the time he had found the porter, and had a long and dispiriting talk with him, it had frozen to despair. The porter was new – the other man had gone sick – nothing was known of the daily woman, not even her address: in the two days that he'd been on the job five tenants had asked the porter if he knew of a daily woman; he hadn't known one and he didn't know one now. It was not his responsibility to see to the inside of apartments – he had enough to do as it was. Someone had just thrown a bunch of dead flowers out of a window – they had fallen on to a very, very sensitive dog who had bitten a truck driver who had been delivering a monkey at the service door. He was sore because he'd been bitten on the sidewalk and his union only insured him in the truck, and the owner of the dog said it was in the middle of analysis and being provoked to aggression just when it was beginning to understand its social responsibilities was very, very bad for it, as if *he* – the porter – was supposed to be responsible for anything tenants threw out of windows: the last block he'd worked in the windows didn't open and things were more civilized. For all he cared the tenants could throw themselves out – then at least the cops could take care of them and he wouldn't have to sort things out. Meanwhile here was the monkey in a basket cage marked: 'I eat four bananas a day please do not give me more out of mistaken kindness' and no address. Had he, by any chance, ordered a monkey? Well, that left him with a cool seventy-four apartments to call up. Emmanuel looked at the monkey, who, grasping the bars of its cage with tiny grape-coloured hands and glaring hungrily at them was clearly longing for some mistaken kindness. It did not seem as though anyone was going to help anybody. He gave the porter a cigarette, and the porter said he guessed they both better sort out their own problems.

He decided to organize a laundry and a cleaner and book an hotel for a couple of nights until everything was sorted out, but he had reckoned without Alberta. He found her methodically at work. The ash trays, glasses, and cups had disappeared from the living room. The flat was light, imbued with fresh air, and she was on the floor sorting and folding dirty linen and making a list of it.

'There's an electric carpet sweeper and quite a lot of soap powder,' she said cheerfully; 'so if we could find a laundry to take this, everything will be all right.'

'I was thinking of booking an hotel until this was cleared up.'

'I really think that would be the most unwarrantable extravagance.'

'Do you?' She looked so earnest about it that he began to feel light-hearted.

'Yes I do. I mean it really *is* my fault that everything is in a mess, and the least I can do is to clear it up. I do know about cleaning houses,' she added anxiously, 'and feel confident of my success.'

'Do you?' He was smiling at her: he found her language sustaining.

'If you'll trust me: it's the least I can do.'

'I must say I've never seen anybody either confident or cheerful about the least they could do before. I trust you implicitly, but you'll have to tell me what to do.' He suddenly found himself viewing the prospect with enthusiasm: the experience was a new one, and she seemed perfectly suited to directing it.

'Find a laundry, wash up, and make a shopping list are the first things.'

'What about lunch? What about our Chinese restaurant?'

But she said that there wouldn't be time, and perhaps they could have sandwiches. So that, in the end, was how they spent the day, and having decided upon it – or consented to it – everything went easily for them. Years of money, travelling, and Lillian's ill health had left him ignorant of housekeeping, and he recognized that he was probably unduly impressed by Alberta's practical intelligence over it, but he was none the less delighted with the pleasant results she made before his eyes. They made a shopping list and he went shopping obediently to buy a great many things that had not occurred to him since he was young and poor. Then, having done all she expected, he bought wine, fruit juices, and whiskey for Jimmy: flowers – tulips, lilac, narcissi, and freesias – for Lillian: then he wanted to find something for her – couldn't think of anything that he was sure she would like him to give her – got desperate, and bought a box of marrons glacés.

The porter, whom he had not seen on his way out, met him at the door of the taxi with suspicious alacrity, and said he'd sure bought a few items for the home. Emmanuel unwisely asked after the monkey; the porter's face took on an expression of hunted sentiment, and said that he'd called all the apartments, and of those that replied, nobody had ordered a monkey. He carted Emmanuel's load to the elevator and then stood in its door looking uncomfortable. Finally he asked if Emmanuel had by any chance a banana handy. No. It was the monkey's eyes that were getting him down. After all, the notice simply said that the monkey ate four bananas a day; it didn't say that it had already eaten them; there was no chart or anything where you could strike off the bananas as the monkey ate them – and meanwhile it sat in that goddam cage looking mournful and blaming him and he wasn't at all sure how much more he could take. Emmanuel pushed him gently out of the way, and advised him to get bananas.

Alberta seemed to have done so much that he was almost shocked. The living room was clean and orderly: it was now the charming room he remembered. Two bedrooms were done and their adjoining bathroom; she was just starting on the other two and she'd made up all the beds. She had a large transparent smudge on her forehead, and her hair was tied back from her head in a tail. He said that they must stop to have lunch, and she said that she wanted to finish all the rooms first excepting the kitchen: he felt it would be dangerous to stop her. So he went and sat in the living room, and wondered vaguely what it would be like to live somewhere – to have some roots that he had never had since he had left home that November morning. The digs, the theatres, the top back rooms, the faded shady little boarding houses, the arty pinched guest houses kept by war widows who had frozen and starved and ground out of him the pittance for their roofs which was their only hope – the miserable appearances which he had contributed towards keeping up – and the rooms themselves, multiplying now out of his memory into myriad icy draughts from sash windows; wardrobe doors that flew open to flush forth sour sweat and moth balls; the spilled powder and hairpins in the top drawers of dressing tables; the threadbare carpets held together by aged dirt and grease; the creaking skeleton beds with fibrous rigid blankets; the chamber pots and sooty lace curtains; the daguerreotypes of Disraeli and Henry Irving and *First Love*; the spotted mirrors and explosive cane chairs; the papers of anonymous flora that roved and climbed, wriggled and wilted over countless walls; the empty grates with paper fans; the cold, the wet feet, the loneliness . . . What had sustained him then? It was easy to remember. The theatres, of course, a new one each week, but above all, the plays; in most of them strong sentimental or melodramatic meat – there was not their equivalent entertainment today even in the cinema – the plots were rich, like dark plum cake, the ideas behind them simple. Right prevailed and there was no doubt about what was right; Love won through; dramatic justice was done to characters who attempted to thwart courage or chastity; motives were declaimed from the start, and the language (except for minor character parts) made no attempt at contemporary idiom. But when he was in his early teens and working with a touring company, these plays and the people in them, this language, these principles, were life – all and more than he had ever asked of it, and for years he lived with this inversion of reality; from the moment each time that the company took possession of an empty dim theatre, and he was on the stage with its menacing odour of size – its dim whiffs of gas – its chalky sweetmeat draughts, he felt, helping to fly backcloths and brace flats, that he was preparing the scene for life. He did not expect to take any part in it: he had been engaged as a general dogsbody – he shifted scenery, did the calling, fetched drinks for the cast, cleaned out dressing rooms, distributed handbills, packed and unpacked clothes and prop baskets, patched flats, made noises off with tea trays, coconut shells, air pistols, and his own voice, and went on the book for rehearsals. Once, they tried him with a one-line part in an historical drama. He was to come on at the end of the second act and announce the sudden death of a main character to the assembled company. He had no rehearsal for this, as he knew the play by heart and was a last-minute substitution – they simply gave him the clothes and told him to make himself up. This had taken a long and exciting time, and the result had been that at the last possible moment he had shot on to the stage, chalk white, with a spectacular and improbably black moustache, creaking boots, and a cloak several sizes too large for him. He stood for a moment, intoxicated by the dazzling, powdery light, delivered the line, and then, feeling that this was not enough for the occasion, he made a speech – his thin arms whirring inside the cloak like a windmill, his voice, which was breaking, cracked and squeaky with excitement, as he recounted in gory and horrible detail the manner of the character's death. After seconds of paralysis – the hero – a man of considerable, if repetitious, experience, had picked him up and carried him, a small struggling bat, to the wings where he was flung at and fielded by a distraught stage hand. This was his one and only appearance on any stage, and it was good old Elsie who had saved him from getting the sack. Dear Elsie – she was a good woman, and she'd been his first friend. It was she who had tried to explain what came over him to the boss, while he stood speechless and trembling – it was she who gathered him to her exuberant bosom and breathed comfort and stout and Devon violets over him while he cried in an agony of fear and contrition – who made him look at his white and black streaky face in the glass until he gave a watery laugh at the sight – it was she, who, standing like a rock beside him in her corsets, turned the whole thing into a joke with the company . . .

Alberta stood in the open door saying: 'I've had to stop: I'm too hungry.'

She looked like a cross little girl, and then he saw that it was simply another smudge on her face.

'We'll eat immediately.'

He had brought what seemed to him a simple sensible meal; she made a prim admiring remark about it, and ate for some minutes in an awed silence. Then, just as he was wondering why he was wondering what to talk about, she said: 'May I ask you something?'

'Well?'

'Do the people who have auditions for Clemency read the rest of the play?'

He started to say 'of course they do', and then realized that in many cases he didn't know. 'Some of them get the whole script certainly. Whether they read it or not is another matter.'

'But all the ones who are just given that scene we had hectographed. *They* don't?'

'No. But they are mostly the shots in the dark: they are expected to go wide of the mark. Why?'

'Because I don't see how they can be any good in that scene unless they know what it is for. Of course I don't know anything about acting. But I didn't understand the scene in spite of watching so many people read it, until I'd read the whole play. Is it different for actresses?'

'Some people would claim that it was. You see, at the moment, we're not looking for somebody who gives the perfect performance of Clemency, we're looking for a certain quality without which she wouldn't ever be Clemency.'

'I should have thought that that quality would make whoever it was insist on reading the whole play before an audition.'

'Supposing you're right about that. Then what would happen?'

She said simply: 'Then they'd know whether they could be her or not. No, thank you, if I drink any more I'll go to sleep.'

'It isn't quite as simple as that. Do you want to know why?' She nodded. 'A good actress can't always be playing inside her emotional experience. But she must play inside her imagination, which is based on her emotional experience. There is always a margin, you see, beyond actual experience, where the imagination can be pure – untainted by the players' false ideas of themselves. It's their business to keep that margin pure – alive – to enlarge it if possible; it's my business to gauge what it is. I'm talking about good actresses now – artists if you like – not just anybody who happens to act. One doesn't write parts like Clemency for them. Of course, I may be wrong about the play. If I am, then however I cast it, it won't come off. It didn't in London.'

'I thought it was a great success?'

'It's running. I mean it hasn't turned out at all as I meant it to.'

'Does that happen often?'

He smiled: she had an unconscious capacity for his sense of proportion which made him laugh at himself and like her. 'No – it does *not*, and I always talk as though it does, or should. Have some grapes now, and tell me what you thought of the play.'

She put a finger gently on the smoky skin and rubbed it clear. 'Isn't that extraordinary? Imagine collecting bloom; it's something you can't *have* – you can only see it sometimes.'

He looked absently at the grape: he wanted suddenly to hear what she thought about Clemency, and he felt that she mightn't tell him. 'You weren't cloaking your opinions in some sort of whimsical symbolism, were you?'

She looked so startled that he nearly laughed. 'Give me your valuable opinion, Miss Young.'

'I liked it. I like the whole idea: it starts and finishes and seems complete in itself, and there is still something on either side of it.' She was getting pink again, round the smudges. 'My experience of play reading is extremely limited, so I don't think I understood all of it, and therefore my opinion must be of little significance.'

'Do you feel that if your experience of play reading increased the significance of your opinion would go up?'

'It would depend . . .' she began – saw his face and stopped: 'The trouble is that I think I take almost everything seriously, which really only means taking *me* seriously about them. I'm so sorry: it is such a dreary bad habit – Papa says it is the broad highway to being a bore.'

'It's a crowded highway,' he said, as a feeling of affection shifted in his heart, and he wondered what to do with it. 'Is there any more of your insignificant opinion?'

She looked up from the grapes with eyes that were nervous with honesty. 'A bit more. Why do you want me to tell you?'

'I might find something out.'

'About your play.' She did not put that as a question, so he did not deny it. She thought for a moment, and then said: 'About the beginning. You mean her – Clemency – to be beautiful, successful, rich, surrounded by admirers, friends, and achievements, don't you?'

'Yes.'

'And in some ways she is happy like that?'

'Externally.'

'This is the beginning of what I don't understand. After that extraordinary evening she spends meeting the anonymous man outside the theatre, she wants something quite different?'

'Yes. But she can't have it with her existing life. She understands that.'

'*Yes.* To get what she wants she has to give up the success and admiration – all that. But, as she doesn't seem to value them much in the first place, they aren't much to give up, are they? I mean they might be impossibly hard for some people, but they are so shadowy to her that they hardly count. I don't know what you mean by external happiness, but surely you can't cheat by paying for something you want very badly with twopence – it isn't expensive enough – and if she felt she was really rich in the beginning, she'd have something to pay with.'

There was a complete silence: he was looking at her, and he saw her so clearly that in her was his own reflection: he saw so much of himself that there were no words in his mind for it – the few seconds were filled so that they were round and unrecognizable drops of time. She knew something – or understood that there was something for him to know, because she did not break this moment; having furnished him, she was still, and when it was over she waited for him to resume, or assume what he would. It was much as though she had unerringly laid a finger on something that he found it very difficult to find, and left him to count the beats.

When he stirred, she got to her feet, and took their tray into the kitchen, but the sensation of warmth and lightness remained with him. He joined her; she was rubbing her face furiously with a wet handkerchief.

'Aunt Topsy says that to make really light pastry, you should never let the flour get beyond your knucklebones. I don't know how far dirt should go in good housework, but I'm sure it shouldn't get to one's forehead.'

'Are you tired? You've done a great deal of housework.'

'I'm not, thank you. Fortunately I have a magnificent constitution. That was the most delicious lunch; now I'm going to clean up the kitchen.'

'I'd like to help. Shall I dry things?'

'Thank you. There are some rather queer towels, with verses – what Papa calls pupperel on them. Do you think people really *read* their tea towels in America?'

'I expect the poor bored housewife gets something out of them.'

'I know. Everything about food and kitchens is made so dull, they do need something. It's terribly difficult to feel skilful and indispensable with gadgets and pre-stressed food. It's all boiled down to the least you can do, which is so disheartening.'

They washed up: there was a kind of affectionate ease with her that he had only felt before with anybody after making love. She asked him how he had come to write his first play and what it had been about, and these questions which he had so often been asked and answered with a kind of dishonest brevity, got their full reply. He told her about running away – getting frightful toothache the first day; about Elsie finding him sitting in the road outside a pub holding his head and crying; how she took him to her dressing room and got the stage carpenter to pull his tooth out with a pair of pliers, made him rinse his mouth out with eau de Cologne, and then got him a job with the company. He told her about his disastrous appearance on the stage and how good Elsie had been then – how afterwards she had said 'Write it all down ducks – get it out of your system – it will only make trouble for you if you don't and it won't do anybody any good inside. If you can think of all that you said on the spur of the moment, you might write a famous play – with a deevy little part in it for me.' And when he had asked her what deevy meant, she said it was slang, but very refined.

'Tell me about her – what did she look like?'

'There aren't many people like her now – although then she was quite an ordinary type. She had been a blonde, and she'd played ingenues for years until she got too heavy for them. She dyed her hair when it began to fade; she still had a pretty complexion and blue eyes, but I think they'd faded like her hair. She had a fine pair of arms and shoulders – they were much more a point of admiration in those days: women dressed to display them – and for the rest, she enjoyed her food and her stout too much to keep her figure. But besides her ready heart and her practical kindness she combined a sense of adventure with a general cosiness in perfect proportions – at least for a boy of fourteen. She said she was thirty-five, but she must have been well over forty: she only mothered me when I really needed it: the rest of the time she never forgot that she was a woman, and that I would one day be a man. She had a passion for gentility and refinement, but for her they went with high life and romance – she believed in them – she didn't care a damn what the neighbours thought. She'd once had supper with a marquis and it was one of her favourite stories against herself. "Imagine *me*, dear," she used to say, "fancying myself a marchioness because a nice young man liked me figure – the *ideas* we get about ourselves." She thought England was the best country in the world – she loved the theatre, and she was passionately in love with the manager of our company, who treated her pretty badly most of the time, and was frequently unfaithful to her with the string of young women engaged to play the parts she had once had.'

'Did she know about it?'

'She knew. She knew all about him, and it didn't make any difference. You see, she knew a good deal about herself. I only once saw her really down with it, when I burst into her dressing room one evening and found her hunched under her dressing gown struggling into her corsets with tears streaming down her face. "He's off with that Violet Everard now. Each time he says it's never going to happen again; I know it is, but I enjoy him thinking it won't." And when I tried to comfort her, she dropped the dressing gown and said: "Of course he's fond of me, but you help me into these and you'll see what a silly old woman I am to go chasing after what I'm not meant for any more. I've only got to get myself into these to have a good laugh at myself – carrying on like a girl of sixteen inside all this. If I can't learn to be my age, why should I expect him to?" And then she really did laugh at herself, and cleaned up her face and gave her performance – as Violet's mother in the play. It was the only time I ever saw her cry.'

He had forgotten about drying glasses – he was sitting on the table – years away. She took the cloth from him and said gently: 'What about your play?'

He laughed, as though he had caught it from Elsie. 'My play. I wrote it: every single character had a title, and most of them were wicked, except for the part I wrote for Elsie, into which I poured all my ideals of womanhood and goodness, and so the most frightful things happened to her without the slightest effect – she might have been a block of stone, she was so passive, so indestructible, and dull. It took place in an earl's castle: opened with a shrimp tea in the library, and it was called *Evil Does Not Pay*. One of the characters left the stage on a line which ran: "I must leave your blasted presence: you sully the air so that I cannot breathe it," and the hero poisoned a lot of characters in the last act by putting bad oysters in their champagne. They didn't drink anything else, you see, so that was bound to do for them.'

'What happened to it?'

'That was the terrible thing. They did it – as a farce – instead of a pantomime, at Christmas. They let Elsie play the part I'd written for her; they paid me twenty pounds and I was so excited I didn't realize what was going on. I went out and bought a string of pink pearls for Elsie – she loved pink – they were in a box lined with pink velveteen, and I planned to give them to her with a card on the first night. It was she who had given me her bottle of green ink she hardly ever used for writing letters, and her box of notepaper to write the play. They were shifty about letting me see rehearsals, but they were all laughing and saying how good it was – except Elsie, who just kept saying get on with starting another play, and just before they went up on the first night she called me and said she was very proud of me, and if the play didn't go as I expected I must not fret but see it was all for the best and everybody had to get started somehow.'

He stopped, and said: 'I haven't thought about all this for years, and this is the third time today that I've remembered about it.'

'Go on: what happened?'

'They put me in front, in a box all by myself, and for about ten minutes, until the house lights went, I felt no end of a nob. I saw myself wearing a top hat and owning theatres, with Julia Neilson, Lewis Waller, Playfair, Dion Boucicault and others all on their knees to me imploring me for plays. I don't suppose those names mean anything to you, but they meant a lot then – they were the epitome of heroic glamour – thousands of people adored them and collected postcards of them in their famous parts just as avidly as they collect pin-ups today. I'd just got as far as postcards of me, when the house lights went. From the moment the curtain went up, I knew something was wrong; and when I saw the pink flannel shrimps, the size of bananas, and the house laughed at them, my heart dropped like a small burning coal into my boots, where it remained for the whole performance, while I struggled with my feelings. My feelings!' he laughed: 'you've no idea what they were like – resentment, shame, rage, self-pity, sheer, obstinate refusal to accept the situation – shame and rage again. They went round and round, accompanied by a full house in holiday mood, roaring with laughter at what I considered to be my most heartrending speeches, agonizing situations, and beautiful moments. When Elsie came on in a white nightgown several sizes too large for *her*, and a long wig of golden hair streaming down her back, I nearly burst. The conflict was so awful, you see: a bit of me thought she looked wonderful; and a bit wanted to laugh, because she was somehow a caricature of herself, and there was everybody shouting with mirth, and her entrance was one of my beautiful moments – well, I sat there seething until – I don't remember what made me – but I laughed – by mistake, of course: it made me furious; I was crying as well, without any noise – with tears on my scalding face like spit on an iron. And I thought if they could see me now – the author looking like this, they'd laugh more than ever: they were the world, you see, and it would be my fault if I gave them another chance to laugh at me. So I watched the rest of the play with a kind of glassy calm – if I was a failure I was going to be dignified about it. And so I bolstered myself until my nose cleared, and I imagined myself facing the company afterwards, with worldly indifference. I hadn't bargained for the end, at all, when they clapped and the cast started to cry for author; Edward Burton – he was the actor manager – sent for me and they hauled me on to the stage and I found myself standing between him and Elsie, unable to look at either of them, as the bitterness of my failure rolled over me all over again. I had set out to do one thing, and the fact that it had turned out to be something quite different, escaped me. I could only see what I'd failed to do.'

He became aware, as he stopped again, of how much he had been talking; he had talked and talked, and she had finished the kitchen. He made a small conclusive gesture with his hands. 'Well: that was that. But it was the classic example of things not turning out as I had meant them to.' He looked round for a cigarette, and she pushed the packet across the table to him.

'You were fourteen when all this happened?'

'Don't you feel I ever could have been?'

'It just seems so young to write a play and have all that happen, and very hard to bear at fourteen. What did Elsie say to you?'

'Oh, she saved my bacon – or sense of proportion – as usual. She talked to me nearly all night till she was dropping, bless her. Had I realized that lots of people wrote plays who never had them performed at all? Of course I hadn't. Did I realize how much easier it would now be to get another play put on? Of course I didn't. I explained that I wanted to write about life, and she said there was nothing to stop me but I'd have to learn something about it. The best thing she said was that one wasn't born knowing things, but one had a chance to find out what one wanted to know. She – do you *want* to hear all about this?'

'Yes, I do.'

'She said that as I wasn't living in castles with a whole lot of earls, it would be difficult to write a serious play about them and that I'd written a play out of other plays, and not out of what I saw or knew. Then she said: look at her: could I imagine her behaving like Lady Geraldine FitzAbbot? Not her – she wouldn't be so silly: she wasn't pure and high born – she was fat and rather common; she liked her stout and a good laugh and she dyed her hair and she loved Teddy Burton and there was nothing pure or noble about her – but at least I *knew* her. Then I began to see what she meant, and felt so much better that although it was three in the morning, I gave her the pink pearls and asked her to marry me, and she was sweet about it all – the pearls and the proposal.'

'Did you really want to marry her?'

'It may seem absurd to you, but yes – I did, then. She

seemed to me so *good* – such a good, kind creature, and I found that such an attractive quality – I wanted to stay with it. I still feel like that, sometimes.'

'You mean, you still sometimes wish you had married her?'

'Yes – no, that's not what I meant.'

There was a silence, and then she coloured, and said: 'I'm so sorry. Of course that's not what you meant.' She was thinking of Lillian, and her possible implication of disloyalty.

He put his hand on her shoulder – let it rest – and took it away. 'I know it's not what you meant, either.' He understood her – that she didn't know he had not been thinking of Lillian.

In the taxi, driving across town to the piers to meet Lillian, he thought of Alberta arranging flowers and unpacking in the apartment she had so neatly made habitable, and Lillian in the boat locking and unlocking pieces of hand luggage, and worrying about whether he had remembered to meet her. Out of her country family life, Alberta – in the middle of New York – could do what was required of her: she could adapt what she had been bred and brought up to be, because something else in her was steady – was not rocked by outward changes. But if Lillian made physical gestures her body broke down, and he did not think that she recognized any other kind now: her courage was therefore constantly misspent, and sinking into the parched field of her activities. She was as pinned by this fixed image of herself and her desperate efforts to serve it, as Alberta was free to be served by her own imagination. That, he supposed, was the difference – and he hovered above it, uncertain where he should stand . . .

2

LILLIAN

THE restlessness started the night before we were supposed to dock. Up until then, it hadn't entered my head – I don't know why not. Jimmy had been his sweetest – really I'd enjoyed the trip – even when he got seasick, which he always does, poor thing, he was so pathetic and good-tempered about it, and so grateful for being looked after that somehow even his being prostrate for two days hadn't spoiled the journey. I read to him – he still likes C. S. Forester and almost any poetry I choose best, and we had delicious little picnic meals in his cabin although the poor creature couldn't eat much. But he adored being looked after – I think that's never having had parents or a proper home – and it was heavenly to be the nurse for a change. He said I was good at it, and he meant that, which was so warming. He told me about his life in orphans' homes which he's never talked about before, and it sounded awful – much worse than he realized. The sense of being a collection – of everything being based on justice rather than feeling; everybody dressed the same, having the same, acting the same, and knowing everything about each other. He told me that he was sent a tin motor car anonymously for Christmas, and he kept it buried in the garden so that the others couldn't share it and told everybody it was lost and dug it up to touch and look at it by himself. Of course it got all rusted and fell to bits, but he said it was worth it to have a secret. It was the only secret he managed to have, he said, the others all got found out in spite of telling lies. He said that even at the time he felt disconnected from his life – as though he was watching somebody else go through the motions of it. I understand that: that's why he is so useful to Em and adores him so, and I really must *not* be jealous of that. But the night before we were supposed to dock there was fog and we reduced speed and everybody was talking at dinner about how late the fog might make us. It was then: it came over me just like the beginning of a disease or fever that perhaps in a week Em had become attracted to her and seduced her because that would be the easiest thing in the world to do. And immediately I thought what nonsense – think of her – she's just a dull little schoolgirl, and if he wants to seduce somebody, he can do better than that. Then I thought of that horrible Gloria Williams – mincing lethargic creature with those hideous legs – a genteel martyr if ever there was one – if he could get off with *her* he might do anything. The vulgarity of my thoughts about him sometimes appals me, *and* the language in which they are couched, which, of course, is in keeping. After all, *I* picked her, and God knows I have learned to consider this squalid little possibility. After dinner, I asked Jimmy to walk on the boat deck with me, and while he was getting our coats I resisted the urge to confide in him – to share this apprehension: I don't want Jimmy to discover that Em talks to him more than he talks to me, and so I have always pretended to Jimmy that I know everything, and understand, or don't care. But while we were pacing up and down in that curiously heavy, billowing air, I asked him what Em had had to do all the week in New York, and when he told me, I felt much better, because really there would hardly be time to start a new affair as well. Only I do hope we don't get delayed too much by this weather, and nobody will say anything definite about that. After a bit, Jimmy said would I like to go to the movies – they were showing *The African Queen*, which we'd both seen, but it is Jimmy's beloved Forester, and I adore Katharine Hepburn, so we went. Afterwards, Jimmy had a drink and we talked a bit about where we would be in the summer, and I said I wanted to go to Greece, which shook him, but it's quite true – I do, and Em has promised me for years. Jimmy looked miserable, and said he loathed sightseeing, and wouldn't it be too hot, and I explained about my idea of living on an island, and having a really simple life. I also told him that I thought that an island would be a good place for Em to write and be away from the theatre or contacts with it. I begged him not to put Em off, and he looked shocked, and said of course he wouldn't dream of it. Then, suddenly, we had nothing more to say and he suggested going to bed. I couldn't sleep. I read and read: in the end I took a pill, and it was like falling slowly into a heavy warm sea – silent and colourless; dark and empty and immeasurable. At the very beginning of my waking, I dreamed of meeting Em. I could float, which made my movements most gentle, and he was standing on a very small island, with one tree beside him. I felt my hair shining, my skin moist as I rose out of the water and turned to him, nearer and nearer, until our eyes were almost fused in our meeting. Then I saw that his island was floating also – away from me – and that I was not to reach it – that I had come up out of the sea on to my separate island, but with no tree, and I sank on to the pale sand which darkened as the sun went slowly in and I woke. It was late – if there had not been fog we should have docked by now. I rang Jimmy, and he'd had breakfast and knew that we should dock at six. At least we knew. In eight hours I should see him – *if* he was there to meet me – *if* the fog did not get worse – *if* he had news of the time that we were to dock. Jimmy came and talked while I had breakfast and was very calm and stern, and said I was working myself up, and he'd call Em's hotel and make sure that he knew we were due at six. He tried to make the call while I thought how funny it was that I couldn't even *enjoy* being excited any more. The call was no good: everybody was making them, and by the time we were through the delay, Em had checked out – which at least means the apartment is on. I wondered what on earth he and the girl were doing, and started to feel bad about her again. Perhaps I get excited by the wrong things – or perhaps excitement is no good anyway. Really I would like to meet him much more like the first half of my dream – with a kind of beautiful, calm confidence – and very quietly. As it is, I can't keep still: can't eat lunch; get more and more breathless, and a pain inside ticks over like an engine ready to start; the palms of my hands sweat, and I keep thinking that I've forgotten to pack something. And yet, whenever I feel like this – right up to whatever is going to happen – the event seems, as it were, to start without me: I am not in it – all my imagination of it is dislocated and there seems nothing to take its place. Once, I remember him meeting me (also in New York), and within a few minutes, we were having an argument about some dreary people we hardly knew, and I told him how excited I'd been about meeting him, and he said: 'In order to talk about the Smithsons?' And then I remembered thinking that excitement was useless. That's the trouble with me: I hardly have any real feelings – just awful substitutes – intellectual imaginings, and physical anti-climaxes. Yes, but how does one *have* real feelings, and how can I have them about Em if he doesn't have them too? I *did* have them about Sarah. Oh! Sometimes I wish she had lived a little longer so that I would have more of her to remember now; her two years seem so short that I've nearly lost the taste of them: all my memories are coloured with the pain of losing her. Surely that was real – that wrenching, aching loss? Afterwards Em once said to me: 'Only joy is unmistakable: remember your joy in her.' He said it in the kind of way that made me feel it was true, but I couldn't understand him; I didn't accept what he said, because not having been allowed to suffer instead of Sarah, I refused not to suffer as well as she. It's very odd: I think so much about these things – but I hardly ever think about them in this way: it is something to do with the ship being late, and these eight hours being slipped into my life – not how I expected or meant. I understand what people mean when they say: 'I would die for her'; in certain circumstances, not being able to becomes a kind of outrage. There is something weak and dangerous about making a person the centre of your life: people are damaged and die too easily – but *where* is anything indestructible? My chief feeling about Em is fear that I may lose him, and as I've never really had him, this is absurd. It is funny, the way I'm always trying to give things I haven't got, and am terrified of losing something I've never had, but I don't seem to laugh at it enough to do any good. I think it was sometime after lunch, when Jimmy had gone off to tip our stewards and people, that I made a solemn promise to myself that I would honestly try to be kind and generous to Alberta – try to understand and make the best of her; and having made this promise, something of the calm – the dream-like calm was there, and it didn't even seem difficult to do. When Jimmy came back, he went on treating me as though I was terribly strung up – he didn't see any difference: it made me angry that he couldn't see – and that's how I lost my short-lived calm. We had already made the arrangements – I was to go straight off the ship with my dressing case and meet Em, and Jimmy was to wait behind, see all our luggage through the Customs, and follow us – but we made them again. Jimmy said why didn't I have a rest, but I couldn't. In the end, I decided to change; I had a new suit of very pale blue silky tweed which I'd never worn, and a dark blue silk jersey, and some shoes which were very plain, but exactly the same colour. I sent Jimmy away, and he said he was going up to look down on the sea, and he'd meet me at five.

I spun it all out as long as possible: had a bath, painted my nails, massaged my hair – but even so, I wondered how countless women manage to keep quantities of men waiting while they bath and change. Perhaps their minds aren't on it like mine seems to be: as some women are about houses, so am I about my body. It is my house, and I enjoy cleaning and grooming and decorating it; and to do it in an orderly, thorough – almost detached – manner, is pleasant exercise . . .

Time: it fidgeted and jerked; it clung drowning to the last straw of each second; it hung, breathlessly, over my smallest movement. I thought of railway station clocks that move every minute with a comforting convulsion – of slow-motion films, of speedometers, of sand running through an hour glass, of my hair growing, of the sundial at Wilde whose shadow never seemed to move when I watched it, of the only time I saw the Derby, of my forty-five years (I am more than forty-five!), of the way Em can give the illusion of a whole afternoon and evening in a forty minute act, of the seventeen hours with Sara . . . the whole business seemed inexorably elastic.

I tried to read. I thought of all the people in the ship who had expected to arrive this morning – the atmosphere of impatience and frustration had been noticeable at lunch – I thought of the extra drinks that were being consumed to fill in time, of the patient crew answering the same questions for hours, of the New York skyline, the Statue of Liberty, and the number of people who had never seen it before . . . From my porthole, I could see that there was much more wind – the fog had almost cleared, but I would need a scarf for my hair – a white one, if I could find it . . .

The time had its life – somehow – it seemed to me always to have been dead, but in the end, it had to make way for more of itself that had been waiting and that I had waited for. There is the curious sensation in a large ship: when she is moving, her engines, however discreet, pulse like the circulation of blood in a body, and all the people in her seem to move over her with the scurrying, soundless activity of ants – they seem nothing to her mainstream of life and movement: but when she is stopped, these activities break into sounds, she becomes simply a hive for people and their noises; cabin doors, luggage shifted, voices, breaking glass and changing money, greetings and farewells, footsteps going down to collect trunks, and up to the sea gulls. She is no longer moving in the moving water; it heaves and slaps against her with time to repeat itself; the air moves round her with a kind of intricate liberty which was not apparent during her journey.

As I was walking off the boat – leaving the concentrated turmoil of crowded passages and doorways for the spread-out confusion below on the quay, I suddenly saw myself, as though it was the beginning of a film. A tall well-dressed woman picking her way down the gangplank – what is going to happen to her? Is she going to meet somebody, and who will they be? She looks apprehensive, and either she is rich, or it is a very bad film, because she has a mink coat slung over her arm. The camera looks for a moment with her eyes at the scene before her – a casual sweep, and then more searchingly. As it is a film, she is looking for a man: and she is either desperately afraid of him, or desperately in love. There he is – the picture hovers at its distance, and then approaches him; he was in the background, and he does not know we have seen him. He is standing with his weight on one leg, staring at the ship. He is a small man; hatless, wearing a blue muffler, and the breeze is raking up his thick, dark hair. His eyes, screwed up a little against the cold air, are not characteristic like that: they should be still, and very bright, but he does not know he has been seen. The woman – we go back to her – has smiled, and perhaps it is a better film than we thought, because it is not possible to tell from her smile whether she is afraid or in love. Supposing, at this point, as much were to happen to me as must happen to the woman at the beginning of a film; some great change, some violent alteration which illuminates the purpose of itself, so that at the end of it I can see where I am placed . . . While I was waiting for the Customs to clear me, and Em was out of sight, I wondered what change there could be. In a film the change could only fall into one of two categories: the external, and some engagement of the heart or body. I didn't want my externals changed, I suddenly realized, excepting my wretched health – and that would not be merely a change – it would be miraculous. With the help of that miracle, I might even have another child. And yet what were miracles? They seemed generally to be events which the people who benefited from them totally failed to understand. If my health were now suddenly to improve, I should not understand why; I should only know just enough about it not to be able to attribute it to some new drug, because I know that there are no new drugs for me. It was then that I discovered that I had lived all my life on the supposition, the hope, that things would be different; that I lived inside as though I was the person meant for these changes, and was waiting to live in them – in fact, as though I was someone else.

'Have you anything to declare?'

I felt my suspicion reflected in his eyes. He held out his hand for my passport, and I resisted the melodramatic impulse to say: 'I have these papers, but I do not know who I am, except that I am not what I seem: isn't that a declaration?' But he pushed them back into my hand and said: 'You've come to the wrong place, lady. This is for American citizens.'

Still wondering who I was, I asked him where I should go.

'You're an *alien*,' he said, as though that answered everything.

So it was a long time before they let me through to find Em with a taxi, and by the time I did find him, his familiarity was so welcome that I actually ran to him.

'There, darling,' he said, 'there,' and I clung to him knowing all the clothes he was wearing and the smell of his skin, and wanting that moment to tell him everything that I had been feeling and had discovered.

'I wish we ran into each other like two drops of water.'

'Then you wouldn't be able to tell me anything: I'd know it already – you wouldn't like that.'

'Perhaps you do know.'

He signed my face with his finger: he was smiling faintly. 'Is Jimmy going to bring the rest of the luggage on?'

'Yes.' We moved towards the taxi – he was holding my shoulders, and I said: 'Admire my suit.'

'It's charming – I have been.' I looked down myself with him to my shoes. 'They are pretty, too. And you've washed your hair, and look at your hands. You take so much trouble, my darling, do you know why?'

I wanted to tell him, but I couldn't, because I also wanted to surprise him with my answer. Instead, when we were in the taxi, I said: 'Jimmy was terribly sick – for two days.'

He laughed; 'You sound so proud of it. Of course, *you* weren't.'

'Of course not. I looked after him, extremely well. We both enjoyed it.'

He looked pleased. 'I hope he's recovered: he's going to have to go to work here.'

'Have you found anyone for your play?'

'No one. The only possible is tied up with a film contract – she can't leave for long enough.'

'How is Miss Young?'

'I left her covered with dirt. The poor girl has had to clear up the apartment. They'd lent it to some people for a party, and it was a shambles. It's a good thing you didn't come at ten – she's been at it all day.'

'What have you been doing?'

'Oh – buying flowers and things – and walking about.'

'And thinking?'

He looked suddenly guarded, and I added: 'Not about my arrival – I didn't mean that.'

He said: 'I never know what quality one has to reach in one's thoughts to constitute thinking. I have been remembering – do you count that?'

'I do it all the time.' I felt a fleeting contradiction in him, although he had not moved: then he took my hand gently, and said: 'Perhaps "remembering" is the wrong word. I don't mean that I have been recalling exactly what happened: I mean that I have been reminiscing with a selection of events and my impressions of them.'

'Why?'

'I've been trying to find something. The curious thing is that one doesn't just start with revolt – one has a clear, innocent reason for it. At the beginning, something seems valuable: one desires it; it seems necessary and possible and worth fighting for. Then the whole plot of this thickens, and by then one has the experience of activity and struggle and one forgets what the whole thing was for.' He was silent.

'Have you forgotten?'

'Very nearly all the time, but I remembered a little this morning.'

We were both very quiet: then, it costing me, I said: 'Em, I'm not sure that I ever knew.'

He turned to me as though I had said something marvellous, kissed me – and at that moment I could remember his earliest attention and care – 'Yes, you did once; everybody does a little, but they don't make it last, and I don't think I've helped you.'

'It wasn't *you*.'

'It was nobody else,' he said sharply, and Sarah flared up and began to die painfully, as he dismissed her. He took my hand again, and my fingers felt stiff against his. 'Lillian: don't cast yourself on that reef any more. Remember you are here, with me, and that there is more to come. Move in your time: feel what it is – now. You will be so unbearably alone if you live in that other time.'

'I *won't* forget! I don't want to.'

'I'm not asking you to forget anything – only to remember more.'

'Tell me something to remember, then.'

He thought for a moment, put one of his large handkerchiefs into my hands, and said: 'I will tell you. When you were a child – I think you were about ten – you had your tonsils out. Afterwards, your parents sent you away with your nurse for a holiday, and as your nurse came from one of the Scilly Islands, that is where you went. The first evening that you arrived, you were put straight to bed. You were very tired from the longest journey you had ever done – a train from your home to London; from London to Cornwall; a boat to the main island; and finally, a little boat run by your nurse's uncle to the small island which was her home. You didn't notice anything that night: but next morning you woke very early with sun filling the small whitewashed bedroom. You found yourself in a feather bed, which had a kind of bulky, silky softness, and that was as strange as it was charming. You put on your clothes, lifted the squeaking latch as quietly as you could, and went out, because you couldn't wait to start being on the island. Your house was on high ground, and you could see everything. It was rocky, with green turf – like bice, you said, in your paintbox – and gorse, and slender strips of land brilliant with flowers: you had never seen whole fields of flowers growing in your life. The sky was blue, and the sea streamed and creamed round the edges of the island which had rocks and little shell-shaped bays of shining sand. There were no roads, and this made you feel wonderfully free, but not lonely, because there were a few other clusters of cottages and the air above them had delicate veins of chimney smoke. You walked where you liked, up the hill until you came to a smooth grey rock shouldering out of the ground. And there you found a little hollowed place in it, filled with slate-coloured water. You sat down on your heels beside it . . .' He stopped. 'Wait a minute – yes, and put your hands face downwards on the rock. You'd never left England before, and you thought of this island having been here all the time of your life – which seemed a very long time – rooted in the sea, rising up to the sun, complete and the perfect size for an island, and you had never known about it until now. The air smelled of salt and honey: the little basin of water shivered from invisible winds, and you were singing inside as though you had several voices. You looked into the little basin – it was glittering – just containing your face, and you felt so new on the island that you decided to christen yourself. You said your name aloud, and marked the water on to your forehead, and it was softer, and colder, than snow. Later in the day, when you were out with your nurse, you came upon another rock, and it also had a little basin, but with hardly any water, and your nurse said that these rocks were the first places on the island to be touched by the sun, and that the bowls had been made a long time ago for sacrifices. You didn't tell her, or anyone else about your rock, until you told me.' He waited a moment, and then, still in the same, quiet story-telling voice, he said: 'There you are. I remember so well your telling me that, you see, and when you told me I think you meant to share it, but perhaps you gave it to me by mistake.'

'You've kept it very well.' Indeed, he had: the morning

which I had not remembered for years was back with me in its true language – fresh and unfaded, as when I had told him first, as when I had felt it. The taxi stopped: he said: 'We have arrived. Have you arrived, darling?' Before I could reply, the porter had opened the taxi door.

'You read that notice on his cage. So I give him four bananas and what does he do? He *eats* them! He peels them like he's tired and his mind's on something else, but he eats them so quick and hands the skins out to me that in a few minutes it's like there never were any bananas at all, and he's back to his staring at me like I was illiterate. He ***dominates*** me.'

Em finished paying the taxi and took my arm. The porter followed us to the lift, and asked if I wanted a monkey. Em pinched me and said: 'My wife is allergic to monkeys.'

'I adore them,' I said, 'but they give me a rash. Lobsters and monkeys.'

The porter said forget it – he'd still got twenty-three apartments to call.

In the lift Em said: 'He isn't absolutely crazy. He really got landed with a monkey that doesn't seem to belong to anyone, and, as you see, it's preying on his mind.'

I think I smiled at him, but I was in full possession of the peace he had given me in the taxi, and so warm with it that I would have smiled at anything he said. He was saying something else.

'. . . worked to get the apartment straight for you – ever since ten this morning. Will you say something nice to her about it?'

I remembered then that in a moment we would not be alone together, and had to use some of my precious warmth to say: 'Of course I will.' But I had the warmth – and at least I could say it.

3

ALBERTA

New York

My dear Uncle Vin,

I am answering your letter at once, because I feel you are worried, and also because I find the nature of your anxiety distressing – this last, I do promise you, not on my account. You have so often said to me that a great deal of gossip goes on in the theatre, and that if people took less notice of it they would be much happier. I have now spent a week here alone with him – Mrs Joyce arrived this evening – and I don't think anyone could have been kinder, more considerate, or more interesting – in fact the things you say sound incredible. Apart from his charming behaviour to me, you seem to have left out the fact that he is married, and from the trouble that he took today it is clear that he is devoted to Mrs Joyce. He spent hours – while I was tidying up this flat in which we are all to stay – buying her favourite flowers, and champagne, and a box of something called Marrons Glacés (chestnuts in sugar) which she fell upon when she arrived, and said were her favourite sweets. He went to meet her himself, and when they came back, they both looked happy and as though they'd achieved something. I would also like to point out to you, Uncle Vin, that he is sixty-one, and could therefore quite easily be my father, and if it wasn't for Papa I wish he was. I hope it is clear that I like and respect him very much, and that is why I hate your believing those horrible idle rumours about him. As for me, you know I have never been in love in my life, and cannot easily imagine what that would be like, but at least I do know that the kind of vulgar intrigue which you imply has nothing to do with love, and cannot start at all unless both people are disposed towards it. When Papa said to me, 'It doesn't matter what you do, as long as you are thoroughly aware that you are doing it,' I think

I understood him. How could I – even supposing it crossed his mind which I am certain it never would – how *could* I encourage him to make poor Mrs Joyce unhappy when she is ill, and has already had so much unhappiness? If I did, it would not be what Papa meant at *all*, and what good could come out of such idiotic irresponsibility? I am sorry to employ this vehemence, but I do feel so angry and sad that people like him should be subjected to such gossip, and although I know that this is nearly always so of remarkable people, the gap between theory and my experience of it is a very large one. So please, Uncle Vin, if you hear anything more of this kind, say that you know better from first-hand evidence.

Now I've read this to see if I've said what I meant, and realize that I haven't once thanked you for worrying about me, which I know you have done with the best reasons. Please don't worry Papa with any of this, though. I'm writing this in bed: the others have gone out to dinner, including Jimmy Sullivan, who had to wait to get all their luggage through the Customs, and didn't arrive here until half past eight. They asked me if I wanted to go with them, and I said no, because I thought Mrs Joyce would like to have dinner alone with him, but then in the end Jimmy went too so it wouldn't have made any difference. This is a beautiful flat and I have a room with so many cupboards that my clothes get lost in them. Mrs Joyce has two *enormous* trunks full of clothes, apart from suitcases. She is very glamorous, in an interesting way – you feel she really *is* – not that she can sometimes manage to be. I am going to help her unpack tomorrow. Finally, to put your mind thoroughly at rest, I may as well tell you that I am not alone in this room, but am sharing it with an unusually gloomy little monkey. He somehow came up in the lift with Jimmy by mistake, and he glares at me all the time in a moping sort of way. I've given him some grapes, and he ate them as though they were wasting his time, and spitting the pips out over his left shoulder, and now he's bored to death and is sitting in a kind of hunched up elegant heap – although Jimmy said all he needed was company, which clearly I'm not managing to be. He shows one quite simply that material comfort is ***not enough***, which is interesting, because it's much harder to see about people. Mrs Joyce wanted to let him out, and she did – in the sitting room. He broke a lamp, upset three vases of flowers, tore some curtains and made four messes; he did all this frightfully quickly and then ran up the curtains and it took ages to catch him, and even Mrs Joyce said that perhaps he was better off in his cage. It's a pity monkeys can't read, because they look as though they can, much more than a lot of people who actually do. Oh well. Much love, darling Uncle Vin – and please don't worry about me – and I promise I'll tell you if I have any difficulties or get ill or ***anything***.

SARAH

4

JIMMY

LOOKING back, at the end of it, on that first week, I realize that we didn't come to what seemed a crazy decision at any one point of it. I say we, because I'm not even sure now who had the idea, I only know that neither of us would have dreamed of it at the beginning of the week. I didn't have a chance to talk to Emmanuel until the morning after we arrived, because the evening was devoted to Lillian, and somehow everything goes wrong if we talk theatre in front of her, and she'd been so excited at meeting Emmanuel that I'd been afraid of her having another attack – I still was – all evening. She was really lit up – not with drink – pure gaiety, and he was responding. He seemed much better than he was in London: less tired and edgy – serene somehow. I guessed he'd been writing, but I didn't ask, and then when she did, he said yes, and I knew he was lying – so it wasn't that. But at least he seemed to be over Gloria, and I'd been afraid we'd have the dregs of her with us for weeks. The new girl – she really is the new girl personified – seems to have done her job well. He doesn't seem to have broken any dates, got drunk, or trodden on anybody's toes; he's managed to make the apartment *and* the ship on time, and I haven't seen him so smooth with Lillian for years.

I left them after dinner; they wanted to go home, and I wanted to walk the streets a bit and show myself the town. It was too late to go to a theatre, and I walked around looking for a movie, and wondering why, whenever I come back here, I always feel like this. I mean, I know the feeling so well, you wouldn't think I'd have it any more. It's all right in England: I tell myself I'm travelling – I'm a foreigner, and I don't even have to tell myself that in France: but here, I look forward to coming back, and then have a kind of resentment that it isn't my home: I feel it ought to be – it's just that most of the ingredients are missing. Twice a year they send a letter from the home where I wasn't born: they ask for news I don't want to give, and give a whole lot of news I don't want. I had a drink on the way back to the apartment and tried not to feel resentful about not being able to spend the evening with Emmanuel, which would have made everything OK. What was it Annie had said in London? The Father Figure, and I was so nuts about him, transferred, I think she said – she was showing off her Freud – that I'd never have a satisfactory affair with a woman. I don't suppose I shall; it seems to me a dreary, interim arrangement. I'd rather lay a woman and never see her again, or be in love with her. I had another Scotch, and started trying to imagine the kind of girl I could be in love with. Slender, but not too tall, with beautiful hair and a low voice – gentle and ready to trust me; someone to whom I could show the world in exchange for her showing me herself. I looked round the bar and imagined myself waiting for her to walk into it: in a sense, I suppose, I *was* waiting for her – and then I thought of the number they'd written into Emmanuel's musical: 'Fate Made a

Date with You and Me' which they'd scored now to merge into the big first act finale number – a waltz: 'The Time and the Place and the Loved One'. Emmanuel had said it was very good and looked like being a hit number. Well, she hadn't turned up, my girl, whoever she was; no sense in looking for her (after all, most of the time I didn't need anyone else in my life), but one thing I knew, and that was she only had to walk into the bar – any bar where I was, and I'd know it was she. It was a little like finding the perfect actress for a part, which perhaps Emmanuel and I would be doing together tomorrow . . .

The first thing we did when we got shot of the apartment was to go to the drugstore we always went to when we wanted to think aloud together with no chance of being interrupted. There was nothing unusual about it except that we always went to it. We got coffee and I bought a pack of Luckies, and we sat and looked at each other. Then he said: 'Well, Jimmy, it's just as difficult as we thought. Neither of the ones we wanted is available. There are about six whom various people want to star in something – I've seen four of them and they're no good: two to go. And of course they've put us through a lot of the routine stuff – agents who want to give a girl the impression they're working for her – or want her to have the experience of an audition.'

'Have you tried Alex?'

Emmanuel smiled. 'I didn't have to try. He was round at George's office like a flash with what he described as his greatest discovery in years.'

'Was she?'

'Her appearance was memorable. There turned out to be only two small snags. She hadn't one word of English, and she'd done no acting in any language whatever.'

'She must have been some eyeful.'

Emmanuel said impassively: 'It was extremely difficult to look at her for long.'

'What does Mick say?'

'He's sympathetic, but he feels I can't have written a play

with a girl who doesn't exist. He's beginning to take it as a slight on America that I can't pick anyone. He has a new agent on the coast who he says will turn up something if we give him time. The point is this, Jimmy. I like actresses who know their job. I like them professional, at least, with a pinch of dedication about them. But if we can't find one of them who would be right – and with Luise and Katie out of it, we look like not finding one, then I like the field wider open than these people – Mick and George and so on – are prepared to open it. The bunch of models, call girls, and bit-part kids is the wrong kind of wide. I'd rather pick a girl off the street who looked right, and have you teach her to act.'

'Yeah, but we're supposed to open this fall, and I can't teach anyone what they need to know in three months.' I thought a minute, and then added: 'Unless they were exceptional, of course.'

He looked at me, his heavy eyelids belying the amusement in his eyes. 'Well, Jimmy – then they've got to be exceptional.'

I got up to pay our check. I knew better than to argue with him then.

That was our first conversation about it.

We spent the rest of the morning seeing George's two girls – the last of the six that he'd got together. We let the first one do the whole scene. She was tall, with what Emmanuel described as a voraciously wistful expression, but she had a good voice with a lot of colour in it. Then when we got to the bit where she goes around taking the pictures off the walls, he said: 'There's a bird that walks like that – a large bird.' So it was for me to get her a nice bucket of clean sand and hold her head in it; she was out, thanking me in anticipation.

Mick was there, and I could feel the whole situation getting on his nerves. Nobody likes to get into real casting trouble, and Mick likes to do everything fast and brilliantly: if personalities advertised, he'd be the done-overnight, solved-while-you-wait problem man. There was a break after the first girl left, because the second girl hadn't shown up. The actor who had been reading for us lit a cigarette, and finally went to sleep on three chairs which he arranged in a row for the purpose. Mick came over to where we were sitting, and did some sales talk on me, and Emmanuel stared at the top of the proscenium arch where a batten wasn't properly masked, and except that he wasn't listening I didn't know what went on in his mind.

Mick's parents had been Polish, and I think he still thought in that language. He had a head like a bullet, a crew cut, a merry sly smile and he loved you to agree with him, but it brought on such bouts of gaiety and energetic appreciation of you that you couldn't stand it for long. If you didn't agree with him, he sulked, and his enterprise in that direction was such that in the end you were responsible for his never having seen Poland which was palpably killing him. But he was a good fixer if he could fix fast, and the set-up that employed him worked on the principle that almost everything could be decided fast if the right man was taking the decisions. Like almost everyone else in the business, Mick resented Emmanuel's control over his plays, and the fact that by sheer weight and merit he could uphold them. Mick knew that experienced and prolific play-wrights don't grow on trees, but just now he was kicking up. Emmanuel, having borne with it for some time, stopped looking at the corner of the proscenium arch, and speaking under Mick, but distinctly, said: 'Jimmy, take him away and talk to him, he's beginning to take my mind off something else.'

'Mick?'

'Sure, sure I'll talk to you. Let's go.'

We went to a small room that he used as an office, and he let go. He'd been fifteen years in the business – he'd worked with some difficult people; he named them and there was hardly anyone left when he was through; but he'd never had trouble like this. He'd read the play – it was just great, but what had got into *Mister* Joyce that he couldn't seem to visualize anybody in what was after all a straight lead? What was so out of this world about it that he hadn't already catered for? Sure, he understood about quality – if I liked he would agree that Mister

Joyce was a genius – the play was a work of genius – *I* was a genius – so what? Weren't there, wasn't there one single *female* genius who could just play one itsy-bitsy part in one goddam play, or must we all kow-tow to genius Joyce as though he'd written the Bible and nothing less than Sarah Bernhardt would do? Mister Joyce gave him the feeling that we were all wasting time, and whereas it would make him happy – it would make him *delirious* to go on providing Mister Joyce with an endless succession of beautiful girls to look at day after day if it gave his power complex a kick, there was just one little thing that world genius Joyce was not taking into account, and that was that his, Mick's, time *was* money. The stark revelation of this final statement seemed to strike him afresh as he said it, and he had to take in some breath. Then he said there was just one more thing that he wanted to know. Would I just tell him how we had found somebody in London for the part who didn't make Mister Joyce sick in his stomach?

'We didn't,' I said. 'The girl we wanted went sick, and we had to make out with somebody who's upset the whole balance of the play. That's why he's so anxious to have the right girl here. He knows what he wants, and he's quite right.'

'Yeah – with one detail hardly worth mentioning – she just don't happen to *exist*!'

'Snap out of it; you've only been on it a week.'

'A week!' He looked as though he was going to burst. 'He thinks I've been on it just a *week*! I tell you something else. It'll end up by his picking some little girl with no sex appeal, no box office, no record, no nothing. And I'll have to try to sell her to MCA – she's spiritual – Mister Joyce is in love with her – we *all* love her – little Miss Wide Open Spaces 1958 – do you think they'll buy it? I can tell you now what they'll tell me to tell you to tell Mister Joyce to do with her and that won't make a news story, and while he's living happily ever after for five minutes, they'll withdraw and he'll be landed with the play *and* the girl . . .'

'Mick, you're making me tired.' He really was: I could feel

the pricking at the back of my neck which is the beginning of getting angry. 'He can always find backing for a new play and you know it. Don't get too big for other people's boots. Be your age and keep your job.'

They called through to say that Miss Harper had arrived. I slapped him as hard as I could on the back and as he fell against the filing cabinet I grinned at him. 'Maybe this is it.'

Of course it wasn't. She was a nice girl, but dumb as they come – she didn't know what she was doing – she just looked good.

We had a weary lunch with Mick and George. It was agreed that everybody perfectly understood everybody else, and was hopping with confidence over everyone else's ability. George gave Mick the job of lining up a whole lot of screen tests to be run through for us; Mick cheered up quite horribly and started loving us all again, and I watched Emmanuel staring at things and not eating his lunch and going blue under the eyes and I thought goddammit do they *really* think he's in it for his power complex? He was just trying to finish a good job, that's all. When we got to coffee, there was a call through for him: I went to take it, and it was Alberta with a message from Lillian to say that she'd fixed the evening for all of us with the Westinghouses – so would we be back not later than seven? I asked if Lillian was there, but she wasn't – she was out lunching with some Russian princess who knew a lot about herbs – and that meant we'd have to go to the Westinghouses'. Then Alberta said she was sorry if she'd distressed me and rang off. She has a sweet voice, but she says some funny things with it. I told Emmanuel about the Westinghouses and he screwed up his eyes and then said unexpectedly: 'She has a pretty voice – that girl,' and George and Mick became galvanized and said which one, and when he said it was his secretary they lost interest.

After lunch, Emmanuel said: 'I have an overpowering desire to sleep. Where can I go?'

He said it to me and very quietly, so I knew he wanted to get away from George. Then he got up from the table, nodded amiably to Mick and George and walked out. I didn't take time to care for the check, I got up to follow him: 'He'll jay walk himself into hospital,' I said. Mick smiled slyly; George said: 'Or revwire.' I grabbed our coats and caught up with him a few yards down on the sidewalk. 'Lillian's out.'

He looked at me expressionlessly: 'Let's go home.'

In the cab, he said: 'Do you know that girl found what was wrong with Clemency?'

'What girl?'

'My secretary.' He still looked like nothing.

A bit later he said: 'I've a damn good mind to chuck the whole business.'

'Not put the play on at all?'

'Not put any play on.'

'What for?'

He looked at me then, and suddenly smiled. 'That's just it, Jimmy. There has to be a reason one way or another. I haven't found it.' He yawned. 'On with the play.'

I didn't answer. He always started a depression this way: wanting to sleep all the time, and making elliptical damaging little stabs at any project in hand, and if you took him up withdrawing to somewhere you couldn't reach him. But I knew then that something would have to be decided somehow, and thought that I would put a call through to Katie and see if there was no way of hooking her.

When we got to the apartment, he waited while I found a key, and opened the door, and at once Alberta came out of the living room. Emmanuel walked firmly up to her and took her by the arm. 'I want you to do something for me. Would you take the calls, Jimmy? Now – where can we go?' He pushed her gently into the kitchen, and turned back to me. 'I want to try something. Stop Lillian from stopping me, will you?'

I nodded, and went into the living room. A minute later, Alberta came in, picked something off a table and went. I shut the door, and put the call through to Katie in California. The time was half past three. While I was waiting for the first call to come through, I made a list of all the others that could be any use, and wondered how that kid had managed to upset him about Clemency. Of course, she wouldn't have meant to – the people who did, moved him not at all. But this kind of thing had happened before: somebody, something, had shifted his view of a completed work, and then there was the devil to pay until he got it back to his satisfaction. Once or twice he hadn't, and they were the worst times of all. That was when I earned my salary: when he lost money, made enemies, and really got down to influencing people. Then it had to be a case of my country right or wrong, and I had the curious sensation of what it cost to believe in anybody. Then I not only had to stand people calling him a fool – a swollen-headed bum perfectionist – a capitalist who didn't care about the security of the workers in the theatre – a sadist who liked to use his power to revenge himself upon some producer or star he'd fallen out with – I had to stand him agreeing with them. 'Why not?' he once said: 'There is no doubt that I have been a fool: that's a useful word; it will cover almost anything. They are quite rightly worrying about the consequences, as I, too late, concern myself with the cause. A fool is somebody who will not keep still, but cannot possibly be responsible for his actions. I am a fool.'

Oh well – it hadn't come to that.

The call to Katie came through at last. At the end of two minutes she had really convinced me that she was tied up, and after that she was free-wheeling on her reasons. Her studio had suspended her a few weeks back: she was scheduled to make two big pictures: she was suing her third husband for failure to pay alimony, and anyway she couldn't leave her hypnotist who was trying to stop her taking sleeping pills. This took another eighteen minutes of her beautiful voice. She couldn't, she said, even work Las Vegas for a week on account of her studio, when God knew she needed the money, and life was twice as expensive as it had been what with lawyers and the hypnotist who hadn't managed to stop her taking sleeping pills yet so any minute she might be suspended again – for good. We exchanged a lot of abstract emotions and hung up. She was an actress, though: she had the lot: and I knew it, even while I caught myself wondering how on earth we ever thought she could play Clemency. I was just starting to call a couple of people I just liked, and thought I'd call, when I heard Lillian, and put the receiver back just as she came into the room. She was not alone.

'Hi, Jimmy. This is Princess Murmansk – you've met, haven't you, Della?'

'Why yes – we certainly have. How are you?'

The Princess – I didn't remember her – had an accent straight from New Orleans where she must have been some landmark – she was well over six feet tall.

'The Princess has been explaining to me how you can do absolutely everything with herbs.'

The Princess smiled, exposing a large quantity of well-kept teeth. Only Cinerama, I thought, would do justice to her. They exchanged herbal cigarettes, and we all sat down.

'You look at a loose end, Jimmy: where's Em?'

'In the kitchen.'

'What on earth is he doing?'

'He's working with Alberta.'

'Why in the kitchen? Why not here?'

'Because he doesn't want to be interrupted.'

'What's he *doing*?'

'Search me. Working.'

Lillian gave an angry little laugh. 'How extraordinary. Well, Della's dying to meet him, and anyway we came back to make some of her marvellous tea.'

'He specially asked me to take all calls and see that he wasn't interrupted,' I said, and noticed that we had both instinctively got to our feet. I tried to smile. 'Don't say I didn't warn you.'

She went. The Princess stretched out a yard or two of leg and said: 'Does it get to be part of your reflexes protecting the great man?'

'It gets to be.'

Lillian came back followed by Emmanuel: I took one look at him and wished I was somewhere else. Lillian said: 'I've got our secretary to boil water and get a tray together, but the actual *skill* will have to be you, Della. My husband – Princess Murmansk.'

'I'm so happy to meet you.' She extended a hand and Emmanuel shook it.

'I do hope I haven't disturbed your inspiration.'

'I have never been fortunate enough to have any. If I had, neither you nor anyone else would be able to disturb it.'

Lillian said: 'Really Em, that's rude of you.'

'Not rude – just hypothetical.'

I couldn't take it. I went to see how Alberta was making out with the tea. She looked flushed, and when I came in she gave me a quick little smile as though if she didn't smile she'd cry.

'Can I help any?' I said: she was putting cups on a tray.

'I just have to wait until the kettle boils: thank you, Jimmy.'

'I'll stay and watch it with you.' I felt suddenly that she was getting the rough end of something she knew nothing about. She looked at the two chairs where they must have been sitting, and pushed her hair back from her forehead.

'Has he been working you hard?'

She looked bewildered. 'Not working *me*, exactly. He's been making me read to him. He said he wanted to hear something.'

'Yeah – he does that. Has he found it?'

'Some of it, I think – but of course, I haven't asked.' She waited a moment, and then said: 'Mrs Joyce was angry when she came in and then he was very angry.' Her voice was very low. 'I don't understand.'

'He didn't say anything, did he?'

'No – but that made it worse. Jimmy – do you mind me asking you something?'

'Go ahead.'

'Who am I working for?'

'You're working for him, and sometimes that means working for her. Sometimes it doesn't.'

'It isn't that I mind doing ***anything***. But if they tell me to do something, and it makes the other angry that I do it . . .'

'Like this?' I indicated the tea tray, and she nodded. 'Forget it. Listen: they're not beautiful simple people, so they make difficulties from time to time: just don't get involved – it irons out – but whatever they do, you keep it small. OK?'

'OK,' she said carefully. 'Thank you, Jimmy. I expect it sounds stupid to you, but my experience of married people is unfortunately superficial.'

'What about your parents?'

'My mother died when I was nine. The kettle's boiling. Do we take it in, do you think?'

'I'll find out where her highness wants it.'

I strode into an atmosphere you could cut with a knife and said: 'Alberta wants to know where you want the boiling water?'

'Tell her to bring it in here with the tray.'

Well, we had tea – if you can call the sickly bitter stuff that woman made, tea. Lillian chattered – the princess answered questions about her herbal rest home; and Emmanuel sat almost silent, and fidgeting, until he suddenly smiled at her with great charm and said he had to go.

'Darling – you can't go out now. The Westinghouses!'

'Tell them I'll be late.' He'd gone.

Lillian looked desperately at me. 'Jimmy – do explain to him, the party's being given for him. He ***can't*** be late.' As I left the room, I heard her saying: 'He's always like this when he's working on a new play; I do hope you'll forgive him, and understand.'

I caught Emmanuel waiting for the elevator: without looking at me, he said: 'One shouldn't meet that woman indoors: she's too big.'

We both got into the elevator. I said: 'I couldn't have stopped that.'

He gave me a bleak smile. 'I could.' He shrugged. 'Well – it's done now. And the only thing that would put it right again, I can't do.'

I was silent.

'I did it last night. It takes a kind of energy I don't seem to keep for long. Or can't afford. Or won't. I have something else to do.'

Then he said angrily: 'It's like marking *sand*. The tide comes in, and you might never have done it.'

'Are you going to show up at this party?' I asked desperately. I didn't want to ask, but I had to.

'You take her to it. If I'm not coming, I'll call them. I promise.'

I put their number on a piece of paper and put it in his pocket.

'I've lost my temper. It's like getting drunk: you know it's going to poison you, and you don't stop. Freedom! We all talk about it, and don't know the meaning of the word!'

The elevator, which had reached the ground floor some time back, suddenly started up again. He laughed.

'You see, Jimmy? It's just like this. We go up and down, up and down, without the slightest control. Where's the break? What the hell can we *do* about anything at all?'

He spread out his hands – they were shaking – small, nervous, blotched on their backs with large freckles. 'See? I haven't the control of a *cat*!'

'They have a lot,' I said.

The elevator stopped, and a wooden-faced couple got in. Their collective gaze shifted over us and the floor and the walls. They only knew how not to look at each other. I pressed the button for our apartment floor, and said: 'Well, I'll take them both to the party, and hope to see you there. And I'll fix somewhere good to work tomorrow.'

He looked at me, and his look went to my heart. 'Bless you, Jimmy.'

I gave Lillian his message dead pan, and went to my room. Alberta had already gone to hers like a sensible girl. But I knew that Lillian would get rid of her lady friend and come after me. She did.

'What do you mean, Jimmy, he'll call if he's not coming?'

'I don't mean anything at all. It's what he said.' I was lying on my bed with the beginnings of a headache and closed my eyes, but she closed the door and went on: 'Does that mean he *isn't* coming, do you think? Because if so, I must call the Westinghouses . . .'

'He said he'd call: I should leave it to him if I were you.'

'If you were me, of course you wouldn't have interrupted him in the first place when he was "working". And if I were you I wouldn't have interrupted him either.'

'That's true,' I agreed amiably, but that only made her dangerous.

'Doesn't it strike you as odd that I'm the only person who's *capable* of interrupting him?'

'Perhaps you're the only one he cares for.'

She didn't know how to take this. Then she said: 'He wasn't working, anyway. He was just listening to the girl reading.'

She wasn't that stupid – surely? But I looked at her, and saw that the only bit of her that was working at the moment was. I decided to have one real try, and then give up.

'Lillian – honey – you're wrong there. If Emmanuel says he doesn't want to be disturbed that's good enough: we don't decide whether he's working or not – *he* does. It made him mad today because he's got something on his mind, but he'll come back all right if you don't grow the whole thing up meanwhile. Be sweet to him – apologize.'

She looked at me, and I saw she was finding it tough. With an effort, she said: 'I'll think about it.' Then she gave herself a little shake, and said: 'I don't blame you for talking to me as though I was a child: the whole thing has become such a storm in a teacup. I want to leave at seven fifteen.'

'Does Alberta know?'

'She ought to. I told her the arrangements this morning.'

Well – that was not the end of it. I went to tell Alberta: she was sitting on her bed writing in a big book, and she just nodded, and went on writing. I wondered what – and guessed it was a novel. Young girls write novels nowadays like they used to press flowers or make candy. At seven, Emmanuel came back. At eight, we left, in an atmosphere nobody could want to call their own. The party was some blocks down on Park Avenue, and except for Lillian saying how dirty the cab was nobody said anything.

The Westinghouses were a nice couple – around their fifties – with a son in the business and several other grown-up children who usually showed up at parties. He was a good-looking man – always sunburned – with an appearance of nobility that had somehow never got around to attaching itself to anything. The prototype for heroic theory, Emmanuel had once said: but Emmanuel was fond of him – they even went once on a disastrous fishing trip together – Emmanuel was nearly drowned, and the rest of the time so bored that he got drunk and stayed that way for nearly two weeks. Debbie Westinghouse was one of those women you only see here – half doll, half little girl – she'd never had a thought in her head, and that went for the nasty ones too – she was crisp, and silly, and sweet and simple, and so clean you could have eaten off her. She loved her family; the room was littered with snaps of her grandchildren, and she understood that books were for other people. She cried very easily, but not for long, and she told everybody that Emmanuel was a genius with the kind of gasping credulity of a child talking about a magician. Van Westinghouse was always very kind to her, and she certainly made him feel a man.

They had collected about thirty people to meet Emmanuel, and they must have known why they were invited, as nearly all of them turned to look at him when we came in. I knew Van Westinghouse would take care of Lillian – he had a lot of old-world charm for other people's wives – and Emmanuel would be swamped, but the poor kid, Alberta, looked out of it all: she had on a dark blue dress that wasn't right for her or the party, and she looked as though she knew it. There was nothing I could do about it: we were plunged into large scale and paralysingly efficient introductions. A collection of well-groomed, intelligent, successful people – for some reason they made me think of a whole lot of shiny new automobiles – powerful, well serviced, fitted inside with all kinds of modern gadgets – like insomnia, contraceptives, equality, and fright. Emmanuel once said that no talk was too small for opinions, they were only the suburbia of intercourse, and cocktail parties were their rush hour, and I was in a mood this evening for that kind of remark to stick in my mind. I had two drinks rather fast and listened to three people – Debbie Westinghouse admiring Lillian's dreamy clothes, an intense young woman who'd written a book all about emotional freedom, and an old, rather nice guy who seemed stuck on English furniture. Usually at these parties, I do at least get myself an attractive girl, at least to drink with, but tonight there seemed two good reasons why that would not make a gay evening. One was Alberta, for whom I felt kind of responsible, and the other was Emmanuel. Alberta was answering questions about England, and looking like a schoolgirl up for an examination, and Emmanuel was listening to a journalist who'd just been on a three weeks trip to India, and who was telling him what an opportunity the British getting out was for the Indian people. What the hell was a party *for*, I wondered. Van Westinghouse was bringing out a cheap edition of Emmanuel's plays – Johnnie, his son, came over to tell me about it: three volumes to start with, with three plays in each: they had galleys, but they were still waiting for a preface and could I turn on some heat to get it? Not tonight, I said. Who was the girl we'd brought – was she an attachment of mine? For some reason this irritated me: I think because I knew Johnnie thought she looked odd, and because I agreed with him. I explained why she was here, and Johnnie said OK, OK, he'd only been asking and got his sister Sally from across the room. She came over, smiling, and looking so good that I felt better just looking. She'd become a model since last time I'd seen her, and she'd changed. I told her she looked wonderful, and she smiled her wide smile and said clothes certainly did something for a girl. Johnnie said: 'Oh, come on, Sal. Tell him you're in love!' 'He's a photographer – I certainly am. He's a genius!' She said it just like her mother. She gave her glass to Johnnie, and smiled again at me and asked me who was the girl I'd brought. Somehow she didn't irritate me asking – so I told her about Alberta and said she was a sweet kid, and was just going to add how young she was, when I remembered that Alberta was at least a year older than Sally. 'She hasn't been around very much – lived in the country,' I said instead – and wondered why everything I said about Alberta seemed wrong or patronizing. That was just when Johnnie knocked against a bottle which fell over Alberta's dress. Sally saw it, and gave a little throaty gasp and went to the rescue. She took Alberta away at once – Johnnie made me an apologetic face – but at the far end of the room, I caught sight of Emmanuel. A good many people had gone, and I could hear that all was not well. He was leaning against the piano, and I didn't like the easy, angry look on his face. I went over '. . . this *extraordinary* illusion you have that we all know what we are doing?' he finished, and as an afterthought emptied his half-full glass of what looked like Scotch.

The intense dame who'd written the book about emotional freedom gave him a winning, intellectual smile, and said soothingly: 'But surely, Mr Joyce, it is the duty of the more knowledgeable person to inform and guide the common man.'

'If you deal in such an inflated view of humanity, possibly it is. Personally, I have never met anyone in the least knowledgeable, and I don't think I'd recognize the common man if I stumbled up against him in the street where I believe he lives. I think society is made up of cranks and morons.' He smiled pleasantly round the room, embracing us all, and somehow managed to get Johnnie to fill his glass again without a word. There was an indiscriminate outcry – of people claiming to be common etc., out of which the man – whom I recognized as the journalist – said: 'You'll be telling me next that you don't believe in progress!'

Emmanuel smiled brightly: 'That's what I'll tell you next. But *you* think information is progress. You think a lot of cranks telling a lot of morons what they ought to think constitutes education. There are a few little worms turning in England, but that is only because they want even their emotional lives for free – they can't even face paying for *that* – they want it on the basis of free milk and public lavatories and they simply illustrate the rot of private irresponsibility – this is what makes most of us cowards . . .'

The journalist was high anyway, and he lost his temper. 'Is this a social message out of one of your plays?'

'I don't write plays with social messages. It is a misuse of the theatre.'

'But surely, Mr Joyce, you consider yourself knowledgeable?' Emmanuel didn't reply, and the journalist said again: 'I repeat – surely you're under the impression that you're knowledgeable?'

Emmanuel said: 'I am attached to the notion that if one is below an impression, it is a false one.'

'You see? You're just evading my point: you damned artists, you think you can run the world. You just think you know everything – for God's sake. Give me the days when the artist was a workman with a job to do and knew his place in society.'

Emmanuel said smoothly: 'I am sure that we all wish that you had lived two hundred years ago,' somebody laughed, and Emmanuel held out his glass to Johnnie.

At this moment – mercifully – Alberta returned to us: Emmanuel saw her first, and although his face did not seem to change, I knew there was a reason for looking, and turned my head. I don't think I'd ever looked at her before – at any rate, now I hardly knew her. She was wearing a black dress with a high Chinese collar, and very short, tight sleeves; her hair was sleeked back – smooth and shining – and her skin made the other women in the room look as though they'd never been in the air on a fine morning. Even Sally, beside her, looked as though she'd lived it up a bit. Emmanuel said: 'Here, at last, is somebody who will answer your question.' He held out his hand with the glass in it, she hesitated, and came over to us.

'Do you consider that I am a wise man?'

She looked at him with unselfconscious steadiness, and said: 'No I do not.' Then she added gently: 'But I think such men are very rare: it has not been my fortune to meet one.'

Emmanuel smiled and inclined his head to her, and there was something like a triumphant recognition about his face and the movement. The sour smell of calamity seemed to have gone: the journalist offered Emmanuel a cigarette, and Johnnie rushed to get Alberta a drink. Sally winked at me and murmured: 'Clothes certainly make a difference to a man about a girl, anyway' – and then I saw Lillian, with an expression on her face like a stubbed-out cigarette. Whatever Lillian may be, she certainly *isn't* supporting cast. Johnnie had given Emmanuel another slug, and he was reciting something to his host and hostess: Debbie was taking it seriously, and Van looked uneasy. I caught Van's eye, and after exactly the right interval, he moved casually over to me.

'I hate to say it, Van, but do you have any further plans for this evening?'

He looked around. 'When the numbers got to around ten, Debbie wanted us to go some place to eat.'

'They're around that now.'

He made a count, during which I noticed that the journalist had got hold of Lillian and was pouring his opinions over her like a bucket of sand on to a chemical fire.

'If you could include Lillian in your care, and your literary pals, perhaps Johnnie could bring the rest of us in due course.'

'Fine.' He went to tell Johnnie: he knew quite a lot about Emmanuel.

Well – the first part of the arrangement worked. Lillian went quietly – she'd decided to behave well about it all, to invest her anger for private distribution I guessed. But when it came to moving Emmanuel everything broke down. When I got back from seeing the others into the elevator, I found him sitting on the floor, making Sally and Alberta compare their childhoods: they became like a couple of kids telling him, and Johnnie was listening and watching Emmanuel's face respectfully – he was a kid with an eye for memories. As soon as there was a chance, I said: how about moving?

Emmanuel said: 'Where?'

'Johnnie's driving us to Patrick's for dinner. We're joining the others there.'

'Well, at least we know where they *are*.' He turned back to Alberta: 'Have you changed your clothes recently?'

'Yes. This dress belongs to Miss Westinghouse. Mine had an accident.'

Emmanuel looked approvingly at Sally and then at Alberta. Johnnie stood around waiting to go, but nobody seemed to take any notice of him, and then Emmanuel started to tell a story about a dress his mother had told him she wanted, and how it had seemed to cost so much money that he imagined it had been made for Queen Alexandra. 'Of course, she never got it,' he finished, and watched pity bloom on the girls' faces like the moon coming out. But Johnnie began feeling the strap of his wrist watch and looking nervous, so I said again that we should be going.

'Where?'

We went through it all again.

'Call them, and say I'm terribly drunk and it's delaying us. If you point out what an embarrassing evening they would have with me – shouting and spilling my food and breaking things, they might not want us at all.'

When Johnnie and I went to make the call, he said: 'I don't know what Dad will say. He doesn't *seem* drunk, at all.'

'He isn't, but if we join them he'll arrive high without drinking another drop. Put the call through and I'll talk to your father.'

'Gee – if he was really like he said at Patrick's, it sure would be exciting.'

'Just dull,' I said: 'Those evenings are all the same – it's just the audience that changes.'

I told Van Westinghouse that we wouldn't be joining them,

and said to tell Lillian I was sorry but things weren't working out that way. Would he look after Lillian, and I'd call him in the morning? He would. He was, as Emmanuel once remarked, in that minority who were at least wiser after other people's events. I turned to Johnnie, who had the look of an expectant schoolboy about to break bounds.

'No more Scotch for anyone – and some small place to eat.'

And that was it. We did go out and eat at Giovanni's, and it was a good evening. All the strain and tensions seemed to have dropped from Emmanuel and he charmed us all – making Sally tell stories and asking Alberta what she thought of them, improvising a preface for Johnnie in the language of a well-known American weekly: 'Slum-born mongrel-playwright Emmanuel Orchid Race Joyce stabs at self-analytical artistic processes as taking people out of themselves and putting them back wrong' etc. But mostly he listened: every now and then he told a story – something very small, but the way he told them they were irresistibly fascinating, and we sat like a bunch of kids, round-eyed, begging for more.

It was not until after the zabaglione, when we were all drinking coffee, that Sally began asking about the new play. Emmanuel answered her, and I had the feeling that he was having a final conversation with himself, and also with me about it. He told her very simply the kind of play that it was; the difficulty about Clemency – what we had done and how we had failed to find her: Johnnie and Alberta were listening too, but the collective attention seemed not to interfere with our privacy. Johnnie, very diffidently, suggested Katie for the part, and I said yes, but she couldn't do it – I'd tried her again that afternoon. Emmanuel was looking at me now, and I knew the feeling – of private summing up, of conclusion – was true. It came into my mind that he was going to scrap the play; that he'd found the reason for doing so which he had said was necessary, and I blotted up this inky fear until I must have changed colour with it . . .

'. . . and so, I have decided to make an experiment, if the

victim is willing,' and both he and I turned instinctively to Alberta, who had been very still, whose eyes, clear and astonished, were the only sign she gave of this news. There was a long, full silence; then she said: 'You know that I know nothing at all about acting.'

'Jimmy will teach you all you need to know.'

She looked at me: I was seeing her for the second time, and entirely different again.

'I'll teach you,' I said, 'if you're willing to learn.'

'Are you willing?'

She put out her hand, as though she was in a dream, and must touch somebody, and Emmanuel and I both put our hands on the table.

'I will try to learn,' she said. Emmanuel touched her then, and she smiled.

And that was the end – or the beginning – of that.

CHAPTER IV

1

ALBERTA

My dearest Aunt Topsy,

This letter is partly for Papa, because it seems that the moment one is in a position interesting enough to warrant writing letters, one has very little time for them. You are the *most* reliable correspondent, and keep me thoroughly in touch, although I'm sorry to hear about Jemima Facks – I must say I should have thought it was extremely difficult to fall down a well *head* first – I mean one would have to be so neat about it: but then I suppose falling runs in the Facks family, and she has had a good deal of experience. Anyway, it's a good thing she had such presence of mind and thick pigtails.

We have just moved into an apartment and I have spent this morning helping Mrs Joyce who has just gone out to luncheon with a Russian Princess (not a real one – she just married a Russian Prince). You asked me to describe Mrs J., and I'll try, appearance first, because I've seen more of it. She is very tall and thin and extremely *elegant* – with rather knobbly bones and thin blue veins which show out of the sides of her forehead and on the backs of her hands (like Lady Gorge, only not so useful-looking – prettier). She has very fine hair which is a mixture of yellow and white – grey, I suppose, but again, pretty, cut short and waving carelessly about in what turns out to be a very expensive manner, and huge rather pale blue eyes with black pupils. Her skin is very white and looks thinner than most people's – almost papery, and her mouth droops slightly downwards but is a beautiful shape. Her hands and feet are what Clem would call pre-Raphaelite – very long and faint-looking, and altogether, if she had long hair one could imagine her in a garden of carnations, or sitting in some banqueting hall; she is very much like a heroine – someone to be rescued or saved. She is extremely delicate, as she has something wrong with her heart, and she had a daughter who died – it is still all very sad. I had to do her unpacking – goodness! – she has two cabin trunks with hangers for dresses down one side and drawers for clothes down the other – apart from countless suitcases. She also travels with her pictures, drawings and paintings – nearly all portraits, I wondered if any of them were of her daughter, but naturally didn't ask. Most of the morning she was in bed talking to people on the telephone, while I put things away until there wasn't any more room to put them. I suppose they are all the consequence of a glittering life, but it must be rather sad not to have anywhere permanent to keep them. Mrs Joyce said I must buy some clothes here because pretty ones are so cheap. I have got one or two things . . . Then she suddenly *gave* me a summer coat: it is a lemon colour, and a little too long for me, but it is beautifully cut – it is loose and absolutely simple and she said it was a French one but she had cut out the label. This evening we are all going to Mr Joyce's publishers who are giving a party for him. I don't think I could possibly have been more lucky in getting this position. The work is not hard, varied, and nearly always interesting, and the Joyces are so very kind about including me in all the things they do. They seem used to doing things with Jimmy Sullivan, and I just get added on; this is a great help against homesickness, which I'm afraid assails me from time to time. Please tell Mary that I am writing my diary as much as I possibly can, and that I look forward to hers also.

I do not know how long we are to remain in New York – it depends upon the casting of Mr J.'s new play which proves a difficult matter. When that is settled, we are to go somewhere to the country, as Mrs J. wants a holiday and Mr J. has to write

– but no certain plans are made. Tell Papa that I quite agree about experiences knowing their place if only one will let them, and that I am trying to remember this. I must add that I find the vast luxury in which I am now living enjoyable; it is rather like *being* a parrot, instead of just looking at one – but perhaps you don't think parrots are luxurious birds? Humphrey says my taste in birds is vulgar – but I suppose one's taste in anything is conditioned in part by one's curiosity about it, and I have never managed to care for little brown birds one can hardly see. I am saving half my salary: this can be certain, the rest is a constant battle between what I need and what I want. You would not like the food here at all. It is either foreign and tastes like it (which I like) or else it looks like ours, only larger, and does not taste at all, so that you have a kind of dream of what you're eating. It is no good my trying to describe New York as I did in my first letter. It would get dull, because I don't know where to begin or what needs describing and what doesn't. I shouldn't worry too much about Serena wanting to be a doctor – it takes such ages she'll probably end up by being a nurse – think of Florence Nightingale – you wouldn't mind that, and you *have* brought us all up awfully well, and, as Papa says, once we're up there isn't much you can do about it. I do hope your hay fever hasn't started: give my love to everybody – including Napoleon and Ticky, but most of all to you and Papa and Mary and Serena and the boys.

Your loving SARAH

This is after tea, and there is such a feeling of tension, that I have escaped to write this in peace. Even the monkey has gone: his owner has turned up at last, and I am quite alone for a bit, which one certainly couldn't be with him. I don't understand people at all well: or just when I think I'm beginning to, they change into someone else. Or do I change? Everybody has turned out unexpectedly today – so perhaps I have too. Take Papa: anybody who really wanted to meet him could do so, and at the worst he's simply shades of himself: one might say: 'He's rather pale today', but he would still be a recognizable colour. I think this is unusual though – there are fewer people like Papa even than I thought. This morning, helping Mrs J., the thread that seemed to run through her morning was her feeling for him. She asked me endless questions about what he had been doing all the week, and whether I had been with him or not, and when I told her about all the shopping he'd done before her arrival she seemed pleased. (I didn't tell her about his buying me clothes – even when she asked me whether I'd got any new ones. This is another piece of deceit, which begins to sit on me rather too often, I think.) But then, when she came into the kitchen, and I was reading to him, she seemed an entirely different person who neither loved nor cared about him – and he was different as well; I didn't know either of them, and had a miserably insular feeling that I wasn't used to people treating each other like that. I was making tea with these bleak thoughts, when Jimmy came in, and *he* was different too: I suddenly felt I could tell him about it, and did, and he made it all the right size with a flick of consideration. He seems to be both experienced and kind, and I do admire him for that. The pear blossom will be out at home, and the magnolia will be right out. They will be having tea in the dining room with drops of water on the pound of butter and white crystals on Aunt T.'s blackcurrant jam, and Ticky on the picture rail shrilling for sugar. But of course, it isn't the same time at home as it is here. That is a curious separation – the hours as well as the miles. This morning Mrs J. asked me whether I'd ever been to Greece in exactly the same voice as she had asked me earlier whether I had been to Saks – a shop on Fifth Avenue – I haven't been to either. Jimmy has just come in to tell me the time of the party tonight. I have never met a publisher. I did ask Mr J. about them, and he said that nearly all publishers hovered uneasily between a business and a profession, that they suffered from the most unpredictable raw material, and that most writers were like a zoo masquerading as a circus with one or two societies for the prevention of cruelty to authors. Then he laughed and said he was a member of the zoo; but none of this – although memorable – is really illuminating. I have no suitable dress for this party and this makes me wish that I was not going to it. It was so odd, reading the play today, to reach that scene that I have heard so many people read. It made me see how, in a well-made play, everything depends on something else. We got a little way into the third act before we were interrupted – I'd stopped feeling nervous ages before, and when we stopped I realized that my throat was aching, which I hadn't noticed at the time, at all. I have never known *anything like* his attention: it is as though he is listening, seeing, almost breathing in the play – as though the words as I read them were falling into his body, and as though everything outside the play had been turned off and didn't exist. Somehow it is impossible not to be drawn into this attention – not as a person – but as a path between it and him. Sometimes I seemed to be nearer the play, and sometimes nearer his attention to it. He hardly spoke at all: once or twice he repeated a line after me, and I realized that I'd got some of the words wrong – even one word – but he always knew and always repeated them right. Ordinarily, I think I'd have felt confused at being corrected – would have wanted to interrupt with apologies, but as the play grew, these personal feelings diminished, until afterwards I wondered whether all apologies weren't simply to oneself for failing to be the marvellous creature one wanted to appear. It is so much more interesting to be a vehicle – transporting something – because one seems to have a place in relation to so much else, instead of being a tiny over-emphatic full stop. Mary will not understand this, but whom does one write a diary for? I think to save oneself a few conversations with oneself. I do hope he finds the right Clemency. I almost feel that I'd know her now just by looking. I think Jimmy feels this: the best part of Jimmy is his recognition, and that is not a small thing to say of anybody. Must go and put on boring dress for glamorous party.

*

This is twenty past two – too late for opinions or fears, but they want me to be Clemency for the play. They know that I know nothing. I have undertaken to try and learn.

2

EMMANUEL

HE woke in the night – eyes burning, hands clenched – as though he'd been fighting with himself to stay asleep, and lost. I drank a good deal, he thought, as another part of his mind started to fidget and jeer. 'No sooner said than done!' it began; 'now we'll see the result of all that grandiose simplicity!' His body seemed to be stretched, strained out, weightlessly over the bed. Now, if only he knew exactly what to do, he would leap out of bed and it would be done. It was a quarter to five. 'Just think what you can't do at a quarter to five – or a quarter to anything come to that.' By eight o'clock he would be wrapped in lead, his head throbbing like an electric pump, his eyes little pinpoints of self-pity: but now some feverish energy remained from the evening and the decision he had taken in it; now he could tackle Mick, even Lillian – work through the traffic of their reactions to the business of getting the girl right on a large enough scale. In practice that would be Jimmy's job, although he'd keep an eye on it: he wasn't sure whether Jimmy had seen what he saw in Alberta. We can't stay in New York once the news has been broken to Mick and the boys, he thought – they'll scare the lights out of her: that means finding somewhere quiet for a month or two – where Jimmy can work with her, and I can work, and Lillian can – somewhere that Lillian wants to go. That is all that has to be *done*, he reflected irritably; but he wanted the whole thing settled now, while he lay there – to be handed a little public peace so that he could afford some private excitement. I'm getting old, he thought, to need favourable conditions for everything. It's time we lived somewhere: travel as well, of course, but have some point of departure, some deeper shades to our behaviour – a home for Jimmy, some possible responsibilities for Lillian, and a key to his own cage for himself. This idea – suddenly presenting itself from above and beyond any immediate action – coloured his bleak and crowded mind, softening considerations, lighting necessities, touching up his distant, fleeting pleasures; and like magic slides, pictures of Lillian in an element he could provide – hedged in with roses, aired with music, with her own library, with parks and trees and far-off animals – soundlessly, speechlessly – jerked and slipped to his attention and out of it . . . He leapt out of bed.

Her room was grey and cold and smelled faintly of lemons, and he heard her make the small undergrowth movement of someone caught awake in the dark who means to be woken. If she had been very angry, she would have sat up, switched on the light and stared at him until he was breathless . . . Patiently, he roused her.

'What is it?'

He sat on the bed shivering.

'I have a plan. You must hear it now.'

She switched on the light. One thing that always surprised him was how she looked in the morning – fresh and gentle, and years younger than her age. Now, any resentment for his abandoning her at the Westinghouses' was neutralized by her curiosity – her hair was ruffled like silky waves in a primitive picture, and her eyes, shining, were waiting, poised for him to begin.

'We are to live in a house: I have been thinking what we need, and the first thing is for some external structure which does not change. It would give us better chances, and provide us with the necessary sense of commitment. We are living like twentieth-century savages in hotels and boats and aeroplanes. It is bad for your health, and my work, and does not give us any sense of adventure or freedom any more. You are deprived of many things that you love. You could have a garden, and animals, collect your books and gramophone records. I have been thinking most carefully about all this,' he added, and the second time it really felt as though he had, and as though he had never thought of it before.

She laid her hands one upon the other and leaned a little towards him: 'I could have a walled garden.'

'If you like.'

'And a wilderness, and grapes and nectarines – and a proper herb garden and those charming cows with bruised faces . . .'

'You could have anything you like.'

'I think they are Guernseys: and you could have a beautiful room to work in – Oh! what about Jimmy? He hates fresh air.'

'He loves the sun. He'd come and go.'

'He wouldn't count English sun.'

'Are we to live in England?'

'Where else do you want to live?'

He felt her reach the edge of her pleasure and look down. He said: 'I hadn't really thought about that. But I'd thought we might as well pick a good climate.'

'Where had you thought of?'

He said again: 'I hadn't thought of anywhere really. I mean I hadn't even considered whether it should be here or somewhere in Europe.'

'Only not in England?'

'My experience of English country has been as limited as it has been unfortunate. Skies like saucepans and a smell of gumboots and damp tweed. Don't you remember staying with the Maudes and your hot water bottle steaming in the sheets?'

'It doesn't have to be like that – truly.'

'And tremendous damp dogs smelling of haddock, and all the food served at blood heat and mice trying to keep up their circulation at night. Don't you remember that frightful mouse that was running to and fro simply to keep warm?'

'Em, that was just Clarissa. She couldn't run a house anywhere.'

'And servants. The only ones we ever saw were at least ninety and raging hypochondriacs. Don't you remember that dreary butler of Clarissa's who changed all our meal times because of his injections? And the housemaid who was on some kind of diet that made her faint all over the place?'

'You're exaggerating now.'

'Only just. It wouldn't surprise me. Accident is so calamitous in the English countryside. Calamitous and dull.'

'It would be just as difficult to get servants here.'

He made an effort not to be irritated by her gravity. 'You really want Wilde back, don't you, darling?'

And responding to his affection, she answered quite simply, 'Yes.'

There was a silence – then they both spoke at once; both smiled, and he said: 'What little reflections of our own uncertainties we do provide. Yes, of course I want a house. That's why I broke in on you so early. I asked *you* whether it was what you wanted.'

She looked at her hands upon the sheets in another silence before she said: 'The trouble is that I don't know what I'm *for*. That makes it very difficult to know what I want, because I never want the same thing for long. It is different for you.'

'Is it?'

'Isn't it? You have your plays to write.'

'I agree that that means I can get by a good deal of the time in a smug frenzy of activity.'

After a moment, she said: 'But sometimes you can't?'

He nodded. '*Why* I write them – what I'm for, or even what plays are for: there are layers of those two questions about everything, so that one can't answer one layer in terms of another.'

'Do you remember when you were a child saying that you lived in a house in a street, in London, England, Europe, the World?'

He shook his head. 'Our childhoods were not the same.'

'It always stopped at the world. The world was one's total horizon of one's address. Now, it doesn't seem enough.' She sighed, and then smiled to dismiss it.

'Well?' His head was beginning to drum, and his skin felt like a hot, dry leaf. He did not want his fiery resolutions to drift into a haze of her nostalgia.

She looked up again from her hands.

'Shall we start looking for a house?'

'What? Immediately?'

'Yes. Go back to England, hire a car, and start looking.'

'I thought we were here to cast your play, and couldn't leave until we had.'

'That is something else I have to tell you. We've drawn such a blank that Jimmy and I have decided to try out Alberta for Clemency. So we can go anywhere.'

'*Alberta*? The *secretary*?'

He explained, and she was silent. Then she asked questions, and he explained again. It was a little like the course for the Grand National, he thought – twice round, and every obstacle presenting a different problem. Then she was silent again. At last, she said: 'Well, the whole idea seems preposterous to me: I don't think it is fair on the poor girl, who knows nothing of what she is in for. Jimmy, at least, must think very highly of her even to try and sweat her through it. I suppose he's fallen in love with her.'

'What on earth makes you think that?'

'He's susceptible and he's got strong protective instincts, and she's at an age when she'd fall in love with anyone who suggested it to her.'

'Why do you dislike this poor girl?'

'Why should my thinking she'd fall in love with Jimmy mean that I dislike her?'

'I haven't the faintest idea, but it seems to.'

'I'm not against her,' she said after a pause: 'I simply think that what you propose doing with her is silly.'

'I need coffee,' he observed; 'and a hot bath. Could we leave this arrangement, now? I can't think of anything more to say about it.'

'Well – don't say I didn't warn you.'

'About Alberta being no good? I am taking that possibility into account.'

'About Jimmy falling in love with Alberta – and Alberta with Jimmy.'

'So far as Jimmy is concerned, he's much more interested in my play. And Alberta is not a suggestible little schoolgirl.' He said this with an almost venomous conviction which surprised him.

She was lighting a cigarette: he felt in his dressing-gown pocket – then thought that if he smoked now his head would get worse, and squeezed the packet regretfully.

Suddenly, she said: 'Em! *Don't* seduce her – anything else but not that. *Please* make sure of that.'

He looked at her: she had spoken as though it was hopeless – as though it was already important and true. He took out a cigarette, tapped it on his finger nail, reached for her lighter, and used it before he had designed an answer.

'Lillian – I know what put that into your head, but I am old enough to be her father, I am married to you, and I don't think she is in search of sensation. She has told me enough about her family for me to feel responsible to them for her. Will that do?'

He felt the climate between them change.

'No, it won't. The first two reasons are laughable, and the last one frightens me. Do you mean you *respect* her?'

'One hardly ever respects people, does one? It's not such a personal business. Sometimes one can respect what they stand for.'

'And you do?'

'I hadn't considered it before, but yes.'

She said coldly: 'I fail to see the difference between Alberta and thousands of other girls.'

'Then you have no reason to respect her.' He got to his feet:

his head was pounding, and beyond their familiar air of destruction something unknown was building of which he was afraid.

'Em!'

As he moved back to her, he felt her change her mind, and because of this, he said more gently: 'What is it?'

She said rapidly: 'I do agree about the house – but not now – not this summer . . .' He waited.

'Will you do two things for me?'

'What are they?'

'Will you make us both some coffee and take me to Greece?'

And because this made him smile, he promised.

3

JIMMY

IT'S no good saying Greece before seven – they won't change their minds, they've decided, or rather *she* has, and I suppose he had to trade Greece for Alberta. Oh well! Join the Joyces and travel, or travel and see the Joyces – it comes to much the same thing. It's stupid to feel sore about it, when it doesn't matter to me where the hell we go. I suppose I can as well train that girl on a Greek island as I can train her any place else. *If* I can train her at all. It began with Lillian. I was taking a shower and she came into my room and called out to me. I wrapped a towel round me and found her, fresh as a daisy, sitting on my bed with a tray of coffee and orange juice beside her.

'I've come to have more coffee with you: I've had some with Em.'

'Is he up?'

She nodded. 'He's having a long, hot bath.'

'What's the time, for heaven's sake?'

'Just after eight. Em couldn't sleep – he had so much to tell me, and we've made a lot of plans.' She gave me my coffee. Somehow I knew that he *had* told her, so I said: 'He's told you about our plan for Clemency?'

'He has. Jimmy, seriously – which one of you had this idea?'

'It wasn't either one of us. We both had it.'

'But one of you must actually have made the suggestion?'

'We just sort of looked at each other and arrived at it. He asked her if she'd do it. Naturally, I leave that kind of thing to him.' I looked at her carefully. If she started upsetting Alberta, I'd never get anywhere with her. 'It's only an experiment, you know. It may work – it may not. But we had to do something.'

'What do you think of her?'

Wondering exactly this, I said: 'I think she looks as though she may be able to learn. Otherwise she has the intelligence, and I should say, the stamina.'

'Do you think she is attractive?'

'She's got something of what is needed for Clemency – that's the main reason why we are trying her. Lillian – I'm sure you think it's a crazy idea, but you could make a lot of difference to whether it's a success or not.'

'How could I?' She was off her guard – engaged – any appeal would do that to her if there was a shred of truth in it.

'I shall have to work her very hard – voice mostly – to get it to come across and to get it to last for a possible eight performances a week. She'll get tired and depressed and nervous. If you could give her a bit of confidence, be kind to her, help her with her appearance, and so on – it might make all the difference. You know what I mean. Any little thing. Get her hair cut properly – not curled – and tell her what an improvement it is.' There was a pause, and then I added: 'Then if she's no good, help me to help her out of it. She's in for a tough time whichever way it goes.'

She smiled then, took my empty cup away from me, and

looked at her watch. 'All right, Jimmy. I'll help, if you'll tell me what to do. There isn't much time to have her hair cut because we're going to Greece.'

'*When* are we going to do that?'

'As soon as possible. I want her to arrange the tickets this morning.'

'Oh Lord!'

'It doesn't matter to you. You can work as well on an island as anywhere else. You love sun and swimming.'

'It seems crazy to me.'

'It's no more crazy than all of us coming all the way over here in order to make a decision we could perfectly well have made in London. Oh Jimmy, please be nice about it. I *do* so want to go, and Em doesn't mind as long as we find a house to live in and he doesn't have to work in some hotel bedroom.'

'OK.'

'It would be silly to go all the way back to England – think of the *rain*.'

'I see the only solution is Greece,' I said, trying to sound pleasant about it.

Lillian went and I dressed, wondering why her saying 'it doesn't matter to *you*' stung me somewhere – why should it? – I had always prided myself on not caring where we went as long as we didn't go too far away from theatres for too long and I could work with Emmanuel.

I found him sitting on a chair outside my room pretending to read a paperback.

'You can't see to read in that light.'

'I can't see to read in any light; Jimmy, for God's sake, before we do anything – take me to a chemist.'

'Drugstore,' I said gently: 'Stay where you are a minute.'

Alberta was cleaning up the kitchen: when she saw me, she sneezed.

'We're all going for a nice holiday to Greece. That'll mean four plane tickets for Athens as soon as possible. The travel agent's name and number are in the green book. Would you call them? I'll be back in half an hour if you have any trouble.'

She sneezed again, and said: '*Greece!* Goodness! When?'

'As soon as possible. From tonight onwards. Have you got soap powder up your nose?'

'No.'

'Well, I might as well warn you that from now on I shall take a personal and very disapproving interest in any cold you get.'

'I am quite certain that I have not got a cold, but considering the rate at which we are changing climates I may hardly escape.'

'You don't get asthma, do you?' Visions of certain terrible hours with Emmanuel reared up in my mind. She would be no good if . . .

'I don't get anything.' She sneezed again. 'Greece! I simply sneeze sometimes – it is an entirely private and quite insignificant affliction.'

'That's all right,' I said kindly: 'Everybody has to have some private life. Back soon.'

We went out of the apartment, down the elevator, into the street in silence – anxiety and dissatisfaction dividing us: I had begun to feel unduly irritated with Lillian, and I knew that – whatever he was feeling about her – this would annoy him. I sat him down in a corner, got him a draught and coffee for both of us. When he had swallowed the draught, he said: 'How commonplace we are to be sure. Three little mechanisms jostling against one another and ticking away to no purpose. Either we regard the fact of our existence as miracle enough, or we suffer from the delusions of that fool last night. His education and progress don't seem even to improve our mechanism. I could undoubtedly put my foot in my mouth soon after I was born, and I fail to see what I have gained to compensate for the loss of this honest achievement.'

'Perhaps we aren't here for any purpose,' I suggested; 'so it's not surprising that we're commonplace.'

'Do you know, I think that is very unlikely?'

'Why?'

He thought for a moment, and then said slowly: 'Because I detect signs of order wherever anything seems to know its place.' He leaned forward. 'That's the trouble, Jimmy: we don't know our place. We have been told what chaos that used to create in the servants' hall. Lillian said this morning that she didn't know what she was for: I have a nasty feeling that that is true of nearly all of us.'

'Well, how do we find out what we are for?'

He looked at me with amusement. 'Jimmy – you're just stringing along: you don't really want to find out because you think you know, don't you?'

'I suppose I do. I know for myself – I wouldn't go any further than that.'

'But supposing you were wrong. I mean, we take ourselves so fearfully for granted. We allow that certain muscles can be developed, and certain parts of the brain, but all the rest is just dubbed lucky, instinctive, or unlucky: we don't question what else we are besides muscles and brains, and certainly not what we might be. We behave like ready-made products trying to grab at change out of circumstances – as though they were the only variable factors in our lives.'

'Well, they do make a difference. I mean, if I hadn't happened to meet you I would never have been . . .'

He looked at me then – curiously intent. 'You didn't "happen to meet me".'

There was a silence into which I tried to follow him. Then, he said: 'Do you believe in magic?'

I thought carefully.

'I don't mean white rabbits. I mean something marvellous that you can't understand, that as you are, you couldn't understand and if you even began to have a glimmer of its meaning you would already be different. I mean that kind.'

I thought again. 'No,' I said at last: 'I don't think that kind of magic is for me.'

'Quite right,' he said, 'but *you* might be for that kind of magic, and not know it. That might be what you are for.'

'Are you?'

There was a kind of ache in his face as he said: 'I hope so, Jimmy. I can't tell you how I hope that.'

Getting to his feet a minute later, he said casually: 'So you see, Jimmy, it doesn't really matter whether we go to Greece or not. We can make some use of it or not, but it won't make "all the difference" like they say in books.'

It was much later, when thinking over this close talk, I realized that he'd referred to three mechanisms. He'd left the girl out of it.

It was the next morning, in fact, when I thought of his leaving the girl out of it. We were due to fly to Athens that evening – Lillian had taken her shopping and arranged to have her hair cut the day before, and now I had to get her photographed. I still hadn't told Mick and the boys that their worst fears were to be realized, and I wanted to have a picture to warm them up a little. So it had to be a good picture. I had a friend who sometimes took that kind if he liked what he saw: I'd called him and told him what I wanted, and now we were on our way there. I'd done Stanley one or two favours in the past, and he was great on paying up favours or dues – I think he preferred dues – it was how he saw life. Alberta sat beside me in the cab with her hands in her lap and her head a little bent. Lillian had done a very good job on her hair; now that it was cut one could see the shape of her head and the back of her neck. She hadn't said a word since we got into the cab, so I asked: 'Anything on your mind?'

'Not my mind exactly.'

'What is it on?' But she didn't answer.

'If you're nervous or worrying about the part – don't. We'll start on that when we get to Greece. Once we're there, and anything worries you, speak up, and if I can straighten it out for you I will.'

'Thank you, Jimmy.'

'But don't start worrying about it now. Emmanuel said you read the part very well, and understood what it was about: well – that's the main thing.'

'Yes.'

She was so quiet, she made me feel a fool – as though I was the one who was nervous, and perhaps this was true.

'You're not nervous about the picture being taken?'

She shook her head, and said: 'I've never had my photograph taken, excepting for my passport. But there is nothing surprising about that. I hardly do anything nowadays to which I am accustomed.'

'You don't sound happy about it.'

'Oh, I am not *un*happy about it. But it is a little like having meals every day of food you've never seen before in your life. Very interesting,' she added primly, 'but a lot of the time I feel rather full.'

'I must get to know you better, or I'll be a wreck myself. First I think you have asthma, and then I think you're scared, when really all you do is sneeze and have indigestion.' She smiled and did not reply, but just before we arrived at Stanley's studio she said: 'There is one thing that I should very much like to ask you.'

'Go ahead.'

'Is it – would it be possible for me to telephone to my father to explain to him about going to Greece? He is not very young, and I don't want to cause him unnecessary anxiety.'

'Will our going to Greece worry him?'

'Oh no – I don't think so. He may regard it as a bit fidgety – but that's all. But I should like to tell him – if it is possible.'

'We'll put a call in right after your picture has been taken.'

'Thank you, Jimmy.'

Stanley had a curious act, or attitude towards his sitters – I never knew which it was – he never spoke to them – he just didn't say anything at all. All the other times I saw him, he talked all the time: softly, almost inaudibly – but that way he didn't use much breath so he never needed to stop. The moment he saw you, he fixed you with expressionless pale blue eyes and started right in telling you what had happened to him since he woke up that morning. He never expressed an opinion, or asked you what you thought; he just quietly, confidently unrolled a record – it was like hearing a newsreel of someone's life – consecutive events with all the commentator's time-honoured adjectives removed. But whenever I'd taken people to him for pictures, he hadn't said a word. He'd greet us with a soft, absent smile and immediately go to the other end of his studio and fiddle interminably with equipment whilst I and his sitter carried on an uneasy conversation until we'd said again everything that we'd said on the way to him and had subsided into an edgy silence. Then he would advance upon us with an ancient lamp and a slightly menacing expression and the sitter – agog for some notice to be taken of her – would turn to him expectantly . . . This was his cue for dragging out a dirty, hideously uncomfortable chair – half-heartedly upholstered in khaki plush: he patted it invitingly, and the sitter, mesmerized by his indifference, invariably sat upon it. He took his photographs with an air of reckless gloom – if he wanted his sitter to move he came and moved her, but with an expression on his face of it not making much difference. When he had finished, he smiled again and went into the only other room he had which I knew was a bathroom, kitchen and darkroom combined, locked the door very noisily, and turned on all the taps. And that was that.

As we climbed the stairs of the old brownstone house where he lived, I nearly told Alberta; then curiosity about what they would make of each other intervened, and I said nothing, except that he was the best photographer I knew – which was true.

Stanley occupied half of the top floor, and his studio (he called it that) had a kind of anonymously international eccentricity. It was drab and rather dirty – filled with spiteful draughts in winter and hot, dead air in summer. It was packed with incongruous objects nearly all of which were being used for some makeshift purpose not their own – and some seemed to have none at all, except the doubtful chance of their owner having at one time thought them decorative. A small gong hung on a nail on the door, and almost as soon as I struck it, there was Stanley ready in his smile with the overpowering smell of caraway seeds behind him. Inside, he left us to the usual problem of where to sit: today it was a couple of shooting sticks stuck into the wide cracks between the floorboards. He had acquired several new things – a large, old-fashioned birdcage which was stuffed with dead lamp bulbs and his bed in the corner was covered with yards of window-dressing grass – but all the old pots made out of twisted gramophone discs were there and the child's playpen with rocks and sand and the old gopher tortoise: the collection of hats on pegs arranged in a serpentine pattern on the wall, and several volumes of the *Encyclopaedia Britannica* spread open on the floor.

Alberta – unlike anyone else I had brought there – did not walk about in search of a mirror and end by furtively jabbing at herself with a powder puff out of her handbag; nor did she run her fingers through her hair and talk to me with one eye on Stanley – she simply sat and looked round the room with a frank accepting interest. So I lit a cigarette and watched them and didn't talk. The silence was preserved while Stanley took three or four pictures: he moved her for each one, but somehow he was doing it differently – he did not manipulate her as though she was material that he knew all about: once he lifted her chin and looked at her with a kind of tentative searching, and after that, he took three more pictures with – it seemed to me – a tender attention in his treatment of her. I knew then that the pictures were going to be good. When he had finished, he did not immediately escape but stood by his camera staring at the floor, and she sat still with her head bent as she had sat in the taxi. Then at the same moment they both looked up at each other and smiled; he moved and we got to our feet: there was a curious feeling in the room – as though they were talking so privately that I could not even hear them.

I had explained when I called him about our going to

Greece, and now I gave him a piece of paper with 'American Express, Athens', written on it. He read it, patted my shoulder, nodded, and stuffed the paper into a pocket of his filthy old leather jacket. Alberta held out her hand and said 'Thank you.'

He bowed over her hand and replied: 'I recognized you: the pictures should be good.'

'Shall I see you again?'

Still holding her hand, he was absolutely still for a moment before answering: 'I'm not sure,' then he let it go, waved his own and we left.

Outside, I took her arm to guide her across the road, and asked her what she thought of Stanley, and she said: 'I don't think he is an ordinary man.'

'He certainly liked you.' I noticed at the time what a lame reply this was.

I took her to a bar I knew nearby where she could telephone: 'It will be more private for you than the apartment, and we can eat here if we want.'

'Would you mind very much helping me to put through the telephone call? I know it sounds silly when I'm supposed to be a secretary, but I've never made a call like this before.'

'We'll get Frank to put it through for you – all you'll have to do is take it. Write down your father's name and telephone number, and I'll give it to him.'

She wrote down The Reverend William Wyndham Young in full with a place and a number.

I gave the piece of paper to Frank, and sat down opposite her at the small table.

'How long will it be?'

'He's getting through now to find out. What do you want to eat?'

She shook her head.

'You've got to eat. Have some – have some Littlenecks.'

'Some *what*?'

'Clams. Special American food.'

'Oh! Yes please.'

Her immediate enthusiasm made me want to smile. 'Are you very fond of them, then?'

'I've never had them. But I don't suppose they'll have them in Greece, will they? So it would be a waste not to try now.'

We had them, and some beer, and talked. The clams were a success, and while we talked I watched her – trying to feel what she was, what stuff she was made of and how I could use it. She had the most extraordinary dignity: at least I couldn't figure it out alongside her extreme lack of sophistication – her English schoolgirl appearance (except when she had been wearing that black dress, I suddenly remembered) – her funny, prim way of expressing herself, and her admitted inexperience in any field I knew about anyway. It wasn't exactly self-confidence – she was shy except when she was alone with you and even then you had to be careful – it was more as though she was collected – all in one piece – no acts, no exaggerations, no trying to make out she was different: she didn't get in the way of whatever she was talking about. I asked her if she had wanted to be a secretary who travelled – she said she never thought about it – it had just happened. 'If my uncle hadn't taken me to the party where I met Mrs Joyce, I don't suppose I would be a secretary who travelled.'

'And what about becoming an actress?'

'I had not considered that at all. And after all, you may find that I'm not one. In that case, you need have no consideration for my feelings, because I shall probably know myself.'

'Will you be disappointed?'

She looked at me then. 'I don't think so, because I didn't appoint myself. I haven't any imagination of myself as an actress – either way.' She smiled – with her eyes as well – and for a moment I felt connected with her: there was some warmth, and a warning in it . . . Then her call came through, and I watched her in the glass booth talking to her father – talking, listening carefully, explaining, listening – her laugh – her moment's tension before she hung up. She came back.

'Everything all right?'

She nodded, and her eyes filled suddenly with tears.

'He wasn't at all surprised to hear me – not *at all*! He sounded exactly the same and clearer than if I was ringing him up from London!'

'What did he say about Greece?'

'A prodigious piece of good fortune.' Her tears ran down with a kind of momentous ease: then she said: 'It's simply that I've known him all my life.' There wasn't anybody I had known like that, and I felt it then.

I said: 'There isn't anyone I've known all my life.'

'Are you an orphan?'

'I don't even know. My mother died when I was born. She wasn't married to my father whoever he was.' I felt my angry smile splitting my face: 'At least I *know* I'm illegitimate.'

'Are you English or American?'

'You may well ask. I'm not anything, really. I've got a British passport, brought up – if you can call it that – in America.' Something in her practical attention eased me, and suddenly I *wanted* to say it all. 'When my mother died, she kind of left me to her sister. The sister married an Irishman who was emigrating to the States. They took me along – the sister died almost as soon as they got there; her husband married again, they didn't want me, and managed to farm me out to an orphanage. That was when I clung to my having been born in England and being different from the rest of the kids. When I was sixteen and I'd been working in a store for some time saving the money for a trip to England, Emmanuel suddenly wrote to me out of the blue and said he'd pay the expenses for the trip. It didn't seem strange at all. I was crazy on the theatre – I'd known about him for years, I'd saved ninety dollars and thirty-five cents for the trip, and I knew I was going in the end, anyway, but it never struck me what an extraordinary piece of luck it was for me that Emmanuel should have picked me out and offered me exactly that. That was in '39: late summer – the war hadn't started, and Lillian had taken Sarah away for a long seaside holiday – I didn't meet her then. I spent five weeks in an hotel with Emmanuel and he showed me London. They were the best weeks in my life. We went to the theatre every night, and sometimes in the afternoons as well – he gave me wonderful meals with wines which I'd never had before, and in the mornings he showed me London, thoroughly – every single thing I wanted to see, and a great deal that I'd never heard of. And he talked to me! He treated me all the time as though I was human and adult and interesting; he taught me by listening to my resentment, by not arguing with my opinions, by encouraging me to walk down each one of my little dead alleys and waiting for me at the open end. I'd gotten a grudge like a house on my back – I was against pretty well everything you can think of from Mick O'Casey, my aunt's husband, to Dr Heller who ran the Home where my childhood had been spent for me – to the President himself – anything, anyone – but in those five weeks it all peeled off – like having a new skin. He once said to me: "After you've given up something which seemed difficult to give up, you find out it wasn't ever there – you feel much lighter and a little foolish": it was just how I felt about the chip on my shoulder. He showed me the play he was writing, and asked me what I thought of it; he bought me decent clothes; he offered to send me to college or university – it was all set that I could stay in England if I wanted.' I stopped and she said: 'Why have you stopped?'

'I don't know why I started. Oh yes: I was trying to explain why I'm such a mongrel. I don't even have me an accent that either country would call their own. *You'd* think it was American, and most Americans would think it was English.'

'Yes, but what happened next?'

'When?'

'After the five weeks? What happened then?'

'The war. I'd paid no attention to it, you see – I was in such a trance, and it just sneaked up on me. He sent me back to America. I didn't want to go to college, so he sent me to learn my profession with a man he knew in Chicago who owned theatres. He promised me a job after the war, and to keep in touch. He wrote to me and I came straight out of the Army to him.'

'He's really become your family, hasn't he?'

'*He* has. I only told you all this so that you wouldn't cry.' This wasn't true: I had wanted to tell her and liked it. I asked Frank for the check, and she said: 'Did you ever know Sarah?'

'She died that fall. Just after I left. I didn't meet Lillian till after the war.'

She said she wanted to pay for her call. 'No – this is part of the expense sheet: honest. We couldn't abduct you to Greece without your father's agreement – you're under the age for that kind of consenting.'

'And I suppose now you're well over the age of resenting?'

'I do hope so.' I was smiling when I said that, and then I remembered Emmanuel's face when he had said the same thing about his magic.

Outside, she said: 'What do you think Greece will be like? Or do you know?'

'I don't *know*, but I suspect that it will be hot and yellow and dusty with everybody arguing about money, and flies on the food. We shall all get dysentery and sunstroke and be eaten by sharks.'

'*Sharks?* Are there really sharks?'

'The sea is studded with them – all half mad with hunger because there aren't nearly enough fish to go round anywhere in the Mediterranean.'

'Sharks,' she repeated dreamily – she sounded pleased. 'What else?'

'Isn't that enough? Well, ruins, of course. The whole country's lousy with ruins, and a lot of rocks so you're worn out climbing. I just can't wait to get back from Greece. I suppose you're looking forward to it.'

She nodded: 'I really am. It may be better than you think.'

I shrugged, but she persisted: 'Or different.'

'I'll tell you if it is either.'

She laughed: 'You won't have to tell me – I'll know.'

4

LILLIAN

CONTRAST – opposites – extremes – how I am fed by them! New York in the early evening of early summer, shrugging with a moonstone mist, chilled, subdued, chalky; filled with a hurrying irresolution – the business day over, the professional night not begun – slung in this hour of waiting for the end of the end. The time for illicit love, for the uncharacteristic event, for killing with a drink or some duty duologue, for playing with the children: to spend, to lose, or to waste – the travelling is over, but nobody has arrived . . . In the aeroplane we have become a giant: everything below us diminished, cosy, twinkling, melted into the distance of our feet, until, at our giant's level, the sky is our country – pleasing with enormous detail and endless resource. We fly away from the sun which retreats like a beautiful calamity with such majestic movement and tragic colour that I know it is its silence which moves me. When we are above the clouds that reflect this crisis of the sun, they lie in soft apricot waves – the smaller ones sharper hit, red and seedy, like split pomegranate, and above us the fine, blue air is already impregnated with stars who are born into the dying blue with little starts of light. Soon the air will have that unbreathing colourless purity that I love and cannot communicate, and I turn to Em sitting beside me because I wonder whether all communication is, after all, only a refuge? This starts some consideration about silence in my mind – the nearest I get to it is with music, when sometimes I am attending to sound outside myself, and if the attention is enough, I am silent inside. I turn to Em again – illogically, even thinking of silence has made me want to talk to him, but at once an avalanche of food and information pours through the aeroplane, quenching all sparks of hunger or need of any kind. Em asks me something but I only hear 'glad' and 'darling': I lean towards him and he repeats: 'Are you glad that we are going to Greece?' and I smile, and start to imagine Athens – but I get caught by the beautiful name and can see nothing . . .

Athens – stepping out of the plane on to the hot ground into air brilliant, burning at such a pitch of light that my eyes cannot reach it. It is noon; and we walk into the Customs with the heat like an arrow between our shoulder blades, and wait for our luggage amid the usual shuffle of languages and a knot of people becoming resigned to impatience. The stalls sell sham pottery, sham jewellery, and doubtful peasant costumes, real silk and beautiful cigarettes; the airport officials have that Mediterranean inability to look serious in uniform. Alberta is looking at a priest: he wears black boots below his greasy gown, but it is his head that fascinates her. After the wealth of his beard it seems impossible that his long hair can screw into so small a bun – it is no larger than a ping-pong ball skewered below his huge stiff hat. His face is shrewd, savage, and joyous. Then we are in a taxi – a huge old American car which thunders loosely along the coast road into Athens. To our right are mountains bleached and shimmering in the hot distance, and to the left the sea – like a stroke of summer – filling and quenching our eyes. We all look, and say very little – the long flight is beginning to catch up on us: we none of us speak any Greek, and are to depend on my French, but when the cab driver points and says 'Akropolis', and there it is, crowning a hill in actual unwinking splendour, there is a different silence – we smile at one another, and I wonder what the others are thinking until Alberta says: 'My father has a picture of that in his study, but it is rather spotted with damp': and Jimmy says: 'Yes: I've seen pictures of that some place too.'

We are into Athens – the air is white and dusty – every other road seems to be up – buildings are being demolished, being built, and traffic is either charging at full speed or hopelessly jammed. Our driver becomes dramatically concerned with getting us to the hotel – he sweats and sways and groans over his wheel – he hoots and pounces whenever he can take anyone by surprise – he swerves round pot holes and shoots down side streets muttering the breathy, liquid language – his face tragic with resolution – I see Em watching it in the driving mirror and take his hand, but it is too hot to touch hands. The hotel is very cool and dark and antiseptic: the man at the desk speaks English, and Jimmy is visibly cheered. In a spurt of excitement at our arrival, we decide to go out to lunch . . .

Now – in the early evening I lie stupefied in the darkened room. We walk back here from the restaurant after lunch, and suddenly I am so tired that I can hardly bear it – the air feels like a hot curtain falling over my face – I wonder why I wanted to come here and how quickly we can leave this sordid stew of heat and glaring concrete and the ashes of antiquity all casually stirred together and simmering with clouds of dust. The lift does not work and I stumble up three flights of stairs with Em holding my arm – making me wait between each flight – my ankles hurt – I am horribly breathless and I know I am behaving like a weak, angry child. Disappointment! I am encrusted with it like the grit from the streets: I think the pain is starting, and clutch Em's arm, but it is simply that I am aching to cry: I say 'Athens' to myself and remember what I had imagined. 'You are simply exhausted,' Em says and, because I want to scream and hit him for saying it, I know he is right. He puts me to bed – as he shuts the door I start to cry and immediately fall into sleep.

Now – I am slowly waking – remembering our departure from New York, the lovely first minutes in the aeroplane, the long, uneasy night, the early morning stop at Orly – French breakfast and we bought brandy (it was raining there and we all huddled in our overcoats) and then our dazzling arrival in Athens. The word sounded beautiful again; all the afternoon horror had gone, and from the blissful lassitude in my bones now, I knew how tired I had been.

There is a gentle knock on the door and Alberta stands in its entrance saying, 'Mr Joyce told me to wake you at seven. Shall I open your shutters?'

'Please do.'

When we could see each other she came over to my bed: 'Do you feel better now?'

'Much better: marvellous – I must have slept for four hours.'

'We should not have walked back from lunch – it was terribly hot: they say it is unusually hot for June.'

'It's nothing: when I get overtired I just get the horrors, like retired pirates.' I was looking for my bag, and she fetched it saying: '*They* got them from too much rum trying to forget their wicked deeds – not at all the same.'

'Are you fond of Stevenson?'

'Some of him: but I haven't read all. My sister has – she likes him better than anybody – *my* knowledge of him is partly vicarious.

I lit a cigarette, and she said: 'Would you like me to unpack for you? Just what you need for now, I mean.'

'Tell me what has been happening while I've been asleep.'

'Well – quite a lot, really. Jimmy and I have got tickets for the boat tomorrow morning which goes to the island. We've been to American Express and cashed an enormous sum of money. We've arranged for a taxi to take us to the boat – it's quite a long way. Mr Joyce met somebody he knew in the street who said he knew someone who might lend us a house on the island and they went off to somewhere called Monestarike and then to the Acropolis. Then we met them and I've just been having a shower. I think the others are sleeping, and,' her eyes widened, 'apparently we are all going out to dinner to eat fish with our feet in the sea.'

She seemed so pleased at this that I could not help smiling back: 'You sound as though you have been very busy. Did you get a picture for your father?'

'I have sent him a postcard: it's *wonderful* here – I can't possibly thank you enough for bringing me. Shall I get out your pleated silk dress – the one that screws up like rope? that won't be in the least crushed, and it is still hot.'

'That would be a good idea: thank you.' I lay and watched while she unpacked my smaller case: whenever I was alone with her, I felt utterly disarmed into a liking that was almost protective. She was simply a nice child – she could almost have been my daughter – excepting that she was not physically how I imagined Sarah would have become. Sarah had had Em's heavy-lidded eyes and the same curling mouth, and her hair had been dark, but otherwise she had been too young to tell: she might have become anything. This girl had a restful quality which was graceful beside her extreme youth. She could have been drawn by Holbein, I thought – she has that well-bred homespun appearance which he would have translated into beauty. She was unwinding my sea green dress – stroking the fine pleats and laying it on Em's bed. She saw me watching her and said: 'It *is* beautiful – like pale green pearls.'

It was. 'I get them in Venice: there is one man who makes them there, although you're supposed to be able to buy them in New York.'

'It is such astonishing silk. It really would go through the eye of a needle, like the princess's shifts.'

'So it would. Is the gold belt there?'

'Yes; and the shoes – everything. Would you like a bath run, or do you want a shower?'

'I'd like a bath. You're spoiling me, Alberta: I'm not an invalid and you are not meant to wait on me.'

'I really like to do what you need. Shall I go now, or wait and talk to you when you've had your bath?'

'Stay and talk to me. I'll be quick – I want a cool one.'

The dress, which was just a pleated tent from neck to hem, drawn in at the waist by a gold belt, was much prettier than I remembered – I'd only worn it once when it was new – and

Alberta admired it deeply. She watched me doing my face with such solemn interest that I wanted to laugh, until she said: 'I hope you don't mind: there has been next to no opportunity for me to learn anything like this. Do you think my dress will do for this exotic evening?'

She was wearing a brown check gingham, square necked and sleeveless. She was watching me looking at it and said anxiously: 'I took the sleeves out in New York, because my aunt can only make the wrong kind, but perhaps you can see that there *have* been sleeves?'

'What about the white embroidered cotton we got in New York? Wouldn't you like to wear that?'

'Of course. How extraordinary! I'd forgotten its existence. Events in my life have changed scale so much. I'll go and change.'

'If you come back, I'll show you how to do your eyes.'

'*Will* you? Oh thank you. I have not had the courage to try and do them. I'll be very quick.'

When she came back and I had sat her at the dressing table, I said: 'Tell me something. What do you mean – events in your life have changed scale?'

'Well at home nothing very much happened – a new dress would be a tremendous event: the whole family would notice it. Now, so much is happening that a new dress seems a very small size of event. You know – it's the difference between leading a Jane Austen life and a Tolstoy one.'

'But some things stay the same size whatever happens, don't they?' I was thinking of Sarah.

'Perhaps they should,' she answered after a moment; 'but I haven't got far enough to make them: I'm too variable for my liking.' She brushed away at her eyelashes in silence and then went on: 'I don't mean what one *thinks*, exactly,' she frowned: 'Not the size or importance one thinks something should have in one's life: I mean what one *feels or knows it is* – all the time – it's difficult to keep that the same.' She put down the mascara brush I had given her. 'Except my father: I was thinking of him. I don't think anything changes how he is to me. I'm not at all good at this: that's one eye – what do you think?'

'That's quite enough – do the other one.'

'I wanted it to show: and it does, doesn't it?'

'Most alluring.' She looked pleased and brushed away at her other eye until I said: 'Was your father always more important to you than your mother?'

'Yes. My mother died, you see, when Serena was born. Of course, it was like having a kind of earthquake in one's life: afterwards, everything seemed changed – but my father kept some bits of it the same by not changing himself.'

'If he loved your mother very much, that must have been a difficult thing to do.'

'I think it was *very* difficult,' she said with emphasis, and I noticed that her voice was trembling. Because I found myself badly wanting to know, I asked: 'Did you find it helped to pray?' I could not help remembering my bitter failure in this direction. The question did not seem to surprise her and she looked clearly at me in the glass.

'Not much: the trouble is that I can't pray – I don't know how to. I ask and thank for things sometimes, but that isn't the point, is it?'

'What does your father say about that?'

'Oh – he says that hardly anybody does know. He says it is a difficult thing to do; one hasn't a hope of beginning until one knows one can't, and most people think of it as a method of getting something; it's nice of them to pray and they ought to get something back – anything from peace of mind to some useful object. They think prayer is *for them*, that's the trouble: that's some of what he says, but of course he says it much better.'

'But what *is* prayer for? Did he tell you that?'

'Of course I asked him: he said: "What is air for?" I said: "To breathe," and he said: "Well, try thinking of prayer as another breath of another life" – that was all he said about it.'

She looked up at me again in the glass and was silent for a moment before saying: 'I am so sorry that you lost your daughter.'

She said it so quietly, that my face, which had begun to stiffen with its habit of rejection (nobody could possibly know how much I cared – all casual pity is an insult) became calm and I felt at ease with her speaking of Sarah.

When she smiled at me and said: 'Will I do?' I took a handkerchief and evened up the corners of her eyes and we went down to the bar.

Everything went well that evening. For the first time, we seemed all to have achieved the right degrees of intimacy, but our composition had also a freshness, and the place, so old, so new to us, gave us a kind of dream-like gaiety in its evening presence. Evening in Athens: the air is dry and tender; people loiter steadily – not going anywhere – simply content with existing along a street: the cafés are like hives – their interiors violently lit, with customers bunched at tables on the pavements and waiters like worker bees scurrying darkly in and out. We drive to Phaleron, past dusty squares where people drink orange soda under shrill strings of lights threaded through the tired trees: down one long narrow street which had at its end and above us the Acropolis, radiant in the full dress of flood-lighting – out on to a wide highway where one notices chiefly the evening sky with land dark below it pollinated with lights. We turn on to a road which has the harbour on our left – the waters have still a dull sheen on them from the sun – like golden oil. There are a few boats anchored and an air of gentle desertion, but to our right, cafés, booths, restaurants are strung out with irregular bursts of cheap savage light and violent music. As we climb, the curve of Phaleron is below us to our left; pretty, laid out with beady lights like a doll's bay which blots out as we plunge into the quiet town above it. Our taxi takes us down to the waterfront and leaves us and we stand in the road where he has put us, a little dazed, the scene is so full to the brim of the water's edge where everybody is eating under canvas awnings and strings of white lights. The food is rushed to them across the road (full of cars, and spectators) from the cafés, which are almost empty, except for a few old men drinking and thinking alone at large bare tables. The harbour is full of yachts and little boats anchored in rows – some brilliantly lit – others as quiet and dark as a bird on a nest. We smile vaguely at each other – we are not yet in this scene which is so chocked with gaiety and pleasure: Em takes my arm and Jimmy Alberta's, and we walk slowly round the curve to choose where we will eat. It is difficult to choose; the restaurants are not all the same, but we do not understand their differences. Finally we go to one which has a table right on the water – a Greek family are leaving it and we sit round their silted coffee cups to find ourselves staring into the despairing eyes of a very old man in a rowing boat. He wants to take us somewhere, but Em tells him that we don't want to go, and like a disillusioned old dog he understands Em's tone of voice – he waits for us not to change our minds and then rows painfully away. We drink *ouzo*, and poor Alberta doesn't like it, but there are beautiful black olives and long glasses of iced water and slices of bread.

A child has come up to Em – she might be about eight or nine, and she is carrying a huge basket in which there are tiny bunches of white flowers. She stands very close to Em without actually touching him, and thrusts a spindly bunch before us: it is jasmine: she says something in a small, hoarse throaty voice. She is not pretty, but her face has a finesse and pride, so that even her begging – her single gesture and one speech – have a kind of casual distinction. Em buys two bunches from her – she does not smile, but accepts his money impassively and glides away. Each flower of the jasmine has been pulled off and fastened with cotton to a stiff stem: the effect is exotic and enchanting and our table is clouded with their night scent. We eat a great deal – fish and rice, and there is resinated wine which we all, in varying degrees, dislike, and baclava and very good Turkish coffee and the most fiery brandy: the stars come out and a ripe moon. More children come round with baskets and bundles of nuts and sweets and flowers – we cannot buy from all of them, but they all seem to have an ageless detachment from our responses – we buy or we do not buy – either event may occur. At our feet are elegant, desperate cats who eat anything they find with sibilant speed – pieces of bread, the heads and tails of prawns, grains of rice – anything. Our talk has been pleasant, easy, small – the size suited to our remembering all the other aspects of this evening. In the end we manage to pay our bill and find our taxi in the road (he has found where we were eating) and drive back to Athens. We say goodnight to the others and go to our room and I throw myself on to my bed.

'Are you tired now?' I notice how often he looks anxious: how if I think of an expression of his it would be anxiety.

'No – I am just delighted with my evening. Are you glad we came here, darling?'

'If *you* are glad, I am.'

'Oh – more than that, surely?'

He sat down and lit a cigarette. 'Yes, I am. It is the people here that I like – they are different, and it is a good difference.'

'Different from whom?'

'I was thinking of other countries that we have visited. We have looked at buildings and pictures and sculpture, and it has been rather like going to see a woman because she comes of a good family and dresses well, and because she is old and poor, she'll see *you* as long as you give dinner and anything else you can spare. You have to care very much about blue blood and good clothes to do it – there is an exchange, but it is a dull one. But these people don't feel to me sold out in that same degree. I don't feel that they are struggling to be comfortable at all costs; to keep up classic or baroque appearances – they have some separate, present pride in themselves, and this makes them less divorced from their heritage.' He was silent for a minute, and then said abruptly: 'I felt this very much at the Acropolis.'

'Tell me about it: what was it like up there?'

He smiled: 'I can't: fortunately there don't seem to be words for its appearance. But I sat on a stone in the sun for a while, and I had suddenly the feeling of life without time: that these temples were building always – that their whole was implicit in each part of them, that they were never completed, never begun, and never abandoned. It was something to do with the people I had been seeing all the afternoon. Touch the place in them, and they would come up the hill with stone and rope and chisels, and be building under the sun.' He waited a moment, and then said: 'Always.'

'Like the child with these?' I held up my jasmine.

He nodded: 'Do you want water for them?'

'It would be no good.' I showed him how the bunch was made. 'Em. Tell me about the house on the island.'

'It is a house in a village – not the main harbour, but near it. It has two terraces and its own well. But – we do not know whether it is empty or not. There is somebody called Aristo*phánes* who arranges the letting of it and has the keys. We have to disembark and find him.'

'Supposing it is let?'

'Sam says that Aristo*phánes* will find us another house: there are also two hotels. Sam was in the house for a month in May, and said that it was one of the nicest there.'

'*If* we get it.'

'I think we will get it: I might not have run into Sam after all. He's leaving for Paris tomorrow.'

'Is he having a show there?'

'He wouldn't say.'

'How was he?'

'Very gay and shaky: bad.' He got up. 'Darling – you must take off your beautiful dress; we have a very early call tomorrow.'

By the time I had taken off my earrings and my gold sandals and cleaned my face, he was in bed. It was a long while since we had shared a room and the speed with which he put on or took off his clothes struck me again with a kind of affectionate irritation. He looked at me over the sheet, and grinned: 'I've cleaned my teeth as well.'

'Have one more cigarette, because I want to tell you something.'

'Yes?' He switched off the light by his bed and sat up.

'Don't sound so wary: it's nothing awful. I saw Dr MacBride in New York.' I was brushing my hair, and moved the glass so that I could see his face: there was no expression on it. 'About swimming. He said that it would not do any harm, to swim a little – not for too long. He said it was pointless to give up everything I enjoyed simply in order to stay alive. So . . .'

'Those are two quite different things to say – and opposite.'

'No, they're not. What he meant was that it would do me no harm to swim a little – might even do some good – but that if I did overdo it it would be my fault, and that might even be better than giving in about it altogether.'

He looked angry now. 'Lillian, you promised me that you wouldn't go to doctors behind my back. We agreed that I should always go too, and that then we should both be clear about what you might or might not be allowed to do.'

'If I'd asked you to go this time, you would just have said that I was torturing myself, and that there was no point. Anyway, you were busy all the time.'

'What did he say exactly?'

'Exactly what I've told you. Don't you believe me?'

He was silent, and I knew that he did not. The fact that I had had to argue with the doctor came back to me now, so that I said what I had said to him: 'After all, it is *my* life!'

And he answered, just like the doctor: 'It *is* your life; no one can argue that.' He was looking for an ashtray, and I brought him one. He looked up at me peaceably: 'I'll write to Dr MacBride – or send him a cable. Have you brought your painting things?'

'No. It's no use, Em; I'm not a painter, and I can't bear fiddling about with it. I don't see the fun of "enjoying myself" with paints: I like it properly done, or not at all. I'm not a Sam, and there's no point in my struggling about in a welter of therapeutic sentiment just because it's a nice quiet pastime.'

'If you were Sam you wouldn't be painting either.'

'Well he *does* paint. I know it's getting more difficult, as the shaking gets worse, but at least he knows he can do it.'

'That must be a great comfort to him, as he finds himself becoming steadily more incapacitated.'

He was angry because I felt I was worrying enough about Sam and whenever he exposed me as being selfish I became violent.

'Well *I* know what that feels like as well. We aren't talking about either Sam's or my main creative faculties: we're talking about my spending a few minutes in a beautiful warm sea – fewer minutes than anybody else, of course, but still something that I can do too, after you've all finished writing and directing and acting your play – otherwise why have we come here at all? Or why be anywhere, if one can never have any life in the place?' I was going to cry, and I went into the bathroom to do it. When I came back, he was standing by the window which he had opened wide. He held out a hand, and I went into his arms on a high tide of apology – able, but unwilling to say: 'I've been whining *again*; it's inexcusable, and worse when I hide it by shouting at other people. I know exactly what makes me do it: I hate it, and I always always mean never to do it again. Please, just *please*, forget it, and give me one more chance starting from a better point than my reality.'

All I did say was: 'Poor, *poor* Sam.'

And almost at the same time, he said: 'My poor darling. My poor Lillian. I don't remember nearly enough what it is like. You shall bathe; of course I understand about the painting – you're quite right about it. My darling: it is wicked to make you cry when you were so happy: come, you've had a very tiring day . . .'

He put me to bed for the second time that day, and I allowed myself to be stroked and tucked up. What did it matter? He had taken us both down a peg with these allowances he made for me. What was the good of wanting something sharper than this easy pity, if I never changed from behaviour which was designed to get only that? I lay in his arms: in a little while he made love to me, and I lost not only all presence of mind but presence of heart. I fly back to the good times – enough memory of them evokes some echo of response in my body . . . The first time after the separate tensions of fear and longing that I was aware of all of myself – it was like the sun coming out in me, warming and lighting all the cold and dark places into which I'd been divided, so that I was whole, and ready to be part of him. Em's face, looking down on me then, radiant, gentle, knowing what was possible . . . my body was like a field of grass and his hands were the wind – I was bowing ahead of his touch . . .

He is holding my face in his hands, the light is on, and I am aware of his eyes, intent and searching. I know what he is looking for, and I wish that I had it.

The time when we had celebrated our knowledge of Sarah coming; when he had discovered the only courage in me, and I was so steeped in joy at my discovery of this meaning of making love with him that desire seemed to change scale: I felt blessed by him. All the times when I was carrying her, becoming sicker and more unwieldy, and wanting him, and his understanding perfectly how my two loves were growing: he used to put me to bed in the afternoons then, and make very quiet love to me and leave me to sleep . . .

He is kissing me – the taste of fruit and charcoal is over my mouth, and I feel his heart knocking on my breast.

And after Sarah – the great gaiety and affections, and lovely, easy, recognizable times . . .

He says my name – asks me little, tender questions – using my name again for each one. I have no answers, but I think I am smiling.

And after Sarah again – when she was dead – nothing: angry rejection, frozen despair – the sun gone out: nothing but dumb, dark confusion, until that morning when I woke and could say her name to him again – admit that she was dead and that I had lost her and cry to him about her. Then he made love to me, and once it was memorable – as though he was piloting me home after a storm: I was so tired, and he gave me peace. It was very long afterwards that I understood that he had not come to me as Lillian (how I used to love his saying my name – 'like all the pretty flowers at once', he said) but as though I was simply a part of that humanity he found so agonizing, whose pain he wanted to share, to help, to save: that it was then that I began to be an object equally of his ignorance and his compassion. When I remember that, I have to go back to anonymous sunny hotel bedrooms of years ago . . .

He finishes his love and I kiss him: it feels just like greeting him after a separation. I touch his forehead with my fingers and some sense of reality is back again – the affection is real – I am about to say something, but he shakes his head, puts his hand over my mouth, and turns off my light. He is right, there are no words to be said.

CHAPTER V

1

EMMANUEL

ONCE they were on the boat, there was an unobtrusive opportunity of being alone. 'I need it,' he thought; 'I am gasping for silence.' Or peace, perhaps, since his internal life was far from silent. He had found a bit of boat deck, empty and sunlit, and now he sat down on it, leaning against the davits of one of the ship's life boats and shut his eyes . . . 'I am too many small, anxious men' – he could see a procession of them, small, shabby and identical, each holding a placard which yelped 'Joyce will win through'.

'I am one little man who is afraid he's had the best years of his life when he wasn't looking. I am another who, having taken his little secret spring for granted, is now suddenly afraid that it has run dry. I am also a man who has a wife who needs but does not want him. I had no land or house which is mine for no good reason. I care less and less what anyone writes or says about writing, including myself. I have no children to care for, unless you count Jimmy, and he certainly wouldn't count me as his father – it would ruin his whole romantic structure. He works for me because he thinks I'm a wonderful playwright.' He thought for a moment without words. 'I have a good deal of money and I've almost entirely overcome asthma. My best days have a kind of winter sun about them – there is light, but no warmth. I know enough people to fill Drury Lane, but apart from Jimmy, none of them are my friends – perhaps the Friedmanns almost are. I don't care enough,' he thought, 'my emotions nowadays seldom reach beyond anxiety, irritation, and sometimes, pity.' It hadn't always been like this. He could distinctly remember times when he had loved Lillian – when he wanted to use himself and pay for it, he could remember other times too when he had felt that life was marvellous and astonishing, that the future was exciting and unknown, and that he was moving towards it, instead of its overtaking him – whatever happened, he had a hopeful interest in the outcome. Now he felt as though he knew what would happen, and he didn't care. He used to sink himself in some idea – he could leave and lose external problems and live inside a play he was making – he had always been able to draw on that; it gave him his reputation for patience and detachment, for kindness and bad manners. But everything, presumably, had to be fed by something else – there is no absolute everlasting spring in anyone which has no source but itself. Instead of these plays needing him to write them, he was starting to need the plays – or even a play – one idea that would knit these small anxious men together. Twice the thing had unfolded in his mind for a little while, and died – like those white trumpet flowers (what were they called?) that only lived for an hour or two – and the rest of the time he seemed to be travelling at the beginning of some future desert without water or shade. People still moved him sometimes; Gloria's sister, that boy playing his fiddle, and the girl – Alberta. As he thought of her, a scene the previous evening recurred – bringing the same impression, but more deeply cut . . .

It was when the child had brought the jasmine up to him in a basket. He had been looking at Alberta: she had been wearing a white cotton dress with a low, rounded neck and no sleeves, and her skin was warm against the paper-white stuff – her arms like natural silk, smooth and womanly, their outline from her shoulders to her wrists running in pretty leisured curves. Lillian and Jimmy were showing her something – she leaned forward and the edge of her breasts moved and rose to the shape of magnolias. At the same moment the scent of the jasmine struck him – it seemed to come from her, and he was seized and filled with desire so violent and immediate that it was as though all the breath was knocked out of his body. The child was speaking to him, holding out a bunch of her flowers, and the others were all looking at her: Alberta – the jasmine – they were separate – he felt air choking his lungs as though it was water and turned heavily to the child, whose eyes, impassive and intent, were fixed upon his face. He had bought two bunches of jasmine, one for each of the women, and for the rest of the evening he flung his attention in every other direction.

Now, sitting alone in the morning sun, trying to collect and to see himself; discussing his absence of heart as though it was simply a piece of history, he was faced with this accident (for the moment he could not think of anything else to call it); but at least he would not delude himself that it had anything to do with his heart. He knew better than that. When one was twenty – even thirty – one was open to this delusion; that an unexpected onslaught of desire constituted love. There were even people of his age who continued to think so – whose deadly security lay in frequent and entire repetition: they used the same words to blame the same situations which the same part of themselves had taken the trouble to attract. 'He is not better, he is much the same.' The point about these little generalizations was that they ceased to be amusing when they applied to oneself. But he was a little better – he wasn't quite the same. While far from sure that he knew what love was, he did feel that he knew what it was not. And this attack he had had was not love . . . He made himself consider carefully what it had been, forced some discovery of what his mind had been doing inside his romantically breathless body. This was very unpleasant: he could easily remember what he had wanted – a part of him jeered with words like lechery and pictures of very old men fumbling with shoulder straps – disgust, ridicule, the poor old creatures – he had not come to that – was nowhere near that age: a part of him justified, denied, made angrily reasonable explanations . . . good God, where was the harm in an experienced man being attracted to a pretty young girl? something wrong with him if he wasn't, surely – no *harm* had been done, he had been simply, acutely, susceptible to her charms . . . but by far the most frightening part of him simply repeated the feelings of the night before again; the desire, the intoxication, the panic, and the humiliated withdrawal into diffusion: this last part did not seem to have any opinions or views on the subject; given half a chance it just went through the same motions again as though to confirm that they had been real. The effect of this, physically, was of a deep, internal blush which he had then to endure for the third time before he started to gather up some rational shreds of dignity. The points were that he had been extremely stupid about his previous secretary; the thing had never for an instant been worth what everybody had paid for it. Alberta was not only his secretary, she was very very young, very innocent, and she had been discovered by Lillian, who had a bad heart, who seemed to have lost the mainspring of her life, who on top of that had already suffered a good deal from his infidelities, and deserved at the least his consideration: if he pretended to love anybody, it ought to be Lillian. If he seduced anyone, it should not be Alberta, for whom he had great liking, almost affection, and the feeling that she should be protected. The whole thing was out of the question on every possible count, and what was the point of being his age if one did not face up to and understand this? He remembered then Lillian sitting up in bed with her enormous, glistening eyes saying: '*Don't* seduce her – anything else, but not that'; and then, immediately, the picture of Alberta sneezing, saying that excitement made her sneeze – saying, too, that she wanted in the end to give up excitement – no, first, she had said that she wanted to be excited by fewer things – he didn't understand the giving-up part of it, but it struck him now that she was damn well right about being excited over fewer things. He had to write a play because on the whole that seemed to be what he was for, and if he needed to replenish his spring for doing it he must find a way which didn't, so to speak, involve pouring alcohol down his throat. She is on good ground, young Alberta, he thought; she seems to stand in the middle of her territory – she may not have explored it yet, but she's in a better position on it than I am, and he had a sudden picture of himself standing just inside the railings of a municipal park with his back to the well-worn paths holding on to the bars and looking out. I will rest here, help her (meaning Lillian) with her swimming, get some kind of map of this play in my mind, and keep an eye on Jimmy training her (meaning Alberta) for Clemency. And see to it that he doesn't upset her by making passes at her or any other irresponsible behaviour. I'm old enough to be her father, and I am responsible for her, after all. If I want excitement, I must get it out of the play. He felt his mind shift, strain a little at the familiar traces and settle to this decision. 'I'm tired,' he thought; 'this holiday will be a good thing if I keep it calm and simple – we all need some fresh air.'

He opened his eyes – the ship was well away from Piraeus; there were new lands ahead and to the right. There was something lighthearted and dashing about their progress – they had seemed to him to leave Piraeus at full speed from a standstill, and they tore along through the marvellous blue water at the same gay and purposeful pace. The sun was getting steadily hotter, and the air smelled sweet; a warm mountain smell, more feminine than the pure smell of sea. Was there no way of making one aim cover all pursuits? To be left less open to chance and casual requirements? That was what he needed; 'and you won't find it by thinking,' he said sternly to himself. One's thoughts were no better than oneself, and worse, they were no different. He watched the mountainous land – brown and grey rock with deep olive and prussian blue shadows; smelled what might be thyme and verbena, and saw the colours of the sea invariably changing; heard the ship moving the water with a rich creaming hiss above the reassuring bloodbeat of her engines, and felt the hard dry caulked boarding of the deck with his hand. 'Coming to my senses; if I am any kind of artist, it's time I did that.' The senses can help to make a good climate for the heart. This made him suddenly remember writing with a kind of reckless ease when he had been very hungry, and the clutches of hard-boiled eggs that he had used to keep all over the place . . . the sun! He put on his dark glasses and the day changed its mood for him: he was warm and thirsty and nearly asleep . . .

There was Alberta standing hesitantly before him.

'Mrs Joyce wondered whether you would like to come down and have a drink?'

He took off his glasses. 'Perhaps I should: I have been dreaming of hard-boiled eggs which is thirsty work.'

'I don't think they have those. They have things called *tiropetas*: hot cheesy things – thirstier than eggs, I should think. Mrs Joyce has had three, but poor Jimmy can't even watch her eat them – he's lying down. I really came up because Mrs Joyce is worrying about how to get him off the ship.'

'Can't he stand?'

'I don't know, but we don't walk *off* the ship on to the island. We are put into little boats, like a shipwreck, and rowed ashore, and Mrs Joyce is afraid they will throw him at a boat and miss; she does not feel calm about his prospects.'

He got to his feet. 'I'd better infuse some strength into him. When do we arrive?'

'I don't know exactly; poor Jimmy went and lay down first on some boxes stacked along the sides of the boat. They made him feel much worse, and then he found that they were full of chickens who were behaving exactly like his insides felt – lurching and fluttering about and uttering low squawks of misery. It is such a pity for him that he misses all this lovely travelling.'

'Is it lovely travelling? Are you enjoying it?'

'Immensely.' As they went down the ladder, she added: 'I'm so sorry to have woken you up – you looked rather tired.'

He was about to deny this – felt his mouth start to curl like an old sandwich with a wry, dry inner sneer – when he recollected the private collection he had just been making of himself, and ceasing to feel tired he said: 'I was tired: I am restored now.' It was much more comfortable to be in one's place, than to have someone – anyone – put one there.

2

ALBERTA

Hydra, Greece

My darling Papa,

Where shall I begin? Where I am, I think, and work backwards and forwards out of it. I'm sitting on a snow white terrace with my back to a wall eating figs and every now and then looking round me at a scene of unimaginable beauty (unimagined by me at any rate). We are on the island, and the above address *is* a complete one, although you might not think so. We came in a gleaming white boat that was filled and packed and crammed with people and animals. We charged into the harbour and literally stopped on our haunches – in a way, Papa, that you would hardly approve – much worse than how people drive through our village, but I think Greek captains are better than English drivers. He stopped the boat with an anchor which rattled out like gunfire, and then we were collected in little boats – some with motors, some with oars – which they filled until they were practically swamped with old ladies in black and rather tragic-looking men and boxes and chickens and babies and us, suitcases, furniture, everything. The *moment* the last chicken was over the side the ship roared away at full speed. The harbour is small – and the place mountainous; it looks like one huge mountain with rocks right down to the water, and the houses are built a long way up its slope; they are nearly all dazzling white, and look as though someone had spilled a packet of lump sugar from the top of the mountain and most of it had rolled to the bottom. At first there seem to be no trees, but there are, dark spiky cypresses and dusty-looking olives. The harbour front is beautifully paved – I've found out in *pink* marble that comes from a nearby island – and there are wonderful stalls of figs and tomatoes and grapes and peppers, and wineshops and cafés and other shops with sponges hanging in bunches. There are no cars – only a rubbish cart – on the island because after the harbour it is all built in roughly paved steps, but there are donkeys and mules; they were all standing in a row near where we landed. They wear turquoise blue beads and so do children: this is to guard them from the Evil Eye – I don't know why donkeys and children should be so especially prone, but evidently they are. Perhaps grown-ups can take other precautions. We had to wait for a man called Aristopházes who knows all about houses: so we had drinks and olives and white cheese that takes the skin off your mouth if you let it, and very good bread. Aristopházes was rather disappointing when he came, rather fat and nearly bald, but I do see that it is a difficult name to live up to and he was extremely friendly and spoke a great deal of melodramatic English so at least I could understand what was going on, because we embarked upon hours and hours of talking, and waiting, and having various kinds of refreshment. To begin with Aristopházes said that we should at once have the house which we should discover quite perfect for everything we could wish; then he told us so much about it and everything that was happening on the whole island that after we had all had dozens of olives and pieces of bread and cheese and drink we were longing to go to see the house but then he said we must have lunch, as a key was necessary for the house and the key was uncertain. He kept sending little boys off on mysterious errands in Greek – and they always ran off at top speed and came walking back slowly. After lunch he suddenly started suggesting other houses which now he knew us he felt would more perfectly suit our needs – he went on and on about it until he persuaded Jimmy and Mr Joyce to go and look at a house and Mrs Joyce said what a pity he spoke English at all. We agreed that there was something odd in Aristopházes' change of heart about the house, but Mrs Joyce knows a painter who had just been staying in it, so she knew that it existed and was nice, and she said that if we sat there long enough with our luggage round us something would happen about it. We drank little cups of Turkish coffee and longed to bathe. The others didn't come back for hours: and afterwards they told us that the reason Aristophánes didn't want us to have the house was because he was living in it himself rent free, and he wouldn't take money to go: we had to rent another house for him to move into and then it was all right. In case this sounds shocking to you, Papa, I must explain that Aristophánes is an *Athenian* and doesn't live on this island at all. He broke his arm eighteen months ago, and he gets relief for incapacitation (that's what he said); anyhow Mr Joyce managed to get a house arranged for him and he became overjoyed again and rushed off to take his things out of ours. Then two little donkeys were absolutely *laden* with our luggage and we went, with Mrs Joyce on a third donkey. As soon as we left the port there were a great many narrow lanes built in steps for climbing. The houses are *beautifully* whitewashed; they dazzle in the sun; they all have shutters which were closed and there were very few people about during our walk which was in the middle of the afternoon and the hottest walk I have ever been. The donkeys had a kind of delicate, leisurely stumble, and it seemed to take ages to get to our house, but it was so lovely when we got there that even Jimmy cheered up (he does not really like walking in the sun which is most unfortunate for him). Our house is adjoining a little church – everything snowy white: it has two terraces facing east and west. The western one looks over a small ravine – I think that is the right word – leading down to the sea. You can see the mainland quite clearly – just undulating masses of mountain softened by blue shadows – very beautiful and mysterious, and a sea planted with one or two islands in perfect positions. The other terrace has a well – it's the one I'm on now, and a much closer view so that you can see the colours of the rock of the opposite hill, and there is a small field, only it's not like our fields, with olive trees and one or two figs. There are cactus and sea plants, but I haven't explored them properly yet. I have a dark cool little room on the ground floor. It is a small house, one room for the Joyces, one for Jimmy, and one for me, and a sitting room between the two terraces: the kitchen is in a separate place, and the privy which really is one is in another little hut.

Dear Papa, and how are *you*? I do hope Mary is proving of some use with the Magazine, and that Lady G. is not upsetting Aunt T. too much over the Flower Show. I will go to a Greek church as soon as possible, and describe it carefully to you. I wish you were here, and the whole family. If only I was rich I would take you for a wonderful holiday – do you remember telling me the story every night after Mamma died about you and me going to India? Every night I could choose something to go into the story, and in the end we had so many elephants that when I chose a tiger, you had to make him tame to ride on an elephant to use one of them up. The extraordinary thing about travelling is that it *is* quite as wonderful as you made it – not the same, of course – but not disappointing.

It's very odd, Papa, but I never realized, until the other evening when I was talking with Mrs Joyce, how very difficult it must have been for you to keep up that story every night for so many weeks at the time that you did it. You were the most reliable man, and that was what was needed. Perhaps it is the first thing to be, and on the way to anything else? Anyhow, wherever I am, I love to think that you are somewhere, at least, and particularly when I am not at home. Please give my love to everybody, and tell Aunt T. that I will write to her soon. I've finished *Middlemarch*. *Villette* next: it's nice to have home books with me, and I shall always remember that I read them here.

Your loving daughter, SARAH.

I wrote a long letter to Papa in the end – but I couldn't bring myself to tell him about them wanting me to play Clemency – I don't know why – perhaps because it looks as though we shall go straight back to New York, and that may make him sad – that I shall be away so long. But if we *do* go straight back, and I don't go home, won't it be just as sad, or will giving him more time to get used to my being away make it better? This is nonsense: I'm just afraid to tell him because I'm not sure he will approve of my becoming an actress in this manner. But then I may not become one at all, in which case it will save a lot of worry not to tell him now. Jimmy says that we are to have two days' holiday before we start work: I asked him whether I should learn my lines, and he said no. How do we work, I wonder? It is rather useless to go on asking questions in a diary, as who is to answer them? Perhaps I shall in the end, if I really want any answers. Jimmy is a much more interesting person than he appeared to be at first. An extraordinary childhood – not belonging to anybody – and then the tremendous luck of Mr Joyce sending for him to England. I must say it must be pleasant to be rich and famous if one can do things like that: it simply transformed Jimmy's life – almost too good to be true. Both of the Joyces are very kind to him and treat him as one of their family, which I expect is what he needs. He is illegitimate and does not know who his father is: I wonder whether he imagines that he was a duke or a magician or something notable like that. Oh dear. Papa once said that diaries were generally filled with idle speculations or idle introspection, and I begin to see why. One is poor company in them because one hardly ever objects to oneself; it is far worse than a doting mother with her children – there does not even seem to be a last straw.

Portrait of Jimmy. Medium height, very soft brown hair, hazel eyes (heavens, I'm not getting anywhere), a very nice, wide, curving mouth, and hair growing to a peak on his forehead. *Very* surprising and beautiful hands – each finger interesting. Can't remember his nose enough to describe it. Has an authoritative air some of the time, which seems to come out of standing a bit away from people as though he's just there to watch them. But in spite of that, and in spite of his appearance of toughness, there is something vulnerable about him: perhaps he is afraid of being caught up with people, and feels it is safer to watch. He moves about most neatly, with no wasted movements – like a cat, and he has a funny laugh – a sort of shout – as though he surprised himself doing it. He has an *extremely* kind heart, so that if he stops simply watching people, he becomes very protective about them. This is especially true of Mr Joyce: his voice becomes quite different when he talks about Mr J. – he tries to sound elaborately casual, but he isn't, at all. He believes in Mr Joyce, and that's that. I do hope Mr J. never does anything that upsets him – he would find it so hard to bear. I like him: he is very good when he is not enjoying himself, which, since we have arrived in this country, has been too much.

Evening. Principal animals on this island: donkeys, mules, goats, cats and dogs and chickens. I do not think any of them have an enjoyable time by English standards, but perhaps, being Greek, they have a different conception of affection and security. The cats come off best, but that is just because they are superior and independent. Jimmy and I went down to the port to arrange about a jar of wine, and on our way we met a very small donkey tied to the third tree in a row. Nothing for him to eat or drink – nothing to do, and no one to talk to. He stood motionless with a slightly lowered head staring at nothing and looking as though that is what happens to him every night. I haven't met any mules yet. Goats look nice from a distance, but when you come face to face with them, they have an expression both cynical and coarse, as though they have just stopped smiling at something unpleasant. Dogs look miserable here – the people seem afraid of them, and they are often tied up. They lie with their heads on the ground, the children kick them and run away. Cats are mostly extremely thin, with large ears and elegant faces; there are all colours, but a lot of black ones. I can think of nothing either kind or revealing to say about chickens. No sign of a shark, but we have not bathed yet, as we have been too busy settling into the house, and the others all slept in the afternoon while I wrote to Papa. Mr Joyce has just asked me to come out on to the other terrace to watch the sunset.

Darling Uncle Vin,

Before I attempt any description of this place, I have to tell you something, and ask what you think about it. Don't laugh, Uncle Vin, but Mr Joyce and Jimmy Sullivan want me to try and act a girl called Clemency in Mr Joyce's last play (the one act you saw in London, which is not yet done in New York). I have agreed to try and learn to do it, and tomorrow we are to start working on it. They could not find anyone they wanted for the part in New York, and Mr Joyce says the girl in London is not right and has turned it into another kind of play from the one he meant. The idea is that we should spend a month or six weeks here as Mrs Joyce needed a holiday, and then go back to New York. The thing is, Uncle Vin, that I have not broached this matter with Papa, because I feel that he may not like it, and also it is likely that they may find I am no good, in which case I might as well not worry him at all. I telephoned him from New York to explain to him about coming here, and he was delighted about it. If only I could see and talk to him I would tell him at once, but I am not used to using letters for this purpose, and am afraid that I shall not know from his reply what he really feels. But I am not used, either, to deceiving him – it's becoming like a smudge on everything else I tell him. Of course if it is found that I can act I should love to do it, and Jimmy has explained that if the play is a success, I would be earning enough money to fly home and see him. What do you seriously think of my chances, as it is your profession after all, and you know me so well? And do you think I should tell Papa, or do you think it would be possible for you to go and see him and tell him about it, or find out what he feels? If Papa really hates the idea, I won't do it, although I shall mind enough to want to know the reason for his disapproval. Please write to me as soon as possible about this, because it is worrying me.

Uncle Vin, I must begin by describing the bathing here,

which exceeds anything I have ever read about. The water is sea green or sea blue, absolutely clear and warm; there are rocks right down to the water, so that one has to go straight in – I can't dive, but I don't mind plunging as it is so warm. We have masks to put over our faces and a tube for our mouths which sticks up in the air so that one can breathe while one is swimming face downwards. You can see the most marvellous things – fishes, and sponges growing to rocks, and anemones, and little octopus and seaweed of many kinds. The colours are far better than on land, or perhaps they are just new to me. The fish do not seem to mind one watching them at all; I found a great cloud of tiny silver ones hanging at all depths in the water like a sequin veil. The rock sometimes goes sheer into the sea, and it is extraordinary to see the sharp division of what grows on it above the water and what below. You do not have to be a good swimmer to do this, thank goodness we have two sets of masks, and take turns – the rest of the time one lies on burning rock. Mrs Joyce has an umbrella, and gave me a lot of sunburn lotion, but I don't think it has done much good, as I feel as though my shoulders are on fire. She can only bathe for a short time which is a pity as she is clearly the best swimmer of the lot of us. We spent the whole morning on this piece of shore – one can't call it a beach, thank goodness – and had a picnic lunch there. We are all beginning to like the wine, which is very odd indeed, but suits the climate. They also have the most delicious orangeade – slightly fizzy – in bottles, and Jimmy says very good beer. Then there is stuff called *ouzo*; it is transparent, but when you put it in a glass and pour water over it, it goes milky – like the stuff you drank in Paris, but I can't remember its name. I tell you all this, because I know you are interested in drinks. People drink in a quite different way, here – I mean they sit for ages at little tables with an enamel mug full of wine: they pour it into small glasses, and they talk a great deal. The foreigners all drink together, but with the Greeks it is only men. The women sit on chairs outside their houses or serve in the shops which never seem to shut, and the children run about, silently, like a crowd of birds. I mean they call and shout and chatter to one another, but the actual running is silent as they luckily do not have to wear shoes. I'm so sorry, Uncle Vin, but I shall have to stop, I am so sleepy, but I will write again soon and try to tell you better what it is like when I am less drunk with the newness and so *much* sun.

Your loving SARAH.

This morning we started Clemency. It is a mysterious business. Mr Joyce and Jimmy were there. They made me sit on a chair and read one little bit two or three times very quietly, and then Jimmy told me what sort of place I was in while I was doing this bit and then he made me walk about while I was reading it which was much more difficult. Then he suddenly said: 'Make as much noise as you can.' I tried, but it felt all wrong, as the things Clemency says are all quiet ones in this bit, and I felt exceedingly foolish. Jimmy just said do it again and I tried – it was even worse. I said the words felt wrong for shouting, and Jimmy said, nonsense the boy stood on the burning deck three blind mice one could say anything – just make a noise. Mr Joyce was staring at the ground and not saying anything. I took a deep breath and tried to shout three blind mice and it came out breathless and squeaky but was apparently no laughing matter to any of us. Then Jimmy said pretend you are a man shouting that, telling five hundred other men about the mice. This was the odd thing. I did: and I had an entirely different voice – heavy and rather hoarse. Then Jimmy smiled at Mr Joyce, and Mr Joyce smiled at me, and Jimmy said, now, don't shout, just tell them about the mice, but be sure they hear. Then Mr Joyce said he'd leave us to it, and the rest of the time was spent on Jimmy making me feel my body while the noise was coming out. We didn't do any more Clemency. Jimmy said that we'd leave her for the moment, but that I would read some of her with Mr Joyce every day, and he and I would practise counting and breathing together. He is quite different when we are working – very businesslike and rather stern, but by the end of the morning I understood that he was right to make this distinction, and that in the end (even of one morning) it made it easier to work if we behaved together as though that was all we did. At the end he said: 'Now, we won't discuss this when we aren't working – there's nothing to say about it. Try during the rest of the day to be aware of how you breathe; that is all you need to do.' Mrs Joyce wants me to go and see if there are any letters as the boat has come in.

3

LILLIAN

I WAS sitting on a rock at the edge of the sea with the sun like a burning fan on my shoulders, and I looked alternately up into the sky and down into the water for the origin of the beautiful reflection one cast upon the other. It was a small bay – almost a semi-circle scooped out from the steep rocks – and the others had swum out of sight round the coast: I sat by myself. I had meant to sit or lie there until their return, and was half-heartedly trying not to feel envious, but inside I was poor Lillian putting a cheap brave face on her disability. I looked down again at the water that was only a few inches below me – lucid, sinuous bulk that heaved and broke its colour against the rock with something between a slap and a stroke: patched in jewelled greens and blues and shot with diamond fish who casually pursued their geometric sense of direction. Looking, I knew that I had only done so to make myself unhappy (really, Lillian, at your age!) and I thought, 'If I wept now the tears would scald on the rock in this heat.' Then, without thinking, I swung my legs over the sea and waited before putting my right foot in the water; it slipped in without seeming to break the surface and gleamed whiter than my leg in the sun. The water was smooth and softly cool after the burning rock: I stretched my foot in it, and as I did this a forgotten, overwhelming sensation began. It started with my foot: I began to feel its length and weight, and the separations of my toes, the water on my skin and my blood under it, and then, through the joint of my ankle this discovery travelled slowly up my body until I reached the palms of my hands pressed down on the rock each side of me and the roots of my hair hot with sun. The difference between *seeing* my hand or my foot, and *knowing* them – feeling absolutely contained within all of my body at once, was marvellously new and clear, and for some unknown quantity of time I remained alive in this way, until my foot – idle and cold in it – turned my attention to the sea. Now it seemed so beautiful that I was freshly struck by its shades of light and mysterious melting depths – its irresistible movement, its enormous, effortless continuity . . . I was still joyfully self-contained, when I flung myself in to meet and join it.

I did not bathe for very long; but it seemed to me then that time was a secondary consideration which I had used to measure partial enjoyment, and now, in the sea, I did not need it. I was out of the water and drying in the sun before the others returned. Jimmy said: 'Lillian, you've been swimming!' and Em came and sat by me to say: 'You weren't in for too long?' and I felt my face relaxed and easy for smiling when I said that I'd had a perfect bathe.

I lost this feeling of my body: I don't know exactly when it went, but I was suddenly aware that it had gone, although now I could remember it, and everything I saw and heard continued to be affected – to be more sharply true. This is a place for sight. Now that we have been here long enough to establish some kind of routine, and I need not be concerned with the order of events, there seems to be even more chance of simply being here. In the morning, early, some of us go and swim – usually then I stay behind on the terrace where the sun has come up over the little nearby hill, and the colours on the rock are soft, and fresh and delicate – cinnamon, tawny, agate, crystalline – with grey-green cactus, signal cypress, and the pure white houses, and the pale blue of the sky glows with morning sunlight. To the left is the sea – denser blue mark and at this distance, still; and to the right, the warm and savage shoulder of mountain, already stripped of mist and naked to its bones for the sun. I look down at the tops of the olive trees in the little field below our terrace; the leaves are like moonshine, oblique, almost apologetic in this young light. The others come back, and Jimmy lights the Primus to boil water for our coffee which we drink black. The island butter is rancid – we eat the bread with honey and melons. Jimmy works with Alberta, and often I persuade Em to walk into the port with me. We buy food for lunch, and beautiful sponges and silk made in the monastery at the top of the mountain. We collect letters and drink more coffee or orange juice at one of the cafés and watch the people and the caiques unloading vegetables and the butcher bringing back scrawny and dripping haunches of goat from the abattoir at one end of the harbour. Em makes me ride home and I acquire a favourite donkey. It is very peaceful; we do not talk much except about what we need to buy or to point out people to each other. Sometimes we meet Aristophánes and then we are chocked full of island gossip and incident. The very old lady who walks slowly up and down in a pale pink coat and skirt and pink high-heeled shoes – bought, Em feels, to match the marble – owns the richest house; it is floodlit at night and she is always trying to fill it with important people, only hampered by continuous and haunting uncertainty as to who they are. Once she turned a man out of her house because his clothes were poor and he was very dirty: he proved to be a painter with an international reputation, and ever since then she has courted the dirtiest and poorest men she could find, with – Aristophánes tells us, contorted with glee – the most murderous results. He would talk to us until the boat came in with fresh hordes of travellers and tourists whom he could waylay with instructions and gossip, but Em gets restive and wants to go back to the house. There are two ways back. One, climbing up through the village, steps and narrow paths and houses all the way; or, round the coast, a switchback path edging the island for the short distance between the port and our village. The first is all whites and stone and shadows on white – enclosed, angled, domestic, made and built and used: the second is wilder, emptier – rock and sea coloured, with few houses, with the air like the clearest honey, and the rocks declining steeply into the water – flowers and sea-birds, and that curious breathless calm that on a fine day lies over the brink of land and sea, but this is the longer way, and we use it more in the evening. We get back to find Jimmy walking up and down the western terrace, smoking, with his worried, professional expression, and Alberta nowhere to be seen. I think he reduces her to tears, poor girl. Em asks how it has gone, and Jimmy shrugs and looks black, Em's tic round his eyes begins, and for a moment there are echoes of the organized tensions that I associated with empty half-lit theatres and hotel bedrooms late at night, but here, suddenly confident and detached, I can say something which disperses them; Jimmy smiles and Em smooths his face with his hand and we all set about preparing for our picnic in the charming bay which we have come to look on as ours. Alberta appears; in shorts and an Aertex shirt she looks about fifteen, and I feel that it is hard that Jimmy should have been making her cry. She looks solemn and subdued; I feel protective and take her to pack the figs and tomatoes and melon and eggs and cheese and bread and wine for lunch.

We go slowly down to the bay. The path is steep and rough, and by now it is very hot – the mainland quivers over the glistening sea – the engines of the daily boat – like a crescendo of heat – can be heard even before she can be seen: it is delicious to feel sweat pricking out all over my skin with the sea so near. The last bit has no path – we simply scramble down with stones rattling ahead of us; they sound shrill and pretentious beside the huge boulders, and some of them even fall into the gentle water waving at our feet. The rocks are so hot that one can hardly walk on them. Jimmy slings our wine bottle into the sea and we float melons in a pool we have made. Jimmy and Alberta swim off with the goggles: Em stays and smokes with me. He is browning more easily than any of us; has never bothered with oil or sunburn, but he still looks tired. I wonder about his new play – whether it is worrying him; but somehow, here, I have learned not to ask about it. We watch the other two until they have swum out of sight round the coast: then, on the third morning, I said: 'Wouldn't you like to join the young? Because I am quite happy in the sun until I have my bathe,' and he said: 'No, no; they're better as they are: I haven't their capacity for swimming – started far too late in life.' After a moment he said: 'Did you notice at what point in your life you began referring to the young?'

'No.'

He said: 'For quite a long time during middle age, the young simply seem to be getting younger – and then there suddenly comes a day when you look at them and see that really they're at least thirty-five and still much younger than you, and then you see what that makes you.'

'Darling, how *morose*. Jimmy's not so very young, he always seems to be one of us. It's the girl who is.'

He heaved a sigh and looked mournfully at me. I said: 'After all, *I'm* younger than you, and you count me as the same age.'

'When really I am an exceptionally old man?'

'Not *old*. Late middle-aged.'

'Late middle-aged,' he repeated: 'how perfectly beastly.'

'Very wise and experienced, of course. And attractive, and successful.'

'Distinguished is the word.' He said it with such distaste that it made me laugh. We lay in silence: I was soaking up sun, and not thinking about anything we'd said, but when I got up to bathe, I saw that he was staring into some distance beyond the rock a few feet away.

'What is it?'

'I was just wondering what the hell I'd *done* with all my time.'

I was sitting with my foot poised above the green bewitching water with the memory of when I had first done this fresh in me. I smiled consolingly – I still felt detached and protective. Poor Em – worrying away in this beautiful place. 'Never mind, darling – you've got lots more time.' And seeing his face, I added: 'Well, at least you've got time to do one splendid thing. What more could you want?'

'What more indeed?' He had turned so that I could not see his face because of the sun. Just then, the others returned, and I wanted to try the goggles. Em made Jimmy go with me as it made him nervous if I was alone and he swam like an old-fashioned frog, he said, which was quite true. Jimmy took me to see a charming fish who lived in a particular crack in the rock with his head sticking out to watch everything that was going on; then I saw a sponge and he tried to dive for it, but it was too far down: then we found a ledge in the cliff large enough to rest on and we sat and talked. Jimmy adores looking under water – I've never known him so enthusiastic about anything. He wants to try with an aqualung and talks earnestly about the possibilities of learning until he suddenly remembers, and turns impulsively to me.

'It's too bad you can't do that when you'd love it so.'

'I don't even want to, Jimmy. I did want to bathe, and that is being so lovely that I am quite content.'

'You look it. You look marvellous. Do you know, you've been looking lately like you were when I first knew you?'

'Have I? Was that a good way to look?'

'It was. You feel good as well, don't you?'

I nearly told him then about my foot in the water, but something warned me to keep that to myself. Instead, I said: 'I feel like a battery being recharged – more and more energy every day.'

'That's fine.'

'The only thing is I don't know what to do with it.'

'Do with it? Why, enjoy yourself, I guess.'

'But I *am* – and it's simply making more energy.'

'Well, that's fine.'

'No Jimmy, you don't understand. If I could write plays, I could write one now. If I was an actress, I could act. If I was a politician I could fight an election, if I was Alberta's age I could fall in love. At the moment I could do so much of anything that I was. The only difficulty is that I don't think I'm anything – in that sense. There's no need here to do more than exist – like a plant or a fish.'

He didn't say anything for a moment but I knew from his face he was thinking. Eventually, he said slowly: 'It's how I think of you, Lillian – not doing anything particular, but just being someone. It's like casting a play and that's the role I see you in. Of course you have to be right – you can't just be *anyone*, but if you were right, you could just be Lillian.'

'Is that what you feel women are *for*?' I was teasing him and he didn't like it, as he said: 'I don't know. I don't express myself very well – that's clearer to me every morning. Come on, let's go back and eat.'

We wetted our masks before putting them on, and as we did it, I realized that usually I would have asked him what he meant, but that I seemed to have lost some of my aimless curiosity; wondered why, and almost laughed. We smiled at each other before setting off and I patted his shoulder. When we got back I found Em gay and peaceful – he and Alberta had unpacked the lunch and were drinking wine. We talked about English picnics, and Em said they were nothing but sand and gooseflesh, and Alberta suddenly said that all her best picnics had been far too hot – and Em said surely not too hot – in *Dorset*? And she said yes, because they'd had them in the boiler house that worked the central heating for the church.

'It was a very old boiler and used too much fuel to be run all the winter, but when it was on, everything steamed with heat and Papa said it was injurious to the church and to people, so whenever it was on we had picnics in the boiler house in order to make the most of it. The fumes were awful, they made Serena cough and none of us wanted to eat much, but Clem said it provided us with a touch of evil so we all did it.'

'Why, were you forbidden to go there?'

'Not exactly, but soon after Clem had asked about it, Papa put "Strictly out of Bounds—Private – Dangerous" on the door in red ink and that made it worth while.'

I knew by his questions that Em was amused, and I remembered how he used to question me, wanting endless details about my childhood, and how much more vivid and desirable a great deal of my youth had seemed when I talked to him about it. I had always thought of his asking about it because he was interested in me, now it occurred to me that he had simply been fascinated by an age of life that he had missed.

'Surely, Em, you're not going to have a lot of children in your next play?'

'It had not occurred to me. Why?' He looked both startled and reserved.

'I thought you were collecting data.' Nobody said anything so I went on: 'They're always ghastly – awful mincing little creatures – not children at all although everybody pretends they are.'

'Well, I promise not to put one in any play,' he said, and lay back with his eyes shut.

Alberta and Jimmy began packing up lunch, and I wondered why I spend so much time talking and thinking about things I disliked, and whether I did this more than other people and whether they had always noticed it.

We climb very slowly back to our house – Jimmy and Em ahead with our baskets, and Alberta with me. Half way up the rock I come upon a few cyclamen growing out of a crevice. They are pale pink, about four inches high, and the flowers are perfectly to scale with their height. I show them to Alberta, who kneels beside them with a cry of delight.

'They are wild,' I say; 'wild cyclamen.'

We both look at them: they are calm and delicate and sweet, and they make me smile with pleasure at finding them, but when I look at Alberta, her eyes have filled with tears. She touches one flower as though it is precious or imaginary, and says: 'I had always thought of them as tremendously looked after, in pots and greenhouses . . .' and I remember feeling just as she is now when I first found some gentians; the same joy at my miraculous discovery of something that has always been there to be found – that's half the miracle – but I do not tell her this because these are her cyclamen. Instead, I ask her whether she wants to pick them? She says no, she doesn't want to, and I remember that I picked my gentians and they wilted before I got them home.

On the coast path we pass a young man – he wears faded cotton trousers and a torn cotton shirt and he is carrying a stick with a string of tiny birds slung to it and a long, thin, archaic-looking gun. We greet him as we have learned to do; he replies, and there are the two shades of our being women, but foreigners, in his voice. I say: 'I don't think I should like being a woman here,' and Alberta thinks that although it would be different, it would be quite all right. I tell her what Aristophánes has told us – about the woman having to provide the house and all its contents for the marriage, which meant that if a man had too many daughters, the younger ones would have little chance of marrying until they were about forty if at all. The man had only to bring his virility to the match, and he was hardly dependent upon his father for that. Alberta says, well, in a way he was, and we agree that Greek fathers had to be strong in every sense. And after all, she points out the moment the man had married, he had to start providing for his daughters – so it came to much the same thing in the end. I wonder what the little birds were, and she says they are quail. We plan to search for them in a port restaurant that evening. 'How did you know they were quail? Do you know about birds?'

'No. A little boy told me. He speaks English and Greek and I met him in the Post Office.'

'What is he like?

'A prodigy,' she answered seriously. 'He said he would take me for a short adventure if I liked, if I would discuss some interesting subject with him while we were on it.'

'What does he consider interesting?'

'He said he would give me a list of topics when we met and I could choose from it. He is compiling it today.'

We have passed the place where I have rested before – our house is in sight . . .

Afternoon . . . I lie alone on the hard bed with all the shutters closed excepting those on the small shady window behind my head: from it there come occasional movements of air smelling of hot fig leaves. The room is very bare and simple; there are curious pieces of stone and rock lying on the window ledges and the chest of drawers to hold down the linen mats which are the only concession to essential detail. Somebody must have collected them, having once found them curious? beautiful? and then perhaps bought the mats to provide a use for their collection. I lie on a sheet – it is too hot for covering of any kind – I am like a larger stone on more linen; my limbs are heavy with sun and exercise – sinking into a rock-like immobility of sleep I am not even a plant or a fish. Fragments of what Jimmy said circle lazily in my mind looking for the roost of my conclusions about them. Looking as I used to look – my energy – my just being Lillian – what did that mean? I try to remember being her, and suddenly, the one time is quite easy because I had been so intensely aware of it then . . .

I was twenty-four; it was December, and I was staying with my uncle and aunt in Norfolk – supposedly for Christmas, but really no term had been set for my visit because nobody knew what to do with me. My parents had left me enough money to provide me with an education as protracted as it was useless; my aunt had eventually presented me, and I had spent a long hectic summer eating cold salmon and strawberries to the seasonal accompaniment of horses, boats, tennis balls, dance bands, and fresh-faced young men who had just changed their size in collars and whose conversation would have read very like an engagement book with a narrow column for remarks. Although nothing was actually said about it there was a tacit admission between my aunt and myself that my season had not been a success. It was known, for instance, that I had been dubbed delicate and brainy, and my only conquest had been an extremely dissolute old peer called Sandlewood who had pinched my thigh most painfully and asked me to go to Majorca with him.

In Norfolk, my cousins shot duck and geese and hunted, whilst I, debarred from these pursuits by ill health and indifference, went for sodden, solitary walks, wondering sometimes, with a kind of numb hysteria, what was to become of me. I had one secret from everyone: I had met the playwright Emmanuel Joyce – twice: once at a party, and once when he had taken me out to lunch and then to Kew Gardens for the afternoon. On both occasions I had been dazzled – aware that I had never met anyone like him, and that there was a different taste to both these times from any that I had had with anyone else. At the end of the afternoon at Kew he had taken me back to the house in Lowndes Square where I had been staying, and said that he hoped to see me again, soon, and gone. Months later, I plodded across frozen ploughed fields remembering Kew at the height of the summer – recalling what he had said and how he had looked when he had said it – wondering whether I had said too much or too little (curiously, I could remember none of my replies to his questions and confidences) for I had heard no more of him and no longer expected to do so. But unwittingly he had opened the world a little to me by showing me something beyond the familiar element that I knew – like being shown the sea for the first time: one is conscious of the end of land and the beginning, but not the end of something new. He had represented change, creation, experience, and freedom to me, and I knew that if I never saw him again, this would still be true: so I hoarded these two meetings as my secret treasure, to be recaptured and examined again and again in private. I lived on this and on Matthew Arnold whose poetry touched some melancholy yearning spring in me. The rest of the time I drifted in the domestic, communal vacuum; large regular meals, violent exercise, amusements made up of repetition and some play on any particular character's idiosyncrasy of the 'Keep still, Sally, there's a spider on you' variety; round games, dancing to the gramophone, everybody changing their clothes, getting bathed and fed, having fun, doing things all together every day, every evening . . . until this particular evening when the telephone rang as usual at half past six, and as usual Sally leapt to her feet, tripped over the setter Moll, and dashed away. Sally was in love and spent twenty minutes on the telephone talking to her young man every evening except at weekends when he came down. But she returned round eyed with curiosity and amazement. 'It's a personal call from *Stockholm* for *Lillian*' – as though she didn't know which surprised her most, and an extraordinary feeling – like an electric shock – ran through me. It must be he, but of course it could not be – nobody else I knew could possibly be in Stockholm; but he did not even know my address in the country. I reached the telephone room and shut the door carefully behind me. If it was he I was right, I had known it was the moment Sally came back; if it was someone else of course I was right, he could never have traced my telephone number – would not want to, had forgotten me.

'Lillian?' he said: his voice was faint, but perfectly clear.

'This is Lillian.'

'This is Emmanuel Joyce. Let me hear you – say good evening to me.'

'Good evening.'

'Thank God. I've been thinking so much about you – I haven't been able to get you out of my mind. How are you? You are not ill, are you?'

'No. Are you really in Stockholm?'

'Only just. I'm catching a plane back tonight. Before I catch it I must know one thing about you.' He paused, and afraid that the line would go dead, I said: 'What thing? What do you want to know?'

There was another pause, and then his voice, still faint, and very deliberate, said: 'Do you think you could possibly marry me?'

Then I heard my own voice simply asking: 'When?' and heard him give a delighted laugh.

'Oh – I *was* right to ask you like this. As soon as anyone will allow us. I'll be back tomorrow. Are you wearing something blue?'

'Yes.'

'I thought you were. Lillian!'

'Yes?'

'I'm forty-one. Is that all right?'

'It's quite all right.'

'Not much background, I warn you – it's all foreground with me.'

'I've got no foreground at all.'

'We can share in that case. Would you like a sapphire?'

'What for?'

'To bind you to me, of course.'

'Yes – yes I would like one.'

'Dark or light?'

'Not dark or light.'

'Not dark or light,' he repeated as though that pleased him. 'Where are we going to live?'

'We are going to live with each other.' (I remember how simple and charming that sounded then.)

We made a plan about meeting; then he said: 'Lillian! Do I have to get anyone's permission to marry you?'

'I'm twenty-four: I'll just tell them. I'm sure they'll be pleased.'

'I shouldn't count on that.'

I said: 'It doesn't matter.'

'Say good night to me now – I've got to go.'

'Good night, Emmanuel.'

There was a pause, and then his voice – faint and gentle.

'Good night, darling Lillian.'

Then he had gone: I put the receiver down, and walked slowly back to the family and told them. We were both right. They were far from pleased: dumbfounded, incredulous, horrified, suspicious, angry, and embarrassed. But they couldn't stop me, and nothing they said mattered in the least. This was when I felt who I was: felt distinct, direct, without choice, calm, and able to do exactly what was needed. Everything they said – and they all said a great deal – simply uncovered more of my own purpose to me, without changing it. I found no need to argue with them; that they did not frighten or divide me, nor make me unhappy or angry. For once I felt something steady, like a firm seed, growing in me – reaching the extremities of my eyes and fingers, so that I saw what a suspended creature patched up of imagination and invention I had always been – the whole of my life until this moment (I was packing my clothes with an economy of neat movement that made even this part of it enjoyable). For once, then, I neither planned nor imagined what marrying Em would be like: I packed all my clothes and dined and slept, breakfasted, said goodbye to the family and caught the train to London, and all the time I was contained in the movement of each minute. I remember feeling almost physically as though my life had suddenly turned towards the sun, and perhaps there is some connection between then and how I am now – so many years later, on this hard bed with the sun striking me on this island of Greece.

But if it is just that there may be some connection, what is it, and what is different between now and then? Surely it is not simply the years? Only the energy is recognizable all this time apart; then there seemed to be so much to do with it, and now? What place is there for my generosity, or target for sacrifice, or time for my patience or – with Sarah gone – person for loving? If I continue as I am, I must find this out or I shall be wrecked and energy will explode in rockets of distress . . . All this makes me unbearably sleepy and sleep now is like a kind of holding my breath in my heart – I can wake, so to speak, where I left off: and so I sleep.

4

JIMMY

THE first time I noticed that something was wrong was in the middle of the night two days after we arrived on the island. There are two small bedrooms at the top of this house we've taken; Emmanuel has one – ostensibly for writing, but he's taken to sleeping there – and I have the other. We all go to bed late, as the evenings are cooler for walking about, and most of us rest in the afternoons. We'd had a good evening; gone down to the port and eaten at one of the restaurants. The food is lousy, but what travel bureaux call the atmosphere – and I don't know what else to call it – is gay; and the brandy although it tastes cheap actually is. There was a young girl playing an accordion; it's a queer instrument for a girl, but she played it very well, and what looked like all her family stood around and shouted and sang and she never said anything back – just smiled and smiled. Well – we walked home along a path overlooking the sea; the fishing boats were out with flare lights to attract the fish and the moon was coming up, shining, someone said, like pewter on the sea; I remembered this because it bothered me, I couldn't think what pewter was. Then Lillian said: 'When we have our house, darling, we'll have pewter in the dining room – it is so much more beautiful than silver.' Alberta asked what kind of house, and where were they going to have it, and Lillian said, England; in the country, but they didn't know where, and Alberta must help to find it, but, oh no, she would be in New

York, wouldn't she – for years and years if the play ran? And Emmanuel said just nothing at all.

When we got back I went straight up and feeling I shouldn't sleep until I heard Emmanuel quiet in his room next to mine, I lay on my bed and smoked. I heard him come up after saying goodnight to Lillian, and waited for him to settle down, but he didn't. It wasn't that he made much noise, or even that I could hear everything (the wall was thin but not that thin); it was just that a strong feeling of restlessness seeped through it to me and made me anxious. I wanted to go into his room, but didn't feel that he'd like that. I lay there arguing that he'd come in to me if he wanted to talk, but he didn't come, and I knew he wasn't asleep and I couldn't sleep either. It was his play, I thought, gnawing at his vitals, and it was then that I realized that I got a kind of vicarious excitement out of Emmanuel starting a play, and didn't like that somehow.

It must have been much later – I realized I'd been dozing – when I came to because I heard his door open and his steps on the creaking stairs. Then another door opened, and then silence. Surely he hadn't woken Lillian? She was sleeping so well these nights that I didn't think he would, and knew I didn't want him to; after all, what was I for? But when, minutes later, I got out of bed and went to my window overlooking the sea terrace, I saw him sitting on the parapet with his knees drawn up and his head on them – he wasn't looking at the moon on the sea. I went down.

When he heard me, he raised his head and made a motion of silence with his hand towards the window a few yards away: Lillian slept there.

'Is the play on your mind?'

'Which play?'

'The new one.'

He shook his head. We were whispering, which seemed to make us say less.

He made another motion, and we moved further along the terrace away from Lillian's window. I offered him a cigarette, and he took it: I waited for him to say something, but he didn't. After a while (I was watching him, and he was looking at the sea) I said: 'This house in England. Is that Lillian's idea, or have you decided to settle down?'

He said: 'She wants the house to be in England.'

There was another pause, and then he broke out: 'Which part of one decides to settle down? That's what I should like to know, and what happens to the rest of one?'

'Lillian wants to do it?'

'*I* think it would be better for Lillian – for both of us.'

'Is that what is worrying you?'

He smiled, and it gave me a shock, because it made me notice his eyes which didn't change – had still a kind of desperate hunger which was accentuated by the smile.

'You know, Jimmy, when I am anxious, anything that comes into my head attaches itself to my anxiety. I'm just Anxiety Inc. People always think that one has a good reason for feeling as one does if philosophy could find it out, and often one has no reason, or a damn bad one. Perhaps that is what philosophy is meant to find out, among other things. More and more I sympathize with Marlowe and his allegorical figures. I could wake up in the morning and say "I'm sloth today" and everything I touched would be affected by what I was.'

He stopped abruptly, but I felt his thoughts going on and on. I was right about this because a minute later he said: 'If I had to describe the whole of life on this earth by marks on a piece of paper, I would make circles.'

'*Circles?*'

He looked at me almost impatiently: 'Yes. The serpent's tail in his mouth, the links of a chain, the sun – the paradox, the fitting connection of one thing with another – the difficulty of understanding what is a beginning and what is an end – dimensions always seem to be scaled down in an attempt to conceal this difficulty, so it's almost impossible to see anything whole – even one's life.'

'Do you want to see that whole?'

He smiled again, and said gently: 'It might help, Jimmy, it might help.'

'Yeah, I see what you mean,' I said, after thinking about it. 'It would make a hell of a difference to what one did.'

'Or a difference to who one was?'

'I suppose so.' I wasn't with him there, and I had thought of something else. 'Look here – what about the girl?'

He drew deeply on his cigarette without replying, and then he gave a curious little start as though he'd only just heard what I'd said.

'She's going to be good, don't you think, Jimmy?'

'I don't know yet. What I do know is that it's no good her being the perfect Clemency inside, if I can't get it to come across, which it isn't doing now.'

'You can't expect that in two sessions. Give her time.'

'Of course I don't expect her to learn everything at once.' I heard the trace of anger in my voice – for some reason I was unaccountably nervous. 'What worries me is that she's unexpectedly self-conscious – and while she's like that she sets up a block and I can't get past it. I can't get her to understand why I want her to do what I want.'

He didn't say anything, so I went on: 'You've seen it: she blushes, and looks miserable, and tries again and it's further off the point than ever.'

'You've established the fact that she's got a big voice.'

'Yeah, I know, but she doesn't know how to use it. She'd lose it in a week the way she is going at present. That's what I've got to teach her. How to relax and keep herself balanced so that she knows what she's doing and where it is coming from.'

'Well? I don't disagree with you, but what am I supposed to say?'

'Well, so I think it would be better if I had her to myself for a bit. I think it's easier to outgrow this self-conscious thing with one other person. Even two people make an audience, and with you there she's worrying the whole time about the sense of the part – the matter rather than the manner.'

'I see.'

'Just for a bit – until I get her loosened up and with more confidence.' Something was wrong about this conversation, but so help me I didn't know what.

He threw his cigarette away, and smiled at me but there was something wrong with that, too. 'Well, Jimmy, if you feel that it would make it easier for you to have her to yourself you must have her to yourself. We must all bear the main point of the exercise in mind, after all. What else are any of us for?'

'Speaking for myself, I have no idea.'

After a bit, he asked: 'Did she say that she didn't want me there?'

'She hasn't said anything at all; it's my idea. Let me have her for a week, and then come and see. She'll need you later on. This isn't an easy way to do things after all – it's forcing someone, like a hothouse plant. She'll need you when she knows a little more how to say the lines; then she'll have to understand why she says any of them.'

'I doubt it. I expect I shoot my bolt when I write a play; the rest is up to the rest of you – producers and the like.'

'Look here,' I said desperately: 'I'm *not* the rest of them – I'm on your side, to do things exactly as you want. If you don't think it's a good idea for me to work on her alone, I *won't* . . .' I was raising my voice, and he made a move for silence.

After we'd both listened for a moment, he said: 'No – you go ahead. You'd better get some sleep if you're going to work in the morning.'

I felt dismissed, and like most people who have got their own way in something, I was anxious to make an irrelevant gesture. 'Sure you wouldn't like a hot drink or something, to help you sleep?'

He smiled again. 'Hot milk, on a Greek island? Don't be absurd, Jimmy. You go up: I shan't be long.'

And that was that.

Well – I started the next morning working with Alberta alone, and he went to the port with Lillian, who was delighted.

Alone with her on the same terrace where we had talked about her in the night, I looked at her carefully – trying to think of the best method . . . She stood in front of me in a cotton skirt and shirt with the sleeves rolled up: she had bare feet. She looked tense and apprehensive, and when she realized I was looking at her she shifted her weight from one foot to another and looked at the ground – like a kid about to recite a lesson she doesn't know. She had nice feet; I hadn't noticed them before.

'Let's sit a while and talk.'

She smiled obediently and sat down: I wasn't getting anywhere.

'Look – what's the matter? When we work on this, you get kind of frightened so I don't know what to do with you.'

She didn't answer at once; then said hesitantly: 'I don't seem able to do anything you tell me to do. I just seem to repeat the same failure again and again. I feel all the time that I am being most trying, but I don't know how to change.'

'Do you think perhaps you are taking it all too personally?'

She looked startled. 'How do you mean?'

'Well what you do or don't do isn't done to please me.'

'But you are the person who's teaching me.'

'That's incidental. *What* am I trying to teach you?'

'To act this part in this play, I suppose.'

'That's it.'

'Yes, *but* – I don't understand all this part of the learning. I don't see what it is for. So I don't know how else to take it but personally – as you say.'

'What don't you understand?'

She looked at me thoughtfully, although she had gone rather pink, and there was a mixture of embarrassment and determination in her voice when she answered: 'You asked me just now what I thought you were trying to teach me. I said to act this part in this play. You agreed. Nothing has been said about turning me into an actress – supposing that to be possible.'

'I agree.'

'But what you are teaching me doesn't seem to have anything to do with Clemency. She doesn't go shouting about breathing deeply with a book on her head.'

She said all this deadpan enough to make me laugh.

'She wouldn't be very convincing if she crept about staring at the floor and muttering under her breath, would she?'

'I don't regard any of this as a laughing matter.'

'Right: well, we'll both try to take a serious, but not dedicated, point of view.'

We looked at each other in wary silence: she didn't know how to take me any more than I knew how to deal with her. Finally I said: 'Look: I know you aren't an actress, and perhaps you don't even want to be one, but you've agreed to try and act this part which, to prevent any further quibbling, is going to involve your doing a little acting. Right?'

She nodded.

'Right. From my point of view, as an actress, or as material, you've got a certain amount of equipment. My job is to teach you how to use it, so that it works as much as possible. You might say that you already know this, one way or another and that it's your own business. It is, as far as you are concerned, while you are being Alberta, but when we come to Clemency – to you being anyone else, in fact – it's not the same. To be Clemency, you've got to act: acting is not life, it gives the impression of life – if you act well, it gives a very strong one. In this part – like all good parts – there are a certain amount of externals pre-arranged: you have to follow them. You have to say certain words, move at certain times, and part of you knows beforehand that this is going to happen. You also have to do this in such a way that apparently intimate words and movements are none the less carried out so that they can be heard and seen at a distance, while preserving their apparent intimacy and spontaneity. You can't start giving these impressions until the knowledge of exactly what you are doing has really sunk into you. I was starting with your body. Until you are aware of that – of your voice and how you move – nobody will be able to take in anything else about you on a stage – however right it is inside you.' I cleared my voice – it was quite a speech for me, and I hadn't known that I had so much to say. 'There are different schools of acting. But you're not a student with several years to learn all about it, and you're not at any of the schools – you've got a couple of months and me. It's urgent, and between us we've got to find the best way of your learning. You must trust me not to be personal or we shall get nowhere.' I stopped, and then said: 'How does that seem to you?'

'Much better: I do begin to understand what you mean. You mean that I probably do understand more at the moment with my mind, and the rest of me is a bit behindhand. Something like that?'

'For this particular work – yes.'

'And it's also a question of scale, I suppose. I mean it all has to be a bit larger than I realized?'

'Yes – but not at the expense of sharpness or depth.'

She was silent for a bit: she still looked nervous, but she was natural with me again. Then she said: 'Jimmy – I don't see why you think I'll be able to learn all I need to learn: it may be a disastrous gamble, and you will be angry and he will be disappointed . . .'

'Who's he? Emmanuel, do you mean?'

'Mr Joyce – yes.'

Something about the way in which she had said 'he' made me watch her now, but she looked back steadily – her face calm. If she developed a crush on Emmanuel, I found myself thinking savagely – *my* relations with her can be as impersonal as hell – it won't make the slightest difference. I decided to narrow the chances any way I could.

'Don't worry about Emmanuel,' I said; 'he understands the situation. He's an old hand at gambling, which means he's prepared to lose out on a hunch, but also that his hunches are often good. He's got a new play on his mind, and the only thing to do then is to leave him alone as much as possible. The best thing we can do for him is to get Clemency into your blood. You've got what it takes all right – believe me – we've just got to get everything working. Let's start – yes?'

She smiled warmly at me. 'Yes: thank you, Jimmy.'

Then I made a fool of myself. 'Anyway – any time he has left over for social intercourse ought to be kept for Lillian. This holiday is largely for her benefit, and heaven knows it's long enough since she had him to herself.'

She started to speak – checked herself, and put her hands in her lap: the colour which had flooded into her face slowly went away again. Already angry with myself, I could not help asking: 'What were you going to say?'

She shook her head.

'Maybe I shouldn't have said that. It sounded disloyal – I was thinking of Lillian: what *were* you going to say?'

'Nothing that has anything to do with Clemency.'

'Forget it,' I said miserably; 'I'd do anything for Emmanuel – you know that.'

She looked at me then with such a kind of sweetness – she didn't say anything, but the cheap, nasty feeling I had just went – she got to her feet and simply said: 'How do we start?'

And that was *that*.

CHAPTER VI

1

EMMANUEL

HE had taken to sleeping on the eastern terrace: it was far enough from Lillian, and out of Jimmy's irritating, anxious clutches. Jimmy had twice followed him down in the night when he had tried to sleep in the room upstairs, and he could not stand any more of it. He had to be alone; he had himself become so crowded that he could not manage these deputations of himself that he seemed forced to meet, if there were other people there: excepting her.

They had been nearly three weeks on the island, and his insomnia had settled to three or four hours' sleep from about two a.m. until the sun slid up from behind the hill gradually gilding the early grey air: the gentle warmth was like a waking caress on his skin – he could not sleep after it. Then he got up and went down to the sea, pausing outside her window, because once she had come too. He went to the beach where they all went each morning for lunch: sometimes he forgot to bathe. A great deal of the time he thought he was mad, and wondered with a kind of reckless irresponsibility what would happen to him next. He lived alternately with her image and her presence: with the first he became a starving rabble, all crying their separate hungers – with the last he seemed to collect into some adoring, accepting unity. Her presence was like air to him; essential at the time, but of no avail as a mere memory; it was only on the rare occasions when he managed to be alone with her that he could store something with which to bear her absence.

Any shreds of control that he still possessed – and perhaps they were substantial shreds – were spent on concealing his state from the others. This meant particularly being a charming, accommodating companion to Lillian during the first half of the morning, and leaving no outward expression of his feelings in Jimmy's way. With her, surprisingly, he found it easy to be 'natural' and passive. Alone, he beat off attacks of terror about the future – the frightful evening when some casual remark had introduced the idea of her being thousands of miles away in New York while he struggled with English country life – attacks of desire that occurred with such sudden force that they ruled out any consideration for anything or anyone else – and attacks of humiliating fear when he felt that if anyone knew of all this, they would simply find it unbearably funny and embarrassing – when even she would laugh. His ability to reason, to analyse the situation with any degree of detachment had vanished: the state of dogged calm which he had reached through his conclusions on the boat might have been reached by someone else, since they seemed to have made not the slightest difference. Alone, he counter-attacked his fears with imagination, invention, and a kind of translation of his memory; these three active ingredients easily idealized the future, transformed the present, and distorted the past. Thus he would declare himself to her, and she, he would reflect with amusement both cunning and tender, she would almost certainly blush and resort to language that she had gleaned from her papa's library . . . she would be deeply sensible of the honour he did her – and she would turn those marvellously clear calm eyes upon him with her consent . . . Later he would confess that he was sixty-two, and ask her whether she minded. She did not mind at all – it was quite all right. (Anxiety in these scenes was like salt – only adding to their taste.) The week in New York with her became encrusted with dreams of moments . . . her head on his shoulder in the taxi, his touching her hair, her smiling peacefully in her sleep. Her confusion when she realized all he had bought her in the store – his taking her hands and explaining to her that there was nothing unseemly in accepting anything if one was loved as he loved her . . . But there were moments, also, which needed no embellishment: her walking into the crowded room at the party and answering his public question – steadily denying his wisdom – he had loved her then, or he had loved something true in her which she had made suddenly recognizable. In the flat, when they had been talking about the play and he had pressed her for her opinion: she had given it and touched some spring in him – illumined some part of himself that he thought had died in his early days . . . The part of him that needed reasons for loving her was satisfied by the purer memories – by this steady core of truth in her – some inner unchanging beauty that he had not recognized in anyone before, and this was the only discovery he made through comparison; the rest of him seemed to forget or ignore any other experience. In the same way, in the scenes with which he decorated his solitude, only he and she were there – and occasionally an anonymous conglomerate crowd – but no single other person; even Lillian seemed not to exist. All this was when he was alone – chiefly the nights, the early mornings, and some of the hot afternoons.

But there were hours without her, spent with Lillian, and sometimes Jimmy, and these he found interminable. Then, all the words that he had read and heard applied to his state were not, he discovered, merely elegant eighteenth-century turns of phrase, but painfully, bitterly apt. Love *was* a fever – it burned and consumed him as he tossed and ached through burning delirious nights: it was a snare, a trap, a gin – injuring and imprisoning those it caught; then, sick with an impatience like pain, he would endure the leisurely mornings with Lillian – the cup of coffee that he did not want and which was too hot to drink, the amble back beside Lillian's donkey. Once, she had a headache, and did not come out to dinner with them: he thought the evening would never end, and when, at last, they were back at the house, Lillian had looked in at her room and said that she was fast asleep, and the disappointment at not seeing her brought unexpected, confounding tears to his eyes.

Time seemed now to have a life of its own – double-edged, airy and malignant. On the few occasions when he was alone with her, it was gathered together into a whole – like a jewel in his hand – each moment with her was a facet reflected in his shining content. When they were four, it flowed over him in a flowery inconsequent manner – neither here nor there so to speak; but when he was alone or without her, it assumed thunderous, sullen, immovable proportions: it hung like a stone round his neck; it was like an eternal black sea with no shore – his restlessness had no relation to it. He would sit in the afternoons at the wooden table in his room at the top of the house while the others slept. This was when he was supposed to be writing. Once, then, he wrote her a letter beginning 'My darling love', and when he had written even that part he wondered how many million letters had been started like that, and how many dozen truths were embedded in the tradition. In spite of his desire to write the letter, he wrote it slowly and painfully – each word of it seemed to be wrenched and wrung from his heart, but also, it seemed a strangely impersonal business. It was extraordinary, but the effort and effect of putting down exactly what he had intended, neither adding nor leaving out anything, somehow removed him from the enterprise: it was necessary that the letter could be to no one but her, but it did not matter who had written the letter – this was the measure of his praise. When it was finished, he read it very carefully to see that it was right, and then burned it. Afterwards he had a feeling that he knew from good writing-days – when he was empty and light with a kind of exhausted peace, until energy from the work done slowly refilled him. But all the other afternoons he did not write anything.

In the late afternoon, when the sun was still simply shining, but the shadows on the Peloponnese – like a giant kneeling on the mountains – had turned violet, he would go down to the western terrace, and often she would come out from her room at one end of it and join him. Sometimes she came only a few minutes before one of the others; sometimes not before them at all, and every day now he was trembling, praying that she would come first. But when she did come, and walked softly on her bare feet across the marble towards him, warm, honey-coloured, entirely unconscious of changing his world, all his tension, his parched breathless waiting and longing for her transformed to a joy like sunlight in his blood.

She would drop down beside him with a brief friendly smile, but unless he asked her a question, they were usually silent.

Sometimes he asked about the child – the prodigy – with whom she went for walks.

'How was Jules Verne today?'

'In a very calculating mood. He was estimating how long the world would last – but it is all done in millions and partly in Greek, so I find him difficult to follow on the subject.'

'Has he references for his calculations?'

'Oh yes, but he says he is a critical statistician, and therefore will take nothing for granted. He said it was a thousand pities that I was not better informed, as our duologue on the subject was unbalanced by my ignorance, and then we talked about other things.'

'What did you talk about next?'

'Fish, and marriage.'

'Has he proposed to you?'

'He had mentioned the matter, but he feels that I am far too old, and he does not approve of too great a discrepancy in age. He is only ten, you see; that makes nine years between us. He feels that looking after his animals – he is very zoophilic – and his children and cooking for him might prove too much for me by the time he is of an age to marry.'

'I see. And what about fish?'

'I was asking him if he had ever seen a shark here. He said yes, he had once, and that there were stories of people being eaten by them from time to time – about four people since the war, he said, which made it a distinguished, though horrible, end.'

'And then what?'

'I told him about learning your play.'

'I should like to meet him.'

'I'm afraid it would be no good. He does not want to meet you as he says that the Greeks wrote far the best plays and it might hurt your feelings if this fact were to emerge.'

That was one kind of conversation that they had. Occasionally, he asked her how she was getting on with Jimmy. Then she was always serious, even when she answered, as once she did: 'He says that I am improving. He has managed to get my head in the air and my feet on the ground, and he says that is something.'

'What does he mean by that?'

'Oh – I hung my head and muttered and shuffled about with my feet all the time whenever he wanted me to stand still.' She stretched out her foot on the parapet as she said this – flexed it, and let it lie. She had the most beautiful feet that he had ever seen – small, with neat round heels and articulate toes, and a pretty arch between them.

'You have Trilby feet,' he said aloud without thinking.

She looked up and smiled, and blushing a little, said: 'Do you think that Jimmy is Svengali then?'

'I don't know. How do you feel about it all? About Clemency, I mean?'

She didn't answer for a moment – she never answered idly, he noticed. 'You see, we've been concentrating on such beginnings that I've rather lost Clemency. Jimmy says this doesn't matter.'

'But it worries you?'

'Yes – it does, rather, I feel that I ought to be learning about her as well, but there doesn't seem to be time for it.'

'Would you like to read her with me again?'

'Very much.' She looked up with sudden gratitude, and her forehead cleared. He wanted to take her face in his hands and shower endearments upon it: he put his hands in his pockets, and said: 'Right: well, we'll do that tomorrow. Afternoon?' When the others were there, they drank *arezinata*, ate the luscious black olives, and watched the evening triumph. Watching the sun set was a long, beautiful sight. It sank with heroic brilliance – the sky a great map of its tumult: they had none of them ever seen sunsets like these. It turned the rocks the colour of a leopard's eyes – the white houses tender, delicate pinks – the sea an inky blue but broken and furred with gold as the evening winds silently echoed over it.

They would sit until the nearby island bloomed mysteriously like a whale in the sea, and a pale crocus cluster of lights trembled from the Peloponnese; the vine against the house was black, and he could watch her face less secretly. Then, sometimes he would cry a private supplication to some god; that it should stay like this – not perfect – she was not his, and she knew nothing of it, but simply that she should be always there. In the flushed calm of the hour, with the long evening before him – even his night alone seemed distant, anything beyond it a dream, and this seemed a possible prayer.

He did not suggest reading Clemency with her until she had had a clear two weeks with Jimmy. This was chiefly because, in some odd way, he was far more frightened of Jimmy discovering about him than he was of Lillian – who seemed safely wrapped up in her own enjoyment. But Jimmy had this streak – which until now he had been grateful for – of acute perception where he was concerned; of anticipating his wishes, of understanding his smallest requirements, of attending him through every kind of crisis. He did not want the precipitation of Jimmy knowing – his intimate blind eye, his almost aggressive loyalty . . . There was, in any case, a slight strain between them – very slight – hardly definable – but something to do with the night when Jimmy had followed him down on to the terrace, clearly expecting him to talk himself into the new play, and he hadn't, because he had had nothing to say about it. Then, quite suddenly Jimmy had switched – to her, and in a few moments of professional reason, had taken his mornings away from him. He had felt then like a child who has had something most precious to it firmly and with maddening kindness put out of its reach. Only Jimmy hadn't even realized what he'd done – poor Jimmy – he was simply trying to do his best with a raw girl in a big acting part. It was absurd, after all these years, to blame Jimmy for doing his job properly. The prospect of reading the play with her sharpened the whole evening and softened the night, when he was actually able to invoke these kinder, more reasoned considerations . . .

The next morning, Lillian remarked as they walked on to the port, was exactly like a Dufy. There was a stiff breeze; the sea was petrol blue and neatly choppy, the coloured caiques – painted pinks and scarlets and greens – were frolicking at their moorings, the sky overhead was crowded with small, hurrying, white clouds; canvas awnings over shops and cafés were flapping with unrhythmic gusto, and the dozen or so harbour cats were all behaving like theatrical gangsters or secret agents. Only the mules and donkeys stood with lowered heads and expressions of cynical calm, looking – as Lillian said – as though they were trying to hold their breath to recover from hiccoughs. They had now a routine for the morning's shopping. They bought all the food together – Lillian choosing, and he carrying the baskets: fruit, vegetables, Nescafé, rice, tinned meat, eggs, and cheese; then she went to buy cigarettes from the ex-sponge diver who had had the bends and was hopelessly crippled, and he went to the Post Office. He was not interested in the possibility of letters, but Lillian – in theory, at least – adored them, and he knew that *her* letters from Dorset were important to her. So he went every day with the bundle of their passports, and helped the internationally crabbed official with 'Young' and 'Joyce' (he clearly felt that one ought to stand for the other, and the other should not exist at all). This morning, there was a good haul: two letters for her – one from Dorset and one from London, a bulky letter for Lillian, two for him, and a packet from New York for Jimmy.

'Darling, what a lot! Anything for me?'

He handed her her letter and she fell upon it.

'It's from Peg Ashley – I wrote and told her about this

heavenly place. I haven't seen her for ten years, but I thought that if we were going to settle down it would be nice to take up with her again. I've asked her to look for a house for us.'

He did not reply – afraid that it might involve actually discussing the future. With one of his own letters in his hand he was looking at the packet for Jimmy which now lay face downwards on the table. On the back of it, in bold sprawling writing, was the name and address of the photographer to whom Jimmy had taken her for pictures in New York. He had an overwhelming desire to see the pictures: he looked at Lillian; she was engrossed in her letter which was a very long one – but the packet was addressed to Jimmy. He opened his own letter and looked at it: it was from Willi Friedmann, and quite short, but difficult to read. With his mind on the packet he skimmed through his letter. Matthias had had an accident of the hand – Friedmann was not thence going to buy the fiddle as it would not be useful – something about destiny (very Germanic, he thought impatiently) and machinery at school – the boy was in hospital – then an almost illegible paragraph about the boy's feelings which he did not read. Bad luck for the boy, he thought absently – and reached for the packet. Lillian was still reading – it would be hours before they were back at the house, and the thought of having to see the pictures with Jimmy suddenly nauseated him. He opened the packet. The pictures were in a folder, and pinned to it was a note from Stanley to Jimmy. 'Roughs – only. She's a natural, your girl: congratulations. Stan.' Trembling, on fire with wordless thoughts, he ripped open the folder, and there she was. There were eight pictures and they gave him another shock. He had not known that anyone else could see her with such clarity and understanding of what she was; he had thought his image a private one made by his love – it was the only sense of possession he had had about her. At the bottom of the set was a small replica of one plate with another note. 'For your pocketbook'. Anger roared in him like a drum roll: he felt when it stopped he would be forced to see something terrible, and clung to the anger, which at least blinded him. He put the small picture in his pocket, and gathered up his own two letters saying savagely to himself: 'Time I did some letters with my secretary.' He must get back to the house; this desire repeated until it became almost a shout: he turned to Lillian. She was wearing a wide-brimmed red hat which particularly suited her complexion, and now she was bent over the photographs . . .

'. . . well – *really* – he is the most astonishing photographer. I mean, she has a nice little face, but who would have thought that this could be made of it!'

He did not reply, but smiled absently at her and looked about for Spiro to pay for the coffee – must get back.

'Whenever you smile at me like that, I know that you aren't listening. Seriously – I should think that she'll get film offers if she's any good at all at acting and photographs like that; wouldn't Jimmy be furious if she accepted them!'

'Why should it make any difference to him?'

'My dear, his *protégée*! He's been one all his life, he's never *had* one. Haven't you noticed how it's changed him?'

'In what way?'

'He's growing up.' Lillian said it with a kind of satisfaction.

Walking up the hill through the village, he kept behind Lillian's donkey. The stone steps – seemingly so shallow, and cut with wide enough treads for the whole donkey to stand on one of them – this morning were endless: as soon as he got his breath on one level, there was another to be climbed. He had never needed to wear a hat, but now the sun was boring down into the back of his neck in painful, uneven pulses – like the electric current of toothache. Beyond these physical discomforts his mind hunted his worst fears; refusing to consider exactly what he would find, it nevertheless pursued some dangerous track started by those confidential scraps of writing which had not been addressed to him. With this there was the most frightful sense of unreality – the feeling that he did not, could not exist in circumstances which had seemed to descend on him from nowhere, without warning or consideration for what he had thought that he was, making him feel old, and irrelevant and disassociated. The sky burned, the houses dazzled, the stones had no flesh on their bones under his feet: he was sixty-two, and his wife sat on a donkey ahead of him. She was nineteen on the cool terrace, and her future stretched illimitable, like the sea round her. The gap between wanting and giving widened with each step that he took, and each step was bringing him nearer the sun, inviting its violence. He walked – his heart like a sledge hammer – collecting panic, as ideas, facts, likelihoods, and comparisons reared up and sheered off in his mind, each one irrefutable, each not to be borne: he clung only to the shreds of his anger and the illusion that whatever he found could be changed.

When the house was in sight, Lillian called back to him and talked the rest of the way – some long reminiscences about something they had done together; he tried to listen, but it made him feel still more unreal. At the door of the house he gave her the wallet to pay for the donkey and told her to get the man to bring the food in: he wanted to find them alone.

Jimmy was alone on the terrace, stretched at full length on the parapet – she was nowhere to be seen. Jimmy heard the door opening and sat up and said 'Hi!', he seemed half asleep.

'Where is your pupil?' Trying to say it lightly made his voice tremble.

'Alberta? She's somewhere around. It got too hot and we called it a day. She said something about writing a letter and she couldn't do it in the sun,' he added.

The donkey man padded quietly across the terrace with their baskets: unreality began to ebb; he noticed that a plant on the terrace had suddenly flowered with one great scarlet trumpet. Then Lillian appeared and paid the man, who received the money in his customary manner made up of indifference almost bordering on compassion, and went, closing the terrace door behind him. It was all the same, and I am a little mad, he thought wearily; he had to sit down. Then Lillian said: 'Have you shown the photographs to Jimmy?'

Jimmy said lazily: 'What photographs?'

'The ones of Alberta that Stanley took.'

Jimmy swung his legs down off the parapet and said: 'Did Stan send them to *you*?'

He said: 'As a matter of fact he didn't, but I couldn't resist looking at them. I hope you don't mind—'

Jimmy did not answer; Lillian had gone into the house. As Emmanuel held out the packet, Jimmy burst out: 'I should think you've enough letters of your own without opening other people's!' He did not take the packet. Then he added: 'It's extraordinary that I shouldn't be expected to have any privacy at all.'

'Sorry, Jimmy. I didn't know you felt so strongly about it, or of course I wouldn't have opened them.'

But they had known each other too well for this kind of lie: Jimmy said: 'You know damn well that you never stopped to think what I might feel.' For the first time they looked at each other. Jimmy had never in his life been like this to him, and as their eyes met he saw Jimmy realizing this; a flicker of astonishment marked the resentment in Jimmy's eyes and disappeared as he turned to his anger again for support, saying: 'I suppose you think that because you pay for the pictures . . .'

'Oh for God's sake, Jimmy, I think nothing of the kind. Idle curiosity – that's all.' Lying made him angrier. He slammed the packet down on to the parapet between them, and stood up: he could never relinquish the small picture now. He turned towards the house, and as he did so, she came out of it.

'Mrs Joyce said there were some letters for me. And she said that my photographs had arrived from America.'

'They have.' Jimmy did not turn his head, but she looked at him and said: 'Are you satisfied with them?'

'Ask Mr Joyce: I haven't looked.'

She looked inquiringly at both of them – sensed something – he felt her retreat, and quickly held out her letters. 'The pictures are very good. Jimmy is angry with me because I opened the packet and it was addressed to him.'

'Oh,' she flushed slightly: Jimmy still didn't turn round.

Then, in spite of himself, he said: 'Jimmy seems to think that pictures of you are his personal property, when really, if they belong to anybody, they belong to you.'

'They're nothing to do with *me*,' she said cheerfully: 'Surely they were taken for Clemency?'

Jimmy said suddenly: 'Has he opened *your* letters?'

'Of course not.'

'Of course not.'

She and he said this at once, and Jimmy echoed satirically: 'Of course not.'

There was the uncomfortable pause which occurs when lack of proportion becomes manifest; then she put her letters into the pocket of her cotton skirt, and said: 'Mrs Joyce has prepared the lunch. Shall we leave the pictures now, and go to bathe?'

It struck him, walking down to the beach with her, that Jimmy had not even realized clearly the cause of his own anger – that *she* had certainly no idea of it: it was almost possible after these two conclusions to imagine that he had been wrong – that Jimmy was sulking on general, harmless grounds. He took the opportunity to apologize again to Jimmy with more truth in his apology. It was accepted.

2

ALBERTA

Darling Uncle Vin,

You are quite right, and what Papa says about life consisting of ranges of molehills is true also: I had forgotten it, as usual, because sometimes one draws far too near a molehill. I will write to Papa forthwith: I am merely charging up energy in agreeing with and thanking you. As you say, the whole question turns on whether I am good enough. I realized suddenly, yesterday, that I am learning a good deal, which was cheering, as I had been in despair. But yesterday Mr Joyce read some of the play with me (I have been working with Jimmy, learning to walk and speak and stand still and listen) and I had thought that the part was getting further and further away, but after one false start I read it much more easily, and didn't get a sore throat or a thumping heart or feel breathless and unreal – *so* – perhaps I shall be suitable in the end. What you say about the salary is staggering, Uncle Vin. Do you think, if I bought him one, Papa would use a little car instead of his awful old bicycle? Or do you think that that would constitute an even greater danger? If you do, at least I could buy him an ageless mackintosh like you have and have some of the draughts in his study stopped up which he has always said would need a team of experts from London. Which do you think would be best for him? It seems extraordinary to think that I could ever earn enough to do anything so *old* with my money – but perhaps this is all some kind of dream – if you saw this island you would see what I mean. It's something to do with everything in my life having changed, except, in some way, me inside it. It should be 'I', I think. I must say that Charlotte Brontë did not write nearly such good English as Jane Austen. Oh, by the way, I quite understand what you say about telling Papa myself, and not hiding behind you – that this is the wrong way of telling things: I should have told you this earlier, or perhaps I don't need to at all, but you know what a hotbed of misunderstanding letters can be – literature has taught me that, at least.

I'm so sorry that you didn't get the part of the card-sharper in the film, what bad luck, it would have made a change – still, I expect it will be very peaceful being the Rev. Clamber in *The Unashamed*, and it will help you with the instalments on your Mixmaster, and your portable canoe.

I have got quite sunburned, although nothing like Mr Joyce or Jimmy, but at least I've passed the shrimp colours and don't burn any more and my swimming has improved immeasurably. Some photographs of me for the play that were taken in New York have arrived; they are very like me, but I don't think they can be much good, as they seemed to make everybody rather cross. I was hoping that they would be rather glamorous, but I daresay that that was not possible in my case (Jimmy said that the man was a first-class photographer). I will remember what you say about a hare's foot, but at the moment that seems a distant piece of equipment. Jimmy is extremely interesting about acting – both sensible and arresting, and it certainly won't be his fault if I am no good. I wish you could be in the play too. What a good idea, it does not smack of corruption as you are a much better actor than I shall ever be an actress.

Love from SARAH.

I have written to Papa, and it was not difficult at all. Only – now that the envelope is lying beside me with his name and address on it – I wish that I was the letter and going there. It was never an address before – even when I went to Paris with Uncle Vin – it was here and home, and now I feel very far away. June is one of the best months at home: grass up to your knees, hedges high and strung with wild roses; buttercups like money in the fields; thick dew in the mornings, a smell of honey and heather on the heath and the bees seem to dance in the air. All the Junes I have ever known there seem to have become one time, so that I don't seem to have any particular age in my memories, and everything I remember seems always to have been happening. Picnics, adventures with the brothers, waiting up for a ghost, putting a hen in Aunt T.'s cupboard, trying to tame a toad; hot stilted afternoons with Lady Gorge's nieces, walking round her garden, asking names, saying what we had been given for Christmas and what we would do when we were grown up; the atmosphere of cautious competition, the marvellous tea and our riotous escape to play what Lady Gorge described to Papa as a very rough and dirty game; reading to

Serena in the apple tree – she always liked sad stories and cried nearly all the time; evening walks with Papa when somehow whatever we talked about touched me and touched something else, so that I remember most clearly the tone of his voice, the feeling that he was giving me something that it was worth my trying to understand, and the smoothing of the ripe grasses against my legs . . . loving him, I love to remember the reasons for it. I've never thought of spending years of my life away from him, which perhaps I shall do – but it doesn't matter how far I am or for how long because I can always remember that he is there – steady and gentle and true, I've thought very carefully about those three words, and they are the best I can find to describe him. The other side of it not mattering – which may be a piece of grandiloquence due to this being my diary – is that I just wish that I was with him *now*. I just wish that.

Friday.

One thing I am learning is the difference between family life and living with other people: the latter is a much more groundless affair, so that sometimes one has to seek reasons for it, and then they seem to be outside reasons like money and work and things to be done. Things are not always easy here, but I don't understand what makes the difficulties. I thought that perhaps either Jimmy or Mr Joyce had decided that I was unsuitable for Clemency and that the other one didn't agree. Reading the play with Mr J. made me think of this. Half way through, Jimmy joined us – he didn't interrupt by saying anything but the kind of way that Mr J. had been listening stopped – like the lights going out – and I couldn't read properly any more. I tried, because I felt it was wrong for me to become hopeless the moment Jimmy arrived, but it was no use, and when I stopped I saw that Mr J. was staring at the ground looking very sad and Jimmy was staring at him, but he didn't look sad, he just had a kind of violence in his face.

Stopping, seeing their faces, I had an extraordinary feeling – almost a smell, like gunpowder after an explosion, only there hadn't been one: I thought that perhaps we were before it, and without knowing why, I said: 'What is to become of all this?'

They both looked at me then, and seeing that they were not startled and had no ignorance in their faces, I thought: 'They *know* that something is wrong, and they're aware of disaster, but they are not avoiding it or telling me,' and I wanted to say that I would not do what they wanted, but I couldn't speak, so I left them. I left the house and went out, starting for the port: I had such a longing for home that without thinking I ran nearly all the way, but when I got to the Post Office, it was too late and shut. Then I saw Julius walking slowly along reading a huge book, and without looking up, he stopped and waited until I caught up with him. We both went and had an orange drink although we hadn't any money, but the man never minds when we pay, and Julius took an envelope out of his *Outline of History* and said: 'I was going to bring this up to you when you had finished your acting work,' and it was a letter from Papa. We finished our drinks and went up the hill of the village where I knew that they wouldn't find me. Julius said: 'I wish to read today but I do not mind your silent company,' and I felt exactly the same, so we went past the houses up a gully where there was a fig tree with enough shade for two people and I read the letter. I read it twice and the second time I could hardly see his beautiful clear writing. Julius looked up and said: 'I hope no member of your family has died?' and when I said no, he apologized most courteously, and said that it had not occurred to him that letters could otherwise distress people, and went on reading. It was not simply that I was so glad to hear from him: it was that I could understand so much from what he wrote. I knew then that he had known that I was concealing things, that he trusted me about the concealments, that he had even foreseen the difficulties and differences which would occur for me; he did not say any of this in outside words – simply made it plain that he had used his thought for me rightly – putting any of his concern into the future.

> You will feel that you have many decisions in this different life that you are leading, but they are always fewer than they seem: it is a kind of obedience to God not to think or imagine yourself into action but to wait until what is true in yourself picks out the reality in your life from any false contrivance or scene of your invention. Very little external action is required – the energy and courage is meant for other uses. You know this, and I know that you know it, I am only wanting at this distance to prune you of unnecessary anxieties such as any you or I might have for each other.

At the end of the letter, he had written out his full blessing to me.

There were no birds, no clouds, no movement of the shadow from the tree, but a yellow and black and white butterfly – the largest I have ever seen – was silently examining the figs on the lower branches of our shade: Julius was watching it too, and said: 'Do you think it remembers when it was a caterpillar? Would you like me to catch it for you?' I said no, because it had such a short life anyway, and he said that I shouldn't be too sure of that – supposing an hour for us was a year for a butterfly – and then he was off on one of his immense calculations in Greek. I felt so calm and happy about the letter that I was hungry, and asked him whether he liked figs, but he only said: 'I prefer condensed milk,' and went on reading. So I picked some figs and a leaf to put them on and ate them very slowly and carefully, and then went to sleep.

When I went back it was about five o'clock. Mr Joyce was by himself on the terrace, sitting at a small table with paper in front of him, but he didn't seem to be writing anything. He looked up and said 'Alberta!' as though I'd been away for days, and I began to feel rather ashamed of having simply run away without saying anything in the morning. He asked me if I wanted anything to eat, and said that the others had gone for a long walk with donkeys; he didn't say anything about the morning. I got some bread and cheese and olives and we both had a glass of wine and he smoked and we didn't talk much, until he asked me whether I would do his letters with him which had been piling up slowly ever since we got here. It took him a long time to find the letters, as he had been opening them himself since we came to the island and they were all stuffed in various pockets of his clothes. In the end he said, well, we had quite enough to be going on with, and dictated in his rapid quiet dictating voice – I have got quite used to it, although I still find the people we have to write to extraordinary. Then, when I folded my notebook and stood up, he said: 'You aren't going to type indoors on such a beautiful evening surely?' so I brought my typewriter out on to the terrace, and after I had done some of the letters I looked up and he was smiling at me and said: 'Were you going to say this morning that you didn't want to play Clemency?' and I said yes: I didn't say any more, and after waiting a moment, he said: 'But I think you've changed your mind since then – haven't you?' I told him that I had decided not to come to any decision about it, but what did he think? Or Jimmy? He thought for a bit, and then said that he'd come to much the same decision as me – not to make one. He explained that there were many other factors besides getting Clemency right, and that he'd been considering our leaving Greece a little sooner than we had planned and all going to London before New York. Then he said that he felt I should have the opportunity of talking to my father and that Mrs Joyce wanted to make inquiries about buying a house in the country. I told him that I had written to Papa, although he would not have got the letter yet, but the prospect of going home before we went to America added to the feeling Papa's letter had given me. I looked out over the sea which was absolutely calm and the colours of a delphinium, and thought that I would bathe when I had finished the letters. Then Mr J. laughed and said did I think that there would be a pretty house in Dorset for him to buy? I said that I would write to Aunt Topsy and inquire, but he said no don't it was really no more than an idle thought. Then I finished the letters. Samples – to a lady who wished to call her champion Boxer puppy Emmanuel Joyce: another who wanted to spend three months with him telling him the story of her life in order that he should make a play of it. A club who wanted him to talk to them about Renaissance drama and poetry for two and a half hours with lantern slides 'and other expenses' provided. Two girls who wanted to be his secretary. A furious man who was collecting copies of a certain play of Mr J.'s and burning them as he went. He had got to one hundred and twenty-two copies and wished to know how many more there were. Another lady who said he looked awfully like somebody she had met on a boat in the Red Sea once and was he? Then there were the ordinary business ones – asking for material, or asking for permission to act or reproduce scenes or bits of plays. Mr J. is tremendously patient and brief with the mad ones, but as he said nearly all his letters were variations on a negative theme. At the end he said he knew that these weren't all the letters, but he couldn't find any more, but would I make a note of Friedmann in my book, and if the letter didn't turn up, we would have to write to him.

I felt nervous of seeing Jimmy again, but he came back from his expedition in tremendous spirits, and so was Mrs Joyce. It was a very hot night, and we ate in the café belonging to our village and didn't go into the port. You go into the back of the café and look at huge black pots on charcoal stoves and choose what you will have. There isn't much choice and nearly everything is fried, but there is always marvellous fruit and I have got very attached to Turkish coffee. After we had sat for a long time, Jimmy suddenly asked me whether I would like to go bathing by moonlight, and not having bathed all day this seemed a delicious proposal. Mr J. said should he and Mrs J. come and watch them, and Mrs J. said, no, she was tired, and wanted to talk to him, so we all went back to the house, and then Jimmy and I went off with our bathing things. It was the kind of night when the moonlight was golden and the stars were like great shining drops: we walked down to the bay and settled on the piece of rock where we usually sit before bathing and Jimmy said: 'Let's talk for a bit before we bathe.'

We sat for what seemed a very long time and he didn't say anything. I nearly asked him if he had any particular subject in mind, but I had a feeling that he had something he wanted to say so I just waited. Eventually, he said: 'You're nineteen, aren't you?' and I said, yes. Then he said: 'I'm thirty-three: I've been thinking about it all afternoon.'

After a bit, he went on: 'I want to talk to you, but if you interrupt I'll get so thrown I won't be able to explain anything to you. OK, you won't interrupt?'

I agreed, and folded my hands so that I could pinch myself if I forgot.

'About your career. I think that you could make it – could be a good Clemency and a success in New York. If you make a hit there it will lead to other things – you won't be a secretary any more. But you'll need help – you wouldn't find New York on your own with a big and tiring part that easy: not if you were all by yourself.'

'But I *shouldn't* be all by myself, surely?'

'Wait.' I wanted to apologize, but that would have meant further interruption, so I didn't.

'Lillian doesn't want to go to New York. And she doesn't want Emmanuel to go either. She wants to buy a house in England and settle down for a bit. She doesn't want him to go either,' he repeated: he was staring at me. I didn't speak until he said: 'Well? Have you thought of that?'

'No I haven't.' I began to feel alarmed at the prospect. 'I had not thought of trying to do new kinds of work without all of you at all.'

'Well, it's probably time you did.'

Something in his voice irritated me, and I said: 'I haven't thought about it, because I didn't think that it was even decided that I should do the part. If I did, I suppose I thought that everything else would be the same.'

'You mean you thought that you'd still be his secretary? We'd still be a nice cosy little foursome?'

I asked him what was the *matter* – he sounded so odd.

He lit a cigarette with exaggerated care before he said: 'I find it difficult to talk to you because I never know what you understand. You floor me every time. Leave the foursome for the moment. It would have to come to an end anyway. Let's concentrate on you in New York. I rehearse the show – perhaps they come over for the opening, and then there you are in a run, with the rest of us maybe on a slow boat to China or some place. You may be there for *years*! You haven't any friends in New York – you don't know your way around – the work is killing – hotel life will get you down – you'll miss your family – awful old men will keep trying to take you up country for a weekend –'

'Jimmy, *don't*!' I was laughing, and then I saw that although he meant me to laugh, he was meaning some of it, and even part of that picture of me alone in New York for years was dismaying. I was just about to broach the question of Uncle Vin possibly having some part in the play, thus providing me with a friend and some family in one stroke, when he said: 'Now I'm coming to the important part – I mean the part I really want you to understand. The best solution seems to me for me to stay in New York with you right through the run. You see, I know how to take care of things for you all round. I know the city, I know theatre people, and I could see to it you have the right sort of time.' He paused, and looked at me expectantly.

'It is exceedingly kind of you. But what about Mr Joyce?'

'What about him?'

'I thought you were supposed always to be working for him – with him, I mean.'

'Yeah – but if you married me the situation would be different, and I might make a change.'

I stared at him. I wanted to say: 'If I *what*?' but felt it would be rude and I couldn't think of anything else to say. Then he said almost angrily: 'I *told* you I had some complicated things to say, and you have interrupted so much that I *have* got them in the wrong order. You don't understand. I'm making you a perfectly businesslike proposition. You need looking after, I know how to do it and it would all be much simpler if we were married. I like you very much,' he added.

I wondered whether this sort of thing happened to a great many people, and what they did about it: it wasn't at all how I'd ever thought of people proposing to each other. He seemed serious – even nervous about it: it occurred to me that possibly he was just trying to be very kind, although it did seem to be carrying kindness a very long way.

'I don't want to marry somebody simply to make things more comfortable: I don't think that is what marriage is for, but it is extremely kind of you to suggest it.' I thought for a bit, but I couldn't think of anything to add.

He was silent for a while; then he said: 'I wish you'd think about it some more before you turn me down. I don't feel I've put it at all well: it's not just what I think about it all, but I've never met anyone like you before and I don't know how to put it – that sounds corny: it's honestly true.'

I said I would – indeed it would be very difficult not to think about it. He said: 'Well, we'd better forget it now, and bathe.'

We bathed; but I found myself unable to put what seemed such an extraordinary matter out of my mind, so that at one moment I found myself floating on my back facing the stars, in the warm dark water which at night seems to be scented more strongly of the sea, and thinking: 'Really, Sarah, here you are bathing at night off an island in Greece, and your thoughts are much of the kind that they have been when you are pleating Papa's surplice on a rainy Saturday morning in Dorset.'

We came out and sat on our towels, and Jimmy had another cigarette. Before I had had much time to consider how to say it, I asked him how he would feel if some time after we had married one of us fell in love with somebody who we would rather have married. If we *were* married, of course. He said: 'I've thought of all that, naturally. I figured you'd have more opportunity to fall in love with me than with anyone else – if you were married to me, of course.' Then he added: 'A lot of phoney marriages happen because the people have the idea that they're wildly in love. Don't you think it might make sense to start with respect and affection – compatibility of interests and a few other things like that?'

When I said, but what about his falling in love with somebody else, the mere thought seemed to embarrass him as he went rather red and said I needn't worry about that – that wouldn't happen to him. We left it at that: it all seemed a bit cold-blooded to me, but to accuse somebody of cold-bloodedness is something which I feel should not be lightly done. He said he wished he'd brought some drink down with him, and we decided to go back.

When we were climbing the cliffs, which seemed much steeper in the moonlight, I said something about worrying about Mrs Joyce climbing them in the heat of the day, and he answered: 'Lillian is pretty good at knowing what she can do really. It would be more like life if Emmanuel cracked up over them. He's not so young as he was, you know. He's in his late sixties.'

'Is he really?' The thought surprised me so much that for a moment I didn't remember that of course he was sixty-one – it was on the potted autobiography sheet that sometimes got sent to people. So I said: 'I don't call sixty-one "late sixties",' and he didn't reply.

Just as we were reaching the house he put his hand on my arm and said: 'That was a terrible lie about Emmanuel's age. I don't know what made me tell it.'

I said it didn't matter and I expected he'd forgotten, but he went on holding my arm, and said no, he hadn't forgotten – he knew perfectly well, and I was the last person he wanted to lie to. He looked quite desperate so there didn't seem any point in telling him what Papa says about the least important part of lying being who you tell the lie to, so I didn't – I simply begged him not to worry. Now I've been back in my room, read Papa's letter again and written all this – an enormous amount. Then I looked at other bits I've written, and I see that I haven't made a portrait of him.

Portrait of Mr Joyce. (This might be very interesting after we are all dead – a bit like planting trees.)

He is quite a small man with a sallow complexion and wiry thick hair which is dark except where it is a shining grey. He has a rather low forehead, but it is quite wide and he has surprisingly delicate eyebrows – they seem to indicate a line rather than be one. He has very dark brown eyes with heavy eyelids: the expressions in them always seem to be more than one at a time and often at variance. He has a jutting, but simple nose, and two lines run from the side of it down to his mouth, which is wide, with clearly cut complicated lips. He has magnificent ears – that sounds rather like an elephant, but they are – large and delicate. He has quite an ordinary chin – I mean it just seems to go with the rest of his face without being a feature on its own. He has veins and freckles on the backs of his hands, and thickish wrists and his shoulders are rather hunched. He has a gentle voice which very occasionally squeaks when he gets indignant: he is also exceedingly good at imitating people – he just does it suddenly for a few seconds, but it is always startlingly accurate. He walks in a rather jerky manner – taking short springy steps – not at all like Papa's silent tread, but he does give one the same feeling of terrific energy. Perhaps it is because I am sleepy, but I really can't think of any more to say about him, except that I quite understand why Jimmy has been so devoted to him; he is such a kind man to people. An *excellent* employer as Aunt T. would say. Enough, but I begin to wonder whether this diary is suitable for Mary.

3

JIMMY

IN the confusion which I seem to have gotten into one question goes on like a drumbeat setting the rhythm to something I don't begin to understand. What does she think of him? What *does* she think of him? I don't feel that asking her would tell me: maybe I don't have the courage to ask her, in case she did tell me and it was the wrong answer. I've never seen Emmanuel show any interest in a girl without its being returned – he's never had to make much effort for his pounds of flesh – all these years I've sat back and watched it, I haven't cared a damn one way or the other: I've protected him, soothed Lillian, and comforted the girl: there was nothing in it for me. I've watched everyone's behaviour rotate, as regular as clockwork – there's a kind of off-beat reliability about people's emotional extremes – so that sometimes I've even known beforehand what was going to happen and have been able to soften the blow for somebody . . . Well, I don't know now . . . His affairs have always been some kind of escape: once or twice he was infatuated – with that wacky girl who was so good in *The Top Drawer*, and with the one with wonderful hair who sang in a night club that awful summer we spent in Cannes – but generally, as he once said gossip columns should say: 'I'm not good friends with her – we're just going to bed' – it was like that. Although he never talked about the situation with Lillian I knew it went round in circles: she wanted children, they weren't possible so she didn't want Emmanuel; he strayed, she got frightened and did anything she could to get him back, and after a short interval it all started again. I've seen all that; it's been the background to nine years' hard work; I've loved working with him, and as he once said to me: 'By God, Jimmy, we don't choose our backgrounds: if we did, mine would be so dull and respectable that nobody would have a word to say about it.' But supposing he isn't seriously interested in her, what does she feel about him? Enough, maybe, to start something she isn't old enough or experienced enough to stop. But he is interested. He waits on that damn terrace every afternoon for her: I've watched his face when she comes out and sits on the parapet. They don't talk much, or she talks a bit and he watches her although she doesn't seem to realize it. They never look up to my window, or even across to Lillian's – you'd think they were the only two people in the house those times. I didn't think much about this – just happened to see them once or twice – until those pictures arrived. That was what triggered the whole thing off. I'd never have believed he'd open Stan's packet to me, and if I had thought of that, I'd never have believed how angry it would make me. In all these years for the first time I felt: 'That's my packet – *my* life you're interfering with – and nobody, not even you, has the right to do it.' It was worse to feel it with him: for the first time with him I felt back in that orphanage – that dead sea of equality; of owning nothing and not being owned. I didn't want to look at the pictures – I just wanted to throw them over the parapet, but when I saw them it was worse – it was as though I'd never seen Alberta in my life – she'd been there all the time and I'd been too blind to see her. I wouldn't have shown them to anybody – just kept them to myself and got Stan to take another lot for everybody else.

She just isn't the kind of girl for a routine seduction – that's all – it wouldn't happen to her unless she mistook it for something else: and that wouldn't happen unless she was deliberately misled. But I can't say I find these conclusions exactly restful, and when I knew she was to spend the morning reading the play with him, I couldn't keep away. I'd got involved with going down to the port with Lillian, but I made an excuse without worrying too much if it was a good one, and came back. That walk, if you're worrying, is murder in the sun – it seems to go on and on, and I had time to remember all the hot marching I'd done in the Army – only then you never seemed to be going to anything, you were just going – forward they liked to say.

I was a fool to go back: she was reading quite quietly, and he was listening in the way he has that makes you think nobody has ever done it before, but when she saw me she tried to raise her voice, his attention snapped, and I thought, 'Now – if he's innocent, he'll be angry – now I'll know,' and waited for him to lash out as I've seen him do to people who've succeeded in interrupting him when he's working. But he didn't: he glanced at me – tried to look at her and stared at the ground, and she stopped, and said something that for a moment made me think she knew everything about us – we hardly had time to stare at her before she had gone. I would have gone after her, but he got to his feet and then stood, listening, as I was, to her footsteps running on the stones outside. He said: 'She's gone': he said it stupidly – as though it was what he was thinking and he was not sure what it meant. Then he said: 'What on *earth* do you think you are doing barging in like that? I keep out of your frequent sessions with her – I should have thought you'd know better than to interrupt my rehearsal?' But it was all a tremendous effort – it didn't wash. I said: 'I think it's time we talked.'

'My dear Jimmy, we've been talking for years. Can't you think of any new means of communication?'

'Not with you I can't. I want to ask you one or two questions.'

'Are they pertinent?'

'I don't know or care. I just have to ask them – that's all.'

He sat down and it made him look very small: I had to remember her face a few minutes ago to get on with it.

'Are you interested in that girl?'

He said at once: 'Naturally. I would hardly be risking her in a leading part if I wasn't.' I was going to interrupt, but he went on: 'Although, at this rate, I don't think I shall be called upon to take the risk.'

'What do you mean?'

'I mean that you are making it so clear to her that you and I have different methods for preparing her that she will be confused and embarrassed into giving up the whole project. I shouldn't blame her at all if she did that now.'

'Look – you know as well as I do that we've worked together for nine years and our methods have never seemed different until now. It would be queer if they were, seeing that you've taught me. The confusion is not coming out of that, and that wasn't the kind of interest I was asking you about.'

'Are you implying that I have other, more personal interests in her?'

'Yes I am! And I'm not implying it, I'm asking a straight question: I'm not even asking any more – I know!'

He was so still that he looked as though he didn't breathe. Then, he said: 'What do you know?'

'You're in love with her. I know that because I've seen it so many times before; I know the signs. You aren't writing, you don't sleep, you hardly exist unless she's around. It's all very well at the moment, because you can see her every day, and it isn't easy for you to be alone with her. Remember Virginia? It was just like this then. All right – so you're in love with her. But what about *her*? She's nineteen – she probably hasn't been in love with anyone – may not even have been kissed, she's led such a secluded life with that family of hers in the back of beyond. You come along and change her whole life – everything is new and glamorous – she travels, she has clothes, she gets the opportunity most girls would give their eyes for – and all because of you. So far she's taken the whole thing very well – she enjoys it, but she doesn't seem to have let it go to her head. I call that a remarkable dignity – do you remember what that Miriam creature was like after you picked her up? But if you make a pass at her, she doesn't stand a chance. She's not old enough, or spoiled enough to do things by halves – she'll be madly in love with you – there'll be nothing she wouldn't do. So then, what? We go to New York – we go into rehearsal; the normal publicity starts up. She'll have the double strain of doing the part and being in love with you. Sometimes this will make her act twice as well – sometimes it won't. Then there'll be more publicity – you'll never get away from that. They'll never come out into the open – just the usual sly little cracks – she'll be hurt and angry, then she'll be hurt and frightened, and finally – and by this time it will have got back to her family, she'll be hurt and ashamed. And then there's Lillian. Have you thought about her, at all? You should have – you ought to know the pattern by now. To begin with, when she kicks up, you'll be clever enough to blind the girl into thinking it's certainly not her fault, and probably not yours. We'll have the whole neurotic story of Lillian's neurotic life trotted out, and everybody will be terribly sorry for everybody else – excepting Lillian. All this time that girl will be playing eight times a week not counting any other public appearances and the gossip columns will really be minding your business for you. You'll find it harder and harder to see her alone, and all the time they'll be saying things – about her, and about you – comparing your interest in her with your interest in various back numbers – mentioning your age and hers whenever possible – they might even get Mary what's-her-name to give the kind of interview they can blow up into an article, 'My Six Weeks with Emmanuel Joyce', if she's hard up and still feels the way she did last time I saw her. Lillian will be ill – the girl will be living on tranquillizers and pep pills and out of all this, at some point, you'll start to write another play. When you get really stuck into it, you'll ease out of the whole situation: you'll take Lillian away somewhere to recover and you'll write, and *she* will be nicely left with a dazzling career and a broken heart.'

I'd run out of breath and felt my heart pounding about, but there had been no choice about what I'd said to him. He had sat like a stone, with his eyes fixed on me and no expression in them that I could recognize or label. I stared back at him until I couldn't bear his silence any more and said: 'It's only because I've seen it so many times before that I know all this.'

After what seemed a long time, he said: 'And this is what "having a private life" has meant to you all these years.'

'I haven't blamed you; I'm not blaming you now. How can I know what is right for you?'

'But you've known that that kind of "private life" was not for you.'

'I don't remember thinking about that. I just feel now that it wouldn't be right for her.'

There was another long silence, and then he said: 'You are quite right, of course. And everything you've said has been quite true: there is no argument.' He fell silent again; then suddenly he yawned, and after it he looked utterly exhausted. Then he blinked, shook himself and tried to smile at me. 'You make me feel my years – or rather my wasted age.'

'I didn't mean to do that.' I wanted to be gentle now, and felt awkward – but he said heavily: 'Oh yes, you did. The whole exercise would have been wasted if you hadn't made me feel that.'

'Then you do agree about it?'

'Agree that I have no business to seduce Alberta, encourage her to love me and then abandon her? I do agree. For what it is worth, I entirely agree with you – it is out of the question. Now you know that I know that: will that do?'

I said: 'Of course.' I didn't feel at all good about him. I was just about to go, when he roused himself to ask: 'Is this the first time that you've felt like this about me – and anyone else?'

I nodded. 'That's what I mean about not blaming you. Hell, that sounds awful, I just mean it's been your business and theirs and certainly not mine. They weren't the same sort of girl as Alberta to start with – that's all.' I didn't want to pursue this, but he went on: 'You feel that she is not someone who should have casual and irresponsible passes made at her by *anyone* – is that it?'

I didn't reply at once, and he repeated more sharply: 'Is that it? Or do you make exceptions below a certain age?'

'It's not a question of making exceptions, and I don't feel that she can't look after herself at all: I don't feel that most people would meet with any response: you would; that's what I mean.'

He regarded me steadily – he still looked sick. 'And if she doesn't do the part, you still feel that?'

'I do – yes.'

He got to his feet. 'Right – Jimmy – that's about all, I think.' He looked about him as though he was trying to think of some place to go and made for the house. At least I knew better than to follow him.

When Lillian came back with plans for an afternoon expedition I told her he'd gone to his room. She went up and came down a few minutes later: 'He's asleep! He's lying on his face with his head under his arm – that usually means he has a headache. Did he say he had one?'

'He said he was tired. How about you and I take the donkeys and leave him to sleep?' So we did just that.

We went to look at a little church Lillian had found, built fairly high up in the village. When we got there, she sent the donkeys away, because she said she couldn't talk to me with the donkey man there. There were old women with white cloths round their heads sweeping in and outside the church which was very small indeed. The inside was entirely covered with paintings of people with rather sad, simple faces, but the whole effect wasn't simple at all. Lillian loved it – she said it was like being inside a casket of jewels. There was a wooden gallery at one end and I climbed up it. That gave me a shock. All around the walls were sacks – open at the top and stuffed with human bones; I knew they were human because of the skulls. I told Lillian who was unexpectedly calm about it, and said yes, she had been told that some favoured people were allowed to keep their family's bones in the church when they had been buried for long enough. She said she thought it was a friendly idea, and I discovered that I hadn't really thought about it at all, and she was right. 'You're just a mass of preconceived notions, darling Jimmy,' she said and we both liked her saying it.

After the church, we wandered slowly down through the paths and streets to the port again, but got lost, and found a small square with a café running along one side of it. There were two old trees growing out of the stones and we sat at a table under one and had a drink, and then, eventually, lunch.

'Well,' I said; 'how's your energy?'

She said: 'I'm storing it up. I've thought what to do with it, you see.'

'*Have* you?' She didn't answer, so I said: 'What are you going to do, Lillian?'

She had her elbows on the table; now she held her face with her hands as though to keep it steady and spoke rather fast.

'I'm going to *find* this house in England, and furnish it, and stock the garden and learn to drive a car again and to be nicer to Em's theatrical friends so that they will all want to come and stay and he won't feel cut off. I'm going to concentrate on this – on somewhere steady for our future – and not think about the past so much. I'm going to take up the piano again, and unpack all my books after all these years: I thought I might even buy a pair of Labradors – they need not worry Em if he doesn't have them in his study – I thought I might breed them – try to get really good at it. Really stop the kind of thinking I do as I am, and try to have some kind of life, if I can find the right place to have it in.'

'What made you come to all this?'

'It started with Em offering me the house. He doesn't really want one – it was a gesture, you know. No – it started with his making me remember something good before Sarah: that's what I've found so difficult, you see – to remember anything good properly before her. Or perhaps it was something that Alberta said – honestly, Jimmy, I just don't know – all those things, I think, and probably more; this is a beautiful place to accumulate in.'

'What did she say to you?'

'Are you curious about that? She said: "I'm so sorry that you lost your daughter" . . .' Her eyes had filled with tears, but they stayed in her eyes. 'That's all. But she said it in the kind of way that didn't detach Sarah's death from everything else – for me, I mean. Isn't it odd? She touched it in exactly the right way and I found it didn't feel the same as I had always thought it would. That's a step, isn't it?'

'Sure. You like her, don't you?'

She smiled, and a tear fell on to the table. 'Not as much as you do, Jimmy, but I do like her. That brings me to something else.'

'Don't rush yourself: the last time we had lunch was in London.'

'So it was. It wasn't nearly as nice as today. Jimmy. You asked me in New York to help in any way that I could about Alberta being tried for Clemency. I haven't helped much, because there haven't been many ways that I could, but what you really meant was "don't sabotage" and I haven't, have I?'

'You certainly haven't.'

'Well – you *could* help me about having the house in England, and you could certainly sabotage it. Don't you think it would be a good thing if Em had a home somewhere to live and work in between trips?'

Remembering what he had said about it that night on the terrace, I said: 'I think it would be a very good thing if *you* had one.'

'I wouldn't want it without him.'

'I didn't mean that. I meant it would be especially good for you. I don't think he minds where he is – it depends what he is doing there.'

'He might *get* to mind,' she said wistfully. 'And it wouldn't stop us going on trips from time to time – once we were settled in.'

'Lillian, I think it's a fine idea, but what about this play? Won't he want to go straight to New York for that?'

'That's what I wanted to ask you.' She leaned forward while I lit her cigarette and I smelled that scent I've known ever since I've known her: something to do with lemons – I've always liked it.

'Couldn't you manage the play, and Alberta, if you're going to use her, with*out* Em? Surely he doesn't have to be there all through rehearsals? We could just fly over for the opening, and fly back, if he wants to go very badly.'

'He may want to be there,' I said – I was beginning to feel trapped.

'But you could manage without him, if he didn't?'

'Yes – yes I think I *could* do that; but I wouldn't want to if he didn't want me to.'

She was watching me carefully for the evasions I was trying to avoid.

'Alberta is going to be good, isn't she? You've really decided to use her?'

'*I* should like to. I don't know what he thinks. I was going to see this morning, but she walked out on us. I think I upset her.'

'That's a good sign anyway.'

'Why? Surely it's better for a producer if an actress holds her ground and keeps on acting.'

'Temperament,' she said vaguely: 'or perhaps Em put her off.' She was thinking of something else. Then she asked suddenly: 'What did you think of those pictures?'

'Very good. Very like her too.' I'd planned what to say about them by now.

'Oh Jimmy, is that all you can find to say?'

'What else would you say?'

'I'd say that Miss Young is going to have quite a time in New York. I think everyone will be after her if she isn't protected. I think you'll have your work cut out to keep her mind on her work.'

'She's always seemed to me reasonably conscientious.'

'My dear, you forget how young she is. She's never lived in a city before, and certainly nowhere where every other young man in town will want to date her. If you don't take pretty drastic steps, you'll find yourself without a lead because she'll have married someone, or be having a breakdown through lack of sleep or something.'

'What steps do you suggest I take?'

She put out her cigarette and started hunting in her bag. 'Well, you could always marry her yourself, couldn't you Jimmy?'

I felt the back of my neck start to burn, which, damn it, I'd give anything to stop. 'She'd never marry me.'

'Oh I don't know. If you made it clear to her that it was for the sake of her career, and pointed out the vicious and dreary alternatives, she might. After all, whatever you are, you aren't a fate worse than death.' Then she stopped, and said: 'Jimmy – I'm teasing you – perhaps in very bad taste. It's *your* life – you do what you want. Only, if you want something, do something about it.'

I said I'd see about paying the bill and walked flaming into the cool café. As I walked I thought – really I could go anywhere just like this and not have left much behind. I didn't seem to have anything excepting nine years' experience at directing Emmanuel's life and his plays. A future as insecure as my past was uncertain, and nothing tangible about the present unless you counted some nice luggage which just about held my clothes. However you looked at it, it wasn't much to offer.

When I got back to Lillian, she gave me her hand to pull her up, and said: 'You should count up your assets one day, Jimmy dear. You'd be surprised.'

I didn't tell her that I had, and I wasn't.

On the way back Lillian said: 'Let's go by the sea'; so we did, and half way home she said: 'Let's bathe'; so we did that too. We were peaceful and didn't talk much; once she said to me: 'I wasn't teasing you in a bitchy way, darling Jimmy. I was trying to infuse you with the kind of courage I'm afraid you haven't got. Like you have kinds I haven't got.' Then she went on dreamily: 'I wonder how many of us it would take to make one whole person? Even the four of us wouldn't do. Hundreds, I expect.' Then she yawned, and it made me remember Emmanuel in the morning and wonder where Alberta was, but I didn't want her to know that I felt anxious about either of them so I waited for her to suggest our return.

We found Alberta kneeling on the terrace with the typewriter in front of her and Emmanuel signing the letters she had finished for him; everything very calm and businesslike, but I noticed that Emmanuel wouldn't look at me, and I felt somehow nervous of meeting Alberta after the morning, although Lillian had so obviously enjoyed herself that she filled any gaps there might have been.

After dinner I took Alberta for a bathe. I'd had what seemed to me at dinner a very good idea, but when we got down on the beach and I was alone with her – although it still seemed good, it seemed much more difficult. I'd decided that the only way to do it was to be perfectly practical and level-headed and not make too much of the whole thing. Then, although that couldn't frighten her, she might see the sense of it, and I might get some sort of line on how she felt. After all, if she said she couldn't bear me, or she was in love with someone else or she didn't want to marry anybody, I'd know where I was. I'd also thought pretty carefully about what Lillian had said, and decided that my only asset was that I did know how to look after people – so I plugged that part of it fairly hard. The only trouble was that she didn't say any of the things back that I'd expected. She didn't say she couldn't bear me, she didn't say that she was in love with anybody else (although she didn't say she wasn't); she kept saying that was extremely kind of me – as though I was offering her a job. I nearly got angry with her, she was so damn polite: she also said something queer about not wanting to marry in order to be more comfortable . . . what the hell does she think I'm for if it isn't to do every single goddam thing I could to look after her in every way I can think of? I suppose I *didn't* put it to her right; once I'd felt that, I felt sure of it and said so – in order to give myself some kind of loophole to raise the matter again. We bathed, and her hair got wet so that it was stuck in little wet triangles on her forehead and the rest of it was like a neat gleaming cap: I spread out my towel for us both to sit on and put hers round her and for one awful moment I wished she was very unhappy so that she wouldn't even notice who was comforting her. Then she asked me if I'd thought what it would be like if she fell in love with someone else after we were married: this was good; at least it meant she was thinking about it, but naturally I answered her very calmly and finished by making a few general (rather good) remarks about marriage, but I've noticed that women aren't much good at generalizations, they always come back to a personal view: she said what about *my* falling in love with somebody. The utter impossibility of this clearly hadn't struck her – I didn't feel that I could go into that so I just brushed it aside. Then I felt we'd said just about as much as I could manage without losing control of the situation, so I said I wanted a drink. I made her climb in front of me in case she slipped: alone, I could say this to her – even with Lillian it would be possible, but somehow, after this morning not with Emmanuel. This made me angry and I told her an idiot lie about him, and she knew it was one although I think even if she hadn't I couldn't have stuck to it. I wanted to take her by the shoulders and stare into her eyes and ask: 'What *do* you feel about him? Just tell me so I'll know and I won't ask any more questions'; because I know she wouldn't lie to me – she's about the most truthful person I've ever met – but I couldn't do it: I just apologized, and went to bed feeling lousy with anxiety that I'd never be worth her the way I was acting. She's the last person in the world I want to lie to, and he's the last person in the world I want to lie about – and so what? I still did it. That kept me awake some time, and I came to the conclusion that what with one thing and another I'd been taking my own character for granted.

4

LILLIAN

APART from giving Jimmy a chance to be alone with Alberta, I really did want to talk to Em. He'd been almost silent at dinner, excepting when he'd done a set piece – one of his film script conference stories with everyone calling him Mannie – I know them all but they still make me laugh; the rest of the time he seemed hardly to be with us. At one point, when we'd been talking about Greek myths I said why didn't he make a play of one – in contemporary terms, and he said the idea had a kind of whimsical vulgarity that nauseated him. And that, as Jimmy said, was that. Alberta asked whether there were any new ideas that hadn't been written about, and he said no, but occasionally somebody discovered something for himself, and then, if he could write, it became a fresh translation, and, to people who hadn't made the discovery, something new. But in three hours that could hardly be described as a fair share of the conversation. It irritated me because I felt he was casting a feeling of gloom on all three of us and the whole day.

After the others had gone for their bathe, I got glasses and our house bottle of brandy which we hardly ever drink because it is so full of fire and vanilla, and lay on the one comfortable chair that we keep on the terrace. 'Really, Em, that was a most tactless suggestion.'

'What was tactless?'

'Couldn't you see that Jimmy wanted to be alone with her? The last thing they want is a pair of old chaperones: I'd have thought you would be the first person to notice that. Give me some brandy, darling.'

He poured the brandy in silence, and lit a cigarette.

'Is something worrying you? Is the new play on your mind?'

'Not in the least.'

'Are you worrying about Alberta?'

'Alberta?'

'Clemency, if you prefer. Jimmy seems quite happy about her.'

'Has Jimmy been pouring out his heart to you?'

'He's much too shy. He doesn't have to tell me – I know.'

He sat on the parapet and turned to the sea – I could hardly hear what he said. 'What do you think she feels about him?'

It was odd, I hadn't thought of that. 'I'm not sure. She's got the kind of reserve that makes it very difficult to tell. It's obvious she *likes* him, and after all, she agreed to go bathing with him. Do you remember that time in France when we found that wonderful little beach one night and took off all our clothes and just plunged in?' He didn't answer, and I knew it was no good getting angry with him when he was like this, so I went on: 'and the next day when we tried to find it again in the light, we couldn't: it didn't seem to be anywhere. Do you remember?'

He said: 'I didn't – but you've reminded me.'

'Darling, do turn round, or I shan't hear a word you say, and could I have one of your cigarettes?'

He bent down to give me one, and when he lit the match I saw his face. He looked dreadful – collapsed and exhausted like he used to look after bad asthma. 'Darling! What is the matter? Are you ill?'

But he only blew out the match and said crossly: 'Not in the least. I'm deadly tired – that's all; I didn't sleep last night.'

'You slept this morning.'

'As you've so often told me, that is hardly the same thing.'

'Do you want to go to bed now?'

He smiled then, and said: 'Oh no – the last thing I want to do is to go to bed.' He drank some brandy and sat on the parapet again. 'What was it you wanted to talk about?'

'I'm not at all sure that you're in the right mood for it.'

He said nothing: I've noticed before that he gets these attacks of silence: they annoy me because I don't understand them – whatever he is feeling doesn't take me like that when I feel it, and the most I can do is to provoke him into a contradiction or a retort. That would be useless now; I was just about to try again, when he said: 'You want to talk about returning to England and buying a house – is that it?'

'Yes. Would they be wildly unsuitable topics?'

'Not if you will do most of the talking.'

I said: 'I've adored being here: it has been a perfect holiday, but I feel it is coming to an end.'

'The perfection?'

'No – the whole thing. I feel that it is time we went back – almost I feel I know we *are* going back. I'm not bored, and it has been wonderful to bathe again and live in this air and the marvellous, continuing sun – but I was wrong about one thing.'

'What thing?'

'I thought that an island would be a good place for you to write, and it hasn't been. I feel this must be depressing for you, and that you would be far happier in one of the old places that you associated with writing. If we went back to London – Jimmy could get you that nice room in Shepherd Market and I could start house hunting, and only take you to see one if it really seemed a desirable residence. If it is humanly possible, I should like to find a house and get a bit settled before we go to the Bahamas in January.'

'Why on earth are we going there?'

'Because Leonard and Jo asked us. Oh, don't start being difficult about that – you said you wanted to go when they asked us. If we've just got a new house it will probably be torture to go, although one can't do anything much to a garden in January, whereas the autumn is the perfect time to start. But it may take months to find the right house.'

'In which case?'

'In which case, the sooner we start the better. Then you'll be able to get on with your play, Jimmy can go on training Alberta until they have to go to America – perhaps she could have a short holiday at home as well, I know that she wants to see her father, and I can look for the house.'

I waited for him to say that he wanted to go to New York, but he didn't: he didn't say anything.

'What I do need to consider much more with you is the kind of house we are looking for.'

'What kind do you want?'

'It isn't simply what I want. I mean do *you* want it to be near or far from London; what sort of size, and how much land – things like that. And also, how much can we afford it to cost?'

He finished his brandy and reached for the bottle. 'My dear, I haven't the slightest idea about any of this. I think you had better get what *you* want. I don't know how to approach such a plan because I cannot think about life in your terms.'

'But it was *your* idea that we should buy a house!'

'I know. But the idea started from something else. I can't explain to you, but the difference is something like you starting to paint a picture by designing its frame, and I wanting to start at whatever is to be the picture's centre and then discovering what surround it may need. Something like that.'

'Well?'

'Do you remember saying to me that the trouble with you was that you didn't know what you were *for*, and that that made it very difficult for you to know what you wanted because you never wanted the same thing for very long?'

'Did I say that?'

'In New York in the morning.' He smiled. 'Isn't it extraordinary – what we remember and what we forget? Well, you assumed then, that it was different for me – that I did know.'

'Yes?'

'I don't, most of the time. That's all. But when I don't, there is nothing I feel I can safely do. I can't fabricate results with no cause.'

He drank some brandy and stood up. 'But *you* go on with it; you find a house that you like: I am not trying to stop you.'

'But I can't possibly do it all by myself!'

'You may have to.' He paused. 'I may have to go – to New York for this play.'

Somehow I had known he was going to say this ever since I had talked to Jimmy, but that just made it worse. It was no good simply being angry, because I wanted him to change his mind – seeing this, I saw how much I really wanted the house with him: so I waited until the worst things I was going to say had cleared off.

'You don't feel that Jimmy could manage on his own just this once?'

'No.'

'But you haven't even decided whether she is going to do the part, have you?'

'No.'

After a moment, he added: 'When I've decided these things I'll tell you, of course.'

It was the 'of course' that did it. 'Do you have to say things like that to me?'

He looked deliberately surprised – I knew that he wasn't and felt suddenly furious.

'Do you have to treat me all the time as though I was a sick child? Can't you ever discuss what we are going to do – or even what you are going to do – reasonably with me? Or does it satisfy your dramatic instinct to have little secrets all the time? I suppose you know that that dreadful Gloria Williams wrote me a mad letter just before she took all those pills? You thought that that was quite all right as long as I didn't know. Well, it wasn't. It was just as awful, and worse in the end when I did. While we're about it, perhaps you'd explain what on earth this means.' I knew the letter was somewhere in my bag, but I couldn't find it: really it would have been better if I hadn't even tried for a second to be reasonable . . . I found the letter and held it out for him to see.

He said: 'Where *did* you find that? I've been looking for it everywhere.'

'It was on the floor in your room. I saw it when you were asleep. I read it while I was changing for dinner. Who are the Friedmanns? You obviously know them well – have known them for years. Don't you under*stand*, Em – I don't mean it is like Gloria Williams – I realize that this is a man writing to you about a boy and that you saw these people when you were in London, but why don't I know anything about them? When you say that you may go to New York when we have something very important to do together in England and that you'll let me know when you've decided about it you make me so angry and *despairing* about us that I lose my head and my temper at once. You don't take me into your confidence at all.'

'Perhaps I have no confidence in your confidence.'

It was exactly like being slapped for hysteria. I found myself staring at him – my hands with the letter dropped back into my lap. He sat down on the bench beside my chair, took the letter from me and said: 'Sometimes you are very stupid and then there is no reason why I should trust you. If I gave you certain confidences, you would do something stupid, and when things turned out badly you would fall back on your good intentions, when, in fact, you had had no intentions of any kind. The Friedmanns are the people who took the two children you would not adopt. They are Jews: they understood what these children had endured, and like you, Mrs Friedmann was childless: but they have given them what was needed. I have continued to see them because when they undertook the children, they had very little money, and although I could not keep the most serious part of the promises I had undertaken I could at least help somebody else to do so. That's all. But remember how we last talked on this subject – years ago now – and see why you are the last person I would consult. Last time I saw her, Mrs Friedmann said children should be above luck – they were beyond your notice – you simply did not consider them at all. What was there for me to tell you about them, if they were only to provide fuel for your resentment and self-pity?'

There was complete silence. It was as though all my blood had turned and was trying to move in a different direction: I heard myself asking something . . .

He smiled then, and gave my hand a little, absent pat. ' . . . do about them? Why nothing, now. They are much better off with the Friedmanns than they would be with us.'

Soon after that, we went to bed – he upstairs, I to my room, the best room in the house, on the ground floor. For the first time in my life at any such moment, I did not cry – just lay – with what he had said printing itself again and again. It was as though a thought, like a piece of paper, was pressed on to me and torn off – painfully – as though I was publishing this truth about me alone in a room, dark, excepting for the shallow, childish strips made by the moon, which seemed only an echo of light. One piece of the letter recurred: about the boy: 'a child who survives what he has survived, and with his gift, only to have it taken away suddenly by a foolish accident – what is his destiny? All day he looks at his hand. He does not speak not even yet has he wept.' I did not need to understand the situation to recognize this.

I woke in the morning feeling wonderfully light-headed and calm, and with a great desire to begin the day; but before getting up, I lay and remembered how I had lain in the night: Em's voice, the shock, the pain which was still not an ordinary kind, as some locked-up part of me had almost welcomed it – the only part which plainly hurt was when he had said: 'Why nothing, now.' I could nearly have again that curious, physical jolt inside me with the feeling that everything, at that moment, was changing direction . . .

It was the most brilliant and beautiful morning: cloudless sky, heraldic sun, and the sea the smoke-blue of distant flowers. I found Alberta in the kitchen hut at the end of the western terrace, making coffee: she had already boiled a pan of water for us to wash. She was the only one of us who could get a full bucket of water out of the well. She was wearing a blue cotton skirt and a pink cotton shirt I had given her; it had faded, but it suited her more like that than it had ever suited me.

'It is remarkable the way you always make very old clothes look their best. Oh dear. That sounds like the remark of a prize bitch – I really meant it: it is a great art – usually only men have it.'

She said: 'I can't tell you what fun it is having such a choice of clothes. I lie in bed and choose them every morning.'

'Did you have a good bathe last night?'

'Yes. The water seems even warmer in the dark – more salt, too. The ants have got the old figs – we'll have to eat the new ones, but there's a new melon as well. The honey is in the washing-up bowl.'

'Why?'

'Ants! There've been more every day since we've been here.' She blew out the stove and said: 'We must get more paraffin today – there's just about enough for one more morning.'

'Are the others awake?'

'I don't know. They usually seem to hear when I take the coffee on to the terrace – it's a bit like the ants when we move the honey.'

We took the breakfast out of the kitchen hut. Already the sun was stronger, and one of the scarlet trumpet flowers was dying. She said: 'Julius said that it would get hotter nearly every day. He is making a list of the advantages of winter. He's going to read them to me this afternoon.'

Jimmy came out: he did not look as though he had slept very well. He and Alberta seemed calm with each other so I am afraid Jimmy cannot have mustered the courage to tell her what he feels.

Em did not join us until the middle of breakfast: he looked as though he had not slept at all, but when I saw him I had such a rush of warmth of affectionate gratitude towards him, that I could not stay where I was. He saw me rise, came over, and pushed me gently down again. Alberta poured his coffee and he asked about the bathe. Jimmy answered him – they looked at each other, and I had the feeling I often have with them, that they are talking to each other without words. The end of breakfast was friendly and serene – as though we had all known each other all our lives, and I thought, 'How well Alberta has fitted in with us—' and then, rather rashly, said so aloud. It was very silly; she blushed, and Jimmy began slowly going scarlet, the way he does, and Em said, 'She has indeed,' in a mechanical sort of voice to fill the gap.

As I didn't have to go to the port to get food for lunch, we agreed to bathe as soon as possible. Jimmy said that Alberta must do her minimum routine stint – he is a great stickler for discipline; Em said that in that case he would go on to the other terrace to read, and I went to the kitchen hut to clear up breakfast and collect our lunch. It was very hot there. I opened its one window and the door: for a moment I considered opening the heavy gate beyond the hut which is our entrance, but when I looked out the sun was already on the gate.

It was so hot by now that I did everything slowly, with half my attention on the exercises that Jimmy was directing. On the steep rocks outside the kitchen hut window a goat was trying to eat bits of cactus – moving with light, uneasy footsteps on the rocks, its bell muttering round its neck. I threw it a piece of bread, but it didn't seem able to find it. I leaned out of the window with another piece; it looked at me with its stuffed animals' eyes and nodded irritably, so I threw that piece too. I was watching it eat, and listening to all the sound of the small valley made lazy by heat when there was suddenly a brief pounding outside – although I had not heard anybody approach – but there was a sense of violence in the sound which made me run to the gate: as I reached it, it burst open, and there was the little boy I knew must be Julius. He wore simply a pair of faded jeans – his face and his shoulders were streaked with sweat. He stared at me with frightful urgency for a second – I just had time to wonder why he was not scarlet after running so hard because he was panting, gasping for breath – when he pushed past me and ran to the terrace. He went straight to Alberta and said: 'Here is a tragic telegram!' gave it to her, and burst into tears.

She seemed to open it very slowly, and to read it for a long time; and then she looked at the boy crying, and he looked at her with tears streaming down his face – then he raised his fist clenched, and shook it in the air, crying: '*That* – to the driver of the car!'

She put the telegram carefully away in the pocket of her skirt: she was still looking at the boy – had gone very pale: she put out her hand and touched his fist – he flung his arms round her with such a cry, that for a moment I thought that the telegram had been his – his grief was so intense, and she was so still. But then – I think it was Jimmy – said: 'What *is* it, Alberta?' and she looked out over the boy's head that she was holding, and said: 'He was knocked down by a car. He is dead: my father.'

Now she was dead white: we all seemed to be frozen: then I saw that she had been speaking to Em, who was standing in the doorway of the house. He was staring at her, and I saw on his face what I had only seen before in the barest shadow at odd seconds of our lives – that he loved her – and I was struck by it.

CHAPTER VII

1

JIMMY

WHAT struck me was the kind of courage she had. She didn't cry, or faint or make a scene or even say anything very much. Emmanuel made her sit down and I got her some brandy, but she didn't want it. She was even soothing the boy who sat shivering beside her. He'd had quite a time, poor kid; apparently they'd called to him from the Post Office because they couldn't make out the message – he'd written it out for them and then run all the way here in this heat. She hadn't talked to me much about her father, but somehow I knew it was far the worst shock she'd ever had in her life, by the way all her reactions seemed to have slowed down, so that it took her time to understand what you said: she stared at the brandy and held the glass for a minute before she said she didn't want it. It was Lillian who drank the brandy. She'd gone a bad colour – for her to have an attack now was just *all* we needed – but she pulled herself together. The only thing Alberta said was that she had to telephone, and the boy said he would help her. Emmanuel said: 'You'd like to go back, wouldn't you?' and she looked up at him as though she hardly knew him and nodded. He wanted me so we went on to the other terrace.

'Jimmy. You'd better go down to the port with them and ring the airport. Get four seats – I don't think there is much point in any of us staying here now.' He thought for a moment and said: 'We might all go to the port.'

So we all went. There followed an hour of sheer nightmare

in the Post Office, when all we did was to put through the call to England and establish the fact that it might take all day to get through again to the airport – I did manage it once, but couldn't find anyone to speak English and then got cut off. There was nowhere to sit; Lillian had to go outside; the boy argued with the operator until they weren't speaking to each other and Alberta leaned against the counter absolutely white and speechless. The place reeked of dust and sweat, and all the windows were closed. Something had to be done about it. I led Emmanuel outside and said that I would catch the boat when it called and call the airport from Piraeus. He said again that we might all go. 'You can ask her, but the only thing she seems to want is that telephone call and it may take all day to come through.' He agreed, and went to tell Lillian, who was waving anxiously from her café table.

I went back to her. She was standing exactly as I had left her, and I remembered how we had waited in New York for the call to come through to her father – and her saying after she had spoken to him 'It's simply that I've known him all my life' as the tears ran down her face. I put my arm round her shoulder and told her that I was going to Athens to get plane seats and she listened with that same strained expression, and said 'That is extremely kind of you, Jimmy' – and then I remembered wishing last night that she would be very unhappy so that she would not notice who was comforting her. I said: 'I'll come and say goodbye before I go,' and let go of her shoulder which seemed somehow light as well as stiff.

When I got outside again, I was going straight up to the house to fetch our passports and tickets, but Emmanuel waved and I went over to them. He looked kind of surprised and very nervous.

'Lillian says she wants to go with you.'

I looked at her. '*She* says so?'

Lillian looked me full in the face and spoke very fast – so I knew something was wrong. 'Yes, Jimmy. If we are leaving so suddenly, there are one or two things that I want to do in

Athens, so I'd rather come over with you today if you don't mind. Em doesn't mind at all, do you darling?'

I didn't catch his reply.

'I shan't hold you up at all. I'll go straight to the hotel, and do my things on my own. Are you going back to the house? Because we haven't got much time, and I don't think I could make it, but I want my light coat and my little square travelling case – it's got most of my toilet things in it.'

'When is the boat due?'

'In about half an hour, I think, because people are already beginning to collect. You'd better go, Jimmy, if you're going.'

She was quite right: there wasn't time to argue with her. I did that walk in the fastest time I've ever made it, and by the time I'd finished packing what was needed, I saw the boat in the distance, and ran part of the way back. How that kid ran the whole way I can't think. I didn't even have time to think why Lillian was so mad to go, but the craziest part of it was that it wasn't till I was back in the port that I realized that her going meant that Emmanuel would be staying with Alberta. For one moment I thought of thrusting all the papers and his wife's bag at him and saying: 'You make the arrangements – just this once!' but I knew I wouldn't when I saw him. I'd always made the arrangements – it was what I was for: it may have been then that I swore I'd be for something else: at least for making my own arrangements or, maybe, hers.

She was standing just as I had left her, with the boy squatting at her feet.

'Any luck at all?'

She shook her head, and the operator clicked his teeth and smiled and closed his eyes, and Julius said: 'Regrettably there is not time about telephone calls.'

The boat was hooting now and very near. I walked down to the quay with Emmanuel and Lillian where the row boats were waiting to take us out.

'I'll get seats any time from tomorrow evening, and I'll either try to call you this evening, or send a telegram.'

'Won't tomorrow be too soon?'

I looked at Lillian grimly and thought that nothing would be too soon for me. Emmanuel said: 'I'll wait in the Post Office from six till seven this evening for you to call. All right?'

'OK.'

Lillian said: 'Well goodbye darling. I hope her call comes through. See you tomorrow.' She climbed into the small rocking boat and I put her case on her knees. She was smiling brightly – the last thing I wanted was a boat trip with her.

'Goodbye, Jimmy. Do your best.'

'And you,' I said; for a moment our eyes met and he had that creature-of-circumstance look I knew so well and had come to dread. But I had to go. I jumped in; I was the last, and we were off. The boat was swooping into the harbour like a great white gull emitting shrill hoots. Emmanuel waved once and walked slowly away, back towards the Post Office, where, I thought, she would still be standing . . .

'Get her a chair!' I yelled suddenly, and he turned round, but I don't think he heard me.

A lot of that day I had to remind myself that the feelings I was having simply didn't count beside Alberta's – and that in a way I was doing something for her that she needed. To begin with, we were no sooner on the boat and steaming away full bat when I discovered that we weren't going straight back to Piraeus at all – far from it, in fact we returned from a protracted tour to our island at about four and then went back to Piraeus. So all our mad rush had been completely unnecessary. The hope that the others would join us on the boat at four was dim – I felt viciously that if the telephone operator didn't succeed in messing up her call until long after that time, Emmanuel would somehow avoid catching the boat. I couldn't tell Lillian why I felt so anxious and frustrated by the whole thing – I knew from repeated experience what it was like being with her when she thought or knew that Emmanuel was with a girl he was interested in. As she didn't know, she took the news about our boat quite calmly. Once, she said: 'Don't worry too much about

Alberta, Jimmy. Em's the best person in the world to be with when you've had a bad shock – he'll look after her.' As if that made it any better. Everybody on the boat was so damn gay – we careered along like some kids' Sunday outing. I put Lillian in a chair and told her I needed some exercise, and mooched around for what seemed like hours. I ended up just leaning over a rail, feeling bluer than the sea, until I felt someone touch my arm, and it was Lillian saying why didn't we both have a drink. 'You can disown me afterwards if you like, Jimmy dear, but I'm parched and I do so hate bars by myself.' I noticed then that she had dark marks round her eyes, and thought that perhaps she hadn't wanted to come at all – she'd honestly thought it would be easier for Alberta to be alone with Emmanuel: somehow that touched me and I found the whole thing better after that.

Going back to our island was a bad time, though. We got there about a quarter to four – we didn't come so far in to the harbour as we had in the morning, and the row boats seemed to take an age to reach us. Lillian and I leaned over a rail on the boat deck watching the small laden boats, but long before they got near enough for us to see people's faces we knew that Alberta and Emmanuel weren't there. The port otherwise seemed deserted, and the Post Office looked shut.

'Perhaps the poor girl didn't get her call through before they shut at midday.' Then she added: 'Probably she didn't.'

I glanced at her face, but she gave no sign that she noticed me. Suddenly she pointed to the top of the mountain. 'We never went up to the monastery. The day we arrived here, I planned to do that, and we never did. That is something we *could* have done.'

'What couldn't we have done?'

The boat was leaving, and she turned away from the rail. 'Oh – anything from preventing her father's death onwards.'

We decided to settle somewhere for the rest of the trip, and found two chairs in the bows which seemed to have the right amount of shade and shelter. As we sat down she said: 'If only one knew at the time what one *could* do!'

'What would happen then?'

'Well, at least one would try to do it; one would be better occupied.'

She gave me a queer little smile – something appealing about it – not at all how I usually saw her.

The journey to Piraeus seemed very long – partly because it started at a time when the light begins to change, from hot afternoon sun – a bright, impartial light on everything – to the beginning of evening when all those colours start up in the sky. We both slept the first part of the journey, and when I woke it was cooler and softer and Lillian was awake and gazing into the distance. I woke with such a strong feeling for Alberta that it was almost as though I was actually with her and it was a real moment in my life – much more than any other – I couldn't remember anything better. I thought: 'So *this is* my life,' and saw Lillian looking at me and said:

'I love her, now. I know it. I don't just want to look after her – I want life with her on any terms at any price. Anything else would just be existing and playing – a waiting game.'

Lillian leaned towards me and took my hands: 'I'm glad you know – I *do hope* you get it.'

She looked like crying and I felt so wonderful – I couldn't bear her to cry. 'There's nothing sad about it – I'll find a way. Everything is different – if one knows something.'

Lillian was very quiet after that, and we sat, hardly speaking, while the light sank slowly into the sea. It was beautiful, and I thought that any one of these things would from now on remind me of her – the sea, the evening sky, a boat, the warm breeze coming off the land – but she would make me remember all these things at once – the whole world could come to life for me because of her.

2

LILLIAN

THE lights of Piraeus were strung out in a shallow half circle in grey dusk like a jeweller's necklace on velvet. They looked pretty, neat, and inaccessible, but somewhere in the future we were going to tie up in a gap between two beads and they would seem far apart. This was a kind of future – the only kind that I could envisage – something already drawing to its past. But my own life stretched out round me like the sea – it seemed illimitable. Jimmy was silent – wrapped in his dreams, and I, knowing so clearly what would shatter them, was at least silent to him.

The morning already seemed another life away: since I had seen Em's face, so radiant with concerning love, I had lived my old life almost out: it had now so many threadbare patches where I could find no substance, that I could see through myself in it. ('You have a kind of indefatigable stupidity – all your life you have been rehearsing for this event when you thought you were playing the lead in an ancient tragedy.') Now, understanding perhaps for the first time in all my years of living with him, something that mattered to Em, I had left him to decide what he would do, and to tell me afterwards what he had decided, of course. Even then, I had hardly done it. Jealousy – no, a searing envy for that girl who had shown me his face – had blasted me so that I had stood on the terrace with the rocks going round me like lumps of brown sugar, and I had had to drink the brandy that she hadn't wanted. Then we had all gone down to the port – in single file, with the boy leading; the boy, Alberta, Jimmy, I, and Em last. All the morning, I knew that what dignity, what resolution I had was stiffened by hers – I could not bear this acknowledgment, but I could not escape it.

Sitting by myself at the café table while the others were in the Post Office (*I* was the one who could not stand the heat and smell of sweat and nowhere to sit) all my resentment and grievances for the string of his infidelities – known and guessed – were stripped off, revealing such a shocking inadequacy that it even seemed astonishing that I should have been given the chance to recall so many. The times that I had stormed at him – the false righteous indignation that I had managed to employ – about his vulgarity, his coarse and partial views of love, his lack of discrimination, all that I had contrived to twist into peculiar insults to me and my marriage with him unravelled, until I saw that the real confusion had always been mine. He, at least, had known what he was doing; it had had nothing to do with his view of love, he must even have used discrimination to make sure of this. But I, standing upon rights which were not mine and a deprivation which had not been his, had refused to recognize any loyalty in his behaviour to me; for, looking back on these affairs, I was forced to understand that he had not sought love from them. He had not sought it with her: the facts that he had looked steadily more and more desperate since we had been here, and had made no attempts to be alone with her all pointed to his having struggled . . . I might never have known; might have gone on thrusting Jimmy down his throat, speculating idly and aloud about his fatigue, if it had not been for the telegram. It had taken the shock of the telegram for me to know anything . . .

I did not plan to go on the boat; I was too raw and confused to have plans, but when he came out to tell me that Jimmy was going to Athens to get tickets for the aeroplane, I suddenly felt that I should go with Jimmy – that it was one thing that I could do for him – to leave him in peace to make his own decision, and I looked at him thinking how much patience he had had with my difficulties. His face had closed to an expression of conventional waiting and concern, and I thought, if I leave him with her and he tells her – what will become of me? Then, because I felt almost intolerably diminished to myself, I wondered what he had ever admired in me, and there was one answer to that. He had admired my courage – the only time that I ever had any – which was when I had gone on carrying Sarah after they had said that it would almost certainly kill me, and had not told him that I knew this. That had been the end of my courage, it seemed. There must have been many occasions for it, but it was too late to regret them: I could, at least, go to Athens, now. I told him I wanted to go: his reply confounded me.

'Jimmy may not want you to go.'

I said what had it got to do with Jimmy, in my most wilful voice – the only difference was that I heard myself this time. But when Jimmy joined us, I could see that Em was quite right, and Jimmy did not seem in the least anxious for my company. That was a final slap: I had not thought of myself as so generally tiresome: the sensation of doing something which I found difficult and having somebody else irritated with me for doing it made it all at once more real, and more unpleasant. I talked Jimmy into agreeing – haven't I had years of practice at getting my own way? – and in no time, it seemed we had left them.

I watched Em walking away from us on the quay, and then Jimmy shouted to him to get Alberta a chair, and I thought, Jimmy loves her too, and he's left her with Em, but then, of course, he doesn't know what he is doing. On the boat, we found that we need not have left the island until the afternoon, and this made poor Jimmy desperate, but I was grateful that we hadn't known, and I hadn't had all those hours in which to change my mind. Jimmy left me in a chair and went off by himself, and I had the whole day again with the stark ungratifying pictures of myself that it presented. There was plenty of time for review; the trouble was that the more ordered I became in it, the more clearly I saw what I was, the less I liked it, and the more inexorably everything I noted or could remember added up to my standing little or no chance now. It seemed to me that presented with the choice of living with Alberta or with me, nobody in their senses would hesitate. In the end this made me think of Jimmy. The relief of finding that I could actually do this was extraordinary, and I went to find him. Knowing more than he, I felt a need to relieve him somehow, if only from the feeling that I would be a deadweight to him in Athens. We had a drink together, and he talked in a guarded, deliberately practical way about her. Did I think that she would now want to give up doing the play? Did I think that she would just want to go back home and stay there? I said all I could think of – that her father's profession meant that the family would no longer be able to live in the vicarage after his death, and that it would also mean that there was far less money so that she might have more incentive than ever for doing the play. He said it surely was tough on her, but he looked reassured.

When we found ourselves returning to the island, we both went to the side of the ship where we could watch the rowing boats. I knew that they wouldn't be there, but I felt him hoping, and when we had both searched the boats and the port for them and found nothing but the Post Office looking absolutely deserted, I had to comfort him. I felt him turn to me, and it seemed another confirmation of what I was, that when I honestly tried to think of someone else it only made them suspicious. But what could I *do now* about it all? I longed then to go back – to have another chance at my opportunities – but then, if I went back, I should not know what I know now; I should be the same clutching, hysterical creature – laying waste to chance – hoarding sensations until they went bad, making my world smaller and smaller in order to keep myself the centre of it . . . I think I was more frightened then than I had ever been; everything else of that kind that I had felt had been only little gestures towards fear – it was the difference between losing one's way and there being no way to lose . . .

Jimmy was saying something about finding somewhere sheltered. I followed him. I said something to him about wanting to know what one could do, and as he always does to any general or thoughtless exclamation, he asked a question of such ruthless simplicity that he made one feel as though one had asked for something which one would not be able to use. But he was there: he was trying to be patient and kind in spite of his own anxieties. It occurred to me that perhaps even my leaving Em on the island with her had been an entirely selfish idea – designed to tell me where I was, without the slightest reference to Jimmy, and that what I had thought was self-control in not spilling out my fears to him was just a kind of self-enlightened cowardice. I shut my eyes and tried to swallow this, but it was too much: I sank into an apathy where thoughts droned and flitted through my mind without my seeming to have anything to do with them, until I suppose even they got tired of the lack of response, and I must have slept.

When I woke it was twilight, and Jimmy was asleep. I thought of us reaching Piraeus – found I couldn't think of anything beyond that – looked at Jimmy's peaceful, trusting face, and decided not to think about anything excepting the sea – its always moving, always remaining – its continuity and comforting size . . .

When Jimmy woke he suddenly told me that he loved her: he was unmistakable and resolute: he said that everything was different if one knew something – *he* said that. I could not warn or protect him; I could only cling to the papery intention of keeping silent.

We arrived. Then we had to find a taxi to take us into Athens: the heat of the day was still in the streets. I lay back in the cab with the hot, dusty air blowing on my face in small, sluggish wafts, thinking, 'Now we are going to an hotel.' But we arrived there, got rooms, and were at the door of them, and then there seemed to be no future at all, until Jimmy said that I had better have a bath while he telephoned the airport and in half an hour we would have dinner. He did not ask me, he simply arranged it, and I fell gratefully upon half an hour with a future of dinner.

At dinner he told me that he had got two seats on a plane leaving the following evening, and two more for the day after that. 'I'll take her back to her family, and you and Em can go together.'

'Good,' I said: I was feeling sick by then. Then he said that he had tried to get through to the island, but had completely failed. I said that of course we were two hours later than we had told Em that we would be, and I thought the Post Office closed at about eight. He said yes, he'd thought of that too: we would call in the morning, but meanwhile he'd sent a telegram.

Some time after dinner he said: 'You look absolutely done in! Don't you think you'd better get some sleep? We don't have to hurry in the morning – except I've got to check on those tickets and take them to the place to be filled in.'

But I didn't want to go to bed. He ordered some brandy for both of us and we had another cigarette. As he was lighting mine, he said: 'I suppose losing a father is just about as tough as anything that can happen to a girl, isn't it?'

'It depends what kind of relationship they had. I think it is hard on Alberta.'

'What was it like for you? Or do you mind my asking?'

I shook my head while I was thinking.

'You see I didn't just lose a father. I lost both parents at once: they were drowned sailing together. So I lost my home at the same time, and it is really impossible to separate the losses. It was just that everything I knew came to an end, suddenly, without warning.'

'That must have been awful.' He looked really concerned.

'It's probably less awful to have had all that and lost it than never to have had it at all. I had a very happy childhood, and I adored our house and its country.' It was odd how distant all that seemed now – I heard myself telling it in the voice I used for talking about other people.

He said: 'It must be a strange feeling: I shall have to think carefully what it is like. You said she will be losing her home too, and her mother died years ago, so it is a little like you, isn't it?'

'Yes.' I realized that until now I would have said, no, it wasn't. I was only fourteen when *my* parents had died – I would have competed with Alberta about loss when it had nothing to do with Jimmy wanting to know how she felt. If there was to be any competition, it was Jimmy who had undoubtedly suffered most, and there he was, thinking about her.

'I've been thinking.' he said: 'Do you think it is about time I struck out on my own? I mean, I've spent years now just sticking around having things handed me on a plate. Your asking me whether I could handle the play in New York on my own started me thinking that maybe it's time I stopped doing just what came easiest; I never thought about the future – when I think of the *dough* I might have saved!'

I could not help smiling at him. 'If that is the only thing you regret about your past, you're not doing so badly. I should think about it, and wait and see.'

'I wouldn't just walk out on Emmanuel, if that's what is worrying you. Unless he wanted me to.'

'He'd never want that.' I tried to sound convincing, but I couldn't look at him.

He said: 'Oh, you never know – he might want a change; people do sometimes.'

Then he said we must get some sleep.

I was halfway through having another bath, before I remembered that I'd had one before dinner. The rising panic that I had felt when Jimmy said good night to me had resulted in my not having the least idea what I had been doing: I came to, as it were, lying in warm water, looking at my body and thinking: 'You washed it all two hours ago!' and feeling faintly irritated and ridiculous, but I also found I was looking at my body as though it belonged to someone else. All my life I had been dominated by this body – poor Lillian's frail and unpredictable frame – however much care I took of it, it never seemed to be enough, and I discovered then that I had always lived with a picture of somebody called Lillian for whom I would do anything – make endless allowances, flatter, soothe, commiserate with, and comfort. She was highly strung, sensitive, intelligent, delicate, deeply emotional, and vulnerable – she was anybody's sickly-romantic picture of a young girl – perpetually in need of protection and encouragement, guarding her damn feelings so carefully that they never had a chance to operate; she was demanding, dishonest, and dull . . . I could just imagine reading about her in a short, brilliantly written novel, but any longer or more direct association was really too tedious and absurd . . . And yet this picture had never left me. Even though my body had changed until it in no way fitted with this picture, I had somehow arranged the split. I had not actually fallen into the crude trap of continuing to dress as though I was eighteen – had adapted myself externally with ingenious taste and managed all the time to put up with, even to nurture this ageless bore, who, if she was anyone else but Lillian, I would not have tolerated for a weekend. Now, whoever 'I' was, I was faced with living entirely alone with her for the rest of my life. I got out of the bath, wrapped myself in a towel, went into the bedroom with its twin beds and sat on the one that had already been turned down for me. Supposing I go back to England alone, she will have to help me find a house and furnish it. It is no good her weeping and wanting everyone to be sorry for her all the time, because nothing will get done like that. I can't take her back to what remains of my family in Norfolk, although they would be delighted to hear that she'd parted with Em, because the moment they stopped being sorry for her, she'd become intolerable. If I found her work, she'd never keep it – she'd be ill, or she'd bore everyone so much that they couldn't work with her. In spite of her 'needing affection so desperately' she's incapable of giving it, or even of engendering it in anyone but me. I wouldn't want her to meet people, she'd let me down so terribly – she simply isn't interested in anything but herself, and although she thinks that I've led her a 'hard life', she hasn't got any experience at all. She has absolutely no sense of proportion, so nothing makes her laugh – she's neurotic to the point of madness, and if we hadn't turned out to have the same name, nothing would have induced me to have anything to do with her. I would really rather be alone. Just because she was so kind and understanding to me about Sarah, doesn't give her the right to drag at me now. And I suddenly realized that if Sarah had lived, I would have just had to get rid of her because she would have been so bad for Sarah. The possibility of ever having been able to get rid of her was extraordinarily bracing: on the strength of it, I got into the other bed without a sleeping pill.

It was good to lie down: I felt my weight making its shape in the bed, and shut my eyes. Immediately, as though in some other sense I had opened them, there was a picture of Alberta – still in her faded pink shirt – thrown into his arms and weeping so bitterly for her father that I longed to comfort her too.

3

ALBERTA

IF I write this out – just what has happened – it may get a little clearer, and if it did, I might know how to bear it. Now that I've spoken to Uncle Vin, I at least *know* what has happened – it's just that I cannot think about it – I cannot think at all: everything looks the same, life goes on from minute to minute and I go with it, only it all feels quite unreal, and just as it begins to feel ominous and odd that everything should all look the same and yet feel so unreal, the fact about him suddenly explodes all over again as though I hadn't known before. He is dead: he was knocked over by a car in the little lane by the church on the corner they were always going to widen. *The car didn't stop.* He was on his bicycle – Aunt T. said he'd been to see old Mr Derwent who was ill, and he'd gone after supper: this happened on his way back – about a quarter to ten, they think, but they don't know, because they didn't find him until some time after eleven. He was dead when they found him. I asked Uncle Vin whether he had been killed at once by the car and Uncle Vin said no, he didn't think that he had been. So perhaps he had a little time which I know he would have wanted

– without too much pain – oh! that part of it *is difficult* – not knowing that, and I may never know. I cannot write about the driver of the car because I know too well what Papa would say about that, and now he is dead and will never speak to me or write to me again, I shall have to remember more than ever what he has said. Otherwise there will be nothing left of him – I shall lose it all.

There seem to be two sides to this. I don't see why Papa of all people should be subject to such an accident; he wasn't old, he was very useful. He must have noticed that Papa was one of the more useful people, he was so much loved and depended upon. I could understand it a little better if he had had to die *for* something – to save somebody's life, or for some greater cause, but it wasn't like that. He simply gets knocked down on an evening because there wasn't a moon and I don't suppose the tail light of his bicycle was working – I was the only person who ever got it to work – and is left to lie in a ditch and die by himself: *why?* This makes me feel violent: the only person who understood about that and ever helped me to get past it was Papa, and this is the second side of it. It seems to me that losing him is something which stretches round me in every direction – there is no end to the loss – starting from quite small things like calling him in the house and hearing him answer, to feeling that wherever I was or whatever happened, he stood in the same relation to me: he said, 'We cannot do without help,' but it was *he* who helped me, and I loved him for that too. Supposing he had not died but I had this aching shock about someone, what would I do? I would go to him and tell him about it – everything that I have put down here: I would say: 'The one person in my life – the only person who is really necessary to me has been killed in a useless, silly accident. There is something wicked here – that somebody so loved and useful should be murdered out of carelessness.' What would he say to that? He would ask me what this person had stood for in my life. I would say that apart from his being a most important part of my family and my having always known him and loved him, he was the only person who gave me any sense of direction, because what he felt and thought and did was founded on what seemed to be an unshakeable integrity which gave them a sense of purpose and proportion. I found this utterly reliable, and loved it.

Now I have had to think most carefully what Papa would say to this – I have to imagine, out of all the other things that he has said to me, what he would say to this; but I don't think he would really say things, he would ask me a hard question: he would say was it reliable of this person to die and leave me so bereft? The answer to that, of course, is that he couldn't help it. He would agree with that, wouldn't he? Yes, he would; I remember now what he said about examples – he said that if one threw one's arms round a signpost one might become so devoted to it that one forgot what it was for – he said this was a discouraging thing that happened to signposts. What he's really meaning is that people aren't designed to be the kind of reliable that I'm talking about: or perhaps they were designed to be but none of them manage it. If somebody gives one a sense of direction that one wants, the direction cannot die – it would still be there even if one lost it. If he gave me that, I don't want to forget what he said or what he was, but somehow, I must try to go on by myself.

Did he feel like this when my mother died? Because all these years *he* hasn't had anybody who meant to him what he has meant to me. I don't think he has even *tried* to make another person reliable – he just went on by himself: I know that, so that in some way it hasn't stopped because he is dead. So: I am supposed to *make use of his death* – that is how he would see it: he once said: 'It takes *far more* love to be impersonal – not less; will you think about that possibility, my dear Sarah?' But I never did: he has actually had to die to make me consider it. I am the last person to try and pick out wickedness when I don't understand what is good. He always said that was a mug's game.

So the real question about Papa, is not what did he die for

at all. It is the opposite, and that is what I must try to understand. Otherwise, it is very like having to be on a cliff with no head for heights.

4

EMMANUEL

HE turned his back on the boat and walked slowly across the quay away from them. He had at once the sensation of being entirely trapped and entirely free. He had just become aware of this when he heard Jimmy shouting to him: 'Better beware!' He turned round, but Jimmy didn't shout anything more. He was free now to make his decision in peace: he was trapped into the necessity for making a decision. He had never expected an opportunity to look after her – from the moment the telegram had arrived he had foreseen nothing but her shock, his responses choked by convention, and endless, wearisome arrangements made by Jimmy. He had fallen in with this – what else could he do? He had got Lillian out of the Post Office before she fainted from the heat, and after that he had simply fallen in with Jimmy's determination and Lillian's whim. Now they were gone, and he was left with her. He had almost reached the Post Office when the certain knowledge that he wanted to marry her and live with her always more than he had ever wanted anything else and more than he cared about deserting Lillian struck him. It had not been tangible before – he had felt suspended, first by the shock of finding that he loved her, then by his circumstances and the need for concealment. But now, in some way, action had been taken for him by her father's death, now if she was ever to be his it was necessary that he make some move, now, whatever she might feel about him had become relevant. He did not have Jimmy's cynical confidence in his powers – about them, he simply felt that it was easy to achieve something that one did not very much want – one was detached enough for the right kind of intellectual consideration – but he did feel that something which was so profoundly and startlingly true for him could not leave her disaffected . . .

In the Post Office he discovered that she was standing exactly where he had left her over an hour ago. The boy, who was sitting on the floor, said: 'We have had one false alarm,' and she tried to smile at him, but he saw from her eyes that she was not seeing him clearly.

'If we go and sit outside for a bit, would you call us if the call comes through?'

Julius nodded, and she made no protest when he took her arm and led her outside, until they were almost at the café table, when she said: 'It will be all right, won't it? I must speak to them.'

'I promise you.' He arranged his chair so that he could see the Post Office door and saw Julius looking through the window to see where they were. 'It's all right: he's seen us. All he need do is wave. Have a cold drink.'

She nodded, and then asked: 'Where are the others?'

'They've gone on the boat,' he said gently: 'to see about the plane tickets.'

'Oh yes.' She said it as though that had nothing to do with her.

When her drink arrived she said: 'I do realize that this has disorganized everybody: I'm so sorry.'

'We were all ready to go back anyway,' he replied with what he hoped was just the right note of callous cheerfulness.

She had not touched her drink; she stared at it quite calmly, and then said: 'I'm afraid I can't drink it: I feel too dizzy.'

He got up, turned her round in her chair by her shoulders and pushed her head down between her knees, catching her just as her body started to go limp.

After a very short time he felt her head pressing up against his hand and released her.

'All right?' She had some colour in her face now, and he realized how white she had been.

'Yes, thank you. I haven't done that for years – I used to know exactly when to put my own head down.'

He handed her her drink. 'You sound as though you have had a great deal of practice. I should drink some of that.'

'Years of it. Nearly every week at Early Service. You need practice to kneel with no food inside you. Could you get some more orange?'

'You haven't finished that one.'

'I should like to take some to Julius; he is a kind boy, and he is exceedingly fond of orange juice.'

'I'll take him some: you stay where you are.'

Julius received the drink gravely – he had picked up a number of Greek manners. There were more people in the Post Office, as the mail from the boat had been sorted, and a letter was handed to him. He asked Julius if there were any more, and Julius asked and there weren't. As he walked back to her he saw her put her hands on each side of the small table and grip it, and he knew that she was using the table to make something real for herself and his throat ached with pity, but when he reached her she looked up and said: 'Was he pleased?'

'I think he was. There was only one letter – for me.' He put it on the table. 'Do you think it would make it any easier for you while you are waiting for this call if you talked about it?'

But she answered stiffly: 'I haven't anything to say.'

A moment later she said: 'I didn't mean to sound ungrateful. It is just that I am trying to get used to the idea: it seems to be all I can do.'

'Telegrams are winding. It will be better when you have talked to your family.'

She said in a low voice: 'It will seem more real, anyway.'

He had never felt so powerless: everything he longed to do was either useless or impossible. He wanted to take her in his arms and hold her head until she wept and released some tension of her feeling: he wanted to tell her that there was nothing that he would not do to help her – now and always; he wanted to tell that he knew how she was feeling, that he loved her and would never allow anything again to hurt her as this was hurting, he would prevent, or at least share it. But he knew that he wasn't even sharing it: he leaned towards her, impelled to say something, and as suddenly, she smiled and looked down to her feet.

'I wondered what this was.' She had bent down and came up with an extremely small, very dirty kitten in her hands. The moment that she put it on her lap, it rose on to its hind legs, climbed up her and thrust its bullet head under her chin, emitting an improbably noisy irregular clockwork purr.

'Oh really! It seems quite frantic for affection. Isn't it a curious colour? Like a black cat dipped in flour. It's rather ugly, in fact.'

But she was still smiling at it: it was a filthy little creature, with long legs, a rat-like tail, and its ears still looked as though they had been stuck on to its head, but he felt so grateful to it for making her smile, that he said: 'I'll get it some food.'

They gave it some bread and cheese on the table, which it ate in frenzied tearing gulps. Two other full-grown cats arrived like magic; one of them jumped on to the third empty chair, but the kitten put one paw over the bread, fluffed out its meagre coat and swore with such appalling violence that the older cat washed a hind leg and retreated. When it had eaten everything, it walked twice round the table for crumbs, neatly avoiding the letter, looked them both in the face, jumped on to Alberta's lap, and went to sleep with hiccoughs. She said: 'It has the most honest expression, quite unlike Napoleon, who always makes one feel rather uncomfortable on purpose. She's our cat at home.'

'This is a little guttersnipe: it's learned all it knows the hard way. It doesn't look as though it has learned much about washing.'

She stroked its back and said serenely: 'No: it is probably covered with fleas. I wonder whether . . .' but even before him she had seen Julius waving. She said: 'Please keep the kitten,' put it on his knee, and went.

He kept the kitten and waited: it seemed a long time. Eventually, because he had to find something to take his mind off waiting for her, he picked up the letter and opened it.

It was from Mrs Friedmann and it was about the boy, Matthias; the writing was enormous, but difficult to read.

> I am needing to explain something which is hard but you are so much the good man that you will have little difficulty of understanding.

There followed a long and pathetic account of Matthias' state of mind. He had lost one finger at the second joint, and damaged two more so badly that playing the violin was out of the question for him. He was shocked, and inconsolable about this – wished to die – he had tried to attack the surgeon and after that seemed to have no interest in anything or anybody. The sight of Mrs Friedmann or Becky reduced him to floods of tears, and the sound or even the idea of music made him hysterical. He was still in a hospital although they had moved him: they had tried to have him at home, but it was clear that he needed continuous attention, and as he seemed not to endure Mrs Friedmann it had not proved practicable to keep him there. Then came her astonishing suggestion.

> You will not know how it is to feel that there is nothing for him I may do his needing so much to be helped and I helpless. Hans too has tried and tried and the doctors talk with him at first they say a little time but now the talking about time have they stopped. We have agreed Hans and I that he must another chance now have and this is why dear Mr Joyce I now write to you – to say that I must ask you now to take Matthias out of his hospital and away with you into life as you have so much more to give in changing scene and full life of peoples and interest than for us is possible. Last night I am speaking with Hans and say I am so sad and

> unhappy because I so much love Matthias and he say 'you love Matthias? Or you love having a son?' *This is true*, Mr Joyce – too *much* – and now I am knowing it so must write and ask you. We are agreed that there is no other person so full of trust because your goodness to us we will never never forget and know we can have no ways of paying to you our deep thanks. I have also to say that for this one time I write the letter instead of Hans as I think you will not believe that I mean to bear giving up Matthias unless you read my writing with your eyes. Hans will be writing as there is much finances to be under discussion as he will be wishing to pay all for Matthias supposing in your great kindness you agree to what I am asking. Forgiving my shocking English and all I am asking which I would not do except for the boy.

She was his faithfully, B. Friedmann. For a while he sat, shocked by the enormous simplicity of her suggestion. That she should calmly – well, not calmly – but that she should simply suggest handing the boy over to him! She had, of course, exaggerated ideas of his goodness since it was he who had provided her with the children and the means to keep them in the first place, and she had wanted them more than anything else. But still – to suggest handing over an hysterical desperate child who had just lost what he clearly felt was the reason for his life just because she felt it would be better for *him* and that he, Emmanuel, was the best person to take on this delicate and trying responsibility because he was such a wonderful character leading such a full, interesting and good life! 'She doesn't know,' he thought grimly, 'that I am in process of trying to get rid of my extremely difficult, sick wife, and marry a girl more than forty years younger than myself – if she'll have me. The uproar that these two moves will create is hardly conducive to the recovery of a highly strung boy.' He would have to go and see the Friedmanns, however, as soon as he got to London, and explain to them. He crammed the letter into his pocket – trying to feel angry, trying to feel amused by Mrs Friedmann's guileless presumptions. Then Alberta returned, with Julius following her. She was very pale again: she didn't say anything – just sat down as though she was very tired.

They walked across the port to a restaurant for lunch – it was only because Julius said he must go home for his, that they realized that it was lunch time. The kitten followed them, and in the end she picked it up and settled down at a table with it. They ate tiny little tepid fried fish and stuffed tomatoes which were served a little cooler than they were themselves. Neither of them ate much, but the kitten gorged and swore until it was a triangular shape and its whiskers were sticky with rice. Then, belching heavily, it settled again on Alberta's lap and tried to clean itself up. She said: 'I like the way its life goes on.' She was holding its wretched little tail for it to wash. They had reached the coffee rather gratefully: their silence, except for talking about the kitten occasionally, had lasted all through the meal. Now he said abruptly: 'Will you tell me what your family said?'

'He was knocked down by a car in the lane by the church – in the evening. He was dead by the time they found him.'

'They? What about whoever was driving the car?'

'They didn't stop,' she said: her voice had no expression at all when she said this, and something about her face checked his angry exclamation.

'My uncle is there – I spoke mostly to him. I told him that I was coming home as soon as possible. Is that all right?'

'Of course. Will you want to stay there for a time?'

But she looked as though the question was utterly beyond her, so he did not pursue it. Then she said: 'I'm glad that I talked to them, anyway. Do you think we could go back to the house now?'

He paid for lunch, and said: 'What about your kitten?'

'I thought I'd take it up to the house with me. It doesn't seem to belong to anybody, so no one will mind where it spends the afternoon. Do *you* mind?'

'I think it is a good idea.' He meant it: it could at least be something real for her for the day, although he had a pang of jealousy that this creature could collect her attention. But on the way home, she said: 'You are being so exceedingly kind and thoughtful to me. I do really notice it, I simply find it difficult to discuss.' Her voice shook a little with the effort of saying this.

He looked at her walking up the hill beside him. 'It is nothing, my dear Sarah – don't try to talk about any of it.' His heart was pounding: she looked at him with a gentle expression when he used her name, and suddenly he could not stop. 'Sometimes,' he said painfully, 'I love you: sometimes you seem a part of something that I love.' He stopped abruptly; it was enough – more than enough. She gave him an odd abstracted little smile and their silence closed over these words, so that a minute later they might never have been spoken. He did not know what she felt; minutes later, he wondered whether she had even heard them.

When they got back to the house, they found Julius sitting outside their door. He was reading a very large book which proved to be Wells' *Outline of History*: he wore his usual jeans supplemented by a huge sheath knife and his back was the smooth and tender brown of an egg.

'I thought you might have further telephoning and would need my services in Greek.'

'Jimmy Sullivan is going to call me between six and seven this evening: will that be difficult, do you think?'

'Is he the man who went this morning on the boat?'

When they said he was, Julius said ho, well he wouldn't arrive in Piraeus until well after eight in the evening, and explained to them about the boat's circuit. When they realized that the boat was due back to their island in about half an hour he asked her whether she wanted to catch it.

'I don't know. We haven't packed – I mean there is everybody's packing to be done . . .'

'If you like, I will try to arrange that a caique takes you over tonight,' Julius offered.

He looked at her. 'Would you prefer that?'

'I would. But if Julius can't manage it, won't we be rather stuck?'

'There are many caiques going over in summer – it will be all right, it will be fine and wonderful and much better than going in the big boat. Is that your cat?'

She had put the kitten down on the terrace and it lay on its side, gazing at them with fierce innocent eyes. 'Not really. I just found it. Does it belong to anyone, do you know?'

'I will find out. I will go now and leave my book here.'

When Julius had gone, he said: 'You're quite right. We couldn't get packed up in time and we'll need at least one donkey to get it down to the port.'

She picked up the kitten, and said: 'If you don't mind, I would rather leave the packing for a bit. Could we do it later?'

Although she said nothing about it, her need to be alone was now so apparent that without a word he opened the door of her room for her and shut her into it.

He went back on to the terrace, and stood a while staring through the hot restful scene before him. It was one of the hours when the age of this country rose up to the eye: sun burning on rock and sea: animals still – people absent – houses shuttered – the few trees still in the windless heat, and the sky so wide – so spread past a vault or a canopy, of such penetrating height, such boundless distance that it was immortally beyond space and eternally above time: he looked up at it, and as his eyes left the sea and rocks of the island a picture of the whole world placed itself naturally between him and the sky; only now the seas were like single drops of water, the lands small crumbs of earth – the sky was loaded with other stars, with invisible suns and unknown moons, and this world was a grain of dust and water, a particle, an incident so small that it would demand absolute attention for its notice. And yet this same earth contained a multitude of life about most of which he knew nothing; it was of an antiquity that he could not honestly envisage; its variety and size seemed too great for him to explore, and his existence upon it was not significant. Inside that insignificance he thrashed and machinated and obeyed an authority made up of tomorrow, the next generation, and once upon a time. Inside that authority he used words from one of many languages for a small specific purpose of communicating – what? only what he could feel or perceive – the fruit from his little personal shrub of knowledge; he did this and expected to be paid for it in happiness collected off other people, a lavish change in his material scenery and any other trappings that helped to make him swell. 'And there I am, in my nutshell,' he thought: 'and I can't write a play about the stars, because I don't understand them; nor can I become a star. I don't even know what it feels like to be a tree, let alone a star. I don't really know what it feels like to be anybody else.'

He was upstairs, in his room: he had not noticed going there, and it seemed to him extraordinary that, in the middle of discovering the minute size of his life, he should fail to be aware of even one moment of it. Some part of him must have decided to go, and his legs then carried him and here he was – almost as though he had missed out a minute of his life by not existing in it. But if one noticed this kind of thing, then one must be living in a more slipshod manner than was intended – he was, perhaps, rattling about in his nutshell. This was too much: insignificance was one thing – inadequacy was quite another – he did not feel that he could afford it: it made any regrets or desires about understanding the stars utterly absurd. Quite suddenly her criticism of Clemency that she had made in New York came into his mind. She had said that all the things that Clemency had to give up didn't seem to matter much, because she hadn't herself valued them. He had been going to rewrite that bit, and he'd done nothing about it. Why? It was partly laziness, of course, but it was also because although he'd agreed with her, and thought she was right, he hadn't felt what to do about it. It wasn't a piece of writing where one could rely on what a lot one knew about how to write a scene. So rightly, in a sense, he had left it. The trouble was that with his experience of doing without, he'd tended to avoid giving up anything – in case that left him utterly deprived.

He felt now extremely restless, and decided to pack. For weeks now he had been longing for a whole day alone with her, and now that he had got it, every single thing was wrong. She was deeply unhappy, unreachable in her present state: and yet for weeks he had thought of nothing but her, and on top of that his recent thoughts had further diminished and disturbed him, until he felt that, without her, his life would cease to have any meaning at all. He packed all his own things with a kind of angry speed. At some unknown point in time he would be packing to go away with her – the tears, the recriminations, the public yelps of disapproval, the years of trying to compensate somebody for something which wasn't his fault – all of it behind him; he would start a new life – he would use everything he had learned to make it different and good for her . . .

He went downstairs quietly, in case she was asleep: her western shutters were closed, but he had such a desire to see that she was there that he went round to the other terrace, where her room had another window. She was sitting on the floor, leaning against her bed, and she slept with her head against her arm. On the bed was a letter, a large open book, and her pen. He was afraid that if he looked at her too long he would wake her.

He went back upstairs and packed Jimmy's things. Jimmy felt curiously distant; like someone he had once known, but had not met for years. It did not take him long to pack up Jimmy's things.

Now – Lillian. She had left a certain amount of luggage in New York, but she still seemed to have brought an incredible amount. He started methodically with her shoes – mostly sandals of every shape and colour: they all had to be packed in separate linen bags embroidered with her initials. The chest of drawers was full to overflowing with underclothes, shirts, sweaters, shorts, scarves – what on earth could she want with forty-eight scarves, he counted wondering, the wardrobe was crammed with skirts, dresses, jackets, duster coats, hats, belts, trousers, and dressing gowns. The top of the chest of drawers was littered with bottles and pots, little fitted cases, brushes and combs, jewellery, sun glasses, scent, toilet water, and all kinds of lipsticks and rouge. There was also the small red leather folder that had the photographs of Sarah which she was usually never without. He opened it: there she was – two pictures of her, one laughing, one serious: they were rather blurred as they had been too much enlarged: Sarah sitting on a table in a pale dress, with a mere coxcomb of hair: her head looking too large for her body, her bare arms just creased at the wrist, her fingers joyfully articulate. In the serious picture her eyes looked dark and enormous, in the laughing one her forehead was charmingly wrinkled: dear little Sarah – but she was dead: she had been dead for fourteen years and Lillian could not let go of her; pined and brooded over these pictures for hours of her life, and never forgot about them. Whatever she thought, she felt about nothing but Sarah. Really, compared with Lillian, Mrs Friedmann's view that naturally he would do anything for Matthias was hardly obsessive . . . Why had he thought of her, of Mrs Friedmann? It wasn't because of Lillian and Sarah, he realized, it was something else – it was nearly everything that had happened since he had read her letter: he hadn't really stopped thinking about her at all – only he hadn't thought in words. A picture of Mrs Friedmann rose before him: fat, a vulgar shape, overdressed, plastered with wildly unsuitable make-up, her rather hoarse but musical voice saying things that made her own eyes fill with easy tears – he realized that some of them had dropped on to the letter that she had written him – he had to read it again. He cleared a place on the bed, and sat down.

He read it very slowly, and sat for a long time afterwards, unable to move: it might have been another letter that he had read in the morning and he another man reading it. Now, he had no words of any kind – he felt simply, entirely exposed, and seized by some unnameable motion as though his heart was blushing a deep red. He did not know how long it lasted, but at the beginning of its end he heard himself finding that past a certain degree emotions did not need separate names – they were all one – or at least a part of all one. This discovery seemed to be tremendously important; it brought with it a sense of truth and triumph: for a moment he was filled with elation like a soundless fire which silently consumed all his dead, heavy rubbish until he no longer felt like a stone inside his body, and his mind was a poised feather rising and falling over the warm breaths below it . . . Afterwards, or perhaps even before it had died, he started to see his life as though he was on some height, and it lay on a distant plain below him; occurring without chronology, but with amazing swiftness and certainty: events – pursuing – caught up with and overcame his imagination of himself. So – the man in New York who had remembered the boy who swore to rescue his mother in a carriage with horses was now faced with the young man who had let her pine until he had had to lift her into it, and now the black plumes on the black horses nodded and told him so. The man who could move Jimmy to a most tender concern for his romantic story of one fine day in the country with a beautiful girl whom he had then lost, was faced now with the man who had lied to the girl, had forgotten her, and only discovered her plight by accident and too late. His implications to Jimmy of his grief, his fate and misfortune were now ruthlessly transplanted – to the girl – to Jimmy himself. The figure he had designed who enjoyed his reputation for patience and loyalty to a woman who had disappointed him, was faced with the man who had chosen – in a fit of curiosity and solitude – to marry her: the little reasons for doing so crept out now from the vault of his true memory where he had kept them incarcerated: she attracted him because ten years before she would have been unattainable – she represented a kind of life that he thought he would never understand and it was flattering at more than forty to have this young beauty turn her first attentions to him. Everything that happened to Lillian with him had been touched by these considerations he employed about himself in their beginning, and he resented their deserts on behalf of a man who did not exist. 'My wife is as good as she is beautiful,' Friedmann had said, and his saying it recurred – the first words spoken in this silent panorama. He had never in his life felt that about anyone until now; and as he understood this, he saw all his desires and intentions and his behaviour about them, like two sharply serrated edges, clash as though they had never been formed to meet, annihilating all possibility of love. But now, as he approached *her* – she who seemed in a sense to have given birth to his heart, who he thought had entirely transformed him – he was halted by pictures of past approaches in his imagination – of holding her bare shoulders in his hands – of her whole body like a young unexplored country – of her youth that could not compare him with another man – she was to give him transfusions of life; she was to nourish him with her impressions; he was to live on the virtue of her discoveries, since he had forgotten or discarded his own. It was then that he saw her separate from himself. He saw her whole – her promise, her dangers, her degree of life, what moved and what slept in her, what shape what colour what sound of a woman she was now; he saw everything that she was, and not she but the truth of this sight made him see both of her and of himself what was eternal and what could be changed. This knowledge of her, which gradually became more and more brilliantly illuminated – endured past his astonishment (was she, who he had thought entire perfection, only this?) – and past his pain, the disorder, the abuse, the entire *lack of necessity* for her, the quantity of suffering which in ignorance of her he would invoke in order to get what he wanted, was suddenly, perfectly plain to him – it endured until its reality met with his acceptance: there was a moment of bliss in this recognition, and then imperceptibly he became aware that it had happened – that it had finished. He was sitting on the bed looking into empty sunlit air with Mrs Friedmann's letter crushed in his hand.

Julius stood in the doorway, and it struck him as an

interesting piece of order that he should arrive just then – not a few minutes earlier, and not much later when, alone, he might have succumbed to bitterness at the difficulties ahead. Julius said: 'Your caique is arranged – it will cost you five hundred drachs. It leaves at somewhere after half past eleven tonight; I have come to an arrangement with my parents whereby I am enabled to see you off. Are you in favour of vengeance?'

'I don't know.' He felt truthful and startled.

'It is very much done here: of course it is dull compared with the old days.'

'What was it like then?'

'Oh – embroidered cloaks stiff with poison and poisoned wine and swords and things – poisons were generally fashionable, but I don't think people are very well up in them any more. I have been told you write plays: it must make that much more difficult. No wonder,' he added kindly.

He did not feel equal to being unfavourably compared with Euripides, so he said: 'It really is kind of you to have made all the arrangements for us: there is one more thing. Do you think when you go back to the port you could arrange a donkey or two for us for the luggage?'

His face fell, but he simply said: 'What time?'

'I thought about nine. Then we'll lock up here and come in and perhaps you would have dinner with us at about half past at whatever restaurant you think the best. Could you do that?' His eyes shone and he gave a little hop, but he said solemnly: 'I should be charmed and delighted and – charmed. I'll meet you at Janni's at twenty past nine.' Then he moved closer and said in a piercing whisper: 'I have paid for that kitten myself as a parting present for her. It will be a surprise to cheer her up: we might have a discussion on English literature at dinner, mightn't we?'

'We easily might.'

He gave a shout of joy and chanted: 'Alternative subjects – astronomy, history of civilizations, or whether it is necessary to get to the moon. The donkeys will come.' And he went.

He folded up Mrs Friedmann's letter and put it carefully away – he felt that one way and another he was going to need it.

By the time she appeared he had finished Lillian's packing and was sitting on the terrace. She walked slowly across the terrace towards him rolling up the sleeves of a faded shirt that he remembered had once belonged to Lillian: he looked at her face – she was a little flushed from her sleep but her eyes had not changed – they had still the distant look of strain about them which made them too large and dark. 'Would you like to have one last bathe?' he said: 'All the plans have been excellently made by Julius, and we are dining with him at nine thirty.'

'What about the packing?'

'It is all done excepting yours and whatever I have forgotten. We have plenty of time. Where is your kitten?'

'It has gone to sleep in my hat.' She stood aimlessly by the parapet. 'It is still very hot. Perhaps it would be a good idea to bathe.'

They walked in silence down to the bay where they had always bathed: he found that he was intensely aware of his surroundings; of the late afternoon sun turning amber on the rocks – the sea below them streaked with dark purple patches – the hot, somehow antique smell from the land – but he felt that she was simply following him – she hardly knew where she was. They had all taken to getting up in their bathing things so she unbuttoned her shirt, pulled carelessly at the zip on her skirt, stepped out of it and moved towards the water. He said: 'Please wait for me,' he was afraid that she would swim miles away, and he was too poor a swimmer to be any help if she needed it. She sat down on the rock with her feet in the water and waited, without answering. When she saw he was ready she slipped in and he followed her. The water was marvellous after all the sweat of the day, and for a few minutes he simply floated and let it wash him, and looked up at the sky, and when he looked he saw that she was swimming furiously to the point where

Jimmy and she used to go with the goggles, and, worrying about her, he started laboriously to follow. When he was less than half way there, he saw that she had climbed on to a ledge and was sitting with her back to him looking out to sea. He had not swum to this point before, and it took him a long time; he was out of breath and exhausted by the time he reached her. He clutched the sharp edge of the rock and painfully hoisted himself out of the water, but she did not turn round.

'Phew!' he said, feeling nervous and absurd; 'that's the longest swim I've done here.'

She didn't answer for a bit, and then said: 'I'm sorry – but I haven't got anything at all to say. I think I'll go in now,' jumped off the rock and swam away.

He watched her go; he was too tired to swim back at once – and she was swimming back to the beach anyway. The sleep had slackened the hold she had over herself and it was the first time she had had to wake with her father's death. He knew about this from seeing Lillian struggle with it, but it had caught her unawares. He watched her land and put her towel round her – he could almost see her tenseness from here: he had to get her over this bit of it. 'My poor darling,' he thought, and it was a simple thought, charged only with gentleness.

The swim back seemed interminable: he tried to take it slowly and easily – but in the end it just became a matter of getting there somehow. He climbed out at last and sat gasping on the rock feeling too weak to reach his towel. She had dressed and was drying her hair.

'Throw me my towel, like a kind girl,' he said. 'I'm not built for swimming and I'm far too old to learn now. Did your father like swimming?'

She stopped towelling her hair, and said: 'He never had much time for it. Besides the water is awfully cold at our nearest bit of sea.'

'Women are supposed to be much better at it than men: especially indoor men like me. Although I don't suppose he had rickets as a child as I did.'

She said: 'I don't think so,' in a muffled voice and tried to go on with her hair.

He continued to talk and to dress as though he was completely unaware of her. 'Do you remember when you first told me about your father? It was on the aeroplane going to New York: you told me all kinds of things that he had said to you, and instead of that being irritating or dull, you made me feel what a delightful man he was.'

She had stopped even trying to dry her hair – her head was bent so that he couldn't see her face, but she was shaking from head to foot. He got up, drew his belt round him and moved closer to her before sitting again.

'I was thinking how difficult it was for you to have this shock without having him to help you about it. I was wondering – if this doesn't sound too strange to you – what as the person who has always helped you most he would say if you told him that your father, whom you loved, had suddenly died. I was thinking that if you could manage to separate these two things at *all* – it might make a difference. What do you think about that?'

She looked up at last – her face white again – a tumult of misery and recognition: he said again very gently: 'What do you think?' and held out his arms . . .

He held her in silence through the worst of it – until he felt her beginning to return from her abandon – to come out of her maze of grief; then when she was quieter and beginning to be aware of him, he pushed her hair out of her eyes and mopped her face with her towel – with an intentional clumsiness so that she smiled like watery sunlight and sat up. When he had found her a handkerchief, she said: 'If one loves somebody very much indeed – it is difficult to be impersonal about them, isn't it?'

'Very.'

She blew her nose again. 'You know what you said about trying to separate the two things?'

'Yes?'

'Well – I agree with it. It is just that I was finding it very difficult to do.'

'Easier now?'

She nodded. 'I just needed to cry for him once.'

'You may need to again: you are very young, dear Sarah; you have a great deal ahead.'

She looked at him uncertainly.

'I mean – cry because you love him – don't feel too bitterly deprived.' That's enough of that, he thought, and got to his feet.

On the way back to the house the thoughts that he had held her in his arms and that tomorrow she would be on her way back to England occurred with random wildness – he couldn't stop them occurring, but he found it possible to jerk his attention to something else: it would be easier when there was some distance to them: when he had to say 'last week, last month, two years ago'.

When she had packed, she joined him on the terrace: she was carrying the kitten – squirming with appreciation – in her arms. Her tears seemed somehow to have cleansed and simplified her face: she was beautiful after them – her eyelids swollen and smooth as cream, her eyes clear as washed slate, her mouth and forehead gentle with the tensions gone. She had changed into a dark blue shirt with the sleeves rolled up – there was a white stripe on her wrist where her watch had been.

'It has slept all the afternoon. It seems so fond of me that I cannot help reciprocating. Do you think it will mind awfully being returned to its guttersnipe life?'

'We'll give it another enormous dinner anyway'; he did not want to spoil Julius's surprise. He had brought out the large wicker-covered jar which was still half full of wine, and now he handed her a glass.

'We might as well drink until the donkey man arrives.'

'And watch our last sun set.'

'Yes.' He wondered painfully what that meant to her. 'You have not got your watch on.'

'I'm going to give it to Julius. It is the only thing I can think of that he would like. I've put it in a box – the one that had my evening bag you gave me in it.'

'Isn't that far too big a box for a watch?'

'Yes, but I've wrapped it in a good many fig leaves, so it doesn't rattle. It's not a very girlish watch. Do you think he will like it?'

'He is sure to. Sarah!'

She pushed the kitten down into her lap and looked up.

'Shall you be going to New York, do you think?'

'Have you both decided that you want me?'

'We have both decided that we want you.' He smiled to ease the words for himself. 'But I may not be able to come over with you as I have things to do in England. You may have to go with Jimmy; will that be all right for you?'

'Would you come and see the play in the end?'

'Oh yes, I expect so. But Jimmy would look after you: or will your family need you at home?'

'I think my family will need me to earn some money more than anything else.'

'Jimmy would look after you,' he repeated, pressing the point.

She blushed a little, and said: 'I know.' She was silent for a moment, and then added suddenly: 'He even said he'd *marry* me in order to look after me better in New York.'

'What did you say to that?'

She spread out her hands. 'Well – nothing – except thanking him. He asked me in the sort of way you advise people to go to your dentist, because he's so much better than the one they've got.'

'I don't suppose he felt like that, at all. He hasn't got much confidence in people liking him, unless he feels he's useful to them. That is probably my fault.' Then, suddenly, he told her about the girl in the country – the whole story, with all its truthful uncertainties: including the search he had made, for years, but too casually, for Jimmy: how he had thought when finally he discovered him and sent for him in London that he would be sure when he saw him, and hadn't been – had never been sure, and had therefore (therefore? he wondered) never told Jimmy. He considered nothing but the truth while he was telling it, not even his own motives for telling it to her, but at the end he was conscious of some lightening of this particular weight on him, and looked nervously to see whether it had transferred to her. But she, who had listened quietly making no sound or sign, now looked back at him with an impersonal friendliness and said: 'I should think anybody would be glad to know that you might have been their father.'

'You mean you think I should have told him?'

She hesitated: 'I don't know whether you *should* have. I meant only that he might be glad to be told.'

They watched the clouds like a veiled chorus, gather and turn iris in a sky flushed to cloth of gold by the brilliant sun which suffused as it sank and left streaks of greens and pinks – both tender and piercing like a lament, in the air – the sea like burnished steel – the land mysteriously shadowed – and the air turning to velvet, sparked with stars and the yellow domestic lights.

'Would *you* tell him for me?' he asked after a long and companionable silence.

'Don't you want to do that yourself?'

'I – no, no I don't. Unless you think I must?'

'The truth, you see,' he said a minute later: 'I should find that peculiarly difficult with him after all these years.' He looked at her almost pleadingly: 'If *I* knew precisely one way or the other whether he was my son it would be different. As it is I am afraid of simply kicking up a lot of dust about his mother – and also, it is my fault that I don't know, of course.'

She said: 'Yes – I will tell him when the right moment comes. If you trust me.'

'I would be very grateful to you.'

'So am I to you. Does it seem to you a very long time since this morning?'

'A very long time.'

'And tonight this house will be as though we were never in it.'

'Oh,' he said, 'shall we have left no mark?'

He felt her looking at him gravely in the dusk: 'I very much doubt it. It may have marked us, but I don't think we have marked it: its time is too long.'

They heard the delicate, hesitant tapping of a mule or donkey's feet on the stone outside. 'This is the end of being really alone with her,' he thought: 'even the boat won't be quite like this: this is an end.' He got to his feet: 'How are you going to manage the kitten?'

'In a sling round my neck. It is the most adaptable creature. It made a very neat mess in a flower pot in my room.'

When the mule was laden, he came out of the house to lock the door, and she was standing where she had stood that morning on the terrace when she had told him the contents of the telegram, and the rush of feeling that he had had for her then recurred. He turned away quickly to lock the door: in the morning he had been silent because he had felt restricted by other people – now, at least, he was restricting himself – and he tried now to stiffen himself with this difference.

They walked behind the mule to the port, facing a young moon that lay couched in little clouds like a young beauty on a bed of feathers. The man spoke to his mule, but they were silent until they met Julius who was waiting for them. He wore a spotless shirt and his bleached and tufted hair had been smoothed, his face was solemn but discreetly decorated by a little smile of excitement.

'I have commanded quail – small roasted birds. Ho! that's a good way to carry a cat. I should think you'd be desolate to part with it, wouldn't you?'

'She's very sad about it,' he said firmly before she could answer Julius.

Dinner was a great success. He found their combined company charming: Julius drank four bottles of orange and the kitten crunched up so many quail bones that it had not even energy to swear at other cats. After dinner she gave Julius the watch: he was very impressed and told her about the kitten. Then he rushed away into the restaurant and came back with a roll of white paper.

'I am also presenting you with this.'

It was an elaborate and spirited picture of marine life – drawn in indian ink with a remarkable assurance and care. In the corner it had 'With love from Julius Lawson' written in red ink. At the top it had 'Some Life in the Red Sea'.

'I drew it this afternoon. It is quite the best of my collection. You did say you were interested in marine life?'

'Yes: it's beautiful.'

'Five of the specimens are not accurate: I haven't seen them, so they are simply how I thought they would look from their names.'

She admired it again.

'You haven't noticed the chart of depths.' He showed her the side of the picture which was neatly ruled out with fathoms marks deepening down the picture. 'Nobody is swimming out of their depths, you see. I think many painters would forget to do that.'

She thanked him very solemnly and he relaxed. 'It is not a slipshod affair – you could easily have it put in a frame, and hang it on a wall if you have one.'

She rolled it carefully up again and promised to frame it when she got home.

When the time came for them to board the caique, he became very silent. He hopped to and fro off the boat like a small bird, helping them to stow their smaller belongings. Finally he shook hands with Emmanuel, and bowed his thanks for the splendid dinner, and when Emmanuel said rather awkwardly: 'I didn't know what you would like, so would you choose something for yourself?' and gave him a hundred-drachma note, he looked at it with awe and muttered: 'Fifty weeks' worth of pocket money! I am speechless with gratitude at your munificence.'

When she said goodbye he clung to her with a sudden intensity, hugged her and whispered something, but the engine had been started and he had to go. He jumped back on to the quay, his eyes blazing with sad excitement, and shouted: 'Come back! Come back!' and not knowing they said, 'Yes!' Then they were cast off and chugging away and leaving him looking much smaller – a small boy – and forlorn.

They were settled on a hatch amidships: there seemed to be several passengers – all Greek – crouched about the boat among boxes of fish and jars of wine, who talked quietly to one another and called to a second boat that was leaving with them. He and she had been looking at Julius; now he turned to see her face which was still turned towards the shore: she looked grave, almost stern, but he felt her give a little inward sigh: he asked: 'What were you thinking?'

Still looking she answered: 'I was just trying to accept our departure. I mean – we're leaving the island *now*; it is a moment. And yet, years from now, we may have difficulty in remembering it.'

He was about to deny this – since leaving the island meant so much to him – but the essential truth of what she said was undeniable. Years hence, he would remember something of what he had felt while they left the island, but he would not remember exactly what this moment was like – it would all be lost in the ashes of other experience. So he said nothing.

They chugged gently out of the small harbour, and then increased speed. Behind them the island loomed in mountainous bulk above the lights of the port which gradually became diminished until they were like stamens at the heart of an enormous flower. Ahead was dark sea and, above, a midnight sky crowded with stars. Voices had lowered in the boat – the other caique remained a constant distance from them. The kitten lay inert in the sling she had made from a cotton head-square. She said: 'You know, Julius has changed this cat's life. Will they let me take it into England?'

'There is a quarantine, I think. We'll have to think what to do.'

They were sitting on the hatch: suddenly she said: 'Now we have left the island.'

'Then we must be in the boat.'

She smiled; then yawned and answered: 'I think I will be asleep in it.'

He made her a pillow of his coat and covered her with her own. The kitten, let out of its sling, stretched, yawned, and lay down round her neck. 'Young creatures,' he thought; 'they have both simply had enough of the day.' She put up a hand to him and said: 'You have been so kind: you've changed it for me so that I see one isn't entirely alone – one does meet people from time to time.'

He took her hand, and knowing what she did not know, he kissed it. She said drowsily: 'Nobody has ever kissed my hand before,' and seemed really, he thought, as they say, to fall asleep. He had time to put her hand back under the coat, and that was all. The kitten lifted its head, and moved itself closer to the shelter of her neck, and they were both gone.

He thought that he wasn't tired: he had imagined himself talking to her for hours: but now this did not seem a deprivation, she was there, herself, and he could see it. He lit a cigarette, and watched the island recede to a blurred murmur of lights and no outline against the sky. They had left it: soon, he would be leaving her – it was all a matter of departure. Where was he going? This was a question all of one's life. They would arrive, leave the boat, and go – to what? For some long time he tried to understand what any arrival had meant in his life – the cigarette was finished: he made a pillow of her bag – slippery and hard for his head. He was tired, tired, tired: the boat throbbed with his tiredness – on and on – getting nowhere, although the sea was all round him and he knew that they were travelling upon it. He looked at her – rapt and attentive to her sleep – and the kitten – its head curled, curved into her neck – its eyes slits of concentration upon the matter in hand, and wanting to join them in this if nothing else, he lay down. He looked up at the stars, and thought: 'They can bear to be there all the time: I can hardly bear to be here at all.' He put his hand on the kitten's back which lay against her shoulder, and shut his eyes . . .

CHAPTER VIII

1

ALBERTA

IN the boat I seemed to wake up suddenly – and completely. It was very cold and grey, with mist and still water round us; all rather ghostly and unreal, and that may have been why I started to think about home, and to imagine myself there. I thought of unhitching the white gate and walking round the weedy curved drive to the front door which is always open in summer and looking up at the house – the stone which is the most beautiful warmed worn grey, and the wistaria and blowzy roses and cracked white paint on the window sills with Serena's tennis shoes drying a toothpaste white on one of them: waiting to look, and walking up the steps into the hall which is the size of an ordinary room and somehow cold even in summer with all its doors and the staircase. The dining room and the drawing room doors are open and the baize door leading to the kitchen is hitched back, but the door of his study is shut, and the thought of opening it and finding his study exactly as it has always been, but without him, is one which I cannot bear. If I go past the baize door and along the stone passage and out of the garden door by the kitchen it will only be to walk round the back lawn to his study window, because perhaps if you look in at a room through a window you half expect to find it empty. And there is everything – his glass-fronted bookcase, his desk covered with papers and presents like ink wipers that we made him as children, the photograph of our mother in a silver frame with blue velvet inside, the leather armchair and the long battered sofa with the springs broken at one end, the coconut matting and the black woolly rug in front of the fireplace which we used to use for bears, and the really horrible jar with metal snakes writhing round its outside that he will keep pampas grass in – he said it was the kind of jar that was made for pampas grass and anything nicer would have been a waste – and the coat rack next to the door which Aunt T. had put there to remind him to wrap up when he went out, and the dark green wallpaper that he couldn't afford to change, and the unfortunate lampshade that a parishioner made him for a Christmas present which he said it would hurt her feelings not to use, and his First Aid box with two divisions, a large one for children and a small one for animals, and the funny smell like stamp albums with a touch of moth balls thrown in . . . every single thing is there as it seems always to have been ever since I can remember – only when I go back to it now, although I can see him sitting in his chair and looking up when he sees me and just smiling without saying a word – he won't be there – and now I have to go back and the feeling of dread that I woke up with on the boat has grown and grown until I don't know how to bear going back.

This is hopeless. It isn't as though I'll ever have to do it again, because we shall have to move to make room for a new vicar. The others have had this ever since he died: it is what Aunt T. would call morbid and it is where Papa would say 'Courage, Sarah' in his firmest voice . . . Oh dear, at least I *know* what he would say perfectly well, and from now onwards I must just say those sort of things to myself. It *is* better having written it out; partly, I suppose, because I can see how silly it looks. It is no good going back in the wrong way; I must be firm and calm and helpful to poor Aunt T., because Humphrey isn't practical, and Clem isn't calm and poor Uncle Vin is in the middle of a film so I don't suppose he can be very helpful. And Mary and Serena are too young. I simply must be my age, as Jimmy would say.

This morning I tried to thank Mr Joyce for everything: it was after we'd left the boat and staggered ashore with all the suitcases and the kitten. We went to a small café and had bread and coffee as we both felt pretty cold and empty: the kitten kept escaping and of course it doesn't understand in the least about traffic. The sailors gave it a garfish out of one of the fish boxes – they are a very long, thin fish with an intellectual expression – and it ate it like somebody typing very fast down a long line. The food seemed to make it frisky which was most unfortunate. I was beginning to despair of its control when Mr J. said: 'We'll have to get it a basket: we'll try and buy one on our way in to Athens,' and it was then that I tried to thank him. The trouble was that trying to say something I really meant and felt simply made me want to cry. He was very patient and sympathetic about it; which nearly made me laugh; for a moment, with his face blue from not shaving and circles under his eyes and a bar of smudge across his forehead, he looked like a clown – funny, and somehow terribly sad at the same time – but of course I didn't tell him that. In a way I've got to love him – not like Papa, of course, but a feeling of considerable affection, and I have a feeling that, unlike Papa, he *minds* his age, so that although with Papa or someone of my own age I could have said: 'You look like a clown, my dear X,' with Mr J. this would be wrong. Papa used to say that I was not nearly sensitive enough to people's feelings, so that is another thing to start remembering. In the taxi driving into Athens to the same hotel where he said we would be sure to find the others, he suddenly asked me to say goodbye to him then. He said he hated airports and collective farewells and anyway it would probably be raining in London which made everything worse. So we solemnly said goodbye: we shook hands and then kissed each other's faces: 'Like French Prime Ministers,' I said, and at first I thought he hadn't heard, but then he said not in the least – they never stopped shaving. Then he offered me help of a practical nature: he said if I found that there was a money crisis at home, I must tell him because financial help was his long suit and he looked both bitter and kind when he said it. I thanked him and he said:

'Now there is nothing more that we need underline; let's look for your basket.' We found it, and came here, and now I've bathed and changed out of island clothes and am waiting to hear the plans which Jimmy is out making apparently, and the dread of the journey home keeps bouncing towards me and away again – it has just come back like a tiresome ball that seems both unerring and silly; there is a considerable difference between knowing what to do and actually doing it, I suppose one spends most of one's life in this gap?

2

LILLIAN

I WOKE late with the telephone ringing, and as I propped myself up to answer it I saw the turned-down bed that had not been slept in beside me. It was Jimmy, sounding harassed.

'I'm at the Air Terminal, we've a problem on. This plane leaves tonight at six thirty. If they catch the boat – and it seems to be the only one – that we caught yesterday, they can't possibly arrive in time. I tried to call the island before I came here this morning, but I can't make any sense out of what they say. They should have gotten the cable by now, but what difference will that make? Should I cancel today's plane, and try to get two more seats for tomorrow?'

This wasn't the kind of thing Jimmy usually asked anybody, and really wondering, I said: 'What do you feel about it?'

There was a pause, then he said: 'That's the funny thing. My instinct is not to, but I haven't explained the practical situation here because it would sound crazy and they wouldn't *let* me book it.'

I said: 'I should stick to your instinct.'

'OK.' He sounded relieved. Then he said: 'I've heard of a place out of town where I thought we might have lunch. Would you like that?'

'Very much. When will you be coming back?'

'After I've been to American Express. Don't go out, Lillian, in case they call from the island, will you?'

'No.' We hung up. I felt sure then that Jimmy was right – although not in the way he thought: they were going to call from the island and say they were going back together, and it was Jimmy and I who would use today's tickets. I got out of bed and went into the bathroom – I suppose that was instinct too because my stuff was in there – but I was caught before I could reach it off the shelf – skewered on a circle of pain that constricts until there's no room for anything but the skewer . . . I was on the tiled floor – still upright, leaning against the bath clutching my left side where the skewer was embedded and waiting for the extraordinary choking gasps to give me air. I'd never reach those capsules now – in any case nothing in the room was keeping still – even the floor was heaving at me so that I couldn't see properly and there seemed to be something cold, heavy, and unpleasant pressing on the back of my neck. I shut my eyes and concentrated upon the gasps and on pushing the skewer right home and that seemed to work, as the pain died down and the gasps brought air. Then it was just a question of time – of waiting until I dared lever myself up to the shelf with the capsules on it. If the telephone were to ring now it would be a pity, but it would not make any real difference. The facts would be the same; it would only be that I shouldn't know them. After one false attempt I thought that by the time I was able to get up to the capsules, I shouldn't need them, and that somehow seemed to fit with everything else just now. I was very thirsty, but that would have to wait too. If they did not get here until after we had left, I would have to leave without my pictures of Sarah. Perhaps that would not make a real difference, either. After that I concentrated upon my breathing and relieving the extraordinary tension in my chest until I was able to get up.

I drank a little water and then took the glass and the capsules back to the bedroom: even that effort made me sweat: there was nothing for it but to lie down. It had been the thought of facing poor Jimmy with these changed plans that had struck me after he had been talking. I felt that he might well have accused me of being both a fool and a coward to have left Em on the island with her, knowing what I knew and not telling Jimmy. This was confusing; I no longer felt able to attach anyone's judgment of me to the last thing I had done, and therefore Jimmy would probably be right. I hadn't meant it like that (had I? I wondered), and with these weak and uncertain reflections I fell asleep.

I woke again as the door opened with a rattling of keys – Jimmy, I thought, let in by the chambermaid – but it was Em. I was so astonished that I lay quite still, looking at him without speaking.

'Lillian? Were you asleep?'

'How did you get here?'

'We came over on a boat last night.'

He stopped, and I waited for him to say something more, but he didn't. I sat up and looked at my travelling clock: it was nearly twelve.

'It is rather stuffy in here,' he remarked and went to open a window. Near the light I saw his face more clearly: he looked calm but absolutely exhausted. He saw the capsules by my bed and said: 'Are you just keeping them by you, or have you been ill?' His voice was sharp, edgy, with anxiety, and remembering how I had used these attacks, I said: 'I'm just keeping them by me. Have you seen Jimmy?'

'No. I've just had a shower in his room and changed, but they said he was out.'

'He's coming back to take me out to lunch,' I said, wishing desperately that he would tell me something.

'You'd better get up then.' He put my dressing gown on my bed, and lit a cigarette. As I got out of bed, he said: 'Why don't you tell me the plans?'

I got into the bathroom before replying – held on to the basin and seeing the glass over it looked myself firmly in the eye: once in the day was enough, for heaven's sake. I looked terrible – with purple circles under my eyes and all my skin too thin. I said: 'What did you say?'

'What are the plans?' I heard him moving restlessly about the room.

'Jimmy has succeeded in getting two tickets for a plane leaving this evening and two for tomorrow. He couldn't get four for today.'

'How on earth did he know we'd be here in time?'

'He didn't. He just got them to be on the safe side.'

'Well – she wants to get back quickly. We'd better go tomorrow.'

I couldn't see the face in the glass any more: everything blurred as though I had been looking into a stream that had been still and was starting to move. He was not going with her – not going . . .

'You're very quiet in there – hadn't you better get dressed?'

He had come to the open door of the bathroom. I seized a sponge and turned on the cold tap: I seemed to wash my face for hours, until it was numb. The water stopped him talking and he retreated. When I came out, I found that he had sent for my luggage.

'You hate wearing the same clothes for two days running. You may want to change into your other scarf.' He tried to smile, and that too, made me want to weep: in that attempt he exposed himself: I knew all over again that I had been right about his face on the terrace.

'Do you think we might have a drink up here while I dress? I missed breakfast and I'll be giddy by the time we get to lunch if I don't have something.'

He ordered drinks. In the top of the first suitcase I opened was the folder which had Sarah's pictures. He was sitting on the unmade bed, and I felt him watching me – knowing that I would pick up the folder and put it, open, on the dressing table; he must have watched me so many times. I picked up the folder and opened it – knowing what I would see by heart – like the print of seaweed against certain kinds of stone, these pictures were indelibly printed into my memory – I did not need them in the folder. I looked round the room: for the first time in my life I realized that certain gestures, if they are to be honest, must be made without any appearance of drama – that they must be quiet and light or they lose any value: but it was an extraordinary feeling, to know quite well what I meant to do, and be at a loss about how to do it. Eventually, I tossed the folder over to him and said: 'Darling – I really don't *need* these any more, but I can't quite bring myself to throw them away: could you dispose of them?'

He said: 'Are you sure you mean me to throw these away?'

'Yes. After all, there is the whole album that I left in New York if I ever want to look at it, but I'm not sure that I do any more. I think I've changed a little in this way.' It was very odd: I could not look at him and felt myself actually blushing: luckily, then, our drinks arrived, and he put the folder into his pocket. I found my shantung suit, and while I was burrowing for a shirt, he brought me my Americano and said: 'When we have a house, I shan't allow you to travel with so much luggage. I'm afraid I didn't pack it very well.'

'Did *you* pack it?'

He got to his feet abruptly. 'Yes. Now, I'm going to see if Jimmy is back so that we can arrange things. Shall I fetch you, or will you meet us in the bar?'

'I'll meet you in the bar; won't be long.'

He went leaving his drink behind: he had not wanted it in the least – it had been simply another concession. Now that I was alone I could afford some of the relief out of this extreme and light-headed change that he had unwittingly made for me – it would not matter if I laughed or cried or became intoxicated by this – it seemed to me – miraculous reversal. But because my fears for myself had melted – had so instantly dissolved – I could turn in their absence, naturally to him . . .

He was very unhappy: he had not said her name and only referred to her when I had told him about the two tickets: had she, I wondered, failed him with no response? Or had he, deeply touched by her, recognized her requirements as separate from his own, and made his decision as the best he could do for her? Whichever it was I felt he had been struck in some different way – that he was suffering a new and difficult pain – and there was nothing inconclusive about it – he had made up his mind. I tried to imagine him making it up: could feel the instant's warmth, almost inspiration that would come when he resolved it – like a new laid fire with its paper burning, before the paper becomes black ash and the fire has to live on its own. How rare it was to live any promise out; how hard to keep every minute of any decision; how painful to reach even to the height of one's own nature . . . Were he and I going to live with the image of her always before us, as we had lived for so many years now with Sarah? If we were to be so haunted, it was I who had taught him the trick of it. But perhaps he was trying to do more than I had ever tried, and this thought gave me a great gentleness for him as I discovered that one does not only want to protect what is weak. This was new, unmistakable, and I could recognize it: a movement and warmth of concern and joy for him that still, I thought, after all these years of my life might be a very beginning of love.

3

JIMMY

ON the way back from American Express, I bought her something. I don't know why I was so sure she would be back in time for the plane, but I was sure, and I bought the bracelet as a kind of proof to myself. Oh, I bought it for other reasons, but the idea of buying it *then* – even if I wasn't going to give it to her for months – came out of the feeling of being so *sure* – how I've never felt about anything before except getting to England when I was a boy. Even not getting a call through to them on the island hadn't thrown me. I'd felt crazy booking the seats and I'd called Lillian because I'd felt mean at going out without seeing her and I suppose I'd wanted backing over my hunch. She's been sweet, Lillian has: more and more I've wondered, since we've been in Athens, whether she doesn't know just as much about Emmanuel's feelings as I do – she's just dumb about them to me because she doesn't want to upset me; but it isn't just her courage – she's been sweet with it, listening to me last night when she was dead tired, being patient and kind of *good* about it all. I'd offered, on the spur of the moment, to take her out to lunch at this taverna out of the city because I know she adores trips and new places to eat, but walking back from American Express I began to regret the offer. I didn't want to go that far away on account of my hunch that the others were going to turn up. That's the trouble in life: you make a plan, or offer something, and you're sincerely thinking of the other person at the time, but then you start thinking of yourself, and if the plan doesn't suit you you're in trouble. But maybe if I was right about her knowing, Lillian wouldn't want to go out to lunch either.

I'd decided to walk back to the hotel to use up some of the morning. It was a wonderful day and in spite of anxieties, uncertainties and wondering how she was I couldn't stop the feeling of being light-hearted and the world all before me and containing her. Just the sheer certainty that I would see her before the day was out was enough to make it a good day: after that, it was up to me, and I found this a new and exciting way to look at anything. I've never had much sense of direction, and wasn't thinking about it anyway: Athens is a small place, and you have the feeling that you can walk to anywhere in it – but after quite some walk I knew I was lost. This made me twist about into narrower streets where an automobile has to hoot and nudge its way through the people, who don't walk like they do in New York, like they're going some place – nor like they do in London where you feel they're taking exercise-never-mind-the-weather, but just as though they are on the street because they like it that way. I started looking in the shop windows and that's how I saw the bracelet. It was just a circle of pale pink beads with pearls fixed in between some of the beads: it was hanging on a nail at the side of the window which was so stuffed with all kinds of jewellery that afterwards I wondered how I'd ever noticed the bracelet. I went in and got the man to show it me. The pearls were pierced by some kind of golden wire which made them hang stiffly – the pink beads were coral. He wanted fifteen hundred drachma for it – when I asked him where it had been made he shrugged and said something which I think just meant that it hadn't been made in Greece. It looked somehow as though it had been especially made for somebody, and, whoever she had been, I felt that it had also been made for Alberta, so I bought it. I did try to argue about the price but it didn't work, and he knew I didn't really care. He wrapped it up in very thin foreign kind of paper, and within a few minutes of seeing it I was outside the shop again with the bracelet in my pocket. Then I just had to get back to the hotel and took a taxi. In the cab I unwrapped the bracelet to be sure it gave me the same feeling of being the right one for her, and it did. I'd never bought a serious present for a girl in my life: flowers and scent and scarves and candy – anyone could buy those for anybody and that was just how I'd bought them. This was different – this was an antique, something that she could always wear; I wanted to laugh out loud, I was so lit up about it.

When I got to the hotel they told me that Mr Joyce had arrived and was using my room. I said I'd go up, and got them to give me her room number – she was a floor above my room; I took the elevator to my floor, waited until it had gone, and walked the last flight. Now that my hunch was proved right, and she was actually here, I found myself breathless – not only with impatience to see her – but fear of the kind that I had had when we left her on the island with Emmanuel. How did she feel about him – all that again, plus her being unhappy – perhaps sobbing her heart out on his shoulder . . . I knocked, and at once she let me in.

She was wearing her prettiest dress – the one Lillian got with her in New York and she looked marvellously fresh and neat and clean.

'How *are* you,' I said, and that was just all I could think of to say. She said she was very well and thanked me – just how I might have known she would.

'Do you mind me coming up? I wanted to know how you were.'

'Not at all.' She seemed nervous. 'Come and see something.'

She led me into the bathroom. There, crouched in the bath, was a small kitten, looking very neat and lost.

'Julius gave it to me as a parting present. Mr Joyce said he thinks there may be trouble about quarantine, but I'm afraid we're committed to this cat now. It is much nicer than it looks, but I'm keeping it in the bath because it can't get out and it won't matter if it makes a mess there. Of course it has been fed.'

'How did you get here?'

She told me, and somehow I felt that everything had been all right. We went back into her room: there was the big book she writes in lying open on the bed.

'Are you writing a novel or something?'

'A kind of diary, but I don't think I shall go on with it.

I won't, in fact.' She shut the book and put it inside her suitcase.

'Aren't you going to ask me about the plans?'

'Yes: what are they?'

I told her: she didn't look as pleased as I'd hoped, although she thanked me in her prim way for all the trouble I'd taken.

'What's the matter, Alberta? You wanted to get home as quickly as possible didn't you?'

'I do, of course.'

In spite of her fresh clothes, her tanned skin and clear eyes, she looked pale and as though something was worrying her, and as though she couldn't decide whether to tell me or not. I waited; if I asked her, I guessed she wouldn't. Then she sat on the bed suddenly, and said: 'It sounds awfully silly, but I simply *dread* going back. I can't explain it. I would have thought that my father being dead would stop anything else mattering – like places, or things one had to do, but it doesn't stop this at all. I just don't want to go back, and see them and hear all the story of him – how they found him and what people think of the driver of the car, and sort papers in his study and write letters to people I don't even know about him and clear up his house and all the traces of him so that somebody else can live in it, and then we all pack up and leave and that's that. I just don't want to go back,' she repeated, and then in a rather shaky voice added: 'and you needn't tell me that all this is both childish and selfish because I know – and that makes it worse.'

'I wouldn't dream of it—' but she interrupted: 'Well, it *is* both childish and selfish,' and stared angrily at the floor.

'I meant I wouldn't dream of telling you anything about it. Except that I'll come with you, if you'd find that any use at all. There's sure to be a pub near where I could stay and not be a worry to your family, but just be around if you needed me?' I was standing in front of her at the end of the bed – there was nowhere to sit so I knelt because I had to see her face. She looked up and simply said: 'Oh Jimmy – it would make all the difference!' Then more and more colour came into her face and she said: 'If you are quite sure that it wouldn't inconvenience you?'

'It wouldn't.' I handed her my handkerchief and she blew her nose.

'It is most odd. It wouldn't have occurred to me that your coming would make all the difference at all. I don't mean to sound rude, of course: I mean I truly wasn't trying to get you to come or anything.' She looked at me anxiously: 'I really do thank you for taking all this trouble. So it won't just be the aeroplane, it will be the train down and everything else?'

I managed to make an airy gesture: 'Aeroplanes, trains, boats – they're all the same to me.'

Her eyes shone: 'And people? Do you find them indistinguishable?'

I put my hand to her head: 'Some of them have wet hair which is one way of telling. If I really want to make it easy for myself—'

She sneezed: I got my packet out and unwrapped it. 'I put a little distinguishing mark on them.' The bracelet exactly fitted, and she wasn't wearing her watch. 'Then it is perfectly easy for me to tell even at a distance . . . ' She looked up from her wrist. 'That they are different from everybody else.'

She looked solemn and sparkling and her head was very close to mine; but it was odd, I was loving her so much that I knew this had to be done in a different way to any way I'd tried or imagined. So I picked up both her hands and kissed them, and then fetched her big book out of her suitcase. I put it on her lap and unscrewed my pen.

'There's just one more thing for you to write.'

'What should I write?'

'All good young diaries end up with a proposal: I'll dictate it. "Today, Jimmy asked me to marry him. He says I may take as long as I like to decide about this as long as I come to the right decision in the end." That's all.'

She wrote it: then she looked at the bracelet and finally said: 'Is that true?'

'Quite true – only it's a secret: it's a secret diary, you see: so nobody else knows.'

She looked awed: 'You see – I'm not quite sure about it: it is rather a momentous step where one should consult all one's feelings.'

'It's a case for considering every single one of them.'

'And that takes time?'

'Well, naturally, I don't know how many feelings you have, but you take your time.'

She sneezed again. 'I love my bracelet: it is truly the most beautiful object. Do you think we could change the subject – I haven't got much presence of mind left about this one?'

'I haven't got another subject to change into right now. But I ought to go and find Emmanuel and tell him the plans.'

'Not our plans? I mean any plans we might make?'

'Not them – no. I'll meet you in the bar.'

When I was at the door, she said: 'Jimmy! About Mr Joyce. He told me that if we go to New York, he may have to stay in England for a while: he sounded very sad about it. I think he has a great devotion to you.' I waited, because I thought she was going to say something else – but she didn't – she just said: 'That's all. I just wanted to tell you.'

Walking down the stairs feeling so rich with life I seemed to float, I suddenly thought of what she'd said about Emmanuel: in all the years I'd lived and worked with him I'd never thought of the devotion as being that way round. I'd thought of him as powerful, casually generous, brilliant, and generally, somehow, a romantic character, and I as painstaking, and faithful, his devoted dog-eyed boy. I'd really lived it that way regardless of results because I'd had no particular sense of direction – but now that I felt this changing I didn't have the need either to make a religion of working for him, or a political cause out of working for myself . . .

4

EMMANUEL

THE whole day had been stamped with finality for him – all the events had the poignant unreality of a dream – of ends and departure. He had burned the pictures of both the Sarahs together down in Jimmy's room which he had found empty, and he had watched the paper curl and discolour ahead of a flame hardly detectable in the bright sunlight. Very soon they were gone, and he was left with the empty red folder and nothing to conceal. Jimmy had arrived, remarked incuriously on the smell, and told him that he was taking her to her home: he was grateful on the whole, not to have to make a gesture to Jimmy about that. They had gone down together to the bar with so much unsaid that the illusion of their being in complete accord returned, or – possibly because he felt that this was an end to a certain kind of relationship with Jimmy – it had merely ceased to be an illusion. They had ordered a drink, and Jimmy had told him more about the arrangements: he had listened as though these motions were already past, and had never had anything to do with him, but he had observed Jimmy's elated confidence and it had touched him somewhere with a sharp sense of separation. Lillian had joined them and her approach across the room was tentative, had a softness about it which marked her behaviour throughout the day – he noticed that in all the time she had spent upstairs, she had not really made up her face.

And lastly, she came down, wearing the dress in which he had first desired her, and carrying the kitten's basket. As she put the basket down on the floor, he saw a new and pretty bracelet clustered on her wrist, about which, throughout the day, nobody said anything. Lillian was introduced to the kitten who responded with ferocious affection – it wasn't until much later in the afternoon that he had realized that Lillian was the first person to notice a new bracelet and remark upon it . . .

They had lunched at a taverna in the country – out of doors in a grove with the mountain of Hymettus behind them. Sprigs of verbena were laid on the table; the hot air was impregnated with their dry lemon sweetness. They were served with a meticulous leisure – the meal ending hours later with a dish of walnuts steeped in honey. He could not remember what they talked about: any gaiety had the quality of an Indian summer, as though, separately, they were all acknowledging the end of something together. He saw each one of them with the clarity of detachment, and with the affection of a farewell, as though their lives together hung upon a thread; they were all going to leave one another and themselves in this hot silent place and were already aware of the changes to come. He thought of the years he had known them and the hours that he had loved them and the moments that he had understood them – and he included himself in this plural. He saw her, a little shy with Jimmy, friendly to Lillian and grateful to himself. He saw Lillian gentle to the girl, almost tender to Jimmy, but here there was a blank – he felt only that she was acutely aware of him – he could put no name to her manner. And he saw himself – the oldest, who in some way had provided the pivot on which they had all turned to one another, whose function where they were concerned might very well now be fulfilled and who had now to discover some private direction for the rest of his life. In these last hours he felt calm, disengaged, and concealed from them. It did not occur to him – until they were standing round their table preparing to leave it – that perhaps there were dimensions to this concealment, and that they might each, separately, have some different thing to conceal from the other one. This, sharpened by the urgency of departure – there was just time now to drive to the hotel, pick up the luggage and drive to the airport – heightened his perceptions. One does not give up anything, he thought, she was never mine: it was a notion I had of myself with her. He remembered years ago telling Jimmy something of the kind – when the boy had his orphanage chip on his shoulder – he'd told him that afterwards he would find that it had never been there, and this would make him feel light, and a bit of a fool. My God, he thought, the difference between what one thinks about how things are and the actual living through of one's discoveries!

He waited in the car with Lillian while the others collected their luggage. He looked at her and she smiled so hesitantly that he said: 'What is it?'

'It is horrid seeing people off. I was wondering whether I'd stay here, perhaps?'

He said: 'I think we should both go.' He did not know why he said it, and sounded perfectly determined. He glanced at her to see whether she was going to demur, but she simply nodded.

He said: 'I burned those pictures,' and she answered: 'Thank you, darling.'

When they came out of the hotel, Jimmy went in front and Alberta sat between them with the kitten's basket on the floor in front of her. After a while and as though she had been thinking carefully, she said:

'I don't really know how to thank you both for the wonderful time that I have had, and your kindness about everything. As it seems likely that I shall be going to New York eventually, I wondered whether you would care to adopt this kitten? I thought perhaps it could live more happily in your house than being carted about the world by me. It isn't that I don't like it – I think it is the most personable and strong-minded cat I've ever met. But there is its future to be considered.'

Lillian looked at him, so he said: 'You must decide, but personally I think all houses should be furnished by at least one cat.'

So Lillian seriously accepted: she seemed to understand Alberta in this matter, who said: 'It will be much more compatible than that eccentric little monkey,' and they reminded each other of its speedy and terrible behaviour, while he watched the road slip past, marking the time in seconds now.

At the airport they all got out and waited while the tickets were checked and the luggage weighed. They were late, they were given to understand: the bus passengers had already been waiting half an hour, and the aeroplane was actually in – they could see it being refuelled. In the hall where all the stalls sold their trivia, they seemed to split up: Jimmy took Lillian's arm and walked her off to buy cigarettes. He was left alone with Alberta. She said diffidently: 'Shall I see you again before we go to New York?'

'I don't know, Sarah. Do you dread going home?' he added abruptly: the idea of her dreading it had suddenly occurred to him.

'I do, rather. But it will be so much of a bridge to have Jimmy.'

'Is he going home with you?'

'If you can spare him?'

'Oh yes. I shan't be needing him – except for the New York production – for some time.'

'Until you write another play in fact.'

'Yes,' he replied discovering this. They were silent until minutes later she said: 'We've said goodbye, haven't we? So we can't say any more.'

'Remember what I asked you.'

'I do: it may well prove possible in the aeroplane.'

Their flight was being called. The others returned. Lillian kissed Alberta and Jimmy. Jimmy looked anxiously at him: he put a hand on Jimmy's arm, and felt himself smiling, heard himself say: 'Take care of her.' And Jimmy said: 'Yes. I'll call you at Claridge's the day after tomorrow.' Then they had to go. He stood by Lillian to watch them walk through the doorways and become diminished by the crowd outside, who already stood with the afternoon sun in their eyes and white dust circling round their feet, waiting to be led to the aircraft. Lillian said:

'I'll join you in the taxi in a few minutes,' and disappeared.

Now they were being led to the aircraft. He walked to the

window in order to see them better. As they reached the steps, Jimmy turned round, saw him, and waved and then she did the same. She was wearing a yellow coat and her head was bare. He raised his hand and dropped it again. Now they were up the gangway and out of sight. He watched the plane taxi out to the head of a runway and crouch there, and he remembered explaining to her that they ran the engines up one by one: he remembered her gravity, her smooth hair with the black band, her friendly excitement, and was wrenched by a moment's anguish as though he was dragging something out of his heart. They were off: he watched the collection of speed until the moment when they actually left the ground when the speed seemed, as it were, to be dropped on to it – they were just airborne, suspended a few feet from the earth, and then – as suddenly – moving again, climbing up into the blue air towards the sun. He watched until they turned away to make the wide circle and head west, the aircraft glinting and small, like a lucky charm in the sky.

They were gone: no longer part of his present: to steady himself, he tried to see this loss as it might be seen. A boy who might be his son, and a girl whom he might have loved – would have married if circumstances had been different. Now, although they would be unstrapping themselves from their seats, they could not leave the aircraft: they could make what they wanted of the journey, but they could not escape it. This balance of what was inevitable, and what could be changed occurred again to him now as he tried to see his own framework; immediately, the taxi outside, containing Lillian whom all day he had scarcely recognized, although all day she had still been his wife, the mother of the Sarah who died . . . What had been her concealment during this day which had begun with her relinquishing her daughter? That had been bravely done and, as he understood this, something more of her revealed with courage in it which amounted almost to the beginning of something else.

When he reached the taxi she was already sitting in the back of it. He climbed in, the driver mentioned Athens, and they thundered off. At the appropriate moment the driver said 'Akropolis' and they both turned to see this eminent beauty. She said then:

'Do you find it astonishing that it has been there all our lives and we have not seen it until now?'

'Tomorrow morning I will take you to see it before we catch our aeroplane.'

'Oh yes,' she said: 'it will be our last chance.'

He put his hand in his pocket for a cigarette, and felt the letter that for the last twenty-four hours he had needed to keep with him: when he turned to her she looked at him steadily, calm with her knowledge of the day, and his spirit rose to her serenity as he recognized that these were his circumstances; opportunities, neither easy nor impossible, lay under his hand – were simply facts of their small matter waiting to be transformed.